Jennifer Roberson

SHAPECHANGERS'S SONG

THE CHRONICLES OF THE CHEYSULI

OMNIBUS ONE

Book One
SHAPECHANGERS

Book Two
THE SONG OF HOMANA

DAW BOOKS, INC.

DONALD A. WOLLHEIM, FOUNDER

375 Hudson Street, New York, NY 10014

ELIZABETH R. WOLLHEIM
SHEILA E. GILBERT
PUBLISHERS
www.dawbooks.com

SHAPECHANGERS:
For all those who believe in fantasy,
and the special few who believed in me

SONG OF HOMANA:
To Marion Zimmer Bradley,
for daydreams and realities
&
Betsy Wollheim,
for making mine better

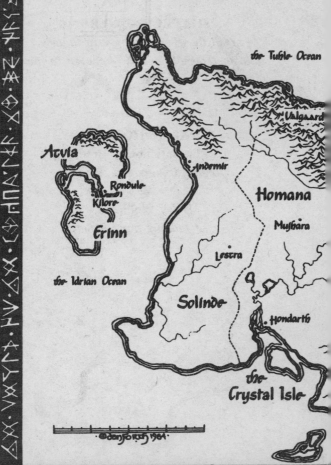

NOT-SO-INSTANT REPLAY
An Introduction
by Jennifer Roberson

I'm very pleased to introduce the first of four omnibus editions of *The Chronicles of the Cheysuli*, an eight-volume series first published from 1984 through 1992. I know by the volume of e-mail I receive that a couple of the original paperback editions are impossible to find. Thanks to DAW Books, the series as a whole will be available again—and take up less room on the bookshelf!

I'm also pleased to present a heretofore unpublished Cheysuli short story, contained in the back of this volume. Set in the days of *Shapechangers,* the first book in the series, "Kinspirit" is the story of Rowan, a young man trapped by the tides of war. Told from Rowan's viewpoint, readers familiar with *Shapechangers* will have the opportunity to revisit some of their favorite characters.

For readers unfamiliar with the series, welcome to the world of the Cheysuli, a race of people gifted with the ability to shift their shapes into animal form at will, and the divine prophecy that orders their lives as well as the survival of a realm.

How did it all begin? Well, in 1979, sick to death of waiting for new books by my favorite authors, I decided to take a shot at writing my own fantasy novel. Certainly I had many years of fantasy reading stored away in my imagination, so it seemed a natural progression for someone who had, at age fourteen, written—and marketed—her first novel. That one, and three others, met with rejection. But none of them had been fantasy, even though it was by far my favorite genre. I was too afraid I couldn't do the genre justice, and so I avoided it.

But it was fifteen years later, and I was willing to accept the challenge. After all, what was one more rejection?

I began jotting down initial notes. I knew it would be a

novel about a race of shapechangers, because the concept had always intrigued me. I'd always felt being able to shift one's shape would be a wonderful ability—possibly because in elementary school I wanted desperately to be someone else—but except for a couple of books by Andre Norton, shapechangers had never been portrayed as benign characters. Certainly not as heroes. So I set out to write a book about *good* shapechangers.

To me, the visual appearance of words on the page is as important as the actual *sound* of the words, and so I began to play with letters and syllables. It didn't take long for the word *Cheysuli* to sort itself out, pronounced Chay-SOO-li, with a hard "ch," as in "chair." And soon enough the word *lir* came to denote the totem animals of the Cheysuli, the magical animals with whom Cheysuli males forged a life-long bond that allowed them to shift shape. (Why limit it to males? Probably because I'd grown up reading adventure, science fiction, and fantasy books where males were always the heroes; it was a natural choice at the time. But I also knew the women would play equally important roles.) And then I created what is a traditional archetype in fantasy fiction: the adolescent human who in fact turns out to be more than human, and must discover a new role in an unexpected life. Generally this character was portrayed by a boy, but I didn't want to write about a boy. My hero-to-be was a hero*ine*, and I named her Calysta. Which was also the manuscript's working title.

I began to assemble a cast of characters. I drew a crude map of Homana—the root word is *home*—and adjoining lands. Once I saw them take shape before my eyes, coupled with the names I concocted, everything began to fall into place. I needed royalty, and a good villain. I also wanted to create internal conflict, the kind that will drive a plot even when enemy nations and races are not at war. And thus the Cheysuli underwent their own ethnic cleansing in a land they founded.

Calysta, which became *The Shapechangers* (the "The" was later dropped by the publisher), was not intended to be the first in a series. I figured a solo fantasy novel was more than enough challenge at the time. But while sitting in a cultural anthropology class one day, playing with the circles and triangles of a generational exercise designed to explain how genetics and dynastic manipulation can change races and cultures, I had a brainstorm. If I played with generations and dynasties in my book, marrying enemy to enemy, race to race, I'd end up with a trilogy.

Thus my version of genetic manipulation, powered by a divine prophecy, was born. So was a trilogy. Which, when I actually plotted it, grew to seven volumes, all because I was marrying people off who had children who in turn married others and had *more* children. But other than trilogies, I preferred even-numbered series, and so I decided I'd write eight volumes instead of seven. Of such inconsequentialities are career decisions made.

At the time I undertook the first volume, I was an adult student at Northern Arizona University. Frustrated with an English department that didn't understand my desire to actually *sell* my work, I was majoring in journalism. I'd already sold a couple of articles, but what I wanted to do with my life was write novels. So I carried eighteen hours a semester, worked twenty hours a week in an on-campus work-study program, and wrote my first fantasy novel.

Then I set about marketing it. I tried several publishers, those who'd published books in my personal library, with editor's names and addresses culled from *Writer's Market* listings, and met with no success. After fifteen years, five novels, and a multiplicity of prayers, I was no better off than I'd been at fourteen. Still a wanna-be.

In 1980, frustrated with rejection, I decided to take a controversial route. I'd received solicitations from a top literary agency offering to read and critique my work for a fee, and to market it if they felt it was saleable. I decided the gamble was no worse than the odds in Las Vegas, and saved up the $200 reading fee.

Not only did the readers at the agency feel my manuscript was unmarketable, but they believed there were so many fundamental flaws in the work that it wasn't even worth rewriting under their direction. The four-page, single-spaced letter proceeded to spell out those flaws.

Some comments I agreed with. Many I did not. I was convinced I *could* make the manuscript saleable. So I started over. I learned what the term "revisions" meant.

Names were changed—too many began with the letter "C"—characters were dropped, characters were altered, whole chunks of the book were cut out. The most significant change was switching from multiple to single viewpoint. This time, instead of telling the stories of a whole slew of characters, I focused on one. I made it the girl's story. Her name was now Alix, and the title had transmogrified to *The Shapechangers*.

I borrowed reading-fee money from a friend and sent the new version back to the agency, where it was plucked from the slush pile by a science fiction author hired to find the wheat among the chaff. This science fiction author read it, and stuck it on the desk of a young, hungry agent by the name of Russell Galen. The science fiction author was frank: the fantasy genre and this particular manuscript were not his cup of tea, but he felt strongly the book was saleable.

And so I was "discovered" by multiple Hugo and Nebula award nominee Barry Malzberg. And so I was taken on as a client by Russ Galen, who had recently negotiated a huge deal on Marion Zimmer Bradley's behalf for a modest work titled *The Mists of Avalon*.

Hollywood ending? Not quite. The first two houses my agent submitted *The Shapechangers* to rejected it. At the time I was too busy to be upset; I was preparing to embark on my final college semester via the American Institute for Foreign Studies, in which a consortium of Arizona's three universities sent students to study in London. I was also in the midst of applying for admission to the Master of Fine Arts in Creative Writing program at the University of Arizona, in Tucson, attempting to get everything lined up before I went to England. I would graduate NAU in December, and start master's work the following semester in a new city.

Off I went to England, a country I had, as a lifelong Anglophile, always wanted to visit. Now I was to *live* there for nearly six months, attending classes three days a week and spending the other four in museums, castles, cathedrals, and hopping the train to historical sites in Wales and Scotland. It was heaven.

Heaven ended when my mother, visiting for two weeks, brought a letter from the University of Arizona. I was denied admission to the MFA program. My work sample, the letter said, was not competitive. It was deemed too "commercial."

Two weeks later, at breakfast, I received a telegram. Arriving two days after my birthday, I assumed someone was wishing me happy birthday. Instead, my agent announced that *Shapechangers* had been sold to DAW Books, and could I stop in New York on my way home to have lunch with the publisher, Donald A. Wollheim?

Apparently my work *was too* commercial.

Six weeks later I landed at JFK and set off for midtown Manhattan to lunch with my new editor, Betsy Wollheim, and her father, Don Wollheim, who was the driving force behind Ace Books at its inception, and who later founded DAW. I landed as a *real author,* no longer a wanna-be—and also a college graduate, as my studies were officially complete that very day. I'd survived a full semester in a foreign country—Americans and Britons do not speak the same language, trust me!—traveled to other foreign countries, and now here I was in New York City for the first time (not counting the connection on my way to London), far more frightened of my countrymen than anyone I met overseas. The Big Apple, after all, was the Big Bad City.

Following explicit directions, I reached the literary agency lugging too much carry-on baggage and vowing never again to wear high-heeled boots in NYC. There I was buzzed in to meet with Barry Malzberg before going off to the DAW offices, as my agent, Russ Galen, was on vacation. In addition to discovering Mr. Malzberg was *extremely* tall and typed faster than anyone I'd ever seen before (and this in the days prior to word processors), I was given a brief verbal "tour" of what I might expect as a published author. He then presented me with an advance copy of *The Mists of Avalon,* allowed me to stow my luggage in his office, and walked me through the mean streets of New York to the DAW offices. After that, I was on my own.

My editor, Betsy Wollheim, was very warm and friendly, welcoming me into the family, but I was too nervous and jet-lagged to do much more than make inane comments when I managed to speak at all. Don Wollheim, with a reputation for being gruff, was less forthcoming. I think my knees were knocking when we walked down the street to a restaurant. Here I was, achieving a dream I'd hoarded for fifteen years—and I couldn't string a semi-articulate sentence together to save my soul.

Fortunately this incoherency was not held against me, and six months later DAW bought *The Song of Homana*. In 1984, at the L.A. World Science Fiction Convention, seven months after *Shapechangers* debuted, DAW bought the third Cheysuli novel—and a new fantasy that had written itself in two weeks, titled *Sword-Dancer*. (That too was intended to be a stand-alone, but I was unsurprised when the two protagonists demanded additional volumes. My brain seems to be hard-wired for fantasy series, not solo works.)

As I write this, it's now twenty-two years after I first conceived a book about a race of shapechangers. In these past two-plus decades, I have honed my craft, refined my style, experimented with new characters, new worlds, new styles, pushed the envelope. *Shapechangers* is by no means my best work, as later and more ambitious novels attest, but it was the best I could do *at the time,* and without doubt is the readers' favorite of all the Cheysuli novels. (Mine actually is *The Song of Homana,* also contained in this edition, because I feel it exhibits a significant improvement in storytelling.) From time to time I flirt with the idea of rewriting *Shapechangers,* of revising the original longer, multi-viewpoint version, presenting it as an author's preferred edition. But *Shapechangers* is a part of my past. It helped shape the writer I am today, but it didn't—and doesn't—define me.

A writer should never stop learning, never stop educating herself, never stop pushing herself to do better with each and every book. Some books are less ambitious than others—at least superficially—and thus perhaps "eas*ier*" to write, but none of them is easy. Even *Sword-Dancer,* an "attack book" I wrote in two weeks (albeit I spent twelve to fifteen hours each day at the typewriter), wasn't truly "easy" to write, because I was inventing new characters, a new world, a new style of writing. I was exploring another compartment in my imagination, attempting to entertain while also writing about sexism, as I'd written about racism and intolerance in the Cheysuli novels. And when I received letters from boys—and men—saying I'd opened their eyes to the value of women as *human beings,* I knew I'd accomplished what I hoped to do: raise some conciousness along the way, as I raised the Sandtiger's. (The moral is: Let no one ever tell you "commercial" writing may not also educate even as it entertains.)

Will I ever write another Cheysuli book? It's a distinct possibility. I've learned never to say "never." But not in the immediate future. There are so many other books that hold my heart, demanding to be written: the *Karavans* series, a new fantasy universe that should begin appearing from DAW next year; a few more big historical fantasy novels such as *The Golden Key,* the collaboration I wrote with Melanie Rawn and Kate Elliott; and additional historicals such as my Robin Hood novels, *Lady of the Forest* and *Lady of Sherwood,* and my personal favorite, *Lady of the Glen,* recounting the Massacre of Glencoe.

So many books . . . so little time.

As always, an author owes many thanks to many people. First, my gratitude to the readers who kept coming back for more—often enough that DAW elected to republish the series in the four omnibus editions appearing this year. I must also thank Betsy Wollheim, initially my editor and now also the publisher, for adding me to the DAW "stable" back in '82. Over the years Betsy and I have formed a very strong working relationship, and it has proved extremely beneficial to my work. We don't always agree, but we definitely challenge one another—and without challenges, the writing never improves. To Russ Galen, now one of the toughest superagents in New York City, head of the Scovil Chichak Galen agency, heartfelt thanks for the guidance and support since 1980. Our strategy sessions are always intense, ambitious, entertaining, enjoyable, and very stimulating. And thank you to Barry Malzberg, who believed in the work and in me even before my agent did. And to Marion Zimmer Bradley, who served as a mentor on many occasions, and published my very first short fiction, a Cheysuli story, in the first volume of her *Sword and Sorceress* anthology.

Lastly, immense gratitude to my late mother, Shera Roberson, who not only raised a kid in a house full of books, but who read to her by the hour; fought for her right to read above her age level in the elementary school library;

challenged her to go for it when, enflamed with a fourteen-year-old's excessive ego, she claimed she could write a better book than another author had; whose conviction that her daughter could and would succeed never, ever flagged. Any success I have achieved, and may yet achieve, is a reflection of her.

—Jennifer Roberson
Flagstaff, Arizona
July 12, 2000

For a complete listing of Jennifer Roberson's novels and short fiction, plus news of upcoming works and appearances, please visit her Web site at: **www.cheysuli.com.**

SHAPECHANGERS

BOOK I

"The Captive"

Chapter One

She sat by the creek, half-hidden in lush grasses. Carefully she twined purple summer flowers into her single dark brown braid, and dabbled bare feet in the rushing water. Stems and crushed blooms littered the coarse yellow gown she wore and damp earth stained the garment, but she paid it no mind. She was purposefully intent on her work, for if she allowed her thoughts to range freely she would be overtaken by the knowledge—and the hope—that he still might come.

A songbird called from the forest behind and she glanced up, smiling at the delicate melody. Then her attention was caught by an approaching rider, and she let fall the flowered braid from limp fingers.

Sunlight glittered off the gold of his mount's trappings and painted the chestnut warhorse bright red. She heard the jingle of bit and bridle and the heavy snort of the big stallion. His rider, who had yet to see her, rode unconcernedly through the meadowlands.

She drew her knees up and clasped her arms around them, resting her chin on their tops. She felt the familiar leap of excitement, anticipation and wonder within her breast, and quickly tried to dismiss it. If she allowed him to see it she would be no different from anyone else to him, and therefore of no account.

And I want to be of account to him, she thought intently.

His tawny-dark head was bent as he rode, blue eyes on the shedding of his gloves. He wore black hunting leathers, she saw, and had thrown a thin green woolen mantle back from broad shoulders. A flash of green and gold glittering at his left shoulder caught her eye: the emerald cloak-brooch he favored. At his heavy belt was hung a massive two-handed broadsword.

The warhorse splashed into the creek, splattering her liberally. She grinned in devious anticipation and straightened in the deep grass, wiping water from her sun-browned skin.

"I did not think you would come," she said, pitching her voice to carry over the noisy horse.

The animal reacted to her unexpected appearance with alacrity. He plunged sideways, halfway out of the creek, then unceremoniously slid down the muddy bank into the water again. His rider, equally startled, reined the animal in with a curse and shot a glare over his shoulder. When he saw her his face cleared.

"Alix! Do you seek to unseat me?"

She grinned at him and shook her head as he tried to settle the horse. The creek bottom offered treacherous footing to any beast, and the warhorse had yet to find a comfortable spot. Finally his rider cursed again in exasperation and spurred him through the water onto the bank, where he stared down at her from the chestnut's great height.

"So, you wish to see Homana's prince take an unexpected bath," he said menacingly, but she saw the amusement in his eyes.

"No, my lord," she responded promptly, very solemn and proper. Then she grinned again.

He sighed and dismissed the topic with an idle wave of his hand. A ruby signet ring flashed on the forefinger of his right hand, reminding her of his rank and the enormity of his presence before her.

By the gods, she whispered within her mind, *he is prince of this land and comes to see me!*

The prince stared down at her quizzically, one tawny eyebrow raised. "What have you been doing—harvesting all the flowers? You are fair covered with them."

Hurriedly she brushed her skirts free of clinging stems and blossoms and began to pick them from her braid. Before she could strip them away entirely he swung down from the horse and caught her hands, kneeling.

"I did not say you presented an unattractive sight, Alix." He grinned. "More like a wood nymph, I would say."

She tried to draw her hands from his large weapon-callused ones. "My lord . . ."

"Carillon," he said firmly. "There are no titles between us. Before you I am as any other man."

But you are not . . . she thought dimly, forcing a smile even as she let her hands stay trapped. After a moment he released one and lifted her to her feet. He led her along the creek, purposely matching his steps to hers. She was tall for a woman, but he was taller still than most men and twice as broad, for all his eighteen years. Carillon of Homana, even did he ever put on the garments of a common crofter, was a prince to the bone.

"Why did you think I would not come?" he asked. "I have ever done it before, when I said I would."

Alix watched her bare toes as she walked, not wishing to meet his steady blue eyes. But she was honest before all else, and gave him a blunt answer.

"I am only a crofter's daughter, and you heir to Shaine the Mujhar. Why *should* you come?"

"I said I would. I do not lie."

She shrugged a shoulder. "Men say many things they do not mean. It does not have to be a lie. I am, after all, not the sort of woman a prince converses with ordinarily."

"You put me at ease, Alix. There is a way about you I find comforting."

She slanted him a bright, amused glance. "Men are not always seeking *comfort,* my lord. At least, not in conversation."

Carillon laughed at her, clasping her hand more tightly. "You do not mouth idle words with me, do you? Well, I would not have it another way. That is part of the reason I seek you out."

Alix stopped, which forced him to. Her chin lifted and she met his eyes squarely. "And what is the *other* part, my lord prince of Homana?"

She saw the brief conflict in his face, following each emotion as it passed across his boyish features. Carillon, even at eighteen, was an open sort, but she was more perceptive than most.

Yet Carillon did not react as she expected, and inwardly dreaded. Instead of embarrassment or condescension or arrogant male pride, there was only laughter in his face. His hands rested on her shoulders.

"Alix, if I wanted to take you as my light woman and

give you chambers within Homana-Mujhar, I would seek a better way of telling you. For all that, first I would *ask* you." He smiled into her widening eyes. "Do not think I am indifferent to you; you are woman enough for me. But I come to you because I can speak with you freely, and not worry that I have said the wrong thing to the wrong ears; hearing it later from the wrong mouth. You are different, Alix."

She swallowed heavily, suddenly hurt. "Aye," she agreed hollowly. "I am an unschooled crofter's daughter with no fine conversation. I am very unlike the sleek court ladies you are accustomed to."

"The gods have made a place for every man and woman on this earth, Alix. Do not chafe at yours."

She scowled at him. "It is easy for a man of your rank to say such a thing, my lord. But what of the poor who live in Mujhara's streets, and the tenant crofters who must live on the questionable bounty of their lords? For all that, what sort of place has Shaine left to the Cheysuli?"

His hands tightened on her shoulders. "Do not speak to me of shapechangers. They are demons. My uncle's purge will rid Homana of their dark sorcery."

"How do you know they are demons?" she demanded, arguing out of fairness rather than conviction. "How can you say when you have never met one?"

Carillon's face went hard and cold before her; aloof. Suddenly she longed for the even-tempered young man she had known and loved but a few weeks.

"Carillon—" she began.

"No," he said flatly, removing his hands to stand stiffly before her. "I have no need to see demons to know they exist. The breed is accursed, Alix; outlawed in this land."

"By your uncle's doing!"

"Aye!" he snapped. "Punishment for a transgression which required harsh measures. By the gods, girl, it was a Cheysuli who stole a king's daughter—my own cousin—and brought civil war to this land!"

"Hale did not *steal* Lindir!" Alix cried. "She went willingly!"

He recoiled from her, though he did not move. Suddenly before her was an angry young man who was more prince than anything else, and therefore entitled to a short temper.

"You freely admit you are an unschooled crofter's daughter," he began coldly, "yet you seek to lesson me in my House's history. What right do you have? Who has said such things to you?"

Her hands curled into fists. "My father was arms-master to Shaine the Mujhar for thirty years, my lord, before he became a crofter. He lived within the walls of Homana-Mujhar and spoke often with the Mujhar. He was there when Lindir went away with the Cheysuli she loved, and he was there when Shaine called curses on the race and outlawed them. He was there when the Mujhar *started* this war!"

Muscles moved beneath the flesh of his jaw. "He speaks treason."

"He speaks the truth!" Alix whirled from him and stalked through the grass, stopping only to remove a thorn from her bare foot. Her slippers, she recalled glumly, were back where they had begun this discussion.

"Alix—" he said.

"By the gods, Carillon, it was the Cheysuli who settled this land!" she said crossly. "Do you think they seek this—purge? It is Shaine's doing, not theirs."

"With just cause."

Alix sighed and set down her foot. They stared at one another silently a long moment, both recognizing they jeopardized the tenuous friendship they had built. She waited for his curt dismissal.

Carillon's hand idly smoothed the hilt of the sword at his belt, caressing the glowing cabochon ruby set in gold. He was silent, thoughtful, not the blustering or coldly arrogant prince she anticipated.

Finally he sighed. "Girl, for all your father had my uncle's ear, he was not privy to all things. He could not know everything about the beginnings of the war. Nor, for that matter, can I. I am but newly made heir, and Shaine treats me as little more than a child. If you will listen, I will tell you what I know of the matter."

She opened her mouth to reply, but a third voice broke into their conversation.

"No, princeling. Let someone who has experienced Shaine's purge tell her what *he* knows of the matter."

Alix jerked around and saw the man at the edges of the

forest; leather-clad in jerkin and leggings, black-haired and dark-skinned. For a moment she stared speechlessly at him, astonished, then her eyes widened as she saw the heavy gold bands on his bare arms and the gray wolf at his side.

"Carillon!" she cried, backing away from the man. She heard the hissing of Carillon's sword as he drew it from its sheath, but saw only the streaking gray form of the wolf as it hurtled silently across the space between them. The animal's jaws closed on Carillon's wrist.

Alix turned to run but the stranger caught her easily. Hands grasped her shoulders and spun her; she stared wide-eyed into a laughing face with yellow eyes.

Beast-eyes! she cried silently.

"Come now, *meijha,* do not struggle so," her captor said, grinning. A gold ornament gleamed in his left ear, flashing against black hair and bronzed skin. Alix was conscious of his soft sleeveless leather jerkin and bare arms as he held her against him. "You championed my race but a moment ago, *meijha.* Surely you do not lose your principles so quickly."

She froze in his hands, staring into his angular, high-planed face. "You are *Cheysuli!*"

"Aye," he agreed. "Finn. When I heard you defending my race to the heir of the man who nearly destroyed us, I could not bear to let the princeling force your beliefs against us. Too many will not hear the truth." He grinned at her. "I will tell you what truly happened, *meijha,* and why Shaine has called us accursed and outlawed."

"Shapechanger! *Demon!*" Carillon called furiously.

Alix twisted so she could see him, afraid he had been badly injured, but she saw only an angry young man on the ground, hitched up on one elbow as he cradled his wrist against his chest. The wolf, a big silver male, sat at his side. There was no question in Alix's mind the animal stood guard.

The Cheysuli's hands tightened on Alix and she winced. "I am no demon, princeling. Only a man, like yourself, though admittedly the gods like us better. If you would have us called demon-spawn and consign us to the netherworld, you had best look to the Mujhar first. He cried *qu'mahlin* on us, not the other way." The contempt in his voice sent a shiver through Alix. "And you make me think you wish to be his heir, princeling, in all things."

Color raced through Carillon's face and he moved as if to rise. The wolf tautened silently, amber eyes slitting, and after a moment the prince remained where he was. Alix saw pain and frustration in his face.

"Let me go to him," she said.

"To the princeling?" The Cheysuli laughed. "Are you his *meijha,* then? Well, and I had thought to make you mine."

She stiffened. "I am no man's light woman, if that is what your barbaric word means."

"It is the Old Tongue, *meijha;* a gift of the old gods. Once it was the only tongue in this land." His breath warmed her ear. "I will teach it to you."

"Let me go!"

"I have only just got you. I do not intend to let you go so quickly."

"Release her," Carillon ordered flatly.

Finn laughed joyously. "The princeling orders *me!* But now the Cheysuli no longer recognize the Mujhar's laws, my young lord, or his wishes. Shaine effectively severed our hereditary obedience to the Mujhar and his blood when he declared *qu'mahlin* on our race." The laughter died. "Perhaps we can return the favor, now we have his heir at hand."

"You have me, then," Carillon growled. "Release Alix."

The Cheysuli laughed again. "But it was the woman I came for, princeling. I have only got you in the bargain. And I do not intend to lose either of you." His hand slid across Alix's breast idly. "You both will be guests in a Cheysuli raiding camp this night."

"My father . . ." Alix whispered.

"Your father will come looking for you, *meijha,* and when he does not find you he will assume the beasts of the forest got you."

"And he will have the right of it!" she snapped.

His hand cupped her jaw and lifted it. "Already you join your princeling in cursing us."

"Aye!" she agreed. "When you behave like a beast there is little else I can do!"

The hand tightened until it nearly crushed her jaw. "Who is to blame for that, *meijha?*" He turned her head until she

was forced to look at Carillon. "You see before you the
heir to the man who drove us from our homeland, making
outlaws of warriors, denying us our rights. Is not Shaine the
Mujhar a maker of beasts, then, if you would call us that?"

"He is your liege lord!" Carillon hissed through gritted
teeth.

"No," Finn said coldly. "He is not. Shaine of Homana is
my persecutor, not my liege lord."

"He persecutes with reason!"

"*What* reason?"

Carillon's eyes narrowed. "A Cheysuli warrior—liege
man to my uncle the Mujhar—stole away a king's daughter." He smiled coldly, as angry as the Cheysuli. "That
practice, it seems, is still alive among your race. Even now
you steal another."

Finn matched Carillon's smile. "Perhaps, princeling, but
she is not a king's daughter. Only her father will miss her,
and her mother, and that will pass in time."

"My mother is dead," Alix said, then regretted speaking
at all. She took a careful breath. "If I go with you, willingly,
will you free Carillon?"

Finn laughed softly. "No, *meijha,* I will not. He is the
weapon the Cheysuli have needed these twenty-five years
of the *qu'mahlin,* for all he was born after it began. We
will use him."

Alix's eyes met Carillon's, and they realized the futility
of their arguments. Neither spoke.

"Come," said Finn. "I have men and horses waiting in
the forest. It is time we left this place."

Carillon got carefully to his feet, cradling the injured
wrist. He stood stiffly, taller than the black-haired warrior,
but somehow diminished before the fierce pride of the man.

"Your sword, princeling," Finn said quietly. "Take up
your sword and return it to its sheath."

"I would sooner sheathe it in your flesh."

"Aye," Finn agreed. "If you did not, you would not be
much of a man." Alix felt an odd tension in his body.
"Take up the sword, Carillon of Homana. It is yours, for
all that."

Carillon, warily eyeing the wolf, bent and retrieved the
blade. The ruby glinted as he slid the sword home awkwardly with his left hand.

Finn stared at the weapon and smiled oddly. "Hale's blade."

Carillon scowled at him. "My uncle gifted me with this sword last year. It was his before that. What do you say?"

When the Cheysuli did not answer immediately Alix looked sharply at him. She was startled to find bleakness in his yellow beast-eyes.

"Long before it was a Mujhar's blade it was a Cheysuli's. Hale made that sword, princeling, and gifted it to his liege lord, the man he had sworn a blood-oath of service to." He sighed. "And the prophecy of the Firstborn says it will one day be back in the hands of a *Cheysuli* Mujhar."

"You lie!"

Finn grinned mockingly. "*I* may lie, on occasion, but the prophecy does not. Come, my lord, allow my *lir* to escort you to your horse. Come."

Carillon, aware of the wolf's silent menace, went. Alix had no choice but to follow.

Chapter Two

Three other Cheysuli, Alix saw apprehensively, waited silently in the forest. Carillon's warhorse was with them. She cast a quick glance at the prince, judging his reaction, and saw his face was pale, jaw set so tightly she feared it might break. He seemed singularly dedicated to keeping himself apart from the Cheysuli even though he was in their midst.

Finn said something in a lyrical tongue she did not recognize and one of the warriors came forward with a strange horse for Carillon. He was being refused his own, and quick color rising in his face confirmed the insult.

"We know the reputation of Homanan warhorses," Finn said briefly. "You will not be given a chance to flee us so easily. Take this one, for now."

Silently Carillon accepted the reins and with careful effort was able to mount. Finn stared up at him from the ground, then moved to the prince and without a word tore a long strip of wool from Carillon's green cloak. He tossed it at him.

"Bind your wound, princeling. I will not lose you to death so easily."

Carillon took up the strip and did as told. He smiled grimly down at the yellow-eyed warrior. "When I am given the time, shapechanger, I will see the color of *your* blood."

Finn laughed and turned away. He grinned at Alix. "Well, *meijha,* we lack a horse for you. But mine will serve. I will enjoy the feel of you against my back."

Alix, both furious and frightened, only glared at him. His dark face twisted in an ironic smile and he took the reins of his own horse from another warrior. He gestured toward the odd gear on the animal's back. It did not quite resemble a Homanan saddle, with its large saddletree and cantle designed to hold in a fighting man, but served an identical purpose. Alix hesitated, then placed her bare foot in the leather stirrup and hoisted herself into the saddle. Before she could say anything to prevent him, Finn vaulted onto the horse's rump behind her. She felt his arms come around her waist to take up the reins.

"You see, *meijha?* You can hardly avoid me."

She did her best. The ride was long and she was wearied from riding stiffly upright before him when at last Finn halted the horse. She stared in surprise at the encampment before her, for it was well hidden in the thick, shadowed forests.

Woven tents of greens, browns, grays, and slates huddled in the twilight, nearly indistinguishable from the trees and underbrush of the forest and the tumbled piles of mountain boulders. Small fires glowed flickeringly across the narrow clearing.

Alix straightened as Finn reined in the horse. She turned quickly to search for Carillon, lost among the black-haired, yellow-eyed Cheysuli warriors, but Finn prevented her. His left arm came around her waist snugly, possessive as he leaned forward, pressing against her rigid back.

"Your princeling will recover, *meijha.* He is in some pain now, but it will pass." His voice dropped to a provocative whisper. "Or I will *make* it."

She ignored him, sensing a slow, defiant—and somehow frightening—rage building within her. "Why did you set your wolf on him?"

"He drew Hale's sword, *meijha.* Doubtless he knows how to use it, even against a Cheysuli." He laughed softly. "Perhaps *especially* against a Cheysuli. But we are too few as it is. My death would not serve."

"You set a *beast* on him!"

"Storr is no beast. He is my *lir.* And he only did it to keep Carillon from getting himself slain, for I would have taken his life to keep my own."

She glanced at the wolf waiting so silently and patiently by the horse. "Your—*lir?* What do you say?"

"That wolf is my *lir.* It is a Cheysuli thing, which you could not possibly understand. There is no Homanan word for our bond." He shrugged against her. "Storr is a part of me, and I him."

"Shapechanger . . ." she whispered involuntarily.

"Cheysuli," he whispered back.

"Is any wolf this—*lir?*"

"No. I am bonded with Storr only, and he was chosen by the old gods to be my *lir.* They are born knowing it. Each warrior has only one, but it can be any creature." He picked a leaf from Alix's hair, even as she stiffened. "It is too new for you to understand, *meijha.* Do not try."

She felt him slide from behind and a moment later he pulled her from the horse. Alix stifled a blurt of surprise and felt each sinew tighten as his hand crept around her neck.

"You may release me," she said quickly. "I can hardly run from a wolf."

His hand slid from her. She felt her braid lifted from her neck and his lips upon her nape. "Then you are learning already, *meijha.*"

Before she could protest he turned her face to his and bent her head back as his mouth came down on hers. Alix struggled against him with no effect except to feel herself held more securely. He was far too strong for her, stronger than she had ever imagined a man could be.

You should not, lir, said a quiet voice in Alix's mind.

She stiffened in fear, wondering how Finn spoke without saying anything. Then she was pushed from him unexpectedly as he moved back a single step. She saw he had not spoken, silently or aloud, but whatever had formed the words had greatly upset him. His eyes, watching her warily, were slitted. Slowly he looked at the wolf.

"Storr . . ." he said softly, in amazement.

You should not, said the tone again.

Finn swung back to her, suddenly angry. "Who are you?"

"What?"

His hand clasped her braid and tugged sharply, jerking at her scalp. "What manner of woman are you, to draw *Storr's* concern?"

The wolf? she wondered blankly.

Finn peered closely at her, fingers painfully closing on her jaw until she had no choice but to look directly into his shadowed face. The wolf-shaped gold earring gleamed.

"You are dark enough for one of us, but you have not the eyes," he muttered. "Brown, like half of Homana. Yet

why else would Storr protest my pleasure? It is not for the
lir to do."

"I am none of yours!" she hissed, profoundly shaken. "I
am daughter to Torrin of Homana. Do not *curse* me by
naming me Cheysuli, shapechanger!"

His hand tightened and she cried out. Faintly she heard
Carillon's worried tone carry across the way. "Alix!"

Finn released her so curtly she stumbled back. "Go to
your princeling, *meijha.* Tend his wound like a proper
light woman."

She opened her mouth to protest his unseemly words,
then bit them back and whirled, hastening to Carillon. He
stood by his Cheysuli mount, unsteady, cradling his bound
wrist against his chest. His face, even in the shadows, was
drawn with pain.

"Did he harm you?" he asked harshly.

Alix shook her head, recalling the anger in Finn's hand
upon her chin. "No, I am well enough. But what of you?"

He half-shrugged. "It is my sword arm. Without it I am
not much of a prince, nor even a man. Otherwise I would
not speak of it."

She smiled and touched his uninjured arm gently. "We
have nowhere else to go, my lord. Let us move into the
firelight where I can see to your wrist."

Finn came to them silently and gestured toward a green
tent not far from where they stood. Mutely Alix followed
the Cheysuli leader, keeping one hand on Carillon's arm.
That he had said anything at all about his wound worried
her, for it indicated the wolf bite was worse than she
suspected.

Finn watched them kneel down on a blue woven rug
before his tent and then disappeared within, ignoring them.
Alix cast a quick glance around the small encampment,
seeking a way out, but there were too many warriors. And
Carillon's face was already fever-flushed and warm when
she set her hand against it.

"We go nowhere, yet," she said softly.

"We must," he answered, carefully unwrapping his injured wrist. The flesh was scored with teeth marks. The
bleeding had stopped, but the wound was open and
seeping.

"We have no choice," Alix whispered. "Perhaps in the morning, when you are better."

Light from the small fire cairn built before the tent flickered over his jaw. She saw the stubborn set to the prominent bones. "Alix, I will not remain in a shapechanger camp. They are demons."

"They are also our captors," she agreed wryly. "Do you think to escape them so easily? You could hardly get half a league with this wolf-wound."

"*You* could. You could reach your father's croft. He could ride to Mujhara for help."

"Alone . . ." she whispered. "And so far . . ."

He rubbed his unwounded forearm across his brow. "I do not wish to send you into the darkness alone, no matter how far the distance is. But I have no choice, Alix. I would go myself, willingly, as I think you know." He lifted his bloody arm. "I do recognize my own limitations." His smile came swiftly, and left as quickly. "I have faith in you, my girl, more so than in any man who might be with me in this."

Pain squeezed her heart so that it nearly burst. In the brief weeks she had known him he had become everything to her, a hero she could worship from the depths of her romantic soul and a man she could dream of in the long nights. To have him look at her so warmly and with such trust nearly undid her convictions about not allowing him to see her vulnerability.

"Carillon . . ."

"You must," he said gently. "We cannot remain here. My uncle, when he learns of this, will send mounted troops immediately to destroy this nest of demons. Alix, you must *go.*"

"Go where?" demanded Finn from the tent's doorflap.

Alix twitched in surprise at his stealth, but Carillon glared at the Cheysuli. Somehow Finn seemed more substantial, a thing of the darkness, illuminated by the firelight dancing off the gold on his arms and in his ear. Alix forced herself to look away from his yellow eyes and stared instead at the earring half-hidden in thick black hair. It, like the armbands he wore above the elbows, bore a skillful figure of a wolf.

For his lir . . . she realized blankly, and wondered anew at the strangeness of his race.

The Cheysuli smiled mockingly and moved to stand over them. His steps were perfectly silent and hardly left a mark in the dirt.

He is like the shadows themselves . . .

"My prince," he said vibrantly, "you must doubtless believe this insubstantial girl could make her way through a hostile forest without aid of any sort. Were she Cheysuli she could, for we are creatures of the forests instead of cities, but she is not. And I have gone to far too much trouble to lose either of you so quickly."

"You have no right to keep us, shapechanger," Carillon said.

"We have every right, princeling! Your uncle has done what he could to slay every Cheysuli in Homana—a land *we* made! He has come closer than even he knows, for it is true our numbers are sadly reduced. From thousands we are hundreds. But it has been fortunate, lately, that Shaine is more concerned with the war Bellam of Solinde wishes to levy against Homana. He needs must steep himself in battle plans again, and forget *us* for a time."

"So," Carillon said on a sighing breath, "you will ransom me back to the Mujhar?"

Finn stroked his smooth jaw, considering, grinning at them both. "That is not for me to say. It is a Cheysuli Clan Council decision. But I will let you know how we view your disposition."

Alix straightened. "And what of me?"

He stared sightlessly at her a long moment. Then he dropped to one knee and lifted her braid against his lips in a seductive manner. "You, *meijha,* will remain with us. The Cheysuli place much value on a woman, for we have need of them to breed more of us." He ignored her gasp of shock and outrage. "Unlike the Homanans, who may keep a woman for only a night, we keep her forever."

Alix recoiled from him, jerking her braid free of his hand. Fear drove into her chest so quickly she could hardly breathe, and she felt a trembling begin in her bones.

He could do this, she realized. *He could. He is a demon . . .*

"Let me go," she pleaded. "Do not keep me with you."

His black brows lifted. "Do you sicken of my company so soon, *meijha?* You will injure me with such words."

"Alix is none of yours," Carillon said coldly. "If you seek to ransom me, you will do the same for her. And if her father cannot meet your price, the Mujhar will pay it from his own coffers."

Finn did not bother to look at Carillon. He stared penetratingly at Alix. "She is a prize of war, princeling. My own personal war against the Mujhar. And I would never take gold from a man who could order his men to slay an entire race."

"I am no *prize!*" Alix cried. "I am a woman! Not a broodmare to be judged by her ability to bear young or bring gold. You will not treat me so!"

Finn caught one of her hands and held it, browned fingers encircling her wrist gently. She tried to pull away, but he exerted just enough force to keep her hand imprisoned.

"I treat you how I choose," he told her. "But I would have you know *meijhas* are honored among the Cheysuli. That a woman has no *cheysul*—husband—and yet takes a man as mate does not make her a whore. Tell me, is that not a better life than the light women of Mujhara receive?"

Her hand jerked in his grasp. "Let me go!"

"You are not the first woman won in such a fashion," he said solemnly, "and doubtless you will not be the last. But for now, you are mine to do with as I will."

Carillon reached out to grab Finn's arm, cursing him angrily, but the pain of his wrist prevented him. His face went horribly white and he stopped moving instantly, cradling the wounded arm. His breath hissed between his teeth.

Finn released Alix. "If you will allow it, I will heal the wound."

"Heal!"

"Aye," the Cheysuli said quietly. "It is a gift of the old gods. We have healing arts at our beck."

Alix rubbed at the place he had held on her arm. "What do you say, shapechanger?"

"Cheysuli," he corrected. "I can summon the earth magic."

"Sorcery!" Carillon exclaimed.

Finn shrugged. "Aye, but it is a gift, for all that. And used only for good."

"I will not suffer your touch."

Finn moved and caught Carillon's wounded arm in a firm grasp. The prince winced away, prepared to make a furious protest, but said nothing as astonishment crept across his face.

"Carillon?" Alix whispered.

"The pain . . ." he said dazedly.

"The earth magic eases pain," Finn said matter-of-factly, kneeling before the pale prince. "But it can also do much more."

Alix stared open-mouthed as the Cheysuli held the lacerated arm. His yellow eyes had gone oddly piercing, yet detached, and she realized her escape lay open before her. He had somehow gone beyond them both.

She moved as if to go, coiling her legs to push herself upright, but the expression on Carillon's face prevented her. She saw amazement, confusion, and revulsion, and the beginnings of a protest. But she also saw acknowledgment of the truth in Finn's words, and before she could voice a question, afraid of the sorcery the shapechanger used, Finn released Carillon's wrist.

"It is done, princeling. It will heal cleanly, painlessly, though you will have scars to show for your foolishness."

"Foolishness!" Carillon exclaimed.

Finn smiled grimly "It is ever foolishness for a man to threaten a Cheysuli before his *lir*." Finn nodded his head at the silver wolf who lay silently by the tent. "Storr will let no man harm me, even at the cost of his own life." He frowned suddenly, eyes somber. "Though that has its price."

"Then one day I will slay you both," Carillon said clearly.

Alix felt the sudden flare of tension between the two, though she could not put a name to it. And when Finn smiled ironically she felt chilled, recoiling from his twisted mouth.

"You may try, princeling, but I do not think you will accomplish it. We are meant for something other than death at one another's hands, we two."

"What do you say?" Alix demanded.

He glanced at her. "You do not know the prophecy of the Firstborn, *meijha*. When you have learned it, you will have your answers." He rose in a fluid motion that put her in mind of a supple mountain cat. "And it will give you more questions."

"What prophecy?" she asked.

"The one which gives the Cheysuli purpose." He stretched out his right hand in a palm-up, spread-fingered gesture. "You will understand what this is another time. For now, I must see my *rujholli*. You may sleep here or within my tent; it is all one to me. Storr will keep himself by you while I am gone."

He turned and walked away silently, fading into the shadows, lost to sight instantly. Alix shivered as the wolf rose and came to the blue blanket. He lay down near them, watching them with an odd equanimity in his amber eyes.

Alix recalled Finn's odd words earlier; his strange reaction to the gentle tone she had heard in her mind. Carefully, apprehensively, she formed her own.

Wolf? she asked. *Do you speak?*

Nothing echoed in her head. The wolf, called *lir,* did not seem so fierce now as he rested his jaws on his paws, pink tongue lolling idly. But the intelligence in his feral eyes, so unlike a man's, could not be ignored.

Lir? she questioned.

I am called Storr, he said briefly.

Alix jerked and recoiled on the blanket, fighting down nausea. She stared at the animal, horrified, but he had not moved. Something like a smile gleamed in his eyes.

Do not be afraid of me. There is no need. Not for you.

"By the gods . . ." she whispered.

Carillon looked at her. "Alix?"

She could not take her eyes from the wolf to look at Carillon. A shiver of fear ran through her as she considered the madness of her discovery. It was not possible.

"Alix," he said again.

Finally she looked at him. His face was pale, puzzled; fatigue dulled his blue eyes. But even were he alert and well, she could not tell him she heard the wolf speak. He would never believe her, and she was not certain *she* did.

"I am only confused," she said softly, mostly to herself. "Confused."

He shifted the arm into a more comfortable position, running a tentative finger over the puffy teeth marks left by the wolf. But even she could see it had the look of healing to it.

"You must leave," he said.

She stared at him. "You still wish me to go, even after what the shapechanger said?"

Carillon smiled. "He sought only to frighten you."

"The wolf . . ."

"The shapechanger will not leave him with us forever. When you have the chance, you must go."

She watched Carillon ease himself down on the blue blanket, stretching out long legs booted to the thighs and wrapping the green cloak over his arm.

"Carillon . . ."

"Aye, Alix?" he asked on a weary sigh.

She bit at her lip, ashamed of her hesitation. "I will go. When I have the chance."

He smiled faintly and fell into an exhausted slumber. Alix looked at him sadly.

What is it about an ill or injured man that turns a woman into an acquiescent fool? she wondered. *Why is it I am suddenly willing to do anything for him?* She sighed and picked at the wrinkles in her gown. *But he would go himself, were he well enough, so I will do as he asks.*

She looked curiously at the wolf, wondering if he could hear her thoughts. But the animal only watched her idly, as if he had nothing better to do.

Perhaps he does not, she decided and drew up her knees to stare sightlessly into the flames.

Chapter Three

The fire had died to glowing coals when she felt an odd touch in her mind, almost like a probing. It was feather-light and very gentle, but terrifying. Alix jerked her head off her knees and stared around wide-eyed, afraid it was some form of Cheysuli torture.

Nothing was there. The camp was oddly empty, for, like Finn, each warrior had gone to a single slate-colored tent at the far end of the small encampment.

Alix looked at the wolf and found his amber eyes fastened on her. "No," she whispered.

The faint touch faded from her mind. Alix put a trembling hand to her ear. "You cannot speak to me. I cannot hear you."

You hear, said the warm tone.

"What do you do to me?" she demanded violently, struggling to keep her voice down so as not to waken Carillon.

I seek, he answered.

She closed her eyes but was still intensely aware of his gaze. "I am gone mad," she whispered.

No, said the tone. *You are only weary, and frightened, and very much alone. But there is no need.*

"You said you sought something, wolf." Alix took a trembling breath, giving in to her madness for the moment. "What do you seek in me?"

Storr lifted his head from his paws. *I cannot say.*

His clear gaze made her uneasy. Carillon slept soundly, lines of pain washed from his face, and she wished he could give her the words she needed to banish this strangeness from her mind. She wished also she could lose herself in such soothing sleep, but every fiber in her body was stretched taut with apprehension and a longing to run away.

Wolf? she asked silently.

He said nothing. After a moment he rose and shook himself, rippling his silver coat. He sent her an oddly intent glance, then padded away into the darkness, as deliberate as any dog among his people.

Alix stared after him. A quick glance told her no one was near; she saw no other animals. She looked longingly at Carillon's unmoving form a moment, wanting to smooth the hair from his hot brow, but she kept herself from it. Such intimacy, if it ever occurred, would have to begin with him. She was too far from his rank to initiate anything.

She released a rushing breath, trying to control the raggedness of it, and got to her feet. She shook her skirts free of folds, curling her bare toes away from the cool ground. Her feet were cold, bruised, but she could waste no time regretting her lost slippers.

Silently Alix slipped into the darkness of the encampment. She was no shadow-wraith like the Cheysuli, but she was forest-raised and could move with little noise. Carefully she eased past the last tent and entered the clustered trees.

Needles and twigs snapped beneath her feet, digging painfully into her flesh. Alix bit her lip against the sharp, nagging pain and went on, ignoring the fear in her soul. A shiver coursed down her body as she moved through the silent forest. She longed for the warmth and safety of her father's croft and the hot spiced cider he brewed.

It is for Carillon, she whispered silently. *For him. Because a prince has asked me.* Irrationally she nearly laughed aloud. *But he does not have to be a prince to bid me serve him. I would do it willingly.*

She grasped a tree and felt the rough bark bite into her palms as she dug fingernails into it. Her forehead rested against the tree as she smiled, inwardly laughing at her conflicting emotions. Fear was still the primary element in her soul, but so was her wish to do as Carillon asked. She was fair caught in the trap that bound so many women.

A twig snapped. Alix jerked her head up and stared into the trees, suddenly so badly frightened she lost all track of other emotions. Her fingers clutched spasmodically at the bark and she sucked in a ragged breath.

The wolf stood in the shadows, little more than a faint outline against the darkness beyond. For a moment she felt fear slip away, for somehow Storr did not threaten her;

then she realized it was not Storr. This one was larger, ruddy instead of silver. Its yellow eyes held a gleam of invitation.

The fear came back. Alix pressed her body against the tree, seeking its protection. A broken bough jabbed into her thigh but she ignored it, wishing only she could somehow scale the tree into branches far above the ground.

The wolf moved slowly forward into a small clearing. Moonlight set its rich red pelt to glowing, pinpointing yellow eyes into an eerie intelligence. Teeth gleamed, and Alix saw its taunting smile.

The wolf began to change.

Cold, primitive fear crawled through her mind. The form before her eyes altered, subtly blurring outline and color into a shapeless void. And then Finn stood before her.

"I said you would not win free of us," he told her calmly. "*Meijha,* you must stay."

Alix shivered. Finn was whole again, a man, with yellow eyes glinting in high good humor and heavy gold bands gleaming faintly against folded bare arms.

She gripped the tree. "You . . ."

He spread his hands slowly, unaggressively. "Do you question what you have seen, *meijha?*" His smile was mocking. "Do not. Your eyes have not deceived you."

Alix felt nausea roil her stomach and send bile into her throat. She choked it back down. "You were a *wolf!*"

"Aye," he agreed, unoffended by her horror. "The old gods gifted us with the ability to take *lir*-shape, once properly bonded with an animal. We can assume a like shape at will." He sounded very serious, incongruous in him. "It is something we honor the gods for."

"Shapechanger!"

Finn's mouth twisted wryly. "Aye, that is the Homanan name for us, when they do not call us demons. But we are not sorcerers, *meijha;* we are not servants of the dark gods. We leave that to the Ihlini." He shrugged. "We are merely men . . . with a god-gift in the blood."

Alix could not deal with it; with him. She stared fixedly at him a moment, still stunned by the enormity of what she had seen. Then she scraped herself around the tree and ran.

Underbrush tore at her gown and welted skin was already prickling with fright as she raced through the trees.

A limb slashed across her face. Alix ignored it all in her panicked flight, seeking only to escape the man, the *demon,* who was everything Carillon had said.

She could hear no pursuit over the noise of her own flight, but it served only to increase her fear. A shape-changer would hardly make noise as he stalked his prey.

Alix stumbled over a log and fell across it, stomach driven against her spine. Breath left her in a whooping rush but she tried to lift herself frantically. Pinpricks of light flashed before her eyes as she struggled to her feet, lungs sucking at air she could not find.

She was driven down again by a hard body from behind.

Alix lay half-stunned, still out of breath. Her face burned from a bleeding welt on her cheek. She lay pressed against the cool ground, sobbing, as she tried to regain her breath, and helpless in his arms.

Her body was lifted from the forest floor and turned over. She lay very still as he set her on her back, unable to close her eyes as he knelt over her. Faint light filtered through the trees. His earring winked coldly.

"Have I not already said escape is impossible?" he asked. "I am Cheysuli."

Her chest hurt, but air was beginning to creep into it again. Alix swallowed painfully. "Please . . . let me go."

"I have said before how much trouble I have gone to get you, and to keep you. At least let me have some repayment for it." His fingers touched the cut on her face and she winced. "You did not need to run from me, *meijha.*"

She shivered. *This man becomes a wolf at will.* She looked at his hands for signs of the wolf-mark. Finn grinned at her with a man's teeth in a wolfish leer.

"When I wear a man's shape, *meijha,* I am all man. Shall I prove it to you?"

Alix stiffened as he leaned closer, hands spread across the ground on either side of her shoulders. If she pushed upward it would be to place herself directly in his arms, and he knew it.

"No!" she cried as he leaned closer.

His eyes, oddly feral, looked directly into hers. "I have watched you for some time, *meijha.* It was a simple raiding mission we came on days ago, to replenish our Keep. But I found prey of a different sort."

She closed her eyes. "Please . . ."

His knees were on either side of her thighs, holding her prisoner. He bent over her until his lips were nearly touching her face.

"Shaine's soldiers have slain nearly all of us, *meijha,* and they have not spared our women. What is a proud race to do when it sees its own demise? We must get more of us on the women we have, and take others where we can, even if they be unwilling."

Her mind flinched from his words, denying them even as she heard the ring of truth in his voice. The Mujhar's purge had begun twenty-five years before. She had grown up knowing the Cheysuli must die, for all she believed the Mujhar's actions unfair in the wake of what her father had said. But now she was faced with a shapechanger who spoke of force, and she was more than willing to forsake her principles to win free of him.

Her fingers on his arm were no more than a feather touch, instinctively seductive. She saw sudden wariness in his eyes and the intensity in his body poised over her.

"Must you make the tales of your savagery and bestial appetites true?" she whispered. "Must you so readily prove to me you are no better than the demon-spawn others name you?"

Finn scowled at her. "Soft words will not gainsay me, *meijha.*"

Her fingers tightened. "Please . . . let me go free."

He smelled of leather and gold and demand. *"Meijha,"* he said roughly, "I cannot . . ."

She opened her mouth to cry out as he pressed a knee between her thighs. But before she could make a sound the familiar tone she associated with Storr came quietly into their minds.

Lir, *you should not.*

It drove Finn from Alix. He shoved her harshly against the ground as she hitched up on one arm, cursing violently beneath his breath, and she winced against the force of his hand against her shoulder. He knelt by her, stiff with tension, and she saw he looked at the wolf.

Storr waited in a thick copse of trees, staring unwaveringly at Finn. Alix could only bless the wolf's timely appearance and intervention, for all she could not comprehend it. Slowly she eased herself onto one elbow.

"Storr!" Finn hissed.

She is not for you.

Finn turned on her, furious. "Who are you?"

She kept her voice steady with effort. "I have said."

He settled one hand around her vulnerable throat. It rested without pressure, promising only, but she felt the violence in his body.

"You have said nothing! Who are you?"

"I am a croft-girl! My father is Torrin and my mother was Leyda. He was arms-master to Shaine the Mujhar before he turned to the land." She glared at him. "I am his daughter. Nothing more."

Finn's eyes narrowed. "Arms-master to the Mujhar. When?"

Alix took a weary breath. "I am seventeen. He left the Mujhar's service a year before I was born, and took a valley girl to wife. But I cannot say how long he served Shaine. He does not speak of those days."

"Does he not?" Finn said musingly, taking his hand from her throat. He sat back on his haunches and frowned thoughtfully, pushing heavy black hair from his face.

Alix, feeling safe for the moment, sat upright and straightened her twisted gown. The welt on her face stung, as did the scratches and bruises on her legs, but she touched none of them. She would not give him the satisfaction.

Finn stared at her impassively. "Do you know the story of the *qu'mahlin?*"

"There are two of them." She covered her legs decorously.

He grinned. "Aye. And I heard you speak of one to the princeling, even when he would dissuade you of it. Which do you believe?"

His change in attitude made her wary, but also relieved. No longer did she fear he would pounce on her like a mountain cat taking a rabbit. With renewed confidence she told him.

"Shaine's daughter broke the betrothal made between Homana and Solinde. It would have allied the lands after centuries of warfare, but she would have none of Bellam's son, Ellic. She went instead with a Cheysuli."

"Hale," Finn agreed. "Shaine's sworn liege man."

Alix shrugged. "I cannot say. I only overheard my father speaking of it once, to my mother, when he thought I could not hear."

"It is true, *meijha*," he said seriously. "Hale took Lindir with him into the forests of Homana, but only because she asked him to, and only because she wanted no marriage with Ellic of Solinde."

She scowled at him, strangely confident in the face of his new self. "What has this to do with me?"

"Nothing," he told her bluntly. "It has to do with me, and why you are here. What I said before is true. The *qu'mahlin* has slain most of the warriors and many of the women. As a race we are nearly destroyed, because of Shaine. And now the daughter of the Mujhar's former arms-master—who witnessed the very beginnings of the *qu'mahlin*—is in my hands." He smiled slowly, gesturing. She saw again the spread fingers and lifting palm. "It is *tahlmorra*, perhaps."

"What do you say?"

"Fate. Destiny. It is a Cheysuli word meaning what is meant will happen, and cannot be gainsaid, for it is in the hands of the gods." Finn smiled ironically at her. "It has to do with the prophecy."

"Prophecy," she muttered in disgust, weary of his attitude and hinted-at knowledge. She looked at the patient wolf. "What has Storr to do with me?"

Finn scowled. "I cannot say, but it is something I would learn. Now." He fixed her with a baleful glare. "Why does he keep me from you?"

She glared back. "That *I* cannot say, shapechanger, save to compliment his actions."

He startled her by laughing. Then he got to his feet and reached for her, pulling her up. She stood stiffly, wary of him, ignoring the provocative appraising look in his eyes.

Storr yawned. *I think she is not as frightened of you as she would have you believe, lir.*

Finn smiled at the wolf, then looked back at her. His dark brows rose. "Are you so brave, *meijha?* Do you dissemble before me?"

Alix slanted a reproving glance at the wolf. "He knows me not at all, shapechanger. Do not listen to him."

"To my own *lir?*" He laughed. "If I forsake Storr, I forsake my soul. You will learn that, soon enough."

Storr shook himself and padded into the clearing. *Enough,* lir; *you do not understand the girl. And she does not understand what is in her blood.*

"My blood?" Alix asked, shaken.

Finn's eyes narrowed as the equanimity left his face. He turned slowly to her, reaching to close a wide hand on her jaw. "What do you say?"

She swallowed, suddenly frightened again. She fought back a shudder at his touch. "The wolf. He said something of my blood. What does he say?"

The hand tightened until she winced. "My wolf?" he hissed. "You *heard* him?"

She closed her eyes. "Aye."

Finn released her. Alix opened her eyes and found him staring at her speculatively. The gold in his ear glinted as he shoved hair back from his face. Slowly he smiled.

"Then the story is true."

"Story?"

He folded his arms over his chest and grinned at her. "Your crofter father did not tell your mother all he knew, or else you did not hear it."

"What do you say?"

Finn flicked a glance at Storr. "Do I have the right of it, *lir?*"

Can you not see it for yourself?

The warrior laughed to himself and turned back to her. Playfully he caught her braid in one hand and threaded blunt fingers into the loosened plait.

"You hear Storr, *meijha,* because you are only half Homanan. The other half is Cheysuli."

"No!"

He frowned. "But even for all that, it is strange. The women do not take *lir,* nor do they converse with them. Yet it only serves to make me certain who you are."

Alix felt a renewal of fear. "I have said who I am. You speak lies to me."

He tugged on her braid. "You have much to learn, *meijha.* You have grown up apart from your clan. You are sadly lacking in the wisdom and customs of the Cheysuli."

"I am *Homanan!*"

"Then say to me how it is you can hear my *lir* when no other can, save myself."

She opened her mouth to reply angrily but no sound came out. After a moment she jerked her braid free of him and turned away, hugging herself for warmth and security. She stiffened as his hands came down on her shoulders.

"Meijha," he said softly, "it is not so bad a fate. We are children of the Firstborn, who were sired by the old gods. The Homanans are nothing when you understand the heritage *we* claim."

"I am not a shapechanger!"

Fingers dug into her shoulders. "You are Cheysuli. *Cheysuli.* Else Storr would not offer you his protection."

"You accept the word of a wolf?" Abruptly Alix clapped hands over her mouth and spun, staring at him. "What do I say? What do I hear from my own tongue?" She swallowed heavily. "He is a wolf. A *beast!* And you are demon-sent to make me believe otherwise!"

"I am not a demon," Finn said, affronted. "Nor is Storr. I have said what I am, and what he is, and—by all the old gods!—what *you* are. Now, come with me."

She wrenched away from his reaching hand. "Do not touch me!"

Finn glared at her. "Your blood has saved you from my attentions, *meijha,* for a time. Do not seek to anger me, or I may renew them."

Alix stiffened as he took her arm and led her through the trees. He brought her to a slate-colored tent set in a tumbled circle of stone. The fire cairn still burned next to a blood-red rug, and she dragged her eyes from it in time to come face-to-face with a hawk perching on a staff before the tent. She stumbled back, gasping.

The bird was large, even with wings folded. He was a myriad of rich browns and golds, with dark eyes that watched her, half-lidded. His deadly, curving beak shone in the muted firelight, and she felt a whisper of awe and appreciation in her mind.

A man who has such a lir *is powerful indeed . . .*

"Cai," Finn said quietly. "This is my brother's pavilion. He is clan-leader, and needs to be told who you are."

Wearily Alix rubbed a grimy hand across her brow. "And what will you tell him, shapechanger?"

"That Hale's daughter has come back to us."

She felt the strength pour out of her limbs. "Hale's . . ."

His eyes were bright and mocking. "What do you think I told you of Lindir and the Cheysuli she wanted? You are their daughter."

Alix felt very cold. She hugged herself against his words. "No."

"You have only to ask my *lir*."

"A wolf!"

"The *lir* are kin to the old gods, *meijha*. They know many things we do not."

"No."

He sighed. "Wait here, *rujholla*. I will speak to Duncan first."

Anger spurred her out of her immobility. "What do you call me *now*, shapechanger?"

"*Rujholla?*" His smile faded into regret. "It is Cheysuli—the Old Tongue—for sister." He sighed. "Hale was my father, also."

Chapter Four

When Finn at last pulled the pavilion doorflap aside and motioned her inside, Alix went numbly, without protest. She had considered, briefly, running again, but his words had dulled her senses. She was incapable of making a decision. She answered his beckoning hand.

First she saw only the torch in the corner, squinting against its acrid smoke. Then Alix's eyes fell on the seated man who held a compact bow in his hands. Transfixed, she stared at his hands; firm and brown, long-fingered and supple. Slowly he smoothed fine oil into the dark wood, rubbing it to a gleaming patina of age and richness. As she stared he put aside the bow and waited.

He was much like Finn, she saw, recognizing characteristic features of the Cheysuli race. But there was something more in the bones of his face. Promised strength, calm intelligence, and the same inherent command she saw maturing in Carillon.

He rose smoothly to his feet and she saw he was taller than Finn; long-boned and less heavy. His face was wide-browed with a narrow nose, with the same high cheekbones and smooth planes as Finn's. Like his brother he wore a sleeveless jerkin and leather leggings, but his gold armbands bore the sweeping image of a magnificent hawk, lined with odd runes. At his left ear hung a golden hawk with wings outspread.

Alix straightened under his calm perusal, lifting her chin as she tried to regain some of her vanished composure. He put out a hand and turned her head so the torchlight fell on her cheek.

"What has happened to your face?"

His voice was untroubled, smooth and low. Alix was taken aback by his question. "A tree limb, shapechanger."

Something glinted in his eyes as she used a purposely rude tone. For a moment she was very afraid.

This man is more subtle than Finn, she thought apprehensively, *and far less predictable.*

He released her chin. "How did a tree limb come to desire the taste of your skin?"

She slid a look at Finn, who remained exceedingly silent. But the other man saw the exchange and laughed softly, surprising her. It also drew quick resentment from her.

"Do *you* propose to force me, shapechanger, as your brother intended?"

He studied her solemnly. "I force no woman. Did Finn?"

Alix gritted her teeth. "He tried. He wished to. The wolf would not allow it."

"The *lir* are often much wiser than we," he said significantly.

Alix was shocked as she saw dark color move through Finn's face. For a moment her perception of him altered through the eyes of his older brother. Alix saw him as a rash young man instead of a fierce, threatening warrior. The image surprised her.

"Shapechanger . . ." she began.

"My name is Duncan. Calling me by it will not make you accursed, girl."

She recoiled from his reprimand and answered glumly, "What is it you want of me, now I am made prisoner?"

Duncan's lips twitched. "If you are indeed Hale's daughter, you are no prisoner. You are of the clan, girl."

"No."

Finn shifted. "Do you see, *rujho?* She will not listen."

"Then I will have to convince her."

Alix blanched and drew away from him. He let her get as far as the doorflap, then smoothly reached out and caught her arm.

"If you will remain with me, I will answer the questions in your mind. This is new for you. Understanding, I promise, will come with time."

His hand pulled her steadily away from the doorflap. Alix was frightened again. "I do not believe what he has said. I am Homanan. I am not Cheysuli."

"If you will be seated, I will tell you a story," Duncan said quietly. "I am no *shar tahl* to give you the birthlines and the prophecy, but I can tell you much of what you must know." His eyes flicked to Finn. "Leave her with me. You had best tend to Carillon."

Finn smiled crookedly. "The princeling sleeps, *rujho*. The earth magic has removed his cares for a time." He straightened under the silent command. "But I will see to him, for all that. Tend her well, *rujho;* she was gently reared."

His departure left Alix alone in the pavilion with Duncan. She waited mutely, unable to force her mind into coherent thought.

Duncan gestured to a spotted gray pelt on the floor and she assented silently, gathering her skirts about her knees as she sat. "What will you do with me?"

He stood over her, arms folded. The torch painted his dark angular face and danced in his yellow eyes. Like Finn, he wore his black hair cut to his neck, where it fell loosely. Unlike Finn, he did not seem so inherently violent.

Duncan settled himself cross-legged before her, hands resting on his knees. "I do nothing with you save welcome you to your clan. Do you expect to be slain?"

She stared at her own hands, clasped tightly in her lap. "You are shapechangers. I have been raised to fear you. What else can I expect?"

"Finn said your *jehan* was arms-master to Shaine when the *qu'mahlin* began. Surely he has not raised you to believe the lies." His calm voice forced her to look at him. "Torrin was a faithful man, and honorable. He would not plant the seeds of untruth, even at Shaine's bidding."

"You speak as if you know my father."

Duncan shook his head. "I never met him. I know few Homanans, now, because of Shaine's *qu'mahlin*. But Hale spoke of him when he came to the Keep."

"I do not understand."

He sighed. "It will take much time. But first you must believe *Hale* is your father. Not Torrin."

Her chin rose stubbornly. "I cannot accept that."

Duncan scowled at her, suddenly very like Finn. "Foolishness has no place here. Will you listen?"

"I will listen."

But it does not mean I will believe.

He seemed to hear her rebellious, unspoken words. For

a moment Alix was nonplussed by the feeling but dismissed it quickly as Duncan began the story.

"Hale took Lindir into the forests. Her *jehana*—Shaine's wife, Ellinda—died soon after. Shaine took another wife, who miscarried three times and then bore him a stillborn son, which made her barren. The Mujhar claims it was Cheysuli sorcery that stole his daughter, slew his first wife, and denied his second living children." Duncan paused. "And that began the *qu'mahlin.*"

"War," she said softly.

"The *qu'mahlin* is more than war. It is annihilation for the Cheysuli race. The Mujhar wants every last one of us slain; the race destroyed." His yellow eyes met hers. "His decree touches even his granddaughter."

Alix felt color drain from her face. "Shaine's granddaughter . . ."

"Your *jehana* was Lindir of Homana. You are the Mujhar's granddaughter."

"No. No, you tell me lies."

Duncan smiled for the first time. "I do not lie, small one. But if you wish, you may ask my *lir.* Cai has told me you have a gift of the gods, and can converse with all the *lir.*"

"The hawk . . ." she whispered.

A golden tone stirred within her mind, softly. *You are Hale's daughter,* liren, *and bloodkin to us all. Do not deny your heritage, or the gift of the gods.*

Duncan saw the anguish and fear in her face. He touched her trembling hands gently. "If you wish to rest, I can finish the story another time."

"No!" she said wildly. "No, I will listen! What more can you say that will not destroy what comprehension I have left to me?"

He took his hand away. "Hale was slain in the *qu'mahlin* by Shaine's troops, as he sought from the beginning. Lindir, carrying a child, returned to her *jehan* to beg his understanding. She wanted shelter for her child." Duncan's face was grim. "The Mujhar needed an heir. He had no son, and his lady-wife made barren. Lindir's child, were it a boy, would be that heir."

A chill washed through her, leaving apprehension in its wake. "But there was no son . . ."

"No. Lindir bore a daughter, and died. The Mujhar, still

dedicated to his purge, ordered the halfling girl-child taken to the forests and left to die."

"But it was only a child . . ."

"A shapechanger. A demon." His voice was rough as he said the Homanan words. "A halfling best left to the beasts."

Alix looked up into his impassive face. She saw it soften into understanding and sympathy and sternness. He had told her, she realized, and he expected her to believe him.

"How do you know this?" she asked. "You?"

"It has been told to the *shar tahl,* who has given it to the clan."

"The *shar tahl?*"

"Our priest-historian, the Homanans would call him. He keeps the rituals and the traditions, and makes certain all know the proper heritage of the Cheysuli. Mostly he tends to the words of the prophecy."

"What *is* this prophecy you prate of?" she asked, irritable. "Finn speaks of little else."

"That is not for me to say. The *shar tahl* will speak with you when it is the proper time." He shrugged, lifting his spread-fingered palm. *"Tahlmorra."*

Alix looked at him in the flickering shadows of the slate-colored pavilion. He was alien to her, part of the vague dreams she had dreamed over the years, growing up knowing the Cheysuli were accursed and outlawed and sentenced to death by the Mujhar. But she knew he did not lie to her, for all she wished to believe it. There was no deceit in his eyes.

"If what you tell me is true, there is one more thing," she said hollowly. "You are my brother, like Finn."

Duncan smiled. "No. Finn and I share a *jehana,* but Hale was to me what the Homanans call foster-father. My *jehan* died when I was very young."

She smoothed the weave of her skirts. "I do not entirely understand. You said Hale took Lindir away and got a child on her. Me." The word was dry in her mouth. "But if he was father to Finn, and foster-father to you . . . I do not understand."

"Hale was liege man to Shaine. It is a Cheysuli thing; hereditary service to the Mujhars and their blood. Until the purge, the Mujhars of Homana ever had a Cheysuli liege man." Duncan smiled faintly. "Hale spent most of his time at Homana-Mujhar, serving his lord, according to custom. Lindir was a golden child who took great joy in teasing her *jehan's* fierce liege man; it was a game to her. Then she was no longer a child, and Hale was no longer indifferent to the promise of her beauty. She had fulfilled that promise." He saw Alix's shocked face and laughed softly. "The Homanans hide their *meijhas* and call them light women. The Cheysuli keep *cheysulas* and *meijhas*—wives and mistresses—and honor them both."

"But Hale *left* your mother!"

"He did what he wished. That is understood among us. Men and women have the freedom to take whom they choose, when they choose." He grimaced. "Though now we have few warriors, and fewer women."

Alix swallowed with effort. "I would rather be Homanan."

Duncan's eyes narrowed. "But you are half Cheysuli. In our clan, that is counted whole."

But her mind had gone past that, grasping the slippery strands of comprehension. She put the relationships together until she had an understanding of them. Then she looked at Duncan.

"Lindir bore a daughter and Shaine lost the heir he wanted."

"Aye," he agreed.

"So he turned to his brother, Fergus, who had a son."

"Aye."

Alix took a shaking breath. "He made that son—his nephew—heir. Prince of Homana."

Duncan watched her closely. "Aye."

She felt her heart begin to hurt. "Then Carillon is my *cousin!*"

"Aye," Duncan said softly, understanding.

Alix drew up her knees and clasped her arms around them tightly. She pressed her forehead against them and squeezed her eyes shut in denial and realization.

Before I was only a croft-girl, but one who put him at ease. Now I am Cheysuli—shapechanger!—accursed, and his bastard cousin. Grief surged into her throat. *He will never come to me again!*

She hugged her knees and keened silently in the shapechanger's tent.

Chapter Five

Alix, at dawn, sat warmly wrapped in a brown blanket, numbly aware she had slept in the shapechanger's presence. She had not meant to. She vaguely recalled her silent tears and his urging of her to sleep, but no more. Now she sat alone in his pavilion, bereft of the heritage she had known all her life.

The doorflap stirred and Alix glanced up, expecting Duncan. Instead she saw Carillon and stood up with a cry, letting the blanket slide to the ground.

Then she froze. His eyes were withdrawn from her, strange, and she saw none of the warm welcome she had come to expect.

They have told him . . .

Alix's arms dropped to her sides. Desolation swept in to fill her soul. She would not look into his face and see his rejection of her.

"Alix . . ."

"You need say nothing, my lord," she said remotely. "I understand how a prince must feel to learn the croft-girl he has kept company with is a shapechanger."

He moved into the pavilion. "Are you so certain they have the right of it?"

Her head jerked up. "Then you do not believe them?"

He smiled. "Do you think I am so easily manipulated, Alix? I think they lie to you. There is nothing Cheysuli about you. Your hair is brown, not black, and your eyes amber. Not beast-yellow."

Carillon let her melt against his chest, sobbing quietly. Her fears of suggesting an intimacy she was not due faded away as she sought solace in his strength. His arms slipped around her and held her close, for the first time since they had met.

"You will come with me when I am released," he said into her tangled hair. "They cannot keep you."

She lifted her face. "Duncan has said I must stay."

"I will take you back with me."

"How do you know they will let *you* go?"

He smiled wryly. "I am worth too much to my uncle for them to keep me long."

"And I?"

"You, Alix?"

She wet her lips. "If I am what they say, then I am the Mujhar's granddaughter. Lindir's daughter."

"So you will admit to shapechanger blood if only to get royal blood as well," he said, amused.

Alix pulled away from him. "No! I only seek acknowledgment . . . the truth! Carillon, if I am Shaine's granddaughter—will he not free me from this place?"

"Do you think the Mujhar will acknowledge a half-shapechanger bastard granddaughter?"

She recoiled from the cruel question. "Carillon—"

"You must accustom yourself. If what the shapechangers say is true, we are cousins. But Shaine will never claim you. He will never offer a single coin for your return." Carillon shook his head. "They are harsh words, I know, but I cannot let you expect something you cannot have."

She set cold hands against her face. "Then you will leave me here. . . ."

He caught her arms, pulling her hands from her face. "I will not leave you here! I will take you to Homana-Mujhar, but I cannot say what your reception will be."

"You would not have to tell him who I am."

"Do I say you are my light woman, then? A valley-girl I have been seeing?" He sighed as he saw her expression. "Alix, what else would I tell him?"

"The truth."

"And have him order you slain?"

"He would *not!*"

His hands tightened on her arms. "The Mujhar has declared the Cheysuli accursed, outlawed, subject to death by anyone's hands. Do you think he will gainsay his own purge for the daughter of the man who stole *his* daughter?"

Alix jerked away from him. "She was not stolen! She

went willingly! Duncan said—" she broke off abruptly, horrified.

Carillon sighed heavily. "So, you accept their words. With so little a fight, Alix, do you deny your Homanan blood and turn to the shapechangers?"

"No!"

You are Cheysuli, liren. Came the hawk's golden tone. *Do not deny yourself the truth. Remain.*

Alix ripped the doorflap aside and stared into the sky. Cai drifted far above, floating on a summer breeze.

"I must go!" she cried.

This is your place, liren.

"No!"

"Alix!" Carillon moved to her and grabbed her arm. "To whom do you speak?"

Homana-Mujhar is not for you, the bird said softly.

"I cannot stay," she insisted, amazed at her willingness to speak to a bird. "I cannot!"

"Alix!" Carillon exclaimed.

She gestured wildly. "The bird! The hawk! There."

He dropped her arms instantly, staring at her in alarm. Slowly his eyes went to the graceful hawk.

"Let me go with Carillon," she pleaded, knowing only that the bird sought to keep her.

I cannot gainsay you, liren. *I can only ask.*

Alix tore her eyes from the hawk and looked beseechingly at Carillon. Frantically she reached out to catch her hands in his black leather doublet.

"Take me with you. Tell the Mujhar whatever you choose, but do not make me stay in this place!"

"You understand what the *bird* says?"

"In my head. A voice." She could sense his shock and sought to convince him. "Not words. A tone . . . I can understand what he thinks."

"*Alix* . . ."

"You said you would take me," she whispered.

He put out a hand to point at Cai, ruby signet flashing. "You converse with *animals!*"

Alix closed her eyes, releasing him. "Then you *will* leave me."

"Shapechanger sorcery . . ." he said slowly.

She looked at him, judging his face and the feelings re-

flected there. Then his hands grasped her shoulders so hard
it hurt.

"You are no different," he said. "You are still Alix. I
look at you and see a strong, proud woman whose soul is
near to destroyed by these shapechanger words. Alix, I will
still have you by me."

You are meant for another, the hawk said gently. *The
prince is not for you. Stay.*

"By all the gods," she whispered, staring blindly at Carillon, "will none of you let me be?"

"Alix!"

But she tore herself from him and ran from them both,
seeking escape in the forest.

She fled to a lush grassy glade lying in a splash of sunlight. There Alix sank to her knees and sat stunned, trying
to regain control of her disordered mind. She shook
convulsively.

*Shapechanger! Spawn of a shapechanger demon and a
king's daughter!* she cried within her soul.

Alix scrubbed at her stinging eyes with the heels of her
hands, fighting back tears. She had never been one for crying, but the tension and fear of the past hours had taken
away her natural reserve. She wanted security and solace
like a child seeking comfort at a mother's breast.

Mother! she cried. *Was I birthed by a Homanan valley
girl, or a haughty, defiant princess?*

Alix felt the conflict in her soul. She longed for Carillon's
confidence in her Homanan origins, yet felt the seductive
tug of mystery attending the legendary magic of the Cheysuli. And though Torrin had raised her to be fair to all men
in her thoughts, even the Cheysuli, he had also instilled in
her the apprehension all felt concerning the race.

She heard a rustle in the leaves and glanced up swiftly,
frightened Finn had followed her again. She did not entirely
trust his intentions, for all he claimed to be her half-
brother. Alix sensed something elemental in him; untamed
and demanding.

A hawk rested lightly on a swinging branch, feathers ruf-
fling in the breeze. Though its coloring was the same, she
realized it was not Cai. This hawk was smaller, more
streamlined; a swift hunting hawk able to plummet after
small prey and snatch it up instantly.

Alix shivered involuntarily as she thought of the deadly talons curving around the branch.

Have you decided to stay? it asked.

She stared at it, astonished to discover the great distinction between its tone and Cai's. It regarded her from bright eyes, unmoving on the branch.

Do you stay? it asked again. *Or do you go?*

Resentful and defiant, Alix started to push the tone away. She would not allow the Cheysuli so to manipulate her mind. She would keep herself apart from them and their sorcery, regardless of the seductiveness of their power.

But even as she decided she felt the fear slip away, replaced by wonder. First she had spoken with a wolf who seemed perfectly capable of speaking back; then Cai. And now this smaller hawk.

By the gods, the animals are mine to converse with! She took a trembling breath. *If this is sorcery, it cannot be demon-sent. It is a true gift.*

The hawk regarded her approvingly. *Already you begin to learn. The lir-bond is truly magic, but does harm to no one. And you are special, for no other can converse with all the lir. Through you, perhaps, we can win back some of our blood-pride and esteem.*

"You lost it through Hale's selfish action!" she retorted, then winced at her audacity. Carefully she looked at the hawk to see if it was offended.

It seemed amused. *For the Cheysuli, aye, it would have been better had he never set eyes on Lindir. But then you would not live.*

"And what am I?" she shot back. "Merely a woman a foolish warrior wanted for his own."

Finn does, occasionally, allow his emotions to overrule his judgment. But it makes him what he is.

"A beast," she grumbled, picking a stem from the grass.

He is a man. Beasts have more wisdom, better sense and far better manners. Do not liken him to what he cannot emulate.

Alix, startled by the hawk's wry words, laughed up at him delightedly. "I am sorry he cannot hear you, bird. Perhaps he would reconsider his rash actions."

Finn reconsiders very little.

She stared at the bird, eyes narrowing shrewdly. The

stem she had picked drooped in her fingers. "If you are not Cai, who are you? Show yourself."

Another time, perhaps, the bird said obliquely. *But know I am one who cares.*

It detached itself from the swinging branch and flew into the blue sky.

Alix dropped the stem and stared after the fleet bird dispiritedly. For a moment she had felt an uprush of awe and amazement that she conversed with the *lir;* now she was a frightened and confused girl. Slowly she got to her feet and wandered back to the Cheysuli encampment.

She was startled to find the tents pulled down and rolled into compact bundles. The warriors tied them onto their horses and made certain the fire cairns were broken up and scattered. Alix stood in the center of the naked clearing and realized her soul and self-image had been as neatly swept clean.

Carillon came to her as she stared blindly at the swift alteration of the camp. He touched her hand, then folded it into his much larger one.

"I will be with you," he said softly. "They have said I must go with them." He grimaced. "They say I am not yet strong enough for the ride to Mujhara, but they did not lie about the wound. It is near healed, and I feel strong enough to fight any of them."

She looked at the wrist and saw healing ridges marking the wolf bite. The swelling and seepage was gone, replaced by new skin.

They have healing arts at their beck, she said silently, unconsciously echoing Finn's words.

"Well, my lord, perhaps it is best," she said aloud. "I do not seek to lose you so soon."

"I have said you will come with me to Homana-Mujhar."

She smiled sadly into his face. "As your light woman?"

Carillon grinned and lifted her hand to brush his lips across her wrist. "If it must be done, Alix, I will not prove unwilling."

She blushed and tried to withdraw her hand, but he held it firmly. He shook his head slightly and smiled. "I do not seek to discomfit you. I have merely said what is in my mind."

"I am your cousin." She did not entirely believe him.

Carillon shrugged. "Cousins often wed in royal houses, to secure the succession. *This* bond would not be a thing Homanans disapprove of."

Alix tried to answer. "My lord . . ."

His brows lifted ironically. "Surely you can dispense with my title if we discuss our futures in this way."

Alix wanted to laugh at him but could not. She had longed for such thoughts and words from him all through their brief acquaintanceship, though she had never thought them possible. Now she could not comprehend it. The revelation of her ancestry destroyed the roots she had depended on.

"I will wed a princess, one day," he said lightly, "to get heirs for the throne. But princes have mistresses often enough."

She heard the echo of Duncan's voice in her mind, explaining the casual Cheysuli custom of wives and mistresses. An open practice she could not comprehend.

Yet Carillon offers me much the same . . . She shivered convulsively. *Who has the right of it—the Cheysuli or the Homanans?*

"Alix?"

She carefully freed her hand from his and met his blue eyes. "I cannot say, Carillon. We are not even free of this place yet."

He started to say something, but Finn's approach drove him into silence. Carillon glared at the Cheysuli warrior, who merely laughed mockingly. Then Finn turned to Alix.

"Will you ride with me, *rujholla?*"

She noted the change of address and felt a mixture of gratitude and resentment. She would acknowledge no blood relationship to him; nor would she accept the sort of physical commitment he wanted from her.

She moved closer to Carillon. "I ride with the prince."

"And likely have him fall off the horse from in front of you."

Carillon glared at him. "I will keep to my horse, shapechanger."

Finn's earring winked as he laughed. "You had better change your name for us, princeling, or you insult your cousin as well."

"*You* seek to do that, not him!" Alix snapped.

He grinned at her, then shot a mocking glance at Carillon. "Have you forgot? You have gained more than just your light woman as a cousin this day. You also have kin among the rest of us."

"Kin among you?" Carillon asked disparagingly.

"Aye," Finn said equably. "Myself. She is my *rujholla,* princeling, though only by half. But it makes you and I cousins, of a sort." He laughed. "I am kin to Homana's prince, who would serve his liege lord by slaying us all. But to do that you would have to slay *her,* would you not?"

Color surged into Carillon's face. "If I slay any shape-changer, it will be you. I leave the rest to my uncle the Mujhar."

"Carillon!" Alix said, horrified.

Finn laughed at them both, spreading his hands. "Do you see, princeling? What you say of us concerns her. Beware your intentions, do you seek to keep her safe."

Carillon's hand dropped to the heavy sword belted at his hips; Alix was still amazed the Cheysuli had let him keep it. But he did not draw the blade. Finn smiled at them both and walked away, calling to another warrior in the Old Tongue.

"He only seeks to goad you," Alix said softly. "To satisfy his own craving for a place."

Carillon glanced at her in surprise. Then he smiled. "Do you prophesy for me, Alix? Can you see into my heart as well as his?"

Inwardly she flinched away from the reference to sorcery, and that at her own command. "No. I only say what I feel in him. As for you . . ." She hesitated, then smiled. "I think you will be Mujhar, one day."

He laughed at her and pulled her into his arms, lifting her into the air. "Alix, I thank the gods I rode my warhorse through your garden that day! Else I would not have you sharing such wisdom with me."

She grinned down at him, delighting in the feelings spilling through her body. His hands on her waist were firm and sure, possessive, betraying no signs of weakness from the wolf-wound. Alix let one hand curve itself around his neck, tangling in his tawny hair.

"And did I not share my wisdom with you when you trampled all my fine young plants?"

He spun her again, then set her down with a rueful grin. "Aye, that you did. You near made me ashamed of my birth."

Alix laughed at him. "Even a prince can manage to go around a garden when his prey avoids it. I cared little for the fine clothes you wore or the gold you threw at me to pay for the damage." She lifted her head haughtily, mimicking the actions of a highborn court lady. "I cannot be *bought*, my lord prince, for all you are heir of Homana."

"But can you be won?" he asked steadily.

Her smile faded. She averted her face. "If I can be won, it is something left to me to discover. I cannot say."

"Alix—"

"I cannot say, Carillon."

Duncan came up before Carillon could speak again. He led a bay horse and carried the oddly compact bow he had polished the evening before. Carillon, looking sharply at it, sucked in his breath.

Duncan frowned at him. "My lord?"

"Your bow."

The Cheysuli held it up. "This? It is not so much. I have better at the Keep. This is for raiding and hunting, and expendable."

"But it is still a Cheysuli bow," Carillon said seriously. "I have heard of them all my life."

Duncan smiled briefly and held it out. "Here. But keep in mind it is not the best I have made."

Carillon disregarded the modest statement and took the bow almost reverently, fingering his enemy's weapon. It was finely crafted, age-polished hardwood. The grip was laced with leather to cushion a man's palm. Odd runic symbols ran from top to bottom, winding around the bow like a serpent.

Carillon looked at Duncan. "You know what is said of a Cheysuli bow."

Duncan smiled ironically. "That an arrow loosed by one cannot miss. But that is all it is, my lord; a legend." His eyes narrowed in cynicism. "Though it serves us well. If Shaine's troops fear a Cheysuli bow, it is all the better for us."

"Do you say a man *can* miss with this bow?"

Duncan laughed. "Any arrow can miss its mark. It is

only rare for a Cheysuli to loose one with poor aim." His smile faded into implacability. "It comes from fighting for survival, my lord. When you are hunted down like a beplagued animal by the Mujhar's guardsmen, you learn to fight back how you can."

Carillon's face tautened. "The legend of these bows was known *before* the purge, shapechanger."

Duncan's mouth twisted. "Then let us say the skill was *refined* by it, prince."

Carillon thrust out the bow. Duncan took it without comment and looked at Alix. "It is time to go. Will you ride with me?"

Her head lifted. "I told your brother—I ride with the prince."

Duncan handed the reins of the bay horse to Carillon. "Your warhorse will be returned when you are better, my lord. For now you may have mine."

Carillon mounted silently. Before Alix could attempt a scrambling mount Duncan lifted her up behind the Cheysuli saddle. She looked down into his impassive eyes and felt a faint tug of familiarity. But he walked away before she could question it.

Finn, mounted on a dun-colored horse, rode up beside them. "Should the princeling falter before you, *rujholla*, I will be more than happy to take you onto my horse."

Alix looked directly into his angular, mocking face and said nothing at all, ignoring him as pointedly as she could.

Finn merely grinned and fell into place before them.

Chapter Six

The long ride took the heart from Alix as she clung to
Carillon. She drooped dispiritedly against his broad back,
longing for respite from the steady motion of the horse.
Whenever Finn rode by she straightened and arranged her
face into an expression of determined spirit, but when he
left them she returned to her haze of weariness.

The Cheysuli did not tell either captive where they rode,
only that their Keep lay at the end of their journey. When
Carillon demanded his instant release and that of Alix,
threatening the Mujhar's displeasure and retribution, Duncan refused courteously. Alix, watching him silently during
much of the day's ride, wondered at the difference so evident in the brothers. Finn seemed the more aggressive of
the two; Duncan kept his own counsel and gave nothing
away to supposition. Though Alix wanted nothing more
than to leave the shapechangers' presence with Carillon
accompanying her, she far preferred Duncan's company
to Finn's.

In the evening she sat before a small fire with Carillon,
staring into the flames in exhaustion. The prince had shed
his green cloak and draped it over her shoulders. She
folded it around herself gratefully. He looked tired and
worn as he stretched his hands out to the fire's warmth; for
all it was the beginning of summer, the nights were still
cold. Alix knew her own appearance was no better. Her
braid was loosened and tangled and her gown showed the
results of too long a time spent in it. Her face felt grimy
and the welt left by the tree limb stung.

The Cheysuli, she marked, took little with them on a
raiding mission. Their mounts were packed lightly and the
warriors carried only a belt-knife and the hunting bows for
weaponry. Alix eyed them glumly as they quickly set up a

small camp, spreading blankets where they would sleep and building tiny fires to heat their evening ration of journey-stew. The colored pavilions were kept packed away; Alix realized she would spend the night unprotected by anything save a blanket.

Uneasily she slanted a glance at Carillon, seated next to her on Duncan's blood-red blanket. "I would near give my soul to be safe in my own bed in my father's croft."

Carillon, gazing blankly into the fire, looked over to her with an effort. Then he smiled. "Had I a choice, I would be in my own chambers within Homana-Mujhar. But even your croft would do me well this night."

"Better than here," she agreed morosely.

Carillon shifted and sat cross-legged. The flames glinted off the whiteness of his teeth as he smiled maliciously.

"When I have the chance, Alix, these demons will regret what they have done."

A strange chill slid down her spine as she looked sharply at his determined face. "You would have them all slain?"

His eyes narrowed at her reproving tone. Then his face relaxed and he touched her ragged braid, moving it to lie across her shoulder. "A woman, perhaps, does not understand. But a man must serve his liege lord in all things, even to the slaying of others. My uncle's purge still holds, Alix. I would not serve him by letting this nest of demons live. They have been outlawed. Sentenced to death by the Mujhar himself."

Alix pulled the cloak more tightly around her shoulders. "Carillon, what if there was no sorcery used against your House? What if the Cheysuli have the right of it? Would you still see to their deaths?"

"The shapechangers cursed my uncle's House when Hale took Lindir away with him. The queen consequently died of a wasting disease, and Shaine's second wife bore no living children. If not sorcery, what else could cause these things?"

Alix sighed and stared at her hands clasping the green wool. She pitched her voice purposely low, almost placating. But what she said had nothing to do with placation.

"Perhaps it was what the Cheysuli call *tahlmorra*. Perhaps it was no more than the will of the gods."

His hand moved from her braid to her jaw and lifted her

face into the light. "Do you champion the demons again, Alix? Do you listen to them because of what you have learned?"

She looked at him steadily. "I do not champion them, Carillon. I give them their beliefs. It is only fitting to acknowledge the convictions of others."

"Even when the Mujhar denounces them as sorcerers of the dark gods?"

Alix touched his wrist gently and felt the ridged scars of the bite from Storr. Once again the image of Finn shifting his shape before her eyes rose into her mind, and it was only with considerable effort she kept the frightened awe from her voice.

"Carillon, will you allow him to denounce *me?*"

He sighed and closed his eyes, withdrawing his hand. He rubbed wearily at his brow and irritably shoved hair from his eyes.

"Shaine is not an easy man to convince. If you go before him claiming you are a shapechanger, and his granddaughter, you touch his pride. My uncle is a vain man indeed." Carillon smiled at her grimly. "But I will not allow him to harm you. I will have that much of him."

Alix drew up her knees, clasping her arms around them. "Tell me of Homana-Mujhar, Carillon. I have ever been afraid to ask before, but no more. Tell me of the Mujhar's great walled palace."

He smiled at her wistful tone. "It is a thing of men's dreams. A fortress within a city of thousands. I know little enough of its history, save it has stood proudly for centuries. No enemy force has ever broken its walls, nor entered its halls and corridors. Homana-Mujhar is more than a palace, Alix; it is the heart of Homana."

"And you have lived their always?"

"I? No. I have lived at Joyenne, my father's castle. It is but three days from Mujhara. I was born there." He smiled as if reminiscing. "My father has ever preferred to keep himself from cities, and I echo his feelings. Mujhara is lovely, a jeweled city, but I care more for the country." He sighed. "Until my acclamation as formal heir last year, I lived at Joyenne. I spent time at Homana-Mujhar; I am not indifferent to its magnificence."

"And I have not even seen Mujhara," she said sadly.

"That is something I cannot understand. The city belongs to the Mujhar and it is well-protected. Women and children go in safety among its streets."

Alix kept her eyes from his. "Perhaps it was a promise made to the Mujhar by Torrin; that he would not allow Lindir's shapechanger daughter to enter the City."

Carillon stiffened. "If you are that child."

Alix closed her eyes. "I begin to think I am."

"Alix . . ."

She turned her head and rested her unblemished cheek against one knee, looking solemnly into Carillon's face. "I converse with the animals, my lord. And I understand. If that is not shapechanger sorcery, then I must be a creature of the dark gods."

His hand fell upon her shoulder. "Alix, I will not have you say this. You are no demon's get."

"And if I am Cheysuli?"

Carillon's eyes slid over the shadowed camp, marking each black-haired, yellow-eyed warrior in supple leathers and barbaric gold. He looked back at Alix and for a moment saw the leaping of flames reflected in her eyes, turning them from amber to yellow.

He swallowed, forcing himself to relax. "It does not matter. Whatever you are, I accept it."

Alix smiled sadly and touched his hand. "Then if you accept me, you must accept the others."

He opened his mouth to deny it, then refrained. He saw the bleakness in her eyes and the weariness of her movements as she shifted into a more comfortable position. Carillon put a long arm out and drew her against his chest.

"Alix, I have said it does not matter."

"You are the heir," she said softly. "It must matter."

"Until I am the Mujhar, what I believe does not matter at all."

And when you are the Mujhar, will you slay my kin? she wondered.

In the morning Duncan led Carillon's chestnut warhorse to them. Alix looked from the horse to the clan-leader and marked his solemn expression. Finn, standing with him, smiled at her suggestively. Alix colored and ignored him, watching Duncan instead.

"You rode well enough yesterday, my lord," he said quietly. "You have our leave to go. Finn will accompany you."

Carillon glared at him. "I can find my own way back, shapechanger."

Duncan's lips twitched. "I have no doubt of that. But the Cheysuli have spent twenty-five years fleeing the unnatural wrath of the Mujhar, and we would be foolish indeed to lead his heir to our new home. Finn will see you do not follow us to the Keep."

Carillon reddened with anger but ignored the Cheysuli's dry tone. He took the scarlet leather reins from Duncan and turned to Alix.

"You may ride in the saddle before me."

Duncan stepped swiftly between the horse and Alix as she moved to mount. His eyes were flat and hard. "You remain with us."

"You cannot force me to stay!" she said angrily. "I have listened to your words, and I respect them, but I will not go with you. My home is with my father."

"Your home is with your father's people."

Alix felt herself grow cold. Without thought she had spoken of Torrin, but the clan-leader reminded her, in a single sentence, she was no longer a simple Homanan croft-girl.

She steadied her breath with effort. "I want to go with Carillon."

His hawk earring swung as he shook his head. "No."

Finn laughed at her. "You cannot wish to leave us so soon, *rujholla*. You have hardly learned our names. There is much more for you to learn of the clan."

"I am still half Homanan," she said steadily. "And free of any man's bidding save my father's." She challenged Duncan with a defiant glance. "I will go with Carillon."

The prince moved beside her, setting a possessive hand on her shoulder. "By your own words you have said she is my cousin. I will have her with me in Homana-Mujhar. You cannot deny her that."

Finn raised his brows curiously. "Can we not? Your fates were decided in Council last night, while you slept. It was my position we should keep you both, forcing you to see we are not the demons you believe, but I was overruled. My *rujholli* would have you returned safely to your uncle, who will send guardsmen to strike us down." He shrugged.

"Some even believed you would be won to the belief we are only men, like yourself, did you spend time with us, but I think you would only plan to harm us how you could." Finn smiled humorlessly. "What would you have done, princeling, had you stayed with us?"

Carillon's fingers dug into Alix's shoulder. "I would have found my escape, shapechanger, and made my way back to Mujhara. You have the right of it. I would aid my kinsman in setting troops after you."

"At the risk of her life?" Finn asked softly.

Alix shivered. Carillon's hand dropped to his sword hilt. "You will not harm her, shapechanger."

"We do not harm our own," Duncan said coldly. "But does Shaine bid his men spare the life of a single Cheysuli? They are not discriminating men. If you allow them to follow us and attack, you risk the girl."

"Then let me go," Alix said. "Perhaps the Mujhar would not send his troops."

"Alix!" Carillon said sharply.

Finn grinned cynically. "Do you see, *meijha,* what manner of man your princeling is? Yet he would have you believe *we* are the bloodthirsty demons. I say it was the Homanans who began the *qu'mahlin* and the Homanans who perpetuate it. It was none of Cheysuli doing."

"No more of this!" Alix cried. "No more!"

Carillon stepped from her and drew his sword hissing from its sheath. He stood before them with the massive blade gleaming, clenched in both hands. Alix saw the ruby wink redly in the sunlight, then drew in her breath. Down the blade ran runic symbols very similar to those on Duncan's bow.

"You do not take her," Carillon said softly. "She comes with me."

Finn crossed both arms over his chest and waited silently, armbands flashing in the light. Alix, frozen in place, felt an odd slowing of time. Carillon stood next to her with blade bared, feet planted, his size alone warning enough to any man. Yet Duncan stood calmly before the weapon as if it did not concern him in the least.

Her skin contracted with foreboding. *Will I see a man die this day because of me?* She swallowed heavily, wishing she could look away and knowing she could not. *Lindir's actions set the purge into motion; if I am truly her daughter, does this not add to it?*

Duncan smiled oddly. "You had best recall the maker of that blade, my lord."

Finn's teeth showed in a feral smile. "A Cheysuli blade ever knows its first master."

Alix looked again at the runes on the sword, transfixed by their alien shapes and the implications of them.

Carillon held his ground. "You do not even use swords yourselves, shapechanger!"

Finn shrugged. "We prefer to give men a close death. A sword does not serve us. We fight with knives." He paused, glancing at Alix. "Knives . . . and *lir*-shape."

"Then what of your bows?" Carillon snapped.

"They were for hunting, originally," Duncan said lightly. "Then the Mujhars of Homana began requiring our services in war, and we learned to use them against men." His yellow eyes were implacable. "When the *qu'mahlin* began, we used them against those we once served."

Finn moved forward, so close to Carillon the tip of the broadsword rested against his throat. "Use it," he taunted in a whisper. "Use it, princeling. Strike home, if you can."

Carillon did not move, as if puzzled by the invitation. Alix, sickened by the tensions, bit at her bottom lip.

Finn smiled and put his hand on the blade. His browned fingers rested lightly on the finely honed edges. "Tell me, my lord, whom Hale's sword will answer. The heir of the man who began the *qu'mahlin*, or Hale's only blood-son?"

"Finn," Duncan said softly. Alix thought he sounded reproachful.

Her fingers twined themselves into the folds of her yellow skirts, scraping against the rough woolen fabric. She knew she would see Finn die; even with his hand on the blade the warrior could never keep Carillon from striking him down. She owed no kindness to Finn, who had stolen her so rudely, but neither did she wish to see him struck down before her eyes. The sour taste of fear filled her mouth.

"Carillon . . ." she begged. She swallowed back the constriction in her throat. "Do you begin your uncle's work already?"

"As I can," he said grimly.

Finn's fingers on the blade shifted slightly. Alix thought he would drop the hand and move into a defensive posture, but he did not. Before she could cry out he twisted the sword aside with only a hand. His own knife flashed as he stepped i.to Carillon.

"No!" she cried, lunging forward.

Duncan's hand came down on her arm and jerked her back. She tried to pull free and could not, then stood still as she saw the Cheysuli blade against Carillon's throat. The broadsword was in his right hand, but she realized the weapon was too bulky to draw back and strike with in close quarters, particularly with Finn so close.

"Do you see, lordling, what it is for a man to face a Cheysuli in battle?" Finn asked gently. "I do not doubt you have been trained within the walls of your fine palace, but you have not faced a Cheysuli. Until that is done you have not learned at all."

Carillon's teeth clenched as they shut with a click. The muscles of his jaw rolled, altering the line of his face, but he said nothing at all. Nor did he flinch before the knife at his throat.

Finn slid a bright glance at Alix. "Will you beg me for his life, *meijha?*"

"I will not," she said clearly. "But if you slay him here, I myself will see to *your* death."

His eyebrows shot up in mock astonishment. Then he grinned into Carillon's still face. "Well, princeling, you have women to argue for you. Perhaps I should respect that." He shrugged and stepped away, returning the knife to his belt. "But she *is* Cheysuli, and my *rujholla,* and I will not risk it."

Duncan bent and picked up the scarlet reins Carillon had dropped. He held them out. Silently the prince slid his sword home in its silver-laced leather sheath and took them.

"Finn will escort you to Mujhara."

Carillon looked only at Alix. "I will come back for you."

"Carillon . . ."

"I will come back for you."

Alix nodded and hugged herself, hunching her shoulders defensively. She knew he could not win her freedom without sacrificing himself, which would give her no freedom at all. The Cheysuli had disarmed both of them.

Carillon turned away from her and mounted the big chestnut. From the horse's great height he looked down on them all.

"You are foolish," he said stiffly, "to free me without requiring gold."

Finn laughed. "You seek to instruct us at the risk of your own welfare?"

"It is only that I do not understand."

Duncan smiled. "The Cheysuli do not require gold, my lord, save to fashion the *lir*-tokens and the ornaments our women wear. We desire only to end this war the Mujhar wages against us, and the chance to live as we once did. Freely, without fearing our children will be slain because of their yellow eyes."

"If you had not sought to throw down Homanan rule—"

Duncan interrupted sharply. "We did not. We have ever served the blood of the Mujhars. Hale, in taking Lindir from her *jehan,* freed her of a marriage she did not desire. In doing that he performed the service to which he bound himself—he served the Mujhar's blood." He smiled slightly. "It was not what Shaine expected of his service, perhaps, for Hale was his man. It was only he wanted Lindir more."

"Your *jehana* was a willful woman," Finn said to Alix, deliberately distinct as if to hammer the point home. "Do you echo her?"

She brought her head up haughtily, defying him. "Were *I* within Homana-Mujhar, I would not leave it to go into the forests with a Cheysuli warrior. Do not judge me by my mother."

Finn grinned, triumphant. "If I have at last got you to admit to your blood, *meijha,* I will judge you by anything."

Before she could retort he turned and faded into the trees. Alix glared after him, then scowled as he returned a moment later on his dun-colored horse.

Duncan moved to Carillon's horse, looking up at the prince. "I would send greetings to Shaine the Mujhar, did I think he would accept them. We do not desire this war."

Carillon smiled mirthlessly. "I think the Mujhar has made *his* desires clear, shapechanger."

Duncan put a hand on the warhorse's burnished shoulder

idly. "If you seek to continue the *qu'mahlin,* my lord, you are not the man I believe you are. The prophecy has said." He smiled and stepped away, using the spread-fingered gesture. "*Tahlmorra,* Carillon."

"I renounce your prophecy," the prince said flatly.

The clan-leader reached out and caught Alix's arm, drawing her close. "If you do that, my lord, you renounce her."

Alix shivered once under his hand. "Let me go with Carillon."

"No."

Finn moved his horse alongside the chestnut and smiled sardonically at the prince. "Waste no more time. I would not wish the Mujhar angrier than he must be. Come, princeling. We ride."

He brought his hand down on the chestnut's wide rump and sent him lunging forward. Finn crowded his mount behind so that Carillon could not wheel back, and the last Alix saw of the prince was his tawny-dark head ducking a low branch.

She made an involuntary movement to follow and again Duncan's hand held her back. After a moment he released her.

"It is not so bad," he said quietly. "You have much to learn, but it will come quickly enough when you have accepted your blood."

Alix drew a shaky breath and stared hard at him. "I will not claim you a liar, shapechanger, but neither will I submit to your rule. If I accept this as your—*tahlmorra,* I do it on my own terms."

A tall warrior smiled at her. "A Cheysuli could do it no other way."

Alix scowled at him. Mutinously, she followed him through the trees to his waiting horse.

Chapter Seven

Alix was so weary by the time the evening fell she let Duncan lead her to his fire and push her down onto a thick tawny pelt without saying a word. A crofter's daughter spent little time on horseback; her muscles ached and her legs had raw sores rubbed on them. She huddled on the pelt numbly and pulled her tattered skirts around her bare feet as best she could. When Duncan put a bowl of hot stew into her hands she thanked him shakily and began to spoon it into her mouth.

He sat down on another pelt across from her and picked up the bow Carillon had praised. Silently he began to rub it with an oiled cloth, eyes on his work.

Alix sipped at the cup of honey brew he had given her, nearly choking on its vitriolic taste. She kept her reaction from him by covering her mouth with a hand, trying not to gasp aloud. She did not wish him to see her disability, or her weariness.

He seemed oblivious to her as she scraped up the last of the stew and set the bowl aside, rattling the wooden spoon. She felt better for a full stomach, but it also made her more alert to the dangers she faced. She could no longer take refuge in the haze of exhaustion and helplessness that had dogged her during the long ride. Now she could look across the small campsite and see the dark warriors so intent on taking her away from her people.

Alix was still apprehensive, but most of the overpowering fright had left her. Duncan had treated her with calm kindness all day, and with Finn gone she sensed no threat to her person or her equilibrium. She had the chance to consider her plight from a more sensible angle.

"Will you answer my questions, shapechanger?"

Duncan did not look up. "I have told you my name. Use it if you would speak with me."

Alix studied his bowed head, marking how the black hair fell forward into his face as he worked. The gold earring winked through thick strands. Then she glanced at the hawk who sat so silently in the nearest tree.

"How does one get himself a *lir?*"

The bow gleamed in his supple hands. "When a Cheysuli becomes a man he must go into the forests or mountains and seek his *lir*. It is a matter of time, perhaps even weeks. He lives apart, opening himself to the gods, and there the animal who will become his *lir* seeks him out."

"Do you say the *animal* does the choosing?"

"It is *tahlmorra*. Every Cheysuli is born to a *lir*, and a *lir* to him. It is only a matter of finding one another."

"Yet not all animals are *lir*," Finn said.

"No. Just as all men are not Cheysuli."

Unwillingly she smiled at his wry tone, though he did not look at her. "What happens if the *lir* is not found?"

His hands stopped their work as his eyes came up to meet hers. "A Cheysuli with no *lir* is only half a man. We are born with it in our souls. If it lacks, we are not whole."

"Not whole . . ."

"It is a thing you cannot comprehend, but a man who is not whole has no purpose. He cannot serve the prophecy."

Alix frowned at him thoughtfully. "If you are not whole . . . what happens to you if Cai is slain?"

Duncan's hands tensed on the bow. First he looked at the hawk perching in the tree, then he set the bow aside and gave her his full attention. He leaned forward intently and Alix felt the full power of his strength.

"You do not ask out of mere curiosity. If you seek to escape by slaying my *lir* you will be Cheysuli-cursed. It is not a simple thing to live with." A flicker passed across his face. "But you would not live long enough to truly suffer."

Alix recoiled from the deadly promise in his voice. She shook her head in speechless denial.

"I will tell you, regardless of your intent," he said quietly, "so you will know. I put my life in your hands." He watched her closely; judgmental. "If a man seeks to slay a Cheysuli, he need only slay his *lir*. Does he imprison that *lir*, he imprisons a Cheysuli. He is powerless, without recourse to the gifts the gods have given us." He relaxed minutely. "And now you know the price of the *lir*-bond."

"How can it be so consuming?" she demanded. "You are a man; Cai a bird. How is it you keep this bond?"

Duncan shrugged as he smoothed the leather of his snug leggings. "I cannot say clearly. It is a gift of the old gods. It has been so for centuries, and will doubtless continue." He grimaced. "Unless the Mujhar slays us all. Then Homana will lose her ancestors."

"Ancestors!" she exclaimed. "You would have me believe *you* made this land what it is, if you speak so."

Duncan smiled oddly. "Perhaps."

Alix scowled at him. "I do not believe you."

"Believe what you wish. If you ask, the *lir* will tell you."

Her eyes went to the hawk. But she refused to hear it from the bird. She preferred to draw Duncan out. "And if you are slain, what becomes of the *lir?*"

"The *lir* returns to the wild. For the animal the broken link is not so harsh." He smiled. "Creatures have ever been stronger than men. Cai would grieve for a while, perhaps, but he would live."

Do not dismiss my grief so lightly, the bird chided. *Else you ridicule our bond.*

Duncan laughed silently and Alix, surprised by his response, stared at him. The solemnity she had learned to associate with him was not as habitual as she had assumed.

After a moment she put out her arms and stretched them, cracking sinews. "What truly becomes of you if the *lir* is slain?" she asked lightly.

Duncan grew very still. "A Cheysuli without a *lir,* as I said, is not whole. He is made empty. He does not choose to live."

She froze, staring at him. "Does not choose . . ."

"There is a death-ritual."

Her arms dropped. "Death!"

Duncan looked again into the trees, eyes on Cai. "A Cheysuli forsakes his clan and goes into the forests to seek death among the animals. Weaponless and prepared. However it comes, he will not deny that death." He shrugged, making light of the matter. "It is welcome enough, to a *lir*less man."

Alix swallowed back her revulsion. "It is a barbaric thing. Barbaric!"

Duncan was impassive. "A shadow has no life."

"What do you say?" she snapped.

He sighed. "I cannot give you the proper words. You must accept what I say. A *lir*less man is no man, but a shadow. And a Cheysuli cannot live so."

"I say it is barbaric."

"If it pleases you."

"What *else* must I think?"

He leaned forward and placed more wood on the small fire. It snapped and leaped in response, highlighting his pale eyes into a bestial glow.

"When you have learned more of your clan, you will think differently." Duncan relaxed, setting the bow aside as he studied her impassively. Then a faint flicker of curiosity shone in his eyes. "Would you wed Carillon?"

Alix stared at him. "Carillon!"

"Aye. I have seen what is between you."

For a moment she could find no proper answer. The question stunned her, both for its audacity and the implications. In all her dreams of the tall prince, she had never considered marriage with him. Somehow the thought of it, and the regret that it could never be, hurt.

"No," she said finally. "Carillon would never take me to wife. He is meant for a foreign princess; some highborn lady from Atvia, perhaps, or Erinn. Perhaps even Solinde one day, if this war between the realms ends."

"Then you will be his light woman. His *meijha.*"

She disliked his easy assumption. "That is difficult to do if I must stay with this clan you prate about."

Duncan grinned, suddenly so much like Finn it startled her. But the similarity vanished when she looked closer, for there were none of Finn's roguish ways about Duncan.

"You are not a prisoner, though it must seem so to you. As for the prince . . . I think he means what he says. He will come back for you." He sighed, losing the animation in his face. "I cannot say when, but he will do it."

"I will welcome it, shapechanger."

Duncan regarded her solemnly a moment. "Why do you fear us so much? I have said we do no harm to our own."

Alix looked away from him. "*I* have said. I was raised

to fear you, and to acknowledge the sorcery in your blood. All I have ever known is that the Cheysuli are demons . . . dangerous." She looked back at him. "You raid crofts and steal the livestock. People are injured. If that is no harm, you have a strange way of showing your peaceful intentions."

Duncan smiled. "Aye, it would seem so. But do not forget . . . Shaine has forced us to this. Before we lived quietly within the forests, hunting when we would and having no need to *raid* for our food. The *qu'mahlin* has made us little more than brigands, like those who ply the tracks to steal from honest folk. It was never our nature—we are warriors, not thieves—but Shaine has left us little choice."

"Had you the choice . . . would you return to your former way of life?"

He fingered the gold hilt of the long-knife at his belt absently, eyes gone oddly detached. When he answered Alix heard the echos of prophecy in his voice.

"We will never regain our former way of life. We are meant for another way. The old gods have said."

She shivered, shrinking from the implications of his words. She picked up the wooden cup, intending to drink to cover her confusion, saw it was empty and set it down.

"You will be Carillon's light woman?"

The cup fell over as her fingers spasmed. "I will be no man's light woman."

Duncan's smile was crooked; disbelieving. "I have been led to believe most women would slay for a chance to be so honored."

"I am not most women," she retorted. She sighed, picking at the twigs caught in her tangled braid. "I cannot conceive of it ever happening, now, so there is no need for me to consider it."

"Then you give him up so easily?"

Alix dropped the braid and stared at him despondently, forgetting he was her enemy and thinking only of the sympathy in his voice.

"I cannot say what I will do. I cannot even say what I *want!*"

He grunted. "Those are the restraints put on you by your Homanan upbringing. Among the Cheysuli, a woman takes what man she will." A fleeting shadow passed across his face as he frowned. A shrug banished the expression. "A woman of the clan may refuse one man and take another, easily."

"My father did not bring me up to be a light woman," she said firmly. "One day I will wed a crofter, like my father, or a villager." She shrugged. "One day."

"You father did not bring you up at all," he said bluntly.

Alix opened her mouth to protest *yes, he most certainly did,* then realized Duncan referred to Hale. Once again she recalled the astonishing story behind her own birth—if she would accept that story as truth. But she could not tell him what she thought, so she settled for the familiar litany she had repeated each evening.

"Carillon will wed a princess. Of course."

"Of course," he mocked. "If he lives at all, he will wed a princess."

"Lives!"

Duncan stretched one eyelid and rubbed at it. "The Ihlini will see to it Carillon does not live to wed."

"The Ihlini!" Alix stared at him, horrified. "The sorcerers who serve the dark gods? But why? What do they care for Carillon? Is it not Bellam who dictates what Solinde will do?"

Duncan picked up his bow and studied it, then began to oil it once more. His voice, deep and quiet, took on an instructive tone. "Solinde has ever been a strong land, but her kings are greedy. They are not satisfied with Solinde; they also want Homana in vassalage. Bellam has sought to achieve that all his life, but these constant skirmishes at the borders—and the full battles that slay so many—have won him nothing. He seeks to gain Homana how he can, now."

"By turning to the *Ihlini?*"

"Already Solinde is much stronger than before. Bellam seeks the unnatural power of Tynstar, who rules the Ihlini—if a sorcerer can be said to rule his own race." He bent his head over his work. "Tynstar is the might behind Solinde, not Bellam."

"Tynstar . . ." she whispered. For a moment she allowed her mind to recall the tales she had heard as a child, when her mother—despairing of winning Alix's attention to chores—had threatened her with Ihlini retribution.

Until my father said she should not, for to speak of Tyn-

star and the Ihlini was to invite his power over you. Alix shuddered once, seeking to throw off the specter, but Duncan did not seem to notice.

"Tynstar. called *the Ihlini*," he said, "perhaps the most powerful of all those who serve the dark gods of the netherworld. He has arts at his command no man should have, and he uses them for Bellam's gain. This time Homana cannot stand against her enemies."

Alix sat upright, flushed with affrontedness and defiance. "Homana has never fallen! Not in all the years the kings of Solinde have sought to defeat us." She thrust her chin up. "My father said."

Duncan looked across the fire at her, showing her an expression of such amused tolerance she longed to throw the cup at him. "And in all those years the Mujhars of Homana had the Cheysuli by their sides. We used our own god-gifts to defeat the Solindish troops. Not even the Ihlini could halt us." The tolerance faded. "Twenty-five years ago we helped Shaine hold his borders against Bellam, putting down a massive force that might have destroyed Homana. The peace that resulted from our victory would have been solidified by a marriage between Lindir and Bellam's son, Ellic. When that was broken, so was the peace. Now Shaine slays us, and Homana will fall to the Ihlini."

"Twenty-five years . . ." she echoed.

"Lindir remained hidden with Hale for eight years of the *qu'mahlin,* fleeing her *jehan*'s wrath. When he was slain she returned, and bore you but weeks later."

"Well . . . if the Ihlini are so powerful, how is it you have withstood them before?"

"That is a thing between the races. I cannot say." He frowned faintly. "The Ihlini have no real power before us. Oh, they have recourse to some of their illusions and simple arts, but not the dark magic. But we also suffer, for though the Ihlini cannot overcome us with their arts, neither can we take *lir*-shape before them, or hear our *lir*. We are as other men before them."

Alix, stunned by his words, said nothing. All her life she had known the Cheysuli had awesome arts at their call, though she could not have named what they did; to hear Duncan speak of the Ihlini as the demons she had ever thought a Cheysuli characteristic upset her preconceived notions of the order of things. Already Finn had destroyed her innocently confident childhood. Duncan had further shaken her foundations by speaking of a prophecy and the future she faced with his clan. Now, to think of the Ihlini as a real threat to the land she loved, Alix felt a desperation building in her soul.

Too much is being shattered . . . she thought abstractedly. *They are taking too much of me, twisting me, promising things I have ever feared . . .*

"Here," Duncan said gently, "you have suffered long enough."

She dragged her eyes from the fire, blinking at the residue of flames that overlay his dark face. He held something in his hand, offering it to her. She saw it was a silver comb, gleaming in the firelight. Slowly she put out a hand and took it, fingering the intricate runic devices that leaped and twisted in the flickering shadows.

"You may have it," Duncan said. "I carried it for a girl in the Keep. But you have more need of it."

Alix hesitated, staring at him. She could not, even as she tried, view him as her enemy. Finn's threat was very real, substantial; Duncan's was not.

Or else he hides it from me . . .

"Use it," he urged gently.

After a moment she set the comb down and began to undo her tangled braid. Duncan stirred the fire with a stick, coaxing life back to the rosy coals.

She picked twigs and leaves from the heavy plait, gritting her teeth at the pain of snarls set so deeply she would have to rip most of them out. To cover her grimaces she spoke to Duncan.

"You have a wife?"

"No, I have no *cheysula.*"

She dragged the comb through her hair. "Then you have a . . . *meijha?*"

He glanced at her briefly, face closed. "No."

She scowled at him as she ripped at a tangle. "Why did you go to such effort to explain the freedom of your race, if you do not subscribe to it yourself?"

Duncan continued to stir the fire, though it did not particularly require it. "I am clan-leader. It came on me eight months ago, when Tiernan died. With it comes much responsibility, and I chose not to divide myself between a *cheysula* and the leadership this year." He waved the stick idly. "Perhaps next year."

Alix nodded absently as she freed the last tangle from her hair. Her attention was not really focused on Duncan, but she sensed an odd tension in him as he watched her silently. His eyes followed her hands as she pulled the silver comb through the heavy length of her dark hair.

The exercise improved her disposition and her feelings toward the clan-leader. No man, did he want to sacrifice her to some unspeakable god, would allow her the amenities common to courtesy. She was grateful to him.

"My thanks," she said gravely, then smiled warmly at him across the fire.

Duncan was on his feet in one movement, muttering something in the lyrical Old Tongue. His lips compressed into a thin line and his eyes were suddenly hostile as he stared at her, transfixed.

"What have I done?" she cried, aghast.

"Can you not feel it?" he demanded. "Can you not hear the *tahlmorra* in you?"

Alix dropped the comb. "What do you say?"

He swore and turned from her, hands curling into fists. Then he gathered up a bundled blanket and tossed it at her violently.

Alix caught it before it could fall into the fire, recoiling from his cold anger until she felt a tree against her back. As he continued to stare at her with an unwavering, bestial glare, Alix pushed herself to her feet and hugged the blanket as if it would protect her.

"What do you say?" she whispered.

"*Tahlmorra* . . . and you know nothing of it," he snapped.

"No!" she cried, illogically angry when she should be frightened. "I do not! And do not mutter to me of it when I cannot comprehend what it is. How am I to conduct myself if you tell me nothing?"

Duncan took a trembling breath and visibly controlled himself, as if he knew he had frightened her. "I had forgot," he admitted quietly. "You cannot know it. But I question that you feel nothing."

"Feel *what?*"

"We serve the prophecy," he said with effort, "but we

cannot know it perfectly. The *shar tahls* tell us what they can, but even they cannot know everything that the gods intend. The *tahlmorra,* as a whole, is unknown to us. But we feel it. Sense it." He sighed constrictedly and ran a stiff hand through raven hair. "I have come to face a part of my *tahlmorra* I did not know. I should welcome it . . . but I cannot. I cannot accept it. And that, in itself, is a denial of my heritage."

Alix felt a measure of his pain, amazed at the depth of his turmoil. His solemnity had vanished; the man she had thought so controlled and implacable was no different from herself. But she did not understand, and said so.

Duncan relaxed minutely. "No. You cannot. You are too young . . . and too Homanan." His eyes, focused on the heavy curtain of her hair, were bleak. "And Carillon has already won your heart."

"Carillon!"

He gestured to the blanket still clasped in her arms. "Sleep. We ride early."

Alix watched him walk into the shadows, disappearing as easily as if he were a part of the night. She wondered, as she shook out the blanket and lay it by the tree, if he were.

The gods sent her a dreamless sleep.

Chapter Eight

Alix rode with Duncan the next day, hands clasping the saddle and body held carefully upright so she would not touch his back. With Finn she had kept herself from him because of his undisguised interest in her; Duncan's dignity seemed to demand such behavior on her part. She could not imagine hanging onto him or otherwise interfering with anything he did. And he had closed himself to her since their conversation of the evening before. For all he was still courteous, he was also cool toward her.

When evening came and the band of Cheysuli stopped to set up camp, Alix found herself delegated to tend Duncan's fire as if she were a servant. She disliked the sensation. It made her feel a true prisoner, even though she was treated mostly like a visitor.

Alix dumped a tree limb onto the fire and scowled at it blackly, angry with herself for remaining so acquiescent to orders and angry with the circumstances in general. When she sensed a presence on the outer fringes of the firelight she straightened, then gasped and stumbled back a step as she saw the baleful gleaming eyes of a ruddy wolf.

It came closer, into the light, and blurred itself before her. Alix released her breath and gritted her teeth as she saw the form shape itself into Finn.

"Do you seek to frighten me to death?"

Finn laughed at her and squatted to pour himself a cup of honey brew from the pot Duncan had set over the fire. After several restorative swallows he fixed her with a bright gaze and scratched idly at his cheek.

"Well, I have returned your princeling to safety."

Alix knelt down on a thick dark pelt, disgruntled enough to speak rudely even to him. "You did not slay him?"

"Carillon is meant for a death, like all men, but it will not come at my hands."

She shot him a dubious glance. "You would do whatever you could in this personal war you wage against the Mujhar. Even to slaying his heir, were you given the chance."

"But Duncan would not let me do it." He laughed at her startled glance. "No, I would not slay Carillon. He has a part in our own prophecy, if we are to believe he is the one the runes show us. There is no name; only his deeds are written down. The prophecy does not foretell the prince's death so soon, so you may take comfort in that. First he must be Mujhar." Finn studied her over the cup as he drank from it, still squatting by the fire. "You do not seem to fret for him, *meijha.* Have you retrieved your heart from him so soon?"

Alix lifted her chin defiantly. "I will be with him soon enough, when he returns for me."

"Your place is with us," he said seriously. "We are your people. You do not belong with valley crofters *or* the majesty of the Mujhar and his heir."

She knelt on the thick fur, leaning forward in supplication. "You took me from my people. You *stole* me, as the Homanans say Hale did to Lindir. Can you not understand how I feel about the race you say is mine? By the gods, Finn, you even threatened to force me!"

"I did not think you would have me willingly."

Alix released a breath in frustration. "Why will you not hear me? Are you ever so witless as you seem?"

"Witless!"

"Do you do anything with any thought put to the consequences?"

"The *qu'mahlin* has left us little time for thought. Most of the time we act because we must."

"You use that as an excuse!" she cried. "You prate about the *qu'mahlin* as if only you have suffered. Yet you leave me no room to think perhaps your race has the right to curse Shaine, because you behave as if you are free to do what you wish. Duncan would have me see you are men like any other, yet you behave as if the Cheysuli *are* demons with no understanding of what you do to others."

"You need learning," he said bluntly. "When we have

reached the Keep and you have spoken to the *shar tahl,* you will understand better what it is to be Cheysuli. You will understand what the *qu'mahlin* has done. Until then you are lost."

"Take me home," she said softly. "Finn, take me home."

He set the cup down and looked at her levelly. "I do."

Alix ground the heels of her hands against her eyes, feeling the grittiness of exhaustion and tension. Her desperation was growing, swelling up inside her until it threatened to burst her chest and force tears from her eyes. She had no wish to cry before Finn of all people, and the sensation of futility and helplessness hurt so bad she could think only to hurt back.

"I will escape," she said firmly. "When I have the time, and the opportunity, I will win free of you. Even does it come to putting a knife into you."

He smiled. "You could not."

"I could."

"You have neither the spirit nor the strength to do it."

Furious, Alix snatched up the pot of bubbling honey drink and threw it at him. She saw the contents strike his upraised arm and part of his face, then she was on her feet running.

Finn caught her before she reached the edge of the firelight. Alix cried out as he caught one arm and twisted it behind her back. Then he jerked her around until she faced him, and she was suddenly terrified as he bent over her.

"If you would be so bold as to do that, *meijha,* and yet be caught, you had best be prepared to suffer the consequences."

Alix cried out again. She could feel his breath on her face; the dampness of the spilled drink as it stained her gown. She felt her lip caught in his teeth, then stumbled back as Finn was jerked away from her.

Alix gasped in pain and shock as Finn came off the ground, hand to his knife. Then he froze, staring angrily at his assailant.

"You will not force a Cheysuli woman," Duncan said coldly.

Finn took his hand from his knife. "She may have our blood, Duncan, but she has been reared Homanan. She wants humbling. If you leave her to me, I will see to it she behaves with more decorum."

"We do not humble our women, either," Duncan snapped. "Leave her be."

"Why?" Finn demanded, all affronted male pride. "So you can take her?"

"No."

"If she is what you want as *cheysula,* clan-leader, then you had best follow tradition and ask for her clan-rights in Council."

Duncan smiled thinly. "I ask no clan-rights of any woman this year, *rujho.* But if you are so hot to take her, you should hear your own words. She is no light woman, Finn. Ask for her clan-rights, when she has been proven to have them."

Finn glared at him. "I have no need of formal clan-rights where a woman is concerned. There are enough to be had without taking a *cheysula.*"

"Stop!" Alix cried, so loudly they both stared at her in surprise. Self-consciously she swept back her loose hair and scowled at them. "I know nothing of these traditions you speak of, or clan-rights, or Council .. or *anything!* But you had best know I will do *nothing* against my will! You may have forced me to come with you now, but there will be a time when you do not watch me, and I will get free of you all. Do you hear? You cannot keep me!"

"You will stay," Duncan said calmly. "No one escapes the Cheysuli."

Finn smiled. "The clan-leader has spoken, *meijha.* We may disagree, my *rujho* and I, but not on this."

Alix felt the tears welling in her eyes. She widened them instinctively, trying to take back the moisture, but the first tear fell. On a choked sob she spun and ran from them, wondering what animal they would send to fetch her back.

She found a damp mossy area beneath a huge beech tree not far from camp and sat down quickly, loose-limbed and awkward. For a moment she gazed blindly at the shadows and wondered forlornly if she would ever see her home again. Then the enormity of her plight crept upon her. Alix pulled her knees to her chest and hugged them, hiding her face in her torn and stained skirts.

Liren, said a gentle voice, so empathetic it nearly undid her. *Liren.*

Alix turned her head against the rough weave of her gown and saw Storr waiting quietly in the moonlight. For a moment resentment replaced her grief, then it faded. She knew, somehow, Storr had come on his own, not because he was sent to take her back to camp.

I was not sent, he said. *I came because you are in pain, and in need.*

"You speak as a wise old man," she whispered.

I am a wise old wolf, he said, sounding amused. *But there is not so much difference, for all that.*

Alix smiled at him and put out a hand. Storr moved to her and allowed her to place a hand on his head. For a moment she was stunned at what she did; *touching a wolf,* she thought silently. But Storr was patient and very gentle, and she did not fear him.

"You are Finn's *lir,*" she murmured. "How can you be so wise and trustworthy and belong to *him?*"

Storr's eyes closed as she ran fingers through his thick pelt. *My* lir *is not always so hasty and unwise. You have confused him.*

"I!"

He saw you and wanted you. Then he found you were Cheysuli, and his rujholla. *He has had no one but Duncan for too long.*

"Well, he will not have me."

You must take someone . . . someday.

"I will not have a beast like him!"

Storr sighed. *Remember, what name you give him fits you also. You are Cheysuli. It may seem strange now, but you will be happier among us than elsewhere.*

"I would sooner go home. *Home* home; not this Keep."

Even knowing you are not like others?

"Aye. And I am no different."

But you are. Knowing yourself different makes you different. Think of the qu'mahlin. *The Mujhar's decree applies also to you.*

"I am his granddaughter."

And Cheysuli. You do not know Shaine. But know this— if your kinship to him were more important than your race, you would be in Homana-Mujhar.

She knew he was right. But she could not say it, even when he nudged her hand and went away.

"I am sorry for my *rujholli.*" Duncan moved softly out of the shadows. "You must not give credence to his words. All too often Finn speaks without thought."

Alix looked at him and wished herself as far from Duncan and his brother as could be. But since the wish did not work, she answered him.

"You are nothing alike."

"We are. You have not seen it yet."

"You cannot make me believe you are as angry, or as cruel." She sighed in surrender and picked at the moss. "Or else you do not show it."

Duncan squatted before her, hands hanging loosely over his knees. "Finn was but three when the *qu'mahlin* began. He has little memory of the peace in our clan—or in the land—before it. He knows only the darkness and blood and pain of Shaine's war."

"What of you?"

He stared at the moss she was destroying with rigid, nervous fingers. "I was five," he said finally. "Like him, I awoke in the middle of the night when our pavilion fell under the hooves of Homanan horses. It was set on fire even though the Mujhar's men saw we were only children, and too small to do much harm. They did not care." He caught her hand suddenly, stilling it as if its movements disturbed him. His eyes were pale in the moonlight. "You must understand. We were small, but such things remain clear."

"What do you say?" she whispered, sensing his need to have her comprehension.

"That you should understand why he plagues you. He is bitter toward Shaine, and Homanans in general. Carillon is the Mujhar's heir." He paused. "And you want *him* . . . not Finn."

"But if your story is true, Finn is my brother!"

Duncan sighed. "You were raised apart. Why should he not desire a woman, even *after* he has learned she is blood-kin to him?"

Alix stared at him, hand still caught in his. The stubborn conflict she felt rise at Finn's name faded beneath a new—and more frightening—comprehension. She saw before her a solemn-faced warrior who seemed to be waiting for something from her.

For a moment she nearly rose and fled, unable to face the conflict. But she restrained the instinct. There was the faintest whisper of knowledge within her soul, the realization of a power she had never thought she might have, and it astonished her.

"Duncan . . ." she said softly, "what is this *tahlmorra* you say I should feel?"

"You will know it."

"How?"

"You will know it."

"And do you say . . . do you say every Cheysuli has this *tahlmorra?*"

"It is something that binds us all, as tightly as the prophecy. But it has weakened in many of us because so many of us have been lost and forced to take Homanan women to get children." His mouth twisted into a wry smile. "I am not proud of that. But it must be done, if we are to survive. But there are some of us who feel *tahlmorra* more clearly than others." He brought her hand up, smoothing his thumb over the back of her palm. "Mine has told me what will come. When we reach the Keep I will seek out the *shar tahl* and have him show me the prophecy runes to be certain. But I know it already."

Alix withdrew her hand, uneasy. "It has nothing to do with me."

"It is never wrong. The prophecy was given to us by the Firstborn, who were sired by the old gods. It unveils itself in the fullness of time, and to those who listen and understand. I am one of those who follow its path, Alix. I would give my life to see the prophecy fulfilled." He smiled suddenly. "I *will* give my life to see the prophecy fulfilled. That much is clear."

"You know your own death?" she whispered.

"Only that I will die as I am meant, serving the *tahlmorra* of the prophecy. The Firstborn have said."

Alix looked away from the steadiness of his gaze. "You confuse me."

"When you have spoken with the *shar tahl*, the confusion will leave you. Be sure of that."

"And does Finn serve this same *tahlmorra?*"

Duncan laughed. "Finn follows a *sort* of *tahlmorra*. I think he makes his own."

"I am no part of it," she told him severely.

His eyes were gentle. "Of Finn's . . . no. The threads of your *tahlmorra* are entwined with those of another man."

"Carillon?" she asked in a blaze of sudden hope.

He did not answer. She understood him then. Her head came up until she met his gaze squarely. Then she got to her feet and shook out her tattered skirts.

"If I am Cheysuli, I make my own *tahlmorra*. Like Finn." She looked down on him. "You cannot force me, Duncan."

"I would not." He shook his head and rose, looming over her in the darkness. "There is no need."

"You will not force me!"

His hand touched her face gently. "I would not, small one. Your own *tahlmorra* will."

Alix stepped away from him, holding his eyes with her own and denying him what she saw in his face. Then her resolution wavered.

She turned and fled into the shadows of the camp.

Chapter Nine

The warning came as the warrior band rode through the thick forest, making their own track. Cai broke through the thin veil of tree limbs and foliage to seek out Duncan. Alix, glancing up in surprise, saw the hawk wing down and light upon a branch.

They come, lir, the bird said. *Mounted men in the Mujhar's colors. Half-a-league; no more.*

Duncan pulled his horse to a halt. Alix, seeking to remain upright on the animal, caught at Duncan's waist. She felt the tension in his body as if it were her own.

He half-turned in the saddle, muttering something under his breath. Then, "I must find a place for you."

"You will fight them?"

"They will give us no choice, Alix. Why do you think they come, save to slay us all?"

Alix opened her mouth to retort but suddenly could find no words. Her mind was ablaze with sound so intense she knew it was not something she heard with her ears. She thought her head would burst with words, and it was only grabbing at Duncan's waist that kept her on the horse. She mumbled something, closing her eyes against the weight of voices, and vaguely heard the approach of a horse. Duncan took no note of her sudden weakness.

"Well, *rujho,*" Finn's voice said, "the princeling did not lie. He has given us little time."

Alix forced her eyes open and glared at him, though a part of her attention was still claimed by the multitude of voices.

Do they not hear them? she wondered.

Duncan reached around and caught her arm, easing her down from the horse until she had to scramble to stay upright. "Take her," he told Finn.

Alix forcibly detached her mind from the other voices.
"No! Not with him!"

"See to her, *rujho*," Duncan said calmly. "I will not have
her harmed. These men will see only a shapechanger
woman, and would do her injury. I leave her to you."

Finn grinned down at her. "Do you see, *meijha?* The
clan-leader passes you back to me."

"I will have none of you," she said with effort, trying
to speak beneath the weight of words in her mind. "Do
you hear?"

Duncan said something to her but Alix heard nothing;
she saw only that his mouth moved. She clapped hands
over her ears and bowed her head, trying to withstand the
patterns and tones in her mind.

Finn's hands came down on her shoulders. Dimly she
saw Duncan lead his horse away, leaving Finn on foot with
her. She peered at him uncertainly.

"You have been given into my keeping," he announced.
"I do not intend to let you out of it."

"Is it sorcery?" she gasped. "Do you seek to take my
mind from me?"

Finn scowled at her. "You do not make sense, *meijha*.
But I have no time to listen to you now . . . can you not
hear them?"

"I hear their voices!" she cried, trembling. Finn's look
on her was strange. "I speak of their horses, *meijha*. I hear
no voices."

For a moment she pushed away the soundless words and
listened to reality. Through the forest came the sounds of
men battering their way through delaying brush. Her eyes
flew to Finn's.

"They will slay you," he said gently.

The weight began to fall from her mind. Faintly she
heard echoes of the tones and patterns, but she did not feel
so bound by them. Her strength was spent. She nodded
wearily at Finn and did not protest as he led her deeper
into the forest.

"Storr?" she asked softly.

"He is behind, watching. He—like the others—will fight
the Mujhar's men."

Finn pulled her down under cover of a broken tree trunk
leaning drunkenly against another. Quickly he set deadfall

over them, weaving a rapid shelter. When it was done he pushed her down on her stomach and knelt beside her. Alix, still shaken from the silent voices, watched from a distance as he loosened his belt-knife and effortlessly nocked a yellow-fletched black arrow to his compact, powerful bow.

Alix put her head down on one arm and longed for the security of her father's croft.

"Watch my back, *meijha*," Finn said roughly. "I have no time for women's fears."

She wrenched her head up and glared at him. His back was to her, presenting an excellent target for a furious fist, but the precariousness of their position was uppermost in her mind. She put away the urge to do him harm and turned instead to watch behind him, as he had bidden.

Alix's head ached. She scrubbed at her forehead as if to drive the pain away, but it did no good. The voices were gone, only a figment of memory, but it was enough to leave a residue. Her entire body ached with the indignities she had been forced to endure: sores remained on her legs from continued riding; bruises dotted her flesh and her bones and muscles felt like rags. Her mind, she knew dimly, was as exhausted. For all they insisted they would do her no harm, the Cheysuli had accounted for more pain and fatigue than she had ever thought possible.

At first she thought it was a Cheysuli horse crashing through the brush toward their thin shelter. Alix stared silently up at the man a moment before she realized he was a mailed man-at-arms in the scarlet-and-black tunic livery of the Mujhar, sword drawn.

Relief flooded through her. She would escape Finn and the others now, putting herself into the care of a Mujharan guardsman, who would surely rescue her from her plight. Alix sighed in relief and crawled forward as the man's eyes fell on hers. The beginnings of her smile of greeting faded.

The sword lifted in a gloved hand, swinging back over his shoulder. Transfixed, Alix stared at the bright blade. It hung over her, poised to fall, and in a blinding flash of realization she knew Duncan's words were true. They would slay her where she stood, and call her shapechanger.

Alix lunged backward into Finn. He turned sharply and hissed something, then saw why she moved. He said noth-

ing more. The arrow's flight was unmarked in passing, but
Alix saw the feathered shaft quiver out of the guardsman's
throat. He fell back in the saddle, crying out something in
a gurgling voice. Then he tumbled from his bolting horse.

She stuffed a fist into her mouth to keep from screaming,
aware only that Finn had left her and was fighting hand-
to-hand with yet another guardsman. Alix recoiled, staring
open-mouthed at the straining men. A bough jabbed her
in the small of her back, tearing through the woolen fabric
and into her flesh, but she was oblivious to the pain.

Finn bent the man's knife arm away from his throat, a
fearful rictus of concentration baring his teeth. Muscles
bulged beneath his armbands as he fought to keep the
blade from his throat.

Alix mumbled something to herself, unaware she spoke.
Finn drove his knife upward into the guardsman's stomach,
but not before the man managed to bring his own weapon
down in a slashing motion that penetrated Finn's rib cage.

Alix cried out again, then heard a strange moaning sound
and saw the Cheysuli blur himself into his wolf-shape. Before her horrified eyes the wolf leaped on the man and
bore him to the ground, ripping his throat away.

Sickened, she leaped to her feet and fled the shelter.

"Alix!"

She ran on, ignoring Finn's human cry.

"Alix!"

An agonized glance over her shoulder showed him coming after her, bloodied knife in one hand. She blurted out
a garbled denial and ran on, breaking her way with outstretched hands.

A horse drove through the brush before her, pawing
hooves flailing at her head as its rider jerked it to a halt.
Alix ducked down and threw a beseeching hand up, expecting a blow from one of the hooves. She saw an enraged
face hanging over her as the guardsman drew his broadsword.

"Shapechanger witch!"

"No!" she shrieked. *"No!"*

"You'll not live to bear more of the demons!" he cried,
lowering the blade in a hideous slash.

Alix threw herself flat onto the ground and heard an

eerie whistle as the blade flew past her head. Then she scrambled up and instinctively dashed directly at the horse.

The wolf-shape hurtled past her, leaping, and took the man from the horse in one sweeping lunge. Alix heard the guardsman cry out. The horse screamed and reared, striking out.

The guardsman's broadsword fell at her feet as she stumbled away from the terrified horse. The man, now on foot, lifted his knife to slash at the wolf leaping toward his throat. The point slid sideways and tore open one furred shoulder, driving the wolf back.

The soldier bent for his sword, caught it up and advanced on the snarling animal. "Demon!" he hissed. "Know what it is to *die* in that shape!"

Alix threw herself forward and grabbed at his arm, thwarting his blow. The mail bit into her hands and face as she hung onto the arm. One jerk knocked her to the ground so hard she lay there, half-stunned.

Gloating, the man turned back to the wolf. But the animal was gone. In its place stood a Cheysuli warrior whose knife found a new sheath in the guardsman's throat. His blood splattered Alix as the body fell next to her.

Finn stood over her, clasping his left shoulder. His jerkin was heavy with blood from the wound in his ribs. Amazed, Alix saw a grin on his battered face.

"So, *meijha,* you feel enough for me to risk your own life."

Burgeoning panic and the sickening smell of blood drove her to her feet. Alix stood before him unsteadily, trembling with rage and reaction. She wiped a hand across her face and felt the dampness of the man's blood.

"I wish death on no one, shapechanger. Not even you."

Another horse crashed through the trees, leaping mailed bodies as they lay scattered on the forest floor. Alix swung around in panic and saw Carillon on his chestnut warhorse. He wore his Cheysuli sword but had not unsheathed it.

"Alix!" He jerked the horse to a halt, staring down at the man Finn had slain. The Cheysuli warrior, weaponless, glared wrathfully at the prince.

"Do you slay me now, lordling?" he demanded, lowering his hand from the wound in his shoulder.

Carillon ignored him and reached out to Alix. "Quickly. Climb up behind me."

She moved forward, stunned by the suddenness of her rescue, but Finn's bloody hand on her arm stopped her.

"Meijha . . ."

She wrenched her arm free. "I go with Carillon," she said firmly. "As I told you once before."

"Alix, waste no time," Carillon urged.

"Meijha, stay with your clan," Finn said.

Alix grasped Carillon's hand and pulled herself onto the horse's broad hindquarters. Her arms settled around the prince's hips, resting on his swordbelt. She sent Finn a significant look of triumph.

"I do not stay. I go home . . . with Carillon."

Finn scowled blackly up at them. Carillon, smiling oddly, tapped his sword hilt. "Another time, shapechanger." He spun the chestnut and sent him leaping back the way he had come.

Alix, clinging to him, saw with horror the carnage as they passed. Liveried guardsmen lay scattered through the forest, some displaying the marks of beasts. She shuddered and pressed herself against Carillon's back, sickened by the results of the forest battle.

Carillon's horse broke into a clearing and galloped across a lush meadow. The edge of the forest fell behind them, and with it the grim toll of dead.

"I said I would come," Carillon said above the sound of pounding hooves.

"So many are slain . . ." she said.

"The Mujhar's vengeance."

Alix swallowed and put a hand to her tangled, blood-matted hair. "I saw only slain *guardsmen,* Carillon. There were no Cheysuli."

She felt him stiffen and expected a curt reply, but the prince said nothing. The golden hilt of his sword pressed against her left arm as she hung on, and she stared at its huge ruby and the golden Homanan lion crest in wonder.

Hale's sword . . . she whispered within her mind. *My father?*

A hawk broke free of the trees and flew to catch them. It circled over them, drifted a moment, then drove closer.

The warhorse, shying as the bird neared his head, plunged sideways.

Alix saw the hawk as it streaked by them, circling to return. It was the smaller one she had conversed with in the forest, and she nearly fell from the plunging horse as her grip loosened in shock. Carillon, cursing, tried to rein the stallion into control.

The hawk drove close again, wings snapping against the horse's head. Alix felt the smooth hindquarters bunch and slide from beneath her, though she grabbed at Carillon's leather doublet. She cried out and tumbled awkwardly to the ground.

Carillon called her name but the frightened horse would not allow him to approach. The prince wrestled with the reins, muttering dire threats under his breath, but Alix saw no good come of his words. She sat up dazedly and fingered the lump on the back of her head.

Stay with me, the bird said. *Stay.*

"Let me go!" she cried, getting unsteadily to her feet.

Stay.

"No!"

I ask, small one. I am not Finn, who takes. The bird hesitated. *I ask.*

Realization flooded her. "Duncan!"

Stay with me.

"Duncan . . . let me go with him. It is what I want."

It does not serve the prophecy.

"It is not *my* prophecy!" she cried, lifting a fist into the air. "It is not mine!"

And the tahlmorra?

Alix was conscious Carillon had calmed the warhorse somewhat. The prince jumped off the chestnut and dragged him behind, crossing to her with long steps.

"Alix!"

She stared at the hawk drifting idly in the sky. "It is not my prophecy," she said, more quietly. "Nor is it my *tahlmorra.*"

But it is mine . . .

Alix turned to Carillon, shoving tangled loose hair out of her face. "I go with you. If you can keep your horse in check, I will stay aboard."

She saw questions in his eyes but he did not ask them. Eloquently, silently, he gestured toward the hawk.

Alix stared up at it, aware of a sensation of regret. "If you would stop me, shapechanger, you must do as your brother. And to do that earns you my enmity."

The bird paused in mid-flight. *That,* it said after a moment, *is not entirely what I seek.*

"Then let me go."

The hawk said nothing more. It circled a last time, then soared higher into the sky and flew away.

Carillon touched her shoulder. "Alix?"

Strangely defeated and somehow bereft, she turned to him. She spread her hands. "You may take me to Homana-Mujhar, my lord, and to my grandsire."

His hand tightened on her shoulder. "I have warned you what he may feel when he sees you."

She smiled grimly through her dirt and blood stains. "I will take that chance."

Carillon caught her waist and swung her up on the quieted horse. He put her in the saddle and she clutched at it, surprised. He mounted behind her and took up the reins, setting his arms around her waist.

"I think the Mujhar may find his granddaughter is no simple crofter's child."

Alix smiled wearily as the stallion moved on. "He raised a willful daughter. Let him see how that spirit serves Lindir's child."

BOOK II

"The Meijha"

Chapter One

Carillon took Alix first to the croft so she could see Torrin and show him she was well. As they rode down the hills into the valley Alix had known all her life, she felt a strange sense of homecoming mixed with loneliness. Her relief at seeing the lush valley again was tinged with sadness and regret, for she realized her few days with the Cheysuli had altered her perceptions forever.

"It seems odd," Carillon said quietly as he guided the chestnut toward the stone crofter's cottage built along the treeline.

"Odd?"

"Torrin lived among the halls of Homana-Mujhar, privy to much of Shaine's confidences. Yet he gave it up to work the land like a tenant-crofter owing yearly rents to his lord."

Alix, slumped wearily in the saddle, nodded. "My father—" She broke off, then continued in a subtly altered tone. "*Torrin* has ever been a man of deepness and dark silences. I begin to see why, I think."

"If the story is true, he has carried a burden on his soul for many years."

Alix straightened as the whitewashed door of the croft squeaked open. Torrin came out and stood staring as Carillon took the horse in to him.

"By the gods . . ." Torrin said hoarsely, "I thought you taken by beasts, Alix."

She, seeing him through different eyes, marked the seams of age in his worn face and the thinning of his graying hair cropped close against his head. His hands, once so powerful, had callused and gnarled with crofter's work over the years, so different from an arms-master's craft. Even his

broad shoulders had shrunk, falling in as if the weight of
the realm rested on them.

*What manner of man was he before he took me from the
Mujhar?* she wondered. *What has this burden done to him?*

Alix slid free of the horse as Carillon halted him, standing straight and tall before the man she had called father
all her life. Then she put out her hand, palm up, and spread
her fingers.

"Know you what this is?" she asked softly.

Torrin stared transfixed at her hand. Color leached from
his weather-burned face until he resembled little more than
a dead man with glistening eyes.

"Alix . . ." he said gently. "Alix, I could not tell you. I
feared to lose you to them."

"But I have come back," she said. "I have been with
them, and I have come back."

He aged before her eyes. "I could not tell you."

Carillon stepped off his horse and walked slowly forward,
skin stretched taut across the bones of his face. "Then it is
true, this shapechanger tale. Lindir went willingly, forsaking
the betrothal because of Shaine's liege man."

Torrin sighed and ran a gnarled hand through his hair.
"It was a long time ago. I have put much of it away. But
I see you must know it, now." He smiled a little. "My lord
prince, when last I saw you, you were but a year old. It is
hard to believe that squalling infant has become a man."

Alix stepped up to Torrin and took one of his hands in
hers. She felt the weariness and resignation in his body.

"I will go to my grandsire," she said softly. "But first I
will hear the truth of my begetting."

Torrin led them inside and gestured for Carillon to seat
himself at a rectangular slab table of scarred wood. Alix
paced the room like a fretful dog, seeking security in the
familiarity she had ever known.

Finally, knowing it eluded her, she stopped before the
fireplace and faced Torrin. "Tell me. I would know it all."

He nodded, pouring a cup of thin wine for Carillon and
another for himself. Then he sat down on a stool and stared
fixedly at the beaten dirt floor.

"Lindir refused Ellic of Solinde from the very first. She
would not be marriage bait, she said, to be given to Ellic
like a tame puppy. Shaine was furious and ordered her to

do his bidding. When she remained defiant, he said he
would place her under guard and sent her to Lestra, Bellam's city. Lindir was ever a determined woman, but she
also recognized the strength in her father. He would have
done it."

"So she fled," Alix said softly.

"Aye." Torrin blew out a heavy breath. "Hale did not
steal her. That was a tale the Mujhar put out, to justify the
affront to his pride. Later, when Ellinda died and Lorsilla
bore no living children, he decided it was a curse laid
against his House by the Cheysuli. What Lindir did made
him half-mad, I thought. She had kept her secret well. None
knew of her feelings for Hale."

"He had a woman at the Keep," Alix said. "Yet he left
her for Lindir."

Torrin looked at her steadily. "You will understand such
things one day, Alix, when you have met the man you will
have. Lindir was the sort all men loved, but she would have
no one, until Hale." He shrugged. "She was eighteen, and
more beautiful than anything I have ever seen. Had she
been born a boy—with all her pride and strength—she
would have made Shaine the finest heir a king could want."

"But she *refused* Ellic."

Torrin snorted. "I did not say she was acquiescent. Lindir
had a way about her that ensorcelled all men, even her
father, until he would wed her to the Solindish heir. Then
she showed her own measure of the Mujhar's strength and
stubbornness."

Carillon sipped his wine, then set the cup down. "My
uncle never speaks of it. What I have heard has come
from others."

"Aye," Torrin agreed. "The Mujhar was a proud man.
Lindir defeated him. Few men of so much pride will speak
of such things."

"What happened?" Alix asked, hugging herself before
the fire.

"The night of the betrothal, when all the lords of Solinde
and Homana gathered in the Great Hall, Lindir walked out
of Homana-Mujhar in the guise of a serving woman. Hale
went as a red fox, and no one knew either of them as they
left the city. He was not seen again."

"What of Lindir?" Carillon asked.

Torrin sighed. "She disappeared. Shaine sent troops after them, of course, swearing Hale had stolen her for himself. But neither was ever found, and within a year the Lady Ellinda was dead of a wasting disease. Shaine's second wife, the Lady Lorsilla, was made barren when she lost the boy who would have been prince. But I have told you that. Shaine began his purge the morning after the boy was born dead, and it has continued since."

Alix shivered. "But . . . Lindir came back."

Torrin's hands clenched against his knees. "She came back eight years after Shaine began the purge. Hale was dead and she herself was ill. The Mujhar accepted her only because he needed an heir, and when Lindir died after bearing a girl he would not accept it. He said the purge would continue. The Lady Lorsilla and myself pleaded with him not to have the child left to die in the forests. He said I could take the girl, if I left his service and swore never to allow her in Mujhara. I agreed."

Alix stared at him. "You did all that for a halfling girl-child . . ."

He swallowed heavily. "Had Shaine cast you out, I could not have served him again. Taking you was the best thing I have ever done."

"Then they are not demons?"

Torrin shook his head slowly. "The Cheysuli have never been demons. They have arts we do not, and most of us fear them for it, but they do not use them for ill."

"Why did you allow me to believe they were?"

"I never called them demons, Alix. But neither could I tell you differently, or your own innocence in defending them would draw suspicion. Had Shaine ever heard of you, he might have called you to him. He might have rescinded his decision to let me keep you as my own."

"And Hale?" she asked softly.

Torrin's head bowed. "Hale served his lord with a loyalty no other man could hope for. It was Lindir who twisted that loyalty. Hale was a good man. You have no need to fear the memory of your father."

Alix went to him and knelt before him, placing soft hands over his hardened ones. She put her forehead down on his knee.

"*You* will ever be my father!" she said brokenly.

Torrin placed one hand on her bowed head. "You are my daughter, Alix. If your blood begins to show you another way, I understand it. There is magic in a Cheysuli soul." He sighed and smoothed her hair. "But you will be my daughter as long as I live."

"I will never leave you!"

He cradled her head, lifting it so she could see his face. "Alix, I think you must. I served with the Cheysuli years before your birth; I know their strength and dedication and their magnificent honor. They did not ask for this *qu'mahlin*. But they realize it is a part of their *tahlmorra*."

"*You* speak of that!"

He smiled sadly. "I have reared a Cheysuli girl-child in my house, and in my heart. How could I not?"

A chilling sensation rippled through her body. "Then you knew . . . one day . . ."

"I have ever known." He leaned forward and kissed her brow softly. "A Cheysuli can never deny his *tahlmorra*. To do so angers the gods."

"I did not want this," she said dully.

Torrin removed his hands and sat back from her as if to illustrate the sacrifice he made. "Go with the prince, Alix. I would keep you, if I could, but it is not the will of the gods." He smiled, but the pain remained in his eyes. "The path to your *tahlmorra* lies another way."

"I will stay," she whispered.

Carillon rose quietly and moved to her. "Come, cousin. It is time you met your grandsire."

"You have brought me home, Carillon. It is enough."

He bent and grasped her arms, pulling her upright. Alix jerked around and glared at him. "You would have me think you no better than Finn—ordering me this way and that!"

He grinned at her. "Then perhaps he has the right of it. What else can a man do when a woman defies him, save force her?"

She took a step away from him. "I will see the Mujhar another time."

"If you do not come now, you will never do it." Carillon glanced at Torrin and saw the confirmation in his eyes. The prince smiled faintly and took her arm once again.

"You will come here another time," Torrin said.

Alix, testing Carillon's grip tentatively, gave it up. She looked down on the slump-shouldered man who had been a king's arms-master before taking a halfling girl-child to his heart.

"I have loved you well," she whispered.

Torrin rose, looking at her as if he hurt. Then he cradled her head in his gnarled hands and kissed her forehead.

Carillon led her from the croft.

The prince took her out of the forests and the valleys into Mujhara, and through its cobbled streets. Alix sat behind him silently, clinging to his waist as if his closeness would give her confidence. The gleaming city with its winding, narrow streets took away her powers of speech. Alix was acutely aware of her torn and stained garments and bare feet.

"I do not belong here," she muttered.

"You belong wherever you wish to be," Carillon said. He gestured. "Homana-Mujhar."

She looked past his arm and saw the stone walls rising before her. The fortress-palace stood on a gentle rise within the city itself, hidden behind time-worn walls of rose-colored, undressed stone. Before them towered massive bronze-and-timber gates, attended by eight men liveried in the Mujhar's colors. Alix saw red tunics over light chain mail, emblazoned with a rampant black lion. It was the proud coat-of-arms she had seen etched into Carillon's ruby seal ring; and stamped into the heavy gold of the sword hilt.

The guardsmen swung open the huge gates, acknowledging Carillon with brief salutes. As their incurious eyes fell on her she let go of Carillon's waist, blushing in shame.

"Carillon . . . take me back to the croft! I should not be here!"

"Be silent, Alix. This place is your legacy."

"And Shaine sent me *from* it!"

He did not answer her. She was forced to sit quietly on his warhorse and ride inexorably toward the huge palace. Alix closed her eyes as they entered the bailey and wished herself elsewhere.

Duncan was right . . . Homana-Mujhar is not for me.

Carillon stopped the horse before a flight of marble steps that led up to the palace of Homanan kings. A groom raced over to catch the reins and bowed reverently; Carillon jumped down and lifted Alix from the horse before she could protest. She kept her head lowered as he took her up the smooth, dark-veined steps into the rose-colored palace, until she saw the first servant stare at her with undisguised contempt. Carillon did not see it, but Alix was instantly aware how her arrival would be regarded. Everyone would think her some lice-ridden woman of the streets if she behaved as one, so she resolutely lifted her head. She summoned her pride and confidence and went with Carillon as if she belonged with him.

She saw magnificent tapestries picked out in rainbow colors; candleracks holding fresh candles glowing with flame; thick rugs and clean rushes; ornaments and heavily embroidered arrases at doorways. Liveried servants bowed respectfully to Carillon and included her in their homage. Inwardly she smiled at the change in attitude a little arrogance brought.

But when Carillon escorted her up a winding stairway of red stone to a doorway of hammered bronze, Alix halted abruptly. "Where do you take me?"

"These are the chambers of the Lady Lorsilla."

"Shaine's *wife?*"

"She will see to it you are bathed and dressed as befits a princess, before you meet the Mujhar." He smiled at her. "Alix, I promise you will be safe."

She swallowed and glared at him. "I do not wish to be safe. I wish to go back to the croft."

Carillon ignored her and rapped on the bronze door. Alix closed her eyes and consigned herself to the netherworld. The defiance she had held in abundance when first learning of her heritage fled, leaving her cold and lonely within the massive palace.

"Carillon!" cried a woman's voice as the door swung open. "You are returned so soon?"

Alix opened her eyes. She saw a chambermaid at the door, curtsying to Carillon, and beyond her a tiny blonde woman in a silken blue robe banded with white fur.

"I have brought back what I said I would," Carillon said gravely. "Regardless what my uncle wishes."

The woman sighed and smiled wryly. "You are more like Shaine than you know, at times. Well, let me see her."

Carillon led Alix forward. She heard the door shut behind them and swallowed against the sudden fear in her throat.

The woman sat on a cushioned bench of dark stone. She settled the rich robe more comfortably around her shoulders. "Alix, you are well come."

"No," Alix said. "I am not. Shaine cast me out before; I have no doubt he would do so again."

Lorsilla, queen of Homana, smiled warmly. "He must see you, first. And I think he will hold his tongue, if only from sheer amazement."

"Or hatred."

"He cannot hate what he does not know," Lorsilla said gently. "Alix, he is your grandsire. His anger was never at you, but at himself for losing Lindir. Had he treated her more gently when she refused Ellic, she might have remained here."

Alix gestured helplessly, indicating her tatters and blood-streaked face. "I am not the sort a king would acknowledge."

Carillon laughed. "You will be, when *she* has done with you. As for me, I will leave you to the lady. When I come for you, you will be ready to face even the harshest of men."

Instinctively she whirled and caught his hand. "Carillon!"

He detached himself gently. "I must go, Alix. It is not my place to see you bathed and dressed." His grin was amused. "Though I would not mind it so much, myself."

Lorsilla lifted a delicate brow. "Carillon, conduct yourself with more decorum."

He laughed at her and bowed, then took his leave.

Alix stood before the queen of Homana and shivered once, involuntarily. Her feet ached and her face burned with shame.

Lorsilla rose and moved forward. She touched a soft hand across the healing welt on Alix's face and brushed away the dried remains of the guardsman's blood. Her voice was very gentle.

"You have no need to fear me, Alix. I am your grand-dame."

Alix's voice shook. "But I am a *hafling* . . ."

The tiny woman smiled sadly. "I will have no children

of my own, and no grandchildren. Let me at least have Lindir's daughter, for a time."

She bowed her head and nodded, hiding the welling of grief in her heart. She heard the woman order a bath drawn and clothing to be prepared. Then Lorsilla laughed softly.

"You have been raised a croft-girl, Alix. Now you will know what it is to claim the heritage Shaine denied you. I will make you a princess, my girl."

She swallowed painfully. "But I am Cheysuli."

Lorsilla's delicate face grew stern. "It does not matter. You are Shaine's granddaughter, and that is enough for me."

But what of him? she wondered apprehensively. *What of the Mujhar himself?*

Chapter Two

Alix went before her grandsire in silks and velvets, girdled with gold and garnets. The rich brown fabrics whispered against her legs and fine slippers hugged her bruised feet. Her head felt heavy with the weight of her hair, laced with pearls and tiny garnets. Her ears ached dully with fresh piercing, but the gems glittering in them assuaged her pain.

The croft-girl was gone as she stood before the Mujhar of Homana, and she wondered if that girl would ever return to her.

Carillon, standing next to her in the huge audience hall, radiated pride and confidence. But Shaine dominated the hall with inborn power and strength of will.

"My lord," Carillon said quietly, "this is Alix. Lindir's daughter."

The Mujhar stood on a low marble dais that spread the entire width of the hall. Behind him, raised on grasping lion's claws, stood a carved throne banded with bronze and silver; cushioned in silks and velvets. Etched deeply within the throne was scroll work of gold paint, and the wood gleamed with polishing. The scent of beeswax and power hung in the air. Shaine himself wore black and gold, and the harsh pride of an arrogant man.

His gray eyes narrowed at Carillon's announcement. Alix stared at him, concentrating on the fact he was her grandsire and not Homana's king. It did not help.

A wide circlet of emeralds and diamonds set in gold banded his brow, smoothing his silvering dark hair. He was bearded, but it did not hide the determination of his jaw or the tight line of his lips.

There is no forgiveness in this man . . . Alix realized.

Accordingly, she lifted her head proudly and firmed her own mouth. Carillon stepped away from her, renouncing his right to speak for her, but it did not disturb her. She was beyond fear or reticence and let the instincts she had only sensed rule her actions. Her defiance flashed across the Great Hall to strike Shaine like a blow.

"I see nothing of Lindir in you," the Mujhar said quietly. "I see only a shapechanger's stamp."

"What does it tell you, my lord?"

He stared at her, face taut and remote. "It tells me you have no place here. It speaks to me of treachery and sorcery, and a Cheysuli curse."

"But you admit it is true I might be Lindir's child."

A flicker shadowed the gray eyes a moment. Alix could sense Shaine's consideration of rejecting her outright, but she knew his pride too well for that. He would not quail before acknowledging his wish to rid himself of a halfling child, even at birth.

"Carillon says you are that child," he said finally. "Also that Torrin had the raising of you. So you may call yourself Lindir's child if you wish—it does you no good. I will not acknowledge you."

"I did not come expecting acknowledgment."

His dark brows rose. "You did not? I find that difficult to believe."

Alix kept her hands away from the golden girdle with effort, fighting down her nervousness. "I came because I wished to see the man who could cast out a child and curse an entire race. I came to see the man who began the *qu'mahlin.*"

"Use no shapechanger words to me, girl. I will not have it in this place."

"Once you welcomed them."

His gray eyes burned with inward rage. "I was deceived. Their sorcery is strong. But I will take retribution for it."

Alix lifted her head in a reflection of his arrogance. "Is what Lindir did worth the destruction of an entire race, my lord? Do you seek to be no better than Bellam of Solinde, who wants only to humble this land?"

Carillon drew a quick breath of dismay but she paid it no heed. She held Shaine's eyes with her own and felt the power in the man. She began to wonder, deep within her soul, if she had not her own measure of it.

"You are Cheysuli," the Mujhar said harshly. "You are subject to death . . . like all of them."

"You would have me slain, then?"

"Cheysuli are under penalty of death."

Carillon moved closer to her. "What Lindir did was long ago, and best forgotten. You cast Alix away once. Do not do it again."

"You have no place in this, Carillon!" Shaine lashed. "Take yourself from this hall."

"No."

"Do as I bid."

"No, my lord."

Shaine glared at him, hands knotting on his gold belt. "The Cheysuli took you prisoner and set a wolf on you. This girl is one of them. How can you defy me like this?"

"Alix is my cousin, my lord. Bloodkin. I will not see her treated so, even by you."

The Mujhar's breath hissed through his teeth as he stepped wrathfully from the dais. He stood before the empty firepit running the length of the hall.

"You do not speak to *me* so! I am your liege lord, Carillon, and I have made you my heir. Am I to believe the shapechangers have used sorcery on you, to win you to their side? Must I disinherit you?"

Alix looked sharply at Carillon and saw his face go bloodless, jaw clenched as tightly as Shaine's.

"You may do as you will, my lord, but it seems futile to disinherit the only possible heir to Homana's throne. Did you not live through too many empty years in hopes of getting one before?"

"Carillon!"

"You have made me your heir," he said steadily. "But it does not take my humanity from me."

"Get yourself from this hall!"

Alix stepped forward. "So you may deal with me alone? So you may have me taken from this place and slain on the altar of your pride?"

Shaine's face blanched white. "*You* do not speak freely in this hall, shapechanger witch! You will do as I bid you!"

Alix opened her mouth to answer but a sudden chiming tone within her mind banished the words. Stunned, she stared blindly at the Mujhar. Cai's gentle tone wove its familiar pattern in her mind.

I am here, liren. *Should the man grow too full of himself, we shall show him something; you and I.*

Cai! she cried silently.

I am here for you, liren. *This petty lord cannot harm you.*

Alix began to smile. "Cai."

Carillon stiffened. "Alix, what do you say?"

She ignored him. She looked steadily at the Mujhar and spoke softly, with renewed confidence. A sense of power and resolve was growing within her.

"My lord, you rule here through the sufferance of the Cheysuli. You owe them more than you will admit."

"I will drive them from this land!" he roared, face congesting. "They are demons! Sorcerers! Servitors of the dark gods . . . no better than the Ihlini. I will see they are destroyed!"

"And you will destroy the very heart of Homana!" she shouted. "Foolish man—you do not deserve to be king of an honorable land!"

He raised his hand to her, stepping forward. Alix, unflinching, stood before him, but before the blow could fall she felt a flaring of power within her mind. It reached out, seeking, and the magnificent hawk answered it.

The velvet arras hanging at a narrow casement rippled and billowed aside as the *lir* winged into the hall. His passage set the candles guttering, throwing eerie shadows against the stone walls. Many of the tapers winked out, plunging the hall into flickering relief. Wall sconces flared and smoked as his wingspan flurried them.

Shaine turned as he felt the beat in the wind. His raised hand fell to his side as he stared speechlessly at the hawk. A garbled sound broke from his throat as Cai whipped a slash of air across his face.

The bird of prey circled the lofty hammer-beamed hall gracefully; eloquently powerful. Alix felt a welling of pride so sharp it hurt. As she watched him she began to understand the magic of her blood, and to understand what it was to be Cheysuli.

They have not lied . . . she whispered silently. *They have said the truth—that it is better to be part of an accursed race with a god-gift in the blood, than to be a* lir*less Homanan.*

Cai circled and flew toward them again, dark eyes brightened by the flames of the sconces and candleracks. He slowed, stalling with broad wings, and settled himself upon the back of the throne. He mantled once, then perched in perfect silence on the dark lion throne of Homana.

There, liren; have we made the man take notice?

Alix laughed joyously within her mind, welcoming her god-gift, and felt the hawk's approval.

Shaine stumbled away from her, but neither did he go near the throne with its hawk headpiece. The Mujhar's hand raised and pointed at the bird.

"Is this your doing? Do you summon the familiars of demons?"

"He is a *lir*, my lord," she said evenly. "Surely you recall them. Hale had one, did he not?"

"Go from here!" Shaine cried hoarsely. "Leave this place! I will not suffer a Cheysuli within Homana-Mujhar!"

"Willingly, my lord grandsire," she said clearly. "Nor will I suffer a foolishly vain man longer than I must."

His face contorted. "Leave this place before I have my guard take you!"

Alix was so angry she ached with it. She turned her rigid back on the Mujhar and walked to the open doors at the end of the hall. There she swung around once more.

"I see now why Lindir took her leave of you, my lord. I only wonder she did not do it sooner."

Alix went unaccosted into the darkness of the cobbled bailey courtyard. As she picked up her skirts to hasten toward the tall gates she heard the clash of gold and gems at her girdle and realized she fled with some of the Mujhar's riches. Then she hardened her heart and determined to keep them, if only to have a legacy of her mother. She had no coin; the gems would serve.

Alix glanced over her shoulder apprehensively, expecting to be followed. From all accounts Shaine was too vain to let such an affront to his pride go unremarked; if she did not win free of Homana-Mujhar quickly she might soon taste the hospitality of his dungeons. When she turned back, hitching her skirts higher, she saw a shadow detach itself from the wall and come at her.

She stumbled back in alarm as the looming figure caught

her. Before she could cry out a hand fastened firmly over her mouth.

"Be silent!" hissed a whisper.

By the gods, Shaine will have me slain! She struggled against the hard body, fighting the guardsman with all her strength. The hand clenched against her jaw painfully, restraining her teeth as she sought to bite. Her free hand clawed for his face and missed, dragging across a bare arm and stopping against the warmth of embossed metal.

Alix froze.

"*Now* will you be still?" the man asked. He removed his hand from her mouth.

"Duncan. *Duncan!*"

He shook her, hissing at her vehemently. "Be silent! Will you give us both away?"

"This is *Homana-Mujhar!* Shaine will have you slain!"

"Only if he learns I am here," Duncan said grimly. "But that should not be difficult if you persist in shouting."

"I am not shouting," she said sullenly, lowering her voice.

He dragged her toward the wall, ignoring her protests. When they reached the shadows he set her against the cold stone and stood before her, blocking out the torchlight from the palace.

"Have you learned what you wanted?" he demanded, not bothering to hide his anger. "Have you seen what it is to be Cheysuli in Shaine's presence?"

She could not make out his features in the darkness, but his odd violence told her what he felt. "Duncan, it was a thing I had to do."

He sighed, still gripping her arms. "You are no better than Lindir. The Mujhar's get are willful women."

"Why are you here?" she whispered, peering at his shadowed face. *"Here?"*

"I will give you answers later. First we must leave this place. I have horses waiting outside the walls."

Alix planted her feet as he sought to lead her toward a small wooden gate hidden in shrubbery. She felt his startled hesitation and nearly laughed. But she did not let him see her amusement.

"Duncan, I told you to let me be when Carillon came for me. Why have you come?"

He shifted slightly. Faint torchlight illuminated his face and showed her an odd glint in his yellow eyes. He smiled coldly.

"You said I must do as my brother to stop you. I let you go then. I will not do it again."

"Let me be!"

"You are Cheysuli," he said flatly. "You have a place with your clan."

"I *refuse* it!"

His hands clamped on her arms, hurting her. He ignored her wince of pain. "Alix, you will have us found if you persist. What sense is it to have us both slain in the name of Shaine's purge?"

"If you do not explain yourself I will shout for the guardsmen. I am surprised they have not found you already, if they are so skilled."

He laughed softly. "The Cheysuli move in silence, small one." He paused significantly. "Except, perhaps, for you."

She glared at him. A strange sense of defiance and exhilaration crept into her heart and nearly consumed her. She smiled at him in vindictive joy and opened her mouth as if to cry out.

Duncan silenced her instantly. This time he did not use his hand. Alix, shocked to the core, felt herself caught in a harsh embrace and kissed as if he would take the soul from her.

She stiffened instantly, pressing palms against his chest to push him away. In that moment she realized the absolute strength of a determined man and was amazed by it. She sought to escape but was trapped within his arms.

Alix shuddered once, recalling Finn's harshness and the instinctive fear he had provoked. Then, oddly, the thought fell away.

A new awareness slid through her as Duncan's mouth moved on hers. It was imperceptive, yet she felt it, and he no longer forced her. The pain he had inflicted at first was gone, altering in some subtle fashion. When a second shiver coursed through her it was of another origin.

Duncan is not his brother, she thought dazedly, *and I do not fear this man . . .*

Alix felt the wall at her back as he lifted his mouth from hers. An odd expression of inner conflict moved through his pale eyes, tautening his face into blankness. Alix, wanting only to see the possessive determination in him again, touched his chin.

"Is this your *tahlmorra?*" she asked breathlessly. "Is this why?"

The tight line of his mouth relaxed. "Perhaps it will not be so long a time to wait after all."

"Duncan . . . I do not understand."

"I have come to you as Finn, forcing myself on a woman who does not wish it," he said grimly. "Have I earned the enmity you promised?"

"I have forgot what I said."

His lips twitched. "Forgot? You?"

Alix turned her head away, realizing she still clung to him. Her wantonness made her ashamed, but when she tried to slide away he kept her pressed against the wall.

"Alix, you have only to listen to what is in you. Heed it. I will not force you again." Duncan moved away from her, releasing her to stand in solitude against the wall. Alix sensed impatience in him and the slow rising of an odd anxiety and urgency in herself.

By the gods, what has this man done to me? Why do I want him by me? She closed her eyes. *It is* Carillon *I want, not this Cheysuli warrior I have known so brief a time.*

"Alix," he said gently, "I am sorry. You are too young to understand."

Her eyes opened. The torchlight from the palace painted his shoulders and glinted off the gold on his arms. Suddenly she wanted the warmth of him against her again.

"Duncan, I think no woman is too young to understand."

He blinked in surprise. Then he laughed silently and relaxed visibly. His hand slid around her neck and caught in the braids coiled against her head, cradling her against his chest. He murmured something in the Old Tongue, and Alix wished she spoke it.

Hastening footsteps echoed across the bailey, scraping on the cobbles. "Alix!" Carillon cried.

Duncan cursed and jerked around. His hand slipped to the knife at his belt.

"No!" Alix cried, grasping at his hand.

"Alix!" Carillon shouted again.

"Here," she answered, and heard Duncan's swift in-drawn breath.

The prince found them in the darkness. For a moment he stiffened as he saw Duncan, but he made no hostile movement. His mouth was a grim line as he looked at Alix.

"You have driven the Mujhar into a rage. He swears he will have the hawk hunted and slain, and you exiled upon the Crystal Isle. Imprisoned." He sighed. "Alix, I have spoken with him. It does no good. I will take you to Torrin's croft."

"She comes with me, Homanan," Duncan said ominously.

"Does she?" Carillon snapped. "Do you speak for her, shapechanger?"

"You have no place in this," Duncan answered. "She is not for you."

Alix moved between them. "Carillon, something happened to me in the hall. Something . . . came to life in me. When the Mujhar called me witch and cursed me for my blood, I felt no shame. I felt no horror; no fear. I felt only anger that a man could hate so powerfully, and do so much harm to a race. It was as if the Cheysuli in me finally came to life." She touched his arm beseechingly. "I want no more of this place."

"I have said I will take you to Torrin. When I can, I will come to you."

She shook her head slowly. "I think—I think what is between us must stay unknown, or unnamed." She pressed his arm. "Do you know what I say?"

"No," he said, so harshly she knew he did.

"The Cheysuli are not your enemy," Alix said softly. "It is the Solindish, and the Ihlini. Turn your anger on them. Do not let Shaine's madness infect you also. You said once you would accept me whatever I was. Now I ask you to accept the others of my race."

"Alix, I cannot."

"Do you sentence yourself to serve the Mujhar's insanity?"

He reached out and clasped her shoulders. "Alix, I want you where you will be safe."

She smiled at him, certain of her words. "Duncan will see I am kept safe."

His fingers tightened painfully. "Do you go willingly with

him, then? Or has he ensorcelled you with shapechanger arts?"

"No," she said softly. "I think it is something within myself. I have no words for it, but it exists."

Duncan, eloquently silent, stretched out his hand. She saw the familiar gesture of spread fingers and bared palm.

And she understood.

Alix stepped away from Carillon. His empty hands fell limply to his sides. He looked at Duncan, then at her, eyes shadowed with pain and confusion. But she also saw acknowledgment.

"I will get you mounts," he said quietly.

"I have horses," Duncan answered.

"How do you propose to get over the walls with her? Alix cannot fly in the guise of a hawk."

Duncan's face tightened. "No. But the eight guardsmen are simple enough to put out of my way, if I must."

Carillon sighed wearily. "Shapechanger, I begin to understand the arrogance of your race. And its strength, as Torrin said. Do you know Shaine sent fifty men against you in the forests and only eleven survive?"

"I know."

"How many did you lose?"

"Of twelve men, we lost two. One to death; one to the soulless men."

Alix shivered at the relentless tone in his voice. She sensed the purpose and determination in the man and realized had she refused to go with him he could easily have forced her.

Carillon nodded. "I will escort you through the gates. The guard will not stop me, even do I walk with a shapechanger."

Duncan laughed harshly. "Once we walked *freely* within this place, prince. But you will have my gratitude, regardless."

Carillon turned to lead them to the bronze-and-timber gates. Before he could move away Duncan reached out and caught his arm. The prince stiffened.

"Carillon. There is much you do not understand. Perhaps you cannot, yet. But Shaine will not always be Mujhar."

"What do you say, shapechanger?"

"That we are not your enemy. We cannot alter the

qu'mahlin while Shaine lives. He has struck well and quickly, reducing us to less than a quarter of what we were. Even now we grow fewer with each year as the *qu'mahlin* continues. Carillon, it is in you to stop this."

The prince smiled. "I have been raised on tales of your perfidy. Stories of your demon ways and cruel arts. Tell me why I should halt my uncle's purge."

Duncan's hand rested on Alix's shoulder. "For her, my lord. For the woman we both want."

Alix stood immobile, unable to answer the resolve in Duncan's voice. Something in him had reached out to her, seeking something from her, and she wanted very much to give it to him.

Carillon swallowed. "It is true the Mujhar alarms me with his vehemence in dealing with your race. He does not even curse Bellam or the Ihlini as he does the Cheysuli. There is an unnatural anger in him."

Duncan nodded. "Hale served him for thirty-five years, my lord, with a loyalty only the Cheysuli can give. They were more than brothers. It is a binding service which our race had honored for centuries. Hale shattered that bond and hereditary service by his actions. Any man would take it ill and swear revenge, but Shaine also lost a daughter and consequently found his realm plunged into war once again. I understand why he has done this thing, Carillon, even as it destroys my race."

"Then you are more forgiving than the Mujhar."

"What of you?" Duncan asked calmly. "Do you serve the *qu'mahlin* when you are king?"

Carillon smiled crookedly. "When I am king," he said gently, "you will know."

He turned and walked to the gates. The guards, answering his bidding, opened them instantly. Duncan took Alix's arm and led her silently from Homana-Mujhar.

Chapter Three

Duncan took her through the shadows of tall buildings to the horses. From his saddlepack he pulled a dark hooded cloak and gently draped the folds around her.

"You wear fine clothing and rich jewels, my lady princess," he said quietly. "I am only one man, and thieves may think it a simple matter to slay me and steal your wealth. Or even you."

He pinned the cloak at her left shoulder with a large topaz brooch carved into a hawk shape and set in gold. Silently he pulled the hood over her garneted hair and settled it.

"Duncan," she said softly, trembling even at his lightest touch.

"Aye, small one?"

"What is this thing? What is this within me?" She swallowed and tried to hide the hesitation in her voice. "I have lost myself, somehow."

He smoothed back a strand of dark hair from her cheekbone, fingertips lingering. "You have lost nothing, save a measure of your innocence. In time, you will understand it all. It is not my place to tell you. You will know." He removed his hand. "Now, mount your horse. We have a long way to ride."

She was muffled by the weight of the unaccustomed gown and the folds of the cloak. Duncan's firm hands held her close as he lifted her into the saddle. Alix settled her wrappings as he turned to his own mount, then dutifully set out to follow him through the city streets. She was well aware of what she did, though days before she would never have admitted she could act so strangely. But something within her told her she would be safe with him, and that it was the will of the gods she go with him.

"Duncan," she said quietly, "you spoke of losing someone to the soulless men. What did you truly say?"

Torchlight caught and flashed on his armbands, but he remained shadowed and indistinct as he led her through Mujhara. She thought again how easily the Cheysuli melted into the darkness.

"I have said what it is to be *lir*less," he said at last, pitching his low voice to carry over the tap of hoof on stone. "A *lir* was lost, and Borrs seeks the death ritual in the forests."

"And you let him go?"

"It is our way, Alix. Our custom. We do not turn our backs on what has been within the clan for centuries."

Wearily she pushed the hood off her face and let it fall to her shoulders. "Duncan, where do you take me?"

"To the Keep."

"What will happen to me there?"

"You will see the *shar tahl*, and learn what it is to be Cheysuli."

"You are so certain your clan will accept me?"

He cast her a sharp glance over a shoulder. "They must. I have little doubt of your place in the prophecy."

"Mine!"

"The *shar tahl* will explain it to you. It is not my place."

Frustration rose within her, sharpening her voice into a demand. "Duncan! Do not shroud your words in obscurity and expect me to meekly accept them. You have taken me from all I have ever known, and even now you lead me into *more* I cannot comprehend. Tell me what is before me!"

He reined in his horse and allowed her to catch up. Faint illumination showed his face clearly to her, limning rigid determination. His mouth was a taut line.

"Must you know all before its time?" he asked harshly. "Can you not wait?"

She glared at him. "No."

His eyes, beastial in the torchlight, narrowed into pale slits. "Then I will speak plainly, so plainly even you may understand."

She nodded.

"What I have seen in my own *tahlmorra* is that the old gods intended you and I for one another. From us will come the next link in the prophecy of the Firstborn. You are Cheysuli. You have no choice."

He was a stranger suddenly. The gentleness he had used before fled beneath the hardness of his voice and words and Alix nearly quailed from it. Then the full meaning and implications of what he had said flared within her mind.

"You and I . . ."

"If you would feel your own *tahlmorra,* you would see it as clearly as I."

Alix's breath came harsh in her throat. Her hands tightened compulsively on the reins. "Ten days ago I was a valley girl tending her father's animals. Now you tell me I must accept the will of this crooked prophecy and serve it accordingly." Her voice wavered, then grew firm again. "Well, I will not. I choose my own way."

"You cannot."

She glared at him through angry tears. "I have been cast from my grandsire's palace; threatened with imprisonment and death. Even *Torrin* says I must follow this *tahlmorra,* as you do. But I will do as I choose! I am not an empty vessel to be filled with other men's desires and plottings! I am more!"

Duncan sighed. "Have you not yet learned all men are no more than empty vessels for the gods? *Cheysula,* do not rail so at your fate. It is not so bad."

"What do you call me?"

He stiffened, rigidly upright in the saddle. "I have some honor, girl. I will accede to the dictates of my own *tahlmorra,* but I will also honor yours. I know how it is with Homanans and their propriety, so I will renounce my vow of solitude. You I will take according to Cheysuli custom, and make you a wife."

"You will *not!*"

"Alix—"

"No! When I become a wife it will be because I wish it, and to a man I can be at ease with. You frighten me with your shadowed soul and mutterings of prophecy I cannot even understand. Leave me to *myself!*"

He pressed his horse closer and caught her arm. Alix struggled against him as he pulled her effortlessly out of her saddle and sat her upright against his chest. In one terrifying instant she saw the echo of his brother in him, and all of Finn's fierce determination.

"Duncan—*no!*"

"You have asked for it!" he snapped, settling her across his lap.

Cai, drifting down from the rooftops, circled over them. *You should not,* lir.

Alix, trapped within the hard circle of Duncan's arm and fearful of his intentions, saw the conflict in his face. His hand was on her jaw, imprisoning it, but he made no further move against her. She waited stiffly, not breathing; afraid even to move.

Abruptly he kneed his horse to hers again and deposited her roughly into her own saddle. Alix grabbed at the reins and pommel, fighting to stay upright. When she cast an anxious glance over her cloaked shoulder she saw him visibly constrain the force of his emotion. Then his face was a mask to her.

"It seems," he began stiffly, "you have all the *lir* at your bidding. First Storr gainsays my *rujholli* from forcing you; now Cai does so with *me*. There is more within you than I thought."

"Perhaps you should heed it!"

Duncan's face twisted. "I think the gods laughed when they determined we should serve the prophecy together. It will be no simple task."

She glared at him. "It will be no task at all, shapechanger. *I* have determined that."

He swore something in the Old Tongue, forsaking the control he had so recently won back. Alix, startled by the savagery in his voice, reined her horse back two steps.

Lir! Cai cried in warning.

Duncan turned swiftly in the saddle, hand to his knife, but the men were on him. Three of them, clothed in dark garments, dragged him from his mount.

Alix gasped as she saw him stand braced against his horse, knife drawn to face the men. Suddenly her anger and frustration evaporated, replaced by stark fear for his life.

A swift feathered weight plummeted from the night sky, wingtips brushing her hair. Cai shrieked into the darkness and fell, talons outstretched. Alix's horse, terrified by the bird, reared.

She cried out and scrabbled for a solid handhold, tangling reins and mane in her rigid fingers. She had little knowledge of horses; always before she had ridden with someone. Now she struggled to keep the horse from striking Duncan with its pawing hooves.

A hoarse outcry followed Cai's attack. Alix tried to see if Duncan was safe, but her horse denied it to her. It reared again and danced backward, then spun and bolted.

Shod hooves slid on cobbles, striking sparks. The horse cared little for obstacles in its path, leaping anything in its way. Alix clung to the animal with all her strength, unable to control its flight, and sought the mercies of the gods.

The horse leaped a bushel and slipped badly on landing, sliding spread-legged, nearly throwing Alix from the saddle. The cloak, whipping back, dragged at her. She felt the woven strands of garnets and pearls break free of her hair, spilling loosened braids over her shoulders in disarray. She took two trembling wraps in the reins, snugging them around her hands, and pulled the horse's head sideways in an instinctive bid to slow it.

Dimly she heard the animal's wheezing breath and felt the lash of bloodied saliva against her face. The horse slid and thrashed all four legs in an effort to maintain momentum, but Alix kept her painful grip on the reins. She felt the cloak torn from her, whipped back into the darkness.

The horse folded beneath her suddenly, without warning, and tumbled her painfully into the street.

Stunned, knocked dizzy with the force of her sprawled landing, Alix felt the tug at her left arm. The twisted reins still wrapped themselves about her wrist, threatening to drag her as the animal fought to regain its feet. Dazedly she picked at the taut leather with her other hand, freeing her wrist at last.

She heard a rattle of pebbles and dimly realized the jeweled lacings in her hair had broken, scattering garnets and pearls across the cobbles. A searching hand at her hips told her the girdle was also gone, and her skirts were torn and stained. But she dismissed that and got painfully to her hands and knees.

The horse, defeated in its attempt to rise, lay wheezing on its side near her. Alix stared at it blankly, wanting to go to it; afraid of what she might find if she did.

Hair tumbled over her shoulders into her bruised face, dragging on the cobbles. Wearily she pushed it behind her ears and discovered the garnets in her ears remained. Alix got to her feet and waited for the pain to begin. When she found she could stand it, she picked up her heavy skirts and moved slowly back the way she had come.

Duncan was missing when she found the place. Alix moved into the pool of faint torchlight and stared vaguely at the cobbles, seeing two bodies. One man lay on his back with a deep knife wound in his abdomen. The other, clawing hands clasped to his face in death, had had his forehead rent by talons. He bled freely from a wound in his throat.

The third man was nowhere. Alix wobbled unsteadily and put both hands over her mouth to force back the sour bile rushing into her throat.

A lantern flared in a door across from her as it opened. Alix squinted against it, trapped in the spilling illumination. An old man peered out, one hand grasping the collar of a growling dog. He lifted the lantern to shed more light into the street and Alix instinctively shrank from it, pressing herself against the wall.

But he saw her. His dark eyes widened, then narrowed as he stared at the slain men. His voice came harsh as he looked back at her.

"Witch! *Shapechanger* witch!"

Alix put a trembling hand to her face, realizing how deeply she bore her father's stamp. In the darkness, illuminated by the lantern light, she was branded by the Mujhar's hatred.

"No," she said clearly.

His hand loosened on the dog's collar. Alix, fearing he would set the animal on her, gathered up her skirts and fled.

She ran until her lungs screamed their protest and her legs faltered. Breathlessly she fell against a stone well set in the intersection of cobbled streets. She clutched at the cross-beams of the well and held herself upright, gasping from knifing pain in her chest and sides.

When some of the breath-demand had gone she cranked up the bucket. The cool water was sweet on her raw throat, trickling down to soothe her heaving stomach. It splashed over the rim and stained the velvet of her fine garments, but she did not care.

"Could you spare some water for a thirsty horse, my lady?" asked a quiet voice.

Alix jerked upright, dropping the bucket down the well. Her hands clenched spasmodically in her skirts as she stared at the man.

He moved softly, silently, forsaking the shadows like a wraith. She saw a dark cloak falling to his booted feet. An oddly twisted silver brooch pinned it to his left shoulder, but he had pulled the folds back from a silver sword hilt at his hips. Somehow, though he moved in darkness, he brought the light with him.

His face was smooth, serene. Strength of a sort she had never seen shone from the fine features, and his smile was gently beguiling. His hair and beard were inky dark, carefully trimmed, and flecked with silver. His eyes, black as the horse who followed him, were soothing and sweet.

"Do not fear me, my lady. I seek only water for my horse." He smiled gently. "Not some light woman for the evening."

Alix, even bruised and weary, felt the insult keenly. She drew herself up and glared at him, disdaining to answer. But as her eyes met his the defiance slid away, leaving her powerless before him.

She gestured weakly. "The well is yours, my lord."

He cranked up the bucket and held it steady in gloved hands, letting the horse take its fill. He watched her in a manner almost paternal.

"You have seen trouble this night, lady," he said quietly. "Are you harmed?"

"No. I am well enough."

"Do not seek to hide the truth from me. I have only to look at your eyes."

She swallowed, aware of her loose hair and stained clothing. "We were set upon by thieves, my lord."

"You are alone now."

"The man I rode with stayed to fight the thieves. My horse was frightened, and ran. In order to stop him I was forced to put him down on the stones." She shrugged slightly, dismissing the remembered fright. "So now I walk."

"What of your escort?"

Alix looked away from him. "I cannot say, my lord. Perhaps he is slain." The vision rose before her eyes, showing her Duncan twisted on the cobbles, slain. She shuddered and felt the horrible anguish in her soul.

"With such words you place yourself in my hands," he said gently.

A chill of apprehension slid through her, but she was aching and weary, too dazed to care. "If it be so, my lord, what will you do with me?"

He sent the bucket back to the depths of the well and caressed the horse's silky jaw. "Help you, lady. I will give you my aid." His beguiling smile soothed her. "Come into the light and look upon me. If I truly seem treacherous, you have only to leave me. I will not gainsay you. But if you find me honest in my intentions, you are welcome to come with me."

Slowly Alix answered his summons, moving into the torchlight. His appearance was calm, gentle-seeming, and his affection for the horse indicated goodwill. She met his eyes for a long moment, searching for an answer there.

At last she sighed. "I am so wearied from this day and night I care little what your intentions may be. Where do you go, my lord?"

"Where you wish, lady. I serve you."

Alix looked into his smooth face, seeking an indication of his true intent, but she saw only serenity. He was richly clad, though not ostentatious, and his manner was that of some high lord.

"Do you serve the Mujhar?" she asked, suddenly apprehensive.

He smiled, white teeth gleaming. "No, lady, I do not. I serve the gods."

It relieved her past measure. Silently Alix took the gems from her ears and held them out.

But he would not take them. "I have no need of your jewels, lady. What I do for you requires no payment." He gestured smoothly. "Where do you go, lady? I will take you there."

"A croft," she said quietly. "In the valley. It is perhaps ten leagues from here."

His eyes glinted in gentle humor. "You do not have the

appearance of a croft-girl, lady. I see more in you than that."

Her hand gripped the garnet earrings. "Do you seek to humble me, my lord? There is no need. I know my place."

He moved closer. The light seemed to follow him. His eyes were soft, sweet, like his voice, and deep as the well from which they drank.

"Do you?" he asked softly. "Do you truly know your place?"

Alix frowned at him, baffled by his manner, and lost herself in the dominance of his black eyes.

He lifted his right hand. For a moment she thought he would make the Cheysuli gesture of *tahlmorra,* but he did not. Instead a hissing line of purple light streaked out of the darkness and pooled in his hand, throwing a violet glare over her face and his.

"So you have learned your legacy," he said quietly. "After all this time. I had thought Lindir's child lost, and of no more account."

Alix gasped.

The flame leaped in his hand. "You hold more of the prophecy within you than any I have yet seen. And I have watched for years . . . waiting."

Her voice hurt. "What do you say?"

Black eyes narrowed and held dominion over her. "Can it be you do not fully understand? Have the Cheysuli not yet bound you to their *tahlmorra?*"

"Who are you?"

He smiled. "I have many names. Most are used by petty men who fear me. Others are revered, as they should be."

Alix shivered. "What manner of man are you?"

"One who serves the gods."

She wanted to leave him but the power in his fathomless black eyes held her. Purple light glowed in his palm.

"What do you want of me?"

"Nothing," he said calmly, "if you remain unknowing. It is only if you recognize the *tahlmorra* within yourself that I will be forced to gainsay you. In any way I can."

Her palm burned where the earrings bit into her flesh. "You are not Cheysuli."

"No."

"Yet you speak of their *tahlmorra*, and the prophecy. What is it to you?"

"My bane," he said softly. "The end of me, should it be fulfilled. And the Cheysuli know it."

Cold knowledge crept within her mind. Consciously she forced her body to relax, then lifted her head. "I know you. I *know* you." She took another breath. *"Ihlini."*

"Aye," he said softly.

"Tynstar . . ."

His eyes smiled. "Aye."

"What do you do here?" she whispered.

"That is for me to know. But I will tell you this—already Bellam breaks Shaine's borders and invades. Homana will fall, lady . . . soon. It will be mine." He smiled. "As it was ever meant."

"Shaine will never allow it."

"Shaine is a fool. He was a fool when he sent the Cheysuli from their homeland and sentenced them to death. Without them, he cannot win. When he does not, the prophecy will fail. And I will be lord of this land."

"By your unnatural arts!" Alix cried.

The sorcerer laughed softly. "You are party to your own unnatural arts, lady . . . you have only to learn them. But until you do, you remain insignificant, and of no account to me." He shrugged. "So I will let you live."

"Let me live . . ." she echoed.

"For now," Tynstar agreed lightly.

A winged shadow passed over them, blotting the violet glow a moment. Tynstar glanced up and watched the shadow, then looked at Alix.

"You summon the *lir,* lady, even though you do not know it. Perhaps you are not the naïve child you would have me believe."

Cai! she cried silently, staring up at the hawk.

Tynstar's hand was on his horse. The other still held hissing purple flame. He smiled at her across its glow and sketched a twisted rune in the air. Its path glowed against the darkness a moment, then flared into a column of cold fire. When it had gone, so had he.

"Alix."

She spun and stared at Duncan. He stood silently with his horse at his back, left arm streaked with blood. A bruise darkened his cheekbone and he bore a shallow slice across his forehead, but he seemed whole.

Alix looked at him. The defiance she had struck him with earlier had faded. Her words then, angry and frightened, had no more meaning. Something whispered in her soul, tapping at her mind, and she began to understand it.

"The horse ran away," she said unsteadily.

His eyes were fixed on her. "I found him. He is lamed, but will recover."

"I am glad he was not badly hurt." She knew the words they said held no meaning. Their communication lay on another level.

"Will you suffer to ride with me?" he asked. "I cannot waste more time seeking another horse. The clan has need of me."

Alix walked slowly toward him, eyes dwelling on every visible wound and bruise. A strange trembling weakness crept into her limbs as his yellow gaze remained on her in a calm, deliberate perusal. The hawk-earring glittered in the strands of his black hair.

She halted before him. "It was Tynstar."

"I saw him."

She put out a hesitant hand and gently touched the drying blood on his arm. "Duncan, I did not mean to hurt you."

He flinched at her soft touch but she realized it was not from pain. Something told her this man was hers to hold, to keep, and the enormity of it stunned her.

"Duncan . . ." She swallowed heavily and met his blazing eyes. "Duncan, please hold me so I know I am real."

He whispered something in the Old Tongue and took her into his arms.

Alix, hair spilling down her back, melted against his firm warrior's body until she was boneless. The strange weakness was new to her, but she welcomed it.

Duncan sank a hand deep in her hair and jerked her head back. "Do you deny it? Do you deny the *tahlmorra* in our blood?"

She did not answer. She caught her hands in the thick hair curling at his neck and dragged his mouth down on hers.

Chapter Four

Duncan found them a cave in the hills beyond Mujhara and spread furred pelts over the stone floor. Alix sat on one, pulling his red blanket around her shoulders, and watched him build a small fire. When it was done he took the small grouse he had caught, spitted it, and set it over the fire.

"Does your arm hurt?" she asked.

He flexed the scabbing forearm. "No. The men were not skilled with their weapons."

"Finn has said you can heal. Will you not do it?"

"Not for myself, or for so trivial a wound. The healing arts are used only in great need, and usually only on others."

"Finn healed Carillon's wrist."

"Because Carillon required convincing we were not the demons he believed."

She shifted, easing a sore hip. Her entire body ached with the fall from the horse. "What did you mean when you spoke to Carillon as we left? It sounded as if you spoke from certain knowledge."

He tended the sizzling grouse and sipped at a cup of honey brew. "I spoke from the knowledge of the prophecy. Carillon is not named in it—no man is—but I think he is the one."

"Speak plainly with me."

Duncan smiled crookedly at her. "I cannot. You have no knowledge of the prophecy. That will be given to you by the *shar tahl,* and then you will know."

"Why must you shroud your words in so much darkness? You would have me think it is some sorcery you seek to do."

"It is no sorcery to serve the gods."

"As does Tynstar?"

He stiffened. "Tynstar serves the dark gods of the nether-world. He is evil. He seeks only to end the prophecy before its time is come."

"So he said." Alix sighed and rubbed at her brow. "Where did you go when my horse ran?"

"First I slew two of the thieves. The third ran. I went to find you."

"Why did you not simply send Cai? Or seek *lir*-shape?"

"I could not take *lir*-shape. I sensed the presence of an Ihlini, though I did not know who. As for Cai . . . him I sent to Homana-Mujhar."

"Homana-Mujhar!"

"I thought you had returned to Carillon."

She stared at him, astonished, then felt a strange bubble of laughter welling within. "You will have me think you are jealous of him."

He scowled. "I am not jealous."

Alix smiled in wonder, then laughed outright. "So, I am to think the Cheysuli are not capable of such a Homanan emotion? Yet your brother—who is also mine—seems well able to display it."

"Finn is young."

"And you not much older."

Color came into his face. "I left my youth behind the day my first Keep was invaded by the Mujhar's men. It was only the will of the gods I was not slain, as so many others were."

"Duncan—"

"You will see when we have reached the Keep."

"Are so few left?"

"Perhaps fifty women, half of which cannot bear children. The rest are old men, girls, and boys. Of warriors . . . there are perhaps sixty."

The horror of the *qu'mahlin* swept into her for the first time. "Duncan . . ."

He looked old suddenly. "Once this land was ours. More than fifty clans ranged Homana, from Hondarth on the Idrian Ocean into the mountains of the north, across the Bluetooth River. Now they are all slain, leaving only my own clan. And we are not so strong as we were."

"Shaine's doing . . ."

He reached out and caught one of her arms, eyes beseeching her. "Do you see it now? Do you understand why we steal women and force them to bear our children? Alix, it is the survival of a race. It is not *you* the Council will see, but your race and your youth. You must serve your race, *cheysula*."

She sat straight upon the pelt. "And will they hear you have called me that?"

He released her arm. "I will ask for you. It is my *tahlmorra*." Duncan gestured slowly, spreading his fingers. "You are Hale's daughter. I think they will not deny me."

She felt chilled. "But—they *could?* They could refuse you?"

His hand dropped. "Aye. First you must be acknowledged within the clan, given the knowledge in the old fashion, made aware of your birthlines. The *shar tahl* will say if you are truly Cheysuli."

"But—*you* have said!"

Duncan smiled sadly. "There is no doubt, small one; it is only custom. But you have been raised Homanan. In the eyes of the Council, you are tainted. Until the *shar tahl* has declared you free of it."

Desolate, she closed her eyes. Her growing security in him was destroyed with but a few words. Then her eyes snapped open.

"They would not give me to *Finn!*"

Duncan's face was a mixture of surprise and amusement, then consideration. He frowned.

Alix was suddenly frightened. "Duncan, they would not!"

He turned the spitted bird slowly. "I am clan-leader, but not the sole power in the clan. It is Council that says what will be."

She leaped to her feet and stumbled to the rock wall facing her. She stared at it blindly, hugging the blanket around her aching body. The new knowledge of what Duncan meant to her twisted in her entrails like a serpent, setting jagged teeth into her spirit.

To lose him when I have only just found him . . .

Duncan's hands settled on her shoulders. "I will not let you go so easily."

Trembling, she turned to him. "Could you gainsay it, if they wished to give me to another man?"

Muscles rolled beneath the smooth flesh of his jaw. "No."

"Then what of this *tahlmorra* you prate about?"

"It is mine, Alix," he said somberly. "It does not mean it is the clan's."

She whispered his name. Then she lifted her face and touched his arm. "If I went before this Council already carrying your child . . . ?"

His eyes flickered in surprise. Then he smiled faintly. "If you made such a sacrifice, small one, there would be little they could say about the match."

Alix let the blanket drop. The gown beneath, ungirdled, hung loosely. Slowly she undid the fastenings at the neck. Duncan watched her mutely, held by the strength in her eyes. His breath came harsh.

When the gown was undone she let it fall to her feet. Her hair, unbound, streamed over her shoulders like a mantle.

"I am new to this . . ." she whispered, trembling with something other than fear. "Duncan . . . it cannot be so very difficult to conceive . . ."

"No," he breathed, reaching for her. "It is not so very difficult."

He took her from Homana into Ellas, the realm bordering Homana's eastern side. Alix, clasping his lean waist with a new and wonderful possessiveness, felt regret and anger stir within her that her grandsire could so malignantly drive her race from their homeland into a strange realm.

When at last Duncan halted Alix saw before her a large half-circle wall of piled stone. The wall ran a distance before circling back, and at the wide opening she saw three warriors with their *lir*. They waited silently, and she realized they were guards.

"The Keep," Duncan said, and rode past the warriors.

Huge oiled pavilions billowed in a faint breeze. All were dyed warm colors, dwarfing the small tents she had seen at the raiding camp. Each had its own firepit before flapped entrances, but smoke drifted from the poled peaks and she realized smaller fires were tended within. Each pavilion, regardless of its color, bore a painted animal on its sides. By the shapes she could know what *lir* lived there.

The curving wall of undressed, unmortared stone hugged the shoulder of a craggy mountain. The half-circle blended into thick, sheltering trees. Alix realized such anonymity was the safety of the Cheysuli.

Duncan halted the horse before a green pavilion. She looked for the hawk painting on its side but saw only a wolf.

She stiffened. "Why do we stop here?"

"I would see my *rujho*," he said quietly, slipping from the horse. He turned to lift her down.

"Why? I want nothing to do with Finn."

Duncan eyed her thoughtfully. "When last I saw him, he was feverish from the wounds gotten in the forest battle." His mouth was firm. "Wounds won protecting you."

Chastened, Alix slipped silently into his arms and allowed him to lead her into the pavilion.

Finn was stretched out on a pallet of thick furs, wrapped in a soft woven blanket. As he saw them he hoisted himself up on one elbow and grinned at her.

"So, my *rujho* managed to win you away from the wealth of Homana-Mujhar . . . and Carillon."

She had been prepared to wish him well, feeling guilty over his injuries gotten in her behalf. But now, facing his mocking eyes and words, her good intentions evaporated.

"I came willingly enough, when my grandsire called me shapechanger witch and threatened to have me slain."

"I *said* your place was with us, *meijha;* not among the walls of Shaine's palace . . . or within the princeling's arms."

She glared at him. "You do not look feverish to me."

He laughed. "I am fully recovered, *meijha.* Or nearly. I will be plaguing you soon enough, when I am on my feet."

"You do not require feet to do that!" She scowled at him. "You need only be in my presence."

Finn grinned and ran a hand through his hair. She saw his eyes were alert and unclouded by illness, though his color was not as deep as usual. Inwardly she was grateful he had not been badly injured, but she would not say it to him.

"Will you two never admit peace between you?" Duncan growled. "Must I ever seek to placate you, one at a time?"

"She is a woman, *rujho*," Finn said airily. "And they are ever the cause of much agitation."

Before Alix could answer Duncan put a firm hand on her shoulder, pressing gently. She said nothing, but saw

Finn's eyes narrow suspiciously. Alix could not keep her face from turning bright red.

He smiled slowly, watching her, eyes very bright. He was not stupid, she knew. He looked at Duncan with a blank mask on his face. "Malina has conceived."

Duncan's hand bit into Alix's shoulder. She stared at him in surprise, seeing him go pale beneath his Cheysuli coloring. She was new to a woman's intuition for her mate, but understood instantly that something had deeply shaken him.

"Is it certain?" Duncan asked in a peculiar voice.

Finn nodded. "She is four months gone." His face twisted mockingly. "Was it not four months ago when she turned from you to Borrs, and took him as her *cheysul?*"

"I count, Finn!" Duncan said angrily.

The younger man looked at Alix's uncomprehending face. He smiled more broadly. "And now Borrs is among the soulless men, seeking his death-ritual. Malina is free again."

Instinctively Alix reached for Duncan's clenched fist. But he withdrew his hand from her seeking fingers and stepped away, putting distance between them.

"Has she declared the unborn child before Council yet?" he asked harshly.

Finn, solemn again, shook his head. "She has been in formal mourning for the last three days, since she learned of the news. But it will have to be a brief mourning, if she is to take another *cheysul.*"

"Did Borrs know of the child?"

Finn hunched a shoulder. "He said nothing of it to me. But then he knew you and I are close, *rujho,* and he would hardly speak of such a thing to the *rujholli* of the man who first had his *cheysula.* Would he?"

"Then she has not named the *jehan.*"

A mocking glint crept back into Finn's eyes. "Perhaps even Malina does not know the *jehan* of her unborn child, *rujho.* Do you?"

Alix stepped toward him. "What do you say? What has this to do with Duncan?"

"It would be better, perhaps, he told you himself."

"Tell me!"

Finn slid a glance at his silent brother, then nodded slightly. His smile was wolfish and triumphant. "Duncan would have asked for formal clan-rights of Malina next year, taking her as his *cheysula*. She had been his since I can say . . . in the clans children are close and often wed when they are of age." He scratched at an eyebrow. "But Borrs also wanted her, and when Duncan wished to wait because of becoming clan-leader, Malina did not. I cannot account for a woman's whim to punish one man by taking another, but it is what she did." He looked intently at Duncan. "Yet now Borrs is among the soulless men, clanless, and she is free to choose again." He paused significantly. "Or *be* chosen."

Alix, aware of Finn's natural perversity, sought the truth in Duncan's eyes. He turned from her and went out the flapped entrance, saying no word.

Finn's low laugh stung her. Alix turned on him, furious, fist uprasied in his direction. But he laughed again, amused by her action, and she dropped the hand back to her side.

"Why?" she asked. "Why do you punish me this way?"

He sat up, crossing his legs beneath his blanket. He wore no jerkin and she saw the bronze of his broad chest was ridged with scars. The wound in his shoulder was unbound but healing, and she recalled again his savagery as he slew the guardsman who would have slain her.

"So," he said in a low, taunting voice, "you recognize the *tahlmorra* in yourself at last. I see you have chosen my *rujholli* after all, forsaking even Carillon. Only now Duncan returns to his first woman." He clucked his tongue. "Poor little *meijha*."

"I require no pity from you!"

"Duncan differs from me in many ways, *meijha;* particularly in his women. He has long been satisfied with Malina, requiring no others." He shrugged. "I take a woman where I will; freely. Save for you, they have never denied me."

"What do you say!"

"That Duncan makes a life-bond when he takes a *cheysula*. If Malina is offering clan-rights with proven fertility, he would be a fool to deny her." He stretched idly, cracking tough sinews. "My *rujho* is many things, but he is not a fool." Finn grinned at her. "Do not worry, *meijha* . . . I will still have you. You will not be lonely."

She longed to scream at him but did not. Somehow she

summoned a regal elegance, even in a torn and stained gown.

"I am Hale's daughter . . . I believe it now. Therefore I am Cheysuli. Therefore I have free choice of any man, *rujholli,* and I tell you now—you would be the last warrior I would ever consider. The *last.*"

Alix left him feeling a strange satisfaction that she had so easily bested him. The look on his face had assured her victory. But the satisfaction faded as she recalled the cause of it. Outside Finn's green pavilion, Alix hugged herself and longed for Duncan.

Cai drifted down from the skies. *Come with me,* liren.

Where? she asked dully.

To my lir.

Your lir *seeks the company of another woman.*

Cai's tone was exceedingly gentle. *You are weary and filled with sorrow and confusion. Come with me.*

Silently Alix followed the bird across the Keep to a slate-colored pavilion embellished with a painted gold hawk. As Cai settled on his polished wooden perch she pulled the doorflap aside and went in.

Duncan had filled his pavilion with thick soft pelts and a richly embroidered tapestry. Alix stared at it blankly, unable to decipher the runes and odd symbols stitched in the blue pattern. Then she knelt before the ash-filled fire cairn.

She felt very small. An ague seemed to have settled in her bones, rattling them even as she sought to calm herself. Her breath seemed to have gone completely; repeated gasps only worsened her need for air. Finally she bowed her head and clutched at it, pressing against her temples.

"By the gods . . ." she whispered, "what have I done?" She drew in a deep breath. "I have left my croft . . . I have been sent from Homana-Mujhar . . . I have ridden into a strange realm with a man I cannot understand, and he has forsaken me as easily as Shaine." Alix clenched her fists as if to drive demons from her skull. "I have *given* myself to him . . . and now he seeks another!" She lifted her head and stared blindly at the tapestry. "What have I done?"

The tapestry did not answer her; nor did Cai. Alix longed for his warm tone and reassurance, but the hawk remained silent. She became aware of other whispers in her mind. They formed patterns and tones like the ones she had heard before the forest battle, but did not oppress her as much.

"I am gone mad," she whispered.

The whispers and tones continued, rising and falling as any ordinary conversation. She began to separate the sounds, frowning in concentration as she tried to understand the implications. Alix dragged fingers through her hair as if to untangle the threads of the patterns and realized how tangled her hair was. She took the silver comb Duncan had given her from her bodice and began to drag it through the snarls, hoping the pain would rid her of what she could not understand.

When her hair was smooth again she braided it into a single plait, tying the end with a strip of velvet torn from her gown. Its splendor was ruined; the silken overtunic was in shreds and the hem ragged and stained. But she cared not at all for the vanished elegance of her clothing; she wanted only to win back Duncan's regard.

When he came it was silently, without the warmth she was accustomed to. His face was drawn as he settled the door-flap behind.

"You must come with me."

"Where?"

"To Raissa."

"Who is Raissa?" she asked, knowing it was not truly the answer she sought.

"She is the woman who will keep you until you go before the *shar tahl,* and Council."

"Can I not stay with you?" she asked softly, hands folded in her lap.

Duncan knelt and shifted the wood resting in the small pavilion fire cairn. He took up a flint and fired the kindling.

"No," he said at last. "You would do better to stay elsewhere."

Alix bit at her lip to fight back tears. "Then what Finn said is true . . . there is another woman you would have."

His hand snapped a stout branch. After a moment he tossed the pieces on the fire, settling on his knees to face her through the rising smoke.

"When I came for you in Homana-Mujhar, Malina was *cheysula* to another man. I had put her from my mind. I thought only of you."

She swallowed painfully. "But now you can no longer put her from your mind."

He moved to her, still kneeling, and took her face in his browned hands. "I will not give you up."

Alix stared at him, holding back the trembling in her bones. "Then what do you say, Duncan?"

"Our *tahlmorra* is one, Alix. I feel it, even if you do not. I will not give you up." He sighed, brow creased. "Malina will be my *cheysula,* as I promised her when we were children, but you hold a place in my soul. *Meijhas* have honors and rights within the clan . . . there is no disgrace among the Cheysuli. I will keep you by me."

Alix reached up and grasped his wrists firmly. Then she jerked his hands away. "What did you promise *me!* What did you say to me in the cave, when I offered to conceive your child so we would never be separated, even by your Council?"

"Alix—"

"I will be no man's light woman, Duncan . . . not even yours. It is a thing I cannot consider . . . perhaps it is my *tainted* Homanan upbringing!" She glared at him. "Do you think what I did is so easy for an untried girl?"

"Alix—"

"No."

His hand reached for her but she avoided it, sitting back on her heels. After a moment he let his hand drop back to his thigh.

"What would you do, were you free to do it?" he asked.

She scowled at him, understanding what the delicate question asked. He was perfectly capable of denying her the right to leave the clan; she expected it. But she would try it nonetheless.

"I will go back to Carillon."

Duncan stared at her. His face was a mask but he could not quite hide the cold anger in his yellow beast-eyes.

"To be light woman to a prince."

"No. For his help." Alix picked at a tear in her skirt, avoiding his eyes. "He would help me in whatever I asked."

"You cannot leave, small one," he said gently. "I understand your feelings, but I cannot allow you to go."

Her hand clenched in the soft velvet. "And your reason, clan-leader?"

Duncan's face softened. "You might have conceived."

Realization flooded her. Angrily she pressed a fist against her stomach. "If I have conceived by you, I will name the child fatherless and raise it myself!"

Duncan went white, bolting to his feet like a wounded man. He caught her arm cruelly and dragged her to her feet, ignoring her cry of pain.

"If you have conceived by me, it is *mine!*"

She gritted her teeth and hissed at him. "And do you not already have an unborn child, shapechanger? In the belly of the woman you will take as *cheysula!*"

"If it is mine I will keep it by me, just as I will if *you* bear me a child."

She paled beneath the pain of his hand on her arm. "You cannot take a child from its mother!"

"Here you live among the Cheysuli," he said grimly. "You will abide by our customs. If you will not have me then you will not, but if you have conceived the child is mine . . . and a link in the prophecy."

Alix spoke through the pain. "And will you force me to do what my mother did . . . run away? And bear my child in solitude?"

He drew her near. Alix stiffened rigidly as his arms went around her. It was no gentle lover's kiss. He was forcing her, as Finn had once, and she hated it. Warring emotions filled her soul and she struck out in bitterness, but her fist was trapped between his chest and her own. Slowly, against her will, it crept up to grasp his hair and pull him closer. Whatever power he had to inflict pain on her also inflicted something deeper, and instinctively she recognized her need of him.

"Cheysula," he whispered against her lips.

Alix jerked free of him. "I am *not!* You have said you will choose another . . . and I *will not* be your light woman!"

His mouth was compressed into a thin line. "Then you will be *cheysula* to no man."

She lifted her head. "I will not."

"Nor *meijha.*"

"Nor *meijha.*"

His eyes glittered strangely. "Do you hold with your Cheysuli blood, Alix? Do you follow our customs?"

"I have little choice!"

"Do you accept them?"

"Aye!" she cried bitterly.

A muscle twitched in his jaw. "Then you must accept *all* customs as your own."

She glared back at him defiantly. "I do."

His hand darted to his belt and came up with his knife. Alix, terrified, spun to flee.

Duncan caught her by the heavy braid and in one slash severed it at her neck.

Alix, stumbling, gasped in shock as the hair fell away. Her hands clasped the ragged edges left to her. Duncan stood silently, dark braid hanging from his hand.

"What have you done?"

"A Cheysuli custom," he said, deliberately casual. "When a woman refuses her place within the clan as *cheysula* or *meijha,* her hair is shorn so all men know her intent. This way she cannot change her mind."

"I see a stranger before me . . ." she whispered.

He dropped the braid to the fire. It caught and smoldered, filling the pavilion with the stench of burning hair.

Duncan returned the knife to his belt and gestured toward the doorflap. "Now, *rujholla,* I will escort you to Raissa."

Chapter Five

Duncan took her to a brown pavilion that bore a gold-colored fox on its sides. He pulled the doorflap aside and gestured her to go in; Alix did so without meeting his eyes. She felt horribly shamed without the braid, for though she still felt more Homanan than Cheysuli Duncan's disparagement of her brought the implications of her braidless state home with real impact.

A woman stepped from behind a curtain dividing the pavilion into two sections. Her black hair was generously threaded with gray, but she had woven silver laces into multiple braids cunningly, fastening them to her head with an intricate silver comb. Her dress was fine-spun black wool threaded with scarlet ribbons at collar and cuffs, and a delicate chain of silver bells clasped her waist. She was no longer young, but she was a handsome woman. Her face reflected her Cheysuli blood with its high cheekbones, narrow nose and wide, smooth brow. Her yellow eyes were warm as she looked at Alix.

"Raissa, this is the girl," Duncan said. "Alix."

The woman smiled at Alix and then looked steadily at Duncan. "Who has shorn her hair?"

His jaw tightened. "I have."

Her brows lifted. "But it is for Council to decide if she remains solitary."

Alix heard the unspoken reproach and stole a glance at Duncan, surprised to see him bow his head in acceptance. Then it lifted again.

"She had made the decision for herself . . . I merely acquiesced."

"He did not tell me he would cut off my hair," Alix said bitterly.

Raissa moved forward. The tiny bells chimed and winked

in the folds of her black gown. Her slender hand touched the ragged curling tendrils at Alix's neck and jaw.

"I am sorry he acted so hastily. He should have explained the custom to you." Her lips twitched with a half-hidden smile. "I have never known Duncan to act without reason, so he must have been driven to it."

"He did it out of jealousy."

Raissa withdrew her hand. "Duncan? Why do you say so?"

Alix slewed her eyes sideways to look at him. "He told me he would ask for me in Council . . . as his *cheysula*. Then—finding his former consort had conceived and was free again—he refused me honorable marriage and offered only to have me as his light woman." She looked back at Raissa. "Of course I refused."

The woman was solemn. "Among us a *meijha* has honor, Alix. Here she is not treated like filth, as are the whores of Mujhara. We are too few, now, to place so much value on a woman's married or unmarried status. *Meijha* is not a dishonorable position."

Alix's stubborn chin came up. "I have much left to learn of Cheysuli customs, but this will take the most trouble, I think." She swallowed and set her jaw. "I will not accept a lesser position with any man."

The older woman smiled. "Ah . . . it is everything or nothing, with you. Well, perhaps you are not so wrong. Once I said the same to my *cheysul*." She glanced at Duncan. "All of this will be settled in Council. Until her birthlines are studied and she is formally accepted, I will keep her by me and teach her what she must know. My thanks, Duncan, for bringing a lost one back to us."

He said nothing, merely inclined his head and left the pavilion without looking at Alix. She stood there, bereft, hating Finn all the more for beginning it all with his abduction of her.

Raissa guided Alix to a gray pelt and gestured for her to sit. Alix did so, staring at her hands as they twisted themselves into the fabric of her gown. Raissa arranged her own skirts and sat down before her.

"Duncan would not offer unfairly," she said quietly. "I know the man . . . he is not one to trouble a girl that way."

"He did not know about Malina until we arrived," Alix

admitted. "But Finn wasted no time in making certain his brother learned of it quickly enough."

"Finn has ever been jealous of Duncan," Raissa said. "Why?"

She spread her hands eloquently. "An elder son is ever favored by a *jehan*. It grates particularly hard when your own blood father favors a foster son. Hale treated them equally, but Duncan matured quickly. He felt the weight of the *qu'mahlin* more. And it has cost him, though Finn does not fully understand that." Raissa's eyes were expressive. "And now, Alix, you have given Finn reason for jealousy again."

"*I* have?"

Raissa looked at her solemnly. "Would you have Finn as your *cheysul*?"

"No. Never."

"You see? You will have Duncan, or none. It cannot be easy for Finn to know once again his *rujholli* takes precedence." She smiled. "Wanting Duncan, you could not want Finn. I know that. They are too dissimilar. But Finn is not so bad as he seems, Alix . . . he might make a fine *cheysul*."

"Finn stole me. He would have forced me, had Storr not kept him from it. How can you say he would be a good husband?"

Raissa smiled. "There is much of men you do not understand. But you must learn that for yourself; it is not my place to teach you such things."

Alix recalled the determination in Finn's face when he said he would have her. And now she was no longer promised to Duncan.

"Raissa!" she said, suddenly frightened. "They would not force me to take Finn, would they?"

Raissa glanced down at her skirts, settling the tiny bells into perfect symmetry. "This will be hard for you, I know. Particularly since you were raised Homanan and feel no loyalty for your true race." The yellow eyes came up. "We are too few, now. The clans have been destroyed, save for us, and even now Shaine works to slay what remains of us. We need children . . . we need women who will bear them." Light flashed off the silver in her hair. "You are Cheysuli, Alix. You must take your place in the future of the clan . . . in its *tahlmorra*. You must bear children for us. If you will not have Duncan, or even Finn, then it will have to be another warrior."

"You would *force* me!"

Raissa reached out and grabbed her hands, holding them even as Alix sought to withdraw. "No woman wishes to be used as breeding stock, Alix! Children are a gift of the gods . . . not coin with which to barter! But we have too few . . . we are dying. You will not be forced to lay with a man you cannot abide, but the censure of the clan is no light burden to bear."

"Then I will go back," Alix said flatly. "I will go back to the croft."

Raissa squeezed her hands. "No. You must stay. By the gods, Alix, you are Hale's daughter! We need his blood."

"Through Finn?" Alix disengaged her hands. "He is my half-brother."

"Aye, but you were raised apart. Hale's blood must come back into the clan."

"Then tell *Finn* to get himself children!" she said angrily.

"He would do so willingly enough . . . were you his *cheysula*. Or *meijha*," Raissa said steadily.

"What if I have already conceived?" Alix asked in desperation.

Raissa's eyes sharpened. "Already conceived . . . you have lain with Duncan?"

Alix nodded silently, suddenly apprehensive. "Was it wrong?" she whispered. "Is it wrong to lay with a clan-leader while he rules?"

The older woman smiled. "A clan-leader does not rule . . . we have no kings, Alix. And no, it was not wrong. Do you think Duncan keeps himself chaste? It would be a burden no man should carry."

Alix looked away, embarrassed. "Then what will happen?"

Raissa sighed. "Well, it would change things. The Council might be willing to let you remain solitary . . . they would respect your shorn hair, regardless of the reasons for it. You would have the freedom you desire if you refuse to take a *cheysul,* and have already conceived. But that is still a Council decision."

"I should never have come," Alix said. "I should never have allowed Duncan to take me out of Mujhara."

"This is your home."

"I should have let Carillon take me back to the croft."

"It will not be so harsh—I promise—when you are accustomed. Alix, we are your people."

Alix looked at the woman and saw the innate strength and pride reflected in her Cheysuli face. She put a hand to her own, tracing the identical high cheekbones. Her skin was not so bronze; her hair not so dark; and her eyes amber, not beast-yellow . . . but she knew herself Cheysuli.

She sighed. "Where is Malina's tent?"

Raissa's eyes flickered but she said nothing of her surprise. "Near the gates. The blue one with Borrs' *lir*-symbol, a mountain cat. There is only one."

Alix took the silver comb out of her bodice and stared at it. Then she met the woman's eyes and smiled. "I have something to return. My thanks for your kindness."

Raissa nodded and Alix left the brown pavilion.

Alix found the blue tent and jerked the entrance flap aside, somehow not surprised to find Duncan there. But Malina did surprise her.

The girl did not look Cheysuli. Her hair was dark blond and her eyes blue. She lacked the feral, feline grace of the true Cheysuli woman, but she was beautiful nonetheless.

Duncan rose to his feet. Alix moved swiftly to the woman and held out the comb. "This is yours."

"Mine?" Malina asked in surprise.

Alix saw she did not show her pregnancy yet; no swelling belly evident beneath the soft green gown banded with amber beadwork and bronze platelets.

"He let me use it because I had none . . . when I still had hair enough to need it." She glanced at Duncan a moment, then looked back at Malina. "But it is yours. He said so, once." Alix put the comb into the girl's hand and silently left the pavilion.

Duncan caught her before she had gone more than five steps. He swung her gently to face him, one hand going tenderly to her shorn hair.

"*Cheysula,* forgive me. I had no right."

His gentle voice nearly finished her. "I have no claim to that title, Duncan. You have given it to another."

His hands cupped her jaw and lifted her face so he could

see her welling tears. His own face was stark and tight. "You have only to say it, Alix. It is yours to decide. We would not be happy apart."

"I would not be happy sharing you." She swallowed heavily. "I doubt Malina would care for it, for all that."

"Malina knows I have asked for you as *meijha*."

"She *knows?*"

His hand smoothed back a ragged tendril of hair. "It is often done among us, Alix."

"I cannot." A tear spilled over and slipped down her cheek.

"And if you have conceived?"

She closed her eyes and put her forehead against his chest. "Why must you take her back? What I have done is no light thing for me, and now it is all for naught. Duncan . . . I did not know I would have to fight a woman and an unborn child. I thought I had only to think of the Council."

"I am sorry, small one. I did not intend this."

Alix sucked in a trembling breath. "They will try to make me take Finn as a husband."

His hands stiffened. "What do you say?"

"Raissa told me. It is doubtful I can keep my wish to remain apart." Alix shivered. "Unless I have conceived. Raissa said it would change matters."

"Aye, you could live apart with the child . . . or become *meijha* to me. Which would you choose?"

She lifted her head. "I have said I will be *meijha* to no man, Duncan. Even you."

"And Finn?"

"I want no one but you."

"I have said how you may have me."

"And *I* have said no." She stepped back from him and smiled sadly. "Perhaps Finn will have the forcing of me yet."

"Alix . . ."

"Duncan, I know there is much of the Cheysuli I cannot comprehend. But there are things in me *you* cannot comprehend. Do not ask me again to be your *meijha,* for I will not."

She waited for his answer. When he said nothing at all, remote and unattainable before her, Alix turned and walked away.

Alix felt the weight of her decision as she walked slowly back to Raissa's pavilion. She knew, instinctively, Duncan wanted her as much as she him, but the pride inherent in his race would not allow him to come after her.

Nor will mine allow me to accept his offer.

She considered it carefully again, as she had since Duncan first suggested she be his *meijha*. The shiver of distaste that ran briefly through her body once more told her she could not be so free with the man she loved. It was not a Homanan custom.

If I cannot have him to myself, I will not have him at all.

But the decision, once made, gave her no contentment.

She slowly became aware of the voices as she walked. They were different from those she heard spoken by Cheysuli in the Keep; these were not sounds her ears heard but what her mind sensed. Alix fingered her brow as if touch might tell her what it is, but no answer came. Whispers floated through her awareness, drifting in wisps of tonal patterns similar to what she heard as words from Cai and Storr.

Alix stopped abruptly, staring around to search for those who tormented her, but no one seemed to pay her mind except passing curiosity. The Cheysuli, she had learned, did not exhibit the open emotions of the Homanans.

She pressed hands against her head as the oppression increased. No one said anything to her, yet she was so sensitized to the gentle waves of sound in her mind that she thought she had gone mad. Alix stopped walking and waited for the madness to take her completely.

Liren, do not fight so, said Storr's gentle voice.

Alix opened her eyes and saw the wolf before her. She gasped and knelt, putting grasping hands to his neck ruff.

Storr, is this a punishment? she wailed silently. *A curse?*

It is a gift, liren, from the gods. It is only new to you.

Alix glanced up as a shadow passed over her. Cai circled in the air, dipping and playing among the currents.

Liren, he said, *you must learn to control your gifts.*

Control them! she cried, startled.

Come with us, Storr said gently. *Come with us, liren, and we will teach you.*

They took her out of the Keep, to a huge oak scored with an old lightning-wound. The charred hole left behind was enough to hide her, and Alix crawled into it as if seeking security in a mother's womb. Storr lay down at her feet and Cai perched on an overhead limb.

"What must I learn?" she asked aloud.

To accept, Cai said. *Not to rail against your* tahlmorra.

"You are Duncan's *lir,*" she accused. "You will support whatever he says."

I am his lir *but I am also myself. I am not a dog,* liren, *who answers its master's voice with unthinking loyalty. I am of the* lir, *and we are chosen by the gods.*

Storr's tone agreed. *We are not echoes of those we bond with, or I would have all of my* lir's *faults.*

Alix laughed softly and stretched out a hand to caress Storr's silver pelt. "You have none of Finn's faults."

Then will you listen?

Her hand fell away. "Aye."

Cai mantled once and settled more comfortably. *You bear the Old Blood,* liren. *It has gone out of the clan. You will bring it back.*

"By bearing children."

Aye, Cai agreed. *How else does a female give more to the world?*

Alix scowled at her bare feet.

Storr's eyes glinted. *It is not that you do not want children,* liren, he said. *It is that you wish to choose who will father them.*

"Aye!" she shouted. "Aye, you have the right of *that!*"

We cannot tell you who to take, Cai said calmly, ignoring her outburst. *That is for you to decide. But we can aid you accept your* tahlmorra, *and the gifts the gods have given you.*

"What have they given me?"

The ability to hear us.

Alix frowned. "I have ever heard you. From the beginning."

But you hear us all, liren, Storr said. *Each* lir *in the Keep.*

You are not mad, Cai said reassuringly. *It is only you hear what no one else hears.*

"I hear . . ." she whispered distantly.

The weight in your mind, Storr told her. *It is the voices you hear, when the* lir *converse. You must set it aside until it is needed.*

"And if I cannot?"

Then it could *drive you mad,* Cai said at last.

Alix closed her eyes. "It *is* a curse."

No, said Storr. *No more than the ability to take* lir*-shape.*

Her eyes snapped open. "I could *shapechange?*"

You have the Old Blood, Cai said quietly. *And with it comes all the old gifts.*

Alix set a hand against the tree as if to steady herself. Her thoughts ranged far ahead of what she had just heard, conjuring visions of herself in the shape of any animal she wished. Then she frowned.

"I have no *lir.*"

You need none, Storr told her. *That is what the Old Blood means . . . freedom to speak with all* lir *and assume any shape.*

"By the gods!" she whispered. "How is it possible?"

Others have also asked that, Storr said, sounding suspiciously like Finn. *But they have not been the get of the gods.*

She slanted him a sharp glance. "No one else in the clan can do this?"

No. It is a thing long lost to us, for the Cheysuli have taken Homanan women to increase their numbers. It has weakened the gifts. Storr paused. *It is for you to bring the Old Blood back.*

"We begin again," she said suspiciously. "You have said this before."

That does not make it less true, Cai commented.

She craned her head to stare up at the hawk. "Then teach me," she said. "Show me what it is to shapechange."

First you must decide which of us to bond with.

She considered it. "Flight must be difficult. Perhaps it would be better if I remained earthbound, this first time."

You are wise, liren. *My* lir *near broke his arm his first time in the air.*

Alix, struck by a vision of Duncan having difficulties, laughed aloud and nodded. "Then I will be a wolf."

Storr approved. *Then listen,* liren. He paused. *Your sight, while good, has become secondary to your ability to smell. Allow yourself to judge the world by scent,* liren. *The earth, trees, insects, worms, birds, leaves, pollen, breezes. And more. Do not depend solely on mere sight, for it can fail. Think with your nose.*

She concentrated, closing her eyes and trying to separate individual scents.

Now you must feel the damp earth beneath your paws; mud clinging to your claws. Be wary of sharp stones that can trap themselves between your pads, and thorns that pierce the tender webbing between toes.

Alix put her hands to the moldy, leafy ground and felt the dampness.

Winter is coming. Your coat must be thick and warm. A heavy layer of fat forms beneath your skin, thickening your undercoat. It itches, but you know it will mean added warmth in the coldest season. Your tail grows bushier, more luxuriant, and you are lovely, liren.

She was.

You have the endurance to travel many leagues in a single day, without food and little water. Your sinews and nerves are strongly knit and your heart is large. You are young and strong and joyous in life.

Alix felt warm blood pulsing through her veins; felt the vibrancy and exhilaration of youth. She opened her eyes and met Storr's on a level, realizing she knelt in the leaves like any four-footed creature.

The world spun. It picked her up like a leaf on a whirlwind and turned her upside down.

Alix put a hand out toward Storr, silently asking his help, but she saw only a padded, furred paw with black nails.

She cried out, and heard her voice echoing in the woods like the howl of a lonely wolf.

Disorientation took her. Dizzily she clasped her head in her hands, conscious they were human once more.

"Storr . . ." she said weakly.

It was too fast, liren. *You must not fear the shapechange. You cannot harm yourself in* lir-*shape, but it is not wise to shift too quickly. The mind cannot adjust.*

Slowly her stomach settled itself. Her eyes saw clearly again and the ache in her head died to nothingness. She smiled wearily, triumphantly, and looked into the wolf's wise eyes.

"I have done it."

It will be better, after this.

Perhaps, Cai said gently, *you will amaze even my* lir.

Chapter Six

Alix sat hunched on the broken stump of a felled tree, toes digging through the velvet of her court slippers into the soft ground. The slippers were torn and stained, nearly useless, for they had been made for Shaine's palace and not the wildness of a Cheysuli Keep. Her ruined gown had been changed for a woolen dress of palest orange; her ragged hair trimmed so that it did not straggle so much, but she had retained the slippers to recall her brief moment of glory.

The glory had gone. Only in her dreams did she recall the richness of Homana-Mujhar and the fine glittering city surrounding its rose-colored walls. Her days left her no time to think, for the hours were filled with Raissa's words as she taught Alix the customs she must know. Her hands were never still; she needs must learn how to weave a tapestry, how to tend two fires at once, how to cook Cheysuli dishes . . . and how to prepare herself to take a *cheysul*. The *shar tahl* had yet to see her personally but Raissa said there was no need; the man spent his time researching the birthlines to trace her history and ancestors so that no one could question her birth.

They bind me . . . she thought. *They seek to bind me tightly within the coils of their prophecy, so I have no choice but to do as they wish.*

Alix smoothed the soft wool over her knees, fingering the nap. She had been shocked to find the skill so evident in Cheysuli craftsmanship. She had grown up believing them little better than barbarians without the niceties of Homanan culture and crafts, but five days with the clan had already altered her perceptions. Their fabrics were close-woven and fine, dyed muted shades of every color and often beaded with semi-precious stones or brightened with gleaming metals.

And the jewelry . . . Alix realized even the finest of Mujhara's goldsmiths could not match the skill of Cheysuli craftsmanship. The warriors wore thick *lir*-bands on their arms and a single earring, but their talents stretched farther than that. Already Alix had seen small casks filled with delicate ornaments fit to bedeck any king or queen.

A strange thing . . . she thought, *that a race so dedicated to war can also make such delicate, beautiful things.*

The hands came over her shoulders and rested there, one thumb caressing her neck. The intimacy of the touch brought home all the longing she felt for Duncan, for he had not seen her except in passing. Alix lowered her head and stared blindly at the leaf-carpeted ground, wishing Duncan would not play with her emotions so.

"I have missed you," he said.

Alix stiffened and spun out from under the hands, leaping up and stumbling away. Finn's hands slowly dropped back to his sides.

Her breath came harshly, whistling through her constricted throat. One hand spread across her neck, guarding it; the other tangled itself in her skirts.

"What is it you want of me?" she asked.

Finn's lips twitched. "That, I think, you know already."

Alix lowered her hand and stood stiffly before him. "Why have you come?"

"To speak with you." He sat down on her deserted stump and stretched out his legs. Thigh muscles bunched and rolled beneath the snug fit of his leather leggings. His face still bore the thread of pinkish scar tissue over one black eyebrow.

"What would you and I have to speak about?"

"You and I," he said quietly.

Alix frowned at him. "I do not understand."

Finn sighed and gestured. "I will not leap on you, *meijha*, I promise. But I cannot speak to you if you persist in being so frightened of me. Your eyes are like those of a doe when facing a hunter." He smiled. "Sit, if you will."

Alix hesitated, still defiant before him, but she was caught by the lightness in his tone. He had shed the ironic

mocking she hated so much. Carefully she settled down in
the leaves and spread her skirts around her folded legs.

"Council has been called for this night."

She felt blood leave her face. "Council . . ."

"At sunset."

"What is the subject of it?"

"All manner of things; many of which concern you."

Alix bit at her lip. "I thought it might be that."

"I have come to save you some trouble."

Her chin lifted. "You do not save trouble, Finn; you
make it."

He had the grace to color. "For you . . . perhaps I did.
I admit it." He smiled crookedly. "But admitting is not an
apology, and I will never apologize for following my
judgment."

Alix stared at him, growing more baffled by the moment.
"Finn, you had best be plain with me."

He pulled his legs in and sat upright on the stump. "You
did not conceive."

Heat coursed through her face as she went rigid. "What
do *you* know of it?"

His eyes were amused, though he did not laugh at her.
"Among the Cheysuli such things are not kept locked behind doors. We are too few to look upon it as a woman's
mystery. It is a reason to rejoice, Alix, when a Cheysuli
woman has conceived." He paused as she stared hard at
the ground. "Raissa told me when I asked this morning.
There is no child."

"Raissa had no right to tell you anything, nor you the
right to ask."

"I had every right. I intend to ask for your clan-rights in
Council this night."

Alix's head jerked up. "No!"

"Duncan will not have you," he said ruthlessly. "That
has been made plain to all of us. He will take Malina, as
he has ever intended. There is no hope left to you."

"There is ever hope," she said fiercely, though she knew
he was right.

He moved off the stump and knelt in the leaves before
her, catching her hands before she could escape his
closeness.

"You have said you will be no man's *meijha*. That is your

Homanan blood speaking, but I will respect it. I am not entirely blind to your needs, Alix." He smiled at her ironically. "I will sacrifice a part of my freedom."

She tried to break free of his clasping hands but could not. Once again she felt helpless, trapped, and the familiar fright rose up. She knelt before him, trembling, hands icy cold in the warmth of his.

"Finn . . . I cannot. There can never be peace between us. You made that impossible from the very first day. I would hardly be a docile, accommodating *cheysula.*"

His grin flashed. "If I wanted that sort of *cheysula,* I would never ask for you."

She managed to glare at him. "Then why *do* you ask for me?"

"I have wanted you from the beginning," he said deliberately. "I will take you however I can get you."

Alix recoiled from him, finally breaking free. "I would never take you . . . *never!* By all the gods, Finn . . . you are my half-brother! You *stole* me! You took my life and destroyed it, and now you seek to make a new one I want no part of. It is Duncan I want . . . *not you!*"

His face remained set and closed, but the color drained slowly until he resembled a dead man. But the intensity in his eyes showed his blood still ran beneath his flesh.

"Duncan wants Malina," he said coldly. "Not you. Else he would renounce the old oath he made to her so long ago, and take you as his *cheysula.*" He shrugged dismissively. "You will grow out of wanting Duncan, my Homanan *rujholla,* if only because such desires die if not fed."

"There is ever hope," she said blankly.

"There is none," he told her. "You turned from Carillon to Duncan. In time, you will turn from my *rujholli* to me."

"You cannot *make* me!" she cried.

"I will not have to." Finn glanced down at his hands as he idly separated the leaves by colors. "I spoke to the *shar tahl.* You will be acknowledged at Council, and formally accepted into the clan. With that acceptance comes clan-rights, which any warrior may ask for." He looked at her. "Others may ask for you, Alix, because you are young and healthy and new to the clan. But I think you will take me, because—for all that has happened between us—you *know* me."

"I will take Duncan," she said firmly, knowing it as a weapon against Finn. "Duncan."

Finn's mouth twisted. "I also spoke with Duncan about your clan-rights, *rujholla*. He is clan-leader. It is his place to know what clan-rights will be asked, and who will do the asking."

She stared at him. "I do not understand."

"A clan-leader can ever deny a warrior the woman he wishes. Taking a *cheysula* is a formal thing. The clan-leader must give his permission."

Alix felt cold and hollow, and very much alone. "And Duncan . . . ?"

"He gave me permission, Alix. He will not interfere."

Duncan! she cried within her soul.

"If it is not me, it will be another," Finn said gently.

Alix looked at him. For the first time he spoke softly to her, without the mocking mannerisms she had come to expect. She summoned up the image of him shapechanging before her, but it no longer frightened her. She had her own ability, though no one knew of it yet. Part of him, she knew, must be like Duncan. If he was harsh and taunting and impulsive, it was because Duncan was not, and Finn must make his own way.

She moved forward on her knees, sitting before him with leaves spread all around them. Alix slowly touched his hand, then pulled it into her own. She saw the startled flicker in his eyes.

"Finn," she said softly, *"Rujho . . ."* She swallowed and smiled. "Take me home."

His hand stiffened and jerked away. "Home . . ."

"To the croft," she said. "To Torrin. To the life I know."

His face masked itself. "This is your home. I will take you nowhere."

"Finn . . ." she said softly, "I give you a chance to pay back what you took from me. Take me home."

Finn got to his feet and looked down on her as she knelt in the leaves. "I could not let you go," he said clearly. "Not now, when you are nearly mine. You forget, *rujholla* . . . I stole you because I wanted you. I will not give you up so easily."

"But if Duncan said no—"

"Duncan said aye," he reminded her. "Duncan has said I may have you."

She stared up at him. "And if I refuse you? If I stand up in Council and say I will not have you?"

The mocking smile was back. "Do not forget our third gift, *meijha*. What you will not do willingly, you may be forced to do."

"Please," she said.

Finn looked down on her pleading face. "No," he said, and left her.

Alix stood outside the slate-colored pavilion and closed her eyes, summoning her courage. Finally she scratched at the doorflap and waited. Duncan called for her to enter.

She hesitated, then pulled the doorflap aside. It dropped behind her as she stood there, letting her eyes adjust to the dim light. Duncan was hunched over a low worktable, a slender metal stylus held in one hand as he scraped carefully at gleaming gold.

"Aye?" he asked, without looking up.

Alix wet her lips. "Duncan."

The line of his shoulders and arms stiffened. For a moment he continued working on the gold ornament, then he set it aside and dropped his tool down. It rattled against the gold and wood, rolling across the table. Alix watched it move, unable to meet his eyes.

"I have come to you because you are clan-leader," she said carefully.

"Sit down, Alix."

She knelt on the other side of the worktable, still not looking at him. Her heels dug into her thighs as she folded her legs under her. Finally she brought her head up.

"Finn came to me. He said he has spoken to you; that he will ask for my clan-rights at Council."

He wore his solemn clan-leader face. "Aye."

Her breath was unsteady as she drew it in. "Duncan . . . I do not wish for Finn. You know that."

"It has been settled," he said remotely. "And if you bring this up again, I cannot be only a clan-leader to you."

Alix smiled at the unspoken warning. At least he was not totally indifferent to her. "I have not come to ask you to reconsider your offer to me," she told him. "You have made it plain what you will do, and I am done begging for more."

His eyes flickered. "Then what do you seek, Alix?"

"I want you to withdraw your permission to Finn. I want nothing to do with him. We could never make a marriage between us . . . and I think it might be the death of one of us if we were forced. I think it would be *his* death . . . not mine."

Duncan smiled briefly, though he banished it quickly enough. "It would not be a tedious match."

"It will not be a match at all," she said darkly. "Duncan, withdraw your permission."

"On what grounds?"

She scowled at him. "I do not want him!"

He shrugged. "Those are not grounds. That is merely contrariness speaking, and women are prone to that."

Alix stared at him. "You cannot *want* me to take him!"

His face twisted. "No," he said at last. "I do not want you to take him. But to refuse him because of that speaks of prejudice, and a clan-leader cannot be so petty. Alix, the match will be good for the clan."

"Is that all you can say?" she demanded. "Can you only see the clan, and not me? By the gods, Duncan, I thought we had more between us. What has become of this precious *tahlmorra*?"

Color surged into his face, then slowly fell away. "Will you accept another warrior?"

"You know there is only one warrior I will accept."

"Then the choice is yours," he said softly. "Be *meijha* to me . . . or *cheysula* to another man."

"*Why?*"

"I promised Malina when we were eight years old," he said quietly. "A Cheysuli oath is binding."

"*She* broke it."

"She did not think I meant what I said." Duncan touched the golden ornament on his table. "She went to Borrs because she thought I would change my mind. When I did not . . . she was fairly caught. The clan-leader had given his permission for Borrs to ask for her clan-rights, and once done that is not rescinded. It is binding." He looked at her bleakly. "I did what you have done. I asked the clan-leader to withdraw his permission to Borrs, so that I could ask for

Malina. He would not do it . . . and they were formally acknowledged before Council."

Alix frowned. "But I thought you were clan-leader, and that was why you would not take a *cheysula*."

He looked weary. "Tiernan died of a sickness. It took months. All knew I would be his successor, so I made my decision to remain solitary before he died. But he was still clan-leader. And when he died, Malina was already *cheysula* to Borrs."

"But the child . . ."

"It could be mine. It could be Borrs'." He sighed faintly. "We are not a race that places much honor on fidelity."

She recoiled. "She was *wed* to him!"

Duncan smiled. "I did not think you would understand."

"Do you mean you are willing to take Malina and myself, and yet may also seek other women?"

He frowned thoughtfully. "I cannot say what I will do. What man could?"

This new side of him shocked her. She peered into his face uncertainly. "Duncan . . . do you mean this?"

He shrugged. "I have never been a man for all women. One suffices. I doubt I would trouble you that way."

"Duncan!"

"Alix, she carries a child that may be mine."

"And I do not," she said dully.

"Alix—"

"If she had not conceived, would you be so ready to make her your *cheysula?*"

He looked away. "If Borrs had lived, and the child still mine . . ." Duncan sighed deeply. "I think I would have said nothing."

She stared at him. "Then it is the *child* . . ."

"I have ever cared for Malina," he said steadily.

"And if the child is not yours?"

His jaw tightened. "I cannot take that chance."

"Yet she is willing to share you with me?"

"I made it a condition," he said softly. "I said I would take her for the sake of the child . . . and if she would accept you as my *meijha*."

"Duncan!"

"Small one, had she said no I would have made you my

cheysula. But there is much between Malina and myself, and I could not forsake her so easily."

"But you forsake me . . . you give me to *Finn!*"

"Because he has asked, and there is no reason to deny him. It is not for me to do."

"I will not have him. I have told him that, and now I tell you." She fisted her hands in her skirt. "I am Cheysuli, clan-leader, and you cannot compel me."

"We will do whatever we must, Alix," he said gently. "Even to one of our own."

She rose slowly, shaking her skirts into order. Somehow she summoned a smile. "You cannot force *me,* Duncan. That you will see."

She turned on her heel and left him.

BOOK III

"The Cheysula"

Chapter One

Alix stood before Raissa's pavilion and called Cai and Storr to her. The *lir* came and accompanied her to the lightning-scored tree, saying nothing, though she was sure they knew what she planned to do. She needed practice in assuming *lir*-shape; if she wanted to impress upon the Council the magnitude of her abilities, she had better do it competently.

Cai perched above her on a stout limb, preening his feathers into perfection. Storr sat down and watched her from wise amber eyes.

"Help me," she said.

You need only think yourself a wolf, he said, *and you will be one.*

She recalled the words he had used before, the sensations coursing through her body as she made the transition. A part of it still frightened her, but she also recognized it for the gift it was. And it might keep her from Finn, if she showed Council what she could do.

Alix opened her eyes and crawled out of the deep hollow, shaking her shaggy red-gray coat. Sounds came more sharply to her twitching ears, and her nose told her more than she dreamed possible. She smiled, baring gleaming teeth.

Storr and the young wolf-bitch shouldered through the underbrush. Alix delighted in the feel and sensation of things she normally paid no mind to. She found she did not lose awareness of herself as a person, rather that knowledge and awareness were enhanced and extended until she could comprehend both life processes. Her intelligence was neither diminished nor improved; she merely understood things as both human and wolf.

She had lost her human speech but needed no words

with the *lir*. Thoughts from Cai and Storr still formed themselves in patterns easily comprehended. With an uprush of pride and ecstasy she knew in full measure what it was to be Cheysuli.

And in that same instant she understood why Shaine the Mujhar hated her race.

He thinks the Cheysuli will use their arts in retribution for the qu'mahlin. *He will* never *rescind it!*

Now you fully understand, liren, Cai chimed. *Shaine cannot forgive himself his own pride, or his own fear.*

Alix, new to her wolf senses and lost in contemplation, did not hear the snapping of twigs in the underbrush. Cai winged higher and Storr slipped into the shadows, but she—glowing ruddy-gray in vibrant health—provided an inviting target to the mounted hunter.

A bough cracked beneath the horse's hooves. Alix spun around. Alarm spread through her sinews and charged her thudding heart with shock.

She twisted, leaping into the air, yelping in fear and pain as the arrow sliced into the ruff at her neck.

The hunter, dismounting to locate the downed wolf-bitch, parted the underbrush and found himself looking into the dilated eyes of a woman.

He stumbled back a step as she clasped the flesh at the top of her left shoulder, blood welling between her fingers. She gripped the arrow in her free hand and threw it at him, trembling with shock and pain.

Alix's words tumbled over themselves as she cursed him, hardly able to speak through the violence of clenched teeth. He turned and crashed back through the underbrush to his horse.

She moaned softly and rocked on her knees, one arm clasping her bleeding shoulder, the other stretched across her roiling stomach.

You must return to the Keep! Storr said in alarm as he melted out of the trees.

"I c-cannot . . ." she gasped.

Cai came down to a nearby branch, agitated and mantling. Liren, *you must get to the Keep.*

Alix could only force out a weakened denial and slipped bonelessly to the leafy ground, blood spilling rapidly from her shoulder.

*   *   *

She was aware of pain when the arms took her from the ground and cradled her against a broad chest. Alix fought to open her eyes, achieved it, and stared dimly at Duncan's face. It was drawn and pale, and in his eyes she saw fear.

"Duncan . . ."

"Be silent, small one. I will take you to the Keep."

"How did you know?" she asked weakly.

"The *lir* came. Cai told me."

"What of Council?"

His arms tightened. "Be silent, Alix! I will not have you weaken yourself with such worries."

He took her to Raissa's pavilion and settled her on her thick furred pallet, shifting her limbs carefully. Though her mind was sluggish and strangely dull she was conscious of his gentleness and concern. But when she tried to ask him another question he placed a hand over her mouth.

"If you will allow it, small one, I will let you feel the healing arts of the Cheysuli. But it must be soon."

Her ears rang and her bones felt heavy as stone. Her eyes saw only fuzziness. "I would not consign myself to death," she whispered as he removed his hand. "Do what you will."

He settled himself next to her pallet, crossing his legs. He did not touch her, but his eyes were fixed on her with absolute possessiveness and determination.

Suddenly she found herself trembling, unable to feel the soft furs beneath her or the warmth of the blood still spilling from her shoulder. Only air was beneath her, and when she tensed against its feather touch she felt the earth under her hands. Her fingers curled against it, clawing into its softness. It enveloped her in rich gentleness, entering the pores of her skin.

She opened her mouth to scream but could find no voice. A blurring came into her mind, fogging her eyes, stopping her ears. She sought to lift a trembling hand and found her body would not answer her.

Duncan's hand smoothed hair from her damp forehead. "It is done, small one. Rest yourself. I promise you will be better."

Her eyes cleared slowly. She saw him by her, himself again, though he looked weary. "Duncan . . ."

"Hush," he said softly, running a gentle hand over the wounded shoulder. "It is healed, but it will take time for you to recover your strength. The earth magic does not give back everything."

"What did you do?"

"I summoned the healing touch of the earth. It is magic that resides in all the lands, but only the Cheysuli may summon it."

"I will miss Council," she said.

"Aye. It will take time for your strength to return."

Her eyes closed. "It is better so. I have no wish to see you ask for Malina."

"Or have Finn ask for you?"

Her eyes flew open. "Duncan . . . do not tease me. Not about this."

"I do not tease," he said gently. "And I should not long prolong this for either of us." He took her right hand and laced his fingers into hers. "Finn will not be asking for your clan-rights this night. Or ever."

"You have refused him?"

"There is another warrior who takes precedence over Finn."

"Another!" Her fingers stiffened. "Duncan—"

His free hand covered her mouth again. "Listen to me, small one; do not be so ready to fight me when there is no need." He smiled at her. "I went to see Malina after you had left. I had every intention of asking for her clan-rights this night. But she let fall the truth of the child . . . that it was Borrs', and she knew it. She said nothing because she did not wish to lose me to you." His expression was wry. "I had not thought myself the sort of man two women would want so badly, but I will not task myself over it. I will simply accept the wisdom of the gods."

Alix grinned at him, amused by his masculine assurance. Her fingers tightened in his. "If you will not have Malina—"

"—I will have you." He bent and kissed her tenderly. "If you will take me."

"There is no question," she whispered, fighting against drowsiness. "None."

He put something in her hand, curling her fingers around

the coolness of metal. Alix opened her eyes and stared at the thing. It was a curving neck torque of purest gold, beaten into hundreds of gleaming facets. At the lowest point stretched the fluted wings of a soaring hawk, and in its talons was clasped a glowing lump of dark amber.

"It is Cheysuli custom," he said. "The warrior offers the woman a torque, to signify the bond, and if she accepts it they are considered wed."

"What of these clan-rights you speak of?"

Duncan smiled. "I will ask for them formally in Council, but it would not hurt anything if we preceded the formality a little. If you are willing."

She ran a trembling finger over the gleaming hawk, down to the amber. "I must ask it, Duncan."

"Then ask."

"You said your race does not place so much honor on fidelity."

He smiled. "I thought it might be that. Small one, you need fear nothing. While it is true the Cheysuli do not often keep themselves to one woman, it does not mean we *cannot*. I respect your Homanan ideals, *cheysula*. I do not intend to give you reason to cast me out of your heart."

She closed her eyes to hide her tears. "Duncan . . . if this is the *tahlmorra* you spoke of . . . I think I can follow it faithfully."

He bent and kissed her brow. "Hush. I must leave you now, for Council, but I will return. Rest, *cheysula*."

She wanted to keep him by her but let him go. When he had left her Raissa came and knelt, covering her with a soft blanket.

"Now you see the strength in him, Alix. For all Shaine's *qu'mahlin* changed his life, it has made him a warrior."

She felt herself drifting. "You speak as if you have known him longer than any."

Raissa smiled. "I have. I bore him."

Alix's eyes snapped open. "You are Duncan's mother?"

"And Finn's."

She stared at the woman blankly. "You did not say . . ." She thought it over. "Nor did they."

"There was no need. But have I not proven a good ear for you to rant of Finn's arrogance while you silently longed for Duncan?"

Alix closed her eyes. "You shame me, lady. I have said things no mother should hear."

Raissa laughed. "I know all of Finn's faults, small one. And you fool yourself if you think Duncan has none."

"I have not seen any," Alix said distinctly.

The woman laughed again and smoothed back her shortened hair. "Only because you will not let yourself. Have you not lost most of your hair because of his jealousy?"

Alix smiled through her exhaustion. "Perhaps that is one fault I can accept."

"Rest now, small one," Raissa said gently. "He will come back to you."

Alix struggled for awareness a moment longer. "I am Hale's daughter, lady. How can you show kindness to the daughter of the man who left you for another?"

"It does not matter, Alix. That is all in the past."

"I know how Finn hates," Alix said quietly. "I would not have you hate me like that."

"Hale was a Cheysuli warrior. He conducted himself according to his lights. It is the custom among us. Alix, you are welcome in my pavilion. If I can have Hale back through you, I am glad of it."

"Raissa—"

"Hush. If you wish, we will speak of this another time. Perhaps there are things you would like to know about your *jehan*."

Alix slid farther into dreamless sleep, lost within the realization she would be Duncan's woman after all.

But she also wondered at the magic in Lindir's soul to so ensorcel a man.

And she wondered if she had not her own measure of it.

Two days later she was installed in Duncan's pavilion, propped up on her pallet by mounds of rolled furs. It seemed strange to be in his place, knowing it was now hers as well, but as he stood over her solicitously she knew only she was the happiest she had ever been.

"I am well, Duncan," she said softly.

He looked down at her sternly. "Then tell me how you came by an *arrow* wound."

Alix laughed at him. "It was a young hunter. Ellasian, I must believe."

He frowned at her. "Tell me why a hunter would *shoot* you, rather than seek other things with you."

She looked down at her blanketed legs, wiggling her toes beneath the wool. Finally she glanced back up. "Because," she said gently, "he thought I was a wolf."

Duncan's brows lifted. "I hardly see how he could mistake you for a *wolf*, Alix. Perhaps he saw Storr, and simply missed."

The time had come for an admission. She had missed Council, when she would have shown her skill to them, and had not said anything to Duncan regarding the accident. She had cradled her knowledge to her like a child, keeping it secret and anticipating the joy in telling him. Now it proved more difficult than she had imagined.

"He did not miss," she said finally, fingering the healing wound in her shoulder. "He mistook me for a wolf because I *was* one."

Duncan made a skeptical sound and sat down at his low worktable, picking up his tools and a gold brooch she had watched him work on for two days. The *lir*-torque rested against her throat, warmed by her skin.

"You do not believe me?" she asked.

"You weave me a tale, *cheysula*,"

"I am telling you the truth. Duncan . . . I can do more than speak with the *lir*. I take *lir*-shape, too."

For a moment he continued to work on the brooch. Then, when she said nothing more, he looked at her from beneath lowered brows.

"Alix, would you truly have me believe—"

"You had better!" she flung at him. "I would hardly lie about something so close to a Cheysuli warrior. I will even prove it to you."

She moved as if to get up. Duncan, rising rapidly from his cross-legged position as he dropped his tools, reached her bed and stood over her. "You go nowhere, *cheysula*, until you are better."

"I *am* better."

"Better than you are now." He grinned. "It will not be long, I think."

She settled back against the furs. "I am not lying. Ask Cai. He and Storr taught me how to do it."

Duncan dropped to his knees beside her. "Is this true?

Alix, you are unique enough that you converse with the *lir*. Can you truly assume *lir*-shape as well?"

"Aye," she said softly.

He sank back on his heels. "But this has not been done for *centuries*. Our history says once all Cheysuli could assume any *lir*-shape, but since before my grandsire's time this was only done by men. And then only when bonded by a single *lir*. It was the Firstborn who had the old abilities."

"Those who made the prophecy."

"Aye," he said absently, eyes clouded with thought. "The Firstborn took any *lir*-shape at will, and conversed with them all. But their blood has been gone from us for a long time." He looked at her sharply. "Unless, somehow, you have a measure of it." Duncan got to his feet rapidly, startling her. "I will be back."

Alix stared after him, baffled by his sudden withdrawal, but she assumed he knew what he was doing. She pulled the blanket higher around her shoulders and snuggled down against the pallet, drowsily content. But part of her was still amazed at the new course her life had taken.

Duncan returned with a Cheysuli Alix did not know; a much older man whose hair was pure white and held back by a slender bronze fillet. Alix, struggling to sit upright again, saw he did not wear the leather of the warriors; instead he clothed himself in a fine white wool robe, clasped with a leather belt mounted with bronze platelets. Like Raissa, he wore silver bells at his belt that sent a shiver of sound through the pavilion whenever he moved.

Alix sent a puzzled glance at Duncan, who gestured with all deference for the man to seat himself on a brown bear pelt placed before the small fire cairn. The man did so with great dignity, carefully settling brittle bones into a comfortable position. He put a rolled deerskin on the pelt before him and waited.

Duncan sat down at Alix's side. "This is the *shar tahl*. He keeps the rituals and traditions for the clan, and passes the history down to each generation. Each child born learns his ancestors and what has gone before from this man. You have come late to your clan, but you are here now, and he will tell you what you must know." He smiled faintly. "He may also have the answer to my question."

The *shar tahl* nodded to her, then untied the rolled deerskin. It was soft and supple, bleached white as snow, and as it unrolled before him Alix saw the runic symbols and lines twisting on the floor of the pavilion like a snake. He tapped the deerskin with a gnarled finger.

"Your birthline," he said. "You are here as surely as your *jehan,* and his *jehan* before him." The finger moved. "All the way back to the Firstborn."

"But what does it mean?" she asked softly.

His finger moved off the main line of runes and traced a second line, like the branch of a tree. Alix followed the movement until it stopped. The finger tapped again.

"There."

"Where?" she asked.

He looked at her sternly from rheumy yellow eyes. "There. The answer lies there."

She looked helplessly at Duncan. He maintained his solemn clan-leader demeanor, though she had come to know he had flashes of Finn-like irreverence. He simply kept it quieter.

"If you know so little of your clan, you had best come to me for instruction," the *shar tahl* intoned.

Alix nodded meekly. "I will learn."

The *shar tahl* touched a red symbol gone dark with age. "It is here in the birthline. Five generations ago the Mujhar took a Cheysuli *meijha,* whose clan was so pure it could name members of the Firstborn as direct ancestors. All could assume *lir*-shape, even the women." His thin shoulders stiffened. "That clan has since been destroyed by the *qu'mahlin.*"

Alix ignored his controlled bitterness, counting back in her head. Then she shot the *shar tahl* a startled glance. "Shaine's great-great grandsire?"

"The woman who was *meijha* to a Mujhar bore him a daughter. She was raised at Homana-Mujhar and wed to a foreign princeling, from Erinn. Shaine the Mujhar first took an Erinnish princess to wife, and so the blood came back."

"Then I am Cheysuli on both sides." Alix sat upright. "There is Cheysuli blood in Shaine!"

"It has been thinned," the *shar tahl* said firmly. "Marriage with foreigners has overcome any Cheysuli traits left." He pushed a wisp of white hair from his brow. "It is the

women who have done this. It is in their blood. Ellinda
bore Lindir, who has gifted you with the Old Blood long
lost to us all."

Duncan touched her shoulder and pressed her down
upon the furs. "Perhaps Lindir, unknowing, had her own
tahlmorra. Perhaps Hale did not forsake his fate for a *Homanan* princess, but followed what the gods have set for
us." He smiled. "If Lindir has passed this gift to you, you
can bring it back into our clan."

She sank back. "I do not understand."

The *shar tahl*, surprising her, smiled. "It is time you
learned the prophecy. If you will be silent, I will tell it
to you."

She felt Duncan's silent amusement and shot him a grimace of resentment. But she settled herself upon the pallet
and nodded at the old man.

"I am more than ready."

He sat upright before her, aged yellow eyes taking on
the brightness of youth and wisdom. "Once, centuries ago,
Homana was a Cheysuli place. This land was gifted to us
by the Firstborn, who were sired by the old gods. Do you
hear me?"

"I hear," she said softly.

"The Cheysuli ruled Homana. It was they who built
Mujhara and the palace of Homana-Mujhar. It was the
Cheysuli who held sovereignty over all men."

"But the Mujhars are Homanan!"

He fixed her with a stern glare. "If you will hear me,
you must listen."

She subsided, chastened.

"Mujhar itself is a Cheysuli word. So is Homana. This
was our place long before it came into the hands of the
Homanans."

Alix nodded reluctantly as he looked at her. A faint smile
curved his creased lips.

"The Ihlini rose up in Solinde and began to move against
us. The Cheysuli were forced to use their own arts to defend the land. The Homanans, ever doubtful of such sorcery, began to fear.

"Within a hundred years the fear turned to hatred; the
hatred to violence. The Cheysuli could not convince the

Homanans of their foolishness. We gave up the throne to them so they might know peace and security, and took up the bond of service to the Homanan Mujhars. Nearly four centuries ago."

Alix groped with the knowledge, unable to absorb it all. Finally she nodded to him, silently bidding him continue.

"Until Hale took Lindir away, the Mujhar had ever kept Cheysuli advisors and councilors, and warriors who protected this land in battle. A Cheysuli liege man dedicated his life to the Mujhar. Such was Hale's service."

"And Shaine ended it," she whispered.

"He began the *qu'mahlin.*" The *shar tahl*'s face tightened. "Even that was spoken of in the prophecy, but we chose to ignore it. We could not believe the Homanans would ever turn on us. We were foolish, and we have paid the price."

"What is the prophecy?"

The bitterness vanished, replaced with pride and great dignity. "One day a man of all blood will unite four warring realms and two races bearing the gifts of the old gods."

Alix stared at him. *"Who?"*

"The prophecy does not name a name. It only shows us the way, so we may follow it and prepare Homana for the proper man. But it seems we grow closer to the path."

"How do we follow it?" she asked softly.

"We have the Old Blood in our clan again, because of you. The prophecy speaks of a Cheysuli Mujhar ascending the throne of Homana again after four centuries. It is nearly time."

"But Carillon will be Mujhar," Alix said.

"Aye. It is his *tahlmorra* to prepare the way for the prophecy's proper path."

"Carillon?" she asked incredulously. "But he distrusts all Cheysuli!"

The *shar tahl* shrugged. "It has been foretold."

Duncan sighed. "This is what I meant when I spoke to him in Homana-Mujhar, *cheysula.* He must be turned from this hatred Shaine has put in him, and be made to see Homana's need of us. It is time we served the prophecy of the Firstborn . . . as it was meant."

She looked at him blankly. "But what have I to do with it?"

"It is up to you to give us back our pride and ancient magic."

"How?"

He smiled gently. "By bearing more of us."

Chapter Two

Alix, tongue clenched firmly between her teeth, wrestled with the knee-high furred boots. Duncan had brought her the black pelt of a mountain cat, cut it to shape with his knife, then handed the remains to her with instructions to begin a pair of winter boots. Aghast, Alix had stared at him and hoped he was teasing. He was not, she found, and now she cursed within her mind as she tried to work the thick hide and fur into something resembling boots.

She worked until her fingers were awl-pricked and sore, troubled by her inability to fashion the boots. She was slowly learning her place within the clan and her responsibilities as a clan-leader's *cheysula,* but her experience was sorely lacking. The warm gray wolfskin boots she wore had been made by Duncan for her when the weather turned cold, and she wished he would consent to making them all.

But he has things of more import to concern himself with! she thought sourly, throwing her half-done black boot aside to stare at the pavilion across the way. *He spends his time hunting or conversing with the Council, speaking ever of the war with Solinde!*

Instantly she was ashamed, for she knew as well as anyone how seriously concerned the Cheysuli were about the war. Increasingly alarming messages arrived from *lir*-couriers sent from Cheysuli secreted with Mujhara, seeking to learn of Shaine's actions. The Solindish, buttressed by Tynstar's Ihlini and troops guided by Keough, Lord of Atvia, had made inroads upon the Mujhar's defense of Homana.

And I said Bellam could never take this land, she thought hollowly. *I, like all the others, have been too impressed with past victories.*

She sucked idly at a bleeding finger and recalled Duncan's summing up of the threat to their homeland.

"Homana will fall if Shaine does not commit himself to this war," he had said one evening, staring gloomily into the flames of the pavilion fire cairn. "He recalls the victory against Bellam twenty-six years ago, and trusts to the might of his armies. But then he had the Cheysuli, and now he does not."

Alix had shifted closer to him, resting one hand upon his thigh. "Surely the Mujhar understands this Solindish threat. He has ruled for many years, and won many battles."

"He concerns himself more with the *qu'mahlin* than the Solindish war. I begin to think his fanaticism has made him mad." Duncan's hand idly caressed her arm. "He sends his brother, Fergus, into the field as commanding general, keeping himself safe within the walls of Homana-Mujhar."

"He has fought before," she said softly. "Perhaps he realizes Fergus is a better soldier now."

Duncan leaned forward and placed more wood upon the fire. "Perhaps. But perhaps it is also he prefers to avoid the sacrifices a man makes in war. Shaine is not one who wishes to sacrifice anything."

Alix stared at the brown pelt beneath them and pushed rigid fingers through the bear fur. "To send your heir into battle is a sacrifice," she said quietly, trying to hide from Duncan the fear it brought. "He has sent Carillon to fight."

Duncan was not fooled. "If Carillon is to be Mujhar, he must learn what it is to lead men. Shaine has trusted to his own council too long; he has neglected Carillon's education." He grimaced. "I think the prince could make a good Mujhar, but he has been given little chance to learn the responsibilities." Duncan slid Alix a carefully blank glance. "It is no wonder he took to speaking soft words to innocent croft-girls in the valley, to while away his time."

Alix flushed deeply and withdrew her hand. But when she saw the glint in his eye she realized he only teased, and laughed at him.

"But I am no longer so innocent, Duncan. *You* have seen to that."

He shrugged, purposefully solemn. "Better a clan-leader, I think, than a mere warrior."

"Warrior . . . *what* warrior?" ·

"Finn."

"You beast!" she cried, striking him a glancing blow on

the shoulder. "Why must you remind me of him? Even now he calls me *meijha* and torments me by suggesting I be his light woman."

Duncan arched his brows. "He seeks only to irritate you, *cheysula.* Even Finn knows better than to seek a clan-leader's woman, when she is unwilling." His brows lowered. "I think."

"Finn would dare anything," Alix said darkly.

He smiled. "But if he did not, small one, he would be a tedious *rujholli* indeed."

"I would prefer him tedious."

"You, I think, would prefer him slain."

She looked at him sharply, startled. "No, Duncan! Never. I wish death on no man, not even one like Shaine who would have all Cheysuli slain." She recalled the guardsmen killed in her behalf. "No."

His hand was gentle on her head, caressing her shorn hair. It had grown, but still barely touched her shoulders. "I know, *cheysula;* I only tease." He sighed heavily as his hand fell away. "But if we join this war, there may be many deaths."

"But the Mujhar will not have you with his armies. You have said."

"In time, perhaps, he may *have* to."

Alix, hearing the weariness of reluctant acceptance in his tone, leaned her head against his bare shoulder and tried to think of other things.

Now, as she took up the black boot again, she wondered how Carillon fared.

She had not lost her affection for the prince, even though she had spent nearly three months with the clan in Ellas. Carillon had been the first man she had fastened her fancy on; though it had been an impossible dream, she dreamed it with great joy. Duncan had replaced Carillon in her dreams, dominating her thoughts and desires, but she did not forget the first one she had loved. That love had been childish, immature and unfulfilled, but it had been true.

Alix fingered the thick black fur absently, lost within her thoughts. Duncan had showed her what it was to be a woman; what it was to be Cheysuli; what it was to have a *tahlmorra.* Already her roots had twined themselves around his own so deeply she knew she could never be herself again without him. She wondered if that was what it was to have a *lir*.

The adjustment had not been easy. Alix missed Torrin and the croft; missed the green valleys she had ever known. At times she awoke in the night sensing an odd disorientation, frightened by the strange man at her side, but it always faded when full awareness came back. Then she would press herself against Duncan's warmth, seeking comfort and safety, and always he gave it; and more.

She thought again of Carillon. She had heard only that the prince was in the field with his father, fighting the Solindish and Atvian troops. Duncan—sensing her loyalty—was unusually reticent with her when speaking of Carillon. Finn was not. He taunted his brother with the fact the prince had shared a place in Alix's heart first, and relished giving her news of Carillon if only to tease Duncan. His attitude irritated Alix, but it was a way of getting news.

As if hearing her thoughts, Finn walked up to her and sat down on the gray pelt spread before the large fire cairn. Alix glared at him, expecting his normal mocking manner, but she saw something else in his face.

"It has come, Alix," he said quietly.

"What do you say?" she asked in dread.

"It is time the Cheysuli defied the *qu'mahlin* and went again into Mujhara."

"Mujhara!" She stared at him, shaken by his somber tone. "But the Mujhar . . ."

Finn smoothed the nap of the pelt absently, staring at his hand. "Shaine will be too occupied with real sorcerers to waste much time on us." His eyes lifted to hers. "The Ihlini have broken into the city."

"No . . . oh, Finn! Not Mujhara!"

He stood. "Duncan sent me for you. Council is calling all into the clan pavilion." He put out a hand to help her up. "We go to war, *meijha*."

Silently she took his hand and rose, shaking out her green skirts. She looked at Finn for more information, apprehensive, but he said nothing else. He merely led her to the Council pavilion, a huge black tent painted with every *lir*-symbol imaginable.

Duncan sat before the fire cairn on a spotted pelt, watching his clan file into the black interior in pensive silence.

At his right lay an ocher-colored rug, and it was to this
Finn took Alix. The heaviness of the silence fell on her like
a cloak. She sat down on the rug, watching Duncan's face
closely. Finn sat beside her.

Duncan waited until the pavilion was filled, ringed with
dark faces and yellow eyes. Then he looked to the *shar
tahl,* seated across from him, and nodded to himself. Slowly
he got to his feet.

"Vychan, in Mujhara, has sent his *lir* to us. The message
is one we have expected these past months. Tynstar has
led his Ihlini sorcerers into Mujhara, and they have taken
the city."

Alix, sickened with fear, swallowed against the foreboding in her soul. The others, she saw, waited mutely for
Duncan's words.

"The western borders fell three months ago. Keough of
Atvia fights for Bellam, marching toward Mujhara where
the Ihlini await them. Only Homana-Mujhar has not
fallen."

Alix closed her eyes and conjured the Great Hall with
all its candleracks and rich tapestries.

And Shaine . . .

"If Homana-Mujhar falls, Homana herself falls. We, as
the descendants of the Cheysuli who built both palace and
city, cannot allow it to happen."

Finn shifted. "So you will send us into the Mujhar's city,
rujho, and have us fight two enemies."

Duncan shot him a sharp glance. "Two?"

"Aye," he said briefly. "Do you forget Shaine? He will
set his guardsmen against us, when he would do better to
use them against the Ihlini."

Duncan's mouth was a thin line. "I do not forget Shaine,
rujho. But I will set aside our personal conflicts to save
Homana."

"Shaine will not."

"Then we will give him no choice." Duncan looked
slowly and deliberately around the pavilion, marking each
attentive face. "All of us cannot go. We must leave warriors
to defend the Keep. But I have need of strong men willing
to go into the city and fight the Ihlini with any method at
hand. We are not many. Any force we send will have to
be selectively efficient. Open warfare will result in too high

a death toll. We must answer the Ihlini with stealth of our own." His eyes returned to Finn. "I send the best and the strongest. And some will be lost."

Finn smiled crookedly. "Well, *rujho,* you say nothing I do not already know. It is ever so, I think." He shrugged. "I go, of course."

Other warriors echoed Finn's words, committing themselves to a war the Mujhar would not welcome them to. Alix, listening blankly to them, realized why Duncan had wanted to remain solitary. He had known all along the Cheysuli would risk their few numbers to save their ancestral home.

It is tahlmorra, she whispered within her mind. *Ever* tahlmorra.

Alix walked back to the pavilion alone, lost within fears and worries. In her time with Duncan she had learned of his strength of will, determination, and selfless dedication to serving the prophecy. Nothing would deter him from leading his warriors into Mujhara. She knew better than to ask him to remain in safety with her, and though she wished he did not have to involve himself so deeply, she also knew he would lessen himself in her eyes if he did choose to stay. Duncan was, perhaps, less aggressive than Finn in his desire to fight, but his pride ran just as deep.

The fire cairn had burned itself to ash, so Alix spent her time rekindling it for warmth and illumination. The pavilion was her security now, as much as Torrin's croft had been. Even the tapestry meant much to her, for Duncan had carefully explained each runic device and the designs stitched within the patterning of rich blue yarns. The tapestry contained much of Cheysuli lore, highlighting the strengths and traditions of the race. She wondered, as she knelt by the fire, if more history would be added with the warriors' return to the city.

Duncan came in softly, easing aside the doorflap. Alix, seeing the quietude in his eyes, met him with a measure of her own solemnity.

"Duncan," she began softly, "how soon do you leave for Mujhara?"

He went to his weapons chest and took out his war bow, a compact instrument of death similar to his plain hunting bow. But this was dyed black, polished, inlaid with gold and tiger-eye. The string also was black, humming tautly as he strung the bow and tested it.

He dug his black arrows out of the chest and sat down cross-legged, beginning the laborious examination of each one. The arrows were fletched with yellow feathers, and the obsidian heads gleamed.

Alix waited silently, patiently, and finally he answered her. "In the morning."

"So soon . . ."

"War does not wait for men, *cheysula*."

Carefully she smoothed her green skirts over her thighs as she knelt upon the spotted pelt. "Duncan," she said at last, "I wish to go."

He meticulously inspected the fletching of each arrow. "Go?"

"To Mujhara."

"No."

"I will be safe."

"It is no place for you, small one."

"Please," she said clearly, not begging. "I could not bear to remain here, waiting out each day without knowing."

"I have said no."

"I would not hinder you. I too can assume *lir*-shape. I would be no trouble."

He studied her impassively a moment, half his attention on his arrows. Then he smiled. "You are *ever* trouble, Alix."

"Duncan!"

"I will not risk you."

"You risk *yourself!*"

He set down one arrow and picked up another. "The Cheysuli," he said slowly, "have ever risked themselves. For Homana, it is worth it."

"But for Shaine?"

"The Mujhar *is* Homana. Shaine has held these lands safely for more than forty years, Alix. Our race has not benefited from him, perhaps, but all else have. If he requires help to hold the land now, we must give it to him." His eyes dropped. "And we must think of the one who will succeed him."

Alix took a trembling breath. "Let me give my aid as well. Shaine is my grandsire . . . and Carillon my cousin."

He set the arrow aside and clasped his hands loosely in

his lap. Alix found herself avoiding his eyes, focusing instead on the heavy gold banding his bared, bronzed arms. She saw the embossed, incised hawk-shape of his *lir* and the runic designs worked into the gleaming metal on either side of the hawk. When she could look at his face again, she saw pride and warmth in his eyes.

"*Cheysula,*" he said gently, "I know your determination. I am thankful for it. But I will not have you risking yourself, especially for the man who cast you out at birth and then again so many years later."

"Yet you risk yourself," she repeated hollowly, sensing defeat.

He sighed minutely. "It is a warrior's place, *cheysu'a,* and a clan-leader's *tahlmorra.* Do not deny me it."

"No," she said. She reached for the bow and picked it up, caressing the smooth patina and gleaming ornamentation. She slid careful fingers down the taut bowstring, testing its tension and vibrancy. "Will you be careful?" she asked in a low voice.

"I am usually little else, as Finn often tells me."

"*Very* careful?"

He smiled wryly. "I will be very careful."

Alix gently set the bow in front of him. "Well, I would not want your first son born without a father."

He was silent. Alix, eyes downcast in a submissive position unfamiliar to her, waited for his astonishment and joy.

But Duncan reached out and grabbed her shoulders, jerking her upright onto her knees. He glared at her wrathfully.

"And you would *risk that* by coming to an embattled city?"

"Duncan—"

"You are a fool, Alix!" He released her abruptly.

She stared at him open-mouthed as he rose stiffly and stalked from her, halting at the open doorflap to stare out.

"I thought you would be pleased," she told his rigid back.

He turned on her. "Pleased? You beg to go to war and then tell me you have conceived? Do you wish to *lose* this child?"

"*No!*"

He glared at her. "Then remain here as I have said, and conduct yourself as a a clan-leader's *cheysula.*"

Alix, driven into speechlessness by the intensity of his anger, said nothing at all as he turned away from her and left the pavilion.

She shivered once, convulsively, then folded both arms across her still-flat belly and bent forward, hugging herself tightly.

She let the tears come unchecked and rocked back and forth in silent grief.

Chapter Three

When the doorflap was pulled aside Alix sat up hastily and wiped the tears away. She was prepared to meet Duncan with dignity, but when she saw Finn staring in at her she lost her composure.

"Duncan is not here," she said shortly.

Finn studied her a moment. "No, I know he is not. He passed me but a moment ago, black of face and very black of mood." He paused. "Have you had your first battle, *meijha?*"

She scowled at him, fighting back the impulse to cry again. "It is none of your concern."

"He is my *rujholli;* you my *rujholla.* It is ever my concern."

"Go away!" she cried, and burst into tears.

Finn did not go away. He watched her in ironic amazement a moment, then stepped inside the pavilion. Alix turned her back on him and cried into her hands.

"Is it truly so bad?" he asked quietly.

"You are the last person I would tell," she managed between sobs.

"Why? I have ears that hear as well as anyone's."

"But you never *listen.*"

Finn sighed and sat down next to her, carefully avoiding any contact. "He is my *rujho,* Alix, but it does not make him perfect. If you wish to tell me how abominable he is being to you, I will listen readily enough."

She shot him a repressive glance. "Duncan is never abominable."

His brows lifted. "Oh . . . he can be. Do you forget I grew up with him?"

Something in the lightness of his tone broke her down farther, destroying her last reservation. Most of the tears had gone, but she was still upset.

"He has never been *angry* with me before," she whispered.

Finn's mouth twitched. "Did you think Duncan beyond it? Most of the time he loses himself in the burdens of being clan-leader to a dwindling race, but he is like any other. He has ever been more solemn than I, but he has just as much anger and bitterness. It is only he hides it better."

She thought of the cause of Duncan's anger, but could not tell Finn. It was too new; too private.

"It is too hard," she said, pushing away the last of the tears.

"Being his *cheysula?*" he asked in surprise. "Well, there was a way out of that . . . once." He grinned sardonically. "You had only to be *meijha* to me."

"I did not mean that," she said sharply. "I spoke of learning new customs, and conducting myself the way a Cheysuli woman does."

Finn thought about it. "Perhaps that is true. I had never thought of it." He shrugged. "This is the only life I know."

"I know two," she told him heavily. "The one you stole me from, and this. There are times I wish you had never seen me."

"So you could dally with the princeling and grow up to be his light woman?"

Alix glared at him. "Perhaps. But *you* ended any chance of that."

"You had best not say that where Duncan can hear it," Finn said tonelessly.

Alix was startled. "Duncan knows how I felt about Carillon. How could he not?"

Finn dragged at his boot, as if delaying his answer. Then his mouth twisted. "He still fears you may go back to the princeling."

"Why?"

"Carillon offers more than we can." His eyes were expressionless. "The magnificence of Homana-Mujhar, wealth, the honor in being a prince's light woman. It is more than any Cheysuli can give."

"I do not take a man for what he gives me," she said firmly. "I take him out of love. Duncan can say it was *tahlmorra* that brought us together—perhaps it was—but it is not that which keeps us together."

Finn seemed suddenly uncomfortable. "Then you will re-main with the clan?"

"Duncan would not let me go; nor, I think, would you." Alix held his eyes. "I have no real wish to go back . . . now. My place is with Duncan."

"Even though it be hard to learn our ways?"

Alix sighed resignedly. "I will learn . . . eventually."

Finn lifted her hand, encircling her wrist with his fingers as he had done so long before. "Does what you feel for him pall, Alix, or he dies in this war we face . . . you may come to me." He silenced her before she could protest. "No. I do not mean it out of my own desire for you, though that is unchanged." He shrugged, dismissing it. "I mean for you to come to me in safety, should you ever need it."

"Finn—"

He released her wrist. "I am not always so harsh, *rujholla*. But you never gave me the chance to show you otherwise."

He left before she could say anything more. Alix, staring after him, wondered if perhaps she had done him an injustice in her thoughts.

Duncan said little to her in the morning as they parted. Though he had come back to the pavilion much less angry and sorry he had frightened her, he was still determined she would do nothing to endanger the child or herself. Aloud she agreed with him, admitting her foolishness; inwardly she calmly considered when would be the best time to assume *lir*-shape and go by herself.

But when Duncan bid her farewell she clung to him in helpless anguish, silent, and made no reference to her secret plans.

Alix found, to her anguish, Cheysuli women did not say good-bye in the privacy of the pavilion. Instead a *cheysula* or *meijha* stood outside, before the tent, bidding her warrior safe journey in the open. The custom, Duncan said, came from a wish to make parting easier on the warriors. It was difficult to leave a sobbing woman with any degree of confidence.

She stared fiercely after them as they rode out of the stone Keep. The winged *lir* flew ahead, scouting; the four-footed beasts paced beside the horses. Alix saw Cai swoop above the treetops; Storr lope easily beside Finn; and the others go silently with their *lir.*

And I will be them all, she thought in grim satisfaction.

She was calm in her decision, acknowledging the difficulties. She had been a wolf only twice, and then with disastrous results, but that was hardly her fault. She would do better. Yet she was concerned with the knowledge she would have to go as a bird, an unknown shape, for a wolf would move too slowly for her to catch up to the party of warriors.

I wish Cai were here to teach me to fly, she thought uneasily. *It must be frightening to seek the air for the first time, trusting your life to fragile wings.*

But she knew she would go.

Alix prepared rapidly, wanting to leave no later than afternoon. She drew a pair of Duncan's worn leggings and a soft jerkin from a chest, cutting both garments to her smaller size. The jerkin she put on over the top half of the gown she had worn at Homana-Mujhar, using it as a rough shirt to cover her arms and hide her figure. A leather strap served as a belt, and she pulled on her wolfskin boots, cross-gartered to the knees. Grimly she looked down at herself.

I look no more a warrior than some Cheysuli boy playing at it. Well, it will have to do. I cannot go to war wearing skirts.

She sat down on the spotted pelt by the fire cairn and stared sightlessly into the coals.

How to make oneself a bird . . . ?

Carefully Alix detached her mind from her surroundings, dismissing the familiarity of soft pelts and colored tapestries and the mundane tools of daily life. The coals blurred before her eyes into a collage of rose and gray, transfixing her mind.

She thought of treetops and fields and clouds. She thought of a falcon, swift and light; of feathers and talons and hooked beak; bright eyes and hollow bones and the marvelous freedom of flight.

When she broke out of the pavilion and air rushed gloriously through her outstretched wings she knew she had succeeded, and rejoiced.

At first she wheeled in exultation, dipping and circling,

playing among the currents. Below her lay the Keep, spreading to shelter the last of Homana's ancient race. The pavilion was a speck of slate against the neutral tones of the Keep and surrounding forest.

Then Alix put away the joy of such freedom and flew on to seek a *lir*.

But she wearied quickly. Unaccustomed to prolonged flight, Alix at last admitted defeat and perched herself upon a tree. She was weary and hungry, tense with the effort to keep *lir*-shape, and realized she had nearly reached her limit.

She flew again to the ground and blurred herself from her falcon-shape into human form. Again she marveled at the gods-given ability of the *lir*-bond, for her clothing changed with her when she assumed *lir*-shape, and returned when she shifted back.

That is fortunate, she thought wryly. *I would not care to be caught in the middle of a forest unclothed.*

Alix climbed up a gentle spill of dirt packed against the mountainside and halted as she found a brush-covered hollow half-hidden in the shadows of dusk. Carefully she moved closer, peering through the boughs. The limbs and leafy branches had been woven together roughly, as if to form a cover, and as she inspected it closely she knew it could only be human-made. She pulled the covering aside and crept into the shallow cave.

She discovered a coarse, poorly woven brown blanket spread on the uneven floor of the rocky cave. Next to it lay a leather bag fastened with a wooden pin, and a small fire snapped at freshly piled kindling. She hesitated, wondering suddenly if she would not be welcome. Perhaps she trusted too easily.

The sound of breaking twigs sent her whirling on hands and knees, eyes widened in fear.

The man ducked his head as he crawled into the cave through the narrow opening, eyes on the stone floor. Over his shoulder he wore a crude bow, but the long-knife at his belt looked more efficient. Under one arm he held the drooping body of a slain rabbit.

Alix withdrew farther, stone wall biting at her back as she pressed against it. The sound penetrated the silence like an enemy's shout. The man dropped the rabbit and drew his long-knife in a single motion, bracing himself on one knee as he came up from the floor to strike.

Then she saw shock and amazement flare in his brown eyes as he realized she was a woman.

He swore softly in wonder and shoved the knife back into its sheath. Carefully he eased into a squatting position, as if he feared to frighten her.

"Lady, I will not harm you. If you seek shelter here, you must be a refugee from Bellam's troops also."

"Refugee!"

He nodded. "Aye. From the war." He frowned. "Surely you have heard of the war, lady."

"I have heard." She stared blankly at his crusted, age-cracked leather-and-mail, and the soiled scarlet tunic bearing the Mujhar's rampant black lion. His mail was rusted, as if washed with blood, and she shivered against the sudden foreboding in her bones.

"My name is Oran," he said, rubbing a dirty hand through matted, lank brown hair. "I am a soldier of Homana."

She frowned at him. "Then why are you here? Should you not be with your lord?"

"My lord is slain. Keough of Atvia, Bellam's foul accomplice, overran the army twenty days ago like a pack of savage dogs." His eyes narrowed angrily. "It was night, moonless and dark. We slept, wearied from a three-day battle. The Atvian host crept upon us in all stealth, and routed us before the dawn."

Alix wet her dry lips. "Where, Oran? Mujhara?"

He laughed. "Not Mujhara. I am not one of the Mujhar's fine guard. I am a common soldier who once was a tenant crofter for Prince Fergus, the Mujhar's own brother."

"Fergus." She eased herself away from the rocky wall, kneeling before him. "Then it was Fergus you served in the field?"

"Aye, seven days' ride out of Mujhara." He hawked and spat, turning his head from her. He wiped the spittle from his lips and looked at her bleakly. "Prince Fergus was slain."

"Why did you not stay?" she demanded. "Why did you forsake your lord?"

His grimy, stubbled face was ugly. "I sickened of it. I

was not meant to slay men like beasts on the order of a man who keeps himself safe behind the ensorcelled walls of Homana-Mujhar." Oran spat again. "Shaine has set wards, lady; instruments of sorcery to keep the Ihlini out. He keeps himself safe, while thousands die in his name."

Alix drew a trembling breath, clenching fists against her knees. "What of Carillon? What of the prince?"

Oran's mouth twisted. "Carillon is prisoner to Keough himself."

"Prisoner!"

"Aye. I saw him slay two who sought to take him, fighting like a demon, but it was Keough's own son who broke his guard and disarmed him. Thorne. The Atvian prince took Carillon's sword, then Carillon himself, and marched him to his father." Oran stared at her narrowly. "They will slay him, lady, or take him to Bellam in Mujhara."

"No . . ."

He shrugged. "It is his lot. He is the Mujhar's heir, and valuable. Keough will keep him close until he is in Bellam's hands. Or Tynstar's."

Alix closed her eyes and summoned up his face, recalling his warm blue eyes and stubborn jaw. And his smile, whenever he looked on her.

Oran shifted and she opened her eyes. He grinned, displaying broken, yellowed teeth, and took up the leather pouch. He undid the pin and spilled the contents across the blanket.

It was a stream of gems glowing richly in the shadowed cave. Brooches, rings of delicate gold and silver, and a wristband of copper. Oran prodded the cache with a finger.

"Solindish, lady. And fine, as you can see."

She frowned at them. "Where did you get them?"

He laughed crudely. "From men who no longer had need of such things."

She recoiled. "You stole them from dead men?"

"How else does a poor soldier make his way? I am not one of your rich lordlings, like Carillon; nor am I a Mujhara noble born to silks and jewels. How else am I to get such things?"

Avarice glinted in his eyes. She saw them travel her body expectantly. She wore the golden *lir*-torque Duncan had given her and delicate topaz drops hung at her ears.

"So," she said on a long breath, "you will slay me for my wealth as well."

He grinned. "There need be no slaying, lady. You have only to give them to me." He stroked his bottom lip. "I have never seen your like before. Are you some lord's light woman?"

The insult did not touch her. Oran, in his commonness, did not recognize it as such. And the Cheysuli had begun to change her perceptions of such things.

Alix slowly tensed. "No."

"Then how came you by such things?"

Enlightenment flared within her mind. Carefully she damned the sudden realization of her power and looked at him calmly.

"My *cheysul* gave them to me."

He scowled at her. "Speak Homanan, lady. What do you say?"

"My husband, Oran. He made me these things."

He grinned. "Then he can make more. Here, lady; give them to me."

"No." She looked at him levelly. "It is not wise for a Homanan to seek that fashioned by a Cheysuli."

"Cheysuli!" His brows slid up. "You live among the shapechangers?"

"I *am* one."

For a moment fear flashed in his eyes. Then it faded, replaced with determination and greed. "The shapechangers are under the Mujhar's death decree. I should slay you, and then all you have would be mine."

It angered her past caution. "I doubt you could accomplish it."

His hand flashed to his knife. "Can I not, shapechanger witch? You do not frighten me with your sorcery. Only your warriors shift their shape, so you offer little threat." He grinned and lifted the knife. "What do you say now, witch?"

Alix said nothing. He effectively blocked the cave entrance with his mailed bulk, and as he moved slowly toward her she saw she had no chance to avoid him. The wall curved snuggly against her back.

"Do not," she said softly.

Oran laughed silently and put his hand on the torque at her throat.

Alix summoned the magic and blurred herself into a wolf.

He gaped at her, then fell back with a cry of terror. The knife fell from limp fingers as he scrabbled on the floor. The wolf-bitch snarled and leaped over him, avoiding his body, but forcing him flat on his back as she moved. She heard his scream of horror as she drove past his trembling body and into the darkened forest.

She paused a moment, free of the place, and sent an exultant howl soaring to the dark heavens.

Then she went on in *lir*-shape.

The wolf-bitch, silvered by moonlight, sifted out of the trees into the Cheysuli camp. She saw the huddled forms of blanketed, sleeping warriors and the shadowed lumps of *lir* scattered throughout the camp. She sent soothing patterns to the animals so they would not give the alarm and moved smoothly toward the fire. She heard Cai, perched in a tree, send a single word to his *lir*.

Duncan rolled over instantly and sat up. His movement awoke Finn, next to him, and they got to their feet in silent unison. They parted smoothly, unsheathing knives, watching the wolf-bitch carefully.

Alix, realizing they thought her some wild creature, laughed within her mind.

And Duncan named me helpless . . .

She sensed his attentiveness. Finn, moving silently, stepped closer to her. She considered leaping at him in mock attack, but gave it up as she realized he would very likely slay her.

Instead, she blurred herself into human form.

Duncan blinked, then frowned.

Finn laughed. "Well, *rujho,* I have not given you proper credit. You are powerful indeed if she cannot even part with you for two days."

Alix, suddenly chilled and wearied by the exertion and tension of the past hours, ignored him and walked to the glowing bed of coals. There she dropped to her knees and stretched her hands over the embers.

Duncan slid his knife home in its sheath. He said nothing.

Finn laughed again and gathered up his blanket, dropping it over her shoulders as he moved softly to her. "There, *rujholla*," he said mockingly. "If he will let you freeze, at least I will not."

She slid him a resentful glance and gathered the folds about her. Finn shrugged eloquently and returned to his sleeping place, settling himself cross-legged on the flattened earth.

Duncan stepped behind her, so close she could feel his knees against her back. "I suppose you will tell me why . . . eventually."

"It was *not* what Finn said!"

"Well," Duncan said, sighing, "it was too much to expect you to obey me. I should have put a spell on you."

She jerked around so hard the blanket slid off a shoulder. "You can do that?"

He laughed and moved next to her, squatting down. He took a stick and stirred the coals. "You do not know all of our gifts yet, *cheysula*. There are three. The Cheysuli can assume *lir*-shape, borrow the earth magic to heal, and also force submission on any save an Ihlini." He smiled. "But that we save for extremity."

"Duncan!"

He grinned at the coals. "I would not truly do it, *cheysula*. But you tempt me, with your forward ways."

She scowled at him. "You know I have come mostly because of you, Duncan." She took a breath. "But also because of Carillon."

His hand stopped stirring the coals. "Why?"

"He requires our help."

"How would you know that? Or can you also read the minds of men in addition to the *lir*?"

She disliked the mocking glint in his eyes. "You know I cannot. But I met a man who says he saw Fergus slain and Carillon taken by Thorne, Keough of Atvia's son. It was a bloody battle, from the appearance of his garments."

"War is often bloody, Alix. Why else would I seek to keep you from it?"

"We must find Carillon."

"The prince is no half-grown boy, Alix. And he is valuable. His captivity may well be unpleasant, but it will not be the death of him. Bellam—perhaps even Tynstar—will want him alive, for a time."

She stared at him. "I begin to think you will allow this jealousy to prevent his rescue."

"I am jealous of no one!" he snapped, and reddened as he heard Finn's spurt of laughter.

"Duncan, we must go to him."

"We go to Mujhara, to fight the Ihlini. They are a bigger threat than Keough."

"Then you sentence Carillon to death!"

Duncan sighed heavily. "If his death is meant, it will happen. Carillon may not be Cheysuli, but he has his own sort of *tahlmorra.*"

"Duncan!" she cried incredulously, aware the others watched in silent interest. "You cannot mean to forsake him like this!"

He looked at her harshly. "The Ihlini have taken Mujhara. If the palace falls, Homana is in the hands of Tynstar. Do you not see? Carillon will be kept alive while Bellam wants him, but if Homana-Mujhar falls he will slay all threats to his control. First Shaine, then Carillon." He released a weary breath. "I know you care for him, *cheysula,* but we cannot seek out a single man when an entire city may be destroyed."

"He is your prince," she whispered.

"And I am your *cheysul.*"

She scowled at him. "Do you send me back, then?"

"Would you go if I did?"

"No."

He grunted. "Then I will save my breath." He raised her, removed Finn's blanket and led her over to his pallet. He pressed her down with a hand on her shoulder. "Sleep, *cheysula;* we ride early."

"Sleep?" she inquired impishly as he lowered himself next to her and encircled her with his hard arms.

He laughed softly. "Sleep. Would you give my *rujholli* more to make sport of?"

"It is ever Finn," she said grumpily, pulling a blanket over them both.

Duncan settled her head upon his shoulder. After a moment he sighed. "If it pleases you, small one, I will send Cai to the prince. He can bring word of Carillon's welfare."

"Well," she said after a silence, "it is something."

His hand tightened threateningly on her throat. "Can you never be satisfied, Alix?"

"If I told you aye, you would cease trying to please me." She spread her fingers against the hollow of his throat, feeling its pulse. "Duncan," she whispered after a moment, "why have you never said you loved me?"

He was very still. "Because the Cheysuli do not speak of love."

Alix sat bolt upright, dragging the blanket from him. "What do you say?"

His hand reached out and caught hers, pulling her back down against his chest. "I said we do not *speak* of love. It weakens a warrior, who should think of other matters." He smiled into the darkness. "For all that, words do not always serve."

"Then am I supposed to *guess*?"

He laughed softly and settled the blanket over them again. "There is no need for you to guess. I have given you answer enough, before." His hand slid down to rest across her stomach as he whispered. "You bear my son, Alix. Is that not enough?"

She stared into the darkness. "For now . . ."

Chapter Four

Alix spent her days behind Duncan on horseback, clasping his lean waist and anticipating what they would do when they reached Mujhara. She had decided not to bother Duncan with entreaties to go instead to Carillon, for he had sent Cai as promised four days before, and his arguments made sense. For all she still held great esteem and affection for Carillon, she knew even the prince would be more concerned with the welfare of Homana-Mujhar than himself.

Duncan was unusually solicitous of her, so much so that Finn, riding next to them, finally demanded an explanation. Alix, looking at him in surprise, realized Duncan had said nothing of the child.

"Well *meijha?*" he asked. "Have you sickened, or does my *rujho* simply worry himself over women's things, now he has a *cheysula?*"

She felt color rise in her face. "I have not sickened."

Duncan shot Finn a dark glance. "Do not plague her, *rujho*. You have done enough of that in the past."

Finn kneed his horse closer. "Do you seek to tell me something without speaking?"

"No," Alix said quickly.

Duncan laughed softly. "Perhaps it is time, *cheysula*. You will not be able to be silent about it much longer."

"Duncan . . ." she protested.

Finn scowled at them. "What do you say?"

"Alix has conceived. She bears me a son in six months."

She waited for Finn's mocking words and twisted mouth, dreading what he might say. But he said nothing. He glanced at her quickly, then away, head bent as if he studied the ground beneath his horse's hooves. His face was masklike, as if he feared to set free an emotion he could not control.

Duncan frowned. "Finn?"

Finn glanced up and smiled at his brother. His eyes slid to Alix, then away. "I wish you well of it, Duncan. It is a good thing to know the Cheysuli increase, even if only by one."

"One is enough for now," Alix said firmly.

His grin crept back. "Aye, *meijha,* perhaps it is. I will be glad enough to be uncle to one."

She watched him, puzzled by his manner. He was a different man. She saw his yellow eyes settle broodingly on Duncan, then a strange regretful smile twisted his mouth. He glanced up and saw her watching him, then gestured expressively with a hand.

Tahlmorra.

Alix opened her mouth to ask a question, sensing something she could not quite understand. But she said nothing as Duncan stiffened before her. She felt the sudden tensing of his muscles as he shuddered once, violently.

"Duncan!"

He did not answer her. Instead he jerked the horse to a stop so unruly it slid Alix along smooth hindquarters until she clutched helplessly at Duncan, trying to stay horseback. It was futile. She landed awkwardly on her feet, hanging onto the stirrup to steady herself.

"Duncan!"

The horse side-stepped nervously. The reins were slack in Duncan's hands as he bent over the pommel and shuddered again.

Alix stumbled back as the horse moved against her, nearly stepping on her. She grabbed Duncan's leggings and tugged, trying to gain his attention.

Finn, on the other side, wrenched his mount to a halt and reached out. *"Rujho?"*

Duncan pushed himself upright and slid awkwardly off the horse. He hung onto the stirrup helplessly, unaware of Alix's presence. He set his forehead against the saddle and sucked in air like a drowning man.

"Duncan . . ." she whispered, putting a hesitant hand on his rigid arm. *"Duncan!"*

Finn dismounted rapidly and moved around the riderless horse to Duncan's side. He gently pushed Alix out of the way, ignoring her protests, and took Duncan's arm.

"What is it?" he asked.

Duncan turned his head, gazing blankly at Finn. His eyes were dilated and oddly confused. "Cai . . ." He gasped hoarsely, shuddering again.

Finn steered him away from the fretting horse to a tree stump, pushing him down on it as Duncan swayed on his feet. There he knelt in the leaves and looked into his brother's face.

"Slain?" he whispered.

Alix, still standing by the horse, understood the implications of the question instantly. She fell to her knees next to Finn.

"Duncan . . . *no!*"

His face was strained and pale. His head dropped until he stared sightlessly at the ground, hands hanging limply against his thighs.

Alix touched his cold hand softly. "Duncan, say you are well."

Finn set his hand on her shoulder, silencing her without a word. Then he grasped Duncan's tensing forearm.

"*Rujho,* is he slain?"

Duncan raised his head and stared at them. His eyes were strange, dangerously feral in a hollowed face. Tautness moved through his body like a serpent, knotting sinews into rigidity. But color began to flow slowly back into his face.

"No," he said at last. He swallowed against another shudder. "He is—injured. And far from this place." He shoved a shaking hand through his black hair. "His *lir*-pattern is so weak I can barely touch him."

Alix sent out her own call, trying to discover the hawk, but nothing answered. She had spent time working on screening out the other *lir* so she could think in peace; perhaps it worked against her now.

Finn glanced over his shoulder at the gathered warriors. "We camp here until morning." He turned back and looked at Alix out of a face suddenly old and weary. His smile held little reassurance, though he sought to soothe her. "Cai is not slain. Duncan will be well."

She swallowed and felt some of the horrible fear slide out of her bones. But much of it remained, and when Finn pulled Duncan to his feet she nearly cried to see his spirit so diminished.

This is what it is to have a lir, she thought miserably. *This is the price of the old gods' magic . . .*

Duncan was made to lie down, wrapped in blankets before a hastily laid fire. But he came out of his shock long enough to stare frowningly at his brother.

"We should go on, *rujho*. We do not reach Mujhara like this."

Finn smiled and shook his head. "I know what you feel. When Storr nearly died of an arrow wound, I was close to death myself with the shock of it. You have never had to deal with it, so keep silent until you are better. I am second-leader, after you."

Duncan pulled the blankets more closely around his shoulders, worn to the bone. "You have never led men, Finn," he said crossly. "How can I know you will not get us into trouble?"

Alix smiled faintly, relieved to hear the brotherly banter. Finn, standing over his elder like an avenging demon with a newly won soul, grinned and crossed his arm over his chest.

"You will simply have to find out, *rujho*. It may be *I* am better suited, even, than you."

Duncan scowled blackly at him a moment, then closed his eyes and sank against the ground. Alix watched him fade into sleep as she knelt beside him. She gripped his war bow in her hands.

"He will be well?" she asked softly.

"He is full of Cai's pain," Finn told her. "When a *lir* is injured, the Cheysuli feels all of it in the first moments. It will pass." He sighed. "He only needs rest."

"And Cai," she said softly.

Finn's face tightened. "Aye. And Cai."

Duncan recovered rapidly, though his attention seemed elsewhere most of the time, seeking Cai. Alix remonstrated with him to rest longer than a single night, but Duncan declared himself fit enough and ready to go on to Mujhara. Finn, after grumbling about his brother's foolishness, gave in and agreed. So Alix climbed aboard the horse once again and hung onto Duncan more firmly than usual, making certain he was well.

They were two days out of the city when Cai appeared in the sky, winging slowly toward them. She felt Duncan's instant tension and smoothed a hand across his back, as if to quiet a fretful child. Duncan halted the horse and waited.

Lir, the bird sent, sounding pleased, *I was not certain how far you rode from me.*

Alix smiled in relief at the hawk's healthy tone. But Duncan sat stiffly on his horse. He reached out his left arm and let the hawk alight. Talons closed, gripping tightly, and Alix saw a trickle of blood thread its way across the vulnerable flesh. Duncan seemed not to notice.

The bird settled himself. *I am sorry,* lir, *that I troubled you. I am better now.*

Finn guided his horse to Duncan's and waited mutely, watching Duncan's face. Alix realized once more how special her gift was. The others must wait for Duncan to pass on Cai's speech, but she could hear the hawk's warm tone easily.

Duncan draped the reins over the pommel and put his free hand to Cai's head, stroking the shining feathers gently.

"I would not lose you," he murmured.

Nor I, you. The bird's eyes sharpened. *I bring news,* lir. *The war goes badly for Homana. The Mujhar's armies are near destroyed, scattered by the Solindish troops. What men did not flee were taken by Keough of Atvia, who rules the field. It was Atvian archers who loosed arrows at me for sport, and nearly brought me down. But the wing was hardly touched, and I am strong again.* Cai lifted from Duncan's arm and circled the forest clearing. Then he perched himself on a low branch. *You see?*

Relief loosened the constraints of Duncan's muscles. Alix felt him relax for the first time since Cai had been injured. But she also felt his concern for the army's welfare as Cai continued.

It is bad, lir. *Of the thousands Shaine sent, only hundreds remain alive. Most are captives of the Atvian lord. Like Carillon.*

Alix stiffened so quickly her fingers dug into Duncan's back. "What of Carillon?"

Cai hesitated. *He is well enough, for a man kept chained*

*night and day and plagued by Atvian and Solindish soldiers
who wish to ridicule him.*

"He is not hurt?" she asked breathlessly.

*Liren, I did not see him well. But he was in a tumbril,
heavily chained so he could not move. No man, even uninjured, can bear such close bonds for long without suffering.*

She set her forehead against Duncan's back in anguish,
vividly picturing the prince a prisoner to the enemy. She
hardly heard Duncan telling the others what Cai said.

Finn smiled grimly. "So, the princeling learns what it is
to be a man."

Alix jerked her head up and glared at him. "How can
you say that? Carillon is a warrior, a *prince!* He was a man
before ever you took me captive!"

Finn lifted a placating hand, grinning at her vehemence.
"*Meijha,* I speak no ill of him. I mean only he has not
fought for his realm before, and it is a hard thing to learn
when one is taken prisoner."

"Fergus is slain," she said in a deadly tone. "Mujhara is
in the hands of the Ihlini. And now Carillon is prisoner to
this Atvian lord. It seems more than enough for any *man.*"

"Aye," Finn said gently.

She glared at him, expecting more. But he said nothing.

Duncan glanced at the waiting warriors. "We must go to
the city."

"No!" Alix cried.

Cai agreed with Duncan. *Even now the Atvian lord
moves his men toward Mujhara. If you go there, you will
be able to defend the ancient city.*

"No," Alix said firmly. "We must go to Carillon."

Duncan sighed. "Nothing has changed, *cheysula.* Mujhara
is taken. Shaine waits within the palace. It is there we
must go."

"But he is a *prisoner!*"

"You knew that days ago," he said shortly. "And you
agreed I had the right of it."

"I did not know he was chained! He deserves our help."

Finn snorted. "He wanted nothing to do with us before,
meijha. Why should I believe differently now?"

"By the gods!" Alix swore. "You would have me believe
you *desire* his death!"

"No," Finn said, unsmiling. "It would not serve the prophecy."

That silenced her. Finn never spoke of the *tahlmorra* contained within the prophecy of the Firstborn, and to hear his serious tone made her realize he was not always the disruptive warrior. Alix scowled at him, disliking the unfamiliarity of his new attitude.

Duncan kneed his horse forward. "We go on to Mujhara."

"Duncan!"

"Be silent, Alix. You are here because I have allowed it."

She gritted her teeth and spoke through them. "If it were *you*, Duncan, and Carillon could come to *your* aid, would you be content to let him go elsewhere?"

Duncan laughed. "The prince does not even know we move to aid the Homanans. He can hardly miss us."

"It is not fair," she muttered.

"War rarely is," Duncan agreed, and led the warriors on.

Alix did not sleep. She lay stiffly under Duncan's sleep-loosened arm, thinking deeply. The Cheysuli camp was silent save for the settling of the coals and the shifting of a *lir*. She had longed to question Cai more closely about Carillon, but could not for fear Duncan would hear. So she pretended sleep when he would speak softly to her, and smiled grimly when he fell asleep himself. Then she began to plan.

If I go to Carillon, they also will have to go. Duncan would not allow me to remain alone in an enemy camp for long. She smiled wryly, half-pleased with the thought. *Not bearing this child who may give the Old Blood and its gifts back to the clan.*

She snuggled more deeply under the blanket. *I will go, and then Carillon will have the help he needs.* She scratched at a bug bite on her neck. *And if the others desire it another way, perhaps I will be enough to win Carillon free of Keough and his Atvian demons.*

Storr, lying at Finn's side, stirred and lifted his head. *You should not, liren. There is danger.*

She peered through the darkness but could not see the wolf's silver form. *Storr, I must do this. Carillon would do it for me.*

Your cheysul *will not approve.*

Then he may beat me, if he wishes, when he comes to find me.

He would never beat you. Storr was silent a moment. Liren, *you are stubborn.*

Alix smiled into the darkness. *I am Cheysuli.*

Cai settled his wings more comfortably. *Perhaps it will be enough.*

It will be, she said firmly, and waited for the dawn.

Chapter Five

Just before sunrise, when the stillness of the night lay heaviest on her soul, Alix slipped carefully from beneath the blanket. Duncan made no movement as she folded the blanket so the chill would not give away her absence. Cai, perched in the nearest tree, startled her with his resigned tone.

Still you go, liren?

She straightened the twisted jerkin and tightened her belt. *I go. Carillon is deserving of it.*

You carry a child.

Her mouth twisted. *I do. And I will keep it safe.*

The hawk's tone saddened. *I cannot gainsay you,* liren.

She looked at him sharply, peering at his huddled form. *Do you tell your* lir *of this?*

He will have to know.

But not yet, she pleaded. *First, let me go. Then you may tell him.*

It is not my place to keep things from my lir.

Cai, I will go. Even if Duncan wakens and seeks to gainsay me, I will go. Do you see?

The great bird seemed to sigh. *I see,* liren. *Then go, if you must.*

Alix smiled fondly in his direction, then blurred herself and went unto the skies as a falcon.

The journey took time, and Alix tired as she soared over the forests. But she ignored the tension in her wings and kept on, determined to reach Carillon. When at last she broke free of the trees into bare plains, she was near exhaustion. Already it was twilight, and she feared she would not reach the armies until after dark.

Suddenly the Atvian host was below her. Alix circled and drifted over the army, seeking knowledge of the true state

of affairs. She saw strange bearded men in red-painted
leather-and-mail, wearing keyholed helms that hid their
faces. There were archers, she saw, and soldiers bearing
heavy broadswords. Among the red-mailed men were Solindish troops in chain mail and breastplates.

She kept one keen eye on the archers, fearing they would
shoot at her as they had Cai. But most of the troops seemed
more concerned with food, for they squatted around fires
with bowls and mugs in their hands. No one paid a lone
falcon any mind.

Alix dared closer, drifting in an idle pattern toward a
blue field pavilion. Carefully she settled on the ridgepole,
seeking the proper place for a prince held captive.

Her body trembled. She mantled once, settled her feathers and tried to recoup her lost strength. Alix was afraid the
exhaustion in her hollow bird-bones might sap her ability to
hold *lir*-shape, and she could not risk discovery.

If I am caught, I will be named witch, she thought uneasily. *Shapechanger witch.*

She waited until some of her strength returned. Then she
lifted from the ridgepole and drifted over the sprawling
encampment.

Alix saw no sign of Carillon. She found the Homanan
prisoners, harshly tied and guarded by Atvian men, but
Carillon was not among them. She closed her mind to the
cries and moans of the wounded, for if she listened their
pain would become hers, and she would fail.

She dipped closer when she saw the post set before a
scarlet pavilion. For a moment she feared the figure lashed
to it was Carillon, but she saw it was a boy. His body was
slumped against the post, arms and legs tied securely on
the other side. His forehead was pressed against the rough
wood and his eyes were closed. The soiled tunic he wore
was in shreds, hanging from his back. She saw, with a quickening of revulsion, he had been flogged.

His eyes were shut tight in a pale, grimy face, and his
black hair hung limply to his shoulders. She could not tell
if he was alive or dead.

Alix flew on, passing over a two-wheeled tumbril near
the picket-line of horses. A glance down showed her the
figure slumped in it, and the familiar tawny-dark hair.

She sucked in her breath and turned back, driving toward

the tumbril. Carillon sat against the front of the cart, legs stretched to hang from the opening. The setting sun glinted off the iron banding his legs and hands.

Like the boy, his eyes were closed. And, like him, he showed no signs of life. Alix flew closer.

He moved. She heard the clash of iron as he shifted his arms, settling the chain links against his chest. His eyes opened, half-lidded, staring out at the tumbril blankly. His face was badly bruised and smeared with blood. But he lived.

Alix felt the fear abate and anger rise in its place. She nearly shrieked her rage aloud but refrained as she realized it would be better not to draw attention to herself. Instead she dropped to the tumbril and settled on its rim.

Carillon stared at her. Now she could see the gauntness in his face; the blackened eyes and poor color. But there was also life in his eyes, and burning resentment.

She could not speak to him in *lir*-shape, and she dared not change back yet. She could only sit by him, and wait.

The prince shifted in the tumbril. The chains clashed and rattled against the wooden flooring, driving empathetic pain into her own heart. The heavy shackles bound his wrists mercilessly, and she saw the ridged, seeping sores beneath.

Keough is a demon! she raged within her falcon-soul. *A demon!*

Carillon raised his shackled hands and rubbed wearily at his eyes. Blood ran up the right side of his face like a flag, but she could not tell if it was his or another man's. His lips were pale and compressed.

"Well, bird," he rasped, "do you come to witness my death? Do you seek my flesh like the carrion crows?"

No! she cried silently.

Carillon sighed and rested his head against the tumbril. "You may not have long, then. Keough has slain hundreds of Homanan soldiers. It is only time before he puts me up to take my head as well." He grimaced. "Unless he means me for Bellam, in Mujhara."

Alix stared at him in anguish, unable to speak to him, knowing he saw only a bright-eyed falcon.

Carillon's smile was that of a man who sees his own death. "Keep your vigil, then. I can use the company, no matter what sort it may be. The nights are long."

Alix held her position on the tumbril rim, waiting for the long night to come.

When it did she slipped off the tumbril and blurred herself into human-form. The guard stood far away, as if a chained prince was of little account. She was unable to hold *lir*-shape any longer and slipped back into her human shape with a sigh of relief. Carillon, eyes closed, did not see it.

She moved carefully to him and put a gentle hand on his booted leg. "Carillon." He did not stir. "Carillon," she whispered again.

He opened his eyes and stared at her. For a long moment he remained expressionless, as if he saw nothing at all, and she feared he was too dazed to acknowledge her presence. Then she saw sense come into his eyes, and the incredulity.

"Alix . . ." he hissed. He sat bolt upright, wincing as the shackles bit into his raw wrists. *"Alix!"*

She raised a hand. "Be silent, Carillon, or at least quieter. Would you have me made prisoner also?"

He gaped at her. Slowly his mouth closed and he wet his lips. "Alix . . . have I discovered madness? Is it truly you?"

"Aye," she whispered. "I have come to give you what aid I can."

He shook his head slowly. "This cannot be. No man could walk into Keough's camp undiscovered. How is it *you* have done this?"

She smiled, suddenly calm and exultant at the same time. "You have cursed my race, Carillon, but now see how it serves you. I came to you in *lir*-shape."

"You!"

She glanced around anxiously, hushing him with a quick gesture. "Carillon, there is something in me that allows me to assume any animal form I wish. The *shar tahl* says it is the Old Blood in me, gotten from Lindir." She saw the scowl begin on his face and slid into the tumbril, covering his mouth with her hand. "*Lindir,* Carillon. She had Cheysuli blood in her, from her mother, though it was little enough. Yet it gave me the magic of the Firstborn."

"I do not believe it."

"Shaine's great-great grandsire took a Cheysuli *meijha,* who bore him a daughter. Perhaps you also have a drop or two of Cheysuli blood in your veins."

"I *cannot* believe it."

Alix smiled at him. "Were you not attended by a falcon earlier, my lord?"

He scowled at her. "That was a bird."

"*I* am a bird, when I wish it." She sighed and gently touched a bruised cheek. "I have come to get you free of this place. Do you wish to discuss my abilities all this night, rather than escaping?"

He grabbed her before she could move, pulling her down until his mouth came down on hers. Alix, shocked into immobility, smelled his sweat and blood and fear, and wondered at her own lack of response.

Is this not what I wanted for so long?

She pulled away from him, one hand to her mouth. Carillon's face, though shadowed, was not at all repentant. His eyes, looking so deeply into hers, saw the answer she could not speak, and he accepted it.

He lifted his arms, chains clashing. "I go nowhere in these."

Alix looked away from his face; at the iron locked around his boots and the chain so short it denied him slack enough to walk.

"I will get the iron from you," she promised. "I will give you your freedom again."

"I would not ask you to risk yourself, Alix. I have given you my thanks for what you have done—if you wish an explanation—but I could not ask such a dangerous thing of you."

"I *offer*. You do not ask." She smiled. "If I unlock your chains, could you take a horse from here?"

He stared hard at the tumbril floor and at the muscles that quivered in his thighs. His voice, when it came, sounded old and worn thin. "I have been chained as you see me for weeks. I doubt I could stand without aid, let alone ride." His eyes shifted to her face. "Alix, I would be willing to try, but I will not let you do this. I will not risk your life."

"You sound like Duncan!" she accused. "He will not credit my willingness to do this either."

His brows lowered. "What has the shapechanger to do with this?"

Alix sat on her folded legs, forcing her frustration down.

"He is my husband, Carillon, after Cheysuli fashion. He has much to do with this."

He shifted uncomfortably. "You should not have gone with him from Homana-Mujhar. You could have stayed with me, once I had soothed the Mujhar."

"I chose to go with Duncan." She sighed and forced herself to relax. "Carillon, we can speak of this another time. For now, I have come to help you escape. Tell me where the key to this iron is kept."

"No."

"Carillon!" she hissed.

"I will not," he said firmly. "I would rather remain a prisoner than risk you."

She glared at him, teeth and fists clenched. "They will take you to Mujhara! Tynstar is there, with Bellam. Carillon, you will be *slain!*"

He remained silent.

Alix ground her teeth and flung a furious glance around the area. Finally she hunched over, propping her chin on one hand.

"I have come all this way for you, and you will not let me help you. I defied my husband, who said Homana-Mujhar is more important than Homana's prince, and I have risked the life of my child for you, and *still* you will not let me do this."

"Child," he said sharply, straightening. "You have conceived?"

She scowled at him. "Aye. I have assumed the form of wolf and falcon. I have no knowledge what such magic will do to an unborn child, but I did it for you. For *you,* Carillon."

He closed his eyes. "Alix," he said in despair, "you have been a foolish woman."

She picked at the leather of her borrowed leggings. "Aye, perhaps I have. But I cannot go back now." She brightened. "Would it change your mind if I said the Cheysuli will come here?"

He stared at her suspiciously. "Cheysuli?"

She straightened, growing excited. "We were on our way to Mujhara, to aid Shaine. But Duncan will doubtless seek me here, when Cai tells him what I have done." She smiled slowly, proudly. "He will not let me do this alone. He will come after me."

Carillon sighed wearily and fingered the bruise on his cheek. "Alix, if you are anything like your mother, I am not surprised she said no to royal betrothal and fled with a shapechanger. I think you are more stubborn than any woman I have known."

"They will come," she said softly. "The Cheysuli. And you will be freed."

He raised a single eyebrow. "Duncan has no knowledge you are here?"

She averted her face. "No. He would have forbidden it."

"As would I," he retorted. "Perhaps he and I are more like than I thought."

She watched emotion moving in his face, and his struggle to maintain a calm demeanor. She leaned forward and placed a gentle hand on his manacled forearm.

"Carillon, the Cheysuli are not so different from the Homanans. They have only retained the gifts of the old gods." She paused. "Do not curse us for it."

"Alix, you are more eloquent than my uncle's courtiers."

"Will you not admit it?" she asked earnestly. "Will you not see we are not demons and beasts . . . not what men brand us?"

"I cannot say. I have been taught to fear and mistrust them all my life. Alix . . . I have seen what they can do to men in battle . . . what they leave when they kill."

"That is battle," she said quietly. "You should know, now, what price it exacts." Her fingers tightened on his arm. "You know them, now. You know *me*."

Carillon drew up his legs, chains clashing, and stared over his knees at her. "If they come—*if* they come—there is little I can say against them. They will have proven their service to the Mujhar's heir." He smiled bleakly. "But they will not come."

"*I* came."

For a long moment he said nothing, studying her face. She sensed the conflict within him, realizing she had suffered her own measure of it when Duncan first insisted she go to the Keep.

It is not easily done, she reflected. *And he is no kind of*

*man at all if he accedes so swiftly to words he has been
taught not to hear.*

"Alix," he said finally, "perhaps, in time, I will believe
you. But not yet."

She removed her hand and stood. "If I cannot free you,
perhaps there is something else. Can I steal food for you?
Water?"

"I do not hunger. Inactivity and chains take the appetite
from a man." His eyes were grim, hidden in shadow.
"There is only one thing I would ask, and I cannot ask it
of you."

"Tell me."

He pushed grimy fingers through tangled tawny hair, baring his face to the moonlight. Alix saw the glitter in his
eyes.

"There is a boy. Rowan. A Homanan boy no more than
twelve, who came to serve his lord however he could." His
eyes closed a moment. "He told me he acted as a runner
between the captains, carrying messages. But he, like me,
was caught and made helpless. Keough's son took Rowan
from the prisoners—as he did me—and made him serve the
Atvian lords." Carillon's face tightened into bitterness as
he remembered. "I was forced to watch him, in Keough's
field pavilion. His eyes followed me everywhere . . . and I
could see the confusion in his face. I was his prince—why
could I not win his release?"

"Carillon," she said softly.

Chains rattled and glinted in the moonlight. "Rowan did
well enough at first. But he was tired, aching from the cuffs
they had given him all night. They even made him serve
me, though it was done as if I were no better than the
poorest cur." Breath hissed between his teeth. "Rowan
tripped and fell across the table, and spilled wine all over
Keough himself. When they picked him up he was crying
in fear and exhaustion, but his face—when he looked at
me—accepted what they would do to him. He knew." He
swore beneath his breath. "I tried to gainsay it. I tried
to assuage Keough's anger by offering to take the boy's
punishment myself—by the gods, I begged for it! I got on
my knees to Keough . . . when I would not do it before,
when they asked for it! But the boy was worth it."

"They would not accept it," Alix said.

"No. Thorne—Keough's son—took Rowan out and had him flogged until the skin fell off his back . . . and then left him tied to the post."

"I have seen him."

Carillon gave up his breath as if he would breathe no more. "Only a boy, who wished to serve his lord. And do you see what that service has won him?"

She felt for the knife in her right boot and found it. Then she smiled at Carillon. "I will free him for you, my lord. You will see."

"Alix!" he cried, jerking upright, but she had already blurred into the darkness.

Chapter Six

Alix flew to the post and perched upon it. The boy was still slumped at its base, but now she could see the movement of his back that told her he breathed. The flesh had nearly been stripped from his rib cage. She winced to herself, then looked closely at the field pavilions surrounding the area.

The scarlet one was largest, and the finest. Men had set tall torches in the ground before it, illuminating its front. Two other smaller pavilions stood on either side of it, but the torchlight did not extend to them. Alix assured herself there were no guards near the post, then drifted down and blurred into human form.

She drew the knife from her boot and knelt at the boy's side. She put a hand on his shoulder, carefully avoiding his lacerated flesh. He made no movement and she feared his unconsciousness would hinder her ability to get him away safely.

I will take him to the forest's edge, she decided. *Somehow I will get him there, and have him wait. When Duncan comes, I can take him to this boy. Rowan.*

He winced and moaned, stirring under her fingers. His eyes opened wide, dilated, pale in the moonlight. Fear changed his bruised face into a mask of terror.

Alix moved around so he could see her clearly. "No, Rowan," she said softly. "I am not your enemy. I am sent from Prince Carillon, who would have you free of this place."

His face was hidden behind his tied arm, but she could see the gleam of his light eyes. He swallowed visibly. "Prince Carillon?"

Alix set her knife to the rope binding his legs and cut them. "He knows you have served his House," she said soothingly. "He knows what loyalty you have given him.

He would not have you so poorly treated for honorable service."

"I have not served honorably," the boy said miserably. "I ran. I *ran*." His head dropped. "And I was captured."

"Carillon was also captured," she told him. "He fought, but was beaten." Inwardly she flinched at so undermining Carillon's prowess. But it was the truth. "You were here, Rowan. You came to serve. He has seen the honor in you, and he has done what he could to get you free. I have come in his name, because he asked it." She bent closer to him. "He called you by name and told me to come straight here, to release you."

"I am not worthy."

She freed his hands and moved back to his side, sliding the knife into her boot. Carefully she helped him sit up.

"You are more than worthy. Why else would the prince himself insist you be freed?"

The light fell clearly on his face for the first time. It was bruised and grimy, but his eyes, staring at her, were as yellow as Duncan's.

Alix sucked in a breath. "Cheysuli!"

Rowan recoiled from her, then winced. "No!" he cried. "I am not a demon!"

She put a trembling hand toward his face. "No . . . oh no . . . you are not a demon. It is not a curse. Rowan—"

"What do you do?" asked an accented voice from behind.

Alix leaped to her feet and whirled, staring wide-eyed at the man. He stood before her like a demon in shadow, backlighted by the torches. He was dark-haired, bearded, and the color of his eyes was indeterminate. Before she could move he reached out and caught her arm.

"Who are you, boy?"

She was thankful for her warrior's garb. "I am a servant of the prince, my lord. Prince Carillon."

He glanced down at Rowan, shivering against the post. The man smiled grimly and jerked Alix toward the scarlet pavilion, into the torchlight.

She saw he was near Duncan's age, but there the resemblance ended. He was tall and slender; strongly built. She saw cruelty and determination in the lines of his face; glinting in his brown eyes. He was richly dressed in black save for a blue tunic that bore the crest of a scarlet hand clasping a white lightning bolt. His mail, glinting in the light, was little more than ceremonial.

His hand was tight on her arm. "You are no boy," he said, surprised. He turned her face into the light. "No boy at all." And he smiled.

She tugged ineffectually against his grip. When she saw she could not break free she gave it up and waited silently.

"Who are you? Why do you free that worthless child?"

"He is not worthless!" she cried. "He only sought to serve his prince, as befits a loyal man. Yet you punish him for that!"

"I punish him because he threw wine over my father," the man said firmly. "He is fortunate I did not order him slain."

Alix froze. *Thorne . . . Thorne! This man is Keough's heir!*

His dark eyes narrowed. "What do you do here, girl?"

"You saw me. I cut the boy free."

"Why?"

She lifted her chin defiantly. "Because Carillon desired it."

"Carillon is a prisoner." His accent twisted the name. "His desires are nothing to me."

"Let me go," she said, knowing the request was futile.

Thorne arched a dark brow. "I think not. But tell me why you desire to leave a prince's presence so quickly."

"There is another prince whose company I prefer."

He stared at her malignantly. Alix began to regret antagonizing him, for fear of the reprisals that might affect Carillon.

"My father will wish to see you," Thorne said abruptly, and dragged her into the scarlet pavilion.

Keough, Lord of Atvia, sat at a heavy slab table in the shadows of the pavilion. Braziers had been set out to ward off the chill and torches flamed in each corner. Alix stared at him and began to be very afraid for the first time.

He was huge. His massive body dwarfed the chair he sat in, which had been bound with iron to lend it strength. His bared forearms rested on the table. She saw freckles and red hairs bleached golden by the sun. A white ridge of scar tissue snaked across the flesh and up his left arm. His hair also was red, threaded with white, and his beard was bushy. His deep-set eyes watched her in calm deliberation.

"What have you brought me, Thorne?"

"A woman dressed as a boy. You will have to ask her the reason for it."

Keough's eyes narrowed. His Atvian mouth formed the Homanan syllables harshly, without the liquid grace she was accustomed to.

"She does not look like a camp follower. They, at least, wear skirts." His fingers combed his beard. "Are you a woman who prefers those of her own sex?"

"No!" Alix hissed, against her will. She saw Keough's small smile, and it rankled. "I am a Homanan, my lord. That is all you need know."

"Then you are my enemy."

"Aye." It was heartfelt.

The beard and mustache parted as he grinned, displaying discolored teeth as big as the rest of him. "Have you come hoping to fight? If so, you are too late. The battle is already won. Prince Fergus and the generals are slain; executed. Most of the captains are dead, though I save a few for later exhibition. Even Carillon is in my hands." Keough paused. "There is little left for you to champion."

Alix was done with this. She reached for the magic in her bones that would give her *lir*-shape before their eyes. But Thorne, seeming to sense something, twisted the arm he held until the sinews cracked. The sudden pain drove away the concentration the shapechange required.

"What do I do with her?" Thorne asked. "Will you use her, or do I take her for myself?"

Keough looked at her as she hung on her tiptoes. "Leave her with me. See if Carillon is still among us."

Thorne released her and left the tent. Alix cradled her aching arm against her chest, glaring at Keough. For the moment she was helpless, and knew it.

The Atvian lord smiled and sat back in his massive chair. "You are not a light woman. You are not a soldier. What are you?"

"Someone who will seek your downfall, Atvian, when I am given the chance."

"I could have you slain, girl. Or do it myself." He raised

his huge hands. "Your slender throat would not live long in these fingers."

"And your heart will not live long with a Cheysuli arrow piercing it," Duncan said quietly.

Alix swung around, shocked as she saw him standing inside the pavilion. His eyes rested on her briefly, expressionlessly, then returned to Keough. In his hands was the black war bow, its string invisible in the shadows. Eerily, it seemed the bow required no string to send its arrow winging into men's flesh.

Keough made a sound. Alix turned back and saw him stare at Duncan as if demons pursued his soul. His small eyes slid from Duncan to Alix, and she heard the malevolence in his tone.

"So, you are a shapechanger witch sent to distract me while the others work against us."

"No," she said clearly. "I am Cheysuli, aye, but I came only for Carillon. You bind him harshly, my lord. There is no honor in your heart."

Keough laughed at her. "I *have* no heart, witch. None at all."

Duncan moved forward until he stood next to Alix. "My *cheysula* has the right of it. Carillon deserves better."

Keough pressed his hands against the table and rose. He was unarmed save for a sheathed knife at his belt, but he did not reach for it.

"I warn you, shapechanger. I am not an easy man to slay."

Duncan smiled grimly. "You will not be slain this night, my lord. It is not your *tahlmorra*. It would not serve the prophecy."

Keough's red brows lanced down. "What mean you?"

"Nothing, save I desire Carillon's release."

"Your price for leaving me alive?" Keough laughed. "What if I refuse?"

Duncan shrugged. "I have said you will not die this night. I have never lied. Even to my enemies."

The huge Atvian lord smiled. "I give you nothing, shapechanger. What you will have, you must take."

Alix sensed the billowing of the doorflap behind and turned quickly, expecting an Atvian guard. But instead she saw a familiar silver wolf, and Finn beside him.

He grinned at her. "So, *meijha,* you will do for yourself what you cannot convince *us* to do."

"I asked," she said tightly. "You would not come."

"Enough," Duncan said softly.

Thorne burst through the draped pavilion entrance, sword drawn and raised to slash its way into flesh and bone. Finn spun noiselessly and drew his knife, knocking the blade away. Thorne fell sprawling to the ground, a Cheysuli knife pressed against his throat as Finn knelt by him.

Duncan looked solemnly at Keough. "Your son's life, my lord, in exchange for Carillon's release."

Keough spat out an Atvian oath between his teeth and grabbed up the keys from an open chest. He flung them at Duncan.

Alix followed Duncan's silent order and left the pavilion. Duncan followed her out, leaving Finn and Storr to keep the Atvian rulers contained.

"Where is he?" Duncan asked.

"By the horses. Duncan—"

"We will speak of it another time."

Alix winced. "What else could I do?"

"We will speak of it another time."

She stopped to protest, then became aware of the odd stillness shrouding the encampment. She realized not a single Atvian or Solindish soldier moved against the Cheysuli invaders.

Alix turned puzzled eyes on Duncan. "What have you done?"

He smiled grimly. "We have used the third gift of the gods, Alix. We could not force all into submission, but we found the captains and took their minds from them for a time. They, in turn, do as we ordered, and keep the common soldiers from fighting. The Homanan captives have been freed."

She drew back a step. "By the gods . . . you are so powerful?"

"It is a thing we rarely do. It takes the spirit from a man, and that is a thing no Cheysuli would do if there were another way." His eyes were reproving. "You have brought this about, *cheysula.*"

Her hands clenched into fists. "I would do the same for

you!" she burst out. "For you I would give my life. How can you deny me this for Carillon?"

He sighed and jangled the keys against his leg. "Alix, we will speak of this later. You have forced me to free the prince, so let me be about it. Do you come?"

She started to walk on, then stopped stiffly and turned back.

"The boy!"

"What boy?"

"Rowan." She gestured at the post and saw the boy was gone. "He was there. Tied. I freed him." She frowned. "I thought he had not the strength to leave this place." Alix's face cleared. "But if he *is* Cheysuli—"

Duncan took her arm. "Come, *cheysula*. If the boy is free, it is fortunate for him."

She went with him to Carillon.

The prince still sat in the tumbril, legs drawn up. Moonlight spilled across the iron on his legs and hands, illuminating the drawn hollows around his eyes. When he saw Alix he shifted forward, ignoring the clank of chain.

"You are safe!"

She smiled and slid a quick sideways glance at Duncan. "Aye, I am."

Carillon blinked in surprise as he saw the Cheysuli warrior. Then a wariness came into his face. "What have you come for, shapechanger?"

Duncan regarded Carillon solemnly. "I lost something, my lord. I came to recover it." He spread his hands. "But while I am here, I may as well see to your welfare. My foolish *cheysula* has forced me to do her bidding."

Carillon nearly smiled. Alix saw the struggle in his face as he tried to keep his emotional distance from the Cheysuli. But his relief and good nature won out.

"She *is* a foolish woman. I told her so when first she appeared, but she would have none of it." He shrugged. "Women are willful creatures."

Duncan lost his solemnity and grinned. "Aye, especially this one. I think it is the royalty in her."

Carillon laughed. Alix, disgruntled by the amusement in them both at her expense, glared at Duncan.

"Have you brought the keys for nothing, Duncan? See to your prince!"

Duncan banished his smile but not the glint in his eyes. He bent and unlocked the leg shackles. Then he unlocked the heavy bands around his wrists.

The iron fell away. Alix hissed as she saw the raw wounds ringing Carillon's wrists, as if he still wore the shackles. Carefully he stretched out his hands and tried to work them.

Duncan stopped him. "Do not. If you will suffer it, I can take away the pain when we are free of this place." His eyes were very watchful. "*Will* you suffer it?"

Carillon sighed. "It seems I must. Alix has chastised me for my unremitting distrust of your race. Perhaps it is time I listened to her."

A glow came into Duncan's eyes. "If she has caused you to reconsider the feelings most Homanans hold for us, then her foolishness has some merit."

"Duncan!" she cried in frustration.

His brows lifted as he turned to her. "Well, it *was* foolishness. First you left the Keep, where I ordered you to remain; then you joined us when I would have you go back; and now you have come into an enemy camp. What else am I to think of your behavior?"

Alix took a deep breath and glared at him, hands on hips. "My behavior is mine to do. It has nothing to do with you. Because I have wed you according to your barbaric shapechanger custom and carry your halfling child does *not* mean you have the ordering of me."

"Alix!" Carillon cried. He looked first at Duncan, then at her. After a moment he looked back at Duncan. "Does she always speak this way?"

"When it suits her. I have not found her a diplomatic *cheysula*."

Alix scowled at him.

Carillon shook his head slowly. "No, I think not. I had not known of her sharp tongue." He grinned suddenly. "Well, that is not entirely true. I recall her words when I destroyed her garden."

Alix shoved her hair back from her face. "I begin to wish I had not come."

Carillon frowned at her. "Who cut off your hair?"

"Duncan."

Carillon, astonished, looked at the warrior. "Why?"

Duncan's mouth twisted. "She required a lesson." He dropped the keys and stretched out his hand. "Come, my lord; it is time we took you from this place."

Carillon heaved himself from the tumbril with Duncan's help. His face went white and he gasped in pain as his muscles screamed their agony. He remained on his feet only because Duncan held him there.

"Give me a sword," Carillon said between clenched teeth. "I must have a sword. I owe a death to someone."

"I have none." Duncan's eyes were opaque and blank. "The last sword the Cheysuli held was Hale's. You, my lord, have lost it for us."

Carillon blanched beneath the quiet reproach. "I had little to do with it! Thorne disarmed me, and took it." His pale face twisted. "I will slay that man. I have been chained like a beast and treated as common filth. They have made me watch as they ordered my men slain, and Thorne has laughed at it all." He took a slow breath. "But the worst has nothing to do with me. It was the boy. Because of him, and the rest, Thorne will die by my hand."

Alix moved closer. "The boy, Carillon. I saw him closely. Is he Cheysuli?"

Carillon sighed. "I thought so. He had the color for it. But he said no, when I asked him. He was afraid. I think, if anything, he is a bastard got on some Cheysuli woman. He said he was raised Homanan by a man and a woman not his parents." He looked back at Duncan. "If I cannot have a sword, shapechanger, then lend me a knife."

Duncan's eyes narrowed. "I have a name, princeling. You would do well to use it. I have committed my clan to your survival, and that of Homana. You and I have, I think, gone beyond being opponents of any sort. There is more than that between us, now. My lord." Duncan studied him dispassionately. "If you would earn the respect of the Cheysuli—which you must have to keep Homana intact— you would do well to save your hatred for the Ihlini."

Alix feared they might come to blows. Carillon glared angrily at Duncan, as if he would slay him, and Duncan exhibited no intention of retracting his sharp words.

Finally she put a hand on each of their arms. "Come,

my warriors. We should leave this place." When Duncan made no signs of moving she deliberately pressed her nails into his bare arm. "*Cheysul,* do you forget I carry your son? Get me free of this place."

That drove both of them into motion. Carillon wavered on his feet, recovered, and made as if to walk. Duncan caught his arm and led him away from the tumbril. But his other hand was on Alix's wrist, and she felt herself dragged after him.

Satisfied she had achieved her goal, she smiled to herself and went along amicably.

Chapter Seven

Duncan stole an Atvian horse and helped Carillon mount. The prince's face was stretched taut with pain and the struggle to keep it unspoken, but Alix sensed every screaming fiber of Carillon's mistreated body. Silently she watched him compose himself in the saddle, gathering reins with swollen, discolored hands.

Duncan turned to her. "Ride behind him, *cheysula.*"

Carillon glared at him. "I have no need of a woman to keep me in the saddle, shapechanger."

"This *woman* has accounted for your rescue, princeling," Duncan returned. "And as for your ability to keep yourself in the saddle, that is for you to do. It is Alix I am concerned about, and the health of our child."

Carillon, about to say something more, snapped his mouth shut.

Alix shook her head. "I go with you, Duncan."

"The others leave this place in *lir*-shape," he said calmly. "I will walk, leading this horse. Whether you realize it yet, you are doubtless weary. Ride, Alix."

Duncan's words awoke all the trembling in her limbs and the comprehension of what she had accomplished. Alix felt her bones turn to water. Though she longed to protest she withheld it as she saw the understanding in Duncan's eyes. Silently she let him lift her onto the horse, and carefully clasped her fingers into the leather of Carillon's belt.

"Where do we go?" he asked.

"Not far. Perhaps two leagues from here." Duncan took the horse's bridle and led it out. "Come, we will see to your welfare when we are free of this place."

Duncan took them from the open plains into the depths of the shadowed forests, moving so silently Alix heard only the horse's steps muffled against the bedding of the forest floor. Occasionally she saw flitting shapes of animals slipping by and realized the *lir* and their warriors gave the clan-leader and his charges protection. She felt very safe.

At last Duncan turned the horse into a tiny clearing invisible to the untrained eye. Alix pushed free of the horse and dropped to the ground, ignoring Duncan's disapproving comment. She stepped out of the way and watched as he helped Carillon dismount.

"I will be well enough," Carillon said curtly.

Duncan did not remove his steadying arm. "It is no disgrace to require help after so much time spent in close confinement." He met Carillon's eyes. "Or is it only *Cheysuli* aid you spurn?"

Alix sighed wearily and pushed hair from her face. "Must you ever go at one another with no basis other than pride and arrogance?" she asked. "Can neither of you forget your race and simply conduct yourselves as *men?*"

Carillon stared at her. After a moment something softened his expression and twisted his mouth briefly. He looked back at Duncan.

"You have proven your loyalty to *me,* at least, this night. It is not my place to reprove you for it."

Duncan smiled and indicated a fallen log. "Come, my lord. We will see if you are worth saving."

Alix followed as Duncan led Carillon to the log. The prince lowered himself carefully to the ground and leaned against the fallen tree, sighing as his limbs fell once more into the positions they had grown accustomed to in captivity.

"Build a fire, *cheysula,*" Duncan said quietly as he knelt by Carillon's side.

She felt a spasm of fear in her chest. "So close to the Atvians?"

"We must, Alix. Carillon can go no farther this night."

Unhappily she did his bidding, locating stones and building them into a small fire cairn. She lay small sticks and broken kindling upon it, and kept herself from twitching in surprise as a Cheysuli warrior appeared to light it. When she glanced up she saw the clearing was filled with returned warriors.

Flames licked at the kindling and caught, illuminating the clearing into eerie, flickering shadows. Alix saw the dark face of each man and the glowing yellow eyes, acknowledging again her own kinship to the magic of the gods. The *lir*, four-footed and winged, waited silently with their warriors.

Cai? she asked silently.

He rustled in the nearest tree. *Here,* liren.

I accomplished what I said I would.

Aye, liren. He sounded amused. *You are truly Cheysuli.*

Alix grinned. *Those words from you are honor indeed, Cai. Yet once you would not admit it,* liren.

Alix sighed and knelt by the fire, watching her husband at Carillon's side. *But then I was foolish, Cai, and unwilling to learn.*

You have learned much, the bird agreed. *But there is still much left to you.*

She peered into the tree, trying to distinguish the hawk's form from distorting branches. *What do you say?*

In time, you will know.

A stifled exclamation from Carillon took her attention from the bird and she moved closer to the prince. Duncan, she saw in alarm, manipulated Carillon's hands with little regard for his pain.

"Can you not let them be?" Carillon asked between gritted teeth. "They will heal."

"It is worth the pain to let me see to them, my lord. Iron can damage more than flesh. It can take away the little life within the muscles themselves. But you, I think, will hold a sword again."

"And when I hold that sword, I will plunge it into Thorne's black heart."

Alix's eyes widened as she saw Finn step out of the darkness into the ring of firelight. Storr flanked him on one side.

"What sword will you use, princeling?" Finn demanded. "You have lost the one my *jehan* gifted to the Mujhar."

Color flooded Carillon's face. "I admit it."

Finn raised one eyebrow. "Well, I had expected denials and excuses from you. You surprise me."

"This can wait," Duncan said reprovingly.

Finn moved closer and drew a tooled leather sheath from behind his back. The gold hilt of a broadsword gleamed in the firelight, and the brilliant ruby in it glistened like blood.

The warrior lifted it into the light, focusing all eyes on it. "Hale's sword was meant for one man, Carillon. I cannot say if that man is you, but if it is—you had best take care. This is twice you have lost my *jehan*'s sword. Next time I may not see it back in your hands."

Carillon said nothing as Finn held the sheathed weapon down. For a long moment his hands lay still in his lap, where Duncan had released them. Then, when Finn made no move to withdraw it, Carillon closed one hand around the scabbard.

"If you are so dedicated to overcoming my succession," he began, "why, then, do you persist in restoring this blade to me? In your hands it might prove far more powerful."

Finn shrugged, folding bronzed arms across his chest. "A Cheysuli warrior does not bear a sword. And I am that before anything else."

Carillon set the sword across his lap and stared at the Homanan lion crest stamped into its hilt. Then he let the pain and fatigue take his mind, and he fell asleep with Hale's sword held firmly against his chest.

Alix looked on his bruised, gaunt face and suddenly longed for the first days of their meetings in the forest near the croft. His fine clothes were gone, replaced by soiled and scarred leathers and blood-rusted chain mail. His sword-belt was missing and his hair had grown shaggy and tangled in weeks of captivity. The only thing princely about him was the ruby seal ring on his right forefinger, and the determination inherent in his face even in exhausted sleep.

She sighed and felt a hollowness enter her spirit, knowing Carillon's personal *tahlmorra* would take him farther from her yet.

Duncan rose and turned to her, looking down on her expressionlessly. Something in his eyes made her realize her face gave away her feelings, and for an odd moment she saw before her a stern shapechanger warrior who had forced her into his clan against her wishes.

Then the oddness slid away and she saw him clearly.

He is Duncan, she recalled. *Duncan* . . .

Somehow, it was enough.

He moved to her and slowly raised her. She felt the strength in his hand on her arm and marveled again that this man had taken an unschooled croft-girl into his pavilion, when he might have had another.

"Come with me," he said softly, guiding her out of the clearing to the forest beyond.

When he found a shattered tree stump he set her down upon it and stood resolutely before her, dark face unreadable in the shadows.

"Duncan?"

"I cannot fault you for what you have done. You determined what it was that needed doing, and you did it." He shrugged crookedly. "As any warrior does."

Alix stared at the ground, dreading his wrath. Duncan's was ever worse than anyone's.

"I understand what it is to care deeply for someone, so deeply you must do what you can, regardless of outcome," he said quietly. "You know I would sacrifice myself for you, or Finn, or any other warrior of my clan."

After a moment she dared to look up at him. Nervously she wet her lips. "If you mean to be angry, Duncan, do it. I cannot wait for it all night."

His face, still in shadow, showed her nothing. But his voice was surprised. "I am not angry with you. What you did was not *wrong*—only inconsiderate."

She stiffened. "Inconsiderate!"

Duncan sighed and stepped forward, into a shaft of moonlight threading its way through the trees. She saw his smile and warm eyes as his hands settled possessively on her shoulders.

"Do you forget the child? Do you forget the magic in your soul?"

"Duncan—"

"I will not risk losing you because of bearing the child too soon. Such things can take a woman's life. But neither will I risk the child, who deserves to live as a warrior. Alix, you have taken *lir*-shape while carrying an unborn child. Had you not thought what that might mean?"

Instinctively a hand slipped to her stomach. Suddenly she was very frightened.

"Duncan—it will not harm the child? It will not take him from me?"

He traced the worried creases from her brow. "I think it will not harm the child, *cheysula,* but it cannot do it much good. Would you have a poor unformed soul shifting shape before it even knows its own?"

Her fingers tightened spasmodically against her stomach. "Duncan!"

He sighed and pulled her to her feet, wrapping hard arms around her shoulders. She turned her face against him.

"I have not said this to worry you, Alix. Only to make you think."

She clung to him. "I *have* thought, Duncan . . . and I am afraid!"

"The child is Cheysuli, small one, and bears the Old Blood. I think it will be well enough."

She drew back. "But what if I have harmed it? What if it is not whole?"

Duncan muttered something under his breath and pulled her against his chest roughly. "I am sorry I said anything. I should not have put this in your mind."

"You are right to," she said clearly, trying to see his face in the shadows. "I have been foolish . . . as you said."

"Would you say that to Carillon, whom you have freed from captivity?"

"*You* freed him."

"But had you not defied me to begin with, I would not have gone to the Atvian encampment at all. It was Mujhara I was bound for."

Alix sighed, trying to deal with two fears. "Do you send me back, then? Do you forbid me to go with you to the city, and make me wait at the Keep?"

He laughed softly. "Why can you not be as other women? Why must you put on men's garb—my own, I have seen—and act the part of a warrior?"

She scowled. "How can I say? I am myself."

He nodded. "I have seen that. It is not entirely unpleasing, in its place. As for Mujhara, you will have to come with us. I will not have you take *lir*-shape again, and I will not have you return to the Keep alone. I can spare no men to take you." He shrugged, sighing. "So you will come."

Alix said nothing for a long moment. Then she clenched her hands against his ribs. "I cannot say if I am pleased or not. I would not be happy at the Keep, waiting in fear, but neither will I be happy to see you risk yourself for Shaine's city."

He smoothed back her hair. "It is not Shaine's city, small

one. Once it was Cheysuli. We have only to win back what was ours."

She turned her face up to his. "Duncan—had the Cheysuli not given up the throne to Homanans—could you have been Mujhar?"

He smiled. "I am clan-leader, *cheysula*. It is enough."

Something turned in her heart. "But you have lost so much . . ."

His eyes were very clear in the moonlight as he looked into her face. "I have lost something, perhaps, but I have found even more."

"Duncan—"

"Hush, *cheysula*. It is time you let our child rest."

She sighed and felt her left hand clasped firmly in his as he led her back to the tiny camp.

I am not the proper sort of woman for this man . . . she thought in aching regret.

Cai, hidden in the darkness, sent her his warm reassurance. Liren . . . *you are the only woman for this man*.

Alix drew closer to Duncan and hoped the hawk was right.

BOOK IV

"The Warrior"

Chapter One

"I will not subject myself to Cheysuli sorcery," Carillon said firmly in the morning.

He sat upright against his log, hands folded over the scabbarded sword Finn had returned to him. The Cheysuli warriors faced him silently, yet disapproving even in their silence.

Alix saw defiant determination in the prince's battered face. "Carillon," she reproved softly.

His eyes flickered as he looked at her, standing at Duncan's side. "Alix, such sorcery is evil. I cannot deny your own measure of it, but I know you. You would never seek to bring down Homana's heir."

"Nor would we," Duncan said flatly. He sighed. "You would not believe it, perhaps, but the Cheysuli never meant to give up their proper place next to the Homanan Mujhars. Until Hale left, Cheysuli warriors ever served Homanan kings. We seek no quarrel with you."

Finn stood apart from the others, smiling crookedly in his familiar mocking manner. "*You* seek the quarrel, I think."

Carillon's mouth tightened. "I seek only to get to Mujhara and free my city from the Ihlini demons. And Bellam of Solinde." His fingers were bone-white as he clenched them on the sword.

"You will not get there without our aid," Finn said curtly. "Yet last night you were willing enough to let us use our gifts on the enemy."

"Using your magic to release your liege lord is one thing," Carillon retorted. "Subverting my will with it is entirely another."

Finn laughed scornfully. "See how quickly he calls himself our lord! Only months ago you lay in our hands, princeling, and did our bidding. Could we not have forced sorcery on you *then* if we wished it? Or is it that you lift yourself higher, now, because Fergus of Homana is slain?''

"Rujho," Duncan said quietly.

Carillon's eyes were hard as stone as he shook his head. "Let him speak. I have learned much of men because of this war, and I find there are times a man must consider himself first. Long have I allowed the Mujhar to manipulate me, but no longer. My father is slain by Atvian hands and it is my place to do what he would." Carillon smiled slowly, without humor. "You may not like it, shapechanger, but I will be lord of Homana one day. You had better accustom yourself to it."

Color surged into Finn's face as he stiffened. The yellow blaze in his eyes gave away the depths of the rage he felt, and Alix grinned delightedly. She caught his eyes on her and did not hide her reaction, which only angered him further. Finn turned and walked away from the clustered warriors.

Duncan, legs spread and arms folded, smiled ironically down on Carillon. "My lord prince, you may well be our liege lord. But it remains: you cannot ride into Mujhara in this fashion. You would not last the journey."

Carillon placed one hand flat against the ground and pushed himself upright, tensing his body with the effort it took. Alix stifled the movement she longed to make to help him, knowing to do so would diminish the impact of his rising. He stood taller than most of them, though the Chey-suli were a tall race, and his broad shoulders stretched against the leather-and-mail he wore. Only his eyes gave away the immensity of effort it took for him to remain standing erectly before them.

"If I cannot ride into my own city, I have no business attempting to free her from the Ihlini terror."

"Carillon," she said softly, "it will not hurt. It will only strengthen you."

His eyes burned into hers as he stretched out his left hand. The stiff sleeve of his fighting leathers and mail drew back on his arm, baring the ridged purple weals still weeping fluid from the shackle-wounds.

"I care little if it hurts, Alix. Have I not learned to deal with pain?"

Duncan's hand pressed against her shoulder as if bidding

her into silence. Alix longed to answer Carillon's bitterness but refrained. As she listened to Duncan she realized nothing she said could change Carillon's mind. But Duncan's words might.

"Homana lies in her death struggle," he said clearly. "I believe you realize that. It is a harsh thing to comprehend, when you are prince of a land and must someday ascend the throne, but it is something you must deal with. The Cheysuli denied the truth of the prophecy once, Carillon, and suffered because of it. If you deny it, you also will suffer."

"I am not Cheysuli," Carillon said sharply. "A shapechanger prophecy cannot foretell what will become of a Homanan. I have no place in it."

"You cannot know," Duncan said softly. "Nor can any man. You must allow things their own path if you are to survive. This prophecy *has* foretold what will become of you, my lord, even though you be Homanan. I believe you are the Mujhar it speaks of—the one who will end the *qu'mahlin* and restore our race to peace and our homeland." Duncan sighed as Carillon's face expressed patent disbelief. "We cannot turn the flow of the prophecy. But we *can* withstand the dark arts of Ihlini interference."

"You cannot tell me what has happened was *meant!*" the prince snapped. "My father's death?"

"A man must die before his son is fully a man," Duncan said gently. "And the throne of Homana must once again fall into Cheysuli hands."

Alix saw bitterness and resentment wash color from Carillon's face. "Cheysuli hands?" he asked ominously. "You say Homana's throne will be in *shapechanger* hands?"

She stepped from Duncan and stood between them, fearing little would be settled over such an emotional score. Gently she touched Carillon's hand as it clung to the sword.

"I have learned once this land was Cheysuli," she said softly, "before ever the Homanans came. It was the Cheysuli who gave the throne to your ancestors. Duncan does not mean he will deny your right to it. It is only that you must *have* it before it goes again to a Cheysuli Mujhar." Alix took a careful breath. "Carillon, can we not be one race instead of two?"

"You will rule in Mujhara, my lord," Duncan said calmly, "but only if we get you there."

Carillon said nothing. It was Alix who smiled into his face and insisted gently, "I will not let them harm you. I promise."

His free hand slid up to her face and cupped it gently. "Then I leave my fate in your hands."

"No," she said softly. "Your fate is your own. *Tahl-morra.*"

The Cheysuli went into Mujhara under cover of darkness. Carillon, submitting to the summoning of earth magic that renewed his strength and sent vigor sweeping through his bones, rode the Atvian mount stolen for him. Alix sat behind Duncan once more and stared in dismay at the city.

It lay in shambles. The glittering magnificence had shattered beneath the continued onslaught of Ihlini sorcery. Walls lay tumbled, oddly charred as if unholy fire had leached life from stone blocks once raised by Cheysuli hands so many centuries before. Many of the dwellings had been destroyed completely; others showed no signs of life within. Crumbling casements stared blindly at the streets as if the eyes had been plucked from them by unseen hands.

Alix shivered and held more tightly to Duncan. Here and there someone moved out of the shadows to avoid them, as if they feared Ihlini retribution, and Alix longed to tell them differently. But she could not find her voice.

Mujhara . . . she mourned within her heart.

She looked at Carillon and saw him sitting erect in the saddle, Cheysuli sword fastened to his leather belt. His face, as he looked on the city, was perfectly blank. His eyes were not.

Duncan halted his horse and waited until the warriors gathered around him in a narrow alley. Their silence was eloquent.

"We are too late to keep the city from the Ihlini," he said. "It is Homana-Mujhar we must look to. If the palace falls, so falls the realm."

Carillon shifted in his saddle. "The palace has stood against strong foes for centuries, shapechanger. It will not fall to dark sorcery."

Duncan slowly lifted his hand and indicated the charred,

still-smoking ruins of a tall dwelling near them. "There is the smell of death in the air, my lord. Does it matter so much if it is achieved at the hands of sorcerers, or mere men?"

Carillon scowled. "What do you say?"

"That if you continue to believe in the infallibility of Shaine and the palace in which he ·hides himself, you are foolish indeed." He smiled bitterly. "Carillon, once my own race was arrogant enough to believe we would ever hold the regard of Homanans. See how that faith has turned to folly? Tynstar is powerful indeed. If Homana-Mujhar can be taken—and any castle can be—the Ihlini will do it."

The prince's blue eyes were bleak. "I do not deny the demon his arts, nor his strength. I have only to see what he has done already. But it is a hard thing to realize the strength of a land resides in a single Mujhar." His mouth thinned. "I am not so much like my uncle, I think. But I will do what I can to keep this land free of Bellam's grasp."

Finn's dun-colored horse stomped against the ash-covered cobbles, raising fine gray dust. The warrior astride the animal set his hand to the hilt of his knife.

"We accomplish little here, *rujho.* Let us go on to Homana-Mujhar."

Alix felt Duncan's subtle sigh. Then he straightened and nodded. "What we do now may well settle the future of the Cheysuli." He stared levelly at Carillon. "Can you truly cling to the belief that we mean the Mujhar's blood only ill, my lord?"

Carillon slid the sword free of its sheath. The moonlight and dying flames from the burning buildings glinted off the blade and set the ruby to glowing like a crimson eye.

"I have said you will know what I believe when I am Mujhar, shapechanger. Shaine still lives." His grim face softened slightly. "But your aid is welcome this night."

Finn laughed curtly. "That is something, I suppose, from you. Well, princeling, shall you show us how a fine Homanan lord fights to save his land?"

"I will fight how I can, shapechanger. As you will see."

Duncan gathered the reins of his mount. "We go separately," he said quietly. "Cheysuli-fashion, when the odds are so high. When we have reached Homana-Mujhar, we will see to the Mujhar's welfare."

Alix watched as the warriors melted into the darkness.

After a moment only she and Duncan remained with Carillon.

Finn kneed his horse out of the shadows. "Duncan, I hope this is what you have wanted so long," he said obscurely.

Alix frowned at him. "What do you say?"

Finn stared at his brother. "He has ever warned the clan against unrestrained retribution for the *qu'mahlin.* It has ever been Duncan, swaying the Council, who kept us in the forests of Ellas, when we would strike against Shaine's patrols and any other serving the Mujhar." Something glinted wickedly in his eyes. "You do not know, *meijha,* what it is to fight a Cheysuli in all extremity. We might have slain many more who sought to slay us, had Duncan allowed it."

"The prophecy does not speak of utter annihilation, Finn," Duncan retorted. "It speaks of a final peace between warring lands and races. Should it not begin with our own realm?"

"Shaine would sooner see us dead."

"Shaine will see us, *rujho,* but we will not be dead." Duncan kneed his horse forward. "Do you come with us?"

"No." Finn gathered his reins. "I fight alone, Duncan, as ever." His eyes flickered over Alix. "You are a foolish woman, *meijha.* You should be at the Keep, with the others who wait."

"I could not bear it," she said quietly.

Finn stared harshly at her a moment longer, then wheeled his horse and rode into the shadows. A silver wolf loped silently at his side.

Alix wrapped her arms around Duncan and pressed herself against his back as they rode through the streets. "Duncan, I am afraid."

"There is no dishonor in fear. It is only when you fail to do what you must that the dishonor comes."

She sighed and put her forehead against his shoulder. "Do not speak to me as a clan-leader, Duncan. I am in no mood to listen."

Carillon, riding abreast, grinned at her. "Have you ever been in the mood to listen? No. Else you would not be here, and afraid."

She shot him a dark glance and refrained from saying anything for fear it would not be seemly.

They rode through streets unfamiliar to her, and even

Duncan at last gave way to Carillon, who knew the city better than any. The people who passed them went cloaked and hooded, saying nothing. Carillon rode silently but Alix saw the tension in his body and realized what the knowledge of what had happened did to him.

Duncan pulled his horse to a halt at a large recessed stable opening of a deserted dwelling. Alix waited, uncomprehending, as he slipped from the saddle and turned to help her down. When she stood on the cobbles she stared into his face and opened her mouth to speak.

Duncan put gentle fingers across her lips. "I would have you remain here, *cheysula;* out of harm's way. That you have come so far with me is risk enough. I will not have you come farther into the enemy's trap."

She pried his fingers away. "Do you leave me here?"

"Aye. The street is empty, the buildings deserted. I think you will be safe here, if you do as I say."

Alix glanced briefly past him and saw Carillon's silhouette against the shine of moonlight. He had halted his horse near the end of the street, giving them privacy.

"Then I will be waiting again; unknowing," she protested. "It will be no different than at the Keep."

His hands clasped her belted waist possessively. "Alix, I understand what you fear. In your place, I could not do it. But I cannot have you by my side as I go into war. It would divide my concentration, and that is deadly to any warrior."

"By myself?" she whispered.

"I will leave Cai. I would not have you go unattended." He smoothed back her tousled hair. "*Cheysula,* say you will do as I ask."

"Duncan, how am I to deal with this? You leave me in the middle of a fallen city and say I must not worry. That is the cruelest torture I could know."

He glanced over his shoulder and saw Carillon returning. He sighed and left his horse in the street, taking Alix into the building half-destroyed by Ihlini sorcery. Before she could protest, Duncan lifted her and set her on a tumbled wall.

"You will stay here, with Cai."

"Without your *lir* you cannot shapechange."

"There are Ihlini here. I cannot seek *lir*-shape anyway."

"Duncan—"

"Do as I ask. Keep yourself safe here, away from fighting."

He sighed and one broad, long-fingered hand slid to cover her stomach. "I must name the child, *cheysula*."

"Name it . . . now?"

"Aye. It is a warrior's custom to name an unborn as he goes into battle." He shrugged. "So that it is gods-blessed, regardless of the *jehan's* fate."

Cold slid through her bones as she grabbed at his hands. "Duncan, I would sooner have you stay with me!"

"I cannot," he said gently. "It is not my *tahlmorra* to turn my back on Homana's need."

"You will come back for me!"

"Of course, *cheysula*. Do you think so poorly of my warrior skills?"

"But I am not a warrior. I cannot judge."

"You are warrior enough for me." He silenced any protest with a kiss of such longing and poignancy she could say nothing when he at last released her. She stared into his face beseechingly, and saw the pride and strength she had ever loved.

"He shall be Donal," he said softly. "Donal."

Perversely, she scowled at him. "And if I bear a girl?"

Duncan grinned. "I think it will be a boy."

"Duncan—"

"I will come for you, when it is done."

Anguish filled her. *"Cheysul—"*

"It is *tahlmorra*, small one," he said firmly, and left her in the darkness.

Chapter Two

Alix paced through the rubble like a madwoman. For a long time she saw nothing of the place in which Duncan had left her, feeling only the turmoil and anger of her spirit, until at last she stopped in the middle of the tumbled building and stared into its shadowed depths. The emptiness of the place oppressed her until she wanted to run screaming from it. Then she realized it was not the tumbled wreckage that beat at her so much, but the acknowledgment of her own futility.

She wrapped both arms tightly around herself as if they would lend her warmth and security. She attuned her senses to her surroundings and heard the skittering of rats in dark corners, and the creaking of weakened timbers. Slowly she lifted her eyes to the broken roof and stared into the black night sky with its scattered stars.

I am here, liren, Cai said softly. *I am here.*

Her mouth twisted. *I respect you, Cai, but you are not Duncan. You are not the father of this child I carry.*

The bird shifted somewhere above. *He has left me to make certain you fare well. Not to take his place.*

She smiled into the blank open doorway. *Cai . . . sometimes I forget you are a hawk and think of you almost as a man.*

A tiny pebble fell from the timber over her head. *I am not so different,* liren. *Because I have wings and talons does not make me insensitive to a woman's fears.* His tone warmed. *He is a brave warrior,* liren.

"But they die," she said aloud. "Even the bravest die."

The hawk seemed almost to sigh. *I cannot say if he lives or dies this night,* liren. *Only that he fights for his beliefs. Should he die, I will be lirless and you without a cheysul.*

But he would be content he had done what he could for the prophecy.

"Prophecy!" she cried aloud, clutching at the abdomen that carried Duncan's child. "I think it is more like a curse!"

Cai shifted overhead and scattered another handful of pebbles to the floor. Alix stared blindly at the invisible fall.

The prophecy is your tahlmorra, the hawk said at last, gently. *As it is mine, and my* lir's. *Even, I think, your child's.*

Alix jerked her head up and stared at his shadow-shrouded form. "What do you say? Do you tell me you know what will come to all of us? Do you say we are only game pieces the gods move as suits their will?"

Liren, he said softly, *we were the first. The gods made* lir *before they made men. We know many things.*

She wrenched her hands from her abdomen. "Then will you not tell me? Will you not say what road lies before me?"

I cannot, liren. *The prophecy unveils itself in the fullness of time. The* lir *cannot precipitate it.*

"Cai!"

No, he said calmly.

"It is not fair!" she cried. "If he should die, you will tell me it is his *tahlmorra* and I should not grieve. Yet if he lives, and returns to me to see his child when it is born, you will say *that* is meant also! Cai, you speak to me in tangled words and snarled threads. I cannot say I like this tapestry you weave!"

The hawk was silent a long moment. *It is not my tapestry,* he said at last, *but that of the gods. They have said what will come. It is up to the* shar tahls *to show you what has gone before, and what may follow.*

"It is not fair," she repeated.

No, he agreed, *nor ever shall be.*

Alix stared blindly into the darkness and cursed her soul for its unquiet depths. After a moment she went to the wall Duncan had perched her on and climbed up to seat herself on it gingerly.

Repeating the action did no good. Duncan was not there, and she felt only the emptiness of her heart.

"Cai," she said at last, hearing the whisper of an echo in the shattered dwelling, "I am not meant to wait so patiently, or so silently."

You are never silent, liren.

She did not smile. "I will not remain here."

He wished it.

"*I* wish to be with him."

Silence crept into the ruin. Then Cai shifted on the beam and sent a brief shower of debris raining down on her.

Liren, *he has said what he wants from you.*

"I will work myself into a frenzy," she said calmly, "and that will do the child no good at all."

Yet if you go, you risk both of you.

She closed her eyes. "Duncan does what he must, and expects me not to question it. But I do, Cai. I must. There is something—different—in myself. I cannot sit calmly by and wait for him to return to me . . . if he can."

Liren . . .

Alix opened her eyes, decision made. "I must do what I must, bird. Perhaps it is my own *tahlmorra.*"

The great hawk lifted and flew from the timber to the broken wall before her. She saw his dark eyes glinting in the moonlight.

Liren, *it is not for me to gainsay you. I have said what I can.*

Alix smiled. "Cai, you are truly a blessing of the old gods."

The hawk fixed her with a bright eye. *So is the child you carry.*

She slid off the shattered wall and straightened her creased leathers. "Cai, I will carry this child to full term. It is a part of my own *tahlmorra.*"

He sounded oddly amused. *You have only just come to us,* liren, *yet you speak as a learned one who has the magic of the* shar tahls.

Alix walked from the dwelling into the cobbled street and stared down the empty alley. "Perhaps I have a measure of that magic, Cai. Now, do you come?"

The great hawk mantled and took to the air. *I come,* liren.

Alix moved softly, mimicking Duncan's stealth. She was very aware of the knife in her boot, wishing she had better but knowing she would be incapable of using it against another anyway. She was no warrior.

Cai winged overhead silently, saying nothing to her as

she walked carefully through the empty streets and alley-ways. The night sky was clear save for stars, but she felt a heaviness in her bones as if the buildings of the Mujhar's city leaned in on her. And she smelled the stench of death, unable to escape its cloying touch.

Occasionally she passed a tumbled wall still smoldering, still caressed by odd purple fire. She swallowed heavily as she recalled Tynstar and his odd method of departing her presence. A shiver of foreboding coursed through her body as she stepped carefully through the broken fragments of a dwelling, and her right hand dropped instinctively to shield her unborn child.

Alix froze suddenly as a shadow streaked across the street before her, hissing malevolently. Instinctively she pressed herself against the nearest wall, hoping the bricks might provide protection. Then she saw it was only a cat, fur raised and ears flattened as it fled the night terrors. For a moment she held herself against the wall, eyes closed tightly as she tried to still her lurching heart. Cai, drifting over her, sent a burst of his own confidence.

Alix pushed away and moved on, releasing a breath that rasped through her dry throat. After a moment she paused, bending, and took the knife from her boot. The feel of it in her hand gave her a measure of renewed confidence, and she walked on softly.

You can go back, Cai said. *You can wait for my* lir, *as he wished.*

No, she said silently.

Liren . . .

No.

Alix felt better for her determination, recalling the urge that had originally driven her into the streets. For all she was frightened of what might befall her, she was more frightened of what might happen to Duncan. She would far prefer being with him, in danger, than without him in comparative safety.

A stone rattled on the cobbles before her. Alix slipped into a recessed doorway, knife drawn up to her chest in readiness. Another stone skittered across the uneven street and came to rest near her foot. She followed its path with her eyes until she saw the figure move silently through the street.

It was a man, she thought, for the cloaked form was tall and moved with the subtle grace of a warrior. She had seen its like in warriors of the clan, marveling at the body's ability to take on the aspect of animal suppleness while maintaining human form. For a moment she thought the man Cheysuli, then recalled none had gone cloaked on this mission into Mujhara. Alix drew in a breath and waited.

He moved past her, half-hidden in the shadowy folds of his cloak. For a moment he paused, very near her, and she feared discovery. A hand rose and pushed the hood free of his face, sliding the draped material to his shoulders. Alix, certain he somehow knew her presence, waited for him to speak.

But the man said nothing. He glanced into the sky, marked the hawk's idle flight, and smiled to himself. Then he moved on.

Alix waited until he was gone. Then she slipped out of the doorway and hastened from the street, fearing belated discovery. When she reached for Cai's soothing pattern she felt an odd current pushing against her, almost as if it sought to prevent communication with the hawk. She strengthened her call and relaxed as the bird's tone came to her.

Ihlini, liren.

Alix paused, frowning against the effort it took to hear him. *Ihlini?*

Aye, the cloaked man.

She stared into the darkness. *Then why do I hear you at all?*

Perhaps it is the blood in you, liren. *Perhaps whatever power it is that prevents other Cheysuli from seeking their lir does not block you from it.* His shadow drifted over her. Liren, *you are fortunate indeed.*

But she felt the strain within the pattern and sensed a draining of her resources. It frightened her, for she dared not risk the child. She broke off the link to Cai and decided to keep it broken, for fear it might harm the unborn. Cai seemed to approve, and she went on in greater solitude than before.

Alix knew herself lost. Her visit to Mujhara with Carillon had not accustomed her to the twistings and turnings of the narrow streets, and she realized she might be moving farther from Homana-Mujhar instead of going to it. Frustrated and fearful, she turned yet again and kept her steady pace. She longed to question Cai, knowing he could tell her, but fought down the instinct. She would not involve the hawk unless forced to.

She heard a child crying in the distance. As she drew closer the piteous wail drove into her spirit like a shaft, beckoning her. Alix broke into a trot, then a run as the crying seemed to weaken. She was breathless as she rounded a corner and tripped over a body in the street.

It was a woman, clothed in a soiled and torn gown. Alix got to her knees and replaced her knife as she put a trembling hand toward the woman's face. Then she saw the staring eyes were blank, bulging in death, and something elemental curled deeply within her soul. She hesitated, then put gentle fingers to the eyelids and closed them. The cold stillness of the flesh shot a convulsive shudder down her spine.

The crying renewed itself. Alix jerked her head around and stared wide-eyed into the darkness. After a moment she located the focus of the sound and rose, moving quietly to the broken wall of a charred building. Behind the scattered stone, placed carefully beneath a sheltering piece of broken door, lay a naked baby.

Soundlessly Alix cried out. Then her hands were on the infant, lifting it free of its protection. It was a boy-child, cold to the touch, and his chest rose feebly in an attempt to breathe. Alix knelt and cradled him to her breast, feeling a mixture of longing and pain in her soul as she sensed the ambiance of her own unborn child.

She crooned to him softly, smoothing his silken head. He was no more than a few weeks, she knew, and helpless as a blind, newborn rabbit. His slender limbs trembled from exposure and unknown fear, and after a moment Alix lay him down in the street and stripped out of her supple jerkin and belt. The leather was not much, but she realized some wrapping was better than none. Carefully she lifted the child and folded the jerkin around his body, snugging the belt over it to swaddle him as warmly as possible. Chill nipped through the loose weave of her improvised shirt, but she ignored it as she lifted the baby and walked on.

At last Alix turned a corner and saw before her the red

stones of Homana-Mujhar. The walls rose mutely in the
moonlight, throwing dark shadows into surrounding streets.
And she saw the Solindish and Atvian guards surrounding
the place, posted at every gate. She wondered if Tynstar
had yet broken through Shaine's wards, taking the palace
for Bellam.

Alix drew back in the sheltering shadows, suddenly at a
loss for what to do. She had anticipated finding Duncan no
matter how impossible the task seemed, even in the cul-de-
sacs and strange turnings. Now she stared worriedly at the
bronze-and-timber gates and feared she had acted wrongly.

Where are they? she asked fearfully. *Where are the
Cheysuli?*

The child whimpered in her arms. Alix shifted him closer to
her chest and placed gentle lips against his forehead, silently
promising him safety. But she also feared for her own.

She glanced back the way she had come and stiffened.
Through the narrow street walked a cloaked figure, moving
with familiar grace. The hood was drawn up again to hide
the man's features, but she knew him by his movements.
Alix pressed back against the wall.

Then a second figure slid out from the shadows, just behind the cloaked Ihlini. Alix watched in painful silence as
the second man moved into the moonlighted street, then
caught her breath in a gasp as muted light glinted off gold
lir-bands.

"Ihlini!" the Cheysuli whispered.

The cloaked figure spun and froze. Alix saw him push
his hands out sideways, away from his body, as if to indicate
his innocent intent. The Cheysuli moved closer and a shaft
of moonlight slanted clearly across his face.

"Duncan!" she whispered in horror, clutching at the
child.

The Ihlini's voice, quiet but pitched to carry, came clearly
to her. "We should not fight, you and I. The Cheysuli and
Ihlini are much alike. You have your gifts, I mine. We
could use them in concert."

She heard Duncan's soft laugh. "There is no likeness
between us, sorcerer, save equal determination to serve our
own gods."

The Ihlini lowered his hands, then pulled his cloak off

and dropped it to the cobbles. "Then I will serve my gods, shapechanger, by ridding this land of one more Cheysuli."

The fight was sudden and vicious. Alix gasped as Duncan closed with the Ihlini, movements half-hidden. She saw only the glint of knives and heard their grunts of effort as each sought to slay the other.

"By the gods," she whispered to herself, horrified, "it is much worse than I thought. *Much* worse!"

The child whimpered again and she hugged him closer, seeking her own strength in his need for security. But her mind was with Duncan.

She saw the Ihlini stumble back. A metallic glint flashed from his left shoulder and she saw the hilt of a Cheysuli knife stand out from his dark leathers. Duncan, crouched in readiness, straightened. Alix felt overwhelming relief flood her body, then realized how much she had longed for the sorcerer's death. The emotion shocked and sickened her.

The Ihlini did not fall. His back turned to her and she saw his right arm move to pull the knife from his shoulder. Duncan, hands empty, waited warily.

Die, Ihlini . . . she whispered silently, hating herself for desiring another's death. *Die!*

The sorcerer went to one knee. She saw Duncan clearly in the moonlight, feet spread to brace himself against his enemy. Darkness slid down one arm, dulling his *lir*-band, and she realized the Ihlini's knife had found at least part of its target. She bit her lip and fought back the instinct to run to him.

A rattle behind Duncan spun him around. He was unarmed, vulnerable to a second attack, but something in his stance told her he was prepared. Then she saw the Solindish soldier move into the moonlight, sword bared.

Cai! Alix cried. *Cai—do something!*

The pattern was faint. At last Cai answered her. *Liren, I cannot. It is an Ihlini he faces . . . the* lir *do not interfere. It is part of the gods' law.*

The Solindish soldier made no move against Duncan. He stood braced, ready to fight, yet did not step in against his shapechanger enemy. Alix saw the Ihlini come out of his crouch and realized the Solindish man acted only as a decoy.

Her cry of warning was lost in the Solindish soldier's

shout. Alix spun and set the baby down in the darkness near a wall, dragging the knife from her boot. Then she pushed herself free of the wall and ran toward the Ihlini.

She saw Duncan stiffen spasmodically as the sorcerer snaked a gleaming wire around his throat. Both hands flew to the wire and clawed at it, seeking to rip it away. But the Ihlini stood unmoving, slowly tautening the thin garrote until blood broke from Duncan's throat.

"No!" Alix shrieked.

The Solindish soldier stared past the Ihlini and his prisoner in alarm. His sword shifted, rising, and she realized he would move to stop her.

But she could not hesitate. Her fear had been replaced by the overwhelming need to strike down the Ihlini who threatened Duncan. Her veneer of civilization and gentle ways was stripped from her easily, leaving her naked before all men, and she knew herself as capable of slaying a man as any warrior.

Duncan's knees buckled. The Ihlini stood firm, bending slightly as he tautened the garrote even further. Alix was oddly aware of the flash of the Solindish sword as she stumbled to a halt behind the sorcerer. But it did not matter. She lifted the knife, clutching it in both hands, and brought it down with all her strength.

The shock ran through her arms as she drove the knife through leathers and into the flesh of the Ihlini. She felt him stiffen spasmodically, crying out. One gloved hand clawed briefly at his back, fingers stretching and scraping, then it dropped slackly at his side. The sorcerer sagged over Duncan and fell into the street.

Alix heard the soldier swear a violent oath, unable to decipher his words. She saw the malevolent gleam in his eyes as he lifted the sword over one shoulder, preparing to unleash the killing stroke. Somehow, she was unafraid.

"By the gods!" cried a clear voice, "you will *not!*"

Dimly she heard the clatter of hoof on stone and saw the horse rearing behind the soldier. Before the Solindish man could turn, a flashing sword swung through the air in a swift arc and severed head from shoulders.

Alix staggered back, gagging, as blood sprayed from the falling trunk. It splattered over her face and clothing, staining her hands as she raised them to cover her eyes. Then she peered through her fingers into the blazing blue eyes of the prince of Homana.

Instantly she forgot Carillon. She stumbled forward, reaching frenziedly toward the sprawled bodies. Blood ran through the cobbles, muddying the ash and dust, but she ignored it all as she clawed at the Ihlini's still form.

Alix tugged ineffectually at the heavy body until Carillon flung himself from his horse and helped her, dragging the slain sorcerer free of Duncan.

"No!" she cried, falling to her knees. *"No!"*

The wire, she saw, had fallen partially free of Duncan's throat. It had bitten deeply but had not yet sliced into the vulnerable windpipe. Carefully she pulled the wire away and threw it into the street, moaning as she saw the livid discoloring as blood stained his neck.

"He is alive, Alix," Carillon said, kneeling over the warrior. "Alive."

She put gentle fingers to his bloodied throat, feeling the erratic pulse-beat. Carefully she cradled his head in her lap, fighting back the rush of bile into her throat as she realized how close he had come to death.

Duncan's hand twitched and moved instinctively to the empty sheath at his belt. Carillon reached out and stopped the searching hand.

"No," he said clearly. "We are not your enemy."

"Duncan!" she cried. *"Duncan . . ."*

His eyes opened and blinked. For a moment he said nothing, lying limply against her lap, then bolted upright into a sitting position. Carillon moved back, squatting, and Alix hastily wiped tears off her cheeks. Duncan, in all his Cheysuli pride, would not want to see her cry.

Duncan looked silently at the body of the Solindish soldier. Then his eyes traveled to the felled Ihlini, lying so close. After a moment he put bloodstained fingers to his throat.

He looked directly at Carillon. "Tell me I did not hear her," he rasped. "Tell me I somehow imagined she was here."

Carillon began to smile. His eyes slid past Duncan to Alix, and his smile became a grin. Then he shook his head.

"I will not lie to you, shapechanger. You have only to look."

Duncan winced and turned his head. Alix swallowed welling tears away as she saw the sliced welt rising on his throat, still weeping blood. But Duncan ignored it as he looked at her in dismay.

"Alix . . ."

She bit her lip in response to the ragged sound of his voice. Then she shrugged her shoulders uncomfortably.

"I am sorry, Duncan, that you are burdened with such a disobedient woman. I am not at all the proper sort for a clan-leader's *cheysula.*"

She saw his eyes travel over her blood-smeared face to the dark stains on her ragged shirt. One hand reached out and touched her arm, tracing the sticky flesh. Then he drew up his legs into a cross-legged position and sat there. Silent.

"Duncan—" she began tentatively, then broke off as she recalled the infant. She jumped to her feet and ran, ignoring Carillon's startled question.

Alix knelt by the jerkin-wrapped child and smiled, gathering it up carefully. "There is someone you should meet, small one," she whispered. "Someone very special."

She half-rose, cradling the child against her chest. Then something stopped her, cutting through her happiness like a scythe.

The child was cold, too cold. He made no sound as her hand gently touched his face. Carefully Alix knelt back on the cobbles and fought down the sudden painful fear as she slid a hand beneath the jerkin and felt his body.

Horror came slowly. Then the pain. "No!" she cried. "Not the *child!*"

He lay unmoving, unbreathing. Alix shuddered over him, rubbing hands against his cold flesh as if her warmth would bring him back to life. She heard footsteps behind her and the clank of a sword sliding home in its sheath.

"Alix," said Duncan's hoarse voice.

She shook her head violently in denial, still rubbing the child's cold flesh.

Duncan's hand was on her shoulder, pulling her away gently. "There is nothing to be done, *cheysula.*"

She jerked away and knelt over the child. "He is mine. *Mine!* I will not let him die."

Duncan pulled her away. Dimly she saw Carillon kneel

by the infant and touch a hand to its chest. Then he glanced up at Duncan and shook his head.

"He is mine," she repeated.

"No," Duncan said hoarsely. He put his hand against her stomach. "*Here* is our child."

She stared into his face. "I only put him down for a moment. You needed my help. The Ihlini would have slain you. So I put him down to go to you." Her eyes closed. "Why did the gods make me choose between you?"

Duncan sighed. "Do not torture yourself like this, Alix. It does no good."

"It was only a *child!*"

"I know, small one. But he was more fortunate than most. He did not know what he faced, before it claimed him." Something crept through his eyes and she saw the vestiges of remembered horror. "He did not know what it was to look into the eyes of death so close."

Alix shivered and pressed herself against him. "Duncan, I could not bear to lose you. I could not bear it."

"Well, you have made certain I will live a little longer." He smiled crookedly at her and traced the bloodstains on her nose. "I have taken myself a warrior instead of a woman."

Carillon's boots scraped against the cobbles. Alix looked at him and saw the weariness and determination in his face.

He gestured toward the red walls rising in the near distance. "Homana-Mujhar, my friends. It waits for us."

Duncan nodded. Alix slipped from his arms, cast one more longing glance at the jerkin-wrapped bundle in the corner, then turned from it resolutely.

But the pain remained.

Chapter Three

They found shelter in the shadows of the high walls, avoiding the Solindish soldiers who gathered in the torch-light spilling from sconces set into the red brick. Cai perched himself in a nearby tree, for the proximity of Ihlini kept him from conversing with Duncan, and even Alix felt the weakness in her mind. She did not wish to expend energy she might need later, so she kept herself from conversing with the hawk.

Duncan leaned one shoulder against the cool walls and looked at Carillon. "We need a way in, my lord. As normal men. I have no recourse to *lir*-shape here."

Carillon's hand idly caressed the hilt of his massive sword. "There is a way. I played here as a child, and I know all the secrets of this place. I am only glad the Solindish do not."

"Alone?" Alix whispered.

Duncan shook his head and felt gently at his bruised throat. "If you can, Alix, summon the *lir*. They will bring the warriors."

Apprehension flared in her. "But you said I should not use what power I have. Because of the child—"

"We have no choice. If we are to succeed, we must get to Shaine." His hand engulfed and pressed her shoulder. "*Cheysula,* I would not ask it otherwise."

She nodded and leaned back against the wall, detaching herself from immediate awareness. She no longer felt Duncan's hand on her, or heard Carillon's startled question. She was aware only of the heaviness in the air and the great effort it took to reach the *lir*.

At last she felt Storr's familiar pattern questioning her. Alix smiled weakly and told him to bring his *lir*, and the others. His aquiescence came just as her strength failed her.

Alix sagged limply against the wall and felt Duncan catch

her. He swore something in the Old Tongue that broke halfway through his exclamation and set her upright, pressing her against the wall. She heard Carillon's sharp question, but Duncan made no answer. At last she dragged her eyes open and looked into their faces, seeing their mutual fear.

Alix managed a faint smile. "They come. The *lir,* and their warriors."

"I am sorry . . ." Duncan rasped uneasily.

She shook her head. "It—it was only that they are so far. I will be well enough in a moment."

Carillon flicked a dark glance at Duncan. "*I* would not use her so, shapechanger."

Duncan's face hardened. "It is for *your* sake I asked it, princeling."

Alix put a hand up and pushed herself away from the wall, straightening her tired shoulders. "Enough of this. If you wish Homana reconciled with her Cheysuli forebears, you will have to begin with yourselves." She glared at them. *"Yourselves!"*

Carillon looked guilty. Duncan, mouth twisting in Finn's ironic manner, nodded to himself.

Alix sighed and rubbed wearily at an eye. "I think they come. Here is Storr."

The silver wolf came out of the shadows silently, feral eyes gleaming in the darkness. With him came Finn, who had a wide smear of blood across his jerkin and a victorious glint in his eye.

"You wanted me, *meijha?"*

"*Duncan* wanted you. And the others."

Finn glanced at his brother, then frowned. He stepped close and examined the bloody slice in Duncan's throat. After a moment he stepped back and raised his brows.

"Did you tangle, somehow, with an Atvian bowstring instead of an arrow?"

Duncan smiled. "An Ihlini garrote, *rujho.*"

Finn grunted. "They are ever troublesome. We should teach the Ihlini something, someday." His eyes belied the irony in his tone. "*Rujho* . . . you are not badly hurt?"

Duncan shrugged. "I am well enough. Growing voiceless, perhaps, but you may prefer me that way."

Finn's teeth flashed. "Aye, *rujho,* I believe I may."

The others had gathered. Alix saw not a single warrior was missing. She wondered, in remembered horror, how many men lay dead at shapechanger hands.

"We will go in," Duncan said in his broken voice. "We will go in and give what aid we can to Shaine the Mujhar."

"How?" demanded Finn. "We cannot seek *lir*-shape so close to the Ihlini. And we can hardly scale the walls without being seen."

Duncan gestured to Carillon. "The prince has said he can get us in."

Finn's face expressed doubt. No one else moved, but Alix sensed their unspoken disbelief. Then Carillon shifted against the wall and stood upright.

"You have little enough reason to trust me. It would be a simple matter for me to let you in and lead you into a trap of the Mujhar's making." He smiled grimly. "While I have not precisely been your enemy, neither have I been your ally."

"I think we are in agreement for the first time, princeling," Finn said in careful condescension.

Carillon, to Alix's surprise, appeared unoffended. He smiled calmly at Finn. "You need my aid, shapechanger. *Mine.*"

Finn grunted. "I need nothing of yours."

Carillon turned to Duncan. "I will get in, and then I will open one of the smaller gates. I leave it to you to rid yourselves of the Solindish guards." He gestured toward the darkness. "It is but a short distance that way. I will meet you."

He faded into the shadows. Finn spat out a curse between his teeth and looked as if he had swallowed something sour.

Duncan observed him impassively. "I trust him, Finn. He will do as he says."

"He is Homanan."

"They are not our enemy."

Finn's eyes narrowed. "Then what of the *qu'mahlin?*"

"It was begun by a single man, not by a nation. It can also be ended by a single man." Duncan sighed and felt at his tender throat. "Shaine began it. Carillon, I think, is the man who will end it."

"Do not speak so much," Alix admonished him, then

shot Finn a scathing glance. "Carillon expects us, *rujholli.*
Should we not go where he said?"

He grinned at her and gestured with a flourish in the
direction Carillon had indicated. When she did not move
he shook his head reprovingly and went into the darkness.
The others followed.

Alix turned away as the Cheysuli slew the Solindish guards.
Her flesh crawled as she remembered the sensations in her
when she had plunged her knife into the Ihlini's back. She
would have run from the renewed violence had Duncan
not kept her by him.

As the last man died, the narrow gate swung open. Carillon stepped through. His leather-and-mail dripped with
water, pooling at his feet. His hair was plastered darkly
against his head, but his smile was subtly triumphant as
he gestured.

"There is a culvert few know about. Now, through here,
if you please. And you are well come to Homana-Mujhar."

He led them into a small bailey, avoiding the larger one
which opened onto the front of the massive palace. He paused
as Duncan whispered to him, and waited as the clan-leader
turned to his warriors.

"It would be better to go in separately, should the
Mujhar send men against us. Slay only if you must, for
these men are not truly our enemies. When you can, make
your way to the Great Hall." He smiled at Carillon's involuntary start of surprise. "Have you forgot, my lord, that
Hale was my foster-father? I was here as a small child. I
know this place." He looked up at the dark bulk of stone.
"A long time ago, I walked the halls and corridors with
impunity. Shaine once called me by name and bade me
serve him as well as Hale did." His mouth tightened. "A
very long time ago."

Finn stepped between them. "But I was never here,
princeling. I was left at the Keep. You may serve as my
guide."

Carillon turned away and moved toward the palace. The
others melted away. Alix walked at Duncan's side as they
followed Carillon and Finn into the castle.

They went unaccosted, though the servants and guardsmen within the halls grew red-faced or frightened as they
saw the Cheysuli. Only Carillon's presence kept the

guardsmen from moving against them, and Alix saw that Finn marked it. She wondered if it made a difference to him.

At last they reached the hammered silver doors of the audience chamber she recalled so clearly. She felt a shiver of remembered apprehension run down her spine. Shaine had frightened her that day, before he made her angry. Then she smiled as she called to mind the Mujhar's terror as Cai swept into the hall.

"Borrowed glory," Finn muttered. "Borrowed."

Alix glanced at him. "What do you say? This place is magnificent!"

"This place is Cheysuli," he retorted. After a moment his voice softened as he glanced around. "Cheysuli."

Carillon thrust open the unattended doors. Alix would have gone through immediately but Duncan held her back. She looked at him in puzzlement, then saw his gesture toward Carillon. Understanding, she stepped back.

The prince entered the long hall slowly. He left a trail of water behind. For a moment Alix saw a vision of the tall prince forcing his way through the narrow culvert, and smiled. Then she went in with Duncan.

Shaine sat upon the throne, hands clasping the curving lion paws. His eyes stared broodingly into the massive fire-pit. It had died to coals and the hall was chilly. The Mujhar seemed to notice no one as they approached the dais.

Duncan paused at the firepit, allowing Carillon to continue on alone. Alix waited also, as did Finn. They watched as Carillon paced the length of the firepit and halted before the dais.

"You, my lord Mujhar, have been a fool," he said coldly.

Shaine looked at Carillon. Slowly he rose to his feet, taller than his heir only by virtue of the dais, staring at him in amazement.

"*Carillon* . . ." he whispered.

"A fool," Carillon repeated.

But Shaine was not undone by Carillon's unexpected presence. He was a king before all else, and could still command a powerful presence when he chose.

"You will not speak to me until you find the proper words of respect to your liege lord."

The prince laughed openly. "*Respect.* You have earned none of mine, uncle."

Shaine's gray eyes glared. His voice dropped to the ominous tone Alix recalled so clearly.

"I will excuse your poor manners this once. Doubtless you grieve for your father, and you appear to have been poorly treated at Keough's hands. But I will not hear such words from you again."

Carillon smiled grimly. "My father is fortunate in his death, uncle. He does not face the knowledge that the Mujhar has failed Homana. *I* have to deal with that . . . and so must you."

"You call me a fool!" Shaine roared. "What do *you* know of the things I have had to order these past months? What do you know of the harsh decisions I have had to make?"

"Safe within your walls!" Carillon shouted back. "*I* have been in the field with thousands of Homanan soldiers—some of them *boys!* What do you know of *that,* my lord Mujhar? You make the commands—we carry them out. And *we* are the ones who die beneath Bellam and Keough's hordes, uncle—*not you!*"

Shaine's face congested. "You would have me die, then, my lord heir? So you may do better in my place? Is that what you seek?"

Carillon was rigid. "I want Homana safe again, my lord Mujhar. And you alive to see it."

Before Shaine could reply a quiet voice echoed down the hall. "And *I* want you alive as well, Shaine the Mujhar. Else I cannot have the pleasure of taking your life."

Alix stiffened as Finn threw the words down the hall, moving to approach the Mujhar. Storr padded at his side silently. She sensed the wolf's loyalty to Finn more strongly than ever before. She nearly went after them both, suddenly frightened, but Duncan kept her back.

"It is for him to do," he said softly. "It is his *tahlmorra.*"

"He will *slay* him!"

"Perhaps. Be silent, Alix. This is for Finn to do."

She clenched her teeth and turned back, hating the calm acceptance in Duncan's broken voice. Like him, she could only watch.

Finn stopped before the dais. He waited.

Shaine stared at him. Color drained from his face until only a death mask remained. His lips were bluish; hands shaking. An inarticulate sound burst from his throat. Then he swallowed visibly and forced a single word between his lips.

"*Hale.*"

Finn laughed. "No. His son."

"Hale is . . . slain . . ."

"By your order."

"He had to die . . . *had* to . . ." Shaine stiffened before Finn and brushed a trembling hand across his staring eyes. "He had to die."

"*Why?*"

Shaine blinked. "He took her away. Lindir. My daughter." He swallowed. "Took her from me."

"She *chose* to go. You drove her away, my lord Mujhar. You. Lindir left Homana-Mujhar of her own will, because she desired it. Because she desired a Cheysuli"

"No!"

"*Aye, my lord!*"

Carillon stepped toward the Cheysuli. "Finn—"

"Silence yourself, princeling!" Finn snapped. "This is a thing between men."

"Finn!"

"Go, princeling. You have served your purpose. You have delivered the Mujhar to me, as I have long desired." Finn glared at him. "*Go.*"

Alix started forward but Duncan's hand inexorably drew her back.

Carillon turned again to his uncle. "This is *your* doing! Once the Cheysuli served Homanan kings more faithfully than any—now they seek only to destroy the man who ordered the *qu'mahlin*. Is this what you wanted?"

Shaine's face was deathly white. His breath came hoarse and loud. "Hale . . . it is *Hale* . . ."

"No!" Carillon shouted.

The Mujhar's face cleared and sense crept back into his blank eyes. He looked upon Finn a long moment, then reached out to point at the Cheysuli.

"I will not suffer a shapechanger in my presence. In my realm. I have ordered your race destroyed and I will have it done. *I will have it done!*"

The roar swept through the hall. Finn met it with a smile. "He was your sworn man, Shaine the Mujhar. A Cheysuli blood-oath. He fought for you, slew for you, loved you as his liege lord. And you had him slain like some crazed beast.''

"Finn," Duncan said at last.

Shaine's eyes sharpened as he looked past Finn and Carillon. His chest heaved.

"No." He choked. "Not the Cheysuli . . ."

Carillon glanced at him. "My lord?"

The Mujhar's breath was uneven. "I—will—not—have—Cheysuli—*here* . . ."

"It seems you have little choice, uncle."

"I will not have it!" Shaine moved to the throne and drew a scarlet silk bag from its cushioned seat. He turned back to them with an expression of gloating triumph in his eyes. Slowly he poured glowing blue cubes into the palm of one hand.

Carillon stared. "The wards—?"

"Hale's, given to me forty years ago . . . should I ever face harsh odds. There are no more in all of Homana." Shaine swallowed as heavy color rushed into his face. "They have kept the Ihlini from Homana-Mujhar. It is the only thing. And I will willingly destroy them if only to destroy the Cheysuli!"

Surprising them all with his swiftness, the Mujhar moved agilely to the coals of the firepit. Carillon said something incoherently and leaped for him, grabbing for the outstretched hand clutching the blue cubes. Finn drew his knife and advanced.

But the Mujhar was too quick.

Blue flames roared up as the wards burned. Eerie illumination crept across Shaine's tortured features. He stood stiffly before his nephew and Finn.

"I declared *qu'mahlin* on the Cheysuli twenty-five years ago," he rasped. "It has not ended!"

Alix gasped. She saw Shaine look past Finn, and as his eyes fell on her face she saw loathing enter them.

"Shapechanger . . ." he hissed. *"Shapechanger!"* He drew a gasping breath and pointed at her. "My daughter gave her life in exchange for a *halfling witch!*"

Alix stared at him in shock and mute pain, stunned by the virulence of his hatred. Then Finn said something in the Old Tongue and lifted his knife to strike.

Carillon leaped, grabbing the raised arm. Finn spun to dislodge him but a garbled sound broke from the Mujhar's throat and stopped them both.

Shaine fell slowly forward to his knees. His eyes remained locked on Alix, but his face was no longer that of a sane man. It twitched, discolored, and he pitched loosely onto the stones.

Alix was frozen in horror. She saw Finn standing over the Mujhar, still clasping his knife.

Silence reigned. No one moved, as if made immobile by the sudden collapse of Shaine. Then Finn turned a strangely impassive face to Carillon.

"Is he slain, princeling? Is the Mujhar dead at last?"

Carillon knelt by Shaine's side. Carefully he turned the body over and they all saw the twisted travesty of a face. Alix gulped back a sour taste in her throat.

After a moment Carillon lowered the body and rose, facing Finn bitterly. "You have accomplished your goal, shapechanger," he said flatly. "The Mujhar is slain."

Alix began to tremble. She saw an expression in Finn's face that frightened her. It was a mixture of conflicting emotions: pleasure, relief, satisfaction, and something very strange. It turned her cold.

For a long moment Finn looked down upon the body stretched by the firepit. Then he turned and stared at the throne a very long time. Finally he looked back at Carillon and stretched out a restraining hand as the prince moved away.

"No," he said.

Carillon frowned at him. "I go only to tell the guardsmen their lord is slain."

"The *old* lord is slain," Finn said clearly.

"Because of you!" the prince snapped.

Finn looked down at the knife in his hand as if surprised to see it. For a moment he seemed bewildered. Then he glanced back at Duncan.

Alix felt the intensity of their locked gazes and looked from one to the other, shaken. But she did not interfere.

Finn smiled. Something in his face had surrendered. When he looked again at Carillon he seemed resigned. Swiftly he flipped the knife in his hand and slid the point beneath the underflesh of his forearm. Alix winced as blood welled quickly around the blade, staining it.

"Is this expiation for a dead Mujhar?" Carillon asked harshly.

Finn did not answer. He dropped to one knee, head bowed. "It is Cheysuli custom, my lord, that the Mujhar is ever attended by a liege man." A deep breath lifted his shoulders briefly. "Fifty years ago Hale of the Cheysuli swore a blood-oath to take Shaine the Mujhar as his liege lord until death." His eyes moved to Carillon's face as he held out the knife, hilt first. "If you will have it . . . if you will accept it, my lord Carillon . . . I offer you the same service."

Carillon, stating at the kneeling warrior in absolute astonishment, slowly opened his mouth.

"*I?*"

"You are the Mujhar. The Mujhar must have a Cheysuli liege man." Finn smiled without his customary irony. "It is tradition, my lord."

"Cheysuli tradition."

Finn remained unmoving. "Will you accept my service?"

Carillon threw out both hands, flinging water across the dais. "By the gods, Finn, we have never met without railing at one another like jackdaws!"

Finn's mouth twisted. "It is unsettling for a Cheysuli to recognize his own *tahlmorra* when he wants no part of it. What else would you expect me to do?" He waited, then sighed. "Do you accept me, or do you refuse me the sort of honor my *jehan* ever respected?"

Carillon stared down at him. "Well . . . I cannot have you bleeding all over the floor. Although once I said I would see the color of your blood."

Finn nodded. "If you see much more, I will have nothing left to spare in your service."

Carillon smiled and held out his hand. The hilt was placed in it, and he accepted the knife without comment. Then he drew his own, slid Finn's blade home in his sheath, and gave the Cheysuli his own untarnished knife.

"A blood-oath is binding," he said quietly. "Even *I* know that."

Finn rose, shrugging. "It is only binding until it is broken, my lord. But that has only been done once before." He smiled crookedly. "And you have seen the result."

Carillon nodded silently. Then he moved past Finn as one dazed and walked to the huge silver doors. There he paused and looked briefly at Alix, then to Duncan.

"Have you known he would do this? *Him?*"

Alix, who wanted to ask that question for herself, waited expectantly.

Duncan grinned. "Finn does as he chooses. I cannot explain the madness that comes on him at times."

Carillon shook his head and glanced back at the Cheysuli warrior who stood silently with his wolf.

Alix, also staring at Finn, felt a strange bubble of laughter burst in her soul. She grinned at Carillon.

"I think you have your revenge, my lord. How better to overcome a Cheysuli than to appeal to his eternal *tahlmorra?*"

Carillon grinned back. Then he lost it as he heard the first shouts from without the Great Hall. His face turned harsh.

"The Ihlini," he said. "My uncle has destroyed the wards."

"Then it is time we left this place, my lord Mujhar," Duncan said quietly.

Carillon glanced back at Shaine's body. Then he turned on his heel and departed the Great Hall.

Chapter Four

Almost instantly they were surrounded by Solindish and Atvian troops who shouted triumphantly as they made their way past slain Homanan servitors and guardsmen to begin their destruction of the fallen palace.

Alix bit her bottom lip as Duncan thrust her against a wall that blocked an Atvian soldier's cursing attack. She slid back against the wall in horror, seeing only the blood-lust in his eyes and the sudden savagery in Duncan's.

Carillon's sword clanged against another as a Solindish man sought to bring him down. The prince fought well, though badly outweighed and outreached. He fell to one knee, gasping as he tried to bring up his broadsword, but Finn was there before him. Alix saw the royal knife that now belonged to a Cheysuli sink home in a Solindish throat, and bit back an outcry as the man fell at Carillon's feet.

The prince pushed himself upright and turned, staring fixedly at Finn. "Is this what it is to have a liege man?"

Finn, retrieving his new knife, grinned. "I am newly-come to the service, my lord, but I know it is my task to keep you alive." He paused significantly. "When you foolishly engage someone stronger than you."

Carillon scowled at him, but Alix saw gratitude and dawning realization in his blue eyes. She nearly smiled to herself, pleased beyond measure that they could be in accordance after so much discord, but Duncan grabbed her arm and dragged her down the corridor.

"Shaine has done his work well," he said roughly. "We have little time to win free of this place."

"Win *free!*" Carillon called breathlessly from behind. "This place is Homanan! I will not have it fall into enemy hands."

Duncan turned to say something more, saw the approaching enemy soldiers and shouted something to Finn. The younger Cheysuli turned back, shoulder-to-shoulder with the prince, and beat back four soldiers. Duncan grabbed Alix's shoulder and shoved her through a tapestried doorway.

She stumbled into a small ceremonial chamber, protesting inarticulately at Duncan's roughness. He remained at the doorway, holding the tapestry aside as he peered out to search for the enemy. Alix turned from him and surveyed the chamber.

It was deserted but oddly comforting, like the eye of a bad storm. Braziers warmed the room against the chill of mortared stone, and fine rugs and arrases bedecked the floors and walls.

She fingered the back of an ornate wooden chair and wondered at its fineness. Then she heard Duncan expel a sudden breath and whipped around, crying out as the Atvian plunged through the door tapestry with an iron spear.

The flanged head slid easily into the back of the chair and shattered it, spraying her with splinters. She stared speechlessly at the bearded Atvian who clawed at his belt-knife.

Duncan lunged for the man. "Alix! Find a place to hide yourself—I cannot spare the time to watch out for you!"

She retreated instantly, staring as Duncan engaged the man. Finally she wrenched her eyes away and sought a place.

An indigo curtain shrouding a huge casement billowed and she ran for the wide bench of stone sill. Alix climbed up and pressed her back against the cold stone, dragging the velvet around her body. But she left gap enough to watch.

Duncan slew the Atvian soldier and stood over the body, gasping as he tried to recover breath through his torn throat.

"And who prophesied *your* death, shapechanger?" asked Keough from the door.

Duncan straightened instantly, meeting the Atvian's satisfied, expectant eyes. The Cheysuli stood spraddle-legged over the dead soldier as Keough advanced into the room through the only door. Behind him stood his son, blocking the exit.

"Where is your vaunted bow, shapechanger?" Keough challenged. "Where is your animal?"

Duncan said nothing as he stepped around the body and settled into a readied position.

Keough laughed. "Before you had your bow. Now you bear only a knife, and I a sword."

Duncan watched the gleaming blade dance before his eyes. The lord of Atvia was huge and unbelievably swift for a man of his bulk. Thorne, smirking in the door, folded his arms and watched his father drive the Cheysuli across the hall until his back pressed against a colorful tapestry.

Keough smiled in his red beard, sword tip drifting to touch Duncan's neck gently. "It seems someone has already tried to take your head, shapechanger. Shall I finish it for him?"

The sword flashed to the side lightly and Duncan brought up his knife, flipping it to throw.

Keough slapped it from his hand with a frighteningly smooth motion. The sword tip moved again to the bruising on Duncan's throat. A trickle of fresh blood welled in the ugly wire cut.

"Here, shapechanger? Do I strike *here?*"

Thorne cried out as the ruddy wolf flashed from the casement, ripping through the velvet arras. Duncan's yellow eyes widened in unfeigned surprise and Keough, warned by it, whipped the sword around.

He met the snarling jaws of a wolf-bitch, compact body hurling itself against the Atvian's huge chest. Off-balance, Keough went down at Duncan's feet. A terrified cry broke from his wailing throat.

Thorne rushed the length of the hall, sword drawn and raised to strike the wolf from his father's body. Duncan bent swiftly and grasped his knife, thrusting himself forward to block Thorne's furious charge.

Keough's son went down with a cry of pain, clutching at the knife buried in his chest. Duncan straightened and turned, moving unsteadily to the wolf-bitch.

The animal stood across the unmoving lord of Atvia, feral eyes blazing with silent rage. Slowly knowledge crept into them as she saw Duncan staring wordlessly at her, face drawn.

"He is slain," he said hoarsely.

Keough, face congested, bore no wound. But the man lay dead within Homana-Mujhar.

"Cheysula," Duncan whispered.

The wolf-bitch blurred before his eyes and Alix moved to him, arms crossed slackly across her stomach as if to protect the child.

"He would have slain you."

"Aye, Alix."

She blinked empty eyes. "I know you said I should not shapechange, *cheysul,* but you would have died. I think I would be like a *lir*less man if you died, and lose my very soul."

"It was done out of fear and a wolf's fierce protectiveness for its mate. I could not have asked for or expected different, child or no."

"Then you are not angry with me?"

He put out his arms and took her to him, cradling her head against his shoulder. "I am not angry, small one."

"Duncan . . . we are losing Homana-Mujhar."

"Aye. Carillon will have to wait a while longer before he can assume the Mujhar's throne. We must gather ourselves and go before Bellam finishes the *qu'mahlin* Shaine began."

Thorne, at Alix's feet, groaned. She shuddered and whipped her head around to look, hand to her mouth. Duncan took her away from the young Atvian, heading toward the door.

"Duncan—he is still alive!"

"He will have to remain that way. We can spare no more time, Alix. Come."

Getting out of Homana-Mujhar safely proved more difficult than getting in. Twice Duncan had to fend off Solindish soldiers and Alix shrieked once as a wounded Atvian rose from the floor. A thrown knife bearing Carillon's royal crest quivered in the man's back and she looked up to meet Finn's eyes across the corridor.

"So, *meijha,* you still trail after my *rujho.*"

Alix, faced with Finn's obvious exhaustion and blood-smeared features, laughed at him. "Aye, I still do. And ever will."

Finn smiled at her and retrieved the knife that was now

his, shooting his brother a searching look. Duncan gestured for him to follow and they moved down the corridor silently.

"The prince?" Duncan asked hoarsely.

"I left him in Shaine's own chambers, effectively dispatching two Atvians. Our princeling has learned how to kill. He did not need my help."

"Are you ready to go from this place?"

Finn laughed shortly. "Though I hate leaving such work unfinished, I am more than ready. All we do here is die." He sighed. "We will take Homana-Mujhar another time."

"Carillon might not wish to go."

"He will when I have told him. He may be my liege lord, but I have more sense."

"*Do* you?" Alix demanded, grasping Duncan's belt as they moved.

"Aye, *meijha,* I do."

"Well, *rujho,*" Duncan said, "perhaps you have gained some in the past months. You never had any before."

Finn, affronted, followed them as Storr moved closely at his heels.

They found Carillon where Finn had said and convinced him to join their flight from the palace. He was not particularly happy with the idea, but gave in when Duncan explained their chances. Carillon sighed and pushed a forearm across his damp forehead. His hair had dried into unruly curls.

"This way," he said and led them through winding corridors.

Twisting and turning in the bowels of the immense palace, they followed the prince out of Homana-Mujhar, glad of a respite. They found no Atvian or Solindish troops and it gave them all a chance to breathe again.

Alix followed Carillon out of a recessed doorway into the small bailey at the back of the palace. Behind her were Duncan and Finn, murmuring to one another in the Old Tongue she had not yet quite learned. Then she came to an abrupt stop as Carillon halted before her, and stepped around him to question their pause.

She came face-to-face with a cloaked figure very like the man she had slain in the streets of Mujhara, and suddenly she was very afraid.

A gloved hand slid the hood back, baring exquisitely fine

features and a sweetly beguiling smile. "Alix," he said softly. "And my lord prince of Homana. I could not have hoped for better fortune."

"Tynstar . . ." she whispered.

Duncan stepped beside her, keeping her between himself and the prince. Finn stood at Carillon's right hand, making certain the prince had room to use his sword. Storr, hackled and growling, waited at Finn's right side.

Tynstar smiled. "A tableau. I have before me the three men most responsible for attempting to ruin Bellam's bid to take Homana." His black eyes flickered. "And the woman." He moved closer soundlessly, staring into her face. "Alix, I said you should remain insignificant. You have not heeded me."

She swallowed heavily and fought down the fear that threatened to turn her knees to water. The man who had been so kind and unassuming when first they met displayed his true colors to her at last, and she understood the magnitude of his dedication to his dark gods.

Tynstar smiled more broadly. "Shaine is dead. And Keough. Even Prince Thorne lies dying of a Cheysuli knife. You have accounted for a large toll, this night." His voice dropped to a whisper. "But it is for naught."

"Naught!" Carillon echoed.

"Aye. Bellam holds Homana-Mujhar. Homana is his."

"Yours," Alix said softly. "Homana is *yours*."

The Ihlini smiled sweetly.

Carillon's hand settled on his sword hilt. Tynstar's eyes moved from Alix to him.

"Were I you, my young Mujhar, I would leave Homana-Mujhar instantly."

Carillon's hand twitched. "You tell me to *go* . . ."

Tynstar affected a casual shrug. "You are nothing to me. Bellam wants you for parading before his men, and to show the Homanans your defeat, but *I* see no use in that. It only makes a man determined to have retribution." A hand gestured smoothly. "You have seen what such desires have done to the Cheysuli."

"The *qu'mahlin* is ended," Carillon snapped. "Ended. The Cheysuli may come and go as they please, as before."

Alix felt the surge of joy in her chest, but did not move. Before Tynstar, she could not.

The Ihlini gestured toward the small gate in the high walls. "Go, my lord, else I change my mind."

Carillon drew his sword. Before he could complete the action of lifting it against Tynstar he was rudely halted. He uttered a single choked-off cry and the Cheysuli blade clanged to the stones from nerveless fingers. Carillon, collapsing like a drunken man, fell forward to his hands and knees in front of the sorcerer. His head bowed as if in submission.

Alix gasped and moved forward. Duncan caught her arm and pulled her back.

"Wait . . ." he breathed.

Tynstar's eyes were expressionless as he looked on Carillon's taut shoulders.

"I hold your life, Shaine's heir. I could crush your heart in my very hand, yet never touch you. I could steal the very breath from your lungs in an instant. I could make you blind, deaf, and dumb with no more wits than a mewling infant." His teeth gleamed in a terrifying smile. *"But I will not."*

Alix, angered by his words and that neither Duncan nor Finn moved against the sorcerer, jerked free of Duncan and walked toward Tynstar. She stopped at Carillon's side.

"If you take his life, you must also take mine. Do you think I will stand by while you use your dark arts against my kinsman? I am of this House also, Ihlini!"

Tynstar lifted a gloved hand as if in benediction. Another shudder wracked Carillon's body and Alix sucked in a frightened breath.

"I can harm none of *you* with my arts," Tynstar said calmly, "and my strength is lessened within your presence. But there is enough left to me. Carillon is solely within my care. Speak again, Lindir's daughter, and see the result."

"You cannot touch me, Ihlini," she whispered. "My own magic is stronger than any other Cheysuli's. I have only to show you my wolf's fangs, and you will die as Keough did, of fear alone."

Tynstar's eyes narrowed. "It is true, then, that Lindir gifted you with the Old Blood of this land." He smiled and shrugged. "Well, I can wait. Time is nothing to a man who is already three centuries old."

He glanced regretfully at Carillon. Slowly the prince gath-

ered his strength and got shakily to his feet, lifting the
sword loosely as he rose. He stared in cold fury at Tynstar
a moment, then looked at Alix. His hand touched her arm.

"I heard, cousin. And I give you my thanks."

Tynstar stepped back from them smoothly. His beguiling
smile blanketed them all.

"Bellam will hold Homana-Mujhar, Carillon, and you
will have to fight him for it. But not this night."

He raised a hand, called purple flame hissing from the
darkness, and disappeared.

Epilogue

The darkness, illuminated only by eerie Ihlini flames as purple demon fire consumed the magnificence of Homana-Mujhar, was oppressive. Yet somehow they gathered the surviving Cheysuli warriors and left the palace, forsaking the Homanan city Bellam of Solinde had won.

Carillon said very little on the long ride back to the Keep, so many leagues into Ellas, but Alix knew he had not given himself up to depression. Carillon, the boy-prince who had grown into a king, planned.

When at last they reached the Keep and the warriors scattered to their pavilions and women, Carillon solemnly accepted Duncan's invitation to stay in the slate-colored clan-leader's pavilion.

And it was there, six days later, he told them his decision.

Alix shook her head repeatedly. "You should stay here. *Here.*"

He sat before the fire cairn in his scarred leathers and crusted mail. His wrists, though nearly healed, displayed the deep wounds left by Atvian iron.

Carillon's blue eyes were steady. "Bellam sends troops to find me. He is not a man who gives up easily. The Cheysuli have suffered enough at Shaine's hands; I will not have them dying because the Mujhar's heir shelters in their Keep."

"*You* are the Mujhar," Finn said quietly.

Alix glanced at him and saw the odd calmness she had come to acknowledge in him. For all the confrontation within Homana-Mujhar had changed Carillon, it had also worked its power on Finn.

Carillon gestured dismissively. "It is a title, Finn; no more. And empty. Bellam—on the throne of Homana—claims it his."

"Homana knows it false," said Duncan in his husky voice. Alix still winced when she heard it, fearing his normal tone would never return; knowing Duncan, like Carillon, would carry his scars for life.

"Homana is a defeated land," Carillon said quietly. "It is folly to deny it. To survive, Homana must do Bellam's bidding . . . for a time."

"And Tynstar's," Alix said softly, shivering.

Finn shrugged casually. "We need only wait, Carillon. You will take back Homana-Mujhar."

The last surviving male member of the House of Homana sighed heavily. "Not, I think, for a long while. Thorne heals in Atvia, swearing he will avenge his father's strange death." His eyes flicked to Alix, who stared fixedly at the fire cairn. "Tynstar and his Ihlini buttress Bellam's hold on the thrones of Homana and Solinde. This land's strength is diminished, and must renew itself before the battle begins once more." He smiled faintly. "I cannot ask my battered realm to go so quickly into war again."

Alix met his eyes at last. "Where will you go?"

"We are safe here, across the Ellasian border. Your Keep has been left unbothered by High King Rhodri's soldiers for years. I think no one will mind a lone prince wandering through. I will fade into the land for a time." Carillon's faint smile, older now, came quickly. "But I will not risk another Cheysuli life until it benefits us all."

"It matters little that we risk ourselves," Duncan said quietly. "The prophecy says one day you will ascend the throne of Homana. One day . . . you will."

"The Cheysuli throne, Duncan?" Carillon mocked, and grinned. "I have not forgotten."

"Nor have we."

Carillon abruptly got to his feet. He stared down at Alix.

"Cousin, once you told a naïve, arrogant princeling the truth of Shaine's *qu'mahlin,* and he denied it. He even denied you. I am sorry for it. You are wiser than any I have known." He reached down and took her hand, pulling her to her feet. "You have been truer to your blood than I could ever hope."

"Carillon . . ."

He shook his head and released her hand. "I have a

horse. And, I believe, a shapechanger sworn to be the Mujhar's liege man. Like his father."

Finn rose and grinned into Alix's stricken face. "There, *meijha,* you rid yourself of me at last."

She said nothing, unable to speak past the pain closing her throat.

Finn looked at Duncan. "*Rujho,* care for your *cheysula.* She is not one to be treated lightly."

Duncan smiled and rose, sliding a hand around Alix's waist. With the other he held out the black war bow, ornamentation gleaming.

"Here, my lord Mujhar. Finn will show you how to use it."

Carillon hesitated. "But only a Cheysuli may shoot a Cheysuli bow."

"Traditions change," Duncan said softly.

Carillon took it silently. Then he walked from the pavilion like a man turning his back on a past, intent on making a future.

"Storr!" Alix cried.

The wolf's eyes were warm. *Tahlmorra, liren.*

Alix watched in mute pain as Finn followed Carillon, silver wolf flanking him. She was hardly aware of Duncan's hands settling at her hips, pulling her close against him. She was conscious only of the deep anguish and regret swelling in her breast.

"They will be well, *cheysula.*"

"Why must they *both* go?"

He laughed softly. "Have you not longed for Finn's absence from your life?"

She swallowed. "I have . . . grown accustomed to him. That is all."

"The Mujhar is ever served by a Cheysuli, as Finn said in Homana-Mujhar. As Hale served Shaine. And even before."

Alix stared out the open doorflap and wiped quickly at the tears on her face. "I cannot see Finn and Carillon accomplishing much more than *argument!*"

His hands tightened. "Argument, as *you* should know, has its place. I am certain Shaine and Hale argued, on occasion."

"Look at the result."

Duncan moved behind her and gently rested his chin on her head. "Carillon is not his uncle."

"No, he is not." Alix sighed heavily. "He is only Carillon."

"He will come back."

Alix stiffened, but refused to turn to him for fear she would see something she could not bear.

"Duncan . . . do you speak of *tahlmorra?*"

"Perhaps." He turned her until she stared into his face. "Do you think Finn and Storr will allow their princeling to stay long from their home?"

Something fluttered briefly within her. In amazement Alix put a hand to her stomach, then smiled and placed Duncan's hand there as well so he could feel the child move.

"When Carillon returns, *cheysul,* he will have a new kinsman to see."

"And a realm to win back from Bellam," Duncan said gravely.

She stared into his solemn yellow eyes. "Can he accomplish it? Does the prophecy say he will accomplish it?"

He smoothed back her hair with his free hand. "I cannot say, small one. It is Carillon's *tahlmorra.*"

Carillon's tahlmorra . . . she echoed sadly within her mind, and instinctively sought an answer in the power the gods had given her.

There she found it, and smiled.

THE SONG
OF HOMANA

PART I

Chapter One

I peered through the storm, trying to see Finn. He rode ahead on a small Steppes pony much like my own, though brown instead of dun, little more than an indistinct lump of darkness in the blowing snow. The wind beat against my face; Finn would not hear me unless I shouted against it. I pulled the muffling wraps of wool away from my face, grimacing as the bitter wind blew ice crystals into my beard, and shouted my question to him.

"Do you see anything?"

The indistinct lump became more distinct as Finn turned back in the saddle. Like me, he wore leather and wool and furs, hooded and wrapped, hardly a man underneath all the layers. But then Finn was not what most men would name a man at all, being Cheysuli.

He pulled wrappings from his face. Unlike me, he wore no beard in an attempt at anonymity; the Cheysuli cannot grow them. Something in the blood, Finn had said once, kept them from it. But what he did not have on his face was made up for on his head; Finn's hair, of late infrequently cut, was thick and black. It blew in the wind, baring a sun-bronzed predator's face.

"I have sent Storr ahead to seek shelter," he called back to me. "Is there such a place in all this snow, he will find it."

Instantly my eyes went to the side of the narrow forest track. There, parallelling the hoofprints of our horses—though glimpsed only briefly in the blowing snow and wind—were the pawprints of a wolf. Large prints, well-spaced, little more than holes until the wind and snow filled them in. But it marked the path of Finn's *lir* nonetheless; it marked Finn a man apart, for what manner of man rides with a wolf at his side? Better yet, it marked *me,* for what manner of man rides with a shapechanger at his side?

Finn did not go on at once. He waited, saying nothing more. His face was still bared to the wind. As I rode up I saw how he slitted his eyes, the pupils swollen black against the blinding whiteness. But the irises were a clear, eerie yellow. Not amber or gold or honey. *Yellow.*

Beast-eyes, men called them. I had reason to know why.

I shivered, then cursed, trying to strip my beard of ice. Of late we had spent our time in the warmth of eastern lands; it felt odd to be nearly home again, and suffering because of the winter. I had forgotten what it was to go so encumbered by furs and wool and leather.

And yet I had forgotten nothing. Especially who I was.

Finn, seeing my shiver, grinned, baring his teeth in a silent laugh. "Weary of it already? And will you spend your time shivering and bemoaning the storms when you walk the halls and corridors of Homana-Mujhar again?"

"We are not even to Homana yet," I reminded him, disliking his easy assurance, "let alone my uncle's palace."

"*Your* palace." For a moment he studied me solemnly, reminding me of someone else: his brother. "Do you doubt yourself? *Still?* I thought you had resolved all that when you decided it was time for us to turn our backs on exile."

"I did." I scraped at my beard with gloved fingers, stripping it again of the cold crystals. "Five years is long enough for *any* man to spend in exile; it is too long for a prince. It is time we took my throne back from that Solindish usurper."

Finn shrugged. "You will. The prophecy of the Firstborn is quite definite. You will win back the Lion Throne from Bellam and his Ihlini sorcerer, and take your place as Mujhar." He put out his gloved right hand and made an eloquent gesture: fingers spread, palm turned upward. *Tahlmorra.* The Cheysuli philosophy that each man's fate rested in the hands of the gods.

Well, so be it. So long as the gods made me a king in place of Bellam.

The arrow sliced through the storm and struck deeply into the ribs of Finn's horse. The animal screamed and bolted sideways in a twisting lunge. Deep snowdrifts fouled the gelding's legs and belly almost immediately and he went down, floundering. Blood ran out of his nostrils; it spilled from the wound and splashed against the snow, staining it brilliant crimson.

I unsheathed my sword instantly, jerking it free of the scabbard on my saddle. I spun my horse, cursing, and saw Finn's outthrust arm as he leaped free of his failing mount. "Three of them . . . *now!*"

The first man reached me. We engaged. He carried a sword as I did, swinging it like a scythe as he sought to cut off my head. I heard the familiar sounds: the keening of the blade as it slashed through the air, the laboring of his mount, the hissing of breath between his teeth as he grunted with the effort. I heard also my own grinding teeth as I swung my heavy broadsword. I felt the satisfactory jar of blade against body, though his winter furs muffled most of the impact. Still, it was enough to double him in the saddle and weaken his counterthrust. My own blade went in through leathers and into flesh, slowed by the leathers, then quickened by the flesh. A thrust with my shoulder behind it, and the man was dead.

I jerked the sword free instantly and spun my horse yet again, cursing his small size and wishing for a Homanan warhorse as he faltered. He had been chosen for anonymity's sake, not for his war-sense. And now I must pay for it.

I looked for Finn. I saw instead the wolf. I saw also the dead man, gape-mouthed and bleeding in the snow; the third and final man was still ahorse, staring blankly at the wolf. It was no wonder. He had witnessed the shapechange, which was enough to make a grown man cry out in fear; I did not only because I had seen it so many times. And yet I feared it still.

The wolf was large and ruddy. It leaped even as the attacker cried out and tried to flee. Swept out of the saddle and thrown down against the snow, the man lay sprawled, crying out, arms thrust upward to protect his throat. But the teeth were already there.

"Finn!" I slapped my horse's rump with the flat of my bloodied blade, forcing him through the deep drifts. "Finn," I said more quietly, "it is somewhat difficult to question a dead man."

The wolf, standing over the quivering form, turned his head to stare directly at me. The unwavering gaze was unnerving, for it was a man's eyes set into the ruddy, snow-dusted head. A man's eyes that stared out of the wolf's head.

Then came the blurring of the wolf-shape. It coalesced into a void, a nothingness that hurt the eyes and head and made my belly lurch upward against my ribs. Only the eyes remained the same, fixed on me: bestial and yellow and strange. The eyes of a madman, or the eyes of a Cheysuli warrior.

I felt the prickling down my spine even as I sought to suppress it. The blurring came back as the void dissipated, but this time the faint outline was that of a man. No more the wolf but a two-legged, dark-skinned man. Not human; never that. Something else. Something *more*.

I shifted forward in the saddle, urging my horse closer. The little gelding was wary of it, smelling death on Finn's mount as well as on the first two men, but he went closer at last. I reined him in beside the prisoner who lay on his back in deep snow, staring wide-eyed up at the man who had been a wolf.

"You," I said, and saw the eyes twitch and shift over to me. He wanted to rise; I could see it. He was frightened and helpless as he lay sprawled in the snow, and I meant him to acknowledge it. "Speak," I told him, "who is your master?"

He said nothing. Finn took a single step toward him, saying nothing at all. The man began to speak.

I suppressed my twitch of surprise. Homanan, not Ellasian. I had not heard the tongue for five years, except from Finn's mouth; even now we kept ourselves to Caledonese and Ellasian almost always. And yet, here in Ellas, we heard Homanan again.

He did not look at Finn. He looked at me. I saw the fear, and then I saw the shame and anger. "What choice did I have?" he asked from his back in the snow. "I have a wife and daughter and no way to support them. No way to clothe them, feed them, keep them warm in winter. My croft is gone because I could not pay the rents. My money was spent in the war. My son was lost with Prince Fergus. Do I let my wife and daughter starve because I cannot provide? Do I lose my daughter to the depravity of Bellam's court?" He glared at me from malignant brown eyes. As he spoke the anger grew and the shame faded. All that was left was hostility and desperation. "I had no choice! It was good *gold* that was offered—"

The knife twisted in my belly, though the blade did not exist. "Bloodied gold," I interrupted, knowing what he would say.

"Aye!" he shouted. "But *worth* it! Shaine's war got me nothing but a dead son, the loss of my croft and the beggaring of my family. What else am I to do? Bellam offers gold—*bloodied gold!*—and I will take it. So will we all!"

"All?" I echoed, liking little of what I heard. Was all of Homana desiring to give me over to my enemy for his Solindish gold, my life was forfeit before the task was begun.

"Aye!" he shouted. "All! And why not? They are demons. Abominations. *Beasts!*"

The wind shifted. It threw ice into my face again, but I made no move to rid myself of it. I could not. I could only stare at the man in the snow, struck dumb by his admission.

And then I looked at Finn.

Like me, he was quite still. Silent. Staring. But then, slowly, he lifted his head and looked directly at me. I saw the shrinking of his pupils so that the yellow of his eyes stood out like a beacon against the storm. Yellow eyes. Black hair. The gold that hung at his left ear, bared by the wind that blew the hair from his face. His alien, predator's face.

I looked at him with new eyes, as I had not looked at him for five years, and realized again what he was. Cheysuli. Shapechanger. *A man who took on the form of a wolf at will.*

And the reason for the attack.

Not me. Not me at all. I was insignificant. The prisoner did not know that my head—delivered to Bellam—would give him more gold than he could imagine. By the gods, he did not even know who I was!

Another time, I might have laughed at the irony. Been amused by my conceit, that I thought all men knew me and my worth. But here, in this place, my identity was not the issue. Finn's race was.

"Because of me," he said, and that only.

I nodded. Sickened by the realization, I nodded. What we faced now was more impossible than ever. Not only did we come home to Homana after five years of exile to raise an army and win back my stolen throne, but we had to do it in the face of Homanan prejudice. Shaine's purge—the Cheysuli call it *qu'mahlin*—was little more than the petty vengeance of a mad king, and yet it had not ended even with the sundering of his realm.

They had not come to slay me or even take me prisoner. They had come for Finn, because he was Cheysuli.

"What did they do to you?" I asked. "The Cheysuli. What did this man do to you?"

The Homanan stared up at Finn in something akin to astonishment. "He is a shapechanger!"

"But what did he *do* to you?" I persisted. "Did he slay your son? Take your croft? Rape your daughter? Beggar your family?"

"Do not bother," Finn said. "You cannot straighten an ill-grown tree."

"You can chop it down," I returned. "Chop it down and into pieces and feed it to the fire—" I wanted to say more, but I stopped. I saw his face, with its closed, private expression, and I said nothing more. Finn was not one for sympathy, or even anger expressed in his behalf. Finn fought his own battles.

And now there was this one.

"Can he be turned?" I asked. "His need I understand—a desperate man will do desperate things—but his target I will not tolerate. Go into his mind and turn him, and he can go home again."

Finn's right hand came up. It was empty. But I saw the clenching of his fingers, as if he sought to clasp a knife. He was asking for my approval. He was liege man to the Prince of Homana, and he asked to mete out a death.

"No," I said. "Not this time. Use your magic instead."

The man spasmed against the snow. "Gods, no! No! *No sorcery*—"

"Hold him," I said calmly, as he tried to leap up and run.

Finn was on him at once, though he did not slay him. He merely held him on his knees, pressing him into the snow, on one knee himself with an arm thrust around the throat and the other gripping the head. One twist and it would be done.

"Mercy!" the dead man cried. But could I do it, I would leave him alive.

Finn would not ask again. He accepted my decision. I saw the hand tighten against the Homanan's head and the look of terror enter the brown eyes. And then they were empty, and I knew Finn had gone in to do as I had ordered.

It shows in the eyes. I have seen it in the faces and eyes of others Finn has used his magic on. But I also saw it in Finn's eyes each time: the total immersion of his soul as he sought the gift of compulsion and used it on another. He went away, though his body remained. That which was Finn was elsewhere; he was not-Finn. He was something less and something awesomely more. He was not man, not beast, not god. Something—apart.

The man wavered and sagged, but he did not fall. Finn's arm remained locked around his throat. The hand was pressed against his skull, but it did not break it. It did not snap the neck. It waited.

Finn twitched and jerked. The natural sunbronzing of his face was suddenly gone; he was the color of death. All gray and ivory, with emptiness in his eyes. I saw the slackening of his mouth and heard the rasp in his throat. And then, before I could say a word, he broke the man's neck and threw the body down.

"Finn!" I was off my horse at once, thrusting my sword blade down into the snow. I left it there, moving toward Finn, and reached out to grab what I could of his leathers and furs. "Finn, I said *turn* him, not slay him—"

But Finn was lurching away, staggering in the snow, and I knew he had not heard me. He was not himself. He was still—elsewhere.

"Finn." I caught his arm and steadied him. Even beneath the thickness of winter furs I could feel the rigidity in his arm. His color was still bad; his pupils were nothing but specks in a void of perfect yellow. *"Finn—"*

He twitched again, and then he was back. He swung his head to look at me, and only then realized I held his arm. At once I released it, knowing he was himself again, but I did not relax my stance. It was only because he was Finn that I had left my sword behind.

He looked past me to the body in the snow. *"Tynstar,"* he said. "I touched—*Tynstar."*

I stared. *"How?"*

He frowned and pushed a forearm across his brow, as if he sweated. But his face was dusted with snow, and he shivered from the cold. Once, but it gave away his bewilderment and odd vulnerability. "He was—*there.* Like a web, soft but sticky . . . and impossible to shed." He shook himself, like a dog shaking off water.

"But—if he and the others were hunting Cheysuli and not the Prince of Homana . . ." I paused a moment. "Would Tynstar meddle in the *qu'mahlin?"*

"Tynstar would meddle in anything. He is Ihlini."

I nearly smiled. But I did not, because I was thinking about Tynstar. Tynstar, called the Ihlini, because he ruled (if that is the proper word) the race of Solindish sorcerers. Much like the Cheysuli were the magical race of Homana, the Ihlini sprang from Solinde. But they were evil and did the bidding of the demons who served the netherworld. There was nothing of good about the Ihlini. They wanted Homana, and had aided Bellam to get her.

"Then he does not know we are here," I said, still thinking.

"We are in Ellas," Finn reminded me. "Homana is but a day or two away, depending on the weather, and I do not doubt Bellam has spies to watch the borders. It may well be these men were sent to catch Cheysuli—" he frowned, and I knew he wondered what tokens Bellam required as proof of a Cheysuli kill. Probably the earring, perhaps the armbands as well. —"but it may be they sought Homana's exiled prince." He frowned again. "I cannot be sure. I had no time to learn his intent."

"And now it is too late."

Finn looked at me levelly. "If Tynstar is meddling with Homanans and sending them out against the Cheysuli, they must be slain." For a moment he looked at the body again. Then his eyes came back to me. "It is a part of my service to you to keep you alive. Can I not do the same for myself?"

This time I looked at the body. "Aye," I said finally, harshly, and turned back to retrieve my sword.

Finn moved to his dead horse and stripped him of the saddlepacks. I mounted my horse and slid the sword home in the scabbard, making certain the blade was clean of blood. The runes ran silver in the white light of the storm. Cheysuli runes, representing the Old Tongue which I did not know. A Cheysuli sword for a Homanan prince. But then that was another thing the prophecy claimed: one day a man of all blood would unite, in peace, four warring realms and two magic races. Perhaps it would no longer be a Cheysuli sword in the hand of a Homanan prince. It would merely be a sword in the hand of a king.

But until then, the golden hilt with its rampant, royal lion and the huge brilliant ruby in the prong-toothed pommel would remain hidden by leather wrappings. At least until I claimed the Lion Throne again and made Homana free.

"Come up," I told Finn. "You cannot walk in all this snow."

He handed up his saddlepacks but did not move to mount behind me. "Your horse carries enough bulk, with all of you." He grinned. "I will go on as a wolf."

"If Storr is too far ahead—" I stopped. Though the shapechange was governed by the distance between warrior and *lir*, it was obvious this time there was no impediment. The peculiar detached expression I knew so well came over Finn's face. For a moment his body remained beside my horse, but his mind did not. It was elsewhere, answering an imperative call; his eyes turned inward and blank and empty, as if he conversed with something—or *someone*— no one else could hear.

And then he was back, grinning in genuine pleasure and the attack on us both forgotten. "Storr says he has found us a roadhouse."

"How far?"

"A league, perhaps a bit more. Close enough, I think, after days without a roof over our heads." He ran a hand through his black hair and shook free the powdery snow. "There are great advantages to *lir*-shape, Carillon. I will be quicker—and certainly *warmer*—than you."

I ignored him. It was all I could ever do. I turned my horse back to the track and went on, leaving behind three dead men and one dead horse—the others had run away.

I cursed the storm again. My face was numb from the ice in my beard. Even the wrappings did not help.

When Finn at last went past me, it was in wolf-shape: yellow-eyed, ruddy-furred, fleet of foot. And warmer, no doubt, than I.

Chapter Two

The common room was crowded with men seeking respite from the storm. Dripping candles puddled into piles of cooling, waxy fat on each table, shedding crude light and a cruder pall of smoke into the low beamwork of the roadhouse. The miasma was thick enough to make me choke against its acrid odor, but there was warmth in abundance. For that I would share any stench.

The door hitched against the hardpack of the frozen earthen floor. I stopped short, ducking to avoid smacking my head against the doorframe. But then few roadhouse doors are built to accommodate a man of my height; the years spent in exile had made me taller than I had been five years before and nearly twice as heavy. Still, I would not complain; did the added height and weight—and the beard—keep me unknown on my journey home, I would not care if I knocked myself silly against Ellasian doorframes.

Finn slipped by me into the room as I wrestled with the door. I broke it free, then swung it shut on half-frozen leather hinges, swearing as a dog ran between my legs and nearly upset me. For a moment I thought of Storr, seeking shelter in the forest. Then I thought of food and wine.

I settled the latch-hook into place and marked absently how the stout iron loops were set for a heavy crossbeam lock. I could tell it was but rarely used, but I marked it nonetheless. No more did I have room in my life for the ease of meaningless friendships found in road- and alehouses.

Finn waited at the table. Like the others, it bore a single candle. But this one shed no light, only a clot of thick smoke that fouled the air where the flame had glowed a moment before. Finn, I knew. It was habit with us both.

I joined him, shedding furs and leathers. It felt good to be man again instead of bear, and to know the freedom of movement. I sat down on a three-legged stool and glanced around the common room even as Finn did the same.

No soldiers. Elias was a peaceful land. Crofters, most of them, convivial in warmth and the glow of liquor. Travelers as well, bound east or west: Ellasians; Homanans; Falians too, by their accents. But no Caledonese, which meant Finn and I could speak Ellasian with a Caledonese twist and no one would name us other.

Except those who knew a Cheysuli when they saw one, and in Ellas that could be anyone.

Ellasians are open, gregarious folk, blunt-speaking and plain of habits. There is little of subterfuge about them, for which I am grateful. I have grown weary of such things, though I have, of necessity, steeped myself in it. It felt good to know myself accepted for what I appeared in the roadhouse: a stranger, foreign, accompanied by a Cheysuli, but welcome among them regardless. Still, it was to Finn they looked twice, if only briefly. And then they looked away again, dismissing what they saw.

I smiled. Few men dismiss a Cheysuli warrior. But in Ellas they do it often. Here the Cheysuli are not hunted.

And then I recalled that Homanans had come into Ellas hunting Cheysuli and I lost my smile entirely.

The tavern-master arrived at last, wiping greasy hands on a frayed cloth apron. He spoke with the throaty, blurred accent of Ellas, all husky and full of phlegm. It had taken me months to learn the trick, but I had learned. And I used it now.

"Ale," he said, "or wine. Red from Caledon, a sweet white from Falia, or our own fine Ellasian vintage." His teeth were bad but I thought the smile genuine.

"Have you *usca?*" I asked.

The grizzled gray brows rose as he considered the question. "*Usca,* is't? Na, na, I have none. The plainsmen of the Steppes have naught of trade wi' us now, since Ellas allied wi' Caledon in t'last war." His pale brown eyes marked us Caledonese; my accent had won us that much. Or *me;* Finn did not in the least resemble a Caledonese. "What else would you have?"

Finn's yellow eyes were almost black in the dim candle-

light, but I saw the glint in them clearly. "What of Homanan honey brew?"

At once the brows drew down into a scowl. The Ellasian's hair, like his eyebrows, was graying, close-cropped
against his head. A blemish spread across one cheek; some
childhood malady had left him scarred. But there was no
suspicion or distrust in his eyes, only vague disgust.

"Na, none of that, either. 'Tis Homanan, as you have
said, and little enough of Homana comes across our borders
now." For a moment he stared at the gold earring shining
in Finn's black hair. I knew what the Ellasian thought: little
enough of Homana crossed the borders, unless you counted
the Cheysuli.

"No trade, then?" I asked.

The man picked at snags in his wine-stained apron. He
glanced around quickly, judging the needs of his customers
out of long practice. "Trade, after a fashion," he agreed in
a moment, "but not wi' Homana. Wi' Bellam instead, her
Solindish king." He tipped his head in Finn's direction.
"*You* might know."

Finn did not smile. "I might," he said calmly. "But I left
Homana when Bellam won the war, so I could not say what
has befallen my homeland since."

The Ellasian studied him. Then he leaned forward, pressing both hands flat against the table. "*I* say 'tis a sad thing
to see the land brought down so low. The land chafes under
that Solindish lord. *And* his Ihlini sorcerer."

And so we came to the subject I had wanted to broach
all along, knowing better than to bring it up myself. Now,
did I say nothing and ask no questions, I made myself out a
dullard, and almost certainly suspect. The man had proved
talkative; I had best not disabuse him of that.

"Homana is not a happy land?" My tone, couched in
Caledonese-tinged Ellasian, was idle and incurious; strangers passed time with such talk.

The Ellasian guffawed. "*Happy?* Wi' Bellam on her
throne and Tynstar's hand around her throat? Na, not
happy, never happy . . . but helpless. We hear tales of heavy
taxes and over-harsh justice. The sort of thing that troubles
us little enough in Ellas, under our good High King." He
hawked and turned his head to spit onto the earthen floor.
"They do say Bellam desires an alliance with Rhodri him-

self, but he'll not be agreeing to such a miscarriage of humanity. Bellam's a greedy fool; Rhodri is not. He has no need of't, wi' six fine sons." He grinned. "I hear Bellam offers his only daughter to the High Prince himself, but I doubt there will be a match made. Cuinn has better thighs to part than Electra of Solinde's."

And so the talk passed to women, as it will among men. But only until the Ellasian left to see about our food, and then we said nothing more of women, thinking of Homana instead. And Bellam, governed by Tynstar.

"Six sons," Finn mused. "Perhaps Homana would not now be under Solindish rule, had the royal House proved more fertile."

I scowled at him. I needed no reminders that the House of Homana had been less than prolific. It was precisely because Shaine the Mujhar had sired no son at all—let alone *six* of them!—that he had turned to his brother's only son. Ah, aye, fertility and infertility. And how the issues had shaped my life, along with Finn's. For it was Shaine's infertility—except for a defiant daughter—that had left an enormous legacy to his nephew, Carillon of Homana, and the Cheysuli shapechanger who served him. The Lion Throne itself, upon the Mujhar's death, and now a war to fight.

As well as a purge to end.

The tavern-master arrived bearing bread for trenchers and a platter of steaming meat, which he set in the center of the table. Behind him came a boy with a jug of Ellasian wine, two leathern mugs, and a quarter of yellow cheese. I saw how the boy looked at Finn's face, so dark in the amber candlelight. I saw how he stared at the yellow eyes, but he said not a single word. Finn was, perhaps, his first Cheysuli. And worth a second look.

Neither boy nor man lingered, being too pressed by other custom, and Finn and I set to with the intentness of starving men. We were not starving, having eaten at the break of day, but stale journey-loaf eaten in a snowstorm is not nearly as toothsome as hot meat in a warm roadhouse.

I unsheathed my knife and sliced off a chunk of venison, dumping it onto my trencher. It was a Caledonese knife I used now in place of my own, a bone-handled blade wrought with runes and scripture. The hilt had been cut from the thigh of some monstrous beast, or so the king of Caledon had told me upon presentation of it. The blade itself was bright steel, finely honed; the weight of it was perfect for my hand. Still, it was not my own; that one—Cheysuli-made—was hidden in my saddlepacks.

I ate until I could hardly move upon my stool, and ordered a second jug of wine. And then, even as I poured our mugs full again, I heard the hum of rising conversation. Finn and I both looked instantly for the cause of the heightened interest.

The harper came down the ladder with his instrument clasped under one long arm. He wore a blue robe belted at the waist with linked silver, and a silver circlet held back the thick dark hair that curled on his shoulders. A wealthy harper, as harpers often are, being hosted by kings and gifted with gold and gems. This one had fared well. He was tall, wide-shouldered, and his wrists—showing at the edges of his blue sleeves—were corded with muscle. A powerful man, for all his calling was the harp instead of the sword. He was blue-eyed, and when he smiled it was a professional smile, warm and welcoming.

Two men cleared space for him in the center of the room and set out a stool. He thanked them quietly and sat down, settling harp against hip and thigh. I knew at once the instrument was a fine one, having heard so many of the best with my uncle in Homana-Mujhar. It was of rich honey-gold wood, burnished to a fine sheen with years of use. A single green stone was set into the top. The strings glowed gossamer-fine in the smoke and candlelight. They glinted, promising much, until he touched them and fulfilled that promise with the stroke of a single finger.

Like a woman it was, answering a lover's caress. The music drifted throughout the room, soft and delicate and infinitely seductive, and silenced the voices at once. There is no man alive who cannot lose himself in harpsong, unless he be utterly deaf.

The harper's voice, when he spoke, was every bit as lovely as the harp. It lacked the feminine timbre of many I had heard, yet maintained the rich liquid range the art requires. The modulation was exquisite; he had no need to speak loudly to reach all corners of the room. He merely spoke. Men listened.

"I will please you as I please myself," he said quietly, "by giving you what entertainments I can upon my Lady. But there is a task I must first perform." From the sleeve of his robe he took a folded parchment. He unfolded it, smoothed it, and began to read. He did not color his tone with any emotion, he merely read. But the words were quite enough.

"Know ye all men that Bellam the Mujhar,
King of Solinde and Mujhar of Homana;
Lord of the cities Mujhara and Lestra;
Sets forth the sum of five hundred gold pieces
to any man bringing sound word of Carillon,
styling himself Prince of Homana,
and wrongful claimant to the Lion Throne.

"Know ye all men that Bellam the Mujhar
desires even more the presence of the pretender,
offering one thousand gold pieces
to any man bringing Carillon—or his body—
into Homana-Mujhar."

The harper, when finished, folded the parchment precisely as it had been and returned it to his sleeve. His blue eyes, nearly black in the smoky light, looked at every man as if he judged his thoughts. All idleness was gone; I saw only shrewd intensity. He waited.

I wondered, in that moment, if he recruited. I wondered if he was Bellam's man, sent out with the promise of gold. I wondered if he counted the pieces for himself. Five hundred of them if he knew I was here. One thousand if he brought me home to Homana-Mujhar.

Home. For disposal as Bellam—or Tynstar—desired.

I saw what they did, the Ellasian men. They thought of the gold and the glory. They thought of the task and the triumph. They considered, for a moment, what it might be to be made rich, but only for a moment, for then they considered their realm. Ellas. Not Homana. Rhodri's realm. And the man who offered such gold had already swallowed one land.

The Ellasians, I knew, would do nothing for Bellam's

gold. But there were others in the room, and perhaps they would.

I looked at Finn. His face was a mask, as ever; a blank, sun-bronzed mask, with eyes that spoke of magic and myth and made them both quite real.

The harper began to sing. His deep voice was fine and sweet, eloquently expressing his intent. He sang of the bitterness of defeat and the gut-wrenching carnage of war. He sang of boys who died on bloodied fields and captains who fell beneath Solindish and Atvian swords. He sang of a king who hid himself in safety behind the rose-red walls of Homana-Mujhar, half-mad from a crazed obsession. He sang of the king's slain brother, whose son was trapped in despair and Atvian iron. He sang of the same boy, now a man and free again, who lived his life in exile, fleeing Ihlini retribution. He sang my life, did this stranger, and brought the memories alive.

Oh gods . . . the memories . . .

How is it that a harper can know what was? How is it that he captures the essence of what happened, what I am, what I long to be? How is it that he can sing my song while *I* sit unknowing, knowing only it is true, wishing it were otherwise?

How is it done?

The poignancy nearly shattered me. I shivered once convulsively, then stared hard at the scarred wooden table while the shackle weals beneath the sleeves of my leather shirt ached with remembered pain. I could not look at the harper. Not while he gave me my history, my heritage, my legacy, and the story of a land—*my* land—in her death struggle.

"By the gods—" I murmured before I could stop.

I felt Finn's eyes on me. But he said nothing at all.

Chapter Three

"I am Lachlan," said the harper. "I am a harper, but also a priest of Lodhi the All-Wise, the All-Father; would you have me sing of Him?" Silence met his question, the silence of reverence and awe. He smiled, his hands unmoving upon the harp. "You have heard of the magic we of Lodhi hold. The tales are true. Have you not heard them before?"

I looked over the room. Men sat silently on their benches and stools, paying no mind to anyone save the harper. I wondered again what he intended to do.

"The All-Father has given some of us the gift of song, the gift of healing, the gift of words. And fewer of us claim all three." He smiled. It was an enigmatic, eloquent smile. "I am one, and this night I will share what I can with you."

The harp's single green stone cast a viridescent glow as his fingers danced across the strings, stirring a sound that at once set the flesh to rising on my bones. His eyes passed over each of us again, as if he sought to comprehend what each one of us was about. And still he smiled.

"Some men call us sorcerers," he said quietly. "I will not dispute it. My Lady and I have traversed the leagues of this land and others, and what I have seen I have learned. What I will give you this night is something most men long for: a return to the innocent days. A return to a time when cares were not so great and the responsibilities of manhood did not weigh so heavily. I will give you your greatest day." The blue eyes swelled to black. "Sit you still and listen, hearing only my Lady and myself, and I will give you the gift of Lodhi."

I heard the music begin. For a moment I thought nothing of it: it was harpsong as ever, boasting nothing more than what I had already heard. And then I heard the underscore moving through the melody. A strange, eerie tone, seemingly at odds with the smoother line. I stared at the harper's hands as he moved them in the strings, light glittering off the strands. And then I felt him inside my head.

Suddenly I was nothing but music. A single, solitary note. A string plucked and plucked again, my use dictated by the harper whose hands were on my soul. I stared at the eloquent fingers moving, caressing, plucking at the strings, and the music filled my head.

The colors of the room spilled away, like a wineglass tipped and emptied. Everything was gray, dark and light, with no blacks and no whites. I saw a harper in a gray robe with gray eyes and grayish hair. Only the harp held true: honey-gold and gleaming, with a single emerald eye. And then even that was gone . . .

No more war—no more blood—no more wishing for revenge. Only the sense of other days. Younger days, and a younger Carillon, staring with joy and awe at the great chestnut warhorse his father had gifted him on his eighteenth birthday. I recalled the day so well, and what I had thought of the horse. I recalled it all, for on that day I was named Prince of Homana, and heir to the Lion Throne.

Again I clattered down the winding staircase at Joyenne, nodding at servants who gave me morning greeting, thinking only of the promised gift. I had known it was to be a horse, a warhorse, but not which one. I had hoped—

—and it was. The great red stallion had gotten a matching son on my father's best mare, and that son was mine at last. Full-grown and fully trained, ready for a warrior. I was not so much a warrior then, knowing only the practice chamber and tourney-fields, but I was more than ready to prove what I could of my skill. And yet I could not have wished for that chance to come so soon.

I saw then the underside of the harper's spell. It was true he gave me my innocent days, but with those days came the knowledge of what had followed. He could not have summoned a more evocative memory had he tried for it; I think he did it purposely. I think he reached into my mind, digging and searching until he found the proper one. And then he gave it to me.

The memory altered. No more was I the young prince reaching out to touch the stallion. No. I was someone else entirely: a bloodied, soiled, exhausted boy in a man's body, his sword taken from him and his wrists imprisoned in At-vian iron. Taken by Thorne himself, Keough's son, who had ordered the iron hammered on.

All my muscles knotted. Sweat broke out on my flesh. I sat in a crowded common room of a roadhouse in the depths of an Ellasian storm, and I sweated. Because I could not help myself.

And then, suddenly, the colors were back. The grays faded. Candlewicks guttered and smoked, turning faces light and dark, and then I realized I sat still upon my stool with Finn's hand imprisoning my right wrist. It was not iron, it was flesh and bone, holding my arm in place. And then I saw why. In my fist was gripped the bone-handled knife, the blade pointing toward the harper.

"Not yet," Finn said quietly. "Perhaps later, when we have divined his true intent."

It made me angry. Angry at Finn, which was wrong, but I had no better target. It was the harper I wanted, for manipulating me so, but it was Finn who was too near.

I let go the knife. Finn let go the hand. I drew it in to my body, massaging the ridges of scar tissue banding my wrist as if it bore iron still. And I glared at him with all the anger in my eyes. "What did he give *you?* A Cheysuli on the throne?"

Finn did not smile. "No," he said. "He gave me Alix."

It took the breath from my chest. Alix. Of course. How better to get to Finn than to remind him of the woman he had wanted badly enough to steal? The woman who had turned her back on him to wed Duncan, his brother.

The woman who was my cousin, that I wanted for myself.

I laughed bitterly. "A skillful harper indeed . . . or more likely a sorcerer, as he claims." I stared across at the blue-robed man who was calmly refusing to sing again. "Ihlini, do you think? Sent from Bellam to set a trap?"

Finn shook his head. "Not Ihlini; I would know. And I have heard of this All-Father god." He grimaced in distaste. "An Ellasian deity, and therefore of less importance to me, but powerful nonetheless." He shifted slightly on the stool, leaning forward to pour himself more wine. "I will have a talk with him."

He had named himself Lachlan, and now he moved around the room to gather up his payment in coin and baubles and wine. He carried his harp tucked into the crook of one arm and a cup in his other hand. Light glittered off the silver links around his waist and the circlet on his brow. He was a young man still, perhaps my own age, and tall, but lacking my substantial height and weight. Still, he was not slight, and I thought there was strength in those shoulders.

He came last to our table, as I expected, and I pushed the winejug forward so he would know to help himself. And then I kicked a stool toward him. "Sit you down. Please yourself with the wine. And this." I drew forth from my belt-purse a jagged piece of gold, stamped with a crude design. But it was good gold, and heavy, and few men would look askance at its crude making. I slid it across the table with a forefinger, pushing it around the bone-handled knife.

The harper smiled, nodded and sat down upon the stool. His blue eyes matched the rich hue of his robe. His hair, in the dim candlelight, showed no color other than a dull dark brown. It looked as if the sun had never touched it, to bleach it red or blond. Dyed, I thought, and smiled to myself.

He poured wine into the cup he held. It was a fine silver cup, though tarnished with age. The house cup for a harper, I thought, seeing little use. I doubted it was his own.

"Steppes gold." He picked up the coin. "I do not often see payment of this sort." His eyes flicked from the coin to my face. "My skill is not worth so much, I think; you may have it back." He set the coin on the table and left it.

The insult was made calmly and clearly, with great care. Its intent was unknown, and yet I recognized it regardless. Or was it merely a curious man gone fishing for an outsize catch? Perhaps an exiled prince.

"You may keep it or not, as you wish." I picked up my own mug. "My companion and I have just returned from the Caledonese war against the plainsmen of the Steppes—alive and unharmed, as you see—and we are generous because of it." I spoke Ellasian, but with a Caledonese accent.

The harper—Lachlan—swirled wine in his tarnished cup. "Did it please you," he said, "my gift?"

I stared at him over my mug. "Did you mean it to?"

He smiled. "I mean nothing with that harpsong. I merely

share my gift—*Lodhi's* gift—with the listener, who will make of it what he will. They are *your* memories, not mine; how could I dictate what you see?" His eyes had gone to Finn, as if he waited.

Finn did not oblige. He sat quietly on his stool, seemingly at ease, though a Cheysuli at ease is more prepared than any man I know. He turned his mug idly on the table with one long-fingered hand. His eyes were hooded slightly, like a predator bird's, but the irises showed yellow below the lids.

"Caledon." The harper went on as if he realized he would get nothing from Finn. "You say you fought with Caledon, but you are not Caledonese. I know a Cheysuli when I see one." He smiled, then glanced at me. "As for you—you speak good Ellasian, but not good enough. You have not the throat for it. But neither are you Caledonese; I know enough of them." His eyes narrowed. "Solindish, perhaps, or Homanan. You lack the lilt of Falia."

"Mercenaries," I said clearly, knowing it was—or had been—the truth. "Claiming no realm, only service."

Lachlan looked at me. I knew he saw the thick beard and the uncut, sunstreaked hair that tangled on my shoulders. I had hacked off the mercenary's braid I had worn for five years, bound with crimson cord, and went as a free man again, which meant my sword was available. With a Cheysuli at my side, I would be a valuable man. Kings would pay gold for our service.

"No realm," he said, and smiled. Then he pushed away from the table and got to his feet, cradling the harp. He picked up the blackened silver cup and nodded his thanks for the wine.

"Take your payment," I said. "It was made in good faith."

"And in good faith, I refuse it." He shook his head. "You have more need of it than I. I have no army to raise."

I laughed out loud. "You misunderstand mercenaries, harper. We do not raise armies. We *serve* in them."

"I said precisely what I meant." His face was solemn, eyes flicking between us shrewdly. And then he turned away.

Finn put out his hand and gathered up his knife. No, not his precisely; like me, he hid his away. He carried instead a knife taken from a Steppes plainsman, and it served its purpose. In Finn's hand, any knife did.

"Tonight," he said quietly, "I will have conversation with that harper."

I thought fleetingly of the Ellasian god the harper claimed to serve. Would Lodhi interfere? Or would Lachlan cooperate?

I smiled. "Do what you have to do."

Because the storm had driven so many inside for the evening, the roadhouse was crowded to bursting. There were no private rooms. The best I could do was give gold to the tavern-master for two pallets on the floor of a room already occupied by three others. When I went in alone, later than I had intended, they already slept. I listened silently just inside the open door, to see if anyone feigned sleep to lure me into a trap, but all three men were deep asleep. And so I shut the door, set my unsheathed sword on the lice-ridden pallet as I stretched out my legs, and waited for Finn to come in.

When he did, it was without sound. Not even the door squeaked, as it had for me. Finn was simply in the room. "The harper is gone," he said. It was hardly a sound, but I had learned how to hear it.

I frowned into the darkness as Finn knelt down on the other pallet. "In this storm?"

"He is not here."

I sat back against the wall, staring thoughtfully into the darkness. My right hand, from long habit, touched the leather-wrapped hilt of my sword. "Gone, is he?" I mused. "What could drive a man into an Ellasian snowstorm, unless there be good reason?"

"Gold is often a good reason." Finn shed a few of his furs and dropped them over his legs. He stretched out upon his pallet and was silent. I could not even hear him breathe.

I bit at my left thumb, turning things over in my mind. Questions arose and I could answer none of them. Nor could Finn, so I wasted no time asking him. And then, when I had spent what moments I could spare considering the harper, I slid down the wall to stretch full length upon the lumpy pallet and went to sleep.

What man—even a prince with gold upon his head—need fear for his safety with a Cheysuli at his side?

It was morning before we could speak openly, and even then words were delayed. We went out into the ethereal stillness of abated storm, saddled and packed our horses and walked them toward the track. The snow lay deep and soft around my boots, reaching nearly to my knees. The track was better, packed and shallow, and there I waited while Finn went into the trees and searched for his *lir*.

Storr came at once, bounding out of the trees like a dog, hurling himself into Finn's arms. Finn went down on one knee, ignoring the cold, and cast a quick, appraising look toward the roadhouse. I thought it highly unlikely anyone could see us now. Satisfied, Finn thrust out an arm and slung it around Storr's neck, pulling the wolf in close.

What their bond is, I cannot say precisely. I know only what Finn has told me, that Storr is a part of his heart and soul and mind; half of his whole. Without the wolf, Finn said, he was little more than a shadow, lacking the gifts of his race and the ability to survive. I thought it an awesomely gruesome thing, to claim life only through some sorcerous link with an animal, but I could not protest what so obviously worked. I had seen him with the wolf before during such greetings, and it never failed to leave me feeling bereft and somehow empty. Jealous, even, for what they shared was something no other man could claim save the Cheysuli. I have owned dogs and favorite horses, but it was not the same. That much I could tell, looking at them, for Finn's face was transfigured when he shared a reunion with Storr.

Finn's new horse, a dark brown gelding purchased from the tavern-master, pulled at the slack reins. I pulled him back again and got his reins untangled from those of my little Steppes pony. When I looked again at Finn I saw him slap Storr fondly on the shoulder, and then he was pushing back through the snow toward me.

I handed the reins to him. "How does he fare?"

"Well enough." The fond half-smile remained a moment, as if he still conversed with the wolf. I had thought once or twice that his expression resembled that of a man well-satisfied by a woman; he wore it now. "Storr says he would like to go home."

"No more than I." The thought of Homana instead of foreign lands knotted my belly at once. Gods, to go home again . . . I looped my horse's reins over his ears, pulled them down his neck and mounted. As ever, the little gelding grunted. Well, I am heavier than the plainsmen who broke him. "I think we can reach Homana today, does the sky remain clear." I looked skyward and squinted out of habit. "Perhaps we should go to the Keep."

Finn, settling into his saddle, looked at me sharply. He went hoodless as I did, and the early dawn light set his earring to glinting with a soft golden glow. "This soon?"

I laughed at him. "Have you no wish to see your brother?"

Finn scowled. "You know well enough I am not averse to seeing Duncan again. But I had not thought we would go openly into Cheysuli land so soon."

I shrugged. "We are nearly there. The Keep lies on the border, which we must cross. And, for all that, I think we both wish to see Alix again."

Finn did not meet my eyes. It was odd to realize the time away from Homana had not blunted his desire for his brother's wife. No more than it had mine.

He looked at me at last. "Do you wish to take *me* to her, or go for yourself?"

I smiled and tried not to show him my regret. "She is wed now, and happily. There is no room for me in her life except as a cousin."

"No more for *me* except as a *rujholli*." Finn laughed bitterly; his eyes on me were ironic and assessive as he pushed black hair out of his dark, angular face. "Do you not find it strange how the gods play with our desires? You held Alix's heart, unknowing, while she longed for a single word from your mouth. Then I stole her from you, intending to make her my *meijha*. But it was Duncan, ever Duncan . . . he won her from us both." Grimly he put out his hand and made the gesture I had come to hate, for all its infinite meaning.

"*Tahlmorra*," I said sourly. "Aye, Finn, I find it passing strange. And I do not like it overmuch."

Finn laughed and closed his hand into a fist. "*Like* it?

But the gods do not expect us to like it. No. Only to serve it."

"*You* serve it. I want none of your Cheysuli prophecy. I am a Homanan prince."

"And you will be a Homanan king . . . with all the help of the Cheysuli."

No man, born of a brief history, likes to hear of another far greater than his own, particularly when his House has fallen into disarray. The Homanan House had held the Lion Throne nearly four hundred years. Not long, to Cheysuli way of thinking. Not when their history went back hundreds of centuries to a time with no Homanans. Only the Firstborn, the ancestors of the Cheysuli, with all their shapechanging arts.

And the power to hand down a prophecy that ruled an entire race.

"This way, then." Finn gestured and kicked his horse into motion.

"You are certain?" I had no wish to get myself lost, not when I was so close to Homana at last.

Finn cast me a thoroughly disgusted glance. "We go to the Keep, do we not? I should know the way, Carillon. Once, it was my home."

I subsided into silence. I am silent often enough around him. Sometimes, with Finn, it is simply the best thing *to* do.

Chapter Four

The weather remained good, but the going did not. We had left behind the beaten track that led westward into Homana, seeking instead the lesser-known pathways. Though the Cheysuli were welcome within Ellas, they kept to themselves. I doubted High King Rhodri knew much of the people who sheltered in his forests. They would keep themselves insular, and therefore more mysterious than ever. There would be no well-traveled tracks leading to the Keep.

At last, as the sun lowered in the sky, we turned into the trees to find a proper campsite, knowing Homana and the Keep would have to wait another day. We settled on a thick copse of oaks and beeches.

Finn swung off his mount. "I will fetch us meat while you lay the fire. No more journey-loaf for me, not when I have tasted real meat in my mouth again." He threw me his reins, then disappeared into the twilight with Storr bounding at his side.

I tended the horses first, untacking them, then hobbling and graining them with what dwindling rations remained. Once the horses were settled I searched for stones, intending to build us a proper fire cairn. We had gone often enough without a fire, but I preferred hot food and warmth when I slept.

I built my cairn, fired the kindling we carried in our saddle-packs and made certain the flames would hold. Then I turned to the blankets I had taken from the horses. Pelts, to be precise; each horse was blanketed with two. The bottom rested hair-down against the horse, the top one hair-up, to pad the saddle. At night the pelts became blankets for Finn and me, smelling of sweat and horsehair, but warm. I spread them now against the snow; after we ate we could thrust the hot stones beneath them to offer a little heat.

As I spread the blankets I heard the muffled movement in the snow. My hand was on my sword instantly, ripping it from the sheath at my left hip. I spun, leveling the blade, and saw the flash of setting sunlight turn the runes to blinding fire.

Three men before me, running at me out of the thickening shadows. More than that behind me. I wondered where was Finn, and then I did not, for I had no time.

I took the first one easily enough, marking the expression of shock on his face as I swung my blade and cut through leather and furs and flesh, shearing the bone of his arm in two just below the shoulder. The momentum of the blade carried it farther yet, into his ribs, and then he fell and I wrenched the sword free to use it on yet another.

The second fell as well, thrust through the lungs, and then the others did what they should have done at the first. They came at me at once, en masse, so that even did I try to take yet a third the others could bear me down. I did not doubt I would account for at least another death before I died, perhaps even two—Finn and adversity had taught me well enough for that—but the result would be the same. I would be dead, and Bellam would have his pretender-prince.

I felt the cold kiss of steel at the back of my neck sliding through my hair. Yet another blade was at my throat; a third pressed against the leather and furs shielding my belly. Three men on me, then; two were dead, and the last man—the sixth—stood away and watched me. Blood was splattered across his face, but he bore no wound.

"Stay you still," he told me at once, and I heard the fear in his voice. As well as the Homanan words.

I gestured toward my belt-purse. "My gold is there."

"We want none of *your* gold," he said quickly. "We came for something more." He smiled. "But we will take it, since you offer."

I still held my sword in my right hand. But they did not let me keep it. One man reached out and took it from me, then tossed it aside. I saw how it landed across the fire cairn, clanging against the stone. I saw how the hilt was in the flames, and knew the leather would burn away to display the golden lion.

"Whose gold do you want, then?" I spoke Homanan, since they did, but I kept my Caledonese accent.

"Bellam's," he confided, and grinned.

Inwardly I swore. The Solindish usurper had caught me easily enough. And I had not even reached Homana.

Still, I forced a bewildered frown. "What does Bellam want with a mercenary? Can he not *buy* hundreds of them?"

"You travel with a shapechanger," he stated flatly.

Still I frowned. "Aye. What of it? Has Bellam declared it unlawful? I am not Homanan, I am Caledonese. I choose my companions where I will." I looked at the sword hilt and saw how the leather turned black and crisp. In a moment it would peel away, and I would be unmasked. If I were not already.

"Cheysuli are under sentence of death," the Homanan said. "That is one policy Bellam has kept intact since the day of Shaine."

I allowed surprise to enter my face. "You welcome Bellam as king, then? Though you be Homanan?"

He glanced at the others. They were all familiar: I had seen them in the roadhouse the night before. And they had heard Bellam's message the harper had read. But I wondered how I had given myself away.

The man spat into the snow. "We welcome Bellam's gold, since we get none of it another way. While he offers payment for each Cheysuli slain, we will serve him. That is all."

I kept my surprise from showing. Once more, it was not me they sought. Finn again. But it was me they had caught, and worth more—to Bellam—than five hundred Cheysuli warriors.

Except there were not five hundred Cheysuli left in all the world. My uncle had seen to that.

"You have come across the border hunting Cheysuli?" I asked.

He smiled. "They are hard to find in Homana. But the Ellasian king gives them refuge, so we seek them here. How better to earn the gold?"

"Then why," I asked very calmly, "do you disarm *me?* I have no stake in this."

"You came in with the shapechanger. By taking you, we take him. He will not turn beast with your life in our hands."

I laughed. "You count on a bond that does not exist. The Cheysuli and I met on the trail; we owe each other nothing. Taking me wins you nothing except a meaningless death." I paused. "You *do* mean to slay me, do you not?"

He glanced at the others. For a moment there was hesitation in his blue eyes, and then he shrugged. His decision had been made. "You slew two of us. You must pay."

I heard the jingle of horse trappings. The blades pressed closer against my neck, throat, and belly as the man rode out of the trees. In his bare hands was a harp, and the single note he plucked held us all in thrall.

"You will slay no one," the harper said. "Fools, all of you, when you have Carillon in your hands."

The Homanans did not move. They could not. Like me, they were prisoners to the harp.

Lachlan looked at me. "They are Homanans. Did you tell them your name, they might bend knee to you instead of baring steel."

His fingers tangled in the strings and brought forth a tangle of sound. It allowed me to speak, but nothing more. "I am a mercenary," I said calmly. "You mistake me for someone else."

He frowned. His eyes were on me intently, and the sound of the harp increased. I felt it inside my head, and then he smiled. "I can conjure up your life, my lord. Would you have me show it to us all?"

"To what purpose?" I inquired. "You will do what you will do, no matter what I say."

"Aye," he agreed.

I saw how his fingers played upon the strings, drawing from the harp a mournful, poignant sound. It conjured up memories of the song he had played the night before, the lay that had driven a blade into my belly with the memories of what had happened. But it was not the same. It had a different sound. His Lady sang a different song.

The blades moved away from my neck, my throat, my belly. The Homanans stepped away, stumbling in the snow, until I stood alone. I watched, mute, as they took up the men I had slain and bore the bodies away into the trees. I was alone, except for the harper, but as helpless as before.

"Ah," I said, "you mean to claim the gold yourself."

"I mean to give you what men I can," he reproved. "I sent them home to wait until you call them to your standard."

I laughed. "Who would serve a mercenary, harper? You have mistaken me, I say."

Quite calmly he set the harp into its case and closed it up, hooking it to his saddle. Lachlan jumped down from his horse and crossed the snow to me. He knelt swiftly, pulled thick gloves from his belt and folded them, then pulled my sword from the fire cairn. The leather had burned away, and in the last rays of the setting sun the ruby glowed deep crimson. The lion was burnished gold.

Lachlan rose. He held the blade gingerly, careful of the heat even through the gloves, but his smile did not fade. He turned to look at me with subtle triumph in his eyes. "I have leather in my packs," he said quietly. "You will have to wrap it again."

Still I could not move. I wondered how long he meant to hold me. I wondered if he would take me all the way to Mujhara in his ensorcellment, so that Bellam would see me helpless. The thought set my teeth to gritting.

And then I smiled. As Lachlan turned to go to his horse—for the harp, no doubt—Finn stepped around the horse's rump and blocked Lachlan's path. Around the other side came Storr. And the ensorcellment was broken.

I reached out and closed my gloved hand upon the blade of my sword, still in Lachlan's careful grasp. I felt the heat, but it was not enough to burn me. Simply enough to remind me what had so nearly happened.

Lachlan stood quite still. His hands were empty of everything now save the gloves he held, folded in his palms. He waited.

Finn moved closer. Storr followed. I could feel Lachlan's tension increase with every step they took. My own was gone at last; I felt calm, at ease, content to know the confrontation was firmly in our hands. No more in a sorcerous harper's.

"The others are dead." Finn stopped in front of Lachlan.

The harper started. "You *slew* them? But I gave them a task—"

"Aye," Finn agreed ironically. "I prefer to take no chances."

Lachlan opened his mouth to protest, then shut it again. I saw how rigid was his jaw. After a moment he tried again. "Then you have taken five men from Carillon's army. Five men you will miss."

Finn smiled. There was little of amusement in it. "I would sooner take five men from Carillon's army than Carillon himself."

Lachlan looked sharply at me. "You disbelieve me when I say I wish only to aid you. Well enough, I understand it. But he is Cheysuli. He can compel the truth from me. I know of his gifts; I have my own."

"And, having them, you may withstand mine," Finn commented.

Lachlan shook his head. "Without my harp, I have no magic. I am at your disposal. And I am not Ihlini, so you need fear no loss of your own power."

Finn's hands were a blur, reaching to catch the harper's head before Lachlan could move away. He held the skull between both palms, cradling it, as if he sought to crush it, but he did not. Lachlan's own hands came up, reaching to peel Finn's fingers away, but they stopped. The hands fell to his sides. Finn held him there, and went into his mind.

After a moment, when some sense came back to Finn's eyes, he looked at me. "He is a harper, a healer, and a priest. That much I can touch. But nothing else. He is well shielded, no matter that he wishes to claim his innocence."

"Does he serve Bellam or Tynstar?"

"He does not *appear* to." The distinction was deliberate. I looked upon my sword and methodically rubbed the ash and charring from its hilt. "If he is neither Bellam nor Tynstar's man, whose man is he? He had his chance to slay me with that harp, or to take my mind from me. Bellam would give him his gold for a body or a madman." I grimaced. "He might even have used the Homanans as a guard contingent—he has the power with that harp. But he did none of those things."

"Shall I slay him for you?"

I squinted at the ruby, darkening as the sun went down.

"Harpers are traditionally immune from such things as assassination. Petty intrigue they cannot help—I think it is born in them even as the harping is born—but never have I known one to clothe himself in murder."

"Gold can buy any man."

I grinned at him, brows lifting. "A Cheysuli, perhaps?"

Finn scowled. With the fortune in gold on his arms and in his ear, more would hardly tempt him. Or any other warrior. "He is not Cheysuli," was all he said, and the meaning was quite clear.

"No," I agreed, sighing. "But perhaps he is only a spy, not a hired assassin. Spies I can deal with; often they are useful. How else could we have led Bellam this merry dance for five years?" I smiled again. Bellam had sent spies to track us down. Five had even found us. Those we had stripped of their task, giving them a new one instead: to take word to Bellam that we were elsewhere in the world. Usually hundreds of leagues away from where we were. It had worked with three of them.

The others we had slain.

"Then you mean to use him." His tone was perfectly flat, but I knew he was not pleased.

"We will take him with us and see what he means to do."

"You tread a dangerous path, Carillon."

I smiled. "It is already dangerous. This will add a fillip." I laughed at his expression. "It will also keep you in practice, *liege man.* You were slow in coming to my aid."

"I had five men to slay before I could reach the harp." But he frowned a little, and I knew he was not immune to the knowledge that he *had* been slow. Faster than anyone else, perhaps, but slow for a Cheysuli warrior.

"You are getting old, Finn." I gestured. "Set our harper free. Let us see what he intends to do."

Finn released Lachlan. The harper staggered a moment, then caught himself, touching his head with a tentative hand. His eyes were blurred and unfocused. "Have you done?"

"More than done," I agreed. "Now tell us why you wish to aid me."

He rubbed his brow, still frowning slightly. "It is a harper's life to make songs out of heroes and history. You are both, you and your Cheysuli. You should hear the stories they tell." He grinned, his senses restored. "A harper gains his own measure of fame by adding to the fame of others. I could do worse than to ride with Carillon of Homana and his equally infamous liege man."

"You could," I agreed, and let him make of that what he would.

After a moment Lachlan gestured. "Your fire has gone out. Do you wish it, I can give it life again."

I glanced down at the fire cairn. Snow had been kicked into the fire during the scuffle with the Homanans and the weight had finally doused it. "I have flint and steel," I said.

"Your kindling is damp. What I do will take less effort." Lachlan turned to go to his horse for the harp, but Storr was in his way. After a moment a gray-faced harper looked back at me.

I smiled. "Storr does Finn's bidding, when he does not do his own. Look to him."

Lachlan did not move. He waited. And finally Storr moved away.

The harper took down his case from the horse and turned, cradling it against his chest. "You fear I will use sorcery against you?"

"With reason," I declared.

"I will not." He shook his dull, dark head. "Not again. I will use it *for* you, do you wish it, but not against. Never against. We have too much in common."

"What," I asked, "does a mercenary have in common with a harper?"

Lachlan grinned. It was the warm, amused expression I had seen the evening before, as if he knew what I could not, and chose to keep it that way. "I am many things," he said obliquely. "Some of them you know: harper, healer, priest. And one day I will share the rest with you."

I lifted my sword. With great deliberation I set the tip against the lip of the sheath and let Lachlan see the runes, hardly visible in the dying light. Then I slid the sword home with the hiss of steel filling the shadows. "Do you admit to complicity," I said softly, "take care."

Lachlan's smile was gone. Hugging his harp case, he shook his head. "Were I to desire your death, your Chey-suli would give me my own." He cast a quick, flickering glance at Finn. "This is Ellas. We have sheltered the Cheysuli for some years, now. Do you think I discount Finn's skill? No. You need not be wary of me, with him present. I could do nothing."

I gestured. "There is that in your hands."

"My Lady?" He was surprised, then smiled. "Oh, aye, there is her magic. But it is Lodhi's, and I do not use it to kill."

"Then show us how you *can* use it," I bid him. "Show us what other magic you have besides the ability to give us our memories, or to lift our wills from us."

Lachlan looked at Finn, almost invisible in the deepening shadows. "It was difficult, with you. Most men are so shallow, so transient. But you are made of layers. Complex layers, some thin and easily torn away, but in tearing they show the metal underneath. Iron," he said thoughtfully. "I would liken you to iron. Hard and cold and strong."

Finn abruptly gestured toward the fire cairn. "Show us, harper."

Lachlan knelt down by the fire cairn. Deftly he unsealed the harp case—boiled leather hardened nearly to stone by some agent, padded thickly within—and took from it his Lady. The strings, so fragile-seeming, gleamed in the remaining light. The wood, I saw, was ancient, perhaps from some magical tree. It was bound with spun gold. The green stone—an emerald?—glowed.

He knelt in the snow, ignoring the increasing cold, and played a simple lay. It was soft, almost unheard, but remarkable nonetheless. And when his hands grew blurred and quick I saw the spark begin, deep in the damp, charred wood, until a single flame sprouted, swallowed it all, and the fire was born again.

The song died upon the harp. Lachlan looked up at me. "Done," he said.

"So it is, and myself unscathed." I reached down a gloved hand, caught his bare one and pulled him to his feet. His was no soft grasp, no woman's touch designed to keep his harper's fingers limber.

Lachlan smiled as we broke the grip. I thought he had judged me as quickly as I had him. But he said nothing; there was nothing at all to say. We were strangers to one another, though something within me said it would not always be so.

"You ride a blooded horse," I said, looking at the dapple-gray.

"Aye," Lachlan agreed gravely. "The High King likes my music. It was a gift last year."

"You have welcome in Rheghed?" I asked, thinking of the implications.

"Harpers have welcome anywhere." He tugged on his gloves, hunching against the cold. "I doubt not Bellam would have me in Homana-Mujhar, did I go."

He challenged me with his eyes. I smiled, but Finn did not. "Aye, I doubt not." I turned to Finn. "Have we food?"

"Something like," he affirmed, "but only if you are willing to eat coney-meat. Game is scarce."

I sighed. "Coney is not my favorite, but I prefer it to none at all."

Finn laughed. "Then at least I have taught you something in these past years. Once you might have demanded venison."

"I knew no better, then." I shook my head. "Even princes learn they have empty bellies like anyone else, when their titles are taken from them."

Lachlan's hands were on his harp as he set it within its case. "Which title?" he asked. "Prince or Mujhar?"

"Does it matter? Bellam has stolen them both."

When the coneys were nothing but gristle and bone—and Storr demolished the remains quickly enough—Lachlan brought out a skin of harsh wine from his saddlepacks and passed it to me. I sat cross-legged on my two pelts, trying to ignore the night's cold as it settled in my bones. The wine was somewhat bitter but warming, and after a long draw I handed it to Finn. Very solemnly he accepted it, then invoked his Cheysuli gods with elaborate distinction, and I saw Lachlan's eyes upon him. Finn's way of mocking another man's beliefs won him few friends, but he wanted none. He saw no sense in it, with Storr.

Lachlan retrieved the skin at last, drank, then passed it on to me. "Will you tell me what I must know, then? A saga is built out of fact, not fancy. Tell me how it was a king could destroy the race that had served him and his House so well."

"Finn would do better to tell it." If he would.

Finn, sitting on his pelts with Storr against one thigh, shrugged. The earring glinted in the firelight. In the shadows he seemed more alien than ever, part of the nighttime itself. "What is there to say? Shaine declared *qu'mahlin* on us for no good reason . . . and we died." He paused. "Most of us."

"*You* live," Lachlan commented.

Finn's smile was not precisely a smile, more a movement of his lips, as if he would bare his teeth. "The gods saw another way for me. My *tahlmorra* was to serve the prophecy in later years, not die as a helpless child." His hand went out to bury itself in Storr's thick hair.

Lachlan hesitated, cradling his harp case. "May I have the beginning?" he asked at last, with careful intonation.

Finn laughed. There was no humor in it. "What is the beginning, harper? I cannot say, and yet I was a part of it." He looked at me a moment, fixedly, as if the memories had swallowed him.

I swallowed, remembering too. "The fault lay in a man's overweening pride." I did not know how else to begin. "My uncle, Shaine the Mujhar—who wanted a son and had none—tried to wed his daughter to Ellic of Solinde, Bellam's son, in hopes of ending the war. But that daughter sought another man: Cheysuli, Shaine's own liege man, turning her back on the alliance and the betrothal. She fled her father, fled Homana-Mujhar, and with her went the warrior."

"My *jehan*," Finn said before I could continue. "Father, you would say. Hale. He took Lindir from her *tahlmorra* and fashioned another for them both. For us all; it has resulted in disaster." He stared into the fire. "It took a king in the throat of his pride, strangling him, until he could not bear it. And when his *cheysula* died of a wasting disease, and his second bore no living children, he determined the Cheysuli had cursed his House." His head moved slightly, as if to indicate regret. "And he declared *qu'mahlin* on us all."

Lachlan frowned intently. "A woman, then. The catalyst of it all."

"Lindir," I agreed. "My cousin. Enough like Shaine, in woman's form, to be a proper son. Except she was a daughter, and used her pride to win her escape."

"What did she say to the result?"

I shook my head. "No one knows. She came back to her
father eight years later when she was heavy with Hale's
child, because he was dead and she had no other place to
go. Shaine took her back because he needed a male heir;
when the child was born a girl he banished her to the
woods so the beasts could have their shapechanger halfling.
But Alix lived because Shaine's arms-master—and the
Queen of Homana herself—begged the Mujhar to give her
to man instead of beast." I shifted on my pelts. "Lindir
died bearing Alix. What she thought of the *qu'mahlin* I
could not say, but it slew her warrior and nearly destroyed
his race."

Lachlan considered it all. And then he looked at Finn.
"How is it, then, you serve Carillon? Shaine the Mujhar
was his uncle."

Finn put out his hand and made the familiar gesture.
"Because of this. *Tahlmorra.* I have no choice." He smiled
a little. "You may call it fate, or destiny, or whatever Ellasian word you have for such things . . . we believe each
child is born with a *tahlmorra* that must be heeded when
the gods make it known. The prophecy of the Firstborn
says one day a man of all blood shall unite, in peace, four
warring realms and two magic races. Carillon is a part of
that prophecy." He shook his head, solemn in the firelight.
"Had I a choice, I would put off such binding service, but
I am Cheysuli, and such things are not done."

"Enemies become friends." Lachlan nodded slowly, staring fixedly into the fire as if he already heard the music.
"It would make a fine lay. A story to break hearts and
rend souls, and show others that hardships are nothing
compared to what the Cheysuli have suffered. Do you give
me leave, Finn, I will—"

"—do what?" Finn demanded. "Embellish the truth?
Change the story in the interests of rhyme and resonance?
No. I deny you that leave. What I have suffered—and my
clan—is not for others to know."

My hands, hooked loosely over my knees, curled into
fists that dug the bluntness of my nails into the leather of
my gloves. Finn rarely spoke of his past or his personal
feelings, being an intensely private man, but as he spoke I
heard all the pain and emotion in his voice. Raw and unfet-
tered, in the open at last.

Lachlan met his eyes. "I would embellish nothing, with such truth," he said quietly. "I think there would be no need."

Finn said something in the Old Tongue, the ancient language of the Cheysuli. I had learned words and phrases in the past years, but when Finn resorted to it out of anger or frustration—or high emotions—I could understand none of it. The lyrical syllables became slurred and indistinct, yet managed to convey his feelings just the same. I winced, knowing what Lachlan must feel.

But Finn stopped short. He never yelled, having no need, but his quietness was just as effective. Yet silence was something altogether different, and I thought perhaps something had stopped him. Then I saw the odd detached expression in his face, and the blankness of his eyes, and realized Storr conversed with him.

What the wolf said I cannot guess, but I saw Finn's face darken in the firelight with heavy color, then go pale and grim. Finally he unlocked his jaw and spoke.

"I was a boy." The words were so quiet I could hardly hear them over the snap and crackle of the flames. "Three years old." His hand tightened in the silver fur of Storr's neck. I wondered, with astonishment at the thought, if he sought support from his *lir* to speak of his childhood clearly. It was not something he had said to me before, not even when I had asked. "I had sickened with some childish fever, and kept to my *jehana*'s skirts like a fool with no wits." His eyes hooded a little, but he smiled, as if the memory amused him. Briefly only; there was little of amusement in the tale. "Sleep brought me no peace, only bad dreams, and it was hot within the pavilion. It was dark, so dark, and I thought the demons would steal my soul. I was so hot." A heavy swallow rippled the flesh of his throat. "Duncan threw water on the fire to douse it, thinking to help, but he only made it smoke, and it choked me. Finally he fell asleep, and my *jehana*, but I could not."

I glanced at Lachlan. He was transfixed.

Finn paused. The firelight filled his eyes. "And then the Keep was full of the thunder of the gods, only the thunder came from men. The Mujhar's men. They swept into our Keep like demons from the netherworld, determined to destroy us all. They set fire to the pavilion."

Lachlan started. "With *children* inside?"

"Aye," Finn said grimly. "Ours they knocked down with their horses, then they dropped a torch on it." His eyes flicked to Lachlan's astonished face. "We paint our pavilions, harper. Paint burns very quickly."

Lachlan started to speak, as if to halt the recital. Finn went on regardless, perhaps purging his soul at last.

"Duncan pulled me from the fire before it could consume us all. My *jehana* took us both into the trees, and there we hid until daylight. By then the men were gone, but so was most of our Keep." He took a deep breath. "I was young, too young to fully understand, but even a child of three learns how to hate." The eyes came around to me. "I was born two days before Hale went away with Lindir, and still he took her. Still he went from the Keep to Homana-Mujhar, and helped his *meijha,* his mistress, escape. And so Shaine, when he set his men upon us, made certain Hale's Keep was the first."

Lachlan, after a long moment of silence, shook his head. "I have gifts many men do not, because of Lodhi and my Lady. But even *I* cannot tell the tale as you do." His face was very still. "I will leave it to those who can. I will leave it to the Cheysuli."

Chapter Five

When at last we drew near the Keep a day later, Finn grew pensive and snappish. It was unlike him. We had dealt well together, though only after I had grown used to having a Cheysuli at my side, and after *he* had grown accustomed to riding with a Homanan. Now we had come home again, at least to his mind; home again, would Finn put off his service?

It set the hairs to rising on my neck. I had no wish to lose Finn. I needed him still. I had learned much in the years of exile, but I had yet to learn what it was to lay claim to a stolen throne. Without Finn, the task would be close to impossible.

He pulled up his mount sharply, hissing invectives beneath his breath. And then his face went blank with the uncanniness of the *lir*-bond and I knew he conversed with the wolf.

Lachlan, wise harper, said nothing. He waited as I did. But the tension that was a tangible thing did not appear to touch him.

Finn broke free of the contact at last. I had watched his face; had seen it grow hard and sharp and bleak, like his eyes. And now I grew afraid.

"What is it?" I hissed.

"Storr sends a warning." Finn shivered suddenly, though the sunlight that glittered off his earring was warm upon our shoulders. "I think I feel it myself. I will go in. Keep yourself here." He looked at Lachlan a moment, considering something, by the look in his eyes. Then he shrugged, dismissing it. "Keep yourself here, as I said, until I come back for you."

He spoke lightly enough, no doubt for Lachlan's benefit,

but I could not wait for subterfuge. I caught the rein of his horse and held him still. "Tell me. What is it?"

Finn looked again at Lachlan, and then he looked at me. "Storr can touch no *lir*."

"None?"

"Not even Alix."

"But—with her Old Blood—" I stopped. He need say no more. Could Storr touch no *lir* at all, the situation was grave indeed. "There may be danger for you as well," I told him quietly.

"Of course. So I go in *lir*-shape." He dropped off his horse at once, leaving me with a skittish animal at the end of a leather rein. *"Tahlmorra lujhala mei wiccan, cheysu,"* he said to me, shrugging, and then he was no longer a man.

I watched Lachlan. As the space in which Finn stood emptied, swallowed instead by the void, Lachlan's eyes stretched wide. And then they narrowed as he frowned, staring as if he would learn it himself. His fingers dropped to the harp case at his knee, touching it as if to reassure himself he was awake, not asleep. By the time I looked back at Finn the man-shape was completely gone, replaced by the blurred outline of a wolf. I felt the familiar rolling of my belly, swallowed against it, as always, and looked at Lachlan again. His face had taken on a peculiar greenish hue. I thought he might vomit up his fear and shock, but he did not.

The ruddy wolf with Finn's yellow eyes flicked his tail and ran.

"They do not merit fear," I told Lachlan clearly, "unless you have done something to merit their enmity." I smiled as his eyes turned to me, staring as if he thought I too might be a wolf, or something equally bestial. "You are an innocent man, you have said: a harper . . . what have *you* to fear from Finn?"

But a man does not stop fearing the specter of childhood nightmares so easily, no matter how innocent he is. Lachlan—with, perhaps, more guilt than he claimed—might have better reason to fear what he saw. He stared after Finn, seeing nothing now, but the greenish pallor had been replaced by the white of shock and apprehension. *"Wolves* cannot know reason! Does he know you in that shape?"

"Finn, in that shape, knows everything a man knows," I

said. "But he also claims the wisdom of a wolf. A double threat, you might say, for one who deserves careful consideration." I shifted in the saddle, half my mind with Finn and the other half knowing what Lachlan felt. I had felt it myself, the first few times. "He is not a demon or a beast. He is a man who claims a god-gift in his blood, much as you claim it in yours. It is only his gods manifest their presence a little differently." I thought of the magic he made with his music, and then I laughed at his horrified expression. "Think you he worships Lodhi? Not Finn. Perhaps he *worships* no god, or gods, but he serves his own better than any man I have ever known. How else do you think he would keep himself to my side?" Finn's horse tried to wander, searching for grass in the snow, and I pulled him back. "You need have no fear he might turn on you, wolflike, and tear your throat from your body. He would do that only if you gave him reason." I met the harper's eyes steadily, keeping my tone light. "But then you have no wish to betray me, have you? Not with your saga at stake."

"No." Lachlan tried to smile, but I could see the thoughts in his head. No man, seeing the shapechange for the first time, forgets it so quickly. If at all. "What was it he said to you, before he changed himself?"

I laughed. "A philosophy, of sorts. Cheysuli, of course, and therefore alien to Homanans or Ellasians." I quoted the words: "*Tahlmorra lujhala mei wiccan, cheysu.* It means, roughly, the fate of a man rests always within the hands of the gods." I made the gesture, being very distinct as I lifted my right hand and spread my fingers. "It is usually shortened to the word *tahlmorra,* which says more than enough quite simply."

Lachlan shook his head slowly. "Not so alien to me, I think. Do you forget I am a priest? Admittedly my god is singular, and far different from those Finn claims, but I am trained to understand the faith a man holds. More than trained; I believe it with all my heart, that a man may know and serve his deity." His hand tapped the harp case. "My gift is there, Carillon. Finn's is elsewhere, but just as strong. And he is just as devout, perhaps more so, to give himself up to his fate." He smiled. "*Tahlmorra lujhala mei wiccan, cheysu.* How eloquent a phrase."

"Have you any like it?"

Lachlan laughed. "You could never say it. You lack an Ellasian throat." He thumped the harp case. "This one is not so hard: *Yhana Lodhi, yffennog faer.*" He smiled. "A man walks with pride forever when he walks with Lodhi, humble."

And then Finn was back, two-legged and white-faced, and I had no more time for philosophy. I held out the rein as Finn reached for it, but I could ask none of the questions that crowded my mouth. Finn's face had robbed me of my voice.

"Destroyed," he said in a whisper. "Torn down. *Burned.*" His pallor was alarming. "There is no Keep."

I was over the broken stonework before I realized what it was, setting my horse to jumping though he lacked the legs to do it. He stumbled, scrabbling at the snow-cloaked heaps of mortared stone, and then I knew. The wall, the half-circle wall that surrounded every Keep. Shattered and broken upon the ground.

I pulled up at once, saving the horse, but also saving myself. I sat silently on the little gelding, staring at what remained of the Keep. Bit by bit I looked, allowing myself one portion at a time; I could not bear to see it all at once.

Snow covered nearly everything, but scavenger beasts had dug up the remains. I saw the long poles, some snapped in two, some charred. I saw scraps of soiled cloth frozen into stiffness, colors muted by time and harsh weather. The fire cairns that had stood before each pavilion lay in tumbled fragments, spilled by hostile feet and destructive hooves. All of it gone, with only ragged remnants of a once-proud Keep.

In my mind I saw it as I had seen it last: undressed, unmortared stone standing high to guard the Keep; billowing pavilions of varied hues emblazoned with painted *lir.* The perches and pelts existing for those *lir,* and the children who feared nothing of the wild. Save, perhaps, for those who knew to fear Homanans.

I cursed. It came viciously out of my mouth along with the spittle. I thought of Duncan, clan-leader of his Keep, but mostly I thought of Alix.

I rode on then. Directly to the proper place. I knew it well enough, though nothing remained to mark it. And there I slid off my horse, too stiff to dismount with any skill or grace, and fell down upon my knees.

One pole pierced its way through snow to stab out of the ruins like a standard. A scrap of fabric, stiff from freezing, still clung to the wood. I tugged at it and it came away, breaking off in my hand. Slate-colored, with the faintest blur of gold and brown. For Cai, Duncan's hawk.

Not once had I thought they might be dead. Not once, in all the time spent in exile, had I thought they might be gone. They had been the one constant in my life, along with Finn. Always I had recalled the Keep and the clan-leader's pavilion, filled with Duncan's pride and Alix's strength, and the promise of the unborn child. Never once had I even considered they might not be here to greet me.

But it was not the greeting I missed. It was the conviction of life, no matter where it existed. Nothing lived here now.

I heard the sound behind me and knew at once it was Finn. Slowly, suddenly old beyond my years, I stood up. I trembled as if with illness, knowing only a great sorrow and rage and consuming grief.

Gods . . . they could not be dead—

Lachlan made a sound. I looked at him blindly, thinking only of Alix and Duncan, and then I saw the expression of realization in his eyes.

Finn saw it also. As he leaped, still in human form, I caught him in mid-stride. "Wait—"

"He knew."

The words struck me in the face. But still I held Finn. "Wait. Do you slay him, we will learn nothing from him. Wait—"

Lachlan stood rooted to the earth. One hand thrust outward as if to hold us back. His face was white. "I will tell you. I will tell you what I can."

I let go of Finn when I knew he would do nothing more. At least until he had better reason. "Then Finn has the right of it: you knew."

Lachlan nodded stiffly. "I knew. Have known. But I had forgotten. It was—three years ago."

"Three years." I stared around the remains of the Keep. "Harper—what happened?"

He looked steadily at me. "Ihlini."

Finn hissed something in the Old Tongue. I merely

waited for further explanation. But I said one thing: "This is Ellas. Do you say Tynstar has influence here?"

Dull color came up into Lachlan's face. "I say nothing of that. Ellas is free of Ihlini domination. But once, only once, there was a raid across the border. Ihlini and Solindish, hunting the Cheysuli who sheltered in this realm, and they came here." A muscle ticked in his jaw. "There have been songs made about it, but it is not something I care to recall. I had nearly forgotten."

"Remember," Finn said curtly. "Remember it all, harper."

Lachlan spread his hands. "The Ihlini came here. They destroyed the Keep. They slew who they could of the Cheysuli."

"How many?" Finn-demanded.

"Not all." Lachlan scrubbed a hand across his brow, as if he wished to free himself of the silver circlet of his calling. "I—do not know, perhaps, as much as I should."

"Not enough and too much, all at once," Finn said grimly. "Harper, you should have spoken earlier. You knew we came to the Keep."

"How am I to know them *all?*" Lachlan demanded. "The High King gives the Cheysuli shelter, but he does not count them, old or young. I doubt *Rhodri* can say how many Keeps or how many Cheysuli are in Ellas. We merely welcome them all."

This time it was Finn who colored, but only for a moment. The grief and tension were back at once, etching lines into his face. He wore his mask again, the private mask, stark and hard in his insularity. "They may all be dead. And that would leave only me—" He broke off.

Lachlan took a deep breath. "I have heard that those who survived went back into Homana. North. Across the Bluetooth River."

Finn frowned. "Too far," he muttered, looking at Storr. "Too far even for the *lir*-link."

I looked directly at Lachlan. "You have heard much for a man who recalls so little. To Homana, you say. North, across the Bluetooth. Are you privy to information we have no recourse to?"

He did not smile. "Harpers are privy to much, as you should know. Had you none in Homana-Mujhar?"

"Many," I said briefly. "Before Bellam silenced the music."

Finn turned his back. He stared again at the remains of Duncan's slate-gray pavilion. I knew he meant to master himself. I wondered if he could.

"May I suggest," Lachlan began, "that you use my harp skill in trying to rouse your people? I could go into taverns and sing *The Song of Homana,* to test how the people feel. How better to learn their minds, and how they will answer their rightful king's call?"

"The Song of Homana?" Finn said doubtfully, turning to stare at Lachlan.

"You have heard it," the harper said, "and I saw what it did to you. It has a magic of its own."

He spoke the truth. Did he go into Homanan taverns and play that song on his Lady, he would know sooner than anyone else what my people were capable of. Had Bellam cowed them, it would take time to rebuild their spirit. Were they merely angry, I could use it.

I nodded at Lachlan. "The horses require tending."

For a moment he frowned, baffled, and then he understood. Silently he took away our horses and gave us room to speak freely, without fear he might overhear.

"I give you leave to go," I told Finn simply.

Something flickered in his eyes. "There is no need."

"There is. You must go. Your clan—your kin—have gone north across the Bluetooth. Home to Homana, where we are bound. You must go and find them, to set your soul at peace."

He did not smile. "Healing Homana is more important than seeking out my clan."

"Is it?" I shook my head. "You told me once that clan- and kin-ties bind more closely than anything else in Cheysuli culture. I have not forgotten. I give you leave to go, so I can have you whole again." I held up a silencing hand. "Until you know, it will eat at your soul like a canker."

The flesh of his face was stiff. "I will not leave you in companionship to the enemy."

I shook my head. "We do not know if he is an enemy."

"He knows too much," Finn said grimly. "Too much and too little. I do not trust him."

"Then trust me." I put out my gloved hand and spread

my fingers, palm up. "Have you not taught me all you can in the art of staying alive, even in dire adversity? I am no longer quite the green princeling escorted into exile. I think I may have some control over my life." I smiled. "You have said it is my *tahlmorra* to take back the Lion Throne. If so, it will happen, and nothing will gainsay it. Not even this time apart."

He shook his head slowly. "*Tahlmorras* may be broken, Carillon. Do not mislead yourself into believing you are safe."

"Have more faith in me," I chided. "Go north and find Alix and Duncan. Bring them back." I frowned a moment. "Bring them to Torrin's croft. It was Alix's home, and if he is still alive it will be a place of sanctuary for us all."

He looked at the ruined pavilion, buried under snow. And then he looked at Storr. He sighed. "Rouse your people, my lord of Homana. And I will bring home the Cheysuli."

Chapter Six

Mujhara. It rose out of the plains of Homana like an eagle on an aerie, walled about with rose-red stone and portcullised barbican gates. Homana-Mujhar was much the same: walled and gated and pink. The palace stood within the city on a hill. Not high, but higher than any other. Lachlan and I rode through the main gate into Mujhara, and at once I knew I was home.

Save I was not. My home was filled with Solindish soldiers, hung about with ringmail and boiled leather and glinting silver swords. They let us in because they knew no better, thinking Homana's rightful lord would never ride so willingly into his prison.

I heard the Solindish tongue spoken in the streets of Mujhara more than I heard Homanan. Lachlan and I spoke Ellasian merely to be safe. But I thought I could say anything and be unacknowledged; Bellam's soldiers were bored. After five years and no threat from without, they lived lazily within.

The magnificence was gone. I thought perhaps it was my own lack of discernment, having spent so long in foreign lands, but it was not. The city, once so proud, had lost interest in itself. It housed a Mujhar who had stolen his throne, and the Homanans did not care to praise his name. Why should they praise his city? Where once the windows had glittered with glass or glowed with horn, now the eyes were dark and dim, smoked over, puttied at corners with dirt and grime. The white-washed walls were dingy and gray, some fouled with streaks of urine. The cobbled streets had crumbled, decayed until the stench hung over it like a miasma. I did not doubt Homana-Mujhar remained fit for a king, but the rest of the city did not.

Lachlan looked at me once, then again. "Look not so angry, or they will know."

"I am sick," I said curtly. "I could vomit on this vileness. What have they done to my city?"

Lachlan shook his head. "What defeated people do everywhere: they live. They go on. You cannot blame them for it. The heart has gone out of their lives. Bellam exacts overharsh taxes so no one can afford to eat, let alone wash their houses. And the streets? Why clean dung when the great ass sits upon the throne?"

I glanced at him sharply. He did not speak as Bellam's man, saying what he should to win my regard. He spoke like a man who understood the reasons for Mujhara's condition— disliking it, perhaps, as much as I, but tolerating it better. Perhaps it was because he was Ellasian, and a harper, with no throne to make his own.

"I am sorry you must see it this way," I told him with feeling. "When *I*—" I broke it off at once. What good lies in predicting something that may not happen?

Lachlan gestured. "Here, a tavern. Shall we go in? Perhaps here we will find better fortune than we found at the village taverns."

We had better. Failure rankled, though I understood it. It is difficult to ask poor crofters to give up what little they have to answer the call of an outlawed prince. It was soldiers I needed first, and then what other men I could find.

I stared at the tavern grimly. It looked like all the others: gray and dingy and dim. And then I looked at Lachlan.

He smiled, but it lacked all humor, a hooking down of his mouth. "Of course. We will go on to another . . . one you will choose for yourself."

I jumped off my horse, swore when I slipped in some muck, and scraped my boot against a loosened cobble. "This will do well enough. Come in, and bring your harp."

Lachlan went in before me when he had taken his Lady from his saddle. I paused to let him enter alone, then went in behind him, shoving open the narrow, studded door.

At once I ducked. The beamwork of the dark roof was low, so low it made me wince against its closeness. The floor beneath my feet was earthen, packed, but bits of it had been scraped into ridges and little piles of dirt, as if the benches and tables had been dragged across it to rest in different places. I put up a hand to tear away the sticky webbing that looped down from the beam beside my head. It clung to my fingers until I scrubbed it off against the cracked, hardened leather of my jerkin.

A single lantern depended from a hook set into the central beam, painted black with pitch. It shed dim light over the common room. A few candles stood out on the tables, fat and greasy and stinking. There was little light in the place, just a sickly yellow glow and the haze of ocherous smoke.

Lachlan, with his harp, was welcomed at once. There were perhaps twenty men scattered around the common room, but they made way for him at once, drawing up a stool and bidding him begin. I found a table near the door and sat down, asking for ale when the tavern-master arrived. It was good brown ale when it came, hearty and woody; I drank the first cup down with relish.

Lachlan opened with a sprightly lay to liven them up. They clapped and cheered, urging him on, until he sang a sad song of a girl and her lover, murdered by her father. It brought a less exuberant response but no less a liking for Lachlan's skill. And then he picked out the opening notes of *The Song of Homana*.

He got no more than halfway through the tale. Abruptly a soldier in Solindish ringmail and too much wine pushed to his feet and drew his sword. "Treason!" he shouted. He wavered on his feet, and I realized how drunk he was. "You sing *treason!*" His Homanan was poor, but he was clearly understandable. So was his implication as he raised the shining sword.

I was on my feet at once. My own sword was in my hand, but other men had already seized the soldier and forced him down on his stool, relieving him of his sword. It clanged to the floor and was kicked away. Lachlan, I saw, had set down his Lady in the center of a table, and his hand was near his knife.

Four men held the soldier in place. A fifth moved to stand before him. "You are alone here, Solindishman," he said. "Quite *alone.* This is a Homanan tavern and we are all Homanans; we invite the harper to finish his lay. You will sit and listen . . . unless I bid you otherwise." He jerked his head. "Bind him and stop up his mouth!"

The soldier was instantly bound and gagged, propped upon the stool like a sheep held down for shearing. With less tenderness. The young man who had ordered him bound cast an assessive glance around the room. I saw his eyes on me, black in the dimness of the candlelight. They paused, oddly intent though seemingly indifferent, and moved on.

He smiled. He was young, eighteen or nineteen, I thought, with an economy of movement that reminded me of Finn. So did his black hair and the darkness of his face. "We have silenced this fool," he said calmly. "Now we shall let the harper finish."

I sheathed my sword and sat down slowly. I was aware of the men who had moved in behind me, ranging themselves along the wall. The door, I saw, was barred. This was not an unaccustomed occurrence, then; the Solindish were the hunted.

The knowledge made me smile.

Lachlan completed his lay. The final note, dying out, was met with absolute silence. I felt a trickle of forboding run quickly down my spine; I shivered, disliking the sensation. And yet I could not shake it from me.

"Well sung," the black-eyed young man said at last. "You have a feel for our plight, it seems. And yet you are Ellasian."

"Ellasian, aye." Lachlan raised a cup of water to his mouth and sipped. "But I have traveled many lands and have admired Homana for years."

"What is left to admire?" the Homanan demanded. "We are a defeated land."

"For now, aye, but do you not wait only for your prince to return?" Smiling, Lachlan plucked a single string of his Lady. The sound hung in the air a moment, and then it faded away. "The former glory you aspire to have again . . . it may come."

The young man leaned forward on his stool. "Tell me— you travel, as you say—do you think Carillon hears of our need? Do you sing this song wherever you go, surely you have had *some* response!"

"There is fear," Lachlan said quietly. "Men are in fear of Solindish retribution. What army could Carillon raise, were he to come home again?"

"Fear?" The other nodded. "Aye, there is fear. What else could there be in this land? We need a lord again, a man who can rouse this realm into rebellion." He had all the dedication of the fanatic, and yet there was little of the madness in him, I thought. He was desperate; so was I. "I will not lie and say it would be easy, harper, but I think Carillon would find more than a few ready to rally to his standard."

I thought of the crofters, muttering into their wine and ale. I thought of what little success we had had in learning if Homana desired my return.

"What would you do," Lachlan asked, "were he to come home again?"

The other laughed with a bitterness older than his years. "Join him. These few you see. Not many, but a beginning. Still, there are more of us yet. We meet in secret, to plot, and to aid Carillon however we may. In hopes he will come home."

"Bellam is powerful," Lachlan warned, and I wondered what more he knew.

The Homanan nodded. "He is indeed strong, and claims many troops who serve him well. And with Tynstar at his side, he is certainly no weak king. But Carillon brought the Cheysuli into Homana-Mujhar before, and nearly defeated the Ihlini. This time he might succeed."

"Only with help."

"He will have it."

Lachlan nodded idly. "There are strangers among you. Even I, Ellasian though I may be."

"You are a harper." The young man frowned. "Harpers have immunity, of course. As for the soldier, he will be slain."

Lachlan looked at me across the room. "And the other?"

The Homanan merely smiled. And then the men were at my back, asking for my knife and sword. After a moment's hesitation, I gave them into their hands. Two men remained behind me, another at my left side. The young man was taking no chances. "He will be slain, of course."

Of course. I smiled at Lachlan, who merely bided his time.

The knife was given to the young man. He looked at it briefly, frowning over the Caledonese runes and scripture, then set it aside on the nearest table. The sword was given to him then, and he did not at once put it down. He admired the edge, then saw the runes set into the silver. His eyes widened. "Cheysuli-made!" He glanced sharply at me. "How did you get this?" For a moment something moved in his face. "Off a dead man, no doubt. Cheysuli swords are rare."

"No," I said. "From a live one. And now, before you slay me, I bid you do one thing."

"*Bid* me?" He stared, brows rising beneath the black hair. "Ask, perhaps . . . but it does not mean I will answer."

I did not move. "Cut the leather free."

His hands were on the hilt. I saw him look down at the leather, feeling the tautness of it. I had wrapped it well, and would do so again.

"Cut the leather free."

His stare challenged me a moment. And then he drew his knife and did precisely as I asked.

The leather fell free of his hand. He stared at the hilt: the rampant, royal lion of purest Cheysuli gold, the burnished grip, the massive ruby clutched in curving prongs. The magnificent Mujhar's Eye.

"Say what it is, so all will know," I told him quietly.

"The lion crest of Homana." His eyes moved from the hilt to my face, and I smiled.

"Who carries this sword, this crest?"

Color had left his face. "The blood of the House of Homana." He paused. Then, in a rush of breath and words, "But you might have *stolen* this sword!"

I glanced pointedly at my guards. "You have disarmed me. Say I may come forward."

"Come, then." Color was back in his face. He was young, and angry, and afraid of what he thought he might hear.

I rose, pushing away my stool. Slowly I walked forward, looking only at the young man, and then I stopped before him. He was tall, Cheysuli-tall, but I was taller still.

I pushed back the sleeve on my left arm, showing him the scar that ringed my wrist. "See you that? I have another exactly like it, on my right. You should know them both, Rowan." He flinched in surprise. "You were prisoner to Keough of Atvia, as I was. You were flogged because you spilled wine on Keough himself, even though I asked them to spare you. Your back must show signs of the flogging, even as my arms show the mark of the iron." I let go the sleeve. "May I have my sword back, now?"

Stiffly, he lowered his head to look at it in his hands. And then, as if realizing the history of the blade, he thrust it out to me. I accepted it, feeling safer almost at once, and then he dropped to his knees.

"My lord," he whispered. "Oh, my lord . . . forgive me!"

I slid the sword home in its sheath. "There is nothing to forgive. You have done what you should have done."

He stared up at me. I saw how his eyes were yellow in the candlelight; I had always thought him Cheysuli. It was Rowan who denied it. "How soon do we fight, my lord?"

I laughed at his eagerness. "It is late winter now. It will take time to gather what men we can. In true spring, perhaps, we can begin the raiding parties." I gestured. "Get up from there. This is not the place. I am not the Mujhar quite yet."

He remained where he was. "Will you formally accept my service?"

I reached down and caught his woollen shirt and leather jerkin, pulling him to his feet. "I told you to get up from the floor," I said mildly, startled to find him so grown. He had been but thirteen the last time I had seen him.

Rowan straightened his clothing. "Aye, my lord."

I turned to the other men. Rowan's, all of them, intent upon rebellion. And now intent upon the scene before them; not quite believing the prince he had promised had come into their midst.

I cleared my throat. "Most of you are too young to recall Homana before the days of the *qu'mahlin,* when my uncle the Mujhar ordered every Cheysuli slain. You have grown up fearing and distrusting them, as I did myself. But I learned differently, and so must you." I put up a silencing hand. "They are not demons. They are not beasts. They serve nothing of the netherworld; they serve *me.*" I paused. "Has any of you ever even *seen* a Cheysuli warrior?" There was a chorus of denials, even from Rowan. I looked at each man, one by one. "I will have no bloodshed among my men. The Cheysuli are not your foes."

"But—" one man began, then squirmed beneath my eye. "It is not easy to forget a thing you have been taught to believe," I went on, more quietly. "I know that better than you think. But I also think, once you have got over your superstitious fears of something you cannot comprehend, you will see they are no different from any other." I paused. "You had *better*."

Rowan, behind me, laughed once. I thought there was relief in his tone.

"Will you serve me," I asked, "even with the Cheysuli by my side?"

Agreement. No denials. I searched for reluctance and found none.

"And so the *Song* continues," murmured Lachlan, and at that I laughed aloud.

It was Rowan who told me of my kin, what remained of it: my mother and my sister. We sat alone at a corner table, speaking of plans for the army we must gather. He spoke clearly and at length, having spent much of his time considering how best it could be done, and I was grateful for his care. He would make the preparation much easier. But when at last he chanced to say, off-handedly, that my mother no doubt missed my sister's company, I raised my hand to stop him.

"Is Tourmaline not at Joyenne?"

Rowan shook his head. "Bellam took her hostage. Years ago; I think it was not long after you escaped from Homana-Mujhar."

Escaped—Tynstar had *let* me go. I picked at the scarred wood of the table and bid Rowan to continue.

He shrugged, at a loss for what to tell me. "The Lady Gwynneth is kept at Joyenne, well-guarded. Princess Tourmaline, as I said, is at Homana-Mujhar. Bellam seeks to hold anything that might bring you to him. He dares not allow either of them freedom, for fear they could be used as a rallying point for the rebellion."

"Instead of me?" I ran a hand through my beard to scratch the flesh beneath. "Well, Bellam will be busy with me. There is no need for him to hold two women."

"He will," Rowan asserted. "He will never let them go." He stopped a moment, eyeing me tentatively. "There is even talk he will wed the lady, your sister."

I spat out an oath and nearly stood up, hand to my re-

wrapped sword hilt. Instead I sat down again and hacked
at the table with my knife, adding yet more scars to the
wood. "Torry would not allow it," I said flatly, knowing
she would have little to say about it. Women did not when
it came to their disposal.

Rowan smiled. "I had heard she was not an acquiescent
hostage. And with two women in one castle—" He laughed
aloud, genuinely amused.

"Two?"

"His daughter, the Princess Electra." Rowan frowned.
"There is talk she is Tynstar's light woman."

"Tynstar's." I stared at him, sitting upright on my stool.
"Bellam gives his daughter over to *that?*"

"I heard it was Tynstar's price." Rowan shifted on his
bench. "My lord, there is little I can tell you. Most is merely
rumor. I would not dare claim any of it as truth."

"There is some truth in rumor," I said thoughtfully, taking up my ale again. "If she is Tynstar's light woman, there
is a use for her in my plans."

"You wish to use a woman against the *sorcerer?*" Rowan
shook his head. "Begging your pardon, my lord, I think
you are mistaken."

"Princes are never mistaken." I grinned at his instant
discomfort. *"All* men can be mistaken, and fools if they
think not. Well enough, we shall have to consider a plan.
Two of them—to wrest my mother from Joyenne, and
Torry from Homana-Mujhar." I frowned, wishing Finn
were with me. To set a trap without him—I focused on
Rowan again. "For a man who swears he is not Cheysuli,
you are the perfect image of a warrior."

Dark color moved through Rowan's face. "I know it. It
has been my bane."

"There is no danger in it, with me. You could admit it
freely—"

"I admit nothing!" I was pleased he did not hide his
anger, even before his prince. Treacherous are men who
are all obsequious nods and bows, never letting me see
their hearts. "I have said I am not Cheysuli," he repeated.
"My lord."

I laughed at his stiff, remembered formality. And then
the laughter died away, for I heard Lachlan harping in the
background. Making magic with his Lady.

I turned to look at my enigmatic ally. Ellasian. A stranger who wished to be my friend, he said. Bellam's man? Or Tynstar's? Or merely his own, too cunning to work for another? I still doubted him.

Slowly I rose. Rowan rose with me, out of courtesy, but I could see the puzzlement in his eyes. I went across the room and stopped at Lachlan's table, seeing how his blue eyes were black in the yellow light of the tavern.

He stopped playing at once, his fingers still resting upon the gleaming strings. His clustered audience, seeing my face, moved away in silence.

I drew my sword from its sheath. I saw the sudden flaring of fear in Lachlan's eyes. A sour, muted note sang from his harp and then stilled, but the candles and lantern guttered out.

Darkness. But not so dark there was no light. Merely shadows. And the sorcerous green stone in Lachlan's Lady gave off enough brilliance to see by.

His fingers were in the strings. But so was the tip of my sword.

I saw it in his face: the fear I would harm his harp. Slay it, like an animal, or a man. As if the wood and wire lived. "Put her down—your Lady," I said gently, having felt her magic twice.

He did not move. The stoneglow washed across the blade of my sword, setting the runes to glinting in its light. And in that light I knew power, ancient and strong and true.

The blade was parallel to the strings, touching nothing. Slowly I turned it. One string whined its protest, but I held it back from death.

Lachlan bent forward a little, sliding the harp free of my sword. Carefully he set his Lady in the center of the table and took his hands away. He waited then, quietly, his arms empty of his harp.

I put my left hand on my sword, on the blade below the crosspiece. I took my right hand off the hilt. That I offered to Lachlan.

"The Solindish soldier," I said calmly. "Slay him for me, harper."

Chapter Seven

"Forgive me, my lord," Rowan said quietly. "Is it wise you should go, and alone?"

I sat upon a rotting tree stump, high on the hill behind Torrin's croft. Alix's foster father was indeed still alive, and he had been astonished to find me the same when I had arrived at his dwelling some weeks before. He had given me the story of the Ihlini attack much as Lachlan had, verifying that what remained of the clan had gone north across the Bluetooth. So now, using Torrin's croft as a temporary headquarters, I gathered what army I could. Here I was safe, unknown; the army camped in the sheltering forest in the hills behind the valley, practicing with swords and knives.

I stirred, knocking snow off my boots by banging heels against the tree stump. The day was quite clear; I squinted against the sunlight. "Wise enough, does no one find me out." I glanced at Rowan, standing three steps away, in the attitude of a proper servant. I thought it would ease with time, so that he served through desire instead of rigid dedication. "I have told no one but you and Torrin of my plan."

Rowan nodded as the color came and went in his sunbronzed face. He was not accustomed to being in my confidence. It rested ill with him, who thought himself little more than a servant no matter how often I said he was much more. "There is the harper," he offered quietly.

I grunted, shifting my seat on the rotting stump. "Lachlan believes he has proven his worth by slaying the soldier. I will let him think it. He has, to some extent . . . but not all." I bent and scooped up a stone, idly tossing it through the trees. "Say what is in your mind, Rowan. At my behest."

He nodded, head bowed in an attitude of humility. His hands were behind his back. His eyes did not look at me but at the snow-covered ground beneath his boots. "You distrust the harper, still, because you do not know him well enough. My lord—I say you know me little better."

"I know enough," I said. "I recall the thirteen-year-old boy who was captive of the Atvians along with me. I recall the boy who was made to serve the Lord Keough himself, though he be cuffed and struck and tripped." Rowan's eyes came up to mine, stricken. "I was in the tent also, Rowan. That you must surely recall. And I saw what they did to your back."

His shoulders moved, tensing, rippling beneath the leather and wool. I knew what he did, flinching from the lash. He could not help it, no more than I at times, when I recalled the iron upon my wrists.

At that, the flesh twinged. I rubbed at both wrists, one at a time, not needing to feel the ridges to know they were there. "I know what it was, Rowan," I said unevenly. "No man, living through that, would willingly serve the enemy. Not when his rightful lord is come home."

He stared again at the ground. I saw the rigidity in his shoulders. "I will do whatever you require." His voice was very quiet.

"I require you to wait here while I go, and to be vigilant in your watching." I smiled. "Lachlan may fool us all, in the end, by being precisely what he claims, but I would know my enemy before I give him my back. I trust to you and Torrin in this. See to it the harper does not leave and make off for Mujhara, to carry Bellam word of my whereabouts. See to it he cannot give any of us away."

Through the trees came the clashing of swords and the angry shout of an arms-master. The men drilled and drilled until they would drop, cursing the need for such practice even while they knew it was necessary. They had been gone from war too long, most of them; some of them had never known it. Men came from crofts and cities and even distant valleys, having heard the subtle word.

Carillon, it said. *Carillon is come home.*

I stood up, slapping at my leather breeches. The snow was slushy now, almost sodden; I thought the thaw would come soon. But not yet. I prayed not yet. We were nowhere close to being an army, and in spring I wanted to start my campaign against Bellam's men.

I smiled. In spring, when the planting began, so no one would be expecting battle. I would anticipate a summer campaign, and throw Bellam into disarray.

I hoped.

"He will know," Rowan said, "the Solindish king. He will send men."

I nodded. "Take the army deeper into the forest. Leagues from here. Leave no one with Torrin; I do not wish to endanger him. I want no fighting now. Better to hide like runaway children than give ourselves over to Bellam's men. See they do it, Rowan."

He crossed his arms and hugged his chest, as if he were suddenly cold. "My lord—take you care."

I grinned at him. "It is too soon to lose me yet. Does it come, it will come in battle." I turned away to my horse and untied his reins from a slender sapling. The same little dun Steppes gelding, still shaggy and ragged and ugly. Nothing like the warhorse my father had given me five years before.

Rowan's face was set in worried, unhappy lines. All his thoughts were in his eyes: he thought I would die and the rebellion come to an end.

I mounted and gathered in my reins. "She is my lady mother. I would have her know I live."

He nodded a little. "But to have to go where you know there are soldiers—"

"They will be expecting an army, not a single man." I touched the hilt of my sword, wrapped once again and scabbarded at my saddle. "I will be well enough."

I did not look back as I rode away from the young man I had learned to trust. But I knew he stood in the shade of the trees, squinting against the sun.

The walnut dye turned my hair dark and stiff and dull. Grease made it shiny and foul. One braid, bound with a leather lace, hung before my left ear. The beard was already dark, and unknown to any who had seen me at eighteen.

My teeth were good and I still boasted all of them. I rubbed a resinous gum into them to turn them yellow and foul my tongue. My clothes were borrowed, though I doubted I would return them; the man who wore mine no doubt preferred them to his, they being much better than his rags. What I wore now was a threadbare woollen tunic, once dark green, now brown with mud and grease. Matching woollen trews bagged at my knees, reaching only halfway to my ankles. I had put off my boots and replaced them with leather buskins.

Leather bracers hid my wrist scars, something a guard might look for. No doubt Bellam had described me as tall, tawny-dark and blue-eyed, with shackle scars on both wrists. I was still tall, but now walked stooped, hitching a leg, one shoulder crooked down as if a broken bone had been improperly set. There was nothing of Bellam's pretender-prince about me as I walked toward the village surrounding Joyenne. Not even the sword and the bow, for both could give me away. Both I had buried in the snow beneath a rowan tree, marked with a lightning gash. I carried only the knife, and that was sheathed beneath my tunic against my ribs.

I scuffed through snow and slush, kicking out at the dogs who ran up to see the stranger. Joyenne-town was little more than a scattered village grown up because of the castle. There were no walls, only dwellings, and the people passing by. They took no note of me.

I could smell the stink of myself. More than that, I could smell the stink of a broken homeland. The village I had always known had been a good place, full of bustle and industry. Like all villages it claimed its share of reprobates, but the people had mostly been happy. I had known some of it well, as young men will, and I recalled some of the women who had been happy to show favor to their lord's tall son. And I wondered, for the first time in my life, whether I had gotten children on any of them.

The main track led directly to the castle. Joyenne proper, built upon a hill, with walls and towers and the glittering glass of leaded, mullioned casements. My father had taken great joy in establishing a home of which to be proud. Joyenne was where we lived, not fought; it was not a bastion to ward off the enemy but a place in which to rear children. But the gods had seen fit to give them stillborn sons and daughters, until Torry and then myself.

Joyenne was awash with sunlight, gold and bronze and brown. The ocher-colored stone my father had chosen had bleached to a soft, muted color, so that the sunlight glinted

off corners and trim. Against the snowy hill it was a great
blot of towered, turreted stone, ringed by walls and ramparts. There was an iron portcullis at the frontal gate, but
rarely was it ever brought down. At least in my father's
day. Joyenne had been open to all then, did they need to
converse with their lord.

Now, however, the great mortar mouth was toothed with
iron. Men walked the walls with halberds in their hands.
Ringmail glinted silver in the sunlight. Bellam's banner
hung from the staffs at each tower: a rising white sun on
an indigo field.

Because I was a poor man and fouled with the grime of
years, I did not go to the central gate. I went instead to a
smaller one, stooped and crooked and hitching my leg
along. The guards stopped me at once, speaking in poor
Homanan. What was it, they asked, I wanted?

To see my mother, I said civilly, showing stained and
rotting teeth. The scent of the gum was foul and sent them,
cursing, two steps back. My mother, I repeated in a thick
and phlegmy voice. The one who served within the castle.

I named a name, knowing there was indeed a woman
who served the hall. I could not say if still she lived—she
had been old when I had gone to war—but a single question would tell the men I did not lie. She had had a son, I
knew, a son twisted from childhood disease. He had gone
away to another village—her everlasting shame—but now,
I thought, he would come back. However briefly.

The guards consulted, watching me with disgusted, arrogant eyes. They spoke in Solindish, which I knew not at
all, but their voices gave them away. My stink and my
grease and my twisted body had shielded me from closer
inspection.

Weaponed? they asked gruffly.

No. I put out my hands as if inviting them to search.
They did not. Instead they waved me through.

And thus Carillon came home again, to see his lady
mother.

I hitched and shuffled and stooped, wiping my arm beneath my nose, spreading more grease and fouling my
beard. I crossed the cobbled bailey slowly, almost hesi-
tantly, as if I feared to be sent away again. The Solindishmen who passed me looked askance, offended by my stink.

I showed them my yellowed, resined teeth in the sort of grin a dog gives, to show his submission; to show he knows his place.

By my appearance, I would be limited to the kitchens or the midden. It was where the woman had served. But my lady mother would be elsewhere, so I passed by the kitchens and went up to the halls, scraping my wet buskins across the wood of the floor.

There were few servants. I thought Bellam had sent most of them away in an attempt to humble my mother. For him, a usurper king, it would be important to wage war even against a woman. Gwynneth of Homana had been wed to the Mujhar's brother; a widow now, and helpless, but royal nonetheless. It would show his power if he humbled this woman so. But I thought it was unlikely he had succeeded, no matter how many guards he placed on the walls; no matter how many Solindish banners fluttered from the towers.

I found the proper staircase, winding in a spiral to an upper floor. I climbed, sensing the flutter in my belly. I had come this far, so far, and yet a single mistake could have me taken. Bellam's retribution, no doubt, would see me kept alive for years. Imprisoned and humiliated and tortured.

I passed out of the staircase into a hall, paneled in honey-gold wood. My father's gallery, boasting mullioned windows that set the place to glittering in the sun. But the beeswax polish had grown stale and dark, crusted at the edges. The gallery bore the smell of disuse and disinterest.

My hand slipped up between the folds of my soiled tunic, sliding through a rent in the cloth. I closed my fingers around the bone-handled hilt of my Caledonese knife. For a moment I stood at the polished wooden door of my mother's solarium, listening for voices within. I heard nothing. It was possible she spent her time elsewhere, but I had learned that men or women, in trying circumstances, will cling to what they know. The solar had ever been a favorite place. And so, when I was quite certain she was alone, I swung open the oiled panel.

I moved silently. I closed the door without a sound. I stood within the solar and looked at my mother, and realized she had grown old.

Her head was bent over an embroidery frame. What she stitched there I could not say, save it took all her attention to do it. The sunlight burned through the mullioned panes of the narrow casement nearest her and splashed across her work, turning the colored threads brilliant in the dimness of the room. I noticed at once there was a musty smell, as if the dampness of winter had never been fully banished by the warmth of the brazier fires. This had ever been a warm, friendly room, but now it was cold and barren.

I saw how she stitched at the fabric. Carefully, brows furrowed, in profile to me. And her hands—

Twisted, brittle, fragile things, knobbed with buttons of flesh at her knuckles and more like claws than fingers. So painstakingly she stitched, and yet with those hands I doubted she could do little more than thrust needle through fabric with little regard for the pattern. Disease had taken the skill from her.

I recalled then, quite clearly, how her hands had pained her in the dampness. How she had never complained, but grew more helpless with each month. And now, looking at her, I saw how the illness had destroyed the grace my father had so admired.

She wore a white wimple and coif to hide her hair, but a single loop escaped to curve down the line of her cheek. Gray, all gray, when before it had been tawny as my own. Her face was creased with the soft, fine lines of age, like crumpled silk.

She had put on indigo blue, ever a favorite color with her. I thought I recognized the robe as an old one she had given up more than seven years before. And yet she wore it now, threadbare and thin and hardly worthy of her station.

Perhaps I made a sound. She lifted her head, searching, and her eyes came around to me.

I went to her and knelt down. All the words I had thought to say were flown. I had nothing but silence in my mouth and a painful cramping in my throat.

I stared hard at the embroidery in her lap. She had let it fall, forgotten, and saw that the pattern—though ill-made—was familiar. A tall, bearded soldier on a great chestnut stallion, leading the Mujhar's army. I had loved it as a child, for she had called the man my father. It seemed odd that I would look now and see myself.

Her hand was on my head. At first I wanted to flinch away, knowing how foul the grease and dye had made me, but I did not move. With her other hand she set her fingers beneath my chin and turned up my face, so she could look upon me fully. Her smile was brilliant to see, and the tears ran down her face.

I reached out and caught her hands gently, afraid I might break them. They were so fragile in my own. I felt huge, overlarge, much too rough for her delicacy.

"Lady." My voice came out clogged and uneven. "I have been remiss in not coming to you sooner. Or sending word—"

Fingers closed my mouth. "No." She touched my beard lingeringly, then ran both hands through my filthy hair. "Was this through choice, or have you forgotten all the care I ever taught you?"

I laughed at her, though it had a hollow, brittle sound. "Exile has fashioned your son into another sort of man, I fear."

The lines around her eyes—blue as my own—deepened. And then she took her hands away as if she had finished with me entirely. I realized, in that instant, she was sacrificing the possessiveness she longed to show me. In her eyes I saw joy and pride and thankfulness, and a deep recognition of her son as a man. She was giving me my freedom.

I rose unsteadily, as if I had been too long without food. Her smile grew wider. "Fergus lives on in you."

I walked to the casement, overcome for the moment, and stared out blindly to watch the guards upon the ramparts. When I could, I turned back. "You know why I have come."

Her chin lifted. I saw the delicate, draped folds of the silkin wimple clustered at her throat. "I was wed to your father for thirty-five years. I bore him six children. It was the gods who decreed only two of those children would live to adulthood, but I am quite certain they have learned, both of them, what it is to be part of the House of Homana." The pride made her nearly young again. "Of course I know why you have come."

"And your answer?"

It surprised her. "What answer is there to duty? You *are*

the House of Homana, Carillon—what is left for you to do but take back your throne from Bellam?"

I had expected no different, and yet it seemed passing strange to hear such matter-of-factness from my mother. Such things from a father are never mentioned, being known so well, but now I lacked a father. And it was my mother who gave me leave to go to war.

I moved away from the window. "Will you come with me? Now?"

She smiled. "No."

I made an impatient gesture. "I have planned for it. You will put on the clothes of a kitchen servant and walk out of here with me. It can be done. *I* have done it. It is too obvious for them to suspect." I touched my fouled, bearded face. "Grease your hair, sully your skirts, affect the manners of a servant. It is your life at risk—you will do well enough."

"No," she said again. "Have you forgotten your sister?"

"Torry is in Homana-Mujhar." I thought it answer enough as I glanced out the casement again. "It is somewhat more difficult for me to get into Homana-Mujhar, but once we are safely gone from here, then I will turn my plans to Torry."

"No," she repeated, and at last she had my complete attention. "Carillon, I doubt not you have thought this out well, but I cannot undertake it. Tourmaline is in danger. She is hostage to Bellam against just this sort of thing; do you think he would sit and do nothing?" I saw the anguish in her eyes as she looked into my frowning face. "He would learn, soon enough, I had gotten free of his guards. And he would turn to punish your sister."

I crossed to her at once, bending to catch her shoulders in my hands. "I cannot leave you here! Do you think I could live with myself, knowing you are here? You have only to look at this room, stripped bare of its finery and left cold, no doubt to freeze your bones. Mother—"

"No one harms me," she said clearly. "No one beats me. I am fed. I am merely kept as you see me, like a pauper-woman." The twisted hands reached up to touch my leather-clad wrists. "I know what you have risked, coming here. And were Tourmaline safe, I would come with you. But I will not give her over to Bellam's wrath."

"He did it on purpose, to guard against my coming."
That truth was something I should have realized long ago,
and had not. "Divide the treasure and the thieves are defeated." I cursed once, then tried to catch back the words,
for she was my lady mother.

She smiled, amused, while the tears stood in her eyes. "I
cannot. Do you understand? I thought you were dead, and
my daughter lost. But now you are here, safe and whole,
and I have some hope again. Go from here and do what
you must, but go without me to hinder you." She put out
her hands as I sought to speak. "See you how I am? I
would be a burden. And that I refuse, when you have a
kingdom to win back."

I laughed, but there was nothing of humor in it. "All my
fine plans are disarranged. I thought to win you free of
here and take you to my army, where you would be safe.
And then I would set about planning to take Torry—or
take Homana-Mujhar." I sighed and shook my head, sensing the pain of futility in my soul. "You have put me in
my place."

"Your place is Homana-Mujhar." She rose, still clasping
my hands with her brittle, twisted fingers. "Go there. Win
your throne and your sister's freedom. And then I will go
where you bid me."

I caught her in my arms and then, aghast, set her aside
with a muttered oath. Filthy as I was—

She laughed. She touched the smudge of grease on her
crumpled-silk face and laughed, and then she cried, and
this time when I hugged her I did not set her at once aside.

Chapter Eight

I went out of Joyenne as I had gone in: with great care. Stooping and hitching I limped along, head down, making certain I did not hasten. I went out the same gate I had come in, muttering something to the Solindish guards, who responded with curses and an attempt to trip me into a puddle of horse urine pooling on the cobbles. Perhaps falling would have been best, but my natural reflexes took over and kept me from sprawling as the leg shot out to catch my ankle. I recalled my guise at once and made haste to stumble and cry out, and when I drew myself up it was to laughter and murmured insults in the Solindish tongue. And so I went away from my home and into the village to think.

My mother had the right of it. Did I take her out of Joyenne, Bellam would know instantly I had come back, and where. Who else would undertake to win my mother free? She had spent five years in captivity within her own home and no one had gotten her out. Only I would be so interested as to brave the Solindish guards.

It is a humbling feeling to know all your plans have been made for naught, when you should have known it at the outset. Finn, I thought, would have approached it differently. Or approached it not at all.

I retrieved my horse from the hostler at a dingy tavern and went at once, roundabout, to the rowan tree to unearth my sword and bow. It felt good to have both in my hands again, and to slough off the tension my journey into Joyenne had caused me. I hung my sword at my hips again, strapped on the Cheysuli bow, and mounted the gelding once more.

I rode out across the snowfields and headed home again. To a different home, an army, where men planned and drilled and waited. To where Homana's future waited. And I wondered how it had come to pass men would claim a single realm their own, when the gods had made it for all.

I thought of Lachlan then, secure within his priesthood. He had told me how it was for him; how Lodhi's service did not require celibacy or cloistering or the foolishness of similar things. His task, he had said, was merely to speak of Lodhi to those who would listen, in hopes they would learn the proper way. I had acknowledged his freedom to do so, knowing my own lay in other gods, but he had never pressed me on it, and for that I was grateful indeed.

The sun burned yellow in an azure sky, reflecting from the snow. The horse sweated and so did I; the grease stank so badly I wanted to retch and rid myself of its stench. But until I had time to bathe myself I would have to remain as I was.

I saw them then, silhouetted against the skyline. Four men atop a hill, shapes only, with sunlight glittering off their ringmail. All save one, who wore dark clothes instead. No mail. No sword at all.

My heart moved within my chest in the squirm of sudden foreboding. Intentionally I kept my hand from my sword, riding onward along the narrow track beaten into the slushy snow. Men had the freedom to come and go as they pleased; Solindish or not, they had the right to ride where they would. And I had better not gain their attention with a show of arms or strength.

The hill lay to my right, and ahead. I rode on doggedly, round-shouldered and slumped, affecting no pride or curiosity. The four waited atop the hill, well-mounted and silent, still little more than shapes at this distance, yet watching. Watching always.

I did not quicken the gelding's pace. I made no movement to call attention, and yet I could feel their eyes as they watched me, waiting, as I passed the crest of their hill. Still it lay to my right, bulging up out of a rift through which ran the smallest of snow-melt streams. That stream lay to my left; I rode between water and men. The gelding snorted, unimpressed, but I thought he sensed my tension.

The ringmail blazed in the brilliant sun. Solindishmen, I knew. Homanan mail was darker, duller, radiating less light in the sun. Showing less light in the starlit darkness when armies moved to set an ambush. It was something my father had taught me; perhaps Bellam was too sure of his men and saw no need for such secrecy.

I rode on. And so did they.

Three of them. The men in mail. They came directly down the hill toward me, moving to cut me off, and I saw them draw their swords. This was no parley, no innocent meeting of strangers. It was blood they wanted, and I had none to spare.

I doubted I could outrun them. The snow was thick and slushy, treacherous footing to any horse, but to mine in particular: short-legged and slighter of frame. Still, he was willing, and when I set him to a run he plunged through the heavy going.

Snow whipped into the air in a fine, damp spray, churned up beneath driving hooves. I bent low and forward, shifting weight over the moving shoulders. I heard the raspy breathing of my horse and the shouts of men behind me.

The gelding stumbled, recovered, then went down to his knees. Riding forward as I was, the fall pitched me neatly off over his head. It was not entirely unexpected; I came up at once, spinning to face the oncoming men, and stripped the bow from my back.

The arrow was nocked. Loosed. It took the first soldier full in the throat, knocking him off his horse. The next shaft blurred home in the second man's chest, but the third one was on me and there was no more time for a bow.

The sword slashed down to rip the bow from my hands. I stumbled, slipping to my knees in the slushy snow, and wrenched free the sword in my scabbard. Both hands clamped down on the leather-wrapped hilt. I pushed myself up to my feet.

The Solindishman swung back, commanding his horse with his knees. I saw the sunlight flashing off his blade as the man rode toward me. I saw also the badge he wore: Bellam's white sun on an indigo field.

The soldier rode me down. But he paused to deliver what he thought was the death-blow; I ducked it at once and came up with my blade, plunging it into the horse's belly. The animal screamed and staggered at once, floundering to his knees. The soldier jumped off instantly and met me on common ground.

His broadsword was lifted high to come down into my left shoulder. I caught his blade on my own and swung it up diagonally from underneath, wrist-cords tightening beneath the leather bracers. He pulled away at once, dropping to come under my guard; I met his blow with a downward stroke across my body. He changed then, shifting his stance to come at me another way, but I broke his momentum and slid under his guard with ease, plunging my sword to the hilt through his ribs. Steel blade on steel mail shrieked in disharmony a moment, and then I freed my sword as the body slumped to the snow.

I turned at once, searching for the man who wore no ringmail or sword, but saw no one. The crest of the hill was empty. I listened, standing perfectly still, but all I heard was the trickling of the tiny streamlet as it ran down through its channel.

The Solindish warhorse was dead. The horses belonging to the two soldiers dead of arrows had gone off, too far for me to chase. I was left with my shaggy Steppes horse, head hanging as he sought to recover from his flight.

I sheathed my sword, reclaimed my bow and mushed over to him through the snow, cursing the wet of my buskins and the chill of ice against my flesh. The ragged clothing I wore was soaked through from the flight and the fight. And I still stank.

I put out my hand to catch dangling reins and felt something crawl against the flesh of my waist. I slapped at it at once, cursing lice and fleas; slapped again when the tickling repeated itself. I set my hand against the hilt of my Caledonese knife and felt it move.

I unsheathed it at once, jerking it into the sunlight. For a moment I stared at it, seeing blade and bone, and then I saw it move.

Every muscle tensed. The horse snorted uneasily behind me. I stood there and stared, fascinated as the bone reshaped itself.

It was growing. In my hand. The smooth, curving hilt lengthened, pulling itself free of the blade's tang. The runes and scripture melted away into the substance of the bone, as if the pieces carved away to make the shapes were replacing themselves.

And then I knew I was watched.

I looked up at once, staring at the low ridge of the hill from which the Solindishmen had come. There, dark against the blue of the sky, was the fourth man. The one without ringmail or sword. Too far for me to discern his features, save I knew he watched and waited.

Ihlini, I knew instantly.

I threw the knife away in a convulsive, sickened movement. I reached at once for my bow, intending to loose an arrow. But I stopped almost at once, because an arrow against sorcery claims no strength.

The bone. The thighbone of a monstrous beast, the king of Caledon had said. And the Ihlini had conjured the source of the bone, placing it before me in the snowfields of Homana.

The bones knit themselves together. From one came another, then another, until they ran together and built the skeleton. The spine, ridged and long. Massive shoulder joints. And the skull, pearly white, with gaping orbits for eyes.

Then, more quickly, the viscera. The brain. The vessels running with blood. The muscles, wrapping themselves into place, until the flesh overlay it all. And the hide on top of that.

I gaped at the beast. I knew what it was, of course; my House had used it forever as a crest, to recall the strength and courage of the mythical beast, long gone from the world.

The lion of Homana.

It leaped. It gathered itself and leaped directly at the horse, and took him down with the swipe of one huge paw. I heard the dull snap of a broken neck, then saw the beast turn toward me.

I dropped my bow. I ran. So did the lion run. It was a huge flash of tawny golden-yellow; black-maned past his shoulders, tail wiry as if it lived. I ran, but I could not outrun it. And so I turned, unsheathing my sword, and tried to spit the lion on it.

It leaped. Up into the air it leaped, hind legs coiling to push it off the ground, front paws reaching out. My ears shut out the fearful roar so that I heard only the pounding of my blood as it ran into my head.

One paw reached out and caught me across the head.

But I ducked most of the weight; in ducking, I saved my life. The blow, had it landed cleanly, would have broken my neck at once. As it was part of the paw still caught me, knocking me down, so that I feared my jaw was shattered. Blood ran freely from my nose.

Even as I went down I kept my sword thrust up. I saw the blade bite into the massive chest, tearing through the hide. It caught on bone, then grated as the lion's leap carried it past.

I was flat on my back in the snow. I was up almost at once, too frightened to take refuge in the pain and shock. My head rang and blood was in my mouth. My sword was no use against the lion unless I hit a vital spot. To try for that would put me too close, well within its range. I did not relish feeding it on my flesh.

The lion's snarl was a coughing, hacking sound. Its mane stood out from the hide, black and tangled. But the muscles rippled cleanly against the tawny-gold; the wound had done nothing to gainsay it. Blood flowed, but still it came on.

I knew, instinctively, it would not die. I could not slay it by conventional means. The beast had been summoned by a sorcerer.

My foot came down on something hard as I backed away from the lion. I realized I had run in a circle, so that I was back where I had begun. The horse lay where the lion had put it. And the bow lay under my feet.

I dropped the sword at once and caught up the bow. I snatched an arrow from my quiver. As the beast leaped yet again I nocked the arrow and spun—

—let fly. But not at the lion. At the man.

The shaft went home in the sorcerer's chest. I saw him stagger, clutching the arrow, then he slumped down to his knees. He was abruptly haloed in a sphere of purple fire that sprung up around his body. And then the arrow burst into brilliant crimson flames and he was dead.

I swung back. The beast was nothing but bone. A single, hilt-shaped bone, lying in the snow.

I sank down to my knees, slumping forward, until only my arms braced stiffly against the snow held me up. My breath came from deep in my chest in wheezing gasps, setting my lungs afire. Blood still ran from my nose, staining the snow, and my head ached from the blow. I spat out a tooth and hung there, spent, to let my body recover.

When at last I could stand again I weaved like a man too far gone in wine. I shook in every bone. I stumbled to the snow-melt stream and knelt there, scooping cold water and ice to cleanse my face and mouth of blood and filth and my mind of the blanking numbness.

I pushed to my feet again. Slowly, moving like an old, old man, I gathered up bow and sword. The knife hilt I left lying in the snow. That I would never carry again.

The Ihlini was quite dead. His body was sunken within his clothing, as if the arrow had somehow loosed more than life, but a force as well; released, its shell had shrunk. It was a body still, but not much of a man.

The Ihlini's horse stood part way down the backside of the ridge. It was a dark brown gelding, not fine but good. An Ihlini's horse, and ensorcelled?

I caught the reins from the ground and brought the horse closer. Taller than the dun. Shedding his winter hair. He had kind eyes, clipped mane and short tail. One spot of white was on his face. I patted his jaw and mounted.

I nearly fell off again. My head spun and throbbed with renewed ferocity; the lion had rattled my senses. I huddled in the saddle a long moment, eyes shut, waiting for the pain and dizziness to diminish.

Carefully I touched my face and felt the swollen flesh. No doubt I would purple by nightfall. But my nose, for all it ached, was whole. And then, done marking my numerous aches, I turned the horse and rode eastward.

Torrin's dog ran out to meet me. In the weeks since we had come he had grown, now more dog than pup, but his ebullience was undiminished. He loped along next to my horse and warned Torrin of my presence. It was not necessary; Torrin was at the well fishing up the bucket.

In five years, Torrin had not changed much. His gray hair was still thinning, still cropped against his head. He still bore seams in his flesh and calluses on his hands. Crofting had changed his body from the bulk of an arms-master's to the characteristic slump of a man who knew sheep and land, but I could still see his quiet competence. He had been born to blades, not the land, and yet for Alix's sake he had given all of that up. Because Shaine had wanted to be rid of her, and Torrin could not bear to see the infant left to die.

I rode up slowly. The horse made his way to the well and put his head into the bucket Torrin held. Torrin, looking up at me from brown eyes couched in fleshy folds, shook his head. "Was that Solindish-done?"

He meant my face. I touched it and said no. "Ihlini. He summoned a beast. A lion."

The color changed in his leathered cheeks. "Bellam knows—"

I shook my head before he could finish. "He may not. The men who sought to slay me are dead. I have no doubt he knows I am back—most people do but there is no one left to tell him where I am. I think we will be safe a little longer."

He looked troubled, but I had no more time to wonder at it. I bent forward and swung off the horse slowly, wincing from the bruises. I left the horse with Torrin and slowly made my way to the croft. Wood smoke veiled the air.

"My lord, I think—"

I turned back before the door, interrupting in my weariness. "You have a half-cask, do you not? Clothes I left with you. Soap and water? Hot. I wish to boil myself free of this stench."

He nodded, brow furrowed. "Do you wish me to—"

"No." I lifted a hand in a weary wave. "I will see to it myself." It was something I had learned in exile. I needed no servants to fetch and carry.

"My lord—" he tried again, but I went into the croft.

And stopped. It was Alix.

She stood by the table before the fire, with her arms plunged into a bubble of bread dough set out on a board. Flour reached to her elbows. I saw at once her dark brown hair had grown long enough to braid, pinned against her head with silver clasps that glittered in the sunlight slanting in the open door.

I saw again the girl I had befriended, when a prince had so few real friends. I saw again the girl who had been the reason for my capture by Finn and his raiding party. I saw again the girl whose Cheysuli *tahlmorra* was so firmly linked with my own Homanan fate.

But mostly I saw the girl who had become a woman, and I hated the time I had lost.

There was a question in her eyes, and bafflement. She knew me not, in my foul and filthy state, bearded and greased and bruised. I thought of what kind of man I had been five years before, and what I was now, and I laughed.

And then, as her mouth shaped my name, I crossed the tiny room and caught her in my arms.

She hugged me as tightly as I hugged her, saying my name again and again. She smelled of bread dough and wood smoke, and laughed as if she could not stop.

"So *filthy*—" she said, "and so *humble*—"

I had never been that. But I laughed with her, for what she saw was true if, perhaps, to a lesser extent than she thought. Or for different reasons. I was humbled, it was true, by the very thing that elevated so many men: I wanted her. And so, unable to help myself, I cupped her head in my hands and kissed her.

Only once had I kissed her before, and under such circumstances as she could claim it a token of my thanks. I had meant that, then, too, but more as well. But by then, when she rescued me from the Atvians, she had already pledged herself to Duncan. She had carried his child in her belly.

Now, she did not rescue me. There was nothing of gratefulness about what I was feeling; she could not construe it as such. In five years I had had time to think of Alix, and regret what had not happened between us, and I could not hide my feelings.

And yet there was Duncan, still, between us.

I let her go. I still longed to touch her, but I let her go. She stood quietly before me, color high in her face, but there was a calmness in her eyes. She knew me better than I did.

"That much you may have, having taken it already," she said quietly, "but no more."

"Are you afraid what might grow up from this beginning?"

She shook her head once. "Nothing can grow up from this beginning. There is nothing—here." She touched her left breast, indicating her heart. Her gaze was perfectly steady.

Almost I laughed. It was so distinct a change. She had gained understanding and comprehension, aware of what she was. Gone was the virgin, confused by body and emotions. Now she was woman, wife, and mother, and she knew. I was not enough.

"I have thought of you for years," I said. "All those nights in exile."

"I know." Her tone did not waver for an instant. "Had you been Duncan, I would have felt the same. But you were—and are—not. You are yourself. You are special to me, it is true, but it is far too late for more. Once, perhaps . . . but all of that time has passed."

I took a deep breath and tried to regain my composure. "I did not—did not mean to do this. I meant only to greet you again. But it seems I cannot keep my hands from you now any more than I ever could." I smiled wryly. "An admission few men would make to a woman who will not have them."

Alix smiled. "Finn said much the same. His greeting was—similar."

"And Duncan?"

"Duncan was—elsewhere. He is not an insensitive man."

"Nor ever was." I sighed and scratched my jaw beneath the beard. "Enough of this. I came in to wash, as you see."

"Good." Some of the tension vanished and the light came into her eyes. The warm, amber eyes I recalled so well—so perfect a melding of Cheysuli and Homanan, more beautiful to me than either. "I doubt I could stand your stink one more moment." She turned away at once to the fire in the low stone fireplace, kneeling to add wood, then glanced over her shoulder at me. "Perhaps you would fill the cauldron with water?" And then color blazed up high in her face, as if she recalled I was royal and above such lowly things.

I grinned. "I will fetch it and set out the cask. Do you forget?—I have been with Finn all these years. I am not quite the same as you knew me." I left her then, having caught up the heavy cauldron, and went out to fill it with water.

Torrin sat on the edge of the stone-ringed well, smoking his clay pipe. His grizzled eyebrows rose. "I thought to warn you she was here," he said around the stem.

I grunted as I began to crank up the bucket. "I had not thought it was so obvious to everyone."

"To me." Torrin got up to steady the bucket as it came up from the water. He caught it and poured its contents into the cauldron. "She was so young when first you met her. Then so new to her heritage, knowing little of royal things. And finally, of course, there was Duncan."

The name dropped into my soul like a stone. "Aye . . . he had more sense than I. He saw what he wanted and took it."

"He *won* it," Torrin said quietly. "My lord—do you think to win her back from him, think again. I was her father for seventeen years. Even now, I feel she is mine. I will not have her hurt, or her happiness harmed. She loves him deeply." He dropped the bucket down when it was emptied and met my eyes without the flicker of an eyelid. As he had, no doubt, met my uncle's unwavering stare. "You are the Mujhar, and have the right to do what you will, even with the Cheysuli. But I think you have more sense than that."

For most of my life I had been given what I wanted, including women. Alix I had lost before I knew how much I wanted her. And now, knowing it keenly, I knew how much it hurt to lose.

Especially to Duncan.

Alix came to the door of the white-washed, thatch-roofed croft with its gray stone chimney. "The fire is ready." Around her neck shone the golden torque made in the shape of a flying hawk, wings outspread and beak agape, with a chunk of amber caught in the clutching talons. A *lir*-torque and Cheysuli bride-gift. Made for her by Duncan.

I hoisted the cauldron and lugged it inside, hanging it from the iron hook set into the stone of the blackened fireplace. I sat on a stool and waited, aware of her every movement, and stared at the fire as she kneaded the dough again.

"When did you come?" I asked at last.

"Eight days ago. Finn brought us here." A warm, bright smile shone on her face.

"He is back?" I felt better almost at once.

"He brought us down from the North." The silver pins in her coiled braids glittered in the sunlight as she worked.

The folds of her moss-green gown moved as she moved, shifting with the motion of her body. The overtunic, with sheepskin fleece turned inward, was dyed a pale, soft yellow, stitched in bright green yarn. It hung to her knees, belted at her waist with brown leather and a golden buckle. Cheysuli finery, not Homanan; she was all Cheysuli now.

I scratched at my itching face. "He is well?"

"Finn? Oh, aye—when is he not? He is Finn." She smiled again, beating the dough with her hands. "Though I think he has another thing to occupy himself with, now."

"A woman," I predicted. "Has he found someone among the clan?"

She laughed. "No, not a woman. My son." Her smile widened into a grin. "There are times Donal is more like his *su'fali* than his *jehan.* And now they have become close friends as well, I have only Finn to blame for my son's little indescretions. One was bad enough; now there are two."

"Two Finns?" I thought about it, laughing, and saw Alix shake her head.

"Shall I bid them come?" she asked, still kneading. "I have only to speak to Cai and Storr."

I thought again of the power she held, the boundless magic that ran in her veins. Old Blood, it was, a gift reborn of the gods. Alix, and only Alix, could converse with any *lir.* Or take any shape at will.

"No," I said. "I will go up myself, when I have shed my weight of dirt." I checked the water and found it nearly hot. Then I asked for the half-cask; Alix told me where it was and I dragged it out of the tiny antechamber, if a croft could be said to have a proper one. The half-cask was bound with hammered copper. It still smelled faintly of cider, betraying its original purpose. In Homana-Mujhar I had bathed in oak-and-silver cask-tubs polished smooth, so no splinters threatened my flesh. I doubted this one was as good, but it would serve. In exile I had learned to be grateful for anything.

I rolled the cask into Torrin's tiny bedchamber, containing a pallet, chest, and chair. There I tipped the cask on its end, then began filling it from the cauldron. When at last it stood ready I went seeking cloth and soap.

Alix gave me both. "Torrin has changed nothing since I

left," she said with a nostalgic smile, and I wondered if she recalled the day Finn had stolen us both.

How could she not? I did. Too well. And the changes that had occurred since then.

I looked at her a long moment, my hands full of threadbare cloth and hard brown soap. I wished there was more I could say. And then I said it anyway. "I will insult neither you nor your husband by pursuing you where I am not wanted."

Color flared in her face again. I marked how the years had melted away the flesh of youth, leaving her with the characteristic angular, high-planed Cheysuli face. Her face was more like Finn's than ever before; the children showing the father's blood.

"There was no need to say it," she told me softly.

"There was. Otherwise I could not account for my actions." Briefly I touched her face with the backs of two fingers. "Alix—once we might have shared so much. Let us keep of it what we can." I took my hand away and went into the gloomy bedchamber where the water steamed in the air. I pulled the curtain closed and stripped out of my filthy garb.

I could not put her from my mind. I thought of her in the other room, kneading away, knowing she had Duncan close at hand. I thought of her with him, at night. I thought of her as I had known her: a young, sweet-natured girl with coltish grace and an integrity few men possess.

And I thought how odd a thing it is that two people can inhabit a single room, each knowing how the other one feels, and knowing there is no good in it.

No good at all. Only pain.

Chapter Nine

The half-cask, unfortunately, did not accommodate a man of my size. It was an awkward bath. I sat with my knees doubled up nearly beneath my chin and my spine crushed against the wood. But it was wet and hot and I scrubbed with every bit of strength I had, ridding myself of all the dirt and grease. Even that in my hair and beard.

When at last I could breathe again, stripped of the stench of my disguise, I relaxed. I hung my legs outside of the cask and sat back, tipping my head against the wooden rim. The flesh of my face still ached from the lion's blow; the rest of my body hurt as much. I felt older than my years. The lion had drained my strength; that, and the knowledge of Ihlini sorcery.

The water cooled, but not so fast I could not take my time getting out. And so I did. I let go of all my breath, let my muscles turn to rags, and promptly went to sleep.

"Carillon."

I jerked awake. My spine scraped against the rough wood and I cursed, staring in some confusion at Finn, who stood just inside the doorway with the curtain pulled closed behind him. Thoughtful of my modesty, for once; perhaps it was Alix who elicited such care.

I sat upright and pulled my legs back in, scowling at him. Finn merely smiled, amused to find me in such a state, and leaned back against the wall with bare arms folded across his chest. He had put off his winter leathers in deference to the thaw; I saw again the heavy gold that banded his arms above the elbows. Wide, beautiful things, embossed with runes and wolf-shape. He wore snug leathers again: leggings and a sleeveless jerkin. At his belt hung the Steppes knife, and I thought again of the sorcery I had seen.

"When did you get back?" he asked quite calmly.

I stood up, dripping, and reached for the blanket he tossed me from Torrin's pallet. "Not so long ago that I have had time to fill my belly."

"But time for a bath." His tone was perfectly flat, but I had little trouble discerning his intent. I had not had that trouble for some years now.

"Had you seen me—or *smelled* me—you would have pushed me in yourself." I climbed out of the cask and pulled on the dark brown breeches, then bent to jerk on the knee boots. My shirt was green. I put a brown jerkin over it and belted it with leather and bronze. "I thought I would go up to the army. Will you come?"

"Ah, the army." Finn smiled his ironic smile. "Do you wish to call it that."

I scowled at him, combing my fingers through my wet hair. It tangled on my shoulders and dampened the fabric of shirt and jerkin. "Rowan has done what he can to assemble men willing to fight. I will use what I can. Do you expect me to gather the thousands Bellam has?"

"It makes no difference." Finn followed me through to the other room, where Alix knelt to hang the pot of bread dough over the fire. "You will have the Cheysuli, and that is enough, I think." He put out a hand to Storr, seated by the table.

I scoffed. "I have *you*. And no doubt Duncan, and perhaps those he has managed to persuade to join me in the name of the prophecy." I scooped up a clay jug of Torrin's sour wine and poured myself a cup, pouring a second for Finn as he nodded willingness to drink.

"You have more than a few." He accepted the cup without thanks and swallowed half the wine at once. "How many would you ask for, could you have a larger number?"

I returned the jug to its place on the sideboard near the fireplace and perched upon the table as I drank. "The Cheysuli are the finest fighting men in all of Homana." He did not smile at my compliment; it was well known. "And with each warrior I would gain a *lir*, so double the number at once." I shrugged. "A single warrior is worth at least five of another, so with a *lir* it is ten to one." I shook my head. "It is folly to wish for what I cannot have. Nonetheless, I would be more than pleased with one hundred."

"What of *three* hundred?" Finn smiled. "Perhaps even more."

I stared at him, forgoing my wine altogether. "Have you turned sorcerer, to conjure up false men?"

"No." Finn tossed his empty cup to Alix, who caught it and put it with the jug. "I have conjured up men I thought long dead. Shaine, you see, did not slay as many as we feared."

I set my cup down very precisely in the center of the table. "Are you saying—?"

"Aye." He grinned. "While searching for my clan, I found others. The Northern Wastes boast many places where a clan may hide, and I found several of them. It took time, but we have gathered together every warrior we could find." He shrugged. "All the clans are here; we are building a Keep beyond the hill."

He said it so simply: *"All the clans are here; we are building a Keep beyond the hill."*

I stared at him. A Keep. *With three hundred warriors and their* lir.

I whooped. And then I was on my feet, clasping him in my arms as if I could not let him go. No doubt too demonstrative for Finn's sensibilities, but he knew the reason. And he smiled, stepping away when I was done.

"My gift to you," he said lightly. "Now, come with me and I will show you."

We went out at once, leaving Alix to tend her bread, and Finn gave me back my Ihlini horse. His eyes were on it, for he had known me to ride the dun, but he waited until we were free of the croft and riding toward the hill before he asked me about it, and then obliquely.

"Torrin said you had gone to Joyenne."

"Aye. To get my lady mother out."

"You did not succeed?"

"No, but only because she refused to come." The sunlight was bright in our eyes. I put up a hand to block the stunning brilliance. "Bellam holds Tourmaline, my sister. He has for some time. I do not doubt he keeps her safe, being who she is, but I want her free of him." I swore suddenly as the anger boiled over. "By the gods, the man threatens to wed her!"

We rode abreast with Storr leading the way. Finn, frowning, nodded, saying little. "It is the way of kings. Especially usurper kings."

"He will not usurp my *sister!*"

"Then do you mean to dance into Homana-Mujhar as easily as you did into Joyenne?"

And so I knew what he thought of my actions. I scowled at him blackly. "I got in and got out with little trouble. I was careful. No one knew me."

"And did you yourself put those bruises on your face?"

I had nearly forgotten. My hand went to my jaw and touched the sore flesh. "The Ihlini did this. Or rather his conjured beast."

"Ah." Finn nodded in apparent satisfaction. "No trouble at Joyenne, you say, but an Ihlini set a beast on you." He sighed, shaking his head. "Why should I concern myself with your welfare? All you manage to do is tangle with one of Tynstar's minions."

His irony, as ever, galled me. "Enough. It was not my fault the men found me. They could have found me here."

"*Men?* First it was an Ihlini and his beast. Now there are more." He gestured to direct me up the hill.

I glared at him. "Why not just compel me to tell you the truth, as you did Lachlan?"

"Because I had believed you knew enough to tell me willingly."

I sighed and leaned forward as my horse climbed the hill toward the treeline. "You should not worry. I slew them all, even the Ihlini."

"I have no reason to worry," he agreed. "What have I done, save swear a blood-oath to serve you always?" For the first time a hint of anger crept into his voice. "Do you think I waste my time? Do you wish to do this alone? Think how many times over you would have been slain without me. And now, when I leave you to seek my clan—at your behest—you place yourself in such jeopardy even a child knows better."

"Finn—enough."

"*Not* enough." He glared at me openly now. "There is some little of my life invested in you. *All of it,* now. What we do is not entirely for you, Carillon, and for Homana, but for the Cheysuli as well." His mouth tightened as he reined his horse back even with mine. "Were you to die now, in some foolish endeavor of your own devising, the rebellion would fail. Bellam would rule forevermore. He would likely wed your sister, get new sons on her, and put *them* on the throne behind himself. Is that what you wish?"

I reached out and caught his reins, jerking his horse to a halt. All the anger and frustration came pouring out as pride. "I am your *prince!*"

"And I your liege man!" He ignored the jerk of the reins against his hands. "Do you think it is so easy for me to watch you as a father with a son? I am not your *jehan,* Carillon, merely your liege man. And a cousin, of a sort, because my *jehan* saw fit to lie with a haughty Homanan princess when he had a *cheysula* at home!"

He had never said so much before. Had coming home done it? I knew the differences in myself. Perhaps there were some in Finn as well.

I let go his reins and minded my own, though I did not start up the hill quite yet. "Does the service grow so tedious, seek another," I suggested bitterly.

His laugh was a short bark of sound. "How? The gods have tied me to you. Better yet: they have set iron around your neck as well as mine, and locked them together, like oxen in a yoke."

I sat in the blinding gold of the late afternoon sun and said nothing for a long moment. And then when I did, I asked a question I had not thought to ask before: "What do you want from this life?"

He was surprised. I could see it in his eyes. He understood perfectly well what I asked, and probably why, but he went on to step around the question. "I want you on the throne of Homana."

"Given that," I agreed, "what more?"

"The Cheysuli free to live as they would again."

"Given that." Had I to do it, I would ask him until the moon came up.

Finn squinted into the sun, as if the light would shield his feelings from me, or lessen the pain of the question. He appeared to have no intention of answering me, but this once I would make him.

"Finn," I said patiently, with all the solemnity I could muster, "were the gods to give you anything, *anything* at all, what would you ask for?"

At last he looked directly at me. The sunlight, striking through the trees like illuminated spears, was my unwitting servant. All of Finn's soul was bared to me in the light. This once, just once, but enough for me to see it. "You have not met Donal, have you?"

I thought it a question designed to lead me away from the quarry, like a dog led away by a clever fox. "Alix's son? No. I have only just got here. *Finn*—"

But he was serious. "Could I have it, I would ask for a son." He said it abruptly, as if the admission endangered the hope, and then he rode away from me as if he had shared too much.

There were no tracks to mark an army, no pall of smoke hanging above the treeline to mark the army's presence. There was nothing Bellam could use to seek me out. Finn took me into the forest away from the valley and I knew the army was safe. Rowan had done my bidding by taking them deeper into cover; even I could not say there was an army near, and it was mine.

The forest was overgrown with vines and creepers and brambles and bushes. Ivy fell down from the trees to trip the horses and foul the toes of my boots. Mistletoe clustered in the wooden crotches and a profusion of flowers hailed our passing. Homana. At last. Home again, for good, after too long a time spent in exile.

Sunlight spilled through the leaves and speckled the forest floor into goldens, greens and browns. Finn, riding before me, broke a pheasant from cover and I heard the whirring of its wings as it flew, whipping leaves and stirring sunmotes in its passage to the sky. I thought, suddenly, of the last time I had supped on pheasant: in Homana-Mujhar, feasting a guest, when my uncle had been pleased with a new alliance made. Too long ago. Too long being mercenary instead of prince.

I heard the harp and nearly stopped. There was nothing else save the threshing of the horses tearing through the brush and vines and creepers. But the harpsong overrode it all, and I recognized the hand upon the strings. "Lachlan," I said aloud.

Finn, reining in to ride abreast of me, nodded. "He has come each day, sharing his music with us. Once I might have dismissed it as idle whimsy, but no more. He has magic in that harp, Carillon—more even than we have seen. Already he has begun to give the Cheysuli what we have lacked these past years: peace of spirit." He smiled, albeit wryly. "Too long have we forgotten the music of our ancestors, thinking instead of war. The Ellasian has reminded us; he has given us some of it back again. I think there will be music made in the Keep again."

We passed through the final veil of leaves and vines and into the Keep. And yet it was no proper Keep, lacking the tall stone wall that circled the pavilions ordinarily. This was not a true Keep at all, not as I had known it, but a wide scattering of tents throughout the forest. There was no uniformity, no organization.

Finn ducked a low branch, caught it and held it back as I rode by. He saw the expression on my face. "Not yet. It will come later, when Homana is made safe again for such things as permanent Keeps." He released the branch and fell in next to me. "This is easily defensible. Easily torn down, do we need to move on again."

The tents huddled against the ground, like mushrooms beneath a tree. They were the colors of the earth: dark green, pale moss, slate-gray, rust-red, brown and black and palest cream. Small and plain, without the *lir*-symbols I remembered: tents instead of pavilions. But a Cheysuli Keep, for all its odd appearance.

I smiled, though it pained my injured face. I could not count them all. I could not see them all, so perfectly were they hidden, even though I knew how to look. And Bellam? No doubt his men, if they came so far, would miss the Keep entirely.

Defensible? Aye—when an enemy does not see until too late. Torn down fast? Oh, aye—requiring but a moment to collapse the earth-toned fabric. A perfectly portable Keep.

And full of Cheysuli.

I laughed aloud and halted my horse. Around me spread the Keep, huddled and subtle and still. Around me spread my strength, equally subtle and silent and still. With the Cheysuli and an army besides, Bellam could never stop me.

"Tahlmorra lujhalla mei wiccan, cheysu," I said softly. *The fate of a man rests always within the hands of the gods.*

Finn, so silent beside me, merely smiled. "You are welcome to Homana, my lord. And to the homeplace of my people."

I shook my head, suddenly overcome. "I am not worthy of it all . . ." In that moment, I was certain of it. I was not up to the task.

"Are you not," my liege man said simply, "no man is."

When I could, I rode farther into the Keep. And thanked the gods for the Cheysuli.

Chapter Ten

The harpsong filled the forest. The melody was so delicate, so fragile, and yet so strong. It drew me as if it were a woman calling me to her bed; Lachlan's Lady, and I a man who knew her charm. I forgot the warriors Finn had promised and followed a song instead, feeling its magic reach out to touch my soul.

I found him at last perched upon the ruin of a felled beech, huge and satin-trunked. The tree had made its grave long since, but it provided a perfect bench—or throne—for the harper. The sunlight pierced the surrounding veil of branches and limbs like enemy spears transfixed upon a single foe: the harp. His Lady, so dark and old and wise, with her single green eye and golden strings. Such an eloquent voice, calling out; such a geas he laid upon me. I reined in my horse before the beech and waited until he was done.

Lachlan smiled. The slender, supple fingers grew quiet upon the glowing strings, so that music and magic died, and he was merely a man, a harper, blessed with Lodhi's pleasure.

"I knew you would come," he said in his liquid, silken voice.

"Sorcerer," I returned.

He laughed. "Some men call me so. Let them. You should know me better now." For a moment there was a glint of some unknown emotion in his eyes. "Friend," he said. "No more."

I realized we were alone. Finn I had left behind. And that, by itself, was enough to make me fear the Ellasian harper.

He saw it at once. Still he sat unmoving upon the beech trunk, his hands upon his Lady. "You came because I wished you to, and because *you* wished it," he said quietly. "Finn I did not require; not yet. But he will come, and Duncan." The sunlight was full upon his face. I saw no guile there, no subterfuge. Only honesty, and some little dedication. "I am a harper," he said clearly. "Harpers require men of legend in order to do what they do. You, my lord, are legend enough for most. Certainly for me." He smiled. "Have I not proven my loyalty?"

"Men will slay whom they are told to, do they have reason enough for it." I remained upon my horse, for I did not fully trust him with that harp held in his hands. "You slew the man I bid you to, but a spy would do so easily enough, merely to maintain his innocence."

He took his hands from the harp and spread them. "I am no spy. Save, perhaps, your own."

"Mine." I said nothing more; for the moment he had made me speechless. And then I looked deeper into his eyes. "Would you, an Ellasian, serve me, a Homanan, in anything I bid you?"

"Providing it did not go against my conscience," he said at once. "I am a priest of the All-Father; I will not transgress any of His teachings."

I made a dismissing gesture. "I would ask no man to go against his lights. Not in something such as his gods. No. I mean, Lachlan, to see just how loyal you are."

"Then bid me," he returned. "I am here because I wish to be, not because some Ihlini sorcerer or Solindish king has sent me. And if they had, would I not take them the news they wish to hear? Would I still be here, when I could tell them the location of the Cheysuli and your army?"

"A wise spy, spies," I told him flatly. "The hare that breaks too soon is caught quickly by the fox."

He laughed. Lachlan's laugh is warm, generous, a true casement of his soul. "But it is not a fox I fear, my lord . . . it is a wolf. A Cheysuli wolf." His eyes went past me. I did not turn, knowing who stood there.

"What would you do, then?" I asked.

The laughter had died. He looked at me directly. "Spy for you, Carillon. Go into Mujhara, to the palace itself, and see what Bellam does."

"Dangerous," Finn said from behind me. "The hare asks to break."

"Aye," Lachlan agreed. "But who else could do it? No Cheysuli, that is certain. No Homanan, for whom would Bellam admit without good reason? But I, *I* am a harper, and harpers go where they will."

It is true harpers are admitted to places other men cannot go. I knew from my own boyhood, when my uncle had hosted harpers from far and wide within Homana-Mujhar. A harper would be a perfect spy, that I did not doubt.

And yet—"Lachlan of Ellas," I said, "what service would you do me?"

His fingers flew against the strings. It was a lively tune, evocative of dance and laughter and youth. It conjured up a vision before my eyes: a young woman, lithe and lovely, with tawny-dark hair and bright blue eyes. Laughter was in her mouth and gaiety in her soul. My sister, Tourmaline, as I recalled her. At nineteen, when I had seen her last, though she would be twenty-four now.

Tourmaline, hostage to Bellam himself. And Lachlan knew it well.

I was off my horse at once, crossing to the beech in two long steps. My hands went out to stop his fingers in the strings, but I did not touch them after all. I felt a sudden upsurge of power so great it near threw me back from the man. I took a single step backward against my will, all unexpected, and then I stood very still.

His fingers slowed. The tune fell away until only an echo hung in the air. And then that, too, was gone, and silence built a wall between us.

"No," he said quietly. "No man gainsays the truth."

"You do not ensorcell *me!*"

"*I* do not," he agreed. "What power there is comes of Lodhi, not His servant. And do you seek to injure my Lady, she will injure you." He did not smile. "I mean you no harm, my lord, nor my harp; yet harm may come to the man who means *me* harm."

I felt the upsurge of anger in my chest until it filled my throat. "I meant you no harm," I said thickly. "I merely wanted it to *stop*—"

"My Lady takes where she will," he said gently. "It is your sister who lives within you now, because of Bellam's power. I merely wished to show it to you, so you would know what I can do."

Finn was at my side. "What would you do?" he asked. "Free his sister from Bellam?"

Lachlan shook his head. "I could not do so much, not even with all of Lodhi's aid. But I *can* take her any word you might wish to give her, as well as learn what I can of Bellam's and Tynstar's plans."

"Gods!" The word hissed between my teeth. "Could I but trust you . . ."

"Do, my lord," he said gently. "Trust your liege man, if not me. Has he not questioned my intent?"

I let out my breath all at once, until my chest felt hollow and thin. I looked at Finn and saw the solemnity in his face. So much like Duncan, I thought, and at such odd times.

He looked directly at Lachlan. The sunlight set his *lir-*gold to shining like the strings in the harper's Lady. Neither man said a word, as if they judged one another; I found my own judgment sorely lacking, as if I had not the mind to discern what should be done. I was weary and hungry and overcome, suddenly, with the knowledge of what I must do.

"Trust him," Finn said finally, as if disliking the taste. "What is the worst he could do—tell Bellam where we are?" His smile held little humor. "Does he do that, and Bellam sends soldiers, we will simply slay them all."

No doubt he could do it, with three hundred Cheysuli warriors. And no doubt Lachlan knew it.

He stood up from the beech with his Lady clasped in his arms. Slowly he went down on one knee, still hugging the harp, and bowed his head a little. A proud man, Lachlan; the homage was unexpected. It did not suit him, as if he were meant to receive it instead of offer. "I will serve you in this as I would have you serve me, were the roles reversed." His face was grimly set, and yet I saw the accustomed serenity in his eyes. That certainty of his fate.

Like Finn and his *tahlmorra.*

I nodded. "Well enough. Go you to Homana-Mujhar, and tend my service well."

"My lord." He knelt a moment longer, supplicant to a king instead of a god, and then he rose. He was gone almost at once, hidden by the shrubbery, with no word of parting in his mouth. But the harpsong, oddly, lingered on, as if he had called it from the air.

"Come," Finn said finally, "Duncan waits."

After a moment I looked at him. "Duncan? How does he know I have come?"

Finn grinned. "You are forgetting, my lord—we are in a Keep, of sorts. There are *lir*. And gossiping women, I do not doubt." The grin came again. "Blame me, or Storr, or even Cai, whom Storr tells me is the one who told Duncan you had come. He waits, does my *rujho,* somewhat impatiently."

"Duncan has never been impatient in his life." In irritation I turned back to my horse and swung up into the saddle. "Do you come? Or do I go without you?"

"*Now* who is impatient?" He did not wait for an answer, which I did not intend to give; he mounted and led the way.

I saw Duncan before he saw me, for he was intent upon his son. I thought it was his son; the boy was small enough for a five-year-old, and his solemnity matched that I had seen so often on his father's face. He was a small Cheysuli warrior, in leathers and boots but lacking the gold, for he was not a man as yet and had no *lir*. That would come in time.

The boy listened well. Black hair, curly as was common in Cheysuli childhood, framed his dark face with its inquisitive yellow eyes. There was little of Alix in the boy, I thought, and then he smiled, and I saw her, and realized how much it hurt that Donal was Duncan's son instead of mine.

Abruptly Duncan bent down and caught the boy in his arms, sweeping him up to perch upon one shoulder. He turned, smiling a wry, familiar smile—Finn's smile—and I realized there was much of Duncan I did not know. What I had seen was a rival, a man who sought the woman I sought; the man who had won her, when I could not. The man who had led an exiled race back from the edge of death to the promise of life again. I had given him little thought past what he had been to me. Now I thought about what he was to the Cheysuli . . . and to the boy he carried on his shoulder.

The boy laughed. It was a pure soprano tone, girlish in its youth, unabashed and without the fear of discovery. No doubt Donal knew what it was to hide, having hidden for

all of his short life, but he had not lost his spirit with it.
Duncan and Alix had seen to it he had his small freedoms.

The Keep suddenly receded. The humming of voices and
the laughter of other children became an underscore to the
moment. I knew, as I looked at Duncan and his son, I
looked upon the future of Homana. From the man had
come the son, who would no doubt rule in his father's place
when Duncan's time was done. And would my son rule
alongside him? Homanan Mujhar and Cheysuli clan-leader.
Under them would a nation be reborn from war and purge
into life again. Better, stronger than ever.

I laughed. It rang out, bass rather than Donal's soprano,
and for just a moment the voices mingled. I saw the mo-
mentary surprise on Duncan's face and then the recognition, and finally the acknowledgment. He swung his son
down from his shoulder and waited, while I got off my
horse.

It was Donal I went to, not his father. The boy, so small
beside the man, and so wary of me suddenly. He knew
enough of strangers to know they sometimes brought danger with them.

I dwarfed him, taller even than Duncan. At once I went
down on one knee so as not to loom over him like a hungry
demon. It put us on a level: tall prince, small boy; warriors
both, past, present, and future.

"I am Carillon," I told him, "and I thank the gods you
are here to give me aid."

The wariness faded, replaced by recognition. I saw wonder and confusion and uncertainty, but I also saw pride.
Donal detached his hand from his father's and stood before
me, frowningly intent, with color in his sun-bronzed cheeks.
He was a pretty boy; he would make a handsome man. But
then the Cheysuli are not an ugly race.

"My *jehan* serves you," he said softly.

"Aye."

"And my *su'fali.*"

I thought of Finn, knowing he was behind me. "Aye.
Very well."

Donal's gaze did not waver. There was little of indecision
in him, or hesitation. I saw the comprehension in his face
and knew he understood what he said, even as he said it.
"Then I will serve you also."

Such a small oath, from so small a boy. And yet I doubted none of its integrity, or his honor. Such things are in all of the Cheysuli, burning in their blood. Donal was years from being a warrior, and yet I did not doubt his resolve.

I put both hands on his slender shoulders. I felt suddenly overlarge, as I had with my mother, for there was little of gentleness about me. And nothing at all of fatherhood.

But honor and pride I know, and I treasured it from him. "Could I have but one Cheysuli by my side, it would be you," I told him, meaning it.

He grinned. "You already have my *su'fali!*"

I laughed. "Aye, I do, and I am grateful for him. I doubt not I will have him for a long time. But should I need another, I know to whom I will come."

Shyness overcame him. He was still a boy, and still quite young. The intimacy had faded; I was a prince again, and he merely Duncan's son, and the time for such oaths was done.

"Donal," Finn said from behind me, "do you wish to serve your lord as I do, you might see to his mount. Come and tend it for him."

The boy was gone at once. I turned, rising, and saw the light in his face as he ran to do Finn's bidding. My horse's reins were taken up and the gelding led away with great care toward the picket-string in the forest. Finn, like Donal, walked, and I saw the calm happiness in his face as he accompanied the boy. Indeed, he needed a son.

"You honor me with that," Duncan said.

I looked at him. His voice held an odd tone; a mixture, I thought, of surprise, humility, and pride. What had he expected of me? A dismissal of the boy? But I could do nothing so cruel, not to Alix's son.

And then I realized what he meant. He had forgotten none of what lay between us; perhaps he had even dreaded our first meeting. No, not dreaded; not Duncan, who knew me too well for that. Perhaps he had merely anticipated antipathy.

Well, there was that. Or would be. There was still Alix between us.

"I honor you with that," I agreed, "but also the boy himself. I have not spent five years with Finn without learning a little of your customs, and how you raise your children. I will not dishonor Donal by dismissing him as a child, when he is merely a warrior who is not fully grown."

Duncan sighed. I saw a rueful expression leach his face of its customary solemnity. He shook his head. "Forgive me, Carillon, for undervaluing you."

I laughed, suddenly light-hearted. "You have your brother to thank for that. Finn has made me what I am."

"Not in his image, I hope."

"Could you not stand two?"

"Gods," he said in horror, "two of Finn? One is too much!" But I heard the ring of affection in his tone and saw the pleasure in his face; I realized, belatedly, he had undoubtedly missed Finn as much as Finn had missed him. No matter how much they disagreed when they were together.

I put out my hand to clasp his arm in the familiar Cheysuli greeting. "I thank you for him, Duncan. Through him, you have saved my life many times."

His hand closed around my upper arm. "What Finn knows, he learned elsewhere," he retorted. "Little enough of me is in him. Though the gods know I tried—" He grinned, forgoing the complaint. "He did not lie. He said you had come home a man."

That got me laughing. "He would not say that within *my* hearing."

"Perhaps not," Duncan conceded, "but he said it within mine, and now I have told it to you."

Men judge men by handclasps. We held ours a moment, remembering the past, and there was no failing in his grasp, nor none in mine. There was much between us, and neither of us would forget.

We broke the clasp at last, two different men, I thought, than we had been before. Some unknown communication had passed between us: his recognition of me as someone other than I had been, when he had first known me, and my recognition of what he was. Not a rival, but a friend, and a man I could trust with my life. That is not so easy a thing to claim when a king has set gold on your head.

"My tent is too small for Mujhars," he said quietly, and when I looked harder I saw the glint of humor in his eyes. "My tent is particularly too small for *you*, now. Come with me, and I will give you a throne better suited, perhaps, than another. At least until you have slain the man who makes it his."

I said nothing. I had heard the grim tone in his voice and realized, for the first time, Duncan probably hated as well as I did. I had not thought of it before, so caught up in my own personal—and sometimes selfish—quest. I wanted the throne for myself as well as Homana. Duncan wanted me to have it for his own reasons.

He took me away from the tents to a pile of huge granite boulders, gray and green and velveted with moss. The sunlight turned the moss into an emerald cloak, thick and rich and glowing, like the stone in Lachlan's Lady. The throne was one rump-sized stone resting against another that formed a backrest. The moss offered me a cushion. Godsmade, Finn would say; I sat down upon it and smiled.

"Little enough to offer the rightful Mujhar." Duncan perched himself upon a companion rock. The veil of tree limbs hanging over us shifted in a breeze so that the sunlight and shadow played across his face, limning the planes and hollows and habitual solemnity. Duncan had always been less prone to gaiety than Finn; steadier, more serious, almost dour. Seeming old though he was still young by most men's reckoning. Young for a clan-leader, I knew, ruling because his elders were already dead in Shaine's *qu'mahlin.*

"It will do, until I have another," I said lightly.

Duncan bent and pulled a single stalk of wild wheat from the soggy ground. He studied the lime-green plant as if it consumed his every interest. It was unlike Duncan to prevaricate, I thought; unless I had merely gotten old enough to prefer the point made at once.

"You will have trouble reconciling the Homanans with Cheysuli."

"Not with all." I understood him at once. "Some, perhaps; it is to be expected. But I will have no man who does not serve willingly, whether it be next to a Cheysuli or myself." I sat forward on my dais of moss and granite. So different from the Lion Throne. "Duncan, I would have this *qu'mahlin* ended as soon as may be. I will begin with my army."

He did not smile. "There is talk of our sorcery."

"There will ever be talk of your sorcery. It is what made

them afraid in the first place." I recalled my uncle's rantings when I was young; how he had said all of Homana feared the Cheysuli, because he had made them feared. How the shapechangers sought to throw down the House of Homana to replace it with their own.

Their own. In Cheysuli legend, their own House had built Homana herself, and gave her over to mine.

"There is Rowan," he said quietly.

I did not immediately take his meaning. "Rowan serves me well. I could not ask for a better lieutenant."

"Rowan is a man caught between two worlds." Duncan looked at me directly. "You have seen him, Carillon. Can you not see his pain?"

I frowned. "I do not understand. . . ."

A muscle ticked in his jaw. "He is Cheysuli. And now the Homanans know it."

"He has ever denied—" I halted the unfinished comment at once. It was true he had always denied he was Cheysuli. And I had ever wondered if he were regardless, with his Cheysuli coloring.

"Cai has confirmed it," Duncan said. "I called Rowan here and told him, but he denies it still. He claims himself Homanan. How a man could do that—" He broke it off at once, as if knowing it had nothing to do with the subject. "I bring Rowan up because he illustrates the troubles within your army, Carillon. You have Homanans and Cheysuli, and you expect them to fight together. After *thirty years* of Shaine's *qu'mahlin*."

"What else can I do?" I demanded. "I need men—*any* men—and I must have you both! How else can I win this war? Bellam cares little who is Cheysuli and who is Homanan— he will slay *everyone,* do we give him the chance! I cannot afford to divide my army because of my uncle's madness."

"It has infected most of Homana." Duncan shook his head, his mouth a flat, hard line. "I do not say *all* of them hate us. Does Torrin? But it remains that you must fight your own men before Bellam, do you let this hostility flourish. Look to your army first, Carillon, before you count your host."

"I do what I can." I felt old suddenly, and very tired. My face ached from its bruising. "Gods—I do what I can . . . what else is there *to* do?"

"I know." He studied his stalk of wheat. "I know. But I have put my faith in you."

I sighed and slumped down against my mossy throne, feeling the weight of my intentions. "We could lose."

"We could. But the gods are on our side."

I laughed shortly, with little humor in the sound. "Ever so solemn, Duncan. Is there no laughter in you? And do you not fear the Ihlini gods are stronger than your own?"

He did not smile. His eyes appraised me in their quiet, competent way, and I knew again the chafing of youth before an older, wiser man. "I will laugh again when I do not fear to lose my son because his eyes are yellow."

I flinched beneath the bolt as it went cleanly home in my soul. In his place, I might be like him. But in *my* place, what would he do?

"Were you Mujhar—" I began, and stopped when I saw the flicker in his eyes. "Duncan?"

"I am not." No more than that, and the flicker was gone.

I frowned at him, sitting upright again on my rock. "I will have an answer from you: were you Mujhar, what would you do?"

He smiled with perfect calm. "Win back my throne. We are in accord, my lord—you have no need to fear your throne is coveted. You are welcome to the Lion."

I thought of the throne. The Lion Throne, ensconced within Homana-Mujhar. In the Great Hall itself, crouched down upon the marble dais, dark and heavy and brooding. With its crimson cushion and gilt scrollwork, set so deeply in the old, dark wood. How old? I could not say. Ancient. And older still.

"Cheysuli," I said, without meaning to.

Duncan smiled more warmly. The smile set creases around his eyes and chased away the gravity, stripping his face of its age. "So is Homana, my lord. But we welcomed the unblessed, so long ago. Will you not welcome us?"

I set my face against my hands. My eyes were gritty; I scrubbed at them and at my skin, so taut with worry and tension. So much to do—and so little time in which to do it. Unite two warring races and take a realm; a realm held by sorcery so strong I could not imagine the power of it.

"You are not alone," Duncan said quietly. "Never that. There is myself, and Finn . . . and Alix."

I sat hunched, eyes shut tightly against the heels of my hands as if the pressure might carry me past all the pain, past all the battles, past all the necessities of war to the throne itself. Could it be done, I would not have to face the risks and the losses and the fears.

But it could not be done so easily, and a man learns by what he survives, not by passing o'er it.

I felt a hand on my shoulder. I turned my face away from my hands and looked into Duncan's eyes, so wise and sad and compassionate. Compassion, from him; for a man who wished to be his king. It made me small again.

"Tahlmorra lujhalla mei wiccan, cheysu," he said quietly, making the gesture with his right hand. "Now, my lord, come and sup with me. Wars are lost on empty bellies."

I pushed myself off the rock with a single thrust of my hand. *The fate of a man rests always within the hands of the gods.*

My gods? I wondered. Or Bellam's?

Chapter Eleven

Cai sat upon a polished wooden perch sunk into the ground next to Duncan's slate-gray tent. His massive wings were folded with perfect precision; not a single feather was out of place. The great hooked beak shone in the dim firelight and the red glow of the setting sun: dark and sharp and deadly. And his eyes, so bright and watchful, missed not a single movement within the Keep.

I stood outside the tent. Duncan, Finn, and the boy remained within, finishing what supper there was: hot stew, fresh bread, cheese, and Cheysuli honey brew. And Alix, who had come up from Torrin's croft with the bread, had gone off to another tent.

I had put on a Cheysuli cloak, wrapping myself in the harsh woollen folds to ward off the chill of dusk. The fabric was so deep a green I melted into the surrounding darkness, even with the light from the fire cairns on me. No longer did I wonder how the Cheysuli achieved their secrecy; a man, standing still, can hide himself easily enough. He need only affect the proper coloration and wait, and the enemy will come to him.

Cai turned his head. The great hawk looked directly at me, dark eyes glittering in the dying light. He had the attentiveness of a man in his gaze, and yet more, for he was a *lir* and a *lir* is better than a man, or so the Cheysuli claim. I had no reason to dispute it. I had known Storr long enough to acknowledge his virtues, and be thankful for his service.

I shivered, though it was not from the evening chill. It was from the pervasive sense of destiny within the Cheysuli Keep, for a Keep is where a man is, with his *lir,* and here sat a *lir* beside me. Cai, the great dark hawk with the wisdom of the ages, and the knowledge of what was to come.

Divulging it never, to no man, not even Duncan, who
served his gods better than any I had known. Such a harsh
service, I thought, requiring death and sacrifice. What the
Cheysuli bore in their bones was a weight I could not carry.
The shapechange was magic indeed, but I would not pay
its price.

I turned away and pulled aside the doorflap. The dim
light from the small iron brazier filled the tent with shadows, and I saw three pairs of yellow eyes fixed upon my
face.

Beast eyes. . . .

Even friendship does not dampen the residual fear en-
gendered by such eyes.

"I will go up to the army encampment. I have spent
enough time away from my men."

Finn rose at once, handing his cup to Duncan. The light
glittered off the Steppes knife in his belt, and suddenly I
recalled I had none to wear at my own. The bone-hilted
Caledonese weapon lay in the snowfields near Joyenne.

Finn caught up a night-black cloak and hung it over his
shoulders. It hid the gold on his arms entirely, turning him
black from brown in the dim glow of light. His hair swung
forward to hide his earring, and all I saw was the yellow
of his eyes. Suddenly, in the presence of three Cheysuli, I
found myself lacking, and I the Prince of Homana.

Finn smiled. "Do we go?"

I needed no weapon, with him. He was knife and bow
and sword.

"We go." I looked past him to Duncan with his son by
his side. "I will think well on what you have said. I will
speak to Rowan and see what pain is in his heart, so I may
have a man beside me free of such cares."

He smiled. In the dim light he seemed older, but the boy
by his side made him young again. The future of his race.
"Perhaps it will be enough for Homana to know her
Mujhar again."

I stepped aside and Finn came out. Together we walked
through the darkness to our horses, still saddled at the
picket line. The Cheysuli trust no one this close to Mujhara;
nor do I.

"The army will not be far." Finn ducked a low branch.

"I think even Homanans know the value in three hundred Cheysuli."

"They will when we are done with them."

He laughed softly, nearly invisible in the deepening night. I untied and mounted my dark Ihlini horse. Finn was up on his mount a moment later, heading through the trees, and I followed. Storr slipped along behind me, guarding my back as Finn preceded his lord. It is an exacting service, and one they perform with ease.

The moon rose full above us, above the stark black, skeletal trees: a silver plate in the dark night sky. I looked through the screen of trees that arched over my head. Beyond the screen were the white eyes of the stars, staring down. I heard the snap of twigs and branches broken by the hooves and the soft thunk of iron shoe against turf track. The forest sang with scent and the nightsounds I had so long taken for granted. Crickets called out our passage: a moth fluttered by my face on its journey toward the light. But there was no light. Not here, so deep among the trees.

And then such joy at being in Homana again rose up in my chest that I could hardly breathe. It did not last, and for a moment I was taken aback, but then I gave myself over to it. Finn was welcome to his *lir*-bond and the magic of his race. I longed only for Homana. Even an exiled Mujhar can find joy in such exile, does it bring him home again.

We rode along the crest of a hill, rising upward through the trees, and then down it, like water down a cobbled spillway. Finn took me down into a tiny bowl of a valley, skirting the edges so the trees gave cover. Clustered amid the night and darker shadows were pinpoints of flickering light. Tiny lights, little more than the luminance shed by the flame moths. Like the Cheysuli, my army kept itself to subtle warmth and illumination. One would have to look hard to see it; expecting it, it was not so hard for me to discover. A pinpoint here and there, lost within the shadows, screened by trees and brush.

A circlet of light rimmed the bowl-like valley. It crowned the crests like a king's fillet crusted with glowing gemstones, glittering against the darkness. We rode closer, still clinging to the trees, and then I learned how well-guarded was the army.

"Hold!" shouted a voice. I heard the rustling in the leaves and placed each man; a semi-circle of five, I thought. "Say who is your lord." The order was clipped off, lacking the smoothness of aristocratic speech, but Homanan all the same.

"Carillon the Mujhar," I said quietly, knowing Finn's accent would give away his race. In the darkness, the men might slay him out of hand.

"How many?" came the voice.

"Three." I smiled. "One Homanan, one Cheysuli . . . and one *lir.*"

I felt the indrawn breath in five throats, though I heard nothing. Good men. I was grateful for that much, even though I grew cold upon my horse.

"You are Homanan?"

"I am. Would you have me speak more for you, to discern my accent?" I thought it a worthwhile test; the Solindish speech does not mimic ours and would give away an enemy.

"You have said enough. What weapons do you bring?"

"A sword and a bow, and a Cheysuli warrior. Weapons enough, I think."

A grunt. "Come ahead, with escort."

We went on, Finn first, surrounded by the men. Not enough to gainsay Finn did he seek to slay them all; I could account for at least two myself, possibly three. And Storr a few more. It would take ten to stop us, perhaps more. I found I liked such odds.

More rustles in the bushes and the crunching of night-crisped snow. At last we halted near the outer rim of a fire cairn's light, and I saw the glint of weapons. Silent, shadowed men, grave-faced and wary-eyed, watching. Storr they watched the most, as any man will, knowing only a wolf. And Finn, cloaked in black with raven hair, dark-faced and yellow-eyed. Me they hardly marked at all, save perhaps to note my size.

The leader stepped forward into the firelight. He wore a long-knife in his belt and a sword upon a baldric. He was squat, well-proportioned, with close-cropped, graying red hair and bright green eyes. His body cried out for a soldier's leather and mail, though he wore only wool. He had the calm authority of a born leader; I knew at once he was a veteran of my uncle's wars against Solinde.

Other men had gathered around the tiny fire cairn. There was not enough light to see them all clearly, merely arms and legs and faces, shadowed in the darkness. Silence and waiting and wariness, the mark of hunted men. Bellam had made them so.

"What do you call yourself?" I asked the leader.

"Zared," he said calmly. "And you?"

I grinned. "Mercenary. And Finn, with Storr the wolf." I shifted in the saddle and saw hands move to hilts. "Put up your weapons, for I am Homanan-born and wish only to go to war. I am impressed by your competence, but enough of it for now." I paused. "I am Carillon."

Zared's green eyes narrowed. "Come down from that horse."

I did so and stood before the man while he looked closely at my face.

"I fought with Prince Fergus, Carillon's father," he said abruptly. "I saw the son taken by Thorne himself. Do you tell me you are that boy?"

His tone was dubious, but there was no humor in that moment. I put out both hands and pushed back the sleeves from my wrists. In the dim firelight the scars were nearly black; ridged bracelets in my flesh. Zared's eyes were on them, then rose to my face again. They narrowed once more. "Stories have it you were slain in exile."

"No. I am as you see me." I put my arms down again. "Is there more proof you would see?"

"Many men have been chained." An odd argument, but I understood him.

"Take the sword from my saddle."

He flicked a finger. One man stepped to the far side of my horse and unhooked the scabbard, then brought it to Zared. He pulled the blade partway free of the sheath so the runes writhed upon the metal, but the hilt, wrapped again in taut leather, looked an unmade thing.

"Cut it free," I said, yet again.

He did so with his knife, freeing the gold at last. The rampant lion clawed upon the metal as the shadows shifted upon it. The lion of Homana. And in the pommel glowed the ruby.

"That I know," he said in satisfaction. And he gave the sword to me.

"If you thought I was dead, why did you join the army?" I asked curiously.

"I am a soldier," he said simply. "I serve Homana. Even without a Mujhar to follow—a *Homanan* Mujhar—I will fight to defend my land. But I could not do it alone, and before now few were willing to risk themselves." He smiled a little, and it put lines in his rough-worked face. "Now we have more than a thousand men, my lord, and at last a prince to lead them."

I saw the others staring at me. They had just heard their leader admit I was their lord. It is sometimes an awesome thing for men to see who rules, when often he is only a name.

I turned back to my horse and hooked my scabbarded blade to it again. "Direct me to Rowan."

"Rowan?" Zared sounded surprised. "You wish to speak to *him?*"

"Why should I not? It was he who began this army." I swung up into the saddle again. "Would you have it said another has done it, when it was Rowan?"

Dull color flushed his face. "My lord—it is said he is Cheysuli . . . Cheysuli do not lead Homanans." The tone was harsh, the words clipped off; he did not look at Finn.

The nakedness of it stunned me. Zared I judged a fair man, a good soldier, worthy of any rank I chose for him. And he, even knowing the skill of the Cheysuli, could continue to resent their presence.

I drew in a steadying breath and spoke exceedingly calmly. "We will dismiss any man who chooses to hate the Cheysuli. *Any* man. We will not argue with what my uncle's purge has put into your mind—he worked hard enough to do it—but we do not have to tolerate it in our army. Those of you who wish to continue Shaine's policy of Cheysuli extermination may leave now. We will have none of you with us."

Zared stared, openly stunned. *"My lord—"*

"We want none of you," I repeated. "Fight Bellam and Tynstar, but no other. Not Cheysuli. They serve us too well." I gathered in my reins. "Direct us to Rowan at once."

Zared pointed toward a distant flicker. "There, my lord. There."

"Think on what I have said," I told him. "When we have won this war the Cheysuli will know freedom again. We will begin *that* policy now."

"My lord—"

I heard nothing more of his comment, for I left his fire as fast as the horse would take me.

Rowan sat alone by his tiny fire cairn. He was surrounded by clustered trees, as if he had gathered about himself a royal guard, stolid and silent. And yet within his guard he was a man alone, untouched by all save his grief. He had been found out, and no more was the secret kept.

The fire cairn was not enough to warm him, I knew; probably not enough to warm the leathern cup of wine he held in rigid fingers. But the tiny light threw illumination over his face in the thick darkness, and I saw the gaunt expression of loss.

I swung off my horse and moved toward the cairn so that he had to acknowledge me. His head came up. For a moment he stared, still lost in his reverie, and then slowly he moved forward onto his knees. It was an old man's ungainly movement.

I saw past the shock. I saw past the outer shell of loss to the resignation beneath.

He had known.

"How long?" I asked. "And why did you hide it from me?"

"All my life," he said dully, still kneeling on the ground. "As for hiding it from you—what choice did I have? Few Homanans are like you, my lord . . . I thought they would revile me. And they *have*."

I dropped the reins and moved closer yet, motioning him up from his knees. Slowly, he sat again upon the campstool. The cup in his hands shook. "Tell me," I said calmly.

He shut his eyes a moment. In the stark light he was the image of a childhood demon. *Cheysuli.*

"I was five," he said quietly. "I saw the Mujhar's men murder my kin. All save me." A quiver passed over his young face. "They came on us in the trees, shouting they had found a nest of demons. I ran. My *jehan* and *jehana*— and my *rujholla*—could not run in time. They were slain."

The Cheysuli words from Rowan's mouth were a shock to me. He had always spoken with the accent of Homana, lacking the Old Tongue entirely—and now I knew he had more claim to it than most.

I heard Finn come up beside my horse. I did not look at him, but Rowan did. They were as much alike as two leaves from the same vine; like enough to be father and son. Perhaps they were even kin.

"I had no choice," Rowan said. "I was found by a couple who had no children. They were Ellasian, but they had come to live in Homana. The valley was distant, insular, and there were none there who had seen Cheysuli. I was safe. And I kept myself so, until I came here."

"You must have known you would be discovered."

He shrugged. "I knew there was the chance. In Mujhara, I was careful. But the men interested in fighting Bellam were young, like myself, and they had never seen a Cheysuli shapechanger. So I named myself Homanan, and they believed it. It has been so long since the Cheysuli were free to go where they choose—much of Homana does not know her ancient race." Briefly he looked at me. "Aye. I have known what I am. And what I am not." He turned his face to the fire. "I have no *lir.*"

I did not fully understand. And then I thought of Finn's link with Storr and the price it carried, and I knew what Rowan meant. "You cannot mean you will seek out your death!"

"There is no need for that," Finn said. He swung down from his horse and came into the firelight with Storr pacing at his side. "He never had a *lir,* which is somewhat different from losing one. Where there is no loss, a man is not constrained to the death-ritual."

Rowan's face was leached of color, painted bleak by the firelight. "The ritual is already done, though it be a Homanan one. I am named shapechanger, and stripped of what honor once I had."

I thought of the men in the tavern where Lachlan and I had found Rowan. Those men had followed him willingly. It was Rowan who had gathered most of those who were here. Word of mouth had gathered the others and still did, but Rowan had begun it all.

"Not all of them," I told him, ignoring Zared's attitude.

"Those who are men, know men. They do not judge by eyes and gold." I realized, too, he wore no *lir*-gold. He had not earned the right.

"The gods are blind to you," Finn said quietly.

I stared at him in shock. "Do you seek to destroy what is *left* of him?"

"No. I tell him what he knows. You have only to ask him." Finn's voice and eyes were implacable. "He is *lir*less. Unwhole. Half a man, and lacking a soul. Unblessed, like you, though he be Cheysuli instead of Homanan." He went on, ignoring the beginnings of my protest. "He is not a warrior of the clan, lacking a *lir*. He will have no passage to the old gods."

My hand was on his arm. I felt the hard sinews beneath his flesh as my fingers clamped down. I had never before put my hand on him in anger.

He stopped speaking. He waited. And when I took my hand away he explained the words to me. "He gave it up willingly, Carillon. Now he must suffer for it."

"Suffer!"

"Aye." His eyes flicked down to Rowan's hunched figure. "Had it been me with the choice, I would have taken the risk."

"And *died*," I returned angrily.

"Oh, aye," he said matter-of-factly, "but I could not have lived with it, else."

"Do not listen," I told Rowan wearily. "Finn sometimes speaks when he would do better to hide his sentiments."

"Let him speak," Rowan said bleakly. "He says what I have expected all my life. My lord—there is much of the Cheysuli you do not know. Much *I* do not know, having given up my soul." A bitter, faint smile twisted his mouth into a travesty of the expression. "Oh aye, I know what I am. Soulless and *lir*less, unwhole. But it was the choice I made, too frightened to seek my death. And I thought I *would* die, when the time for the *lir*-bond came."

"You knew?" I stared at him. "You knew when the time had come?"

"How could I not? I was sick for days, until my foster parents feared I would die. The longing, the need, the emptiness within me." A terrible grimace twisted his face. "The pain in the denial—"

"You had only to answer that need," Finn said harshly. "The gods fashioned a *lir* for you, and you gave it over into death. *Ku'reshtin!* You should have died for what you did."

"Enough!" I shouted at him. "Finn—by the gods!—I want support from you! Not condemnation for a man I need."

Finn's hand stabbed out to point at Rowan's lowered head. "He lived, while the *lir* died. Can you not see what it makes him? A murderer, Carillon—and what he slew was a gift of the gods themselves—"

"Enough," I repeated. "No more."

"Look at Storr," Finn snapped. "Think how your life would have been had *I* ignored my chance to link with him. He would have died, for a *lir* who does not link when the need is upon him gives himself over to death. It is the price *they* pay, as a warrior does when his *lir* is slain." His teeth showed briefly in a feral baring, like a wolf prepared to leap.

A wolf—Finn.

"Leave Rowan be," I said at last. "You have said more than was required."

"I would say it all again, and more, did I think it would make him see what he has done."

"I *know* what I have done!" Rowan was on his feet at last, his arms coming up as if to ward off the words Finn said. "By the gods, do you think I have not suffered? Do you think I have not cursed myself? I live with it each day, *shapechanger!* The knowledge will never go away."

I saw then that each suffered. Rowan, for what he never had; Finn, for what he could not comprehend: that a Cheysuli could give up his birthright and continue to survive. It was not Rowan who was left out, but myself. Carillon. The Homanan, who could not possibly know what it was to have a *lir,* or what it was to give one up.

"I need you both," I told them finally as they faced one another across the firelight. "I will have no disharmony among my men. Neither Cheysuli-Homanan conflict, nor that between men of a single race, blessed or not." I sighed, suddenly disgusted. "By the gods, do I know anything at all of the Cheysuli? I begin to think I *cannot.*"

"*This* much I know," Rowan said, still looking at Finn.

"No man, unblessed, can ever know the grace of the gods or understand the prophecy."

Finn laughed, though it had a harsh sound. "Not so soulless after all, are you? You have enough blood in you for that much."

The tension lessened at once. They still faced one another like predatory beasts: one a wise wolf, the other a man who lacked the gifts of the *lir*-bond, and yet claimed all the eerie charisma of the race.

"Unblessed," I growled. "By the gods, now there are *two* of you prating this nonsense. . . ." I turned away to my horse, my Ihlini horse, who was as much a stranger as I to the world of the Cheysuli.

I mustered my forces in the valley the following day, Cheysuli and Homanan alike. I watched them come, silent upon my horse, and waited until they filled the bowl-shaped valley. It was a small place and made my army look smaller still; I had so few men beneath my standard. And yet more came each day, trickling in with the thaw.

I thought of haranguing them with all the arguments and commands until all went away with the taste of Carillon in their mouths. I was angry enough that my Homanans could disregard the Cheysuli when we needed every man; did they wish to lose this war? And yet I understood, for I too had been raised to hate and fear the race. I had learned my lesson, and well, by only in adversity. Many of the Homanans I faced had lacked the teacher I had.

Instead of haranguing, I talked. Shouted, rather, since I could not reach them all by merely speaking, but I left my anger behind. I told them what we faced; told them how badly we were outnumbered. I would have none of them saying later I had led them unknowing into war. Did a man go to his death, I wanted him to know the risks.

I broke them into individual units, explaining my strategy to them. We could not afford the pitched battles we had ever known before, there being too few of us, and none I could spare in such futile attacks. Instead we would go in bit by bit, piece by piece, harrying Bellam's patrols. They would be fewer now, with harvest, and we would stand a better chance of catching them unawares.

The units I kept separate, knowing better than to mix

Cheysuli with Homanan. Many of our Homanans were veteran enough to recall the days before the *qu'mahlin,* and they readily accepted the Cheysuli as expert fighting men; these men I put in charge of raiding parties. I counted on them to quash the rumbles of discontent. All men knew the ferocity and incredible abilities of the Cheysuli; I thought, in the end, they would prefer to have them with us than against us.

Few questions were asked. I wondered how many men came out of a true conviction of my goal, or merely desiring a change from daily life. Some, I did not doubt, were like Zared in their desire to free Homana from Bellam's rule. But others likely sought a release from what they had known, wanting merely a different life. I could promise them that much. They would go home vastly different, did they go home at all.

I named my captains. Rowan was one of them. Him I placed with the men he had gathered in the tavern, knowing he could not lead other Homanans until he had proved himself. The Cheysuli would not accept him either, I thought, judging by Finn's reaction.

I dismissed the men into their units, tasking the captains with the goal I wanted: superior raiding parties. Men willing to sweep down quickly on Solindish patrols, slaying as they could, and sweeping away again as quickly as they had come. No time wasted; fewer lives lost. Cheysuli warfare, and more effective than most. I knew it could work, if they were willing to act as I desired.

"You have mastered them." This from Finn, sitting behind me on his horse.

I smiled, watching the army depart. "Have I? Then you are deaf to all the mumbled complaints."

"Men will ever complain. It is the nature of the beast." He kneed his mount forward and came up next to me. "I think you have won their hearts."

"I need that *and* their willingness to fight."

"And I think you will have it." He pulled something from his belt and held it out. A knife. A Cheysuli long-knife hilted in silver, with a gleaming wolf's-head pommel. It was my own, given to me by Finn so many years before. "I took it from your things," he said quietly. "A Mujhar ever carries one."

I thought of the one I had left behind. The piece of bone. I thought of the one I had replaced it with: a Homanan knife of army issue, when there was my own. But I had hidden it so long—Abruptly I put out my hand and accepted the Cheysuli knife. And then I told Finn how it was I had lost the other. I told him of the sorcerer, and of the lion-beast.

His brows drew down as he listened. Gone was the calm expression of the loyal liege man, although even then there was the hint of mockery. Now he listened, thinking even as I spoke, and when I was done with words he nodded a little, as if I had told him nothing new.

"Ihlini," he said on a sigh, as if there were need for nothing more.

"That was obvious."

For a moment his eyes were on me, but he saw something more than myself. Then his gaze cleared and he looked at me, smiling in a grim parody of the Finn I knew. "So obvious?—no. That he was Ihlini, no doubt—but not that he had used so much of his sorcery."

"So much?" It puzzled me. "There are degrees in it?"

He nodded, shifting in the saddle. "There is much of the Ihlini I do not know. They hide themselves in mystery. But it *is* known they have gifts similar to our own."

I stared at him, struck by the revelation. "Do you mean to say they shift their shapes?"

"No. That is a Cheysuli thing." His thoughtful frown was becoming a scowl. "But they can alter the shapes of other things, such as weapons." He looked at the Cheysuli knife I held in my hand. "Had you borne *that,* he could have conjured no beast. Do you see? He touched that which was not alive—nor made of Cheysuli skill—and fashioned it into an enemy for you." He shook his head. "I had heard . . . but I have never seen it."

I felt my gorge rise. I had faced the lion, knowing it was a sorcerous thing, and yet I had fought it as if it had been real, a thing Homanan-born, to be slain before it slew me. I had known it had grown out of the Caledonese bone hilt—how else would it have appeared?—but somehow I had ignored the implications of it. If the Ihlini had such power over objects, I faced a more dangerous foe than I had thought.

"What else can they do?" I demanded. "What magic should I expect?"

A stray breeze lifted a lock of black hair from Finn's left shoulder. The earring glittered. Seated on his dark horse in his dark leathers, he reminded me of the stories I had heard of man-horses, half of each, and inseparable. Well, so was Finn inseparable. From his *lir,* if not from his horse.

"With the Ihlini," he said, "expect anything."

The last of the Homanans disappeared into the trees to gather with their captains. To plan. To do as I wished, which was to strip Bellam of men and power until I could steal it all back from him.

I felt a roll of trepidation in my belly. "I am afraid," I said flatly, expecting ridicule—or worse—from him.

"No man, facing what you face, denies his fear," Finn said calmly. "Unless he lies. And you are not a liar."

I laughed, albeit oddly. "No, not a liar. A fool, perhaps, but not a liar." I shook my head, tasting the sharp tang of apprehension in my mouth. "What we face—"

"—we face," he finished. "As the gods desire." He made the familiar gesture. "*Tahlmorra,* my lord. It will go on." He closed his hand abruptly, the gesture banished. His hand was a fist, a hard brown fist of flesh and bone, and the promise of death to come.

Chapter Twelve

Our first strikes against Bellam were successful. My raiding parties caught the Solindish patrols by complete surprise, as I had intended, slaying everyone rapidly and then departing more quickly than they had come. But Bellam was no fool; soon enough he put up a defense. In two months the Solindish patrols had cut down many of my men. But still more flocked to join me, won over by the knowledge I had come home at last to take back my throne. In those first days I had had thirteen hundred men, Cheysuli and Homanan alike. Now the number was four times that many, and still more came.

Carefully I split my raiding parties and sent them out to harry Bellam from all directions. I took several of my best captains, experienced veterans all, and dispatched them with their men to distant parts of Homana. Slowly, from all four directions, they would work their way toward Mujhara and Bellam's principal forces. Little by little they would gnaw their way inward, chewing holes in Bellam's martial fabric, until the cloth was weakened. Even a large army can be defeated by small insects.

Much of my time was taken up with army matters, allowing me small chance to do any fighting myself, but I was not unready to take the field and I did whenever I could. Finn fought with me, and Storr, along with Rowan and his men. And when I could not fight, too busy with other matters, I practiced when I could against sword and bow and knife.

Zared was often my partner, for the red-haired soldier had proved an invaluable fighter. He had come to me not long after the first few strikes, offering apology for his words concerning Rowan. I had listened in silence, allowing him what he would say, and then ordered Rowan fetched so Zared could say it again to the one who deserved the words. Rowan had come, listened in a silence similar to mine, and accepted the apology. I thought he felt better for it.

Since then Zared and I had been on friendly terms, and I had come to know him better. He knew much of war, having fought for years under my father, and for that alone I was grateful. There were not many left who could recall the man who sired me, for with him had perished thousands. The memory still hurt, for I had been spared where my father had not. And all because I was heir to Shaine the Mujhar. Unexpendable, while my father was not.

Zared and I, between strikes against Bellam's patrols, sparred within a clearing in the forest. We did not maintain the camp in the same place for longer than a few days at the most, knowing more permanency would make us easier to track down. We moved constantly but with little grumbling. The army understood that our safety remained in secrecy.

I had stripped to breeches and boots, bare-chested in the late spring warmth and extra activity. Zared wore little enough as well, concentrating on footwork; I outweighed him considerably and towered over him, so though to most we seemed unevenly matched, it merely afforded us a chance to fight against different styles. He was a superb swordsman, and I still had need of such tutors. Finn had taught me nothing of the sword, for the Cheysuli do not believe in using a sword where a knife will do. What I had learned I had learned from arms-masters within Homana-Mujhar, and from exile in foreign lands.

The bout had gone on for a considerable length of time. My thighs burned and my arms ached. And yet I dared not call halt, or Zared would claim himself the victor. More often than not I won, being younger and stronger, but when he took a bout it was with great finesse and much shouting to let the others know he had beaten his Mujhar. My pride stood it well enough, after the first time, but my battered body did not like it so much. I fought to win.

Zared, on the point of thrusting at me with his sword, suddenly fell back. I followed with a counterthrust, nearly drove the blade through when he did not move to deflect, and stopped short. Zared remained in one spot, staring past me. His sword drooped in his hand. I saw the expression—shock and awe and utter desire—and turned to see what had caused it.

A woman. Women are not unheard of in an army camp—even I had taken my ease in camp followers—but this one was different. This one was no light woman or crofter's daughter seeking a soldier in her bed.

I forgot I held a sword. I forgot I was half-naked and sweaty, wet-haired and smelling of exertion. I forgot who I was entirely, knowing only I was a man, and a man who wanted that woman.

I felt the fist knot up deep in my belly, making me aware of what I needed. Wanted, aye, but needed as well. With the sudden recognition of such things, I knew I wanted to bed the woman before the day was done.

She had not come of her own volition. That much was clear. Finn held her arm roughly, and he brought her to me with infinite satisfaction in his demeanor. I had never seen him so pleased before, and yet his pleasure was not something others—certainly not the woman—could see. It showed only in the deep feral light in his eyes and the set of his mouth, too calm for Finn. He did not smile, but I saw the laughter in his soul.

He brought her to me. I remembered all at once what it was she saw, and for once I was displeased with my liege man. No doubt the woman was a prisoner, but surely he could have done me the courtesy of allowing me time to put on fresh clothing and wipe the sweat from my face. It dripped from my hair and beard to trickle down my bare chest.

She was stiff and clumsy with rage. White-blond hair spilled free of its sheer silken covering, tumbling past slender shoulders clad in slate-gray velvet. Her gown was torn and stained; flesh showed through the rents, but her pride was undiminished. Even as she stood before me in obvious disarray, in the open for all to see, the sight of her pride struck the smile from my face.

Her eyes fixed themselves upon me. Wide-spaced eyes, gray and cool as water, long-lidded and filled with virulent scorn. An apt emotion for the man who stood before her, rank from exertion, a bared blade in his callused hand.

I saw again the wild light in Finn's eyes. "We took a procession out of Mujhara, bound for Solinde."

I looked at the woman again. Her skin was pale as death, but that changed as color crept into her face. Anger, I knew, and defiance.

And then she spoke. "Do you mean to tell me, shape-changer, *this* man is the pretender-prince?"

"Carillon of Homana," I informed her, and a suspicion formed in my mind. I looked at Finn for confirmation and saw his satisfied smile. At that I had to add my own. "Pretender-prince, am I? When I was born to that throne? I think not, lady. I think it is your father who pretends. A usurper king, and you his daughter." I laughed then, into her angry face. "Electra!" I said. "Oh, aye, you are well come to this camp. And I thank the gods for their gift."

Her teeth showed briefly in a faint, feral baring, much as I had seen in Finn from time to time. But there was nothing of the Cheysuli in her. She was pale, so pale, like winter snow. White on white, with those ice-gray eyes. Gods, what a woman was this!

"Electra," I said again, still smiling. Then I gestured toward Finn. "Take her to my tent. Guard her well—we dare not lose this woman."

"No, my lord." I saw the appraisal in his eyes. No doubt it was obvious what I wanted. To her as well as him.

I watched her move away with him, one slim arm still caught in his sun-bronzed hand. The torn gown hid little of her body. It was with great effort that I dispatched Zared for cloth and fresh wine. When he came back I dried myself as best I could, drank down two cups of harsh red wine and put on my shirt and leather jerkin. Little in my apparel made me a prince, but I thought it would not matter. There was more on my mind than rank.

I went into my tent at last. Electra stood precisely in the center, resolutely turned away from Finn, and now myself. The tent boasted little of fine things, being a field pavilion. There was a rude bed, a table and stool, tripod and brazier. There was little room for more.

Except, perhaps, Electra.

Finn turned. He was unsmiling now, but I saw something in the set of his mouth and the tautness of his face. I wondered what she had said or done to set him so on edge. I had seen him like this rarely, especially with a woman.

We measured each other in that moment. But it was Electra who broke the silence by turning to face us both. "This is ill-done, Homanan. You take me from my women and leave me to the shapechangers."

"See to your men," I told Finn briefly. "You may leave with her."

He knew dismissal when he heard it. More often than not we played at lord and liege man, being better friends than most men of such rank, but this time he heard the command. I had not meant it to come out so baldly, but there was nothing for it. There was no room for Finn in this.

He smiled grimly. "Beware your weapon, my lord Mujhar."

The euphemism brought crimson flags to her face as he left and I wondered how much she knew of men. No doubt Bellam claimed his daughter a virgin, but I thought it unlikely. She did not look at me with any of the virgin's fear or curiosity. She was angry still, and defiant, but there was also the look of a woman who knows she is wanted by a man.

The tent was of thin, pale fabric. Though the doorflap hung closed, enough light crept through the gap to lend a dusky daylight to the interior. The roof draped down from the ridgepole, nearly brushing my head, and the breeze billowed the side panels. She stood very still in the center, head raised and arms at her sides, keen-edged as any blade. It reminded me that I bore a sword, unsheathed, and no doubt she took it as a threat.

I moved past her to the table and set the blade upon it. I turned back, watching as she turned, and saw the seductiveness in her movements. She knew well enough what she did: she watched me as well as I watched her.

"Electra." Her eyes narrowed as I spoke. "Do you know what men call you?"

Her head, on her pale, slender neck, lifted. Gold glimmered in her ears and at her throat. She smiled back at me slowly, untouched by the insinuation in my tone. "I know."

I poured a cup of wine and deliberately kept it for myself, offering her none. She made no indication she cared,

and suddenly I felt ludicrous. I set down the cup so hard
the wine slopped over the rim and spilled, crawling across
the parchment map upon the table like a crimson serpent
seeking its lair.

"Tynstr's light woman," I said. "An Ihlini's whore."

Her pale eyes were still and cool in her flawless face. She
appraised me from head to toe, even as I assessed her, and
I felt the heat creep up from my belly to engulf my face.
It was all I could do to keep my hands from her.

"You are a princess of Solinde," I reminded her, perhaps
unnecessarily. "I know it, even if you have forgotten. Or is
it that Bellam does not care what men say about his
daughter?"

Electra smiled. Slowly she reached out and took up the
forgotten wine cup, lifting it to her mouth. She held my
eyes with her own and drank three sips, then threw down
the cup with a gesture of condescension. The red wine colored her lips and made me all the more aware of her, when
I needed no reminding.

"What else have they said, my lord?" Her tone was
husky and slow. "Have they said I am more witch than
woman?"

"You are a woman. Do you require more witchcraft than
that?" I had not meant to say it. It had given her a weapon,
though perhaps she had held it all along.

She laughed deep in her throat. Her accent was exquisite.
"Aye, pretender-prince, perhaps it is. But I will tell you
anyway." One slender, fine-boned hand smoothed a pale
strand of hair away from her face. "How old am I,
Carillon?"

The Solindish accent made the syllables of my name sing.
Suddenly I wanted her to say it again, in my arms, in my
bed, as she assuaged the knot in my belly. "How old?" I
asked, distracted.

"Surely you can give me an age."

The vanity of women. "Perhaps twenty."

Electra laughed. "When Lindir of Homana—your cousin,
I believe?—was promised to my brother, I was ten years
old." She paused. "In case you cannot count, my lord—
that was thirty years ago."

The grue slid down my spine. "No."

"Aye, Carillon." Two fingers traced the gold around her

throat. It was a twisted piece of wire, simple and yet elegantly suitable. "Are not Tynstar's arts impressive?"

My desire began to spill away like so much unwanted seed. Tynstar's arts—Tynstar's light woman. Gods. "Electra." I paused. "I think you have a facile tongue. But you undervalue my intelligence."

"Do I? Do you disbelieve me?" The velvet on her shoulders wrinkled in a shrug. "Ah well, believe as you will. Men do, for all they claim themselves an intelligent race." She smiled. "So—this is what you face: this poor little tent, in your desire to seek my father's throne."

"*My* throne, lady."

"Bellam took it from Shaine," she said calmly. "It belongs to the House of Solinde."

I smiled with a confidence I did not entirely feel, facing her. "And I will take it back."

"Will you? How? By selling me?" Her cool eyes narrowed. The expression did not suit their long-lidded, somnolent slant. "What will you do with me, my lord?"

"I have not decided."

"Ransom me? Slay me?"

I frowned. "*Slay* you—I? Why should I desire your death?"

"Why not? I am your enemy's daughter."

I laughed. "And a woman such as I have never seen. Slay you? Never. Not when there is so much I would rather do."

I saw the subtle change in her mouth; in the shape of her jaw. She had me, not I her, and she knew it. She smiled. It was a faint, slow, seductive smile, and went straight to the knot in my belly. The long-lidded eyes took their measure of me, and I wondered if she found me lacking somehow.

Electra moved swiftly, diving for the Cheysuli sword on the table next to me. I spun and caught her waist as she slipped by; she clawed for the sword even as my hands closed on her. She had it in her hands, both hands, jerking it from the table. The blade flashed in the pale, muted light and I caught her wrist, knocking her arm against my upraised leg. She hissed in pain and lost the sword, dropping it to the hard-packed earth.

The white-blond hair was a curtain across her face, hiding

it from me as the fine strands snagged on the leather of my jerkin. I released one of her arms and smoothed away the hair from her angry face, drawing her inexorably closer. And then, even as she caught my neck in her arms, I ground my mouth onto hers.

She was like the finest wine, subtle and heady and powerful. She went straight to my head, blurring my senses and addling my wits. I could do nothing but drown, drinking more even as I drowned, wanting only to take her with me. I could not think of letting her go. And she did not insist upon it, reaching up to catch my damp hair in two doubled fists. But her teeth sank into my bottom lip, tearing, and I cursed and jerked my face free.

"Rape?" she demanded.

"Who rapes?" I asked. "You or I? I think you have as much interest in this as I."

I had not let her go. I did not, even as I set the back of one hand against my bleeding lip. The other hand was caught in the fabric of her gown, one arm locked around her spine. I could feel every line of her body set so hard against mine. Gods, but it would be easy to simply bear her down and take her here—

"Electra," I said hoarsely, "are you Tynstar's light woman?"

"Does it matter?" Her breasts rose against my chest. "Does it matter so much, pretender-prince?"

My lip still bled. And yet I cared little enough for the pain. I wanted to share it with her. "Oh aye, it matters. For he will pay dearly for you."

She stiffened at once. "Then you will seek ransom—"

"I seek what I can get," I told her bluntly. "By the gods, woman, what do *you* seek to do? Ensorcell me?"

She smiled. "I do what I can." She touched my lip with a gentle finger. "Shall I take the pain away?"

"Witch," I accused.

"Woman." This time she was the aggressor as much as I, and she did as she had offered. She took the pain from my mouth and centered it much deeper, where I could not control myself.

"How much will you ask for me?" she whispered against my mouth.

"My sister."

Her head rose. "Tourmaline?"

"Aye. I care little enough for gold. It is my sister I want."

"My father will never pay it."

"He will. I would." And I knew as I said it, she had had the truth from me.

Electra laughed. "Carillon, oh Carillon—such words from you already? Do you give in to my witchcraft so soon?"

I set her away with effort. I felt unsteady, as if sickening from some fever. I was hot and cold and ringing with the tension as well as the demand.

I realized, with a sense of astonishment, that the sword still lay on the ground between us. I had not recovered it. It had lain there, blade bare, as if in promise of what might lie between us in the future.

Electra stood by the table. Her mouth was still red from the wine and stained by my blood. The long-lidded eyes regarded me calmly, assessively, as if she judged me within her mind. I dared not ask what she saw; I had not the courage.

I bent and picked up the sword. Slowly I slid it home in the scabbard and set it on the table. Within reach. She had only to pick it up again.

Electra laughed. "You are too quick for me, my lord, and far too strong. You are a man, you see, and I merely a woman."

"Merely," I said in disgust, and saw her contented smile. "No rape," I told her, "though I doubt—judging by what I have tasted—you would be so unwilling. But no rape." I smiled. "I do not rape what I will have in marriage."

"Marriage!" she shouted, and I knew I had broken through her guard at last.

"Aye," I agreed calmly. "When I have slain your father— and ·Tynstar—and once again hold *my* throne . . . I will make you Queen of Homana."

"No!" she shouted. "I will not *allow* it!"

"Do you think I care what you will allow?" I asked her gently. "I will take you to wife, Electra. None can gainsay me, now."

"I will gainsay you!" She was so vividly angry I could scare draw breath. "You puling fool, *I* will gainsay you!"

I merely smiled at her, and offered more wine.

*   *   *

Finn, seated on a stool within my tent, nearly dropped his cup of wine. "You will do *what?*"

"Wed her." I sat on the edge of my army cot, boots kicked off and wine in my wooden cup. "Would you have a better idea?"

"Bed her," he said curtly. "Use her, but do not *wed* her. The Mujhar of Homana wed to Bellam's daughter?"

"Aye," I agreed. "That is how alliances are made."

"Alliance!" he lashed. "You are here to take back the throne from the man who usurped it, not win his approval as a husband for his daughter. By the gods, what has put this foolishness in your head?"

I scowled at him. "You name *me* a fool? Are you blind? This is not just a thing between a man and a woman, but between realms and people as well." I shifted on the cot. "We cannot force war on Homana forever. When I have slain Bellam and won back the Lion, there will still be Solinde. The realm is large and strong, and I would prefer not to fight it forever. Do I wed Electra to cap my victory, I may well settle a lasting peace."

It was Finn's turn to scowl. His wine wash untouched. "Do you recall, *my lord,* how it was the *qu'mahlin* was begun?"

"I recall it well enough," I snapped impatiently. "And I do not doubt Electra will also refuse to wed with me, as Lindir refused to wed with Ellic, but she will have no choice when the throne is mine."

Finn said something in a tone of deep disgust, but it was in the Old Tongue and I could not understand it. He reached down and tugged at one of Storr's ears as if seeking guidance. I wondered what the wolf told him.

"I know what I am doing," I said quietly.

"Do you? How do you know she is not Tynstar's minion? How do you know she will not slay you in your wedding bed?"

It was my turn to swear, though I did it in Homanan. "When I am done with this war, Tynstar will be dead."

"What will you do with her now?"

"Keep her here. Bellam will send word concerning Torry's release, and then we shall see to returning his daughter to him." I smiled. "If he is not dead by then himself."

Finn shook his head. "Keeping her I can see, for it is a tool to use against your *rujholla's* captivity. But wedding her? No. Seek your *cheysula* elsewhere."

"Would you have me wed a Cheysuli, then?" I scoffed. "The Homanans would never allow it."

"Cheysuli women wed Cheysuli men," he said flatly. "No woman would look outside her clan."

"What of the men?" I asked. "I have not seen the warriors keeping to their clan. Not even you." I smiled at his wary expression. "There was Alix, only half Cheysuli, and not knowing it at all." I paused. "And now, perhaps, Electra?"

He sat upright so quickly wine slopped over the rim of his cup and splashed across Storr's head. The wolf sat up as quickly as Finn, shaking his head to send droplets flying in all directions. The look he flashed Finn was one of such grave indignation I could not help but laugh, though Finn found little humor in it.

He rose and set the cup down on the table, still scowling. "I want none of Electra."

"You forget, I know you. I have seen you with women before. She touched you, Finn, as much as she touched me."

"I want none of her," he repeated.

I laughed at him. And then the laughter died, and I frowned. "Why is it we are attracted by the same women? There was Alix first, and the red-haired girl in Caledon, and now—"

"A liege man knows his place." The comment overrode me. "Do you truly think he seeks what woman his lord will make his queen?"

"Finn." I rose as he turned away. "Finn, I know you better than that."

"Do you?" His face was uncommonly grave. "I think not. I think not at all."

I put down my cup of wine. "I take her to wife because she is worthy of that much. I will not get her another way."

"Put out your hand and take her," Finn said. "She will come to you like a cat to milk."

The wall went up between us, brick by brick. Where once its name had been Alix, now it was Electra. And, though I thought what he felt for Electra was closer to dislike than anything akin to love, I could not see the way of tearing it down again. Kingdoms take precedence even over friendships.

"There are things a king must do," I said quietly.

"Aye, my lord Mujhar." This time he did leave, and the wolf went with him.

Chapter Thirteen

I jerked aside the doorflap and went out, buckling on my swordbelt with its weight of Cheysuli gold. No longer did I wrap the hilt in leather to hide the crest and ruby. All men knew I had come at last—including Bellam—and no longer did I wish to hide my presence or my identity.

Finn stood waiting with the horses. He, like myself, wore his warbow slung across one shoulder. But he wore no ringmail or boiled leather, trusting instead to his skill to keep him free of harm. No Cheysuli wore armor. But perhaps I too would leave it off, did I have the chance to wear an animal's form.

I took the reins from him and turned to mount. But I stopped the motion and turned back as Rowan called to me.

"My lord—wait you!" He hastened toward me in a rattle of mail and sword. Like us, he prepared to lead an attack against one of Bellam's patrols. "My lord, the lady is asking for you." He arrived at last, urgency in face and voice.

"Electra asks for nothing," I told him mildly. "Surely you mean she has *sent.*"

Color rose in his face. "Aye," he said, "she has sent." He sighed. "For you."

I nodded. Electra sent for me often, usually two or more times in a single day. Always to complain about her captivity and to demand her immediate release. It had become a game between us—Electra knew well enough what she did to me when I saw her. And she played upon that effect.

In the six weeks since Finn had captured her, nothing had been settled between us except out mutual attraction. She knew it as well as I. Ostensibly enemies, we were also eventual bedmates. It was simply a matter of time and circumstance. Did I wish to, I could have her before her internment was done. But I gambled for higher stakes—permanency, in reign and domesticity—and she knew it. She used it. And so the courtship rite went on, bizarre though it was.

"She waits," Rowan reminded me.

I smiled. "Let her." I swung up on my horse and gathered the reins, marking how my men waited. And then I was gone before Rowan could speak again.

Finn caught up to me not far from the camp. Behind us rode our contingent of soldiers: thirty Homanans armed to the teeth and ready for battle once more. Scouts had already brought reports of three Solindish patrols; I would take one, Rowan another, Duncan the third. Such warfare had worked well in the past months; Bellam already shouted impotent threats from his stolen throne.

"How much longer do we keep her?" Finn asked.

No reference was necessary. "Until I have Torry back." I squinted against the sun. "Bellam's last message said he would send Torry out of Mujhara with an escort—and Lachlan also. Electra will be back with her father soon enough."

"Will you let her go?"

"Aye," I said calmly. "It will be no hardship to let her go when I will have her back so soon."

He smiled. "No more hedging, from you. No more modesty."

"No," I agreed, grinning. "I have come home to take my uncle's throne, and I have every intention of doing it. As for Bellam, we have harried him long enough. In a month, or two or three, he will come out of Mujhara to fight. This thing will be settled then."

"And his daughter?"

I looked directly at him, tasting the dust of warfare in my mouth as we moved toward our battle. "She is Tynstar's light woman, by all accounts—including her own. For that alone, I will make her mine."

"Revenge." He did not smile. "I understand that well enough, Carillon, having tasted it myself—but I think it is more than that."

"Political expediency," I assured him blandly. "She is a valuable tool."

A scowl pulled his face into grim lines. "In the clans, it is not the same."

"No," I agreed quietly. "In the clans you take women as you will and care little enough for the politics of the move." I glanced back at my soldiers. They followed in a tight unit, bristling with swords and knives and ringmail. "Men have need of such things as wives and children," I told him quietly. "*Kings* have need of more."

"More," he said in disgust, and his eyes were on Storr. The wolf loped by Finn's horse, silver head turned up so their eyes locked: one pair of eerie, yellow eyes; one pair of amber, bestial eyes. And yet I could not say who was truly the beast.

Or if either of them were.

Our attack swept down on Bellam's patrol and engulfed the guardsmen. I halted my horse some distance from the melee and set about loosing arrow after arrow into selected targets. The Atvian longbow, for all its range was good, lacked the power of my Cheysuli bow; until my arrows were gone, I would be well-nigh invincible.

Or so I thought, until one Atvian arrow, half-spent, struck the tender flesh of my horse's nose and drove him into a frenzy of pain. I could not control him. Rather than lose myself to a pain-crazed horse in place of an Atvian arrow, I jumped from the horse and set about doing what I could on foot.

My Homanans fought well, proving their worth. There was no hesitation on their part, even facing the archers who had so badly defeated them six years before. But we were greatly outnumbered. Bellam's men turned fiercely upon my own, slashing with swords, stabbing with knives, screaming like utter madmen as they threw themselves into the fight. So many times we had swarmed upon them like gnats; at last they swatted back.

I discarded my bow when my arrows were gone, turning instead to my sword. I waded into the nearest knot of men, slashing at the enemy. Almost instantly I was engaged by an Atvian wielding a huge broadsword. I met blade with blade and gasped as the jar ran up through my arms to my shoulders, lodging in knotted muscles. I disengaged, counterthrust, then sank my own blade deep in his chest.

The man went down at once. I wrenched my sword free and staggered across the body, ducking another scything sweep near my head, swung around and cut loose the arm that swung the blade. The Solindishman went down screaming, spraying blood across matted grass already boggy with gore. One glance showed me the battle had turned decidedly in Solindish favor.

The trick was now to get out. My horse had been left behind. But most of the enemy was on foot as well, since we struck first at their mounts, and a foot race is more commonly won by men with greater reason to run. I had reason enough.

I looked for Finn and found him not far from me, as ever, shouting something as he closed with a Solindish soldier. He wore his human form, eschewing the savagery that accompanies the shapechange in the midst of battle. It was a matter of balance, he had told me once; a Cheysuli warrior remains himself even in *lir*-shape, but should he ever lose himself in the glory of a fight, he could lose himself forever. It was possible a warrior, crossing over the boundaries of balance, might remain a beast forever.

I did not care to think of Finn locked into his wolf-shape. Not forever. I needed him too much as himself.

And then I saw Storr running between two men. His tail was straight out as he streaked across the bloodied field. His ears were pinned back against his head and his teeth were bared. I knew then he ran to aid Finn, and I knew he was too late.

The sword came down and bit into the wolf's left shoulder. His yelp of pain pierced through the din of battle like a scythe. Finn heard it at once, or else he heard something more within the link. Helplessly I watched him turn away from his enemy to look for Storr.

"No!" I roared, trying to run through the slippery grass. "Finn—look to *yourself!*"

But he did not. And the Atvian spear drove into his right leg and buried itself in the hillside.

I threw myself over dead and wounded, enemy and Homanan alike. Finn was sprawled on his back against the ground, trying to wrench the spear from his thigh. But it had gone straight through, pinning him down, even as he sought to break the shaft with his hands.

The Atvian spearman, seeing his advantage, pulled his knife from its sheath and lunged.

I brought down my sword from the highest apex of its arc, driving it through leather and mail and flesh. The body toppled forward. I caught it before it fell across Finn and dragged it away, tossing it to one side. And then I cursed as I saw the damage that had already been done; how he had laid open the flesh of Finn's face with his knife. The bloody wound bisected the left side from eye to jaw.

I broke the spear in my hands and rolled Finn onto one side, grateful he was unconscious. I pulled the shaft free as the leg twitched and jumped beneath my hands. Blood ran freely from the wound, pooling in the matted, trampled grass. And then I pulled my liege man from the ground and carried him from the field.

Finn screamed Storr's name, lunging upward against my restraining hands. I pressed him down against the pallet, trying to soothe him with words and wishes alone, but he was too far gone in fever and pain. I doubted he heard me, or even knew I was there.

The tiny pavilion was rank with heat and the stench of blood. The chirurgeons had done what they could, stitching his face together again with silk thread and painting it with an herbal paste, but it was angry and swollen and ugly. The wound in his thigh they had drained and poulticed, but one man had gone so far as to say he thought it must come off. I had said no instantly, too shocked to consider the amputation, but now that some time had passed I understood the necessity of the suggestion.

Did the leg fill with poison, Finn would die. And I did not wish to give him over to such pain.

I knelt rigidly at his side, too stiff and frightened to move away. The doorflap hung closed to shut out the gnats and flies; the air was heavy and stifling. Rowan stood beside me in the dimness of the tent, saying nothing, but I knew he felt his own measure of shock and apprehension. Finn had ever seemed invincible, even to those he hardly knew. To those of us who knew him best of all—

"He is Cheysuli." Rowan meant to reassure me.

I looked down on the pale, sweating face with its hideous wound. Even stitched closed, the thing was terrible. It snaked across his face from eye to jaw, puckering the flesh into a jagged, seeping serpent. Aye, he was Cheysuli.

"They die," I said in a ragged tone. "Even Cheysuli die."

"Less often then most." He moved forward a little. Like me, he was splattered with blood. Rowan and his men had gotten free without losing a single life. I had lost most of my unit, and now perhaps Finn as well. "My lord—the wolf is missing."

"I have dispatched men to search. . . ." I said nothing more. Storr's body had not been found upon the field. And I myself had seen the sword cut into his shoulder.

"Perhaps—once he is found—"

"For a Cheysuli, you know little enough of your customs." Abruptly I cursed myself for my curtness. It was not my place to chastise Rowan for what he could not help. I glanced up at his stricken face, realized he risked as much as I in this endeavor, and tried to apologize.

He shook his head. "No. I know what you say. You have the right of it. If the wolf is already slain—or dies—you will lose your liege man."

"I may lose him anyway." It seemed too much to hope he would live. And if I gave the order to take his leg—

"Carillon." It was Alix, pulling aside the doorflap, and I stared in blank astonishment. "They sent for me." She came into the tent, dropping the flap behind her, and I saw the pallor of her face. "Duncan is not here?"

"I have sent for him."

She moved closer and knelt down at my side, amber eyes fixed on Finn. Seeing him again through her vision, I nearly turned away. He wore a death's-head in place of his own.

Alix put out her hand and touched his bare arm. The *lir*-gold with its wolf-shape was smeared with blood, dulled by grime; it seemed a reflection of his death. But she touched his arm and then clasped his slack hand, as if she could not let him go.

I watched her face. She knelt at his side and held his hand so gently. There was a sudden horrified grief in her eyes, as if she realized she would lose the man who had given her over to her heritage, and that realization broke down the wall between them. Ever had they been at one another's throats, cutting with knives made of words and swords made of feelings. They were kin and yet more than that, so much more, and I think she finally knew it.

She tipped back her head. I saw the familiar detached expression enter her eyes, making them blank and black and odd. Suddenly Alix was more Cheysuli than I had ever seen her, and I sensed the power move into her soul. So easily she summoned it, and then she released a sigh.

"Storr is alive."

I gaped at her.

"He is sorely hurt. Dying." Grief etched lines into her smooth face. "You must go. Fetch him back at once, and perhaps we can save them both."

"Where?"

"Not far." Her eyes were on Finn again and still she clasped his hand. "Perhaps a league. Northwest. There is a hill with a single tree upon it. And a cairn marker." She shut her eyes a moment, as if she drew upon the memory of the power. "Carillon—go *now* . . . I can reach Duncan through Cai."

I stood up at once, hardly aware of the protests of my body. I did not need to tell her to tend him well. I merely went out in my bloody, crusted leather-and-mail and ordered a horse at once.

Rowan came out of the pavilion as I rode up with Storr clasped in my arms. I dismounted carefully, loath to give the wolf over to anyone else, and went in as Rowan pulled aside the doorflap. It was then I was conscious of the harpsong and Lachlan's nimble fingers.

He sat on a campstool at Finn's side. His Lady was set against his chest, resting on one knee, and he played. How he played. The golden notes, so sweet and pure, poured forth from the golden strings. His head was bowed and his eyes were shut. His face was rigid with concentration. He did not sing, letting the harp do it for him, but I knew what the magic he sought.

A healer, he had called himself. And now he tried to heal.

I knelt down and set Storr at Finn's side as gently as I could. Carefully I placed one limp brown hand into the stiffened silver fur, then moved back. The harpsong played on, dying away, and at last there was silence again.

Lachlan shifted a little, as if he awoke. "He is—beyond my aid. Even Lohdi's, I fear. He is Cheysuli—" He stopped, for there was little left to say.

Alix was in the shadows. She had left Finn's side as I entered, making room for Storr, and now she stood in the center of the tent. Her braids were coiled and pinned against her head but glittered not, for it seemed there was no light within the tent. No light at all.

"Duncan comes," she said softly.

"In time?"

"I cannot say."

I crossed my arms and hugged my chest as if I could keep the pain from showing on my face. "Gods—he is my right hand! I need him still—"

"We all need him." Her quiet words reproved me for my selfishness, though I doubt she meant them to.

A single note rang out from the harp as Lachlan shifted again on his stool. He silenced it at once, very grave of face. "How do *you* fare, Carillon?"

"Well enough," I said impatiently, and then I realized he referred to the blood on my mail. "I am unharmed. It was Finn they struck instead." The wolf lay quietly at his side, still breathing; so, thank the gods, was Finn.

"My lord." It was Rowan's tentative voice. "Shall I tell the princess the harper is come?"

For a moment I could not understand him. And then I knew. Lachlan had come from Bellam to direct the exchange. Electra for Tourmaline. And now I could hardly think.

Lachlan's eyes were on me. "Your sister is well, Carillon. Somewhat weary of being held in Bellam's command, but she has taken no harm. None at all." I was aware of an odd note in his voice. "She is well indeed . . . and lovely."

I looked more sharply at him. But I had no time to untangle the subtleties I heard, or the emotions of the moment. There were other things more pressing. "Where is she?"

"Not far from here. Bellam sent her out with a Solindish guard, and myself. They wait with her. I am to bring the Princess Electra, and then escort Torry back." He caught himself at once. "The Princess Tourmaline."

I did not wish to think of Electra, nor even Tourmaline. And yet I must. Impatiently I nodded at Rowan. "Tell her

Lachlan is come, and to ready herself. When there is time, the exchange will be made."

Rowan bowed and left at once, perhaps grateful for a task. There is nothing so helpless as a man who must watch another die.

The flap was ripped aside. Duncan stood in the opening, backlighted by the sunlight, and suddenly the pavilion was filled with illumination. He was a silhouette against the brilliance until he came in, and then I saw how harshly set was his face.

"Alix." She went to him at once. Duncan hardly looked at me, for his attention was fixed on Finn. "Harper," he said, "I thank you. But this is Cheysuli-done."

Lachlan took the dismissal with good grace, rising instantly from the stool and moving out of the way. Duncan pushed the campstool away and knelt down with Alix at one side. He said nothing at all to me.

"I have never done this." There was fear in Alix's voice.

The heavy gold on Duncan's arms glowed in the shadows, reflecting the light that crept in through the gaps in the door-flap. "You have the Old Blood, *cheysula*. You need fear nothing of this. It is the earth magic we seek. You need only ask it to come, and it will use you to heal Finn. And Storr." Briefly he cupped her head in one hand and pressed it against one shoulder. "I promise you—it will be well done."

She said nothing more. Duncan released her and set one hand against the wound in the wolf's side. Of the two, Storr seemed to have a more fragile hold on life. And if he died before they healed Finn, the thing was futile indeed.

"Lose yourself," Duncan said. "Go down into the earth until there is nothing but the currents of life. You will know it—be not afraid. Tap it, Alix, and let it flow through you into the wolf. He is *lir*. He will know what we do for him."

I watched the changes in Alix's face. At first she was hesitant, following Duncan's lead, and then I saw the first indication of her own power. She knelt beside the wolf with her hands clasped lightly in her lap, eyes gone inward to face her soul. For a moment her body wavered and then it straightened. I saw the concentration and the wonder as she slipped from this world into another.

I nearly touched her then. I took two steps, intending to

catch her in my arms, but the knowledge prevented me. What she did was beyond my ken—what she *was*, as well— but I knew Duncan. I knew he would never risk her. Not even to save his brother.

A tiny sound escaped her mouth, and then she was gone. Her body remained, so still and rigid, but Alix was gone. Somewhere far beneath the earth she roamed, seeking the healing arts her race claimed as their own, and Duncan was with her. I had only to look at his face and see the familiar detachment. It was profoundly moving, somehow, that a man and woman could link so deeply on a level other than sexual, and all to save a wolf.

Cheysuli magic goes into the earth, taps the strength of the ancient gods, and lends it to the one who requires the healing. The sword wound in Storr's shoulder remained, but it lacked the unhealthy stink and appearance. His breathing steadied. His eyes cleared. He moved, twitching once all over, and came into the world again.

Alix sagged. Duncan caught her and clasped her against his chest, much as Lachlan clasped his Lady. I saw the fear and weariness etched in his face and wondered if he had lied to her, saying it was safe when such magic took a part of the soul away. Perhaps, for Finn, he *would* risk Alix.

It made me profoundly angry. And then the anger died, for I needed them both. I needed them all.

"No more," Duncan told her. "Storr is well enough. But now it is my task to heal Finn."

"Not alone!" She sat up, pulling out of his arms. "Do you think I will give you over to *that* when I have felt it myself? No, Duncan—call the others. Link with them all. There is no need for you to do this alone."

"There is," he told her gently. "He is my *rujho*. And I am not alone . . . there is Cai." He smiled. "My thanks for your concern, but it is unwisely spent. Save it for Finn when he wakens."

And then he slipped away before she could protest, sliding out of our hands like oil. The shell we knew as Duncan remained, but he was gone. Whatever made him Duncan had gone to another place, and this time he was gone deeper and longer, so deep and so long I thought we had lost them both.

"Alix!" I knew she meant to follow. I bent to pull her from the ground.

She turned an angry face to me. "Do not keep me from him, Carillon! Do you think I could bear to lose him like this? Even for Finn—"

"You risked yourself for me, once, when I did not wish you to," I told her harshly. "When I lay chained in Atvian iron, and you came as a falcon to free me. Do you think I would have given you permission for such a thing?" I shook my head. "What Duncan does is for him to do. Did he want you with him, he would have asked it."

She wrenched her head around to stare again at her husband. He knelt by Finn's side, there and yet not. And Finn, so weak upon the pallet, did not move.

"I could not make a choice," she said in a wavering voice. "I ever thought I would say Duncan before anyone else, but I could not. I want them *both*. . . ."

"I know. So do I. But it is for the gods to decide."

"Has Lachlan turned you priest?" She smiled a little, bitterly. "I never knew you to prate of such things."

"I do not prate of them now. Call it *tahlmorra*, if you will." I smiled and made the gesture. "What is there for us to do but wait and see what will happen?"

Duncan said something then. It was garbled, tangled up in the Old Tongue and his weariness, but it was a sound. He moved as if to rise, could not, and fell back to knock his head against the campstool. Lachlan set down his Lady and knelt at once to give him support, even as Alix wrenched herself free of me.

"You fool," Finn said weakly. "It is not for a man to do alone."

I stared at him, unsure I had heard him correctly. But it was Finn, white as death, and I saw tears in his eyes.

Duncan pushed himself upward with Lachlan's help. He sat half-dazed, legs sprawled, as if he could not come back to himself. Even as Alix knelt down before him he seemed not to know her.

I saw Finn push an elbow against the pallet to lever himself up. And again it was myself who pushed him down. "Lie you still."

"Duncan—" he said thickly, protesting ineffectively.

"Come back!" Alix shouted. "By the gods, you fool—"

And she struck Duncan hard across the face with the flat of her hand.

It set up brilliant color in his face, turning his cheek dark red. But sense was in his eyes again. He looked at Alix, at me, at Finn, and then he was Duncan again. "Gods," he said weakly. "I did not know—"

"No," Finn agreed, with my hand upon his shoulder in case he moved again. "You did not, you fool. Did you think I would wish to trade your life for mine?" He grimaced then, and instantly hissed as the expression pulled the stitches against his swollen flesh. "By the gods—that Atvian—"

"—is slain," I finished. "Did you think I would let him finish what he had begun?"

Finn's hand was in Storr's matted pelt. His eyes were shut in a gray-white face. I thought he had lost consciousness again.

"Rujho," Duncan said, "there is something you must do."

"Later," Finn said through the taut line of his mouth.

"Now." Duncan smiled. "You owe thanks to Carillon."

I looked at him in surprise. Finn's eyes opened a slit, dilated black and glittering with the remnants of his fever. "It was *you* who—"

"Aye," Duncan interrupted, "but it was Carillon who carried you from the field. Else you would still be there, and dead."

I knew what he did. Finn has never been one for showing gratitude, though often enough I knew he felt it. I myself had trouble saying what I meant; for Finn it was harder still. I thought of protesting, then let Duncan have his way. He it was who had had the raising of Finn, not me.

Finn sighed. His eyes closed again. "He should have left me. He should not have risked himself."

"No," Duncan agreed, "but he did. And now there are the words to be said."

I thought Finn was asleep. He did not move; did not indicate he heard. But he had. And at last he looked at me from beneath his heavy lids. *"Leijhana tu'sai,"* he muttered.

I blinked. And then I laughed. "In the Old Tongue, I would not know if you thanked me or cursed me."

"He thanked you," Duncan said gravely. And then, *"Leijhana tu'sai,* Carillon."

I realized I was the only one standing. Even Lachlan knelt, so close to Duncan, with his Lady gleaming on the table. It was an odd sensation to have such people in such postures, and to know one day it would be expected.

I looked at Lachlan. "We have an exchange to conduct."

He rose and gathered his harp. But before we left the tent I glanced back at Finn.

He slept. *"Leijhana tu'sai,"* I said, "for living instead of dying."

Chapter Fourteen

I left the tent, my legs trembling with the aftermath of fatigue and tension. I stopped just outside, letting the door-flap fall shut behind me. For a moment I could only stare blankly at the few pavilions scattered across the turf in apparent confusion, lacking all order. I had taken the idea from the Cheysuli, although here we lacked the trees to hide ourselves adequately. We had camped on a grassy plain, leaving the forests behind as we moved closer to Mujhara; closer to Bellam and my throne. The encampment was little more than a scattering of men with cookfires here and there. But it had served us well.

I sucked in a deep breath, as deep as I could make it, filling my lungs with air. The stink of the army camp faded to nonexistence as I thought how close I had come to losing Finn. I knew perfectly well that had my chirurgeons pressed to take his leg, he would have found another way to die. A maimed warrior, he had told me once, was of little use to his clan. In Finn's case, it was worse; he would view himself as useless to his Mujhar as well, and that would pervert his *tahlmorra* and his very reason for living.

Lachlan slipped through the entrance. I heard the hiss of fabric as he moved, scraping one hand across the woven material. Few of us had tents to claim as shelter; I, being Mujhar, had the largest, but it was not so much. This one served as a temporary infirmary; the chirurgeons had kept all others free of it when I had brought Finn. He would be nursed in private.

Lachlan's arms were empty of harp for once. "Finn will live. You need fear no more."

"Have you consulted Lodhi?"

He made no indication my comment bothered him. "There is no need for that. I asked His help before, but there was nothing in Finn I could touch. He was too far from this world, too lost in his pain and Storr's absence. But when Duncan and Alix worked their magic—" He broke off, smiling a little. "There is much I cannot understand. And until I know more of the Cheysuli, I cannot hope to make songs of them."

"Most men cannot understand the Cheysuli," I told him. "As for songs—I doubt they would wish it. There are legends enough about them." I stared at the tiny field pavilion farthest from where we stood. It was guarded by six soldiers. "How many men are with my sister?"

"Bellam sent a guard of fifty with her." His face was grave. "My lord—you do not intend to go *yourself*—"

"She is my sister." I set off toward the saffron-colored tent as Lachlan fell in beside me. "I owe Tourmaline what honor there is, and of late there is little. I will send no man in my place."

"Surely you will take some of your army with you."

I smiled, wondering if he sought the information for simple curiosity's sake. "No."

"Carillon—"

"If it is a trap, the teeth will close on air." I signaled to the soldiers guarding Electra's tent. They stepped away at once, affording me privacy, though they remained within earshot. "*You* would know, perhaps, what Bellam intends for me."

Lachlan smiled as I paused before the tent. "He did not divulge his plans to me, unfortunately. He welcomed me as a harper, not a confidant. I cannot say he sends men to take you, but I think it very likely." His eyes went past me to study the scattered encampment. "You would do well to take a substantial escort."

"No doubt," I said blandly.

I turned and pulled aside the doorflap, but did not go in at once. I could not. The sunlight was brilliant as it slashed into the interior, illuminating the woman who sat within. She wore a dark brown gown laced with copper silk at throat and cuffs. A supple leather belt, clay-bleached to a soft yellow, bound her slender waist, fastened with a copper buckle. The gown was from Alix, fashioned by her own hands, given freely to replace the soiled gray velvet Electra had worn the day Finn caught her. The new one fit well enough, for they were of a like size, though nothing alike in coloring.

Electra waited quietly, seated on a three-legged camp-stool with the folds of her dark skirts foaming around her feet like waves upon a shore. She sat erect, shoulders put back, so that the slender, elegant line of her neck met the jaw to emphasize the purity of her bones. She had braided her hair into a single loose-woven rope that hung over one shoulder to spill into her lap, coiled like a serpent. The smooth, pale brow cried out for a circlet of beaten gold, or—perhaps better—silver, to highlight the long-lidded, magnificent eyes.

I knew Rowan had been here to tell her. She waited, hands clasped beneath the rope of shining hair. Silently she sat upon the stool as the sunlight passed through the weave of the saffron-colored tent to paint her with a pastel, ocher-ous glow. She wore the twisted gold at her throat, and it shone.

By the gods, so did she. And I wanted so much to lose myself in it. In her. Gods, but what a woman can do to a man—

Even the enemy.

Forty years, this woman claimed. And I denied it, as ever.

I put out my hand to raise her from the stool. Her fingers were still, making no promises, though I had had that of her, as well.

"You have been in battle." Her voice was cool as ever, with its soft, Solindish cadence.

I had not put off the blood-crusted leather-and-mail. My hair, dried now from the sweat of my exertions, hung stiffly against my shoulders. No doubt I smelled of it as well, but I wasted no time on the niceties of such things while I had a war to fight. "Come, lady—your father waits."

"Did you win your battle?" She allowed me to lead her from the tent, making no move to remove her hand from my grasp.

I shook my head. Rowan stood outside with four horses. I saw no good in gaming with her, denying my loss to gain a satisfaction that would not last. I *had* lost, but Bellam still lacked his pretender-prince.

Electra paused as she saw the empty saddles. Four horses only, and no accompaniment. "Where are my women?"

"I sent them back long ago." I smiled at her. "Only you were brought here. But then you were compromised the moment Finn took you captive. What should it matter, Electra—you are an Ihlini's light woman."

Color came into her face. I had not expected to see it, from her. She was a young woman suddenly, lacking the wisdom of experience, and yet I saw the glint of knowledge in her eyes. I wondered, uneasily, if Tynstar's arts *had* given her youth in place of age. "Does it grate within your soul?" she asked. "Does it make you wish to put your stamp upon me, to erase Tynstar's?" She smiled, a mere curving of the perfect mouth. "You fool. You could not begin to take his place."

"You will have the opportunity to know." I boosted her into the saddle without further comment, and felt the rigid unyielding in her body. I had cut her, somehow: but then she had cut me often enough. I nodded at Rowan. "Send for Zared, at once."

When Zared came he bowed respectfully. His gray-red hair was still cropped closely against his head, as was common in soldiery. I had not taken up the custom because it had been easy enough, in Caledon, to braid it and bind it with the scarlet yarn of a mercenary. It had been what I was.

"See to it the camp is dispersed," I told him. "I want no men here to receive Bellam's welcome, for you may be quite certain his daughter will tell him where we have been." I did not look at her, having no need; I could sense her rigid attention. "When I am done with this exchange, I will find the army."

"Aye, my lord Mujhar." He bowed, all solemn servitude, and stepped away to follow orders.

Lachlan mounted next to me, and Rowan next to Electra. She was hemmed in on both sides, closely kept. It would not do to lose her now, before I claimed my sister.

Electra looked at us all. "No army to escort you?"

"Need I one?" I smiled. I glanced to Lachlan and saw his gesture. Westward, toward Mujhara, and Tourmaline, my sister.

*   *   *

The sun beat down upon our heads as we waited on the hilltop. We silhouetted ourselves against the horizon, a thing I had not done in the long months of bitter war, but now I did it willingly. I wanted Tourmaline to see us before the exchange was made, so she would know it was us in truth, and not some trick of Bellam's.

The plains stretched below us. No more spring; it was nearly midsummer. The sun had baked the green from the land, turning it yellow and ocher and amber, and the dust rose from the hooves of more than fifty horses to hang in the air like smoke. Through the haze I could see the men, in Solindish colors, glittering with ringmail and swords. A troop of men knotted about a single woman like a fist around a hilt.

I could not see Tourmaline well. But from time to time I saw the dappled gray horse and the slender, upright figure, wearing no armor but a gown instead, an indigo-colored gown and no traveling mantle to keep the dust off her clothing. Even her head was bared, and her tawny-dark hair hung down freely to tangle across the horse's gray rump.

I heard Lachlan's quiet, indrawn breath. I heard my own as well, but it lacked the note I heard in his. I glanced at him a moment, seeing how avidly he watched the troop approach; how intent were his eyes upon the woman. Not my sister, in that instant, but a woman.

I knew then, beyond any doubt at all, that Lachlan plotted no treachery, no betrayal. I was certain of it, in that instant. To do so would endanger Tourmaline, and that he would never countenance. I had only to look at his face as he looked for hers, and at last I had my answer.

If for nothing else, he would be loyal to me out of loyalty to my sister. And what a weapon he gave me, did I find the need to use it.

The Solindish troop stopped at the foot of the hill. The sun glittered off their trappings; off their ringmail; off their intention. Fifty men bent on taking Bellam's enemy. And that enemy with only a token escort at his side.

It was warm on the hilltop. The air was quite still; the silence was broken only by the jingle and clash of horse trappings and the buzzing hum of an occasional insect. The dust was dry in my mouth and nose; I tasted the flat, bitter salt of summer-swept plains. Come fall, turf would spring up beneath a gentler sun. Come winter, snow would blanket the world. Come spring, I should be King.

If not before.

I looked through the clustered troop to the treasure they guarded so closely. Tourmaline, a princess of Homana. The woman Bellam had threatened to wed; the woman he could not because I had taken his daughter. A princess for a princess.

She sat quite still upon her horse, her hands holding the reins. But she was not entirely free. A soldier flanked her directly on either side; a lead-rope tied her horse to a man who rode before her. They meant not to lose her so easily, did I give them cause to fight.

Lachlan's breath was audible in his throat. It rasped, sliding through the constriction slowly, so that Rowan glanced at him. There was curiosity in Rowan's eyes; knowledge in Electra's. She would know. She would know what he felt: a man in love with a woman, looking at her with desire.

"Well?" I said at last. "Are we to confront one another in silence all day, or is there a thing I must do?"

Lachlan wrenched his attention back to me. "I am to escort Electra down, and bring Torry back with me."

"Do it."

He rubbed at the flesh beneath the silver circlet on his brow. "Nothing more?"

"Am I to think you seek to warn me of some treachery?" I smiled. "Do what you have said must be done. I want my sister back."

His jaw tightened. Briefly he glanced at Electra. She sat very still on her horse, like Torry, hardly moving her hands upon the reins. But I saw her fingers tense and the subtle shift of her weight. She meant to run, with Tourmaline still held.

I reached out and caught one of her wrists, clamping down tightly. "No," I said calmly. "Do you forget I have a bow?"

Her eyes went to the Cheysuli bow at once. And my quiver, freshly filled. "You might slay some," she conceded coolly, "but I doubt you could slay them all before they took you."

"No," I agreed, "but have I spoken of slaying *men?*"

She understood at once. I saw the color move into her

face swiftly, setting flags of anger into her cheeks. The somnolent, ice-gray eyes were blackened with frustration, but
only for a moment. She smiled. "Slay me, then, and you
purchase you fate from Tynstar."

"I do not doubt I have done so already," I told her
calmly. "I think my sister is worth dying for. But are you?"

"So long as *you* do the dying." She did not look at me.
She looked instead at the troop of men her father had sent
to fetch her.

I laughed and released her wrist. "Go, then, Electra. Tell
your father—and your sorcerer—whatever you wish to say.
But remember that I will have you as my wife."

Loathing showed on her face. "You will have nothing,
pretender-prince. Tynstar will see to that."

"My lord." Rowan sounded uneasy. "They are fifty to
our three."

"So they are." I nodded to Lachlan. "Take her down,
and bring my sister back."

Lachlan put out his hand to grasp Electra's rein. But she
did not let him. She pulled the horse away and set him to
walking down the hill. Lachlan fell in close beside her almost at once, and I watched as they rode toward the troop.
I unstrapped the bow so the captain could see it, though I
did not intend to use it. I did not think I would need it.

Electra was swallowed almost at once by the Solindish
soldiers and I was left without a target. Unless one counted
the captain and his men. But Electra had the right of it; I
could not slay them all. Even with Rowan at my side.

He shifted in his saddle. "My lord—"

"Be patient," I chided gently.

Lachlan waited at the edge of the hard-eyed throng. The
sun on his dyed hair treated it poorly, turning it dull and
lifeless. Only the glint of silver on his brow lent him authen-
ticity, and that only won through his harp. I wondered
again what made him the man he was, and how it was to
be a priest.

The troop parted. Tourmaline came forward on her dappled gray horse. Like Electra, she did not hasten, but I saw
the tension in her body. Doubtless she feared the trade
would not be finished.

Well, it was not finished yet.

Lachlan put out his hand to her. Briefly she held it tightly

with her own, as if thanking him for his care; I watched in
bemusement. It was all well and good for a harper to love
a princess—that happened with great regularity, to judge
by the content of their lays—but I was not certain Tourmaline's apparent regard for him pleased me one whit. He
was a harper, and she was meant for a prince.

"They come," Rowan said softly, more to himself than
to me.

They came. Side by side, no longer clasping hands, their
shoulders rigid against the Solindish guard. Dust rose up
from the ground and enyeloped them in a veil; Tourmaline's eyes were squinted against it as she came yet closer
to me. And then she was laughing, calling out my name,
and kicked her horse into a run.

I did not dismount, for all it would have been an easier
greeting on the ground. She set her horse into mine, but
gently, and our knees knocked as she reached out to hug
my neck. It was awkward on horseback, but we got it done.
And then, as she opened her mouth to speak again, I waved
her into silence.

"My lord!" It was Rowan as Lachlan rode up. "They
come!"

And so they did. Almost all fifty of them, charging up
the hill, to swallow us within their ringmailed fist.

I smiled grimly, unsurprised. I saw the frustrated, impotent anger on Rowan's young face as he put his hand to
his sword; he did not draw it because he saw no reason to.
We were too soundly caught.

Lachlan said something in his Ellasian tongue. A curse,
I thought, not recognizing it, or perhaps a plea to his All-
Father; whatever it was, it sounded like he meant to chew
up their bones, did they bother to come close enough.

Tourmaline, white-faced, shot me a glance that said she
understood the brevity of our greeting. What fear I saw in
her face was not for herself, but for me. Her brother, who
had been sought for six long years, was home at last.
And caught.

The Solindish captain wore a mail coif that hid all of his
head but his face. A wide, hard, battle-scarred face, with
brown eyes that had undoubtedly seen everything in war,
and yet now expressed a bafflement born of disbelief. His

Homanan was twisted by his Solindish accent, but I understood him well enough. "Surely a *boy* would know better."

My horse stomped beneath me, jarring my spine against the saddle. I did not answer.

"Carillon of Homana?" the captain asked, as if he could not believe he had caught the proper quarry.

"The Mujhar," I agreed calmly. "Do you mean to take us to the usurper on his stolen throne?"

Tourmaline drew in a sudden breath. Lachlan moved his horse closer to my sister's, as if to guard her. It was for me to do, not him, but I was occupied at the moment.

"Your sword," the captain said. "There is no hope of escape for you."

"No?" I smiled. "My sword is my own to keep."

The first shadow passed over my face, moving on quickly to blot out the captain's face. Then another. Yet a third, and the ground was suddenly blotched with moving darkness, as if a plague of shadows had come to settle across us all. All men, save me, looked up, and saw the circling birds.

There were dozens of them. Hawks and eagles and falcons, owls and ravens and more. With wings outstretched and talons folded, they danced upon the air. Up, then down, then around and around bent upon some goal.

Rowan began to laugh. "My lord," he said at last, "forgive me for doubting you."

They stooped. They screamed. They slashed by the enemy and slapped wings against staring eyes, until the Solindish soldiers cried out in fear and pain. No man was slain; no man was even wounded, but their skill and pride and dignity was completely shredded. There are more ways of overcoming the enemy than merely by slaying him. With the Cheysuli, half the defeat comes from knowing what they are.

Half the birds broke away. They dipped to the ground with a rustle of outspread wings; the soughing of feathers folded away. They were birds no more, but men instead, as the shapechange swallowed them all.

I heard the outcries of utter panic from the Solindish troop. One or two retched and vomited against the earth, too frightened to hold it in. Some dealt with horses threatening to bolt. Others sat perfectly still in their saddles, staring, with no hands upon their weapons.

I smiled. With Rowan, my sister, and Lachlan at my back, I broke passage through the enemy to the freedom outside the shattered fist. And when we were free again, guarded against attack by more than half a hundred warriors, I nodded. "Put them to death," I said. "All but five. They may escort the lady to her father."

"My lord?" It was Rowan, questioning the need for sparing even five Solindishmen to fight us another day.

"I want Bellam to know," I said. "Let him choke upon what I have done."

"Do you leave him his daughter?" Lachlan asked.

I looked past the silent troop to the five men who guarded Electra so closely at the bottom of the hill. I saw the tension in their bodies. Hands rested on their swords. Electra, too distant for me to make out her expression, sat equally still. No doubt she thought I would take her back. No doubt she knew I wanted to.

"I leave him his daughter," I said at last. "Let her spend her time in Homana-Mujhar wondering when I will come." I looked at the Cheysuli warriors surrounding the captured Solindish. Horses trembled; so did men. I thought it a fitting end.

And then I saw Duncan. He stood to one side with Cai upon his shoulder. The great hawk sat quietly, a mass of gold and brown next to the blackness of Duncan's hair. The clan-leader seemed to support him effortlessly, though I could imagine the weight of the bird. In that instant I thought back to the time, six years before, when I had been imprisoned by the Cheysuli; when Finn had held and taunted me. Duncan it was who had ruled, as the Cheysuli are ruled, by numbers instead of a single man. But there was no doubting who held the power in the clan. There was no doubting it now.

Cai lifted and returned to the air, stirring the fine veil of dust with his great outspread wings, and soared into the heavens along with the other *lir*. The shadows continued to blotch the land and the fear continued to live.

Duncan was unsmiling. "Shall I begin with the captain?"

I released a breath and nodded. Then I looked at Tourmaline. "It is time we found the camp."

Her eyes, blue as my own, were wide and staring as she looked upon the Cheysuli. I recalled she had seen none before, though knew of them as I had for so many years. To her, no doubt, they were barbaric. To her, no doubt, they were worse than beasts.

She said nothing, knowing better than to speak freely before the enemy, but I did not doubt she would when we were free.

"Come," I said gently, and turned her horse away.

Chapter Fifteen

The wind came up at sunset as we rode into the newly settled encampment. It blew dust in our faces and tangled Tourmaline's hair, until she caught it in one hand and made it tame, winding it through her fingers. Lachlan muttered something in his Ellasian tongue—it had to do with Lodhi, as usual—and Rowan blinked against the grit. As for me, I relished it. The wind would blow away the taste of blood and loss. For I had led my men into death, and I would not forget.

"A storm," Torry said. "Rain, do you think?"

The cookfires, which pocked the open landscape, whipped and strained against the wind. I smelled the aroma of roasting meat and it set my mouth to watering. I could not recall when last I had eaten—surely it was this morning?

"No rain," I said finally. "Only wind, and the smell of death."

Tourmaline looked at me sharply. I saw a question forming in her face, but she asked nothing. She glanced instead at Lachlan, seeking some assurance, then turned her attention to her horse as I led them to my pavilion when I had asked directions of a passing soldier.

I jumped from my horse by the doorflap and turned to Torry's mount. She slid out of the saddle and into my arms, and I felt the weariness in her body. Like me, she was in need of rest, sustenance, and sleep. I thought to set her down and take her inside, to get her properly settled, but she wrapped her arms around my neck and hugged with all her strength. There were tears, warm against my flesh, and I knew she cried for us both.

"Forgive me," she whispered into my sweat-dried hair. "I prayed all these years that the gods would let you live, even as Bellam sought you, yet when you come I give you thoughtless welcome. I thought you grown harsh and cruel when you ordered them slain, but I—of all—should know better. Was not our father a soldier?"

"Torry—"

She lifted her head and looked me in the face, for while I held her she was nearly as tall as I. "Lachlan told me what odds you face, and how well you face them; it is not my place to reprove you for your methods. Harsh times require harsh measures, and the gods know war is not for gentle men."

"You have not reproved me. As for gentle, no. There is little room in me for that." I set her on her feet and reached out to tousle her hair. It was an old game between us, and I saw she recalled it well. Ever the older sister telling the youngest child what to do. Except the boy had grown up at last.

"In my heart," she said softly, "I reproved. It is my fault for having expectations. I thought, when you came, it would be the old Carillon, the one I used to tease. But I find it is the new one, and a different man who faces me."

There were strangers among us, though I knew their names, and we could not say precisely what we wished. But for the moment it was enough to see her again and know her safe, as she had not been safe for years. So I said something of what I felt. "I am sorry. I should have come home sooner. Somehow, I should have come—"

She put her hand across my mouth. "No. Say nothing. You are come home now." She smiled the brilliant smile of our mother and the lines of tension were washed from her face. I had forgotten the beauty of my sister, and I saw why Lachlan was smitten.

The wind cracked the folds of the pavilion beside us. Lachlan's horse stepped aside uneasily; he checked it with a tightened rein. I looked up at Rowan and squinted against the dust. "See you she has food and wine. It will be your task to make certain she is well."

"My lord," he said, "your pavilion?"

"Hers, now." I smiled. "I have learned these past years what it is to make my bed upon the ground."

Lachlan, laughing, demurred at once. "Are you forgetting harpers are given their own sort of honor? Pavilions are part of it. Does it not ruffle your Mujhar's pride and dignity, you may share mine with me."

"It ruffles nothing," I retorted. "And will not, so long as you refrain from singing—or praying—in your sleep." I looked at Torry again. "This is an army encampment, rude and rough. There is little refinement here. I must ask you to forgive what you hear."

She laughed aloud with the pleasure of her retort. "Well enough, I shall forgive your men. But never you."

The wind blew a lock of her unbound hair against my chest. It caught on the links of my ringmail, snagging, and I sought to free it without tearing the strands. I felt the clean silk against my callused, blood-stained hands, and knew again what manner of man her brother had become.

It was no wonder she had reproved me, even in her heart.

I pulled aside the doorflap and gestured her within. "Rowan will bring food and wine, and anything else you might require. Sleep, if you will. There will be time for talking later."

I saw the questions in her eyes and her instant silencing of them. She nodded and ducked inside, and I saw the glow of a lighted candle. She would not be left in darkness.

I glanced up at Lachlan, who watched her disappear as the flap dropped down behind her. Inwardly I smiled, knowing the edge of the weapon; outwardly I was casual. "No doubt she would welcome company."

His face colored, then blanched. He had not realized how easily I saw his feelings. His hands touched his silver circlet as if to gather strength. "No doubt. But yours, I think, not mine."

I let it go, knowing I might use it later to bind him to me. Through Tourmaline, at least, I could know the harper's intentions. "Come, then. We must tell Finn what has happened. It was his plan, not mine, and he should know."

Rowan started. "His?"

I nodded. "We made it in Caledon one night, or something like it, when we had nothing better to do." I smiled with the memory. "It was a summer night, like this one, but lacking the wind, and warmer. The evening before a battle. We spoke of plots and plans and strategies, and how it would be a fitting trick to set loose in Bellam's midst." My smile faded. "But that night we did not know if we would one day come home again, or that there would be so many Cheysuli."

Again the pavilion fabric cracked. Lachlan stepped down from his horse, hair tamed by the circlet. "But there *are* Cheysuli, my lord . . . and you have come home again."

I looked at him and saw again the dull brown hair. I thought of him in love with my sister. "Will you harp for me tonight?" I asked. "Give me *The Song of Homana*."

It was the harp I saw first as I entered the infirmary tent; Lachlan's Lady, with her brilliant green eye. She stared at us both as the doorflap fell behind us, and I thought, oddly, the harp was like a *lir*. That Lachlan served her I did not wonder; that she served Lachlan, I knew. I had felt the magic before when they wove it between them.

"Ah," said Finn, "he has not forgotten me. The student recalls the master."

I grinned, relieved past measure to hear his voice so full of life. Yet even as I looked at him I could not help but wince, at least inwardly; the stitches held his face together, but the scar would last forever. It would be *that* men—and women—saw before anything else.

Lachlan slipped past me to gather his harp into his arms. He had spent much of the day without his Lady; I wondered if it hurt.

As for Finn, he did not smile. But, knowing him, I saw the hint of pleasure in his eyes and, I thought, relief. Had he thought I would not come back?

"Have they all left you alone?" I hooked the stool over with a foot.

Finn's laugh was a breath of sound. He was weak still, I could see it. But I thought he would survive. The magic had given him that much, even had it not made him fully well. "Alix has spent all day with me. Only now have I managed to send her away." He shifted slightly on the pallet, as if the leg yet pained him. "I told her I needed time alone, and I do. There is no need to coddle me."

"Alix would hardly coddle *you*." I looked more closely at his face and saw the sallow tinge. It was better than the ashy hue of death, but he lacked the proper color. There was no fever, that much I could tell, but he was obviously weary. "Is there aught I might bring you?"

"A Mujhar, serving me?" This time there was a smile, though it was very faint. "No, I am well. Alix has done more than enough. More than I ever expected."

"Perhaps it is her way of compensation," I suggested without a smile.

"Perhaps," he agreed in his ironic manner. "She knows what she lacks. I have impressed it upon her on several occasions."

Lachlan, leaning against the table, struck a note on his harp. "I could put it to song. How you wooed and lost a maiden; how the brother was the victor."

Finn cast him a scowl, though it lacked its usual depth. "Harper, you would do well to think of your own women, and leave mine to me."

Lachlan's smile froze, then grew distracted, and I knew he thought of Torry. His fingertips brushed the glowing golden strings and I heard the breath of sound. It conjured up the grace and elegance in a woman, and I thought at once of Electra. No doubt *he* thought of my sister; Finn— no doubt Finn remembered Alix. Alix before she knew Duncan.

"The exchange was accomplished," I said quietly. "My sister is safe, and Electra returns to her father."

"I thought you might keep her."

I scowled at the ironic tone. "No. I have set my mind to winning the throne before I win the woman. Did it come to a choice, you know which one I would take."

Finn's brows lifted a bit. "There have been times, of late, I have not been so sure." He shifted a little, restless, and I saw the twinge cross his face. Storr, lying next to him, settled his body closer. One brown arm with its weight of gold cradled the wolf as if Finn feared to release him.

"Will you be well?" I asked it more sharply than I intended. "Has the earth magic not healed you fully?"

He gestured briefly with a limp hand. "It does not always restore a body completely, it merely aids the healing. It is dependent on the injury." For a moment tentative fingers touched the bandage binding the thigh. "I am well enough—for a man who should have died."

I took a deep breath and felt the slow revolution of the

shadows in the tent. I was so tired . . . "The plan we made was ideal. Duncan brought all the winged *lir*. The Solindish stood no chance."

"No," he agreed. "It is why I suggested it."

Lachlan laughed softly. "Does Carillon do nothing without your suggestion?"

For a moment Finn's expression was grim, for a face that was mostly ruined by swelling and seeping stitches. "There are times he does too much."

"As when I decide whom to wed." I smiled at Lachlan's expression of surprise. "The lady who goes to her father will become the Queen of Homana."

His eyebrows rose beneath the circlet. "Bellam might not be willing."

"Bellam will be dead when I wed his daughter." I rolled my head to and fro, popping the knots in my neck. My back was tense as well, but there was no help for that. I would have to work it out with proper sleep and exercise; the former I would not see, no doubt, but the latter was a certainty.

"I had heard she was offered to High King Rhodri's heir." Lachlan's fingers brought a singing cadence from the strings.

I shrugged. "Perhaps Bellam offered, but I have heard nothing of Rhodri's answer. You, being Ellasian and his subject, might know better."

Lachlan's mouth twisted thoughtfully. "I doubt he would stand in your way. What I know of Cuinn I have learned mostly first-hand, from being hosted in the castle. The High Prince is an idle sort, though friendly enough, with no mind to marriage so soon." He shrugged. "Rhodri has strength of his own; I doubt he will demand his heir's marriage as yet. But then who am I to know the minds of kings?" He grinned at me. "There is only you, my lord, and what do I know of you?"

"You know I have a sister."

His face went very still. "Aye. I do." Briefly he glanced at Finn. "But if we speak of it more, you will set your liege man to laughing."

Finn smiled. "Has a princess caught your eye? But what else?—you are a harper."

The golden notes poured forth, and yet Lachlan did not

smile. "So I am, with thanks to Lodhi's power. But there are times I could wish myself more . . ."

So a princess might look his way? No doubt. But though harpers hold high honor in the courts of kings, they do not have enough to wed a woman of Torry's rank.

I leaned forward a moment and scrubbed at my gritty, burning eyes. And then I heard the scream.

Finn tensed to rise and then fell back; no doubt he feared it was Alix. But at once I knew it was not. The sound belonged to my sister.

I do not recall how I got from Finn's tent on my own, nor do I recall Lachlan at my side holding his gleaming harp. He was simply there, clasping his Lady, and the curses poured from his mouth. I hardly heard them. Instead I heard the echo of Torry's scream and the pounding of my blood.

Men stood around my pavilion. Someone had pulled the doorflap aside and tied it. I saw shadows within, and silhouettes; I tore the throng apart and thrust myself inside, not caring whom I hurt.

Tourmaline stood in one corner, clutching a loose green robe of my own around her body. A single candle filled the tent with muted, smoky light; it painted her face rigid and pale and glowed off the gold in her hair.

She saw me and put a hand at once, as if to stay me. As if to tell me she had suffered no harm. It passed through my mind then that my sister was a stronger woman than I had supposed, but I had no more time for that. It was Rowan I looked at, and the body he bent over.

"Dead?" I demanded.

Rowan shook his head as he reached down to pull a knife from the man's slack hand. "No, my lord. I struck him down with the hilt of my sword, knowing you would have questions for him."

I moved forward then, reaching to grasp the leather-and-mail of the man's hauberk. The links bit into my hands as I jerked him over and up, so I could see him clearly. I nearly released him then, for the light fell on Zared's face.

He was half-conscious. His eyes blinked and rolled in his head, which lolled as I held him up. "Well?" I asked of Rowan. "You were set to guard her."

"Against Zared?" His tone was incredulous. "Better to guard against *me*."

I felt the burn of anger in my belly. "Does even *that* need doing, I will do it! Answer the question I asked!"

The color fell out of his face. I heard Tourmaline's sound of protest, but my attention was taken up with Rowan. For a moment there was a flare of answering anger in his yellow Cheysuli eyes, and then he nodded. He did not seem ashamed, merely understanding, and accepting. It was well; I did not want a man who put his tail between his legs.

"I heard her cry out," he said. "I came in at once and saw a man standing over the cot, in the darkness. He held a knife." Rowan lifted a hand and I saw it. "And so I struck him down. But it was not until he fell that I saw it was Zared."

"Tourmaline?" I asked, more gently than I had of Rowan.

"I had put the candle out, so I could sleep," she told me quietly. "I heard nothing; he was very quiet. And then suddenly there was a presence, and a shape, and I screamed. But I think, before that last moment, he knew it was not you."

Zared roused in my hands and I tightened my grip. The ring mail was harsh against my fingers but I did not care. I dragged him up, thrust him out of the pavilion and saw him tumble through the throng. He was left alone to fall; they closed him within a circle of glittering, ringmailed leather but did not touch. They waited for me to act.

Zared was fully conscious. He shifted as if to rise, then fell back to kneel upon the ground as the throng took a single step forward. He knew the mettle of the men. He knew me.

He touched fingers to the back of his neck where Rowan had struck him. Briefly he looked at Torry, standing in the open doorflap, and then he looked at me. "I did not mean to harm the lady," he told me calmly. "I admit freely: it was you I wanted."

"For that, my thanks," I said grimly. "If I thought it was my sister you meant to slay, your entrails would be burning."

"Get it done," he returned instantly. "Give me over to the gods."

I looked at him, kneeling there. At the compact, powerful veteran of my uncle's Solindish wars. My father's man, once, and now he sought to slay his son. "After an explanation," I agreed.

He turned his head and spat. "*That* for your explanation." He sucked in a breath as the gathered men muttered among themselves. "I owe you nothing. I *give* you nothing. There will be no explanation."

I took a step forward, angry enough to strike him as he knelt, but Lachlan's hand was on my arm. "No," he said, "let *me*—"

He said nothing more. He did not need to. His fingers had gone into the strings of his Lady, plucking them, and the sound silenced us all.

The pavilion cracked behind me. I heard the breath of the wind as it whipped at nearby fires. Torry said a word, a single sound, and then not another one was made.

The harp music took us all. I felt it more than heard it as it dug within my soul, and there it stayed. So did I. The wind blew dust into my eyes, but I not blink. I felt the beating of grit against my face, but did not move to wipe it away. I stood quite still as the others did, and listened to Lachlan's soft promise.

"You misjudge, Zared," he said. "But how you misjudge my Lady. She can conjure visions from a blind man . . . words from a dumb man. And put madness in its place. . . ."

Zared cried out, cringing, and clapped his hands to his ears. The song went on, weaving us all in its spell. His fingers dug rigidly into his flesh, as if he could block the sound. But it sang on, burrowing into his mind even as it blanked ours out.

"Lachlan," I said, but no sound came out of my mouth.

Zared's hands fell away from his head. He knelt and stared, transfixed as any child upon an endless wonder: jaw sagging, drool falling, eyes bulging open in a terrible joy.

The harp sang on, a descant to the wind. So subtle, seductive, and sly. Lachlan himself, with his dyed hair blowing and his blue eyes fixed, smiled with incredible power. I saw his face transfigured by the presence of his god; he was no more the harper but an instrument of Lodhi, perhaps the harp herself, and a locus for the magic. Pluck him and she sounded, sharp and sweet. Pluck her and he quivered, resonating in the wind.

I shivered. It ran over me like a grue, from scalp to toes, and I shivered again. I felt the hair stand up from my flesh and the coldness in my soul. "Lachlan," I begged, *"no—"*

The harpsong reached out and wrapped Zared in a shroud. And there he sat, soundless, as it dug into his mind and stripped it bare, to make his memories visible.

A pavilion. The interior. Ocher and amber and gray. One candle glowed in the dimness. It glinted off the ringmail hauberk and tarnished sword hilt. The man stood in silence with his ruddy head bowed. He dared not look upon the lady.

She moved into the light. She wore a brown gown and a yellow belt. She glowed at throat and wrists from the copper-dyed silk. But it was the hair that set her apart, that and her unearthly beauty.

She put up a hand. She did not touch him. He did not look at her. But as she moved her fingers they took on a dim glow. Lilac, I thought. No—purple. The deep purple of Ihlini magic.

She drew a rune in the air. It hissed and glowed, clinging to the shadows, spitting sparks and tails of flame. Fearfully Zared raised his head.

His eyes fastened upon it. For a moment he tried to look away, to look at her, but I could see he had not the power. He could stare only at the rune. The delicate tracery of purest purple glowed aginst the air, and as Electra bid him he put up his hand.

"Touch it," she said. *"Take it. Hold it. It will give you the courage you need."*

Zared touched a trembling fingertip to the rune. Instantly it spilled down across his flesh, consuming his hand in livid flame, until he cried out and shook his arm as if to free it. But by then it was done. I saw the rune, so lively and avid, run up his arm to his face, his nose, and then it slid into his nostrils.

He cried out, but it was a noiseless sound. His body was beset by tremors. His eyes bulged out and blood ran from his nose, two thin trails of blackened blood. And then, as he reached for his knife, the trembling was gone and Electra touched his hand.

"It is done," she said calmly. *"You have watched me so long, desiring me so, that I could not help but give you your wish. I will be yours, but only after this thing is done. Will you serve me in this?"*

Zared merely nodded, eyes transfixed on her face. And Electra gave him his service.

"Slay him," she said. *"Slay the pretender-prince."*

The harp music died. Lachlan's Lady fell silent. I heard the wind strike up the song and the echo in my soul. So easily she had done it.

Zared sat slumped against the earth. His head sagged upon his chest as if he could not bear to meet my eyes. Perhaps he could not. He had meant to slay his lord.

I felt old. Nothing worked properly. I thought to cross to the man and speak to him quietly, but the muscles did not answer my intentions. And then I heard the harp again, and the change in the song, and saw the change in Lachlan's eyes.

"Lachlan!" I cried, but the thing was already done.

He conjured Electra before us. The perfect, fine-boned face with its fragile planes and flawless flesh. The winged brows and ice-gray eyes, and the mouth that made men weak. Lachlan gave us all the beauty, and then he took it from her.

He stripped away the flesh. He peeled it from the bone until it fell away in crumpled piles of ash. I saw the gaping orbits of vanished eyes, the ivory ramparts of grinning teeth. The hinge of the jaws and the arch of her cheeks, bared for us all to see. And the skull, so smooth and pearly, stared upon us all.

No man moved. No man could. Lachlan had bound us all. The music stopped, and with it Zared's heart.

I wavered, caught myself, and blinked against the dust. I put a hand to my face to wipe it free of grit, and then I stopped, for I saw the tears on Lachlan's face.

His hands were quite still upon the strings. The green stone in the smooth dark wood was dim and opaque. And his eyes looked past me to Torry.

"Could I undo it, I would," he said in toneless despair. "Lodhi has made me a healer, and now I have taken a life. But for you, lady, for what he nearly did to you . . . there seemed no other way."

Torry's hand crept up to crush a fold of the green woolen robe against her throat. Her face was white. But I saw the comprehension in her eyes.

"Lachlan." My voice was oddly cramped. I swallowed, clearing my throat, then tried again to speak. "Lachlan, no man will reprove you for what you have done. Perhaps the method was—unexpected, but the reasons are clear enough."

"I have no dispute with that," he said. "It is only that I thought myself above such petty vengeance." He sighed and stroked two fingers along his Lady, touching the green stone gently. "Such power as Lodhi bestows can be used for harm as well as good. And now you have seen them both."

I cast an assessive glance around at the staring throng. There was still a thing to be said. "Is there yet a man who would slay me? Another man willing to serve the woman's power?" I gestured toward Zared's body on the ground. "I charge you to consider it carefully when you think to strike me down."

I thought there was need for nothing more, though something within me longed to cry out at them all, to claim myself inviolate. It was not true. Kings and princes are subject to assassination more often than to death from old age. And yet I thought it unlikely more would strike now, after what had just occurred.

I looked at the body. It resembled that of a child within the womb, for I had seen a stillbirth once; the arms were wrapped around the doubled-up knees, fingers clawed. The feet were rigid in their boots. Zared's head was twisted on his neck and his eyes were open. Staring. I thought I might get myself the reputation of a man surrounding himself with shapechangers and Ellasian sorcerers, and I thought it just as well. Let any man who thought to slay his king think twice upon the subject.

"Go," I said, more quietly. "There are yet battles to be fought, and winejugs to be emptied."

I saw the smiles. I heard the low-voiced comments. What they had seen would not be forgotten, used instead to strengthen existing stories. They would drink themselves to sleep discussing the subject of death, but at least they would sleep. I thought it unlikely I would.

I touched Lachlan on the shoulder. "It was best."

But he did not look at me. He looked only at my sister while she stared at Zared's corpse.

"Does it please you," asked Finn, "to know how much the woman desires your death?"

I spun around. He was pale and sweating, white around the mouth, and his lips were pressed tightly closed. I saw immense tension in the line of his shoulders. The stitches stood out like a brand upon his face. He stood with such rigidity I dared not touch him, even to help, for fear he might fall down.

"It does not please me," I answered simply. "But it does not surprise me, either. Did you really think it would?" I shook my head. "Still . . . I had not known she held such power."

"She is Tynstar's *meijha*," Finn said clearly. "A whore, to keep from dirtying the Old Tongue with her name. Do you think she will let you live? Be not so blind, Carillon—you have now seen what she can do. She will fill your cup with bitter poison when you think to drink it sweet."

"Why?" Torry asked sharply. "What is it you say to my brother?"

I lifted a hand to wave him into silence, then let it drop back to my side. Finn would never let silence rule his tongue when there was something he wished to say.

"Has he not told you? He means to wed the woman."

The robe enveloped her in a cloud of bright green wool as she came from the tent to me. Her hair spilled down past her waist to ripple at her knees, and she raised a doubled fist. "You will do no such thing! *Electra?* Carillon—have sense! You have seen what she means to do—Electra desires your death!"

"So does Bellam and Tynstar and every other Solindishman in Homana. Do you think I am blind?" I reached out and caught her wrist. "I mean to wed her when this war is done, because to do so will settle peace between two lands that have warred too long. Such things are often done, as you well know. But now, Tourmaline, *now*—perhaps we can make it last."

"Alliance?" she asked. "Do you think Solinde will agree to any such thing? With Bellam dead—"

"—Solinde will be without a king," I finished. "She will have me instead, and no more Ihlini minions. Think you what Shaine meant to do when he betrothed Lindir to Ellic! He wanted a lasting peace that would end these foolish wars. Now it is within *my* grasp to bring this peace about, and I have every intention of accomplishing it. I will wed Electra, just as you, one day, will wed a foreign prince."

Her arm went slack in my hand. Color drained from her face. "Carillon—wait you—"

"We will serve our House, Tourmaline, as all our ancestors have done," I said clearly. "Shall I name them for you? Shaine himself wed Ellinda of Erinn, before he took Homanan Lorsilla. And before that—"

"I know!" she cried. "By the gods, Carillon, I am older than you! But what gives you the right to say whom I will have in marriage?"

"The right of a brother," I said grimly, disliking to hurt her so. "The right of the last surviving male of our House. But most of all . . . the right of the Mujhar."

Her arm was still slack in my hand. And then it tightened and she twisted it free of my grasp. "Surely you will let me have some *choice*—"

"Could I do it, I would," I said gently. "But it is the Mujhar of Homana the envoys will approach, not his spinster sister." I paused, knowing how much I hurt her, and knowing whom she wanted, even as he heard me. "Did you think yourself free of such responsibility?"

"No," she said finally. "No . . . not entirely. But it seems somewhat precipitate to discuss whom I will wed when you still lack the Lion Throne."

"That is a matter of time." I rubbed at my aching brow and shifted my attention to Finn. "If I give you an order, will you obey it?"

One black brow rose slightly. "That is the manner of my service . . . usually."

"Then go to the Keep as soon as you are able." He opened his mouth to protest, but this time I won. "I am sending Torry, so she will be safe and free of such things as she has encountered tonight." I did not say she would also be separated from Lachlan, whom I thought might offer too much succor for his sake as well as hers. "You I want healed," I went on. "Alix will no doubt wish to return to Donal, so she can give Torry proper escort. Remain until you are fully recovered. And there, my liege man, is the order."

He was not pleased with it, but he did not protest. I had taken that freedom from him. And then, before I could put out a hand to aid him as I intended, he turned and limped away.

The wind rippled Torry's hair as we watched him go. I heard surprise and awe in her voice, and recalled she knew little of the Cheysuli. Only the legends and lays. "That," she said, "is strength. And such pride as I have never seen."

I smiled. "That," I said merely, "is Finn."

Chapter Sixteen

It was bright as glass as I sat outside my pavilion, and the sunlight beat off my head. I sat on a three-legged camp-stool with my legs spread, Cheysuli sword resting across my thighs. I squinted against the brilliant flashes of the mirrored blade and carefully checked its edges. From elsewhere, close by, drifted the curl of Lachlan's music.

> *Come, lady, and sit down beside me,*
> *settle your skirts in the hollowed green hills*
> *and hear of my song*
> *for I am a harper*
> *and one who would give of himself*
> *to you.*

Rowan stood at my right, waiting for my comment. He had spent hours honing and cleaning the blade. At first I had not thought to set him to the task, for in Caledon I had learned to tend my weapons as I tended my life, but this was not Caledon. This was Homana, and I must take on the behaviors of a king. Such things included in that were having men to tend my weapons, mail, and horse. Still, it had been only this morning that I had trusted my sword to another.

The ruby, the Mujhar's Eye, glowed brilliantly in the pommel. The gold prongs holding it in place curved snuggly around it, like lion's claws; apropos, I thought, since it was the royal crest. The rampant beast depicted in the hilt gleamed with a thorough cleaning, and I thought overall it would do. I touched fingertips to the runes, feeling the subtle ridges beneath my flesh, and nodded. "Well done, Rowan. You should have been an arms-master." ·

"I prefer being a captain," he said, "so long as it is you I serve."

I smiled and used a soft cloth to rub the oil of my fingers from the glory of the steel. "I am not a god, Rowan. I am as human as you."

"I know *that*." Some of his awe had faded, that was obvious. "But given the choice, I would continue to serve the Mujhar. Human or not." I glanced up and saw his smile.

A thin veil of dust hung in the air to layer the men who caused it. I heard the sound of arms-practice, wrestling, argument, and laughter. But I also heard the harp, and Lachlan's eloquent voice.

> *Come, lady, and hear of my harp;*
> *I will sing for you, play for you,*
> *wait for you, pray for you*
> *to say you love me, too . . .*
> *as much as I love you.*

I lifted my swordbelt from the ground and set the tip of the blade against the lip of the sheath. Slowly I slid it home, liking the violent song. Steel against leather, boiled and wrapped; the hissing of blade against sheath. Better, I thought, than the chopping of blade hacking flesh or the grate of steel against bone.

"Hallooo the camp!" called a distant voice. "A message from Bellam!"

The dust cloud rolled across the encampment. Four men rode in: three were guards, the fourth a Homanan I had seen only once before, when I had set him to his task.

The guards brought him up, taking away his horse as he jumped from the mount and dropped to one knee in a quick, impatient gesture of homage. His eyes sparkled with excitement as I motioned him up. "My lord, I have word from Mujhara."

"Say on."

"It is Bellam, my lord. He desires a proper battle, two armies in the field, with no more time and blood spent in pointless skirmishes." He grinned; he knew what I would say.

I smiled. "Pointless, are they? So pointless now he begs me hold back my men, because we have undermined his grip upon Homana. So pointless he wishes to settle the thing at last." I felt the leap of anticipation within my chest. At last. *At last.* "Is there more?"

He was winded, trying to catch his breath. I had taken up the practice of posting men in relays along the major roads, ostensibly iternerants or crofters or traders; anything but soldiers. Some had even been sent to Mujhara to learn what they could firsthand, and to expand on the insight Lachlan had given us as to Bellam's mind.

"My lord," the man said, "it seems Bellam is angry and impatient. He is determined to bring you down. He challenges you, my lord, to a battle near Mujhara. A final battle, he claims, to end the thing at last."

"Does he?" I grinned at Rowan. "No doubt there were assorted insults to spice these words of his."

The messenger laughed. "But of course, my lord! What else does a beaten man do? He blusters and shouts and threatens, because he knows his strength is failing." Color stood high in his face. "My lord Carillon, he claims you fight such skirmishes because you are incapable of commanding an entire army within a proper battle. That you rely on the Cheysuli to ensorcel his patrols, having no skill yourself. My lord—do we fight?"

His eagerness was manifest. I saw others gathering near; not so close as to intrude, but close enough to hear my answer. I did not mind. No doubt all my men felt some of the impatience that nipped at Bellam's heels.

"We will fight," I agreed, rising from my stool. The cheer went up at once. "Seek you food and rest, and whatever wine you prefer. Tonight we will feast to Bellam's defeat, and tomorrow we shall plan."

He bowed himself away and went off to do my bidding. Others hastened away as well to spread the word; I knew the army grapevine would do what I could not, which was speak to every man. There were too many now.

Rowan sighed. "My lord—it is well. Even I would relish a battle."

"Though you may die in it?"

"There is that chance each time I lead a raid," he answered. "What difference to me whether I die with twenty men or two hundred? Or even twenty thousand?"

The hilt of my sword was warm against my palm and the royal ruby glowed. "What difference, indeed?" I stared across the encampment with its knots of clustered men. "Is a Mujhar's strength measured by the number of men whose blood is spilled—or merely that it spills?" Then I frowned and shook the musing away. "Find me Duncan. Last I saw, he was with Finn, now that his brother is back. There are things we must discuss."

Rowan nodded and went off at once. I buckled on my swordbelt and turned to go inside my pavilion, intending to study my maps, but I paused instead and lingered.

Come, lady, and taste of my wine,
eat of my fruit
and hear of my heart,
for I long for you, cry for you,
ache for you, hate for you
to say you will not come.

I grimaced and scrubbed fingers through my beard to scratch my tight-set jaw. It was not Torry who was saying she would not come, but her brother commanding it. And in the eight weeks since I had sent her to the Keep, Lachlan had kept himself to his thoughts and his Lady, forgoing the confidences we once had shared.

"A fool," I muttered. "A fool to look so high . . . and surely a harper knows it."

Perhaps he had, once. He had spent his time with kings. But a man cannot always choose where he will love, no more than a princess may choose what man she will wed.

The harpsong died down into silence. I stood outside my pavilion and heard the hissing of the wind across the sandy, beaten ground. And then I cursed and went inside.

"Carillon."

It was Finn at the doorflap, but when I called to him to enter, he merely pulled the flap aside. He stood mostly in shadow with the darkness of full night behind him.

I sat up, awake at once—for I had hardly slept in the knowledge I would face Bellam at last—and lighted my single candle. I looked at Finn and frowned. Of a sudden he was alien to me, eerie in his intensity.

"Bring your sword and come."

I glanced at the sword where it lay cradled in its sheath.

It waited for me now as much as it waited for the morning; *the* morning. And, knowing Finn did nothing without sound reason, I put on my boots and stood up, fully clothed as was common in army camps. "Where?" I pulled the sword from its sheath.

"This way." He said nothing more, merely waited for me to follow. And so I went with him, following Storr, to the hollow of a hill. We left the encampment behind, a dim, smoky glow across the crest of the hill, and I waited for Finn to explain.

He said nothing at first. I saw him look down at the ground, searching for some mark or other indication, and then I saw it even as he did.

Five smooth stones, set in a careful circle. He smiled and knelt, touching each stone with a fingertip as if he counted, or made himself known to all five. He said something under his breath, some unknown sentence; the Old Tongue, and more obscure than usual. This was not the Finn I knew.

Kneeling, he glanced up. Up and up, until he tipped back his head. It was the sky he stared at, the black night sky with its carpet of shining stars, and the wind blew his hair from his face. I saw again the livid scar as it snaked across cheek and jaw, but I also saw something more. I saw a man gone out of himself to some place far beyond.

"Ja'hai," he said. *"Ja'hai, cheysu, Mujhar."*

The wolf walked once around the circle. I saw the amber glint of his eyes. Finn glanced at him briefly with the unfocused detachment of *lir*-speech, and I wondered what was said.

The night was cool. The wind blew grit against my face, catching in my beard. I put one hand to my mouth, intending to wipe my lips clean, but Finn made a gesture I had never seen and I stopped moving altogether. I looked up, as he did, and saw the garland of stars.

Five of them. In a circle. Like a torque around a woman's neck. A moment before they had been five among many, lost in the brilliance of thousands, and now they stood apart.

Finn touched each stone again with a gentle fingertip. Then he placed one palm flat against the earth as if he gave—or sought—a blessing, and touched the other hand to his heart.

"Trust me." I realized this time he spoke to me.

It took me a moment to answer. The very stillness made me hesitate. "When have I not trusted you?"

"Trust me." I saw the blackness of his eyes, swollen in the darkness.

I swallowed down my foreboding. "Freely. My life is yours."

He did not smile. "Your life has ever been mine. For now, the gods have set me a further task . . ." For a moment he closed his eyes. In the moonlight his face was all hollows and planes, leached free of its humanity. He was a shadow-wraith before me, hunched against the ground. "You know what we face tomorrow." His eyes were on my face. "You know the odds are great. You know also, of course, that should we fail—and Bellam keeps Homana— it is the end of the Cheysuli race."

"The Homanans—"

"I do not speak of Homanans." Finn's tone was very distant. "We speak now of the Cheysuli, and the gods who made this place. There is no time for Homanans."

"*I* am Homanan—"

"You are a part of our prophecy." For a moment he smiled the old, ironic smile. "Doubtless you would prefer it otherwise, given a choice—no more than I, Carillon—but there is none. If you die tomorrow; if you die within a week in Bellam's battles, Homana and the Cheysuli die with you."

I felt the slow churning in my belly. "Finn—you set a great weight upon my shoulders. Do you wish to bow me down?"

"You are Mujhar," he said softly. "That is the nature of the task."

I shifted uneasily. "What is it you would have me do? Strike a bargain with the gods? Only tell me the way."

There was no answering smile. "No bargain," he said. "They do not bargain with men. They offer; men take, or men refuse. Men all too often refuse." He set one hand against the ground and thrust himself to his feet. The earring winked in the moonlight. "What I tell you this night is not what men prefer to hear, particularly kings. But I tell you because of what we have shared together . . . and because it will make a difference."

I took a deep, slow breath. Finn was—not Finn. And yet I knew no other name. "Say on, then."

"That sword." He indicated it briefly. "The sword you hold is Cheysuli-made, by Hale, my *jehan*. For the Mujhar it was said he made it, and yet in the Keep we knew differently." His face was very solemn. "Not for Shaine, though Shaine was the one who bore it. Not for you, to whom Shaine gave it on your acclamation. For a Mujhar, it is true . . . but a Cheysuli Mujhar, not Homanan."

"I have heard something of the sort before," I said grimly. "It seems these words—or similar ones—have been often in Duncan's mouth."

"You fight to save Homana," Finn said. "*We* fight to save Homana as well, and the Cheysuli way of life. There is the prophecy, Carillon. I know—" he lifted a hand as I sought to speak—"I know, it is not something to which you pay mind. But *I* do; so do we all who have linked with the *lir*." His eyes were on Storr, standing so still and silent in the night. "It is the truth, Carillon. *One day a man of all blood shall unite, in peace, four warring realms and two magic races.*" He smiled. "Your bane, it appears, judging by your expression."

"What are you leading to?" I was grown impatient with his manner. "What has the prophecy to do with this sword?"

"That sword was made for another. Hale knew it when he fashioned the blade from the star-stone. And the promise was put in there." His fingers indicated the runes running down the blade. "A Cheysuli sword, once made, waits for the hand it was made for. That hand is not yours, and yet you will carry the sword into battle."

I could not suppress the hostility in my tone. "Cheysuli sufferance?" I demanded. "Does it come to this again?"

"Not sufferance," he said. "You serve it well, and it has kept you alive, but the time draws near when it will live in another man's hands."

"My son's," I said firmly. "What *I* have will be my son's. That is the nature of inheritance."

"Perhaps so," he agreed, "do the gods intend it."

"Finn—"

"Lay down the sword, Carillon."

I faced him squarely in the darkness. "Do you ask me

to give it up?" I weighted my words with care. "Do you mean to take it from me?"

"That is not for me to do. When the sword is given over to the man for whom it was made, it will be given freely." For a moment he said nothing, as if listening to his words, and then he smiled. Briefly he touched my arm with a gesture of comradeship I had seen only rarely before. "Lay down the sword, Carillon. This night it belongs to the gods."

I bent. I set the sword upon the ground, and then I rose again. It lay gleaming in the moonlight: gold and silver and crimson.

"Your knife," Finn said.

And so he disarmed me. I stood naked and alone, for all I had a warrior and wolf before me, and waited for the answers. I thought there might be none; Finn only rarely divulged what was in his mind, and this night I thought it unlikely I would get anything from him. I waited.

He held the knife in his hand, the hand which had fashioned the weapon. A Cheysuli long-knife with its wolf's-head hilt; no Homanan weapon, this. And then I understood.

This night he was all Cheysuli, more so than ever before. He put off his borrowed Homanan manners like a soldier slipping his cloak. No more the Finn I knew but another, quieter soul. He was full of his gods and magic, and did I not acknowledge what he was I would doubtless regret it at once. As it was, I had not seen him so often in such a way as to lose my awe of him.

Suddenly I stood alone on the plains of Homana with a shapechanger waiting before me, and I knew myself afraid.

He caught my left wrist in one hand. Before I could speak he bared the underside to the gods and cut deeply into the flesh.

I hissed between my teeth and tried to pull back the arm. He held me tightly, clamping down on the arm so that my hand twitched and shook with the shock of the cutting.

I had forgotten his strength, his bestial determination that puts all my size to shame. He held me as easily as a father holds a child, ignoring my muttered protest. He forced my arm down and held it still, and then he loosened his fingers to let the blood well free and fast.

It ran down my wrist to pool in my palm, then dropped

off the rigid fingers. Finn held the arm over the patch of smooth earth with its circle of five smooth stones.

"Kneel." A pressure on the captive wrist led me downward, and I knelt as he had ordered.

Finn released my wrist. It ached dully and I felt the blood still coursing freely. I lifted my right hand to clamp the cut closed, but the look on Finn's face kept me from it. There was more he wanted of me.

He took up my sword from the ground and stood before me. "We must make this yours, for a time," he said gently. "We will borrow it from the gods. For tomorrow, for Homana . . . you must have a little magic." He pointed at the bloodied soil. "The blood of the man; the flesh of the earth. United in one purpose—" He thrust the sword downward until the blade bit into the earth, sliding in as if he sheathed it, until the hilt stood level with my face as I knelt. The clean, shining hilt with its ruby eye set so firmly in the pommel. "Put your hand upon it."

Instinctively I knew which hand. My left, with its bloody glove.

I touched the hilt. I touched the rampant lion. I touched the red eye with the red of my blood, and closed my hand upon it.

The blood flowed down the hilt to the crosspiece and then down upon the blade. The runes filled up, red-black in the silver moonlight, until they spilled over. I saw the scarlet ribbon run down and down to touch the earth where it merged with the blood-dampened soil, and the ruby began to glow.

It filled my eyes with crimson fire, blinding me to the world. No more Finn, no more me . . . only incarnadine fire.

"*Ja'hai,*" Finn whispered unevenly. "*Ja'hai, cheysu, Mujhar . . .*"

Five stars. Five stones. One sword. And one battle to be won.

The stars moved. They broke free of their settings and moved against the sky, growing brighter, trailing tails of fire behind them. They shot across the sky, arcing, like arrows loosed from bows, heading toward the earth. Shooting stars I had seen, but this was different. This was—"

"Gods," I whispered raggedly. "Must a man ever see to believe?"

I wavered on my knees. It was Finn who pulled me up and made me stand, though I feared I would fall down and shame myself. One hand closed over the cut and shut off the bleeding. He smiled a moment, and then the eyes were gone blank and detached, so that I knew he sought the earth magic.

When he took his hand away my wrist was healed, bearing no scar save the shackle wound from Atvian iron. I flexed my hand, wiggling my fingers, and saw the familiar twist to Finn's smile. "I told you to trust me."

"Trusting you may give me nightmares." Uneasily I glanced at the sky. "Did you see the stars?"

"Stars?" He did not smile. "Rocks," he said. "Only rocks."

He scooped them up and showed me. Rocks they were, in his hand; I put out my own and held them, wondering what magic had been forged.

I looked at Finn. He seemed weary, used up, and something was in his eyes. I could not decipher the expression. "You will sleep." He frowned in abstraction. "The gods will see to that."

"And you?" I asked sharply.

"What the gods give me is my own affair." His eyes were back on the sky.

I thought there was more he wished to say. But he shut his mouth on it, offering nothing, and it was not my place to ask. So I put my free hand on the upstanding hilt and closed my fingers around the bloodied gold. But I knew, as I pulled it from the earth, I would not ask Rowan to clean it.

"Rocks," Finn murmured, and turned away with Storr.

I opened my hand and looked at the rocks. Five smooth stones. Nothing more.

But I did not drop them to the ground. I kept them, instead.

It was Rowan who held the tall ash staff upright in the dawn. The mist clung to it; droplets ran down the staff to wet the fog-dampened ground, as my blood had run down the sword. The banner hung limply from the top of the staff: a drapery of crimson cloth that did not move in the stillness. Within its silken folds slept the rampant black lion of Homana, mouth agape and claws extended, waiting for its prey.

The tip of the staff bit into the ground as Rowan pushed it. He twisted, worked the standard into the damp, spongy ground until the ash was planted solidly. And then he took his hands away, waiting, and saw it would remain.

A cheer went up. A Homanan cheer; the Cheysuli said nothing. They waited on foot at my back, separated from the Homanans, and their standard was the *lir* who stood at their sides or rested on their shoulders.

I tasted the flat, dull tang of apprehension tinged with fear in my mouth. I had never rid myself of the taste, no matter how many times I had fought. I sat on my horse with my sword in its sheath, ringmail shrouding my body, and knew I was afraid. But it was the fear that would drive me on in an attempt to overcome it; in doing so I would also, I prayed, overcome the enemy.

I turned my back on that enemy. Bellam's troops lay in wait for us on the plains, the dawning sunlight glittering off weapons and mail. They were too far to be distinct, were merely a huge gathering of men prepared to fight. Thousands upon thousands.

I turned my back so I could look at my army. It spread across the hill like a flood of legs and arms and faces. Unlike Bellam's hordes, we did not all boast ringmail and boiled leather. Many wore what they could of armor, that being leather bracers, stiff leather greaves, and a leather tunic. A breastplate, here and there; perhaps a toughened hauberk. But many wore only wool, having no better, yet willing to fight. My army lacked the grandeur of Bellam's silken-tunicked legions, but we did not lack for heart and determination.

I pulled my sword from its sheath. Slowly I raised it, then closed my callused hand around the blade, near the tip. I thrust the weapon upright in the air so that the hilt was uppermost, and the ruby caught fire from the rising sun.

"Bare your teeth!" I shouted. "Unsheathe your claws! *And let the Lion roar!*"

Chapter Seventeen

The sun, I knew, was setting. The field was a mass of crimson, orange, and yellow. But I could not be certain how much of the crimson was blood or setting sun.

The ground was boggy beneath my knees, the dry grass matted, but I did not get up at once. I remained kneeling, leaning against my planted sword, as I stared into the Mujhar's Eye. The great ruby, perhaps, was responsible for the color. Perhaps it painted the plains so red.

But I knew better. The field was red and brown and black with blood, and the dull colors of the dead. Already carrion birds wheeled and settled in their eternal dance, crying their victory even as men cried their defeat. It was all merely sound, another sound, to fill my ringing head.

The strength was gone from my body. I trembled with a weakness born of fatigue that filled my bones, turning my limbs to water. There was nothing left in me save the vague realization the thing was done, and I was still alive.

A step whispered behind me. I spun at once, lifting the sword, and set the point at the man.

He stood just out of range, and yet close enough had I the strength to try for a lunge. I did not. And there was no need, since Finn was not the enemy.

I let the tip of the sword drop away to rest against the ground. I wet my bloodied lips and wished for a drink of wine. Better yet: water, to cool my painful throat. My voice was a husky shadow of my usual tone; shouting had leached it of sound.

"It is done," Finn said gently.

"I know it." I swallowed and steadied my voice. "I know it."

"Then why do you remain on your knees like a supplicant to Lachlan's All-Father creature?"

"Perhaps I am one . . ." I sucked in a belly-deep breath and got unsteadily to my feet. The exertion nearly put me down again, and I wavered. Every bone in my body ached and my muscles were shredded like rags. I shoved a mailed forearm across my face, scrubbing away the sweat and blood. And then I acknowledged what I had not dared say aloud before, or even within my mind. "Bellam is—defeated. Homana is mine."

"Aye, my lord Mujhar." The tone, as ever, was ironic and irreverent.

I sighed and cast him as much of a scowl as I could muster. "My thanks for your protection, Finn." I recalled how he had shadowed me in the midst of the day-long battle; how he had let no enemy separate me from the others. In all the tangle of fighting, I had never once been left alone.

He shrugged. "The blood-oath *does* bind me . . ." Then he grinned openly and made a fluid gesture that said he understood. Too often we said nothing to one another because there was no need.

And then he put out a hand and gripped my arm, and I accepted the accolade in silence only because I had not the words to break it.

"Did you think we would see it?" I asked at last.

"Oh, aye. The prophecy—"

I cut him off with a wave of one aching arm. "Enough. Enough of the thing. I grow weary of your prating of this and that." I sighed and caught my breath. "Still, there is Mujhara to be freed. Our liberation is not yet finished."

"Near enough," Finn said quietly. "I have come to take you to Bellam."

I looked at him sharply. "You have him?"

"Duncan—has him. Come and see."

We walked through the battlefield slowly. All around me lay the pall of death; the stench of fear and futility. Men had been hacked and torn to pieces, struck down by swords and spears alike. Arrows stood up from their flesh. Birds screamed and shrieked as we passed, taking wing to circle and return as we passed by their bounty. And the men, enemy and companion alike, lay sprawled in the obscene intercourse of death upon the matted, bloody grass.

I stopped. I looked at the sword still clutched in my hand.

The Cheysuli sword, Hale-made, with its weight of burning ruby. The Mujhar's Eye. Or was it merely *my* eye, grown bloody from too much war?

Finn put his hand on my shoulder. When I could, I sheathed the sword and went on.

Duncan and Rowan, along with a few of my captains, stood atop a small hill upon which stood the broken shaft of Bellam's standard, trampled in the dust. White sun rising on an indigo field. But Bellam's sun had set.

He was quite dead. But of such a means I could not name, so horrible was his state. He was no longer precisely a man.

Tynstar. I knew it at once. What I did not know was the reason for the death. And probably never would.

It—Bellam was no longer recognizably male—was curled tightly as if it were a child as yet unborn. The clothes and mail had been burned and melted off. Ash served as a cradle for the thing. Ringmail, still smoking from its ensorcelled heat, lay clumped in heaps of cooling metal. The flesh was drawn up tightly like brittle, untanned hide. Chin on knees; arms hugging legs; nose and ears melted off. Bellam grinned at us all from his lipless mouth, but his eyes were empty sockets.

And on the blackened skull rested a circlet of purest gold.

When I could speak again without phlegm and bile scraping at my throat, I said two words: "Bury it."

"My lord," Rowan ventured, "what do you do now?"

"Now?" I looked at him and tried to smile. "Now I will go into Mujhara to claim my throne at last."

"Alone?" He was shocked. *"Now?"*

"Now," I said, "but not alone. With me go the Cheysuli."

We met token resistance in the city. Solindish soldiers with their Atvian allies still fought to protect their stolen palace, but word spread quickly of Bellam's death and the grisly manner of it. It wondered at Tynstar's decision; surely the Solindish would hate and fear him for what he had done. Had he not broken the traditional bond between Bellam and the Ihlini? Or would the sorcery prove stronger even than fear, and drive the Solindish to follow him still?

The resistance at Homana-Mujhar broke quickly enough. I

left behind the bronze-and-timber gates, dispatching Cheysuli and *lir* into the interior of the myriad baileys and wards to capture the turrets and towers along the walls, the rose-colored walls of Homana-Mujhar. I dismounted by the marble steps at the archivolted entrance and went up one step at a time, sword bare in my hand. By the gods, this place was *mine* . . .

By the gods, indeed. I thought of the stars again.

Finn and Duncan were a few steps behind me and with them came their *lir*. And then, suddenly, I was alone. Before me stood the hammered silver doors of the Great Hall itself. I heard fighting behind me but hardly noticed; before me lay my *tahlmorra.*

I smiled. *Tahlmorra.* Aye. I thought it was. And so I threw open the doors and went in.

The memories crashed around me like falling walls. Brick by brick by brick. I recalled it all—

—Shaine, standing on the marble dais, thundering his displeasure . . . Alix there as well, beckoning Cai within the hall, and the great hawk's passage extinguishing all the candles. . . . Shaine again, my uncle, defying the Cheysuli within the walls they built so long ago, destroying the magic that kept the Ihlini out and allowing Homana's defeat . . . My hand tightened on my sword. By the gods, I did recall that defeat!

I went onward toward the dais. I ignored the Solindish coats-of-arms bannering the walls and the indigo draperies with Bellam's crest. I walked beside the unlighted firepit as it stretched the length of the hall with its lofty hammer-beamed ceiling of honey-dark wood and its carven animal shapes. No, not animal shapes. *Lir*-shapes. The Cheysuli had gone from carving the *lir* into castles to painting them onto pavilions. The truth had been here for years, even when we called them liars.

I stopped before the dais. The marble, so different from the cold gray stone of the hall floor, was light-toned, a warm rose-pink with veins of gold within it. A proper pedestal, I thought, for the throne that rested on it.

The Lion. It hunched upon its curling paws and claws, its snarling face the headpiece upon the back of the throne. Dark, ancient wood, gleaming with beeswax and gilt within the scrollwork. Gold wire banded the legs. The seat was cushioned in crimson silk with its rampant black lion walking in its folds. That much Bellam had not changed. He had left the lion alone.

My lion; my Lion.

Or was it?

I turned, and he stood where I expected.

"Yours?" I asked. "Or mine?"

Duncan did not attempt to dissemble or pretend to misunderstand. He merely sheathed his bloodied knife, folded his arms, and smiled. "It is yours, my lord. For now."

I heard the shouts of fighting behind him. Duncan stood just inside the open doorway, framed by the silver leaves. His black hair hung around his shoulders, bloody and sweaty like mine, and he bore bruises on his face. But even for all the soiling of his leathers and the smell of death upon him, he outshone the hall he stood in.

The breath rasped in my throat. To come so far and know myself so insignificant— "The throne," I said hoarsely, "is meant for a Cheysuli Mujhar. You have said."

"One day," he agreed. "But that day will come when you and I are dead."

"Then it is like this sword—" I touched the glowing ruby. "Made for another man."

"The Firstborn come again." Duncan smiled. "There is a while to wait for *him.*"

A soft, sibilant whisper intruded itself upon us. "And shall you wait a while for *me?*"

I spun around, jerking my sword from its sheath. Tynstar, *Tynstar,* came gliding out of the alcove so near the throne.

He put up his hand as Duncan moved. "Do not, shape-changer! Stay where you are, or I will surely slay him." He smiled. "Would it not grieve you to know you have lost your Mujhar the very day you have brought him to the throne?"

He had not changed. The ageless Ihlini was smiling. His bearded face was serene, untroubled; his hair was still thick—black touched with silver. He wore black leathers, and bore a silver sword.

I felt all the fear and rage and frustration well up within my soul. It was ever Tynstar, enforcing his will; playing with us like toys.

"Why did you slay Bellam?" When I had control of my voice, I asked.

"Did I?" He smiled. He *smiled*.

I thought, suddenly, of Zared, and how he had died. How Lachlan had harped him to death upon his Lady. I recalled quite clearly how Zared's corpse had looked, all doubled up and shrunken, as Bellam's had been.

For only a moment, I wondered. And then I knew better than to let Tynstar bait me. "Why?"

An eloquent shrug of his shoulders. "He was—used up. I had no more need of him. He was—superfluous." A negligent wave of the hand relegated Bellam to nonexistence. But I recalled his body and the manner of his going.

"What more?" I asked in suspicion. "Surely there was more."

Tynstar smiled and his black eyes held dominion. On one finger gleamed a flash of blue-white fire. A ring. A crystal set in silver. "More," he agreed. "A small matter of a promise conveniently forgotten. Bellam was foolish enough to desire an Ellasian prince for his lovely daughter, when she was already given to me." Amusement flickered across the cultured, guileless face. "But then, I did tell him he would die if he faced you this day. There are times your gods take precedence over my own."

The sword was in my hand. I wanted so to strike with it, and yet for the moment I could not. I had another weapon. "Electra," I said. "Your light woman, I have heard. Well, I shall forget her past while I think of her future—as my wife and Queen of Homana."

Anger glittered in his eyes. "You will not take Electra to wife."

"I will." I raised the sword so he could see the glowing ruby. "How will you stop me, when even the *gods* send me aid?"

Tynstar smiled. And then, even as I thrust, he reached out and caught the blade. "Die," he said gently. "I am done with our childish games."

The shock ran through my arm to my shoulder. The blade had struck flesh, and yet he did not bleed. Instead he turned the sword into a focus for his power and sent it slashing through my body.

I was hurled back against the throne, nearly snapping my

spine. The sword was gone from my hand. Tynstar held it by the blade, the hilt lifted before my eyes, and I saw the ruby go dark.

"Shall I turn this weapon against you?" His black eyes glittered as brightly as his crystal ring. "I have only to touch you—*gently*—with this stone, and poor Carillon's reign is done."

The sword came closer. *My* sword, that now served him. I slid forward to my knees, intending to dive and roll, but Tynstar was too fast.

And yet he was not. Even as the ruby, now black and perverted, touched my head, a knife flew home in Tynstar's shoulder. Duncan's, thrown from the end of the hall. And now Duncan was following the blade.

I found myself face-down against the marble. Somehow I had fallen, and the sword lay close at hand. But the ruby, once so brilliant, now resembled Tynstar's eyes.

Duncan's leap took Tynstar down against the dais, not far from where I lay. But Tynstar struggled up again, and Duncan did not. He lay, stunned by the force of his landing, sprawled across the steps. One bare brown arm with its gleaming *lir*-band stretched across the marble, gold on gold, and blood was staining the floor.

"Tynstar!"

It was Finn, pounding the length of the hall, and I saw the knife in his hand. How apropos, I thought, that Tynstar would die by a royal Homanan blade.

But he did not die. Even as Finn raced toward him, the Ihlini pulled Duncan's knife from his shoulder and hurled it down. Then he sketched a hurried rune in the air, wrapped himself in lavender mist, and simply disappeared.

I swore and tried to thrust myself upright. I failed miserably, flopping hard against the dais. And so I gave up and lay there, trying to catch my breath, as Finn knelt beside his brother.

Duncan muttered something. I saw him press himself up off the floor, then freeze, and it was Finn who kept him from falling. "A rib, I think," Duncan said between tight-locked teeth. "I will live, *rujho*."

"All this blood—"

"Tynstar's." Duncan winced as he settled himself upon the top step, one hand pressed to his chest. "The knife was mostly spent by the time it reached him, or he surely would have died." He glanced at me briefly, then gestured to his brother. "Finn—see to Carillon."

Finn heaved me up into a sitting position and leaned me against the throne. One curving, clawed paw supported my head. "I thought perhaps I could slay him," I explained, "and save us all the worry of knowing he is free."

Finn picked up the sword. I saw the color spill out of his face as he looked at the ruby. The black ruby. "He did *this?*"

"Something did." I swallowed against the weariness in my bones. "He put his hand on the blade and the stone turned black, as you see it."

"He used it to fix his power," Duncan said. "All of Carillon's will and strength was sucked out through the sword, then fed back with redoubled effect. It carried the sorcery with it." He frowned. "*Rujho,* the sword has ever been merely a sword. But for it to become accessible to Ihlini magic, it had to have its own. What do you know of this?"

Finn would not meet Duncan's eyes. I stared at him in astonishment, trying to fathom his emotions, but he had put up his shield against us all.

"*Rujho,*" Duncan said more sharply. "Did you seek the star magic?"

"He found it. He found *something.*" I shrugged. "Five stones, and blood, and the stars fell out of the skies. He said—" I paused, recalling the words exactly. "*—Ja'hai, cheysu, Mujhar.*"

Duncan's bruised face went white. At first I thought it was fear, and then I saw it was anger. He spat something out in the Old Tongue, something unintelligible to me— which I thought best, judging by the fury in his tone. Having never seen Duncan so angry, I was somewhat fascinated by it. And pleased, very pleased, I was not the focus of it.

Finn made a chopping motion with his right hand, a silencing gesture I had seen only rarely, for it was considered rude. It did not have much effect on Duncan.

He did not shout. He spoke quietly enough, but with such violence in his tone that it was all the more effective. I shifted uneasily against the throne and thought to interrupt, but it was not my affair. It had become a thing between brothers.

Finn stood up abruptly. Still he held the sword, and the ruby gleamed dull and black. Even the runes seemed tarnished. "Enough!" he shouted, so that it echoed in the hall. "Do you seek to strip me *entirely* of my dignity? I admit I was wrong—I admit it!—but there is no more need to remind me. I did it because I had to."

"Had to!" Duncan glared at him, very white around the mouth, yet blotched from pain and anger. "Had the gods denied you—what then? What would we have done for a king?"

"King?" I echoed, seeing I had some stake in this fight after all. "What are you saying, Duncan?"

Finn made the chopping motion again. And again Duncan ignored it. "He asked the gods for the star magic. I am assuming they granted it, since you are still alive."

"Still *alive?*" I sat up straighter. "Do you say I could have died?"

Duncan was hugging his chest. "It is a thing only rarely done, and then only because there is no other choice. The risk is—great. In more than six hundred years, only two men have survived the ceremony."

I swallowed against the sudden dryness in my mouth. "Three, now."

"Two." Duncan did not smile. "I was counting you before."

I stared at Finn. *"Why?"*

"We needed it for Homana." He looked at neither of us. His attention was fixed on the sword he held in his hands. "We needed it for the Cheysuli."

"You needed it for *you*," Duncan retorted. "You know as well as I only a warrior related by blood to the maker of the sword can ask the gods for the magic. It was your chance to to earn your *jehan's* place. Hale is gone, but Finn is not. So the son wished to inherit the *jehan's* power." Duncan looked at me. "The risk was not entirely your own. Had the petition been denied, the magic would have struck you both down."

I looked at Finn's face. He was still pale, still angered by Duncan's reaction, and no doubt expecting the worst from me. I was not certain he did not deserve it.

"Why?" I asked again.

Still he stared at the stone. "I wanted to," he said, very

low. "All my life I have wanted to ask it. To see if I was my *jehan's* true son." I saw bitterness twist his face. "I had less of him than Duncan . . . his *bu'sala*. I wanted what I could get; to get it, I would take it. So I did. And I would do it all again, because I know it would succeed."

"How?" Duncan demanded. "There is no guarantee."

"This time there is. You have only to look at the prophecy."

Silence filled the hall. And then Duncan broke it by laughing. It was not entirely the sound of humor, but the tension was shattered at last. "Prophecy," he said. "By the gods, my *rujholli* speaks of the prophecy. And speaks *to* the gods." He sighed and shook his head. "The first I do often enough, but the second—oh, the second . . . not for a *bu'sala* to do. No. Only a blood-son, not a foster-son." For a moment Duncan looked older than his years, and very tired. "I would trade it all to claim myself Hale's blood-son. And *you* offer it up to the gods. A sacrifice. Oh Finn, will you never learn?"

Finn looked at his older brother. Half-brother. They shared only a mother, and yet looking at them I saw the father in them both, though he had sired only one.

I said nothing for a long moment. I could think of nothing to fill the silence. And then I rose at last and took my sword back from Finn, touching the blackened ruby. I returned the weapon to my sheath. "The thing is done," I said finally. "The risk was worth the asking. And I would do it all again."

Finn looked at me sharply. "Even knowing?"

"Even knowing." I shrugged and sat down in the throne. "What else was there to do?"

Duncan sighed. He put out his hand and made the familiar gesture: a spread-fingered hand palm-up.

I smiled and made it myself.

Chapter Eighteen

I received the Solindish delegation dressed befitting my rank. Gone was the cracked and stained ringmail-and-leather armor of the soldier: in its place I wore velvets and brocaded satins of russet and amber. My hair and beard I had had freshly trimmed, smoothed with scented oil; I felt nearly a king for the first time in my life.

I knew, as the six Solindish noblemen paced the length of the Great Hall, they were not seeing the man they expected. Nearly seven years before, when Bellam had taken Homana, I had been a boy. Tall as a man and as strong, but lacking the toughness of adulthood. It seemed so long ago as I sat upon my Lion. I recalled when Keough's son had divested me of my sword and thrown me into irons. I recalled the endless nights when sleep eluded my mind. I recalled my complete astonishment when Alix had come to my aid. And I smiled.

The Solindishmen did not understand the smile, but it did not matter. Let them think what they would; let them judge me as I seemed. It would all come quite clear in time.

I was not alone within the hall. Purposely I had chosen a Cheysuli honor guard. Finn, Duncan, and six other warriors ranged themselves on either side of the throne, spreading across the dais. They were solemn-faced. Silent. Watching from impassive yellow eyes.

Rowan, who had escorted the Solindish delegation into the Homanan-bedecked hall, introduced each man. Duke this, Baron that; Solindish titles I did not know. He did it well, did my young Cheysuli-Homanan captain, with the proper note of neutrality in a tone also touched with condescension. We were the victors, they the defeated, and they stood within *my* palace.

Essien. The man of highest rank and corresponding arrogance. He wore indigo blue, of course, but someone had picked the crest from the left breast of his silken tunic. I could see the darker outline of Bellam's rising sun; a subtle way of giving me insult, so subtle I could do nothing. Outwardly he did not deny me homage. Did I protest, he could no doubt blame the coffer-draining war for the loss of better garments. So I let him have his rebellion. I could afford it, now.

His dark brown hair was brushed smoothly back from a high forehead, and his hands did not fidget. But his brown eyes glittered with something less than respect when he made his bow of homage. "My lord," he said in a quiet tone, "we come on behalf of Solinde to acknowledge the sovereignty of Carillon the Mujhar."

"You are aware of our terms?"

"Of course, my lord." He glanced briefly at the other five. "It has all been thoroughly discussed. Solinde, as you know, is defeated. The crown is—uncontested." I saw the muscles writhe briefly in his jaw. "We have no king . . . no *Solindish* king." His eyes came up to mine and I saw the bitterness in them. "There is a vacancy, my lord, which we humbly request you fill."

"Does Bellam have no heirs?" I smiled a small, polite smile that said what I wanted to say. A matter of form, discussing what all knew. "Ellic has been dead for years, of course, but surely Bellam had bastards."

"Aplenty," Essien agreed grimly. "Nonetheless, none is capable of rallying support for our cause. There would be—contention." He smiled thinly. "We wish to avoid such difficulties, now our lord is dead. You have proven—sufficient—for the task."

Sufficient. Essien had an odd way of speaking, spicing his conversation with pauses and nuances easily understood by one who had the ears to understand it. Having grown up in a king's court surrounded by his advisors and courtiers, I did.

"Well enough," I agreed, when I had made him wait long enough. "I will continue to be—*sufficient*—to the task. But there was another request we made."

Essien's face congested. "Aye, my lord Mujhar. The question of proper primogeniture." He took a deep breath that moved the indigo tunic. "As a token of Solinde's complete compliance with your newly won overlordship of our land, we offer the hand of the Princess Electra, Bellam's only daughter. Bellam's only surviving *legitimate* child." His nostrils pinched in tightly. "A son born of Solinde and Homana would be fit to hold the throne."

"Proper primogeniture," I said reflectively. "Well enough, we will take the lady to wife. You may tell her, for Carillon the Mujhar, that she has one month in which to gather the proper clothing and household attendants. *If she does not come* in that allotted time, we will send the Cheysuli for her."

Essien and the others understood quite clearly. I knew what they saw: eight warriors clad in leather and barbaric, shining gold, with their weapons hung about them. Knife and bow, and *lir*. They had only to look at the *lir* in order to understand.

Essien bowed his head in acknowledgment of my order. The conversation was finished, it seemed, but I had one final question to ask. "Where is Tynstar?"

Essien's head snapped up. He put one hand to his hair and smoothed it; a habitual, nervous gesture. His throat moved in a swallow, then again. He glanced quickly to the others, but they offered nothing. Essien had the rank.

"I do not know," he said finally, excessively distinct. "No man can say where the Ihlini goes; no man, my lord. He merely *goes*." He offered a thin smile that contained subtle triumph as well as humor . . . at my expense. "No doubt he plans to thwart you how he can, and he will, but I can offer you nothing of what he intends. Tynstar is—Tynstar."

"And no doubt he will be abetted," I said without inflection. "In Solinde, the Ihlini hold power—for now. But their realm—*his* realm—shall be a shadow of what it was, for we have the Cheysuli now."

Essien looked directly at Finn. "But even in Solinde we have heard of the thing that dilutes the magic. How it is a Cheysuli loses his power when faced with an Ihlini." His eyes came back to me. "Is that not true?"

I smiled. "Why not ask Tynstar? Surely *he* could explain what there is between the races."

I watched his expression closely. I expected—*hoped*—I would see the subtleties of his knowledge, betraying what he knew. He should, if he knew where Tynstar was, give it away with something in his manner, even remaining silent. But I saw little of triumph in his eyes. Only a faint frown, as if he considered something he wished to know, and realized he could not know it until he discovered the source. He had not lied.

I moved my hand in a gesture of finality. "We will set a Homanan regency in the city of Lestra. Royce is a trusted, incorruptible man. He will have sovereignty over Solinde in our name, representing our House, until such a time as we have a son to put on the throne. Serve my regent well, and you will find we are a just lord."

Essien shut his teeth. "Aye, my lord Mujhar."

"And we send some Cheysuli with him." I smiled at the Solindishman's expression of realization. "Now you may go."

They went, and I turned to look at the Cheysuli.

Duncan's smile was slow. "Finn has taught you well."

"And with great difficulty." The grin, crooked as usual, creased the scar on Finn's dark face. "But I think the time spent was well worth it, judging by what I have seen."

I got up from the throne and stretched, cracking the joints in my back. "Electra will not be pleased to hear what I have said."

"Electra will not be pleased by anything you have to say or do," Finn retorted. "But then, did you want a quiet marriage I doubt not you could have asked for someone else."

I laughed at him, stripping my brow of the golden circlet. It had been Shaine's once, crusted with diamonds and emeralds. And now it was mine. "A tedious marriage is no marriage at all, I have heard." I glanced at Duncan. "But you would know better than I."

For a moment he resembled Finn with the same ironic grin. Then he shrugged. "Alix has never been tedious."

I tapped the circlet against my hand, thinking about the woman. "She will come," I muttered, frowning. "She will come, and I will have to be ready for her. It is not as if I took some quiet little virgin to tremble in my bed . . . this is *Electra*."

"Aye," Finn said dryly. "The Queen of Homana, you make her."

I looked at Rowan. He was very silent, but he also

avoided my eyes. The warriors avoided nothing, but I had never been able to read them when they did not wish it. As for Duncan and Finn, I knew well enough what they thought.

I will take a viper to my bed . . . I sighed. But then I recalled what power that viper had over men in general, myself in particular, and I could not suppress the tightening of my loins. By the gods, it might be worth risking my life for one night in her bed . . . well, I would.

I looked again at Finn. "It brings peace to Homana."

He did not smile. "Whom do you seek to convince?"

I scowled and went down the dais steps. "Rowan, come with me. I will give you the task of fetching my lady mother from Joyenne as soon as she can travel. And there is Torry to fetch, as well . . . though no doubt Lachlan would be willing to do it." I sighed and turned back. "Finn. Will you see to it Torry has escort here?"

He nodded, saying nothing; I thought him still disapproving of my decision to wed Electra. But it did not matter. I was not marrying Finn.

A sound.

Not precisely a noise, merely not silence. A breath of sound, subtle and sibilant, and I sat up at once in my bed.

My hand went to the knife at my pillow, for even in Homana-Mujhar I would not set aside the habit. My sword and knife had been bedfellows for too long; even within the tester bed I felt unsafe without my weapons. But as I jerked the draperies aside and slid out of the bed, I knew myself well taken. No man is proof against Cheysuli violence.

I saw the hawk first. He perched upon a chair back, unblinking in the light from the glowing torch. The torch was in Duncan's hand. "Come," was all he said.

I put the knife down. Once again, a Cheysuli summoned me out of the depths of a night. But this one I hardly knew; what I did know merely made me suspicious. "Where? And why?"

He smiled a little. In the torchlight his face was a mask, lacking definition. His eyes yellowed against the light, with pinpricks for pupils. The hawk-shaped earring glinted in his hair. "Would you have me put off my knife?"

I felt the heat and color running quickly into my face. "Why?" I retorted, stung. "You could slay me as easily without."

Duncan laughed. "I never thought you would *fear* me—"

"Not fear, precisely," I answered. "You would never slay me, not when you yourself have said how important a link I am in your prophecy. But I do suspect the motives for what you do."

"Carillon," he chided, "tonight I will make you a king."

I felt the prickle in my scalp. "Make *me* one?" I asked with elaborate distinctness, "or another?"

"Come with me and find out."

I put on breeches and shirt, the first things I could find. And boots, snugged up to my knees. Then I followed him, even as he bid Cai remain, and went with him as he led me through my palace.

He walked with utter confidence, as a man does who knows a place well. And yet I knew Duncan had never spent excess time in Homana-Mujhar. Hale had, I knew, brought him to the palace at least once, but he had been a child, too young to know the mazes of hallways and chambers. And yet he went on through such places as if he had been born here.

He took me, of course, to the Great Hall. And there he took down a second torch from its bracket on the wall, lighted it with his own and handed them both to me. "Where we are going," he said, "it is dark. But there will be air to breathe."

I felt the hair rise on the back of my neck. But I refrained from asking him where. And so I watched in silence and astonishment as he knelt by the firepit rim.

He began to pull aside the unlighted logs. Ash floated up to settle on his hair. Suddenly he was an old man without the wrinkles, gray instead of black, while the gold glowed on his arms. I coughed as the ash rose high enough to clog my nose, and then I sneezed. But Duncan was done rearranging my firepit quickly enough; he reached down and caught a ring of iron I had never seen.

I scowled, wondering what other secrets Duncan knew of Homana-Mujhar. And then I watched, setting myself to be patient, and saw him frown with concentration. It took both hands and all of his strength, but he jerked the ring upward.

It was fastened to a hinged iron plate that covered a hole. Slowly he dragged up the plate until the hole lay open. He leaned the cover, spilling its coating of ash, against the firepit rim, then grimaced as he surveyed the ruin of his leathers.

I leaned forward to peer into the hole. Stairs. I frowned. "Where—?"

"Come and see." Duncan took back his torch and stepped down into the hole. He disappeared, step by step. Uneasily, I followed.

There was air, as he had promised. Stale and musty, but air. Both torches continued to burn without guttering, so I knew we would be safe. And so I went down with Duncan, wondering how it was he knew of such a place.

The staircase was quite narrow, the steps shallow. I had to duck to keep from scraping my head. Duncan, nearly as tall, did as well, but I thought Finn would fit. And then I wished, with the familiar frisson of unease, that he was with me as well. But no. I had sent him to my sister, and left myself to his brother's intentions.

"Here." Duncan descended two more steps to the end of the staircase into a shallow stone closet. He put his fingers to the stone, and I saw the runes, old and green with dampness and decay. Duncan's brown fingers, now gray with ash, left smudges on the wall. He traced out the runes, saying something beneath his breath, and then he nodded. "Here."

"What do—" I did not bother to finish. He pressed one of the stones and then leaned against the wall. A portion of it grated and turned on edge, falling inward.

Another stairway—? No. A room. A vault. I grimaced. Something like a crypt.

Duncan thrust his torch within and looked. Then he withdrew it and gestured me to go first.

I regarded him with distinct apprehension that increased with every moment.

"Choose," Duncan said. "Go in a prince and come out a Mujhar . . . or leave now, and forever know yourself lacking."

"I lack nothing!" I said in rising alarm. "Am I not the link you speak about?"

"A link must be properly forged." He looked past me to the rising staircase. "There lies your escape, Carillon. But I think you will not seek it. My *rujholli* would never serve a coward or a fool."

I bared my teeth in a grin that held little of humor. "Such words will not work with me, shapechanger. I am willing enough to name myself *both,* does it give me a chance to survive. And unless you slay me, as you have said you would not do, I will come out of here a Mujhar even if I do *not* to into that room." I squinted as my torch sputtered and danced. "You are not Finn, you see, and for all I know I should trust you—we have never been easy with each other."

"No," he agreed. "But what kept us from that was a woman, and even Alix has no place here. This is for you to do."

"You left Cai behind." Somehow it incriminated him.

"Only because here, in this place, he would be a superfluous *lir.*"

I stared at him, almost gaping. Superfluous *lir?* Had *Duncan* said this? By the gods, if he indicated such a willingness to dispense with the other half of his soul, surely I could trust him.

I sighed. I swallowed against the tightness in my throat, thrust the torch ahead of me, and went in.

Superfluous. Aye, he would have been. For here were all the *lir* of the world, and no need for even one more.

It was not a crypt. It was a memorial of sorts, or perhaps a chapel. Something to do with Cheysuli and *lir,* and their gods. For the walls were made of *lir, lir* upon *lir,* carved into the pale cream marble.

Torchlight ran over the walls like water, tracking the veining of gold. From out of the smooth, supple stone burst an eagle, beak agape and talons striking. A bear, humpbacked and upright, one paw reaching out to buffet. A fox, quick and brush-tailed, head turned over its shoulder. And the boar, tusks agleam, with a malevolent, tiny eye.

More. So many more. I felt my breath catch in my throat as I turned in a single slow circle, staring at all the walls.

Such wealth, such skill, such incomparable beauty, and buried so deeply within the ground.

A hawk, touching wingtips with a falcon. A mountain cat, so lovely, leaping in the stone. And the wolf; of course, the wolf, Storr-like with gold in its eyes. Every inch, from ceiling to floor, was covered with the *lir.*

Superfluous. Aye. But so was I.

I felt tears burn in my eyes. Pain, unexpected, was in my chest. How futile it was, suddenly, to be Homanan instead of Cheysuli; to lack the blessings of the gods and the magic of the *lir.* How utterly insignificant was Carillon of Homana.

"*Ja'hai,*" Duncan said. "*Ja'hai, cheysu, Mujhar.*"

I snapped my head around to stare at him. He stood inside the vault, torch raised, looking at the *lir* with an expression of wonder in his face. "What are those words?" I demanded. "Finn said those words when he talked to the gods, and even you said he should not have done it."

"That was Finn." The sibilants whispered in the shadows of the *lir.* "This is a clan-leader who says them, and a man who might have been Mujhar." He smiled as my mouth flew open to make an instant protest. "I do not want it, Carillon. If I did, I would not have brought you down here. It is here, within the *Jehana's* Womb, that you will be born again. Made a true Mujhar."

"The words," I repeated steadfastly. "What do they mean?"

"You have learned enough of the Old Tongue from Finn to know it is not directly translatable. There are nuances, unspoken words, meanings requiring no speech. Like gestures—" He made the sign of *tahlmorra.* "*Ja'hai, cheysu, Mujhar* is, in essence, a prayer to the gods. A petition. A Homanan might say: *Accept this man; this Mujhar.*"

I frowned. "It does not sound like a prayer."

"A petition—or prayer—such as the one Finn made—and now *I* make—requires a specific response. The gods will always answer. With life . . . or with death."

Alarm rose again. "Then I might *die* down here—?"

"You might. And this time you will face that risk alone."

"You knew about it," I said suddenly. "Was it Hale who told you?"

Duncan's face was calm. "Hale told me what it was. But most Cheysuli know of its existence." A faint smile appeared. "Not so horrifying, Carillon. It is only the Womb of the Earth."

The grue ran down my spine. "What womb? What earth? Duncan—"

He pointed. Before, I had looked at the walls, ignoring the floor entirely. But this time I looked, and I saw the pit in the precise center of the vault.

Oubliette. A man could die in one of those.

I took an instinctive step back, nearly brushing against Duncan just inside the door, but he merely reached out and took the torch from my hand. I turned swiftly, reaching for a knife I did not have, but he set each torch in a bracket near the door so the vault was filled with light. Light? It spilled into the oubliette and was swallowed utterly.

"You will go into the Womb," he said calmly, "and when you come out, you will have been born a Mujhar."

I cursed beneath my breath. Short of breaking his neck— and I was not at all certain even I could accomplish that— I had no choice but to stay in the vault. But the Womb was something else. "Just—go in? How? Is there a rope? Hand holes?" I paused, knowing the thing was futile. Oubliettes are built to keep people in. This one would offer no aid in getting out.

"You must jump."

"Jump." My hands shut up into fists that drove my nails into my palms. "Duncan—"

"Sooner in, sooner out." He did not smile, but I saw the glint of amusement in his eyes. "The earth is like most *jehanas,* Carillon: she is harsh and quick to anger and sometimes impatient, but she ever gives of her heart. She gives her child life. In this case, it is a Mujhar we seek to bring into the world."

"I am *in* the world," I reminded him. "I have already been born once, birthed by Gwynneth of Homana. Once is more than enough—at least *that* one I cannot remember. Let us quit this mummery and go elsewhere; I have no taste for wombs."

His hand was on my shoulder. "You will stay. We will finish this. If I have to, I will *make* you."

I turned my back on him and paced to the farthest corner, avoiding the edge of the pit. There I waited, leaning against the stone, and felt the fluted wings of a falcon caress my neck. It made me stand up again.

"You are not Cheysuli," Duncan said. "You cannot *be* Cheysuli. But you can be made to better understand what it is to think and feel like a Cheysuli."

"And this will make me a man?" I could not entirely hide my resentment.

"It will make you, however briefly, one of us." His face was solemn in the torchlight. "It will not last. But you will know, for a moment, what it is to be Cheysuli. A child of the gods." He made the gesture of *tahlmorra*. "And it will make you a better Mujhar."

My throat was dry. "Mujhar is a Cheysuli word, is it not? And Homana?"

"Mujhar means *king*," he said quietly. "Homana is a phrase: *of all blood.*"

"King of all blood." I felt the tension in my belly. "So, since you cannot put a Cheysuli on the throne—yet—you will do what else you can to make me into one."

"Ja'hai, cheysu," he answered. *"Ja'hai, cheysu, Mujhar."*

"No!" I shouted. "Will you condemn me to the gods? Duncan—I am *afraid*—"

The word echoed in the vault. Duncan merely waited.

It nearly mastered me. I felt the sweat break out and run from my armpits; the stench of fear coated my body. A shudder wracked my bones and set my flesh to rising. I wanted to relieve myself, and my bowels had turned to water.

"A man goes naked before the gods."

So, he would have me strip as well. Grimly, knowing he would see the shrinking of my genitals, I pulled off my boots, my shirt, and lastly the snug dark breeches. And there was no pity in Duncan's eyes, or anything of amusement. Merely compassion, and perfect comprehension.

He moved to the torches. He took each from the brackets and carried them out into the stairway closet. The door to the vault stood open, but I knew it was not an exit.

"When I shut up the wall, you must jump."

He shut up the wall.

And I jumped—

Chapter Nineteen

Ja'hai, cheysu, Mujhar—

The words echoed in my head.

Ja'hai, cheysu, Mujhar—

I fell. And I fell. *So far. . . .* Into blackness; into a perfect emptiness. *So far. . . .*

I screamed.

The sound bounced off the walls of the oubliette; the round, sheer walls I could not see. Redoubled, the scream came back and vibrated in my bones.

I fell.

I wondered if Duncan heard me. I wondered—I wondered—I did not. I simply fell.

Ja'hai, cheysu, Mujhar—

It swallowed me whole, the oubliette; I fell back into the Womb. And could not say whether it would give me up again—

Duncan, oh Duncan, you did not give me proper warning . . . But is there a proper way? Or is it only to fall and, in falling, learn the proper way?

Down.

I was stopped. I was caught. I was halted in mid-fall. Something looped out around my ankles and wrists. Hands? No. Something else; something else that licked out from the blackness and caught me tightly at wrists and ankles, chest and hips. And I hung, belly-down, suspended in total darkness.

I vomited. The bile spewed out of my mouth from the depths of my belly and fell downward into the pit. My bladder and bowels emptied, so that I was nothing but a shell of quivering flesh. I hung in perfect stillness, not daring to move, to breathe; praying to stay caught by whatever had caught me.

Gods—do not let me fall again—not again—

Netting? Taut, thin netting, perhaps, hung from some unseen protrusions in the roundness of the oubliette. I had seen nothing at the lip of the pit, merely the pit itself, yet it was possible the oubliette was not entirely smooth. Perhaps there was even a way out.

The ropes did not tear my flesh. They simply held me immobile, so that my body touched nothing but air. I did not sag from arms and legs because of the ropes at chest and hips. I was supported, in a manner of speaking, and yet remained without it.

A cradle. And the child held face-down to float within the Womb.

"Duncan?" I whispered it, fearing my voice would upset the balance. "Is it supposed to be this way?"

But Duncan was gone, leaving me completely alone, and I knew why he had done it. Finn had said little of Cheysuli manhood rites, since most warriors were judged fully grown by the bonding of the *lir*, but I thought there might be more. And I would remain ignorant of it, being Homanan and therefore unblessed, unless this was the way to discover what made the Cheysuli, Cheysuli.

Tonight I will make you a king.

A king? I wondered. Or a madman? Fear can crush a soul.

I did not move. I hung. I listened. I wondered if Duncan would return to see how I fared. I would hear him. I would hear the grate of stone upon stone, even the subtle silence of his movements. I would hear him because I listened so well, with the desperation of a man wishing to keep his mind. And if he came back, I would shout for him to let me out.

Probably I would beg.

Go in a prince and come out a Mujhar.

Gods, would it be worth it?

Air. I breathed. There was no flavor to it, no stench to make it foul. Just air. From somewhere trickled the air that kept me alive; perhaps there were holes I could use to escape.

I hung in total silence. When I turned my head, slowly, I heard the grating pop of spinal knots untying. I heard my hair rasp against my shoulders. Hardly sounds. Mostly whispers. And yet I heard them.

I heard also the beating begin: *pa-thump, pa-thump, pa-thump.*

Footsteps? No. Duncan? No.

Pa-thump, pa-thump, pa-thump.

I heard the wind inside my head, the raucous hissing roar. Noise, so much noise, hissing inside my head. I shut my eyes and tried to shut off my ears.

Pa-thump, pa-thump, pa-thump.

I hung. Naked and quite alone, lost within the darkness. The Womb of the Earth. A child again, I was; an unborn soul caught within the Womb. It was the beating of my own heart I heard; the noise of silence inside my head. A child again, was I, waiting to be born.

"Duncannnn—!"

I shut my eyes. I hung. The chill of fear began to fade. I lost my sense of touch; the knowledge I was held.

I floated.

Silence.

Floating—

No warmth. No cold. Nothingness. I floated in the absence of light, of sound, of touch, taste, and smell. I did not exist.

I waited with endless patience.

Ringing. Like sword upon sword. Ringing. *Noise—*

It filled my head until I could taste it. I could smell it. It sat on my tongue with the acrid tang of blood. Had I bitten myself? No. I had no blood. Only flesh, depending from the ropes.

My eyes, I knew, were open. They stared. But I was blind. I saw only darkness, the absolute absence of light. And then it came up and struck me in the face, and the light of the world fell upon me.

I cried out. Too much, too much—will you blind me with the light?

It will make you, however briefly, one of us.

"Duncan?"

The whisper I mouthed was a shout. I recoiled in my

ropes and recalled I had a body. A body. With two arms, two legs, a head. Human. Male. Carillon of Homana.

You will know, for a moment, what it is to be Cheysuli.
But I did not.
I knew nothing.
I thought only of being born.

I heard the rustling of wings. The scrape of talons. Cai? No. Duncan had left him behind.

Soughing of wings spread, stretching, folding, preening. The pipping chirp of a falcon; the fierce shriek of a hunting hawk. The scream of an angry eagle.

Birds. All around me birds. I felt the breath of their wings against my face, the caress of many feathers. How I wanted to join them, to feel the wind against my wings and know the freedom of the skies. To dance. Oh, to dance upon the wind—

I felt the subtle seduction. I opened my mouth and shouted. "I am man, not bird! *Man,* not beast! *Man,* not shapechanger!"

Silence soothed me. *Pa-thump, pa-thump, pa-thump.*

Whispering.
DemonDemonDemon—
I floated.
DemonDemonDemon—
I stirred. *No.*
SHAPEchangerSHAPEchangerSHAPEchanger—
NoNoNo. I smiled. *ManManMan.*
YouShiftYouShiftYouShift—
Gods' blessing, I pointed out. *Cannot be denied.*
BeastBeastBeast—
No!No!No!
I floated, And I became a beast.

I ran. Four-legged, I ran. With a tail slashing behind me, I ran. And knew the glory of such freedom.

The warm earth beneath my paws, catching in the curving nails. The smells of trees and sky and grass and brush. The joyousness of playful flight; to leap across the creeks. The hot red meat of prey taken down; the taste of flesh in my mouth. But most of all the freedom, the utter, perfect freedom, to cast off cares and think only of the day. The moment. Not yesterday, not tomorrow; the day. The moment. *Now.*

And to know myself a *lir.*

Lir? I stopped. I stood in the shadow of a wide-boled beech. The glittering of sunlight through the leaves spattered gems across my path.

Lir?

Wolf. Like Storr: silver-coated, amber-eyed. With such grace as a man could never know.

How? I asked. *How is it done?*

Finn had never been able to tell me in words I could understand. *Lir* and warrior and *lir,* he had said, knowing no other way. To part them was to give them over to death, be it quick or slow. The great yawning emptiness would lead directly into madness, and sooner death than such an end.

For the first time I knew the shapechange. I felt it in my bones, be they wolf's or man's. I felt the essence of myself run out into the soil until the magic could be tapped.

The void. The odd, distorted image of a man as he exchanged his shape for another. He *changed his shape* at will, by giving over the human form to the earth. It spilled out of him, sloughing off his bones, even as the bones themselves altered. What was not needed in *lir*-shape, such as clothing, weapons, and too much human weight, went into storage in the earth, protected by the magic. An exchange. Give over excess and receive the smaller form.

Magic. Powerful magic, rooted in the earth. I felt the heavy hair rise upon my hackles, so that I saw the transformation. Of soul as well as flesh.

I knew the void for what it was. I understood why it existed. The gods had made it as a ward against the dazzled eyes of humans who saw the change. For to see flesh and bone before you melt into the ground, to be remade into another shape, might be too much for even the strongest to bear. And so mystery surrounded the change, and magic, and the hint of sorcery. No man, seeing the change for what it was, would ever name the Cheysuli *men.*

And now, neither could I.

The fear came down to swallow me whole and I recoiled against my ropes.

Ropes. I hung in the pit. A man, not a wolf; not a beast.

But until I acknowledged what the Cheysuli were, I would never be Mujhar.

Homana was Cheysuli.

I felt the madness come out of my mouth. "Accept!" I shouted. "Accept this man; this Mujhar!"

Silence.

"Ja'hai!" I shouted. *"Ja'hai, cheysu, ja'hai—Ja'hai, cheysu, Mujhar!"*

"Carillon."

"Ja'hai," I panted. *"Ja'hai!" O gods, accept. O gods, acceptAcceptAccept—*

"Carillon."

If they did not—if they did not—

"Carillon."

Flesh on flesh. *Flesh on flesh.* A hand supporting my head.

"Jehana?" I rasped. *"Jehana? Ja'hai . . . jehana, ja'hai—"*

Two hands were on my head. They held it up. They cradled it, like a child too weak to lift himself up. I lay against the cold stone floor on my back, and a shadow was kneeling over me.

My blinded eyes could only see shape. Male. Not my *jehana.*

"Jehan?" I gasped.

"No," he said. *"Rujholli.* In this, for this moment, we are." The hands tightened a moment. *"Rujho,* it is over."

"Ja'hai—?"

"Ja'hai-na," he said soothingly. *"Ja'hai-na Homana Mujhar.* You are born."

BornBornBorn. "Ja'hai-na?"

"Accepted," he said gently. "The king of all blood is born."

The Homanan was back on my tongue, but the voice was hardly human. "But I am not." Suddenly, I knew it. "I am only a *Homanan.*"

"For four days you have been Cheysuli. It will be enough."

I swallowed. "There is no light. I can barely see you." All I *could* see was the darker shape of his body against the cream-colored walls, and the looming of the *lir.*

"I left the torch in the staircase and the door is mostly shut. Until you are ready, it is best this way."

My eyes ached. It was from the light, scarce though it was, as it crept around the opening in the wall. It gleamed on his gold and nearly blinded me with its brilliance; it made the scar a black line across his face.

Scar. Not Duncan. Finn.

"Finn—" I tried to sit up and could not. I lacked the strength.

He pressed me down again. "Make no haste. You are not—whole, just yet."

Not whole? What *was* I then—?

"Finn—" I broke off. "Am I out? Out of the oubliette?" It seemed impossible to consider.

He smiled. It chased away the strain and weariness I saw stretching the flesh of his shadowed face. "You are out of the Womb of the Earth. Did I not say you had been born?"

The marble was hard beneath my naked body. I drew up my legs so I could see my knees, to see if I was whole. I was. In body, if not in mind. "Am I gone mad? Is that what you meant?"

"Only a little, perhaps. But it will pass. It is not—" He broke off a moment. "It is not a thing we have done very often, this forcing of a birth. It is never easy on the infant."

I sat up then, thrusting against the cold stone floor. Suddenly I was another man entirely. Not Carillon, Something else. Something drove me up onto my knees. I knelt, facing Finn, staring into his eyes. So yellow, even in the darkness. So perfectly *bestial—*

I put up a hand to my own. I could not touch the color. They had been blue . . . I wondered now what they were. I wondered what *I* was . . .

"A man," Finn said.

I shut my eyes. I sat very still in the darkness, knowing light only by the faint redness across my lids. I heard my breathing as I had heard it in the pit.

And *pa-thump, pa-thump, pa-thump.*

"Ja'hai-na," Finn said gently. *"Ja'hai-na Homana Mujhar."*

I reached out and caught his wrist before he could respond. I realized it had been the first time I had outthought him, anticipating his movement. My fingers were clamped around his wrist as he had once clasped mine, preparing to cut it open. I had no knife, but he did. I had only to put out my other hand and take it.

I smiled. It was flesh beneath my fingers, blood beneath the flesh. He would bleed as I had bled. A man, and capable of dying. Not a sorcerer, who might live forever.

Not like Tynstar. Cheysuli, not Ihlini.

I looked at his hand. He did not attempt to move. He merely waited. "Is it difficult to accomplish?" I asked. "When you put your *self* into the earth, and take out another form? I have seen you do it. I have seen the expression on your face, while the face is still a face, and not hidden by the void." I paused. "There is a need in me to know."

The dilation turned his eyes black. "There are no Homanan words—"

"Then give me Cheysuli words. Say it in the Old Tongue."

He smiled. "*Sul'harai*, Carillon. That is what it is."

That I had heard before. Once. We had sat up one night in Caledon, lost in our jugs of *usca*, and spoke as men will about women, saying what we liked. Much had not been said aloud, but we had known. In our minds had been Alix. But out of that night had come a single complex word: *sul'harai*. It encompassed that which was perfect in the union of man and woman, almost a holy thing. And though the Homanan language lacked the proper words for him, I had heard it in his tone.

Sul'harai. When a man was a woman and a woman a man, two halves of a whole, for that single fleeting instant. And so at last I knew the shapechange.

Finn moved to the nearest wall and sat against it, resting his forearms on his drawn-up knees. Black hair fell into his face; it needed cutting, as usual. But what I noticed most was how he resembled the *lir*-shapes upon the wall, even in human form. There is something predatory about the Cheysuli. Something that makes them wild.

"When did you come back?"

He smiled. "That is a Carillon question; I think you are recovered." He shifted. Behind him was a hawk with open wings. The stone seemed to encase his shoulders so that he appeared to be sprouting wings. But no, that was his brother's gift. "Two days ago I came. The palace was in an uproar:

the Mujhar, it was said, had gone missing. Assassination? No. But it took Duncan to tell me, quite calmly, he had brought you here to be born."

I scrubbed an arm across my head. "Did you know about this place?"

"I knew it was here. Not where, precisely. And I did not know he had intended such a thing." His brow creased. "He reprimanded me because I had risked you in the star magic, and yet he brought you down here and risked you all over again. I do not understand him."

"He might have been Mujhar," I said reflectively, feeling the rasp in my throat. "Duncan, instead of me. Had the Homanans never ruled . . ."

Finn shrugged. "But they—you—did. It does not matter what might have been. Duncan is clan-leader, and for a Cheysuli it is enough."

I put up a hand and looked at it. It was flesh stretched over bone. Callused flesh. And yet I thought it had been a paw. "Dreams," I murmured.

"Divulge nothing," Finn advised. "*You* are the Mujhar, not I; you should keep to yourself what has happened. It makes the magic stronger."

The hand flopped down to rest across my thigh. I felt too weak to move. "What magic? I am Homanan."

"But you have been born again from the Womb of the Earth. You lack the proper blood, it is true, and the *lir*-gifts as well . . . but you share in a bit of the magic." He smiled. "Knowing what you survived should be magic enough."

Emptiness filled my belly. "Food. Gods, I need food!"

"Wait you, then. I have something for you." Finn rose and went away, stepping out of the vault. I stared blankly at all the walls until he came back again. A wineskin was in his hand.

I drank, then nearly spat it out. *"Usca!"*

"Jehana's milk," he agreed. "You need it, now. Drink. Not much, but a little. Stop dribbling like a baby."

Weakly I tried to smile and nearly failed in the attempt. "Gods, do I not get *food*—"

"Then put on your clothes and we will go out of here."

Clothes. Unhappily, I looked at the pile. Shirt, breeches, boots. I doubted I could manage even the shirt.

And then I recalled how I had lost control of my body in the oubliette, and the heat rushed up to swallow my flesh.

"Gods," I said finally, "I cannot go like *this*—"

Finn fetched the clothing, brought it back and began putting it on me, as if I were a child. "You are too big to carry," he said when I stood, albeit wobbly, in my boots. "And it might somewhat tarnish your reputation. Carillon the Mujhar, drunk in some corner of his palace. What would the servants say?"

I told him, quite clearly, what I thought of servants speaking out of turn. I did it in the argot of the army we had shared, and it made him smile. And then he grasped my arm a moment.

"*Ja'hai-na.* There is no humiliation."

I turned unsteadily toward the door and saw the light beyond. I wavered on my feet.

"Walk, my lord Mujhar. Your *jehana* and *rujholla* are here."

"Stairs."

"Climb," he advised. "Unless you prefer to fly."

For a moment, just a moment, I wondered if I could. And then I sighed, knowing I could not, and started to climb the stairs.

Chapter Twenty

I stared back at myself from the glitter of the polished silver plate set against the wall. My hair was cut so that no longer did it tangle on my shoulders, and the beard was trimmed. I was less unkempt than I had been in years. I hardly knew myself.

"No more the mercenary-prince," Finn said.

I could see him in the plate. Like me, he dressed for the occasion, though he wore leathers instead of velvet. White leathers, so that his skin looked darker still. And gold. On arms, his ear, his belt. And the royal blade with its rampant lion. Though at a wedding no man went armed save the Mujhar with his Cheysuli sword, the Cheysuli were set apart. Finn more so than most, I thought; he was more barbarian than man with all his gold; more warrior than wedding guest.

"And you?" I asked. "What are you?"

He smiled. "Your liege man, my lord Mujhar."

I turned away from the plate, frowning. "How much time?"

"Enough," he returned. "Carillon—do not fret so. Do you think she will not come?"

"There are hundreds of people assembled in the Great Hall," I said irritably. "Should Electra choose to humiliate me by delaying the ceremony, she will accomplish it. Already I feel ill." I put one hand against my belly. "By the gods—I should never have agreed to this—"

Finn laughed. "Think of her as an enemy, then, and not merely a bride. For all that, she *is* one. Now, how would you face her?"

I scowled and touched the circlet on my head, settling it more comfortably. "I would sooner face her in bed than before the priest."

"You told me it was to make peace between the realms. Have you decided differently?"

I sighed and put my hand on the hilt of my sword. A glance at it reminded me of what Tynstar had done; the ruby still shone black. "No," I answered. "It must be done. But I would sooner have my freedom."

"Ah," His brows slid up. "Now you see the sense in a solitary life. Were you *me*—" But he broke off, shrugging. "You are not. And had I a choice—" Again he shrugged. "You will do well enough."

"Carillon." It was Torry in the doorway of my chambers, dressed in bronze-colored silk and a chaplet of pearls. "Electra is nearly ready."

Something very akin to fear surged through my body. Then I realized it *was* fear. "Oh gods—what do I do? How do I go through with this?" I looked at Finn. "I have been a fool—"

"You are often that," Torry agreed, coming directly to me to pry my hand off the sword. "But for now, you will have to show the others you are not, *particularly* Electra. Do you think she will say nothing if you go to her like this?" She straightened the fit of my green velvet doublet, though my body-servant had tended it carefully.

Impatiently, I brushed her hands aside. "Oh gods, there is the gift. I nearly forgot—" I moved past her to the marble table and pushed back the lid on the ivory casket. In the depths of blue velvet winked the silver. I reached in and pulled out the girdle dripping with pearls and sapphires. The silver links would clasp Electra's waist very low, then hang down the front of her skirts.

"Carillon!" Torry stared. "Where did you find such a thing?"

I lifted the torque from the casket as well, a slender silver torque set with a single sapphire with a pearl on either side. There were earrings also, but I had no hands for those.

Finn's hand shot out and grabbed the torque. I released it, surprised, and saw the anger in his eyes. "Do you know what these are?" he demanded.

Tourmaline and I both stared at him. Finally I nodded. "They were Lindir's. All the royal jewels were brought to me three weeks ago, so I could choose some for Electra. I thought these—"

"*Hale* made these." Finn's face had lost its color, yet the scar was a deep, livid red. "My *jehan* fashioned these with such care as you have never known. And now you mean them for *her?*"

Slowly I settled the girdle back into the ivory casket. "Aye," I said quietly. "I am sorry—I did not know Hale made them. But as for their disposition, aye. I mean them for Electra."

"You cannot. They were Lindir's." His mouth was a thin, pale line. "I care little enough for the memory of the Homanan princess my *jehan* left us for, but I do care for what he made. Give them to Torry instead."

I glanced at my sister briefly and saw the answering pallor in her face. Well, I did not blame her. Without shouting, he made his feelings quite clear.

I saw how tightly his fingers clenched the torque. The silver was so fine I thought he might bend it into ruin. Slowly I put out my hand and gestured with my fingers.

"Carillon—" Torry began, but I cut her off.

"Give it over," I told Finn. "I am sorry, as I have said. But these jewels are meant for Electra. For the *Queen.*"

Finn did not release the torque. Instead, before I could move, he turned and set it around Torry's throat. "There," he said bitterly. "Do you want it, take it from your *rujholla.*"

"No!" It was Torry, quite sharply. "You will not make me the bone of contention. Not over *this.*" Swiftly she pulled the torque from her throat and put it into my hands. Their eyes locked for a single moment, and then Finn turned away.

I set the torque back into the casket and closed the lid. For a moment I stared at it, then picked it up in both hands. "Torry, will you take it? It is my bride-gift to her."

Finn's hands came down on the casket. "No." He shook his head. "Does anyone give over the things my *jehan* made, it will be me. Do you see? It has to be done this way."

"Aye," I agreed, "it does. And is it somehow avoided—"

"It will not be." Finn bit off the words. "Am I not your liege man?" He turned instantly and left my chambers, the casket clutched in his hands. I put my hand to my brow and rubbed it, wishing I could take off the heavy circlet.

"I have never seen him so angry," Torry said finally.

"Not even at the Keep when Alix made him spend his time in a pavilion, resting, when he wished to hunt with Donal."

I laughed, glad of something to take my mind from Finn's poor temper. "Alix often makes Finn angry, and he, her. It is an old thing between them."

"Because he stole her?" Torry smiled as I looked at her sharply. "Aye, Finn told me the story . . . when I asked. He also told me something else." She reached out to smooth my doublet one more time. "He said that did he ever again want a woman the way he had wanted Alix, he would let no man come between them. Not you; not his brother." Her hand was stiff against my chest, her gaze intense. "And I believe him."

I bent down and kissed her forehead. "That is bitterness speaking, Torry. He has never gotten over Alix. I doubt he ever will." I tucked her hand into my arm. "Now come. It is time this wedding was accomplished."

The Great Hall was filled with the aristocracy of Solinde and Homana, and the pride of the Cheysuli. I waited at the hammered silver doors for Electra and regarded the assembled multitude with awe. Somehow I had not thought so many would wish to see the joining of two realms that had warred for so long; perhaps they thought we would slay each other before the priest.

I tried to loosen the knots in jaw and belly. My teeth hurt, but only because I clenched them so hard. I had not thought a wedding would be so frightening. And I, a soldier . . . I smiled wryly. Not this day. Today I was merely a bridegroom, and a nervous one at that.

The Homanan priest waited quietly on the dais by the throne. The guests stood grouped within the hall like a cluster of bees swarming upon the queen. Or Mujhar.

I searched the faces for those I knew: Finn, standing near the forefront. Duncan and Alix; the former solemn, as usual, the latter uncommonly grave. My lady mother sat upon a stool, and beside her stood my sister. My mother still wore a wimple and coif to hide the silver hair, but no longer did she go in penury. Now she was the mother of a king, not the mother of a rebel, and it showed quite clearly in her clothing. As for Tourmaline, she set the hall ablaze with her tawny beauty. And Lachlan, near her, knew it.

I sighed. Poor Lachlan, so lost within his worship of my sister. I had had little time of late to spare him, and with Torry present his torture was harder yet. And yet there was nothing I could do. Nothing *he* could do, save withstand the pain he felt.

"My lord."

I froze at once. The moment had come upon us. *Us;* it was Electra who spoke. I turned toward her after a moment's hesitation.

She was Bellam's daughter to the bone. She wore white, the color of mourning, as if to say quite clearly—without speaking a word—just what she thought of the match. Well, I had expected little else.

She regarded me from her great gray eyes, so heavy-lashed and long-lidded. The mass of white-blonde hair fell past her shoulders to tangle at her knees, unbound as was proper for a maiden. I longed to put my hands into it and pull her against my hips.

"You see?" she said. "I wear your bride-gift."

She did the silver and sapphires justice. Gods, what a woman was this—

Yet in that moment she reminded me not so much of a woman as a predator. Her assurance gave me no room for doubt, and yet I wanted her more than ever. More, even, than I could coherently acknowledge.

I put out an arm. "Lady—you honor me."

She slipped a pale, smooth hand over the green velvet of my sleeve. "My lord . . . that is the *least* I will do to you."

The ceremony was brief, but I heard little of it. Something deep inside me clamored for attention, though I longed to ignore it. Finn's open disapproval kept swimming to the surface of my consciousness, though his face was bland enough when I looked. By each time I looked at Electra I saw a woman, and her beauty, and knew only how much I wanted her.

I spoke the vows that bound us, reciting the Homanan words with their tinge of Cheysuli nuance. It seemed àpropos. Homana and the Cheysuli were inseparable, and now I knew why.

Electra repeated them after me, watching me as she said the words. Her Solindish mouth framed the syllables strangely, making a parody of the vows. I wondered if she did it deliberately. No. She *was* Solindish . . . and undoubtedly knew what she said even as she said it.

The priest put a hand on her head and the other rested on mine. There was a moment of heavy silence as we knelt before the man. And then he smiled and said the words of benediction for the new-made Mujhar and his lady wife.

I had taken the woman; I would keep her. Electra was mine at last.

When the wedding feast was done, we adjourned to a second audience hall, this one somewhat smaller but no less magnificent than the Great Hall with its Lion Throne. A gallery ran along the side walls. Lutes, pipes, tambors, harps, and a boys' chorus provided an underscore to the celebration. It was not long before men warmed by wine neglected to speak of politics and waited to lead their ladies onto the red stone floor.

But the dancing could not begin until the Mujhar and his queen began it. And so I took Electra into the center of the shining floor and signaled the dance begun.

She fell easily into the intricate pattern of moving feet and swirling skirts. Our hands touched, fell away. The dance was more of a courtship than anything else, filled with the subtle overtures of man to woman and woman to man. I was aware of the eyes on us and the smiling mouths, though few of them belonged to the Solindish guests. There was little happiness there.

"Tell me," I said, as we essayed a pass that brought us close in the center of the floor, "where is Tynstar?"

She stiffened and nearly missed a step. I caught her arm and steadied her, offering a bland smile as she stared at me in shock.

"Did you think I would not ask?" I moved away in the pattern of the dance, but in a moment we were together again.

She drew in a breath that set the sapphires to glowing against the pale flesh of her throat. The girdle chimed in the folds of her skirts. "My lord—you have taken me unaware."

"I do not think you are ever taken unaware, Electra." I smiled. "Where is he?"

The pattern swept us apart yet again. I waited, watching

the expressions on her face. She moved effortlessly because she claimed a natural grace, but her mind was not on the dance.

"Carillon—"

"Where is Tynstar?"

Long lids shuttered her eyes a moment, but when she raised them again I saw the hostility plainly. Her mouth was a taut, thin line. "Gone. I cannot say where."

I caught her hand within the pattern of the dance. Her fingers were cool, as ever; I recalled them from before. "You had best content yourself with me, Electra. You are my wife."

"And Queen?" she countered swiftly.

I smiled. "You want a crown, do you?"

The high pride of royalty burst forth at once. "I am worthy of it! Even *you* cannot deny me that."

We closed again within the figure. I held her hand and led her the length of the hall. We turned, came back again, acknowledging the clapping from the guests. The courtship had been settled; the lady had won.

"Perhaps I cannot deny it to you," I agreed. "You will be the mother of my heir."

Her teeth showed briefly. "That is your price? A child?"

"A son. Give me a son, Electra."

For only a moment there was careful consideration in her eyes. And then she smiled. "I am, perhaps, too old to bear your children. Did you never think of that?"

I crushed the flesh and bones of her hand with my own. "Speak not of such nonsense, lady! And I doubt not Tynstar, when he gave you permanent youth, left your childbearing years intact."

Dull color stained her cheeks. The dance was done; no longer did she have to follow my lead. And yet we were watched, and dared not divulge our conversation.

Electra smiled tightly. "As you wish, my lord husband. I will give you the child you want."

I thought, then, the celebration went on too long. And yet I could not take her to bed quite yet. Propriety demanded we wait a little while.

But even a little can be too long.

Electra looked at me sidelong. I saw the tilt of her head and the speculation in her eyes. She judged me even as I judged her. And then I caught her fingers in mine and raised them to my mouth. "Lady—I salute you," I murmured against her hand.

Electra merely smiled.

I thought, later, the world had changed, even if only a little. Perhaps more than just a little. What had begun in lust and gratification had ended in something more. Not love; hardly love, but a better understanding. The recriminations were gone, replaced with comprehension, yet even as we moved toward that comprehension I knew it would not be easy. We had been enemies too long.

Electra's legs were tangled with mine, and much of her hair was caught beneath my shoulder. Her head was upon my arm, using it for a pillow, and we both watched the first pink light of dawn creep through the hangings on the bed.

We had spent the remainder of the night in consummation of our marriage, having escaped the dancing at last, and neither of us had been surprised to find we were so well-matched. That had been between us from the beginning. But now, awake and aware again of what had happened, we lay in silent contemplation of the life that lay before us.

"Do you forget?" she asked. "I was Tynstar's woman."

I smiled grimly at the hangings that kept the chill from our flesh. "You share a bed with *me* now, not Tynstar. It does not matter."

"Does it not?" Like me, she smiled, but, I thought, for a different reason.

I sighed. "Aye, it matters. You know it does, Electra. But it is *me* you have wed, not him; let us leave him out of our marriage."

"I did not think you would admit it." She shifted closer to me. "I thought you would blame me for everything."

I twisted my arm so I could put my fingers in her hair. "*Should* I?"

"No," she said, "lay no blame on me. I had no choice in the matter." She twisted, pulling free of my arm and sitting up to kneel before me in the dawn. "You cannot know what it is to be a woman; to know yourself a prize meant for the winning side. First Tynstar *demanded* me— his price for aiding my father. And then you, *even you,* saying you would wed me when we had lost the war. Do you see? Ever the prize given to the man."

"Tynstar's price?" I frowned as she nodded again. "The cost of Inhlini aid . . ." I shook my head. "I had not thought of that—"

"You thought I *wanted* him?"

I laughed shortly. "You were quite convincing about it. You ever threw it in my face—"

"You are the enemy!" She sounded perplexed I could not understand. "Am I to go so willingly into surrender? Am I to let you think I am yours for the easy taking? Ah Carillon, you are a man, like other men. You think all a woman wants is to be wanted by a man." She laughed. "There are other things than that—things such as power—"

I pulled her down again. "Then the war between us is done?"

The light on her face was gentle. "I want no war in our bed. But do you seek to harm my realm, I will do what I can to gainsay you."

I traced the line of her jaw and settled my fingers at her throat. "Such as seeking to slay me again?"

She stiffened and jerked her head away. "Will you throw *that* in my face?"

I caught a handful of hair so she could not turn away. "Zared *might* have succeeded. Worse yet, he might have slain my sister. Do you expect me to forgive—*or* forget—that?"

"Aye, I wanted you slain!" she cried. "You were the enemy! What else could I do? Were I a *man,* my lord Mujhar, you would not question my intention. Are *you* not a soldier? Do *you* not slay? Why should I be different?" Color stood high in her face. "Tell me I was wrong to try to slay the man who threatened my father. Tell me you would not have done the same thing had you been in *my* place. Tell me I should not have used what weapon I had at hand, be it magic or knife or words." She did not smile, staring intently into my face. "I am not a man and cannot go to war. But I am my father's daughter. And given the chance, I would do it again . . . but he is no longer alive. What good would it do? Solinde is yours and you have made me Queen of Homana. Were you to die, Solinde would be no better off. A woman cannot rule there." A muscle ticked in her jaw. "So I have wed you, my lord, and share your bed, my lord, which is all a woman *can* do."

After a moment I took a deep breath. "There is one more," I said gently. "You can also bear a son."

"A son!" she said bitterly. "A son for Homana, to rule when you are dead. What good does that do *Solinde?*"

"*Two* sons," I said. "Bear me two, Electra . . . and the second shall have Solinde."

Her long-lidded eyes sought out the lie, except I offered none. "Do you mean it?"

"Your son shall have Solinde."

Her chin thrust upward. *"My son,"* she whispered, and smiled a smile of triumph.

I was falling. Another oubliette. But this time a woman caught me and took the fear away.

"Ja'hai," I murmured. *"Ja'hai, cheysu, Mujhar."*

Accept this man; this Mujhar . . .

But it was not to the gods I said it.

PART II

Chapter One

I stared at Finn in anguish. "Why will it not be *born?*"

He did not smile, but I saw faint amusement in his eyes. "Children come in their own time. You cannot rush them, or they hang back—as this one does."

"Two days." It seemed a lifetime. "How does Electra bear it? *I* could not—I could not bear a moment of it."

"Perhaps that is why the gods gave women instead of men the task of bearing children." Finn's tone lacked the dry humor I expected, being more understanding than I had ever heard him. "In the clans, it is no easier. But there we leave it to the gods."

"Gods," I muttered, staring at the heavy wooden door studded with iron nails. "It is not the gods who got this child on her . . . that took *me.*"

"And your manhood proven." Finn did smile now. "Carillon—Electra will be well enough. She is a strong woman—"

"Two days," I repeated. "She might be dying of it."

"No," Finn said, "not Electra. She is far stronger than you think—"

I cut him off with a motion of my hand. I could not bear to listen. I had found myself remarkably inattentive of late, being somewhat taken up with the birth of my first child. All I could think of was Electra on the other side of the door; Electra in the bed with her women around her and the midwife in attendance, while I waited in the corridor like a lackey.

"Carillon," Finn said patiently, "she will bear the child when the child is ready to come."

"*Alix* lost one." I recalled the anger I had felt when I had learned it from Duncan. The Ihlini attack on the Keep had caused her to lose the child, and Duncan had said it was unlikely she would ever bear another. And I thought again of Electra, realizing how fragile even a strong woman could be. "She is—not as young as she appears. She could die of this."

Finn shut his mouth and I saw the lowering of his brows. Like most, Finn forgot Electra was twenty years older than she appeared. My reminding him of it served as vivid notice that she was more than merely woman and wife; she was ensorcelled as well, with a definite link to Tynstar. No more his *meijha,* perhaps, but she bore the taint—or blessing— of his magic.

I leaned against the door and let my head thump back upon the wood. "Gods—I would almost rather be in a *war* than live through this—"

Finn grimaced. "It is not the same at all—"

"You cannot say," I accused. "*I* sired this child, not you. You cannot even lay claim to a bastard."

"No," he agreed, "I cannot." For a moment he looked down at Storr sitting so quietly by his side. The wolf's eyes were slitted and sleepy, as if bored by his surroundings. I wished I could be as calm.

I shut my eyes. "Why will they not come and tell me it is born?"

"Because it is not." Finn put a hand on my arm and pulled me away from the door. "Do you wish it so much, I will speak to her. I will use the third gift on her, and tell her to have the child."

I stared at him. "You can do that?"

"It is no different from any other time I used it." Finn shrugged. "Compulsion need not always be used for harm—it can exact an obedience that is not so harsh, such as urging a woman to give birth." He smiled faintly. "I am no midwife, but I think it likely she is afraid. As you say, she is not so young as she looks—she may fear also she will not bear a son."

I swore beneath my breath. "Gods grant it is, but I prefer simply to have her safe. Can you do that? Make her bear the child in safety?"

"I can tell her to do whatever it is women do while giving birth," he said, with excess gravity, "and I think it likely the child will be born."

I frowned. "It sounds barbaric."

"Perhaps it is. But babies are born, and women go on bearing them. I think it will not harm her."

"Then come. Do not waste time out here." I hammered on the door. When the woman opened it I ignored her protests and pushed the door open wider. "Come," I directed Finn, and he came in behind me after a moment's frowning hesitation.

A circle of shocked women formed a barricade around the bed in the birthing chamber. Doubtless *my* presence was bad enough, but Finn was a shapechanger. To their minds we were both anathema.

I thrust myself through them and knelt down beside her bed. Dark circles underlay her eyes and her hair was damp and tangled. Gone was the magnificent beauty I so admired, but in its place was an ever greater sort. The woman was bearing my child.

"Electra?"

Her eyes flew open and another contraction stabbed through the huge belly covered by a silken bedcloth. "Carillon! Oh gods, will you not leave me be? I *cannot*—"

I put my hand on her mouth. "Hush, Electra. I am here to ease your travail. Finn will make the baby come."

Her eyes, half-crazed by pain, looked past me and saw Finn waiting just inside the doorway. For a moment she only stared, as if not understanding, and then suddenly she opened her mouth and cried out in her Solindish tongue.

I gestured him close, knowing it was the only way to ease her. And yet she cried out again and tried to push herself away. She was nearly incoherent, but I could see the fear alive in her face.

"Send him away!" she gasped. A brief grunt escaped her bitten lips. "Carillon—send him away—" Her face twitched. "Oh gods—*do as I say*—"

The women were muttering among themselves, closing ranks. I had allowed Electra Solindish women to help her through her lying-in because I knew she had been lonely, surrounded by Homanans, but now I wished they were gone. They oppressed me.

"Finn," I appealed, "is there nothing you can do?"

He came forward slowly, not noticing how the women pulled their skirts away from his passage. I saw hand gestures and muttered invocations; did they think him a

demon? Aye, likely. And they Solindish, with their Ihlini
sorcerers.

I saw a strangeness in Finn's face as he looked on Electra. It was a stricken expression, as if he had suddenly realized the import of the child, or of the woman who bore it,
and what it was to sire a child. There was a sudden crack-
ling awareness in him, an awareness of Electra as he had
never seen her. I could feel it in him. In nine months I had
seen him watching her as she watched him, both with grave,
explicit wariness and all defenses raised. But now, as he
squatted down beside the bed, I saw an awakening of wonder in his eyes.

Electra's pride was gone. He saw the woman instead; not
the Ihlini's *meijha,* not the haughty Solindish princess, not
the Queen of Homana who had wed his liege lord. And I
knew, looking at him, I had made a deadly mistake.

I thought of sending him away. But he had taken her
hand into both of his even as she sought to withdraw, and
it was too late to speak a word.

He was endlessly patient with her, and so gentle I hardly
knew him. The Finn of old was gone. And yet, as he looked
at her, I had the feeling it was not Electra he saw. Someone
else, I thought; the change had been too abrupt.

"Ja'hai," he said clearly, and then—as if knowing she
could not understand the Old Tongue—he translated each
word he spoke. *"Ja'hai*—accept. *Cheysuli i'halla shansu."*
He paused. *"Shansu, meijhana*—peace. May there be Cheysuli peace upon you—"

"I spit on your peace!" Electra caught her breath as another contraction wracked her.

Finn had her then. I saw the opaque, detached expression
come into his eyes and make them empty, and I knew he
sought the magic. I thought again of the vault in the earth
and the oubliette that waited, recalling the sensations I had
experienced. I nearly shivered with the chill that ran down
my spine, raising the hairs on my flesh, for I was more in
awe of the magic than ever before. For all the Cheysuli
claimed themselves human, I knew now they were not.
More; so much, much more.

Finn twitched. His eyes shut, then opened. I saw his head
dip forward as if he slept, then he jerked awake. The blankness deepened in his eyes, and then suddenly I knew some-

thing had gone wrong. He was—different. His flesh turned hard as stone and the scar stood up from his flesh. All the color ran out of his face.

Electra cried out, and so did Finn.

I heard growling. Storr leaped into the room, threading his way through the women. I heard screaming; I heard crying; I heard Electra's hissing Solindish invectives. I heard the low growl rising; oh gods, *Storr* was in the room—

Finn was white as death with an ashen tinge to his mouth. I put a band on his arm and felt the rigid, upstanding muscles. He twitched again and began to tremble as if with a seizure; his mouth was slack and open. His tongue was turning dark as it curled back into his throat.

And then I saw it was Electra who held his hand and that he could not break free of her grasp.

I caught their wrists and jerked, trying to wrench their hands apart. At first the grip held; Electra's nails bit into his skin and drew blood, but it welled dark and thick. Then I broke the grip and Finn was freed, but he was hardly the Finn I knew. He fell back, still shaking, his yellow eyes turned up to show the whites. One shoulder scraped against the wall. I thought he was senseless, but he was awake. Too awake, I found.

His eyes closed, then opened, and once more I saw the yellow. Too much yellow; his pupils were merest specks. He stared with the feral gaze of a predator.

He growled. Not Storr. Finn. It came out of a human throat, but there was nothing human about him.

I caught his shoulders as he thrust himself up and slammed him against the wall. There was no doubt of his prey. One of his arms was outstretched in her direction and the fingers were flexing like claws.

"Finn—"

All the muscles stood up from his flesh and I felt the tremendous power, but it was nothing compared to my fear. Somehow I held him, pressing him into the wall. I knew, if I let him go, he would slay her where she lay.

His spine arched, then flattened. One hand fastened on my right arm and tried to pull it free, but I thrust my elbow against his throat. The growl was choked off, but I saw the feral grimace. White teeth, man's teeth, in a bloodless mouth, but the tongue had regained its color.

I gritted my teeth and leaned, pressing my elbow into the fragility of his windpipe, praying I could hold him. "Finn—"

And then, as suddenly as it had come on him, the seizure was past.

Finn sagged. He did not fall, for I held him, but his head lolled forward against my arm and I saw his teeth cut into his bottom lip. I thought he would faint. And yet his control was such that he did not, and as Storr pushed past me to his *lir* I saw sense coming back in Finn's eyes.

He pressed himself up. His head smacked into the wall. He sucked in a belly-deep, rasping breath and held it while the blood ran from his mouth. He frowned as if confused, then caught himself as once more his body sagged. With effort he straightened, scraping his *lir*-bands against the wall. I saw the white teeth bared yet again, this time in a grimace of shock and pain.

"Finn—?"

He said a single word on a rush of breath, but I could not hear it for the exhaustion in his tone. It was just a sound, an expulsion of air, but the color was back in his face. I knew he could stand again, but I did not let him go.

"Tynstar—" It was barely a whisper, hoarse and astonished. "Tynstar—*here*—"

The women were clustered around the bed and I knew I had to get Finn from the room. Electra was crying in exhaustion and fear while the contractions wracked her body. I dragged Finn to the door and pushed him out into the corridor while Storr came growling at my heels, all his hackles raised.

Finn hardly noticed when I set him against the wall. He moved like a drunken man, all slackness, lacking grace. Not Finn, not Finn at all. "Tynstar—" he rasped again. "Tynstar—*here*—"

My hands were in the leather of his jerkin, pushing him into the stone. "By the gods, do you know what you did? Finn—"

If I took my hands away, he could fall. I could see it in his eyes. "Tynstar," he said again. "Carillon—it was *Tynstar*—"

"Not *here!*" I shouted. "How could he be? That was *Electra* you meant to slay!"

He put a hand to his face and I saw how the fingers trembled. He pushed them through his hair, stripping it from his eyes, and the scar stood out like a brand against cheek and jaw. "He—was—here—" Each word was distinct. He spoke with the precise clarity of the drunken man, or the very shaken. A ragged and angry tone, laced with a fear I had never heard. "Tynstar set a trap—"

"Enough of Tynstar!" I shouted, and then I fell silent. From inside the room came the imperative cry of a newborn soul, and the murmur of the women. Suddenly it was there I wanted to be, not here, and yet I knew he needed me. This once, he needed *me*. "Rest," I said shortly. "Take some food—*drink* something! Will you go? *Go* . . . before I have to carry you from this place."

I took my hands away. He leaned against the wall with legs braced, muscles bunching the leather of his leggings. He looked bewildered and angry and completely devoid of comprehension.

"Finn," I said helplessly, "will you go?"

He pushed off the wall, wavered, then knelt upon the floor. For one insane moment I thought he knelt to offer apology; he did not. I thought he prayed, but he did not. He merely gathered Storr into his arms and hugged him as hard as he could.

His eyes were shut. I knew the moment was too private to be shared, even with me. Perhaps *especially* with me. I left them there, wolf and man, and went in to see my child.

One of the women, as I entered, wrapped the child hastily in linen cloth, wiping its face, then set it into my arms. They were all Solindish, these women, but I was their king—and would be, until I sired a second son.

And then I looked at their faces and knew I lacked a first.

"A girl, my lord Mujhar," came the whisper in accented Homanan.

I looked down on the tiny face. It lacked the spirit of a person, little more than a collection of wrinkled features, but I knew her for mine.

What man cannot know immortality when he holds his child in his arms? Suddenly it did not matter that I had no son; I would in time. For now, I had a daughter, and I thought she would be enough.

I walked slowly to the bed, cradling the child with infinite care and more than a little apprehension. So helpless and so tiny; I so large and equally helpless. It seemed a miracle *I* had sired the girl. I knelt down at the bedside and showed Electra her baby.

"Your heir," she whispered, and I realized she did not know. They had not told her yet.

"Our daughter," I said gently.

Sense was suddenly in her eyes; a glassy look of horror. "Do you say it is a *girl*—?"

"A princess," I told her. "Electra, she is a lovely girl." Or will be, I thought; I hoped. "There will be time for sons. For now, we have a daughter."

"Gods!" she cried out. "All this pain for a *girl*? No son for Homana—no son for Solinde—" The tears spilled down her face, limning her exhaustion. "How will I keep my bargain? *This* birth nearly took me—"

I gestured one of the women to take the baby from me. When I could, I slipped one arm beneath Electra's shoulders and cradled her as if she were the child instead. "Electra, be at peace. There is no haste in this. We have a daughter and we will have those sons—but not tomorrow. Be at ease. I have no wish to see you grieve because you have borne a girl."

"A girl," she said again. "What use is a girl but to wed? I wanted a *son*—!"

I eased her down against the pillows, pulling the bedclothes close. "Sleep. I will come back later. There is the news to be told, and I must find Finn—" I stopped. There was no need to speak of Finn, not to her. Not now.

But Electra slept. I brushed the damp hair from her brow, looked again on the sleeping baby, then went from the room to give out the news.

Soon enough the criers were sent out and the bells began to peal. Servants congratulated me and offered good wishes. Someone pressed a cup of wine into my hand as I strode through a corridor on my way to Finn's chambers. Faces were a blur to me; I hardly knew their names. I had a daughter, but I also had a problem.

Finn was not in his chambers. Nor was he in the kitchens,

where the spit-boys and cooks fell into bows and curtseys to see their Mujhar in their presence. I asked after Finn, was told he had not come, and went away again.

It was Lachlan who found me at last, very grave and concerned. His arms were empty of his Lady and with him came my sister. I thought first they would give me good wishes when I told them; instead they had news of Finn.

"He took the wolf and left," Lachlan said quietly. "And no horse for riding."

"*Lir*-shape," I said grimly.

"He was—odd." Torry was white-faced. "He was not himself. But he would answer none of our questions." She gestured helplessly. "Lachlan was playing his Lady for me. I saw Finn come in. He looked—ill. He said he had to go away."

"Away!" I felt the lurch in my belly. "Where?"

"To the Keep," Lachlan answered. "He said he required cleansing for something he had done. He said also you were not to send for him, or come after him yourself." He glanced a moment at Torry. "He said it was a Cheysuli thing, and that clan-ties take precedence, at times, over other links."

I felt vaguely ill. "Aye. But only rarely does he invoke them—" I stopped, recalling the wildness in his eyes and the growling in his throat. "Did he say how long he would stay there?"

Torry's eyes were frightened. "He said the nature of the cleansing depended on the nature of the offense. And that this one was great indeed." One hand crept up to her throat. "Carillon—what did he do?"

"Tried to slay the Queen." It came out of my mouth without emotion, as if someone else were speaking. I saw the shock in their eyes. "Gods!" I said on a rushing breath, "I *must* go after him. You did not see what he was—" I started out the door and nearly ran into Rowan.

"My lord!" He caught my arm. "My lord—wait you—"

"I cannot." I shook loose and tried to move on, but he caught my arm again. "*Rowan*—"

"My lord, I have news from Solinde," he persisted. "From Royce, your regent in Lestra."

"Aye," I said impatiently, "can it not wait? I will be back when I can."

"Finn said you should not follow," Lachlan repeated. "Doubtless he has good reason—"

"Carillon." Rowan forsook my title and all honorifics, which told me how serious he was. "It is Thorne of Atvia. He readies plans to invade."

"Solinde?" I stared at him in amazement.

"Homana, my lord." He let go my arm when he saw I was not moving. I could not, now. "The news has come into Lestra, and Royce sent on a courier. There is still time, Royce says, but Thorne is coming. My lord—" He paused. "It is Homana he wants, and you. A grudge for the death of his father, and Atvians slain in Bellam's war. The courier has the news." His young face was haggard with the implications. "Thorne intends to take Hondarth—"

"Hondarth!" I exploded. "He will not set foot in a Homanan city while *I* am alive!"

"He means to raise Solindish aid," Rowan said in a quiet voice. "To come overland through Solinde, and by ships across the Idrian Ocean, bound for Hondarth."

I thought of the southern city on the shores of the Idrian Ocean. Hondarth was a rich city whose commerce depended on fishing fleets and trading vessels from other lands. But it was a two-week ride to Hondarth, going fast; an even longer march. And the marshes would slow an army.

I shut my eyes a moment, trying to get my senses sorted. First Finn's—seizure; my daughter's birth; now this. It was too much.

I set a hand on Rowan's shoulder. "Where is this courier? And find you what advisors you can. We must send for those who have gone home to their estates. It will take time—ah, gods, are we to go to war again, we must reassemble the army." I rubbed at my gritty eyes. "Finn will have to wait."

When I could, I broke free of planning councils and went at last to the Keep. And, as I rode out across the plains, I came face to face with Finn.

He had left Mujhara without a horse, but now he had one. Borrowed from the Keep, or perhaps it was one of his own. He did not say. He did not say much at all, being so shut up within himself, and when I looked at him I saw how the shadow lay on him, thick and dark. His yellow eyes were strange.

We met under a sky slate-gray with massing clouds. Rain was due in an instant. It was nearly fall, and in four months the snow would be thick upon the ground. For now there was none, but I wore a green woolen cloak pulled close against plain brown hunting leathers. Finn, bare-armed still, and cloakless, pulled in his horse and waited. The wind whipped the hair from his face, exposing the livid scar, and I swore I saw silver in his hair where before it had been raven's-wing black. He looked older, somehow, and more than a trifle harder. Or was it merely that I had not noticed before?

"I wanted to come," I said. "Lachlan said no, but I wanted it. You seemed so distraught." I shrugged, made uncomfortable by his silence. "But the courier had come in from Lestra . . ." I let it trail off, seeing nothing in his face but the severity of stone.

"I have heard." The horse stomped, a dark bay horse with a white slash across his nose and a cast in one eye. Finn hardly noticed the movement save to adjust his weight.

"Is that why you have come back?"

He made a gesture with his head; a thrusting of his chin toward the distances lying behind me. "Mujara is there. I have not come back yet."

The voice was flat, lacking intonation. I tried to search beneath what I saw. But I was poor at reading Cheysuli; they know ways of blanking themselves. "Do you mean to?"

The scar ticked once. "I have no place else to go."

It astonished me, in light of where he had been. "But—the Keep—"

"I am liege man to the Mujhar. My place is not with the clan, but with him. Duncan has said—" He stopped short; something made him turn his head away. "Duncan has not—absolved me of what I tried to do. As the *shar tahl* says: *if one is afraid, one can only become unafraid by facing what causes the fear.*" The wind, shifting, blew the hair back into his face. I could see nothing of his expression. "And so I go to face it again. I could not admit my fear—*i'toshaa-ni* was not completed. I am—unclean."

"*What* do you face again?" I asked, uneasy. "I would rather you did not see Electra."

He looked at me squarely now, and the strangeness was in his eyes. "*I* would rather not see her, also. But you have wed her, and my place is with the Mujhar. There is little choice, my lord."

My lord. No irony; no humor. I felt the fear push into my chest. "Did you truly intend to slay her?"

"Not her," he said softly, "Tynstar."

The anger boiled over. I had not realized how frightened I was that he might have succeeded; how close I had come to losing them both. *Both.* Had Finn slain Electra, there was no choice but execution. "Electra is not Tynstar! Are you blind? She is my wife—"

"She was Tynstar's *meijha*," he said quietly, "and I doubt not he uses her still. Through her soul, if not her body."

"Finn—"

"*It was I who nearly died!*" He was alive again, and angry. Also clearly frightened. "Not Electra—she is too strong. It was I, Cheysuli blood and all." He drew in a hissing breath and I saw the instinctive baring of white teeth. "It nearly took me down; it nearly swallowed me whole. It was Tynstar, I tell you—*it was.*"

"Go, then," I said angrily. "Go on to Homana-Mujhar and wait for me there. We will face whatever it is you have to face, and get this finished at once. But there are things I have to discuss with Duncan."

There *was* gray in his hair; I saw it clearly now. And bleakness in his eyes. "Carillon—"

"Go." I said it more quietly. "I have a war to think of again. I will need you at my side."

The wind blew through his hair. The sunlight, so dull and brassy behind the clouds, set his *lir*-gold to shining in the grayness of the day. His face was alien to me; I thought again of the vault and oubliette. Had it changed me so much? Or was it Finn who had been changed?

"Then I will be there," he said, "for as long as I can."

An odd promise. I frowned and opened my mouth to ask him what he meant, but he had set his horse to trotting, leaning forward in the saddle. And then, as I turned to watch, he galloped toward Mujhara. Beside him ran the wolf.

Chapter Two

I rode into the Keep just as the storm broke. The rain fell heavily, quickly soaking through my cloak to the leather doublet and woolens beneath. The hood was no help; I gave up and pushed it back to my shoulders, setting my horse to splashing through the mud toward Duncan's slate-colored pavilion. It was early evening and I could hardly see the other pavilions, only the dim glow of their interior fire cairns.

I dropped off my horse into slippery mud and swore, then noticed Cai was not on his perch. No doubt he sought shelter in a thick-leafed tree, or perhaps even inside. Well, so did I.

Someone came and took my horse as I called out for entrance. I thanked him, then turned as the doorflap was pulled open. I looked down; it was Donal. He stared up at me in surprise, and then he grinned. "Do you *see?*"

I saw. His slender arms, still bared for warmer weather, were weighted with *lir* gold, albeit lighter than the heavy bands grown warriors wore. And in his black hair glittered an earring, though I could not see the shape. Young, I thought; so very young.

Duncan's big hand came down on Donal's head and gently moved him aside. "Come in from the rain, Carillon. Forgive my son's poor manners."

I stepped inside. "He has a right to be proud," I demurred. "But is he not too young?"

"There is no *too young* in the clans," Duncan said on a sigh. "Who is to say what the gods prefer? A week ago the craving came upon him, and we let him go. Last night he received his *lir*-gold in his Ceremony of Honors."

I felt the pang of hurt pride. "Could *I* not have witnessed it?"

Duncan did not smile. "You are not Cheysuli."

For four days, once, I had been. And yet now he denied me the honor.

I looked past him to Alix. "You must be proud."

She stood on the far side of the fire cairn and the light played on her face. In the dimness she was dark, more Cheysuli than ever, and I felt my lack at once. "I am," she said softly. "My son is a warrior now."

He was still small. Seven, I thought. I did not know. But young.

"Sit you down," Duncan invited. "Donal *will* move his wolf."

I saw then what he meant, for sprawled across one of the pelts carpeting the hard-packed earth was a sleeping wolf-cub. Very young, and sleeping the sleep of the dead, or the very tired. He was damp and the pavilion smelled of wet fur; I did not doubt Donal had been out with the wolfling when the rain began.

Donal, understanding his father's suggestion at once, knelt down and hoisted half of the cub into his arms. The wolf was like a bag of bones, so limp and heavy, but Donal dragged him aside. The cub was ruddy, not silver like Storr, and when he opened one eye I saw it was brown.

"He is complaining," Donal said, affronted. "He wanted to stay by the fire."

"He has more hair than you," Alix retorted. "Lorn will be well enough farther back. This is the Mujhar we entertain."

I waved a hand. "Carillon, to him. He is my kin, for all that." I grinned at the boy. "Cousins, of a sort."

"Taj is weary of Cai's company," Donal said forthrightly. "Can *he* not come in, too?"

"Taj is a falcon and will remain outdoors," Duncan said firmly as he sidestepped the flopping wolf-cub. "Cai has stood it all these years; so will Taj."

Donal got Lorn the wolf settled and sat down close beside him, one small hand buried in damp fur. His yellow eyes peered up at me with the bright intentness of unsuppressed youth. "Did you know I have two?"

"Two *lir?*" I looked at Alix and Duncan. "I thought a warrior had only one."

"Ordinarily." Duncan's tone was dry as he waved me

down on the nearest pelt. Alix poured a cup of hot honey brew and handed it across. "But Donal, you see, has the Old Blood."

Alix laughed as I took the cup. "Aye. He got it from me. It is the Firstborn in him." She sat back upon her heels, placing herself close to Duncan. "I took *lir*-shape twice while I carried him, as wolf and falcon both. You see the result."

I sipped at the hot, sweet brew. It was warm in the pavilion, though somewhat close; I was accustomed to larger quarters. But it was a homey pavilion, full of pelts and chests and things a clan-leader holds. A heavy tapestry fell from the ridge-pole to divide the tent into two areas; one, no doubt, a bedchamber for Alix and Duncan. As for Donal, he undoubtedly slept by the fire on the other side. And now with his wolf.

"How fares the girl?" Duncan asked.

I smiled. "At two months of age, already she is lovely. We have named her Aislinn to honor my mother's mother."

"May she have all of her *jehan's* wisdom," Duncan offered gravely.

I laughed. "And none of my looks, I trust."

Alix smiled, but her face soon turned pensive. "No doubt you have come to see Finn. He is no longer here."

The honey brew went sour in my mouth. I swallowed with effort. "No. I met him on the road. He is bound for Homana-Mujhar. And no, I did not come to speak to him. I came to speak of Homana."

I told them what I could. They listened in silence, all three of them; Donal's eyes were wide and full of wonder. It was, no doubt, the first he had heard of war from the Mujhar himself, and I knew he would always remember. I recalled the time I had sat with my own father, listening to plots and plans—and how those things had slain him. But death was not in Donal's mind, that much I could see. He was Cheysuli. He thought of fighting instead.

"I must have allies," I finished. "I need more than just the Cheysuli."

"Then you offer alliances." Duncan nodded thoughtfully. "What else is there to give?"

"My sister," I said flatly, knowing how it sounded. "I

have Tourmaline to offer, and I have done it. To Ellas, to Falia, to Caledon. All have marriageable princes."

Alix put a hand to her mouth and looked at Duncan. "Oh Carillon, no. Do not barter your sister away."

"Torry is meant for a prince," I said impatiently. "She will get one anyway; why should I wait? I need men, and Torry needs a husband. A *proper* husband." I could not help but think of Lachlan. "I know—it is not a Cheysuli custom to offer women this way. But it is the way of most royal Houses. How else to find a man or woman worthy of the rank? Torry is well past marriageable age; the dowry will have to be increased. There will be questions about her virginity." I looked again at Donal, thinking he was too young. But he was Cheysuli, and they seemed always older than I. "Bellam held her for years; he even spoke of wedding her himself. There will be questions asked of that. But she is my sister, and that will count for something. I should get a worthy prince for her."

"And allies for Homana." Duncan's tone lacked inflection, which told me what he thought. "Are the Cheysuli not enough?"

"Not this time," I answered flatly. "Thorne enters in more than one place. Bellam came at us straight away. But Thorne knows better; he has learned. He will creep over my borders in bits and pieces. If I split the Cheysuli, I split my strongest weapon. I need more men than that, to place my armies accordingly."

Duncan studied me, and then he smiled. Only a little. "Did you think we would not come?"

"I cannot *order* you to come, any of you," I said quietly. "I ask, instead."

The smile widened and I saw the merest glint of white teeth. Not bared, as Finn's had been; a reflection of true amusement. "Assemble your armies, Carillon. You will have your Cheysuli aid. Do whatever you must in the way that you must, to win the allies you need. And then we shall send Thorne back to his island realm." He paused. "Provided he survives the encounter."

Alix glanced at him, and then she looked squarely at me. "What did Finn say to you when you met him on the road?"

"Little."

"But you know why he came . . ."

I shifted on the pelt. "I was told it was something to do with cleansing. A ritual of sorts."

"Aye," Duncan agreed. "And now he has had to go back."

The cup grew cool in my hands. "He said he had no other place to go. That you had, in essence, sent him out of the Keep." I meant to keep my tone inflectionless and did not succeed. It was a mark of the bond between Finn and me that I accused even his brother of wrongful behavior.

"Finn is welcome here," Duncan demurred. "No Cheysuli is denied the sanctuary when he requires it, but that time was done. Finn's place is with you."

"Even so unhappy?"

Alix's face was worried. "I *thought* he should not go—"

"He must learn to deal with that himself." Duncan took my cup and warmed it with more liquor, handing it back. It was high honor from a clan-leader; I thought it was simply Duncan. "Finn has ever shut his eyes to many things, going in the backflap." An expressive flick of his fingers indicated the back of the pavilion. "Occasionally, when I can, I remind him there is a front."

"*Something* has set him on edge." I frowned and sipped at the liquor. "He is—different. I cannot precisely say. . . ." I shook my head, recalling the expression in his eyes. "What happened with Electra frightened me. I have never seen him so."

"It is why he came," Duncan agreed, "and why he stayed so long. Eight weeks." His face was grim. "It is rare a liege man will leave his lord for so long unless it has something to do with his clan- and kin-ties. But he could not live with what he had done, and so he came here to renew himself; to touch again the power in the earth through *i'toshaa-ni.*" He looked tired suddenly. "It comes upon us all, once or twice; the need to be *cleansed.*"

The word, even in Homanan, had a nuance I could not divine. Duncan spoke of things that no Homanan had shared, though once I had shared a fleeting moment of their life. Such stringent codes and honor systems, I thought; could I bind myself so closely?

Duncan sipped at his honey brew. I noticed then that his

hair was still black, showing no silver at all. Odd, I thought; Duncan was the elder.

"I am not certain he was cleansed at all," Alix said in a very low voice. "He is—unhappy." Briefly she looked at Duncan. "But that is a private thing."

"Can he say nothing to me?" I could not hide the desperation in my voice. "By the gods, we have been closer than most. We shared an exile together, and then only because of me. *He* might have stayed behind." I looked at them both, almost pleading to understand. "Why can he say nothing to me?"

"It is private," Duncan repeated. "But no, he can say nothing to you. He knows you too well."

I swore, then glanced in concern to Donal. But boys grow up, and I did not doubt he had heard it before. Finn had taught me the Cheysuli invectives. "He told you what he did, then. To Electra?"

"To Tynstar," Duncan said.

I heard the fire cairn crackle in the sudden silence. A hissing mote of sparks flew up. "Tynstar?" I said at last.

"Aye. It was not *Electra* he meant to slay; did you think it was?" He frowned. "Did he tell you nothing?"

I recalled how he had said it over and over, so hoarse and stricken: *Tynstar was here.* And how I had ignored it. "He said—something—"

"Tynstar set a trap," Duncan explained, echoing Finn's own words. "He set it in Electra's mind, so that anyone using the earth magic on her would succumb to the possession."

My body twitched in surprise. *"Possession!"*

The firelight cast an amber glaze across the face before me. Smoke was drawn upward to the vent-flap, but enough remained to shroud the air with a wispy, ocherous haze. Duncan was gold and bronze and black in the light, and the hawk-earring transfixed my gaze. I smelled smoke and wet fur and honey, sweet honey, with the bittersweet tang of spice.

"The Ihlini have that power," Duncan said quietly. "It is a balance of our own gift, which is why we use it sparingly. We would not have it said we are anything like the Ihlini." Minutely, he frowned, looking downward into his cup. "When we use it, we leave a person his soul. We do little more than *suggest,* borrowing the will for a moment only." Again the faint frown that alarmed me. He was not divulging something. "When it is Ihlini-done, the soul is swallowed whole. *Whole* . . . and not given back at all."

Silence. Duncan put out a hand and touched his son, tousling Donal's hair in a gesture that betrayed his concern as the boy crept closer, between father and *lir.* I thought Duncan knew how avidly the boy listened and meant to calm any fears. The gods knew I had a few of my own.

"Finn reacted the way any Cheysuli would react; perhaps even you." He did not smile. "He tried to slay the trapper through the trap. It is—understandable." His eyes lifted to meet mine squarely. "In that moment she was not Electra to him, not even a woman. To Finn, she was simply Tynstar. Tynstar was—*there.*"

I frowned. "Then Tynstar *knew* it was Finn he had—"

"I do not doubt it," Duncan said clearly. "An Ihlini trap will kill. He did not intend to leave Finn alive. But something—*someone*—prevented the death by shattering the trap-link."

"*I* broke it." I recalled how Electra had grasped Finn's hand, leaving blood in the scratches she had made. How he had been unable to break free.

And I recalled, suddenly, how he had slain the Homanan assassin in the Ellasian blizzard, more than a year before. How he had said he *touched* Tynstar, who had set the man a task—

I stood up. Bile surged into my throat. Before they could say a word I bent down and swept up my damp cloak, then went out of the pavilion shouting for my horse.

Alix, running out into the rain, caught my arm as I moved to sling on the cloak. "Carillon—wait you! What are you doing?"

The hood lay on my shoulders and the rain ran into my mouth. "Do you not see?" I was amazed she could be so blind. "Finn thought he slew Tynstar through Electra. Tynstar thought he slew *him*—" I swung up on my horse. "*If one is afraid, one can only become unafraid by facing what causes the fear.*"

"Carillon!" she shouted, but I was already gone.

*   *   *

I heard the howling when I ran into Homana-Mujhar. *Howling.* Gods, was Finn a wolf—?

The white faces were a blur, but I heard the frightened voices. *"My lord!" "My lord Carillon!" "The Mujhar!"* I pushed past them all and answered none of them, conscious only of the great beating of fear in my chest.

Howling. Gods, it was Storr. Not Finn. But the screaming was Electra's.

Weight hung off my shoulders as I pounded up the twisting red stone stairs. I ripped the cloak-brooch from my left shoulder and felt the fabric tear. Weight and gold fell behind me; I heard the clink of brooch on stone and the soft slap of soaked wool falling to the stairs. *"My lord!"* But I ran on.

I burst through the women and into the room. I saw Electra first, white-faced and screaming though Lachlan suggested she be quiet. No need, he said; no need to scream. Safe, he said; unharmed. The wolf was held at bay.

Electra was whole. I saw it at once. She stood in a corner with Lachlan holding her back, his hands upon her arms. Holding her *back*—

—from Finn. From Finn, who was capably cornered by Rowan with his sword, and another man-at-arms. They caged him with steel, bright and deadly, and the wolf in man's shape was held at bay.

He bled. Something had opened the scar so that his face ran with blood. It stained the leather jerkin and splattered down to his thighs, where I saw more blood. His right thigh, where the Atvian spear had pierced. There was a cut in his leggings and blood on Rowan's blade.

He was flat against the wall, head pressed back so that his throat was bared. Blood ran from the opened scar to trickle down his throat, crimson on bronze; I smelled the tang of fear. Gods, it swallowed him whole and left nothing to spit out.

I looked again at Electra and heard the women's frightened conversation. I understood little of it, knowing it to be only Solindish. But I understood the screams.

I went to her and set a hand on Lachlan's shoulder. He saw me, but he did not let her go. I knew why. There was blood on her nails and she wanted more; she would rip the flesh from his bones.

"Electra," I said.

The screaming stopped. *"Carillon—"*

"I know." I could hear the howling still. Storr, locked somewhere within the palace. Locked away by his *lir.*

I turned away again, looking back at Finn. His eyes were wide and wild. Breath rasped in his throat. Even from here, I saw how he shook; how the trembling wracked his bones.

"Out!" I shouted at the women. "This will be better done without your Solindish tongues!"

They protested at once. So did Electra. But I listened to none of it. I waited, and when they saw I meant it they gathered their skirts and scuttled out of the room. I slammed the heavy door shut behind them, and then I went to Finn.

The man-at-arms—Perrin, I knew—stepped out of my way at once. Rowan hesitated, still holding Finn at sword-point, and I set him aside with one ungentle thrust of my arm. I went through the space where Rowan had stood and caught the jerkin in both hands, pulling Finn from the wall even as he sagged.

"Ku'reshtin!" I used the Cheysuli obscenity, knowing he would answer no Homanan. *"Tu'halla dei!"* Lord to liege man, a command he had to acknowledge.

I felt the shaking in the flesh beneath my hands. Fists clenched and unclenched helplessly, clawless and human, but betrayal nonetheless. I had seen the bruises on Electra's throat.

I heard the labored breathing. The howling filled the halls. Human and wolf, both driven to extremes. But at this moment I thought Storr, at least, knew what was going on.

I thrust Finn into the corner, fenced by two walls of stone. I drew back one fist and smashed it into his face, knocking skull against brick. Blood welled up in a broken lip.

"No!" Rowan caught my arm.

"Get you gone!" I thrust him back again. "I am not beating him to death, I am beating him to *sense*—"

A hand closed on my wrist. Finn's hand, but lacking all strength. "Tynstar—"

At least he could speak again. "Finn—you fool! *You fool!* It was a trap—*a trap*—" I shook my head in desperation. "Why did you go in again? Why did you give him the chance?"

"Tynstar—" It hissed out of his bloodied mouth. "Tynstar—*here*—"

"He nearly slew me!" Electra's voice was hoarse and broken. "Your shapechanger tried to slay me!"

"Tynstar was here—"

"No." I felt the futility well into my chest. "Oh Finn, no—not Tynstar. *Electra*. It was a trap—"

"Tynstar." For a moment he frowned in confusion, trying to stand on his own. He knew I held him, and I thought he knew why. "Let go."

"No." I shook my head. "You will try for her again."

It focused him. I saw sense in his eyes again, and the fear came leaping back to swallow him whole once more.

I slammed him against the wall once more as he thrust himself from the stone. Electra shouted again, this time in Solindish, and I heard the rage in her voice. Not only fear, though there was that. Rage. And wild, wild hatred.

"Finn—" I set the elbow against his throat and felt him stiffen at once. We had done it all before.

"My lord." Rowan's voice was horrified. "What will you do?"

"Tynstar's *meijha*," Finn rasped. "Tynstar was *here*—"

I let him go. I let go of the wrist I held, took my arm from his throat and stood back. But this time the sword was in my hand, my sword, and he stopped when I set the point against his throat. "No," I said. "Hold. I will get the truth from you one way or another." I saw the shock in his eyes. "Finn, I *understand*. Duncan has said what it was, and I recall how you were in the Ellasian snowstorm." I paused, looking for comprehension in his eyes. "Do not make it any worse."

He was still white as death. Blood welled in the opened scar. Now, seeing him in extremity, I saw clearly the silver in his hair. Even beneath the blood his face was harder, more gaunt at eyes and beneath his cheeks. He had aged ten years in two months.

"Finn," I said in rising alarm, "are you ill?"

"Tynstar," was all he said, and again: "Tynstar. He put his hand on me."

When I could I looked at Rowan, standing silent and shocked beside me. "How did you come to be here?"

He swallowed twice. "The Queen screamed, my lord. We

all came." He gestured at Lachlan and Perrin. "There were more at first, but I sent them away. I thought you would prefer this matter handled in private."

I felt old and tired and used up. I held a sword against my liege man. I had only to look at his face to know why it was necessary. "What did you find when you came?"

"The Queen was—in some disarray. Finn's hands were on her throat." Rowan looked angry and confused. "My lord—there was nothing else I could do. He was trying to slay the Queen."

I knew he meant the leg wound. I wondered how bad it was. Finn stood steadily enough *now,* but I could see the pain in the tautness of his gaunt, bloody face.

Lachlan spoke at last. "Carillon—I have no wish to condemn him. But it is true. He would have taken her life."

"Execute him." Electra's tone was urgent. "He tried to slay me, Carillon."

"It was Tynstar," Finn said clearly. "It was Tynstar I wanted."

"But it was Electra you would have slain." The sword, for the slightest moment, wavered in my hand. "You fool," I whispered, "why have you done this to me? You know what I must do—"

"No!" It exploded from Rowan's throat. "My lord—you *cannot*—"

"No," I said wearily, "I cannot—not that. But there is something else—"

"Execute him!" Electra again. "There is nothing else to be done. He sought to slay the Queen!"

"I will *not* have him slain."

It was Lachlan who understood first. "Carillon! It will bare your back to the enemy!"

"I have no choice." I looked directly at Finn, still caged by the steel of my sword. "Do you see what you have done?"

He raised his hands. He closed them both on the blade, blocking out the runes. The ones his father had made. *"No."*

I was nearly shaking myself. "But you would do it again, would you not?"

The grimace came swiftly; bared teeth and the suggestion of a deep growl in a human throat. "Tynstar—"

"Electra," I said. "You would do it again, would you not?"

"Aye . . ." A breathy hiss of sound expelled from a constricted throat. He was shaking.

"Finn," I said, "it is done. I have no choice. The service is over." I stopped short, then went on when I could speak. "The blood-oath is—denied."

His eyes were fixed on mine. After a moment I could not bear to look at them, but I did. I had given him the task; it was mine to do as well.

He took his hands from the blade. I saw the lines pressed into his palms, but no blood. He bled enough already, inside as well as out.

His voice was a whisper. *"Ja'hai-na,"* he said only. *Accepted.*

I put the sword away, hearing the hiss of steel on boiled leather as it slid home. The lion was quiescent; the brilliant ruby black.

Finn took the knife from the sheath at his belt and offered it to me. My own, once; the royal blade with its golden Homanan crest.

It nearly broke me. "Finn," I said, "I cannot."

"The blood-oath is denied." His face was stark, old, aging. *"Ja'hai,* my lord Mujhar."

I took it from his hand. There was blood upon the gold. *"Ja'hai-na,"* I said at last, and Finn walked from the room.

Chapter Three

When I could, I went out into the corridor and moved slowly through the dimness. The torches were unlighted. The hallway was empty of people; my servants, knowing how to serve, left me to myself.

No more howling. Silence. Storr, with Finn was gone. My spirit felt as extinguished as the torches.

I went alone to the Great Hall and stood within its darkness. The firepit was banked. Coals glowed. Here, as well, none of the torches was lighted.

Silence.

I tucked the Homanan blade into my belt beside the Cheysuli knife in its sheath and began shifting the unburned logs in the firepit with my booted feet. The coals I also kicked aside until I bared the iron ring beneath its heavy layer of ash. Then I took a torch, pushed the shaft through the ring, and levered it up until the heavy plate rose and fell back, clanging against the firepit rim. The ash puffed up around it.

I lighted the torch and went down when the staircase lay bare. I counted this time: one hundred and two steps. I stood before the wall and saw how the rain had soaked it from the storm. The walls were slick and shiny with dampness. The runes glowed pale green against the dark stone. I put my fingers to them, tracing their alien shapes, then found the proper keystone. The wall, when I leaned, grated open.

I stood in the doorway. *Lir*-shapes, creamy and veined with gold, loomed at me from the walls. Bear and boar, owl and hawk and falcon. Wolf and fox, raven, cat and more. In the hissing light of the iron torch they moved, silent and supple, against the silken, stone.

I went into the vault. I let the silence oppress me.

FoolFoolFool, I thought.

I took the Cheysuli knife from my sheath. The light glittered off the silver. I saw the snarling wolf's-head hilt with its eyes of uncut emerald. Finn's knife, once.

I moved to the edge of the oubliette. As before, the torchlight did not touch the blackness within. So deep, so soft, so black. I recalled my days in there, and how I had become someone other than myself. How, for four days, I had thought myself Cheysuli.

I shut my eyes. The glow of the torchlight burned yellow against my lids. I could see nothing, but I recalled it all. The soft soughing of shifting wings, the pip of a preening falcon. How it was to go trotting through the forest with a pelt upon my back. And freedom, such perfect freedom, bound by nothing more than what the gods had given me.

"Ja'hai." I reached out my hand to drop the knife into the pit.

"Carillon."

I spun around and teetered on the brink while the torch roared softly against the movement.

I might have expected Finn. But never Tourmaline.

She wore a heavy brown traveling cloak, swathed in wool from head to toe. The hood was dropped to her shoulders and I saw haw the torchlight gleamed on the gold in her tawny hair. "You have sent him away," she said, "and so you send me as well."

All the protests leaped into my mouth. I had only to say them in a combination of tones; impatience, confusion, irritation, amazement, and placation. But none of them were right. I knew, suddenly and horribly; *I knew.* Not Lachlan. Not Lachlan at all, for Torry.

The pieces of the fortune-game, quite suddenly, were thrown across the table from their casket and spread out before me in their intricate, interlocking patterns that double too often as prophets. The bone dice and carven runesticks stood before me in the shape of my older sister, and I saw the pattern at last.

"Torry," was all I said. She was too much like me. She let no one turn her from one way when it was the way she wanted to go.

"We did not dare tell you," she said quietly. "We knew what you would do. He says—" already she had fallen into the easy attribution so common to women when they speak of their men "—that in the clans women are never bartered to the warriors. That a man and woman are left to their own decisions, without another to turn them against their will."

"Tourmaline . . ." I felt tired suddenly, and full of aches and pains. "Torry, you know why I had to do it. In our House rank is matched with rank; I wanted a prince for you because you deserve that much, if not more. Torry—I did not wish to make you unhappy. But I need the aid from another realm—"

"Did you think to ask me?" Slowly she shook her head and the torchlight gleamed in her hair. "*No.* Did you think I would mind? No. Did you think I would even protest?" She smiled a little. "Think you upon my place, Carillon, and see how *you* would feel."

The pit was at my back. I thought now another one yawned before me. "Torry," I said finally, "think you I had any choice in whom *I* wed? Princes—and kings—have no more say than their women. There was nothing I could do."

"You might have asked me. But no, you ever *told.* The Mujhar of Homana orders his sister to wed where he will decide." She put up a silencing hand. Her fingers seemed sharp as a blade. "Aye, I know—it has ever been this way. And ever will be. But this once, *this once,* I say no. I say I choose my way."

"Our mother—"

"—is gone home to Joyenne." She saw my frown of surprise. "I told her, Carillon. Like you, she thinks me mad. But she knows better than to protest." The smile came more freely. "She has raised willful children, Carillon—they do what they will do when it comes to whom they marry." She laughed softly. "Think you that I was fooled about Electra? Oh Carillon, I am not blind. I do not deny she was a pathway to Solinde, but she is more than that to you. You wanted her because like all men who see her—you simply had to have her. That is a measure of her power."

"Tourmaline—"

"I am going," she said calmly, with the cool assurance of a woman who has what she wants in the way of a man. "But I will tell you this much, for both of us: it was not intended." Tourmaline smiled and I saw her as Finn must see her: not a princess, not a gamepiece, not even Carillon's sister. A woman; no more, no less. It was no wonder he wanted her. "You sent him to the Keep to recover from his wounds. You sent *me* there for safety. I tended him when Alix could not, wondering what manner of man he was to so serve my brother's cause, and he gave me the safety I needed. Soon enough—it was more." She shook her head. "We meant to do no harm. But now it comes to this: he is dismissed from his *tahlmorra,* and mine is to go with him."

"*Tahlmorra* is a Cheysuli thing," I told her bleakly. "Torry, no. I do not wish to lose you as well."

"Then take him back into your service."

"I cannot!" The shout echoed in the vault, bouncing off the silent *lir.* "Do you not see? Electra is the Queen, and he a Cheysuli shapechanger. No matter what *I* say in this, they will always suspect Finn of wishing to slay the Queen. And if he stayed, he might. Did he not tell you what he tried to do?"

Her lips were pale. "Aye. But he had no choice—"

"Nor do I have one now." I shook my head. "Do you think I do not want him back? Gods, Torry, you do not know what it was for the two of us in exile. He has been with me for too long to make this parting simple. But it must be done. What else is there to do? I could never trust him with Electra—"

"Perhaps you should not trust *her.*"

"I wed her," I said grimly. "I need her. Did I allow Finn to stay and something happened to Electra, do you know what would happen to Homana? Solinde would rise. No mere army could gainsay an outraged realm. *Murder,* Torry." Slowly I shook my head. "Think you the *qu'mahlin* is ended? No. Be not so foolish. A thing such as that is stopped, perhaps, but never forgotten. For too long the Cheysuli have been hated. It is not done yet." The torch hissed and sputtered, putting shadows on her face. "This time, a race would be destroyed. And with it, no doubt, would also fall Homana."

Tears were on her face, glittering in the light. "Carillon," she whispered, "I carry his child."

When I could speak, albeit a trembling whisper, I said his name. Then, to myself. "How could I not have seen it?"

"You did not look. You did not ask. And now it is too late." She gathered her skirts and cloak with both her hands. "Carillon—hē waits. It is time I left you."

"Torry—"

"I will ʒo," she said gently. "It is where I want to be."

We faced each other in the flickering light in a vault full of marble *lir*. I heard the faint cry of hawk and falcon; the howl of a hunting wolf. I remembered what it was to be Cheysuli.

I dropped the torch into the oubliette. "I can see no one in this darkness. A person could stay or she could go—and I would never know it."

Dim light crept down the stairs behind her. Someone held a torch. Somone who waited for Torry.

I saw the tear on the curve of her cheek as she came up to kiss me. And then she was gone, and I was left alone with the silence and the *lir*.

I let the cover fall free of my hands and slam shut against the mouth. The gust of air sent ash flying. It settled on my clothing but I did not care. I kicked coals and pushed wood over the plate again, hiding the ring in ash, and went out of the Great Hall alone.

I meant to go to bed, though I knew I would not sleep. I meant to drown myself in wine, though I knew it would leave me sober. I meant to try and forget, and I knew the task was futile.

> *Come, lady, and hear of my soul,*
> *for a harper's poor magic*
> *does little to hold*
> *a fine lady's heart*
> *when she keeps it her own.*

I stopped walking. The music curled out to wrap me in its magic and I thought at once of Lachlan. Lachlan and his Lady. Lachlan, whose lays were all for Torry.

> *Come, lady, and listen:*
> *I will make for you music*
> *from out of the world*
> *if you wait with me,*

stay with me,
lay with me, too . . .
I will give you myself
and this harp that I hold.

I followed the song to its source and found Lachlan in a small private solar, a nook in the vastness of the palace. Cushions lay on the floor, but Lachlan sat on a three-legged, velvet-covered stool, his Lady caressed by a lover's hands. I paused inside the door and saw the gold of the strings, the gleam of green stone.

His head was bowed over his harp. He was lost within his music. I saw how his supple fingers moved within the strings: plucking here, touching there, ever placating his Lady. He was at peace, eyes shut and face gone smooth, so that I saw the elegance in his features. A harper is touched by the gods, and ever knows it. It accounts for their confidence and quiet pride.

The music died away. Silence. And then he looked up and saw me, rising at once from his stool. "Carillon! I thought you had gone to bed."

"No."

He frowned. "You are all over ash, and still damp. Do you not think you would do better—"

"He is gone." I cut him off. "And so is Tourmaline."

He stared, uncomprehending. "Torry! Torry—?"

"With Finn." I wanted it said so the cut would bleed more quickly, to get rid of the pain at once.

"Lodhi!" Lachlan's face was bone-white. "Ah, Lodhi— *no*—" He came three steps, still clutching his Lady, and then he stopped. "Carillon—say you are mistaken. . . ."

"It would be a lie." I saw how the pain moved into his eyes; how it stiffened the flesh of his face. He was a child suddenly, stricken with some new nightmare and groping for understanding.

"But—you said she was meant to wed. You meant her for a prince."

"A prince," I agreed. "Never a harper. Lachlan—"

"Have I waited too long?" His arms were rigid as he clasped the harp to his chest. "Lodhi, have I waited *too long?*"

"Lachlan, I know you have cared. I saw it from the beginning. But there is no sense in holding onto the hope that it might have been."

"Get her back." He was suddenly intent. "Take her from him. Do not let her go—"

"No." I said it firmly. "I have let her go because, in the end, there was no way I could stop her. I know Finn too well. And he has said, quite clearly, he will allow no one to keep him from the woman he wants."

Lachlan put one hand to his brow. He scraped at the silver circlet as if it bound him too tightly. Then abruptly, as if discovering it himself, he pulled it from his head and held it out in one fist as the other arm clasped his Lady.

"Harper!" His pain was out in the open. *"Lodhi,* but I have been a fool!"

"Lachlan—"

He shook his head. "Carillon, can you not get her back? I promise you, you will be glad of it. There is something I would say to her—"

"No." This time I said it gently. "Lachlan—she bears Finn's child."

He lost the rest of his color. Then, all at once, he sat down on the three-legged stool. For a moment he just stared at the wooden floor. Then, stiffly, he set his Lady and the circlet on the floor, as if he renounced them both. "I meant to take her home," was all he said.

"No." I said it again. "Lachlan—I am sorry."

Silently he drew a thong from beneath his doublet. He pulled the leather from around his head and handed the trinket to me.

Trinket? It was a ring. It depended from the thong. I turned it upward into the candlelight and saw the elaborate crest: a harp and the crown of Ellas.

"There are seven of those rings," he said matter-of-factly. "Five rest on the hands of my brothers. The other is on my father's finger." He looked up at me at last. "Oh, aye, I know how things are in royal Houses. I am from one myself."

"Lachlan," I said. "Or, is it?"

"Oh, aye. Cuinn Lachlan Llewellyn. My father has a taste for names." He frowned a little, oddly distant and detached. "But then he has eleven children, so it is for the best."

"High Prince Cuinn of Ellas." The ring fell out of my hand and dangled on its thong. "In the names of all the gods of Homana, *why did you keep it secret?*"

A shrug twitched at his shoulders. "It was—a thing between my father and myself. I was not, you see, the sort of heir Rhodri wanted. I preferred harping to governing and healing to courting women." He smiled a little, a mere twisting of his mouth. "I was not ready for responsibility. I wanted no wife to chain me to the castle. I wanted to leave Rheghed behind and see the whole of Ellas, on my own, without a retinue. The heirship is so—binding." This time the smile held more of the Lachlan I knew. "You might know something of that, I think."

"But—all this silence with Torry. And *me!*" I thought he had been a fool. "Had you *said* anything, none of this might have happened!"

"I could not. It was a bond between my father and me." Lachlan rubbed at his brow, staring at his harp. He hunched on the stool, shoulders slumped, and the candle-light was dull on his dyed brown hair.

Dyed brown hair. Not gray, as he had said, pleading vanity, but another color entirely.

I sat down. I set my back against the cold wall and waited. I thought of Torry and Finn in the darkness and rain, and Lachlan here before me. "Why?"

He sighed and rubbed at his eyes. "Originally, it was a game I wished to play. How better to see your realm than to go its length and breadth unknown? So my father agreed, saying if I wanted to play at such foolishness, I would have to play it absolutely. He forbade me to divulge my name and rank unless I was in danger."

"But to keep it from *me* . . ." I shook my head.

"It was because of you." He nodded as I frowned. "When I met you and learned who you were, I wrote at once to my father. I told him what you meant to do, and how I thought you could not do it. Take Homana back from Bellam? No. You had no men, no army. Only Finn . . . and me." He smiled. "I came with you because I wanted to, to see what you could do. And I came because my father, when he saw what you meant to do, wanted you to win."

I felt a sluggish stirring of anger deep inside. "He sent me no aid—"

"To the pretender-prince of Homana?" Lachlan shook his head. "You forget—Bellam encroached upon Ellas. He offered Electra to Rhodri's heir. It was not in Ellas's interests to support Carillon's bid for the throne." He softened his tone a bit. "For all I would have liked to give you what aid I could, I had my father's realm to think of, too. We have enemies. This had to remain your battle."

"Still, *you* came with me. You risked yourself."

"I risked nothing. If you recall, I did not fight, playing the harper's role." He shook his head. "It was not easy. I have trained as a warrior since I was but a child. But my father forbade me to fight, and it seemed the best thing to do. And he said also I was to go to *watch* and learn what I could. If you won the war and held your realm for a twelve-month and a day, Rhodri would offer alliance."

"It has been longer than that." I did not need to count the days.

"And did you not just send to other realms, offering the hand of your sister in marriage?" The color moved through his face. "It is not my place to offer what I cannot. My father is High King. It was for him to accept your offer, and I had to wait for him." He shut his eyes a moment. "Lodhi, but I thought *she* would wait . . ."

"So did I." The stone was cold against my spine. "Oh Lachlan, had I known—"

"I know. But it was not for me to say." His face was almost ugly. "Such is the lot of princes."

"Could you have said nothing to *her*?"

He stared at the cushion-strewn floor. "I nearly did. More times than I can count. Once I even spoke of Rhodri's heir, but she only bid me to be quiet. She did not wish to think on marriage." He sighed. "She was ever gentle with my feelings, seeking to keep me—a harper—from looking too high, as did her brother, the Mujhar." He did not smile. "And I thought, in all my complacency, she would say differently when she knew. And you. And so I savored the waiting, instead."

I shut my eyes and rested my head against the stone. I recalled the harper in the Ellasian roadhouse, giving me my memories. I recalled his patient understanding when I treated him with contempt, calling him spy when he was merely a friend and nothing more.

And how I had bidden him slay a man to see if he would do it.

So much between us, and now so little. I knew what he would do. "You had no choice," I said at last. "The gods know *I* understand what it is to serve rank and responsibility. But Lachlan, you must not blame yourself. What else could you have done?"

"Spoken, regardless of my father." He stared at the floor, shoulders hunched. So vulnerable, suddenly, when he had always been so strong. "I should have said something to someone."

And yet it would have done no good. We both realized it, saying nothing because the saying would bring more pain. A man may love a woman while the woman loves another, but no man may force her to love where she has no desire to do so.

"By the All-Father himself," Lachlan said wearily, "I think it is not worth it." He gathered up his Lady and rose, hooking one arm through the silver circlet. He had more right to it than most, though it should have had the shine of royal gold.

I stood up stiffly and faced him. I held out the ring on its leather thong. "Lachlan—" I stopped.

He knew. He took the ring, looked at the crest that made him a man—a prince—apart, then slipped the thong over his head once more. "I came a harper," he said quietly. "It is how I will leave in the morning."

"Do *you* leave me, old friend, I will be quite alone." It was all I could say to him; the only plea I would ever make.

I saw the pain in his eyes. "I came, knowing I would have to leave. Not when, but knowing the time would come. I had hoped, for a while, I would not leave alone." The line of his jaw was set; the gentleness of the harper had fled, and in its place I saw the man Lachlan had ever been, but showing it to few. "You are a king, Carillon. Kings are always alone. Someday—I shall know it, too." He reached out and caught my arm in the ritual clasp of friendship. *"Yhana Lodhi, yffennog faer."*

"Walk humbly, harper," I said softly.

He went out of the room into the shadows of the corridor, and his *Song of Homana* was done.

I went into my chambers and found her waiting. She was in shadow with a single candle lighted. She was wrapped in one of my chamber robes: wine-purple velvet lined with dappled silver fur. On her it was voluminous; I could see little but hands and feet.

I stopped. I could not face her now. To look at her was to recall what Finn had done, and how it had ended in banishment. How it had ended with Torry and Lachlan gone as well. To look at her was to look on the face of aloneness, and that I could not bear.

"No," she said, as I made a movement to go. "Stay you. Do you wish it, *I* will go."

Still in shadow. The wine-colored velvet melted into the shadows. The candlelight played on her hair—unbound, and hanging to her knees.

I sat down because I had no strength to stand. On the edge of my draperied bed. I was all over ash, as Lachlan had said, and still damp from the storm outside. No doubt I smelled of it as well: wet wool and smoke and flame.

She came and stood before me. "Let me lift this grief from you."

I looked at her throat with the bruises on it; the marks of a crazed man's madness.

She knelt and pulled off my heavy boots. I said nothing, watching her, amazed she would do what I, or a servant, could much more easily do.

Her hands were deft and gentle, stripping me of my clothing, and then she knelt before me. "Ah my lord, do not grieve so. You put yourself in pain."

It came to me to wonder whether she had ever knelt for Tynstar.

She put one hand on my thigh. Her fingers were cool. I could feel the pulse-beat in her palm.

I looked again at the bruises on her throat. Slowly I reached out and set my hands there, as Finn had set his, and felt the fragility of her flesh. "Because of you," I said.

"Aye." Her eyes did not waver from mine. "And for you, good my lord, I am sorry he had to go."

My hands tightened. She did not flinch or pull away. "I am not Tynstar, lady."

"No." Neither did she smile.

My hands slid up slowly to cup her skull with its weight of shining hair. The robe, now loosened, slid off her shoulders and fell against the floor: a puddle of wine-dark velvet. She was naked underneath.

I pulled her up from the stone and into my arms, sagging back onto the bed. To be rid of the loneliness, I would lie with the dark god himself.

"I need you," I whispered against her mouth. "By the gods, woman, *how I need you. . . .*"

Chapter Four

The infirmary tent stank of blood and burning flesh. I watched as the army chirurgeon lifted the hot iron from Rowan's arm, studied the seared edges of the wound and nodded. "Closed. No more blood, captain. You will keep the arm, I think, with the help of the gods."

Rowan sat stiffly on the campstool, white-faced and shaking. The sword had cut into the flesh of his forearm, but had missed muscle and bone. He would keep the arm and its use, though I did not doubt he felt, at the moment, as if it had already been cut off.

He let out his breath slowly. It hissed between his teeth. He put out his right hand and groped for the cup of sour wine Waite had set out on the table. Fingers closed on the cup, gripping so hard the knuckles shone white, and then he lifted it to his mouth. I smiled. Waite had put a powder in it that would ease the pain a bit. Rowan had originally refused any such aid, but he had not seen the powder. And now he drank, unknowing, and the pain would be eased somewhat.

I glanced back over my shoulder through the gap in the entrance flap. Outside it was gray, gray and dark blue, with the weight of clouds and winter fog. My breath, leaving the warmth of the infirmary tent, plumed on the air, white as smoke.

"My thanks, my lord." Rowan's voice still bore the strain, but it lessened as the powder worked its magic.

He began to pull on his fur-lined leathers, though I knew the motion must hurt. I did not move to help because I knew he would not allow it, me being his Mujhar, and because it would hurt his pride. Like all the Cheysuli, he had his pride; a prickly, arrogant pride that some took for condescension. It was not, usually. It was merely a certainty of their place within the boardgame of the gods. And Rowan, though he was less Cheysuli in his habits than Homanan, reflected much of that traditional pride without even knowing it.

I shifted in the entrance, then grimaced in response to the protests of my muscles. My body was battered and sore, but I bore not a single wound from the last encounter earlier in the day. My blood was still my own, unlike Rowan's—unless one counted what I had lost from my nose when struck in the face by my horse's head. The blow had knocked me half-senseless for a moment or two, making me easy prey, but I had managed to stay in the saddle. And it was Rowan, moving to thrust aside the attacker's sword, who had taken the blow meant for me. We were both fortunate the Atvian had missed his target.

"Hungry?" I asked.

Rowan nodded. Like us all, he was too thin, pared down to blood and bone. Because of his Cheysuli features his face was gaunter than mine; because of my beard, no one noticed if I seemed gaunt or not. It had its advantages; Rowan looked ill, I did not, and I hated to be asked how I fared. It made me feel fragile when I was not, but that is the cost of being a king.

Rowan pulled on his gloves, easing into the right one because the movement hurt his arm. He was still pale, lacking the deeper bronze of Cheysuli flesh because of the loss of blood. With his eyes gone black from the drug and the pallor of his face, he looked more Homanan than Cheysuli.

Poor Rowan, I thought: forever caught between the worlds.

He scrubbed his good arm through his heavy hair and glanced at me. He forced a smile. "It does not hurt, my lord."

Waite, putting away his chirurgeon's tools, grunted in disgust. "In my presence, it hurts. Before the Mujhar, it does not. You have miraculous powers of healing, my lord . . . perhaps we should trade places."

Rowan colored. I grinned and pulled aside the doorflap, waving him outside even as he protested I should go first. The mist came up to chill our faces at once. Rowan hunched his shoulders against the cold and cradled his aching arm. "It *is* better, my lord."

I said nothing about the powder, merely gestured toward

the nearest cookfire. "There. Hot wine and roasting boar.
You will undoubtedly feel better once your belly is full
again."

He walked carefully across the hardpacked, frozen
ground, trying not to jar the injured arm. "My lord . . . I
am sorry."

"For being injured?" I shook my head. "That was my
wound you took. It requires my gratitude, not an apology
from you."

"It does." Tension lines marred the youthfulness of his
face. He watched the ground where he walked and the
thick black hair hid most of his face. Like me, he had not
cut it for too long. "You would do better with Finn at your
side. I am—not a liege man." He cast me a quick, glinting
glance out of drug-blackened eyes. "I have not the skill to
keep you safe, my lord."

I stopped at the cookfire and nodded at the soldier who
tended the roasting boar. He began to cut with a greasy
knife. "You are not Finn, nor ever can be," I said clearly
to Rowan. "But I want you by my side."

"My lord—"

I cut him off with a gesture of my hand. "When I sent
Finn from my service six months ago, I knew what I was
risking. Still, it had to be done, for the good of us all. I do
not dismiss the importance his presence held. The bond
between Cheysuli liege man and his Mujhar is a sacred
thing, but—once broken—there is no going back." I
grasped his uninjured arm, knowing there was no *lir*-band
underneath the furs and leathers. "I do not seek another
Finn. I value *you*. Do not disappoint me by undervaluing
yourself." The soldier dropped a slice of meat onto a slab
of tough bread and put it into my hands. In turn, I put it
into Rowan's. "Now, eat. You must restore your strength
so we can fight again."

The mist put beads of water into his hair. Damp, it tangled against his shoulders. His face was bleak, pale,
stretched taut over prominent bones, but I thought the pain
came from something other than his arm.

A pot of wine was warming near the fire cairn. I knelt,
poured a cup and handed it up to Rowan. And then, as I
turned to pour my own, I heard someone shout for me.

"Meat, my lord?" asked the soldier with the knife.

"A moment." I rose and turned toward the shout. In the mist it was hard to place such sounds, but then I saw the shapes coming out of the grayness. Three men on horseback: two of them my Homanans, the third a stranger.

They were muffled in furred leathers and woolen wrappings. The mist parted as they rode through and showed them more clearly, then closed behind them again. "My lord!" One of the men dismounted before me and dropped to one knee, then up again. "A courier, my lord."

The gesture indicated the still-mounted stranger. He rode a good horse, as couriers usually do, but I saw no crest to mark him. He wore dark leathers and darker wool; a cap hid most of his head so that only his face showed.

The hot wine warmed my hands, even through my gloves. "Atvian?" I put no inflection in my tone.

The stranger reached up to pull woolen wraps from his face. "No, my lord—Ellasian." Mouth bared, the words took on greater clarity. "Sent from High Prince Cuinn."

Lachlan. I could not help the smile. "Step you down, friend courier. You are well come to my army."

He dismounted, came closer, and dropped to one knee in a quick bow of homage. Neatly done. He had a warm, friendly face, but was young, and yet he seemed to know his business. He was red-haired beneath the cap, judging by his brows, and his eyes were green. There were freckles on his face.

"My lord, it pleases me to serve the High Prince. He bids me give you this." He dug into a leather pouch at his belt and withdrew a folded parchment. A daub of blue wax sealed it closed, and pressed into it was the royal crest: a harp and the crown of Ellas. It brought back the vision of Lachlan and his Lady, when he told me who he was.

I broke the seal and unfolded the parchment. It crackled in the misted air; its crispness faded as the paper wilted. But the words were legible.

Upon returning home to Rheghed, I was met with warm welcome from the king my father. So warm, indeed that he showered me with gifts. One of these gifts was a command of my own, did I ever need to use it. I doubt Rhodri ever intended me to be so generous as to loan the gift to you, but the thing is already done. My men are yours for

*as long as you need them. And does it please you to offer
a gift in return, I ask only that you treat kindly with Ellas
when we seek to make an alliance.*

> *By the hand of the High Prince,*
> *Cuinn Lachlan Llewellyn*

I grinned. And then I laughed, and set my cup of hot wine into the hands of the courier. "Well come, indeed," I said. "How many, and where?"

He grinned back when he had drunk. "Half a league east, my lord. As to the number—five thousand. The Royal Ellasian Guard."

I laughed again, loudly. "Ah Lodhi, I thank you for this courier! But even more I thank you for Lachlan's friendship!" I clapped the courier on his shoulder. "Your name."

"Gryffth, my lord."

"And your captain's?"

"Meredyth. A man close to the High Prince himself." Gryffth grinned. "My lord, forgive me, but we all know what Prince Cuinn intended. And none of us is unwilling. Shall I send to bring them in?"

"Five thousand . . ." I shook my head, smiling at the thought. "Thorne will be finished in a day."

Gryffth brightened. "Then you are near to winning?"

"We *are* winning," I said. "But this will make the ending sweeter. Ah gods, I do thank you for that harper." I took the cup from Gryffth as he went to remount his horse, and watched him ride back into the fog with his Homanan guides.

"Well, my lord," Rowan said, "the thing is done at last."

"A good thing, too." I grinned. "You are not fit to fight with that arm, and now you will not have to."

"My lord—" he protested, but I did not listen as I read Lachlan's note again.

The map was of leather, well-tanned and soft. It was a pale creamy color, and the paint stood out upon it. In the candlelighted pavilion, the lines and rune-signs seemed to glow.

"Here." I put my forefinger on the map. "Mujhara. *We* are here—perhaps forty leagues from the city: northwest." I moved my finger more westerly. "The Cheysuli are here, closer to Lestra, though still within Homana." I lifted the finger and moved it more dramatically, pointing out the Solindish port of Andemir. "Thorne came in here; Atvia is but eight leagues across the Idrian Ocean, directly west of Solinde. He took the shortest sea route to Solinde, and the shortest land route to Homana." I traced the invisible line across the map. "See you here? —he came this way, cutting Solinde in half. It is here our boundary puts its fist into Solinde, and it is where Thorne was bound."

"But you stopped him." The Ellasian captain nodded. "You have cut him off, and he goes no farther."

It seemed odd to hear the husky accent again, though we spoke Homanan between us and all my captains. There were other Ellasians as well, clustered within my tent; I meant Lachlan's gift to know, precisely, what they were doing.

"Thorne let it be known he was splitting his army," I explained. "He would come overland through Solinde, gaining support from the rebels there. But he also sent a fleet—or so all the reports said. A fleet bound for Hondarth—down here." I set my finger on the mark that represented Hondarth, near the bottom of the map and directly south of Mujhara. "But there was no fleet—no *real* fleet. It was a ruse."

Meredyth nodded. "He meant you to halve your army and send part of it to Hondarth, so that when he came in here—full strength—he would face a reduced Homanan warhost." He smiled. "Clever. But you are more so, my lord Mujhar."

I shook my head. "Fortunate. My spies are good. I heard of the ruse and took steps to call back those I had dispatched to Hondarth; thank the gods, they had not gotten far. We have Thorne now, but he will not give up. He will send his men against me until there is no one left."

"And the Solindish aid he wanted?"

"Less than he desired." Meredyth was older than I by at least twenty years, but he listened well. At first I had hesitated to speak so plainly, knowing him more experienced than I, but Lachlan had chosen well. Here was a man who would listen and weigh my words, then make his judgment upon them. "He came into Solinde expecting to find thousands for the taking, but there have been only hundreds.

Since I sent the Cheysuli there, the Solindish are—hesitant to upset the alliance I made."

Meredyth's expression showed calm politeness. "The Queen fares well?"

I knew what he asked. It was more than just an inquiry after Electra's health. The future of Solinde rested upon the outcome—or issue—of the marriage; Electra would bear me a second child in three months and, if it were a boy, Solinde would be one child closer to freedom and autonomy. It was why Thorne had found his aid so thin. That, and the Cheysuli.

"The Queen fares well," I said.

Meredyth's smile was slight. "Then what of the Ihlini, my lord? Have they not joined with Thorne?"

"There has been no word of Ihlini presence within the Atvian army." Thank the gods, but I did not say it. "What we face are Atvians with a few hundred Solindish rebels." I made a quick gesture. "Thorne is clever, aye, and he knows how to come against me. I am not crushing him as I might wish, not when he uses my own methods against me. No pitched battles, merely raids and skirmishes, as I employed against Bellam. As you see, we have been here six months; the thing is not easily won. At least—it *was* not, until Lachlan sent his gift."

Meredyth nodded his appreciation. "I think, my lord, you will be home in time to see the birth of your heir."

"Be the gods willing." I tapped the map again. "Thorne has sent some of his army in here, where I have posted the Cheysuli. But the greater part of it remains here, where we are. The last skirmish was two days ago. I doubt he will come against me before another day has passed. Until then, I suggest we make our plans."

Thorne of Atvia came against us two days later with all the strength he had. No more slash and run as he had learned from me; he fought, this time, with the determination of a man who knows he will lose and, in the losing, lose himself. With the Ellasian men we hammered him back, shutting off the road to Homana. Atvian bowmen notwithstanding, we were destroying his thinning offense.

I sought only Thorne in the crush of fighting. I wanted him at the end of my blade, fully aware of his own death and who dealt it. It was he who had taken my sword from me on the battlefield near Mujhara, nearly seven years before. It was he who had put the iron on me and ordered Rowan flogged. It was Thorne who might have slain Alix, given the chance, had not the Cheysuli come. And it was Thorne who offered me insult by thinking he could pull down my House and replace it with his own.

When the arrow lodged itself in the leather-and-mail of my armor, I thought myself unhurt. It set me back in the saddle a moment and I felt the punch of a sharpened fist against my left shoulder, but I did not think it had gone through to touch my flesh. It was only when I reined my horse into an oncoming Atvian that I realized the arm was numb.

I swore. The Atvian approached at full gallop, sword lifted above his head. He rode with his knees, blind to his horse, intent on striking me down. I meant to do the same, but now I could not. I had only the use of one arm.

His horse slammed into mine. The impact sent a wave of pain rolling from shoulder to skull. I bent forward at once, seeking to keep my seat as the Atvian's sword came down. Blade on blade and the screech of steel—the deflected blow went behind me, barely, and into my saddle. I spun my horse away and the Atvian lost his sword. It remained wedged in my saddle, offering precarious seating, since an ill-timed movement might result in an opened buttock, but at least I had disarmed him. I stood up in my stirrups, avoiding the sword, and saw him coming at me.

He was unarmed. He screamed. And he threw himself from his horse to lock both hands through the rings of my mail.

My own sword was lost. I felt it fall, twisting out of my hand, as the weight came down upon me. He was large, too large, and unwounded. With both hands grasping the ringmail of my armor, he dragged me from my horse.

I twisted in midair, trying to free myself. But the ground came up to meet us and nearly knocked me out of my senses. My left arm was still numb, still useless.

His weight was unbearable. He ground me into the earth. One knee went into my belly as he rose up to reach for his knife and I felt the air rush out. And yet somehow I gritted my teeth and unsheathed my own knife, jabbing upward into his groin.

He screamed. His own weapon dropped as he doubled over, grabbing his groin with both hands. Blood poured out of the wound and splashed against my face. And yet I could not move; could not twist away. His weight was upon my belly and the fire was in my shoulder.

I stabbed again, striking with gauntleted hands. His screams ran on, one into another, until it was a single sound of shock and pain and outrage. I saw the blindness in his eyes and knew he would bleed to death.

He bent forward. Began to topple. The knee shut off my air. And then he fell and the air came back, a little, but all his dead weight was upon me. His right arm was flung across my face, driving ringmail into my mouth, and I felt the coppery taste of blood spring up into my teeth. Blood. Gods, so much blood, and some of it my own . . .

I twisted. I thrust with my one good arm and tried to topple him off. But his size and the slackness of death undid me, the heaviest weight of all, and I had no strength left to fight it. I went down, down into the oubliette, with no one there to catch me. . . .

Shadows. Darkness. A little light. I thrust myself upward into the light, shouting out a name.

"Be still, my lord," Rowan said. "Be still."

Waite took a swab of bloody linen from me and I realized he tended my shoulder. More blood. Gods, would he turn to cautery? It was no wonder Rowan seemed so calm. He had felt the kiss of hot steel and now expected me to do the same.

I shut my eyes. Sweat broke out and coursed down my face. I had forgotten what pain was, real pain, having escaped such wounds for so long. In Caledon, once or twice, I had been wounded badly, but I had always forgotten the pain and weakness that broke down the soul.

"The arrow was loosed from close by," Waite said conversationally. "Your armor stopped most of the force of it, but not all. Still, it is not a serious wound; I have got the arrowhead out. If you lie still long enough, I think the hole will heal.

I opened one eye a slit. "*No* cautery?"

"Do you prefer it?"

"*No*—" I hissed as the shoulder twinged. "By the gods— can you not give me what you gave Rowan?"

"I *thought* you gave me something," Rowan muttered. "I slept too well that night."

Waite pressed another clout of linen against the wound. It came away less bloody, but the pain was still alive. "I will give you whatever you require, my lord. It is a part of a chirurgeon's service." He smiled as I scowled. "Wait you until I am done with the linens, and you shall have your powder." He gestured to Rowan. "Lift him carefully, captain. Think of him as an egg."

I would have laughed, had I the strength. As it was I could only smile. But when Rowan started to lift me up so Waite could bind the linens around my chest, I nearly groaned aloud. "Gods—are all my bones broken?"

"No." Waite pressed a linen pad against my shoulder and began to bind strips around my chest. "You were found beneath three hundred pounds of mailed Atvian bulk. I would guess you were under it for several hours, while the battle raged on. It is no wonder you feel half-crushed— there, captain, I am done. Let him down again, gently. Do not crack the eggshell."

I shut my eyes again until the sweat dried upon my body. A moment later Waite held a cup to my mouth "Drink, my lord. Sleep is best for now."

It was sweetened wine. I drank down the cup and lay my head down again, trying to shut out the pain. Rowan, kneeling beside my cot, watched with worried eyes.

I shivered. Waite pulled rugs and pelts up over my body until only my head was free. There were braziers all around my cot. In winter, even a minor wound can kill.

My mouth was sore, no doubt from where the ringmail had broken my lip. I tongued it, feeling the swollen cut, then grimaced. What a foolish way to be taken out of a battle.

"I must assume we won the day," I said. "Otherwise I would doubtless be in an Atvian tent with no chirurgeon and no captain." I paused. "Unless you were taken, too."

"No." Rowan shook his head. "We won, my lord, re- soundingly. The war as well as the day. The Atvians are broken—most of them who could ran back into Solinde. I doubt they will trouble us again."

"Thorne?"

"Dead, my lord."

I sighed. "I wanted him."

"So did I." Rowan's face was grim. "I did not heed you, my lord; I went into battle myself. But I could not find him in the fighting."

The powder was beginning to work. Coupled with the weakness from the wound, it was sucking me into the darkness. It grew more difficult to speak. "See he is buried as befits his rank," I said carefully, "but do not return his body to his people. When my father lay dying of his wounds on the plains near Mujhara, and Thorne had taken me, I asked for a Homanan burial. Thorne denied it to him. And so I deny an Atvian rite to Thorne."

"Aye, my lord." Rowan's voice was low.

I struggled to keep my senses. "He has an heir. Two sons, I have heard. Send—send word the Mujhar of Homana asks fealty. I will receive Thorne's sons in Homana-Mujhar—for their oaths." I frowned as my lids sealed up my eyes. "Rowan—see it is done—"

"Aye, my lord."

I roused myself once more. "We leave here in the morning. I want to go back to Mujhara."

"You will not be fit to go back in the morning," Waite said flatly. "You will see for yourself, my lord."

"I am not averse to a litter," I murmured. "My pride can withstand it, I think."

Rowan smiled. "Aye, my lord. A litter instead of a horse."

I thought about it. No doubt Electra would hear. I did not wish her to worry. "I will go in a litter until we are but half a league from Mujhara," I told him clearly. "*Then* I will ride the horse."

"Of course, my lord. I will see to it myself."

I gave myself over to darkness.

Waite, unfortunately, had the right of it. Litter or no, I was not fit to go back in the morning. But by the third day I felt much better. I dressed in my warmest clothing, trying to ignore the pain in my shoulder, and went out to speak to Meredyth and his fellow captains.

Their time with me was done. Their aid had helped me accomplish Thorne's defeat, and it was my place now to send them home. I saw to it each captain would have gold to take back to Ellas, as well as coin for the common soldiers. The war with Thorne had not impoverished me, but I had little to spare. All I could promise was a sound alliance for the High King, which seemed to please Meredyth well enough. He then asked a boon of me, which I gave him gladly enough: Gryffth had asked to stay in Homana to serve Ellas in Homana-Mujhar, more an envoy than simple courier. And so the Royal Ellasian Guard went home, lacking a red-haired courier.

I also went home, in a litter after all—too worn to spend time on horseback—and spent most of the journey home sleeping or contemplating my future. Atvia was mine, did I wish to keep it, although there was a chance Thorne's sons might wish to contest it. I thought they were too young, but could not set an age to them. Yet to try to govern Atvia myself was nearly impossible. The island was too distant. A regent in Solinde was bad enough, and yet I had no choice. I did not want even Solinde; Bellam had, more or less, bequeathed it to me with his death, and the marriage had sealed it. Although I was not averse to claiming two realms my own in place of the single one I wanted, I was not greedy. In the past, far-flung realms had drained the coffers of other kings; I would not fall into the trap. Atvia was Atvian. And did Electra give me an heir this time, I would be happy enough to see Solinde go to my second son.

It was days to Mujhara by litter, and it was well before half a league out that I took to a horse at last. The wound in my shoulder ached, but it was beginning to heal. I thought, so long as I did not push myself too hard, I could ride the rest of the way.

And yet when at last I rode through the main gates of my rose-walled palace, I felt the weariness in my body. My mind was fogged with it. I could hardly think. I wanted only to go to bed, my bed, not to some army cot. And with Electra in my arms.

I acknowledged the welcome of my servants and went at once to the third floor, seeking Electra's chambers. But a

Solindish chamberwoman met me at the door and said the Queen was bathing, could I not wait?

No, I said, the *bath* could wait, but she giggled and said the Queen had prepared a special greeting, having received the news of my return. Too weary to think of waving such protestations aside—and wondering what Electra could be planning—I turned back and went away.

If I could not see my wife, I could at least see my daughter. I went to the nursery and found eight-month-old Aislinn sound asleep in an oak-and-ivory cradle, attended by three nursemaids. She was swathed in linens and blankets, but one fist had escaped the covers. She clutched it against her face.

I smiled, bending down to set a band against her cheek. So soft, so fair . . . I could not believe she was mine. My hand was so large and hard and callused, touching the fragile flesh. Her hair, springing from the pink scalp, was coppery-red, curling around her ears. And her eyes, when they were open, were gray and lashed with gold. She had all of her mother's beauty and none of her father's size.

"Princess of Homana," I whispered to my daughter, "who will be your prince?"

Aislinn did not answer. And I, growing wearier by the moment, thought it better to leave her undisturbed. So I took myself to my chambers and dismissed my body-servant, falling down across my bed to mimic my daughter's rest.

I came up out of the blackness to find I could not breathe. Something had leached the air from my lungs until I could not cry out; could not cry; could not speak. All I could do was gape like a fish taken from the water, flapping on the bank.

There was no pain. Merely helplessness and confusion; pain enough, to a man who knows himself trapped. And does not know why.

A cool hand came down and touched my brow. It floated out of the darkness, unattached to an arm, until I realized the arm was merely covered by a sleeve.

"Carillon. Ah, my poor Carillon. So triumphant in your battles, and now so helpless in your bed."

Electra's voice; Electra's hand. I could smell the scent upon her. A bath, the woman had said; a special greeting prepared.

The cool fingers traced the line of my nose; gently touched my eyelids. "Carillon . . . it ends. This travesty of our marriage. *You* will end, my lord." The hand came down my cheek and caressed my open mouth. "It is time for me to go."

Out of the darkness leaped a rune, a glowing purple rune, and in its reflection I saw my wife. She wore black to swath her body, and yet I saw her belly. The child. The heir of Homana. Did she dare to take it from me?

Electra smiled. A hood covered all her hair, leaving only her face in the light. One hand came up to cradle her belly. "Not yours," she said gently. "Did you really think it was? Ah no, Carillon . . . it is another man's. Think you I would keep myself to you when I can have my true lord's love?" She turned slightly, and I saw the man beyond her.

I mouthed his name, and he smiled. The sweet, beguiling smile that I had seen before.

He moved forward out of the darkness. It was his rune that set the room afire. In the palm of his right hand it danced.

Tynstar set his hand to the wick of the candle by my bed, and the candle burst into flame. Not the pure yellow fire of the normal candle, but an eerie purple flame that hissed and shed sparks into the room.

The rune in his hand winked out. He smiled. "You have been a good opponent. It has been interesting to watch you grow; watch you come to manhood; watch you learn what it is to rule. You have learned how to manipulate men and make them bend to your will without making them aware what you do. There is more kingcraft in you than I had anticipated, when I set you free to leave this place eight years ago."

I could not move. I felt the helplessness in my body and the futility in my soul. I would die without a protest, unable to summon a sound. At least let me make a sound—

"Blame yourself," Tynstar told me gently. "What I do now was made possible by you, when you sent the Cheysuli from your side. Had you kept him *by* you—" He smiled. "But then you could not, could you, so long as he threatened the Queen. You had Electra to think of instead of yourself. Commendable, my lord Mujhar; it speaks well of your priorities. But it will also be your death." The flame danced upon its wick and sculpted his bearded face into a death's head of unparallelled beauty. "Finn knew the truth. *He* understood. It was Finn who saw me in Electra's bed." His teeth showed briefly as I spasmed against the sheets. One hand went to Electra's belly.

I tried to thrust myself from the bed but my limbs would not obey me. And then Tynstar moved close, into the sphere of light, and put his hand upon me.

"I am done playing with you," he said. "It is time for *me* to rule." He smiled. "Recall you what Bellam was, when you found him on the field?"

I spasmed again and Tynstar laughed. Electra watched me as a hawk will watch a coney, delaying its stoop until the perfect moment.

"Cheysuli i'halla shansu," Tynstar said. "Give my greetings to the gods."

I felt the change within my body. Even as I fought them, my muscles tightened and drew up my limbs. Buttocks, feet, and knees, cramping so that I nearly screamed, while my legs folded up to crush themselves against my chest. My hands curled into fists and a rictus set my mouth so that my teeth were bared in a feral snarl. I felt my flesh tightening on my bones, drying into hardness.

What voice there was left to me lost itself in a garbled wail, and I knew myself a dead man. Tynstar had slain his quarry.

Cheysuli i'halla shansu, he had said. *May there be Cheysuli peace upon you.* An odd farewell from an Ihlini to a Homanan. Neither of us claimed the magic the Cheysuli held, and yet Tynstar reminded me of it. Reminded me of the four days I had spent in the oubliette, believing myself Cheysuli.

Well, why could I not again? Had I not felt the power of the race while I hung in utter darkness?

My eyes were staring. I shut them. Even as I felt my muscles wrack themselves against my bones and flesh, I reached inward to my soul where I could touch what I touched before: the thing that had made me Cheysuli.

For four days, once, I had known the gods. Could I not know them again?

I heard the hiss of steel blade against a sheath. And then I heard nothing more.

Chapter Five

Silence. The darkness was gone and the daylight pierced my lids. It painted everything orange and yellow and crimson.

I lay quite still. I did not breathe; did not dare to, until at last my lungs were so empty my heart banged against my chest protesting the lack. I took a shallow breath.

I saw the shadow then. A dark blot moved across the sunrise of my vision. It whispered, soughing like a breeze through summer grass. Like spreading wings on a hawk.

Afraid I would see nothing and yet needing to see, I opened my eyes. I saw. The hawk perched on the chair back, hooked beak gleaming in the sunlight and his bright eyes full of wisdom. And patience, endless patience. Cai was nothing if not a patient bird.

I turned my head against the pillow. The draperies of my bed had been pulled back, looped up against the wooden tester posts and tied with ropes of scarlet and gold. Sunlight poured in the nearest casement and glittered off the brilliance. Everywhere gold. On my bed and on Duncan's arms.

I heard the rasp of my breath and the hoarseness of my voice. "Tynstar slew me."

"Tynstar *tried*."

I was aware of the bed beneath my body. It seemed to press in on me, oppressing me, yet cradling my flesh. Everything was emphasized. I heard the tiniest sounds, saw colors as I had never seen them and felt the texture of the bedclothes. But mostly I sensed the tension in Duncan's body.

He sat upright on a stool, very still as he waited. I saw how he watched me, as if he expected something more than what I had given him. I could not think what it was—we had already discussed Finn's dismissal. And yet I knew he was afraid.

Duncan afraid? No. There was nothing for him to fear.

I summoned my voice again. "You know what happened—?"

"I know what Rowan told me."

"Rowan." I frowned. "Rowan was not there when Tynstar came to slay me."

"He was." Duncan's smile was brief. "You had best thank the gods he was, or you would not now be alive. It was Rowan's timely arrival that kept Tynstar's bid to slay you from succeeding." He paused. "That . . . and what power you threw back at him."

I felt a tiny surge within my chest. "Then I *did* reach the magic!"

He nodded. "Briefly, you tapped what we ourselves tap. It was not enough to keep Tynstar in check for long—he would have slain you in a moment—but Rowan's arrival was enough to end the moment. The presence of a Cheysuli—though he lacks a *lir*—was enough to dilute Tynstar's power even more. There was nothing he could do, save die himself when faced with Rowan's steel. So—he left. But not before he touched you." He paused. "You nearly died, Carillon. Do not think you are unscathed."

"He is gone?"

"Tynstar?" Duncan nodded. "Electra was left behind."

I shut my eyes. I recalled how she had come out of the darkness to tell me the truth of the child. Gods—*Tynstar's child*—

I looked at Duncan again. My eyes felt gritty. My tongue was heavy in my mouth. "Where is she?"

"In her chambers, with a Cheysuli guard at the doors." Duncan did not smile. "She has a measure of her own power, Carillon; we do not take chances with her."

"No." I pushed an elbow against the bed and tried to sit up. I discovered no part of my body would move. I was stiff and very sore, far worse than after a battle, as if all the dampness had got into my bones. I touched my shoulder then, recalling the healing wound. There were no bandages. Just a small patch of crinkled flesh. "You healed me . . ."

"We tried." Duncan was very grave. "The arrow wound was easily done. The—other—was not. Carillon—" For a moment he paused, and then I saw his frown. "Do not think Ihlini power is easily overcome. Even the earth magic cannot restore that which has been taken from a soul. Tynstar has power in abundance. What was taken from you will never be regained. You are—as you are."

I stared at him. And then I looked down at myself and saw myself. There seemed to be no difference. I was very stiff and sore and slow, but a sojourn in bed will do that.

Duncan merely waited. I moved again to sit up, found it every bit as difficult as before, but this time I prevailed. I swung my legs over the side of the bed, screwed up my face against the creaking of my joints, and sat there as all my muscles trembled.

It was then I saw my fingers. The knuckles were enlarged hugely, the flesh stretched thin over brittle bones. I saw how the calluses had begun to soften, shedding the toughness I needed against the use of a sword. I saw how the fingers were vaguely twisted away from my thumb. And I ached. Even in the sunlight, I ached with a bone-deep pain.

"How long?" I asked abruptly, knowing I had spent more than days in my bed.

"Two months. We could not raise you from the stupor."

Naked, I wrenched myself from the bed and stumbled across the chamber, to the plate upon the wall. The polished silver gave back my face, and I saw what Tynstar had done.

Carillon was still Carillon, certainly recognizable. But older, so much older, by twenty years at least.

"It is my father," I said in shock, recalling the time-worn face. The tawny-dark hair was frosted with gray with the beard showing equal amounts. Creases fanned out from my eyes and bracketed nose and mouth, though most were hidden by the beard. And set deeply into the still-blue eyes was the knowledge of constant pain.

It was no wonder I ached. I had the same disease as my mother, with her twisted hands and brittle bones, the swollen, painful joints. And with each year, the pain and disability would worsen.

Tynstar had put his hand on me and my youth was spent at once.

I turned slowly and sat down on the nearest chest. I began to shake with more than physical weakness. It was the realization.

Duncan waited, saying nothing, and I saw the compassion

in his eyes. "Can you not heal me of this?" I gestured emptily. "The age and gray I can live with, but the illness . . . you have only to see my lady mother—" I stopped. I saw the answer in his face.

After a moment he spoke. "It will improve. You will not be as stiff when some time has passed. You have spent two months in bed and it takes its toll on anyone—you will find it not so bad as it seems now. But as for the disease . . ." He shook his head. "Tynstar did not give you anything you would not have known anyway. He inflicted nothing upon you that time itself would not inflict. He merely stole that time from you, so that a month became ten years. You are older, aye, but not old. There are many years left to you."

I thought of Finn. I recalled the silver in his hair and the hard gauntness of his face. I recalled what he had said of Tynstar: *"He put his hand on me."*

The chest was hard and cold against my naked buttocks. "When my daughter is older, I will be old. She will have a grandsire for a father."

"I doubt she will love you the less for that."

I looked at him in surprise. A Cheysuli speaking of love?—aye, perhaps, when the moment calls for an honesty that can bring me back to myself.

My body protested against the dampness of the chamber. I got up and walked—no, limped—stiffly back to my bed, reaching for the robe a servant had left. "I will have to deal with Electra."

"Aye. And she is still the Queen of Homana."

"As I made her." I shook my head. "I should have listened to you. To Finn. I should have listened to someone."

Duncan smiled, still sitting on his stool. "You know more of kingcraft than I do, Carillon. The marriage brought peace to Homana—at least regarding Solinde—and I cannot fault you for that. But—"

"—but I wed a woman who intended my death from the first moment she ever saw me." The pain curled deeply within my loins. "Gods—I should have known by looking at her. She claims more than forty years—I should have known Tynstar could give those years as well as take them." I rubbed at my age-lined face and felt the twinges in my fingers. "I should have known Tynstar's arts would prevail when I had no Cheysuli by me. No liege man."

"They planned well, Tynstar and Electra," Duncan agreed. "First the trap-link, which might have slain Finn and rid them of him sooner. Then, when that did not work, they used it to draw him into a second trap. Finn, I do not doubt, walked in on Tynstar and Electra when he meant only to confront her. He could not touch Tynstar, but Tynstar touched him, then took his leave and Finn had only Electra. And yet when he told you Tynstar had been present, you thought of the trap-link instead." Duncan shook his head and the earring glittered in the sunlight. "They played with us all, Carillon . . . and nearly won the game."

"They *have* won." I sat huddled in my robe. "I have only a daughter, and Homana has need of an heir."

Duncan rose. He moved to Cai and put out a hand to the hawk, as if he meant to caress him. But he did not touch him after all, and I saw how his fingers trembled. "You are still young, for all you feel old." His back was to me. "Take yourself another *cheysula* and give Homana that heir."

I looked at his back, so rigid and unmoving. "You know Homanan custom. You were at the wedding ceremony; do you not recall the vows? Homanans do not divorce their wives. It is a point of law, as well as being custom. Surely you, with all your adherence to Cheysuli custom, can understand the constraints that places on me. Even a Mujhar."

"Is the custom so important when the wife attempts to slay the husband?"

I heard the irony in his tone. "No. But she did not succeed, and I know what Council will say. Set her aside, perhaps, but do not break the vows. It would be breaking Homanan law. The Council would never permit it."

Duncan swung around and faced me. "Electra is Tynstar's *meijha!* She bears his child in her belly! Would the Homanan Council prefer to have you *dead?*"

"Do you not see?" I threw back. "It has been taken from my hands. Had Tourmaline not gone with Finn, wedding with Lachlan instead, I could have sought my heir from her. Had she wed *any* prince, Homana would have an heir. But she did not. She went with Finn and took that chance from me."

"Set her aside," he said urgently. "You are Mujhar—you can do anything you wish."

Slowly I shook my head. "If I begin to make my own rules, I become a despot. I become Shaine, who desired to destroy the Cheysuli race. No, Duncan. Electra remains my wife, though I doubt I will keep her here. I have no wish to see her *or* the bastard she carries."

He shut his eyes a moment, and then I understood. I knew what he feared at last.

I was tired. The ache had settled deeply in my bones. I felt bruised from the knowledge of what I faced. And yet I could not avoid it. "There is no need to fear me," I said quietly.

"Is there not?" Duncan's eyes were bleak. "I know what you will do."

"I have no other choice."

"He is *my* son—"

"—and Alix's, and Alix is my cousin." I stopped, seeing the pain in the face Alix loved. "How long have you known it would come to this?"

Duncan laughed, but it had a hollow, desperate sound. "All my life, it seems. When I came to know my *tahlmorra*." He shook his head and sat down upon the stool. His shoulders slumped and he stared blankly at the floor. "I have always been afraid. Of you . . . of the past and future . . . of what I knew was held within the prophecy for any son of mine. Did you think I wanted Alix *only* out of desire?" Anguish leached his face of the solemnity I knew. "Alix was a part of my own *tahlmorra*. I knew, if I took her and got a son upon her, I would have to give up that son. *I knew.* And so I hoped, when she conceived again, there would at least be another for us . . . but the Ihlini took even that from us." He sighed. "I had no choice. No choice at all."

"Duncan," I said after a moment, "can a back not be turned upon *tahlmorra?*"

He shook his head immediately. "The warrior who turns his back on his *tahlmorra* may twist the prophecy. In twisting it, he destroys the *tahlmorra* of his race. Homana would fall. Not in a year or ten or twenty—perhaps not even a hundred—but it would fall, and the realm would be given over to the Ihlini and their like." He paused. "There is another thing: the warrior who turns his back on his *tahl-*

morra gives up his afterlife. I think none of us would be willing to do that."

I thought of Tynstar, and others like him, ruling in Homana. No. It was no wonder Duncan would never consider trying to alter his *tahlmorra*.

I frowned. "Do you say then that even a *single* warrior turning his back on his *tahlmorra* may change the balance of fate?"

Duncan frowned also. For once, he seemed to grope for the proper words, as if he knew the Homanan tongue could never tell me what I asked. But the Old Tongue would not serve; I knew too little of it. And what I did know I had learned from Finn; he had never spoken of such personal Cheysuli things.

Finally Duncan sighed. "A crofter goes to Mujhara today instead of tomorrow. His son falls down a well. The son dies." He made the spread-fingered, palm-up gesture. "*Tahlmorra.* But had the crofter gone tomorrow instead of today, would the son yet live? I cannot say. Does the death serve a greater pattern? Perhaps. Had he lived, would it have destroyed the pattern completely? Perhaps—I cannot say." He shrugged. "I cannot know what the gods intend."

"But you serve them all so blindly—"

"No. My eyes are open." He did not smile. "They have given us the prophecy, so we know what we work toward. We know what we can lose, if we do not continue serving it. My belief is such: that certain events, once changed, can alter other events. Are enough of them altered, no matter how minor, the major one is changed. Perhaps even the prophecy of the Firstborn."

"So you live your life in chains." I could not comprehend the depth of his dedication.

Duncan smiled a little. "You wear a crown, my lord Mujhar. Surely you know its weight."

"That is different—"

"Is it? Even now you face the overwhelming need to find an heir. To put a prince on the throne of Homana you will even take my son."

I stared at him. The emptiness spread out to fill my aching body. "I have no other choice."

"Nor have I, my lord Mujhar." Duncan looked suddenly weary. "But you give my son into hardship."

"He will be the Prince of Homana." The rank seemed, to me, to outweigh the hardship.

He did not smile. "It was your title, once. It nearly got you slain. Do not belittle its danger."

"Donal is Cheysuli." For a moment I was incapable of saying anything more. I realized, in that moment, that even *I* had served the gods. Duncan had said more than once it was a Cheysuli throne, and that one day there would be a Cheysuli Mujhar in place of a Homanan. And now I, with only a few words, made that prediction come true.

Are men always so blind to the gods, even when they serve them?

"Cheysuli," Duncan echoed, "and so the links are forged."

I looked at Cai. I thought of the falcon and wolf Donal claimed, two *lir* instead of one. Things changed. Time moved on, sometimes far too quickly. And events altered events.

I sighed and rubbed at my knees. "The Homanans will not accept him. Not readily. He is Cheysuli to the bone, despite his Homanan blood."

"Aye," Duncan agreed, "you begin to see the danger."

"I can lessen it. I can take away the choice. I can make certain the Homanans accept him."

Duncan shook his head. "It has been less than eight years since Shaine's *qu'mahlin* ended because of you. It is too soon. Such things are not easily done."

"No. But I can make it easier."

"How?"

"By wedding him to Aislinn."

Duncan stood up at once. "They are children!"

"Now, aye, but children become adults." I did not care to see the startled, angry expression on his face, but I had no choice. "A long betrothal, Duncan, such as royal Houses do. In fifteen years, Donal will be—twenty-three? Aislinn nearly sixteen: old enough to wed. And then I will name him my heir."

Duncan shut his eyes. I saw his right hand make the eloquent sign. *"Tahlmorra lujhalla mei wiccan, cheysu."* All the helplessness was in his voice, and I knew it chafed his soul. Duncan was not a man who suffered helplessness with any degree of decorum.

I sighed and mimicked the gesture, including the Cheysuli phrase for wishing him peace: *Cheysuli i'halla shansu.*

"Peace!" It was bitterly said; from Duncan, a revelation. "My son will know none of that."

I felt the dampness in my bones and pulled the heavy robe more tightly around my shoulders. "I think *I* have known little of it. Have you?"

"Oh, aye," he returned at once, with all the force of his bitterness. "More than you, Carillon. It was to me that Alix came."

The bolt went home. I grimaced, thinking of Electra, and knew I would have to deal with it before more time went by. The gods knew Tynstar had stolen enough.

"I will send for Alix," I said at last, hunching against the chill he did not seem to feel. "And Donal. I will explain things to them both. I would have you send Cai, but there is a task I have for you." I expected a refusal, but Duncan said nothing at all. I saw the weariness in his posture and the knowledge in his eyes. He was ever a step before me. "Duncan—I am sorry. I did not mean to usurp your son."

"Be not sorry for what the gods intend." He gestured the hawk to his arm. How he held him, I cannot say; Cai is a heavy bird. "As for your task, I will do it. It will get me free of these walls." For a moment his shoulders hunched in, mirroring my own, but for a different reason. "They chafe," he said at last. "How they chafe . . . how they bind a Cheysuli soul."

"But the Cheysuli built these walls." I was surprised at the vehemence in his tone.

"We built them and we left them." He shook his head. "*I* leave them. It is my son who will have to learn what it is to know himself well-caged. I am too old, too set in my ways to change."

"As I am," I said bitterly. "Tynstar has made me so."

"Tynstar altered the body, not the mind," Duncan said. "Let not the body affect the heart." He smiled a moment, albeit faintly, and then he left the room.

I went into Electra's chambers and found her seated by a casement. The sunlight set her hair to glowing and made her blind to me. It was only when the door thumped closed that she turned her head and saw me.

She did not rise. She sat upon the bench with the black cloak wrapped around her like a shroud of Tynstar's making. The hood was draped across her shoulders, freeing her hair, and I saw the twin braids bound with silver. It glittered against the cloak.

Tynstar's child swelled her belly. Mine had done it before. It made me angry, but not so angry as to show it. I merely stood in the room and faced her, letting her see what the sorcery had wrought; to know it had been her doing that changed me so.

Her chin lifted a little. She had not lost a whit of her pride and defiance, even knowing she was caught.

"He left you behind," I said. "Was that a measure of his regard?"

I saw the minute twitch of her mouth. I had put salt in the open wound. "Unless you slay me, he will have me still."

"But you do not think I will slay you."

She smiled. "I am Aislinn's mother and the Queen of Homana. There is nothing you can do."

"And if I said you were a witch?"

"Say it," she countered. "Have me executed, then, and see how Solinde responds."

"As I recall, it was Solinde you wanted freed." I moved a trifle closer. "You wanted no vassal to Homana."

"Tynstar will prevent it." Her eyes did not shift from mine. "You have seen what he could do. You have *felt* it."

"Aye," I said softly, approaching again. "I have felt it and so have you, though the results were somewhat reversed. It seems I have all the years you shed, Electra, and like to keep them, I think. A pity, no doubt, but it does not strip me of my throne. I am still Mujhar of Homana— and Solinde a vassal to me."

"How long will you live?" she retorted. "You are forty-five, now. No more the young Mujhar. In five years, ten, you will be old. *Old.* In war, old men die quickly. And you will know war, Carillon; that I promise you."

"But you will never see it." I bent down and caught one of her wrists, pulling her to her feet. She was heavy with Tynstar's child. Her free arm went down to cradle her belly protectively beneath the heavy cloak. "I exile you, Electra. For the years that remain to you."

Color splotched her face, but she showed no fear. "Where do you send me, then?"

"To the Crystal Isle." I smiled. "I see you know it. Aye, a formidable place when you are the enemy of Homana. It is the birthplace of the Cheysuli and claims the protection of the gods. Tynstar could never touch you there. Not ever, Electra. The island will be your prison." I still held her wrist in one hand. The other I put out to catch one braid and threaded my fingers into it. "You will be treated as befits your rank. You will have servants and fine clothing, good food and wine, proper accoutrements. Everything except freedom. And there—with his child—you will grow old and die." My smile grew wider as I felt the silk of her hair. "For such as you, I think, that will be punishment enough."

"I will bear that child in less than one month." Her lips were pale and flat. "A journey now may make me lose it."

"If the gods will it," I agreed blandly. "I send you in the morning with Duncan and an escort of Cheysuli. Try your arts on them, if you seek to waste your time. They, unlike myself, are invulnerable."

I saw the movement deep in her eyes and felt the touch of her power. Color returned to her face. She smiled faintly, knowing what I knew, and the long-lidded eyes drew me in. As ever. She would always be my bane.

I let go of her wrist, her braid, and cupped her head with both hands. I kissed her as a drowning man clings to wood. Gods, but she could move me still . . . she could still reach into my soul—

—and twist it.

I set her away from me with careful deliberation and saw the shock of realization in her face. "It is done, Electra. You must pay the price of your folly."

The sunlight glittered off the silver cording in her braids. But also off something else: tears. They stood in her great gray eyes, threatening to spill.

But I knew her. Too well. They were tears of anger, not of fear, and I went out of the room with the taste of defeat in my mouth.

Chapter Six

The arms-master stepped back, lowering his sword. "My lord Mujhar, let this stop. It is a travesty."

My breath hissed between my teeth. "It will remain a travesty until I learn to overcome it." I gripped the hilt of my Cheysuli sword and lifted the blade yet again. "Come against me, Cormac."

"My lord—" He stepped away again, shaking his crop-haired head. "There is no sense in it."

I swore at him. I had spent nearly an hour trying to regain a portion of my skill, and now he denied me the chance. I lowered my sword and stood there, clad in breeches and practice tunic while the sweat ran down my arms. I shut my eyes a moment, trying to deal with the pain; when I opened them I saw the pity in Cormac's dark brown eyes.

"Ku'reshtin!" I snapped. "Save your pity for someone else! I have no need of such—" I went in against him then, raising the sword yet again, and nearly got through his belated guard.

He danced back, danced again, then ducked my swinging sword. His own came up to parry my blow; I got under it and thrust toward his belly. He sucked it in, leaped aside, then twisted and came toward my side. I blocked, tied up his slash and pushed his blade aside.

The rhythm began to come back. It was fitful and very slow, but I had lost little of my strength. The stamina was blunted, but it might return in time. I had only to learn what it was to deal with the stiffness of my joints and forget about the pain.

Cormac caught his lip between his teeth. I saw the light in his eyes. His soft-booted feet hissed against the floor as he slid and slid again, ducking the blows I lowered. We did not fight for blood, sparring only, but he knew I meant to beat him. He would allow me no quarter, not even if I were to ask it.

It was my hands that failed me finally, my big-knuckled, aching hands. In the weeks that had followed since I had regained my senses, I had learned how weakened they were. My knees hurt all the time, as if some demon chewed upon them from the inside moving toward the outside, but when I was moving I forgot them. Mostly. It was when I stopped that I was reminded of the ache in my bones. But my hands, in swordplay, were the most important, and I had found them the largest barrier to regaining my banished skill.

My wrists held firm, locked against his blow, but the fingers lost their grip. They twisted, shooting pain up through my forearms. The sword went flying from my hands, clanging against the stone, and I cursed myself for being such a fool as to let it go. But when Cormac bent to retrieve it I set my foot upon it. "Let it go. Enough of this. We will continue another time."

He bowed quickly and took his leave, taking his sword with him. My own still lay upon the floor, as if to mock me, while I tried to regain my breath. I set my teeth against the pain in my swollen hands. In a moment I bent down, grimacing against the sudden cramp in my back, and scooped up the blade with one hand.

The sweat ran into my eyes. I scrubbed one forearm across my face and cleared my burning vision. And then, giving it up, I sat down on the nearest bench. I stretched out my legs carefully and gave into the pain for a moment, feeling the fire in my knees. I set back and head against the wall and tried to shut it all out.

"You are better, my lord, since the last time."

When I could, I rolled my head to one side and saw Rowan. "Am I? Or do you merely let me think so?"

"I would not go up against you," he said flatly, coming closer. "But you should not hope for it all, not so soon. It will take time, my lord."

"I have no time. Tynstar has stolen it from me." I scraped my spine against the wall and sat up straight again, suppressing a grimace, and drew in my feet. Even my ankles hurt. "Have you come on business, or merely to tell me what you think I want to hear?"

"There is a visitor." He held out a silver signet ring set with a plain black stone.

I took it and rolled it in my hand. "Who is it, then? Do I know him?"

"He names himself Alaric of Atvia, my lord. Crown Prince, to be precise."

I looked up from the ring sharply. "Thorne is slain. If this boy is his son, he is now Lord of Atvia in Thorne's place. Why does he humble himself?"

"Alaric is not the heir. Osric, his older brother, sits on the Atvian throne." He paused. "In *Atvia,* my lord."

I scowled. "Osric is not come, then."

"No, my lord."

I gritted my teeth a moment, swearing within my mind. I was in no mood for diplomacy, especially not with a child. "Where is this Atvian infant?"

Rowan smiled. "In an antechamber off the Great Hall, where I have put him. Would you prefer him somewhere else?"

"No. I will save the Great Hall for his brother." I stood up, using the wall for a brace. For a moment I waited, allowing the worst of the pain to die, and then I gave Rowan my sword. I shut up the ring in my fist and went out of the practice chamber.

The boy, I discovered, was utterly dwarfed by his surroundings. The Great Hall would have overtaken him completely, and I was in no mood for such ploys. Alaric looked no older than six or seven and would hardly comprehend the politics of the situation.

He rose stiffly as I came into the chamber, having dressed in fresh clothing. He bowed in a brief, exceedingly slight gesture of homage that just missed condescension. The expression in his brown eyes was one of sullen hostility, and his face was coldly set.

I walked to a cushioned mahogany chair and sat down, allowing no hint of the pain to show in my face. I was stifffening after the sparring. "So . . . Atvia comes to Homana."

"No, my lord." Alaric spoke quietly. "My brother, Lord

Osric of Atvia, sends me to say Atvia does *not* come to Homana. Nor ever will, except to conquer this land."

I contemplated Alaric in some surprise. He was dressed as befitted his rank, and his dark brown hair was combed smooth. A closer look revealed him older than I had thought. He was perhaps a year or two older than Donal, but the knowledge in his eyes seemed to surpass that of a grown man.

I permitted myself a smile, though it held nothing of amusement. "I have slain your father, my lord Alaric, because he sought to pull down my House and replace it with his own. I could do the same to your own, beginning with you." I paused. "Has your brother a response to that?"

Alaric's slender body was rigid. "He does, my lord. I am to say we do not acknowledge your sovereignty."

I rested my chin in one hand, elbow propped against the arm rest. "Osric sends you into danger with such words in your mouth, my young Atvian eagle. What say you to remaining here a hostage?"

Angry color flared in Alaric's face, but he did not waver a bit. "My brother said I must prepare myself for that."

I frowned. "How old is Osric?"

"Sixteen."

I sighed. "So young—so willing to risk his brother and his realm."

"My father said you had ever been Atvia's enemy, and must be gainsaid." Grief washed through the brown eyes and the mouth wavered a little, but he covered it almost at once. "My brother and I will serve our father's memory by fighting you in his place. In the end, we will win. If nothing else, we will outlive you. You are an old man, my lord . . . Osric and I are young."

I felt a fist clench in my belly. Old, was I? Aye, to his eyes. "Too young to die," I said grimly. "Shall I have you slain, Alaric?"

Color receded from his face. He was suddenly a small boy again. "Do what you wish, my lord—I am prepared." The voice shook a little.

"No," I said abruptly, "you are not. You only think it. You have yet to look death in the face and know him; had you done it, you would not accept him so blithely." I pushed myself up and bit off the oath I wished to spit out

between my teeth. "Serve your lord, boy . . . serve him as
well as you may. But do it at home in Atvia; I do not slay
or imprison young boys."

Alaric caught the heavy ring as I threw it at him. Shock
was manifest in his face. "I may go home?"

"You may go home. Tell your brother I give him back
his heir, though I doubt not he will have another one soon
enough, when he takes himself a wife."

"He is already wed, my lord."

I studied the boy again. "Tell him also that twice a year
Homanan ships shall call at Rondule. Upon those ships
Osric shall place tribute to Homana. If you wish continued
freedom from Homana, my young lordling, you will pay
the tribute." I paused. "You may tell him also that should
he ever come against me in the field, I will slay him."

The small face looked pinched. "I will tell him, my lord.
But—as to this tribute—"

"You will pay it," I said. "I will send a message for your
brother back with you in the morning, and it will include
all the details of this tribute. You must pay the cost of the
folly in trying to take Homana." I signalled to one of the
waiting servants. "See he is fed and lodged as befits his
rank. In the morning, he may go home."

"Aye, my lord."

I put a hand on Alaric's shoulder and turned him toward
the man. "Go with Breman, my proud young prince. You
will not know harm in Homana-Mujhar." I gave him a push
from my swollen hand and saw him start toward Breman.
In a moment they both were gone.

Rowan cleared his throat. "Is he not a valuable
hostage?"

"Aye. But he is a boy."

"I thought it was often done. Are not princes fostered
on friendly Houses? What would be the difference?"

"I will not take his childhood from him." I shivered in
the cold dampness of the chamber. "Osric is already wed.
He will get himself sons soon enough; Alaric will lose his
value. Since I doubt Osric has any intention of coming so
soon against Homana, I lose nothing by letting Alaric go."

"And when, in manhood, he comes to fight?"

"I will deal with it then."

Rowan sighed. "And what of Osric? Sixteen is neither child nor man."

"Had it been Osric, I would have thrown him into chains." I paused. "To humble that arrogant mouth."

Rowan smiled. "You may yet be able to, my lord."

"Perhaps." I looked at Rowan squarely. "But if he is anything like his father—or even Keough, his grandsire— Osric and I shall meet in battle. And one of us will die."

"My lord." It was a servant in the doorway, bowing with politeness. "My lord Mujhar, there is a boy."

"Breman has taken Alaric," I said. "He is to be treated with all respect."

"No, my lord—another boy. This one is Cheysuli."

I frowned. "Say on."

"He claims himself kin to you, my lord—he has a wolf and a falcon."

I laughed then. "Donal! Aye, he is kin to me. But he should have his mother with him in addition to his *lir*."

"No, my lord." The man looked worried. "He is alone but for the animals, and he appears to have been treated harshly."

I went past him at once and to the entry chamber. There I saw a falcon perched upon a candlerack with all the wicks unlighted. The wolf stood close to Donal, shoring up one leg. Donal's black hair was disheveled and his face was pinched with deprivation. Bruises ringed his throat.

He saw me and stared, his eyes going wide, and I realized what he saw. Not the man he had known. "Donal," I said, and then he knew me, and came running across the floor.

"They have taken my *jehana*—" His voice shook badly. He shut his eyes a moment, blocking out the tears, and tried to speak again. "They have taken her . . . and slain Torrin in the croft!"

I swore, though I kept it to myself. Donal pressed himself against me, hanging onto my doublet, and I wanted nothing more than to lift him into my arms. But I did not. I know something of Cheysuli pride, even in the young.

I set one hand to the back of his head as he tucked it under my chin. I thought, suddenly, of Aislinn, wondering what she would think of him when she was old enough to know. This boy would be my heir.

"Come," I said, rising, "we will speak of this elsewhere."

I turned to take him from the chamber but he reached up and caught my hand. Instantly I forgot my resolution and bent to pick him up, moving to the nearest bench in a warmer chamber. I sat down and settled him on my lap, wincing against the pain. "You must tell me what happened as clearly as you can. I can do nothing until I know."

Lorn flopped down at my feet with a grunt, but his brown eyes did not leave Donal's face. The falcon flew in and found another perch, piping his agitation.

Donal rubbed at his eyes and I saw how glassy they were. He was exhausted and ready to fall, but I had to know what had happened. As Rowan came in I signalled for him to pour Donal a swallow or two of wine.

"My *jehana* and I were coming here," Donal began. "She said you had sent for us. But there was no urgency to it, and she wanted to stop at the croft." He stopped as Rowan brought the cup of wine. I held it to his mouth and let him drink, then gave it back to Rowan. Donal wiped his mouth and went on. "While we were there, men came. At first they gave my *jehana* honor. They shared their wine and then watched us, and within moments Torrin and my *jehana* were senseless. They—cut Torrin's throat. They *slew* him!"

I held him a little more tightly and saw the stark pity in Rowan's face. Donal had come early to his baptism into adulthood, but Rowan earlier still. "Say on, Donal . . . say on until you have said it all."

His voice took on some life. Perhaps the wine had done it. "I called for Taj and Lorn, but the men said they would slay my *jehana*. So I told my *lir* to go away." Renewed grief hollowed his face, blackening his eyes. "They put her on a litter and *bound* her . . . they put a chain around my neck. They said we would go to the Northern Wastes. . . ."

I glanced at Rowan and saw his consternation. The Northern Wastes lay across the Bluetooth River. There would be no reason to take Donal or Alix there.

"They said they would take us to *Tynstar*—" Donal's voice was hardly a whisper.

It came clear to me almost instantly. Rowan swore in Homanan even as I said something in the Old Tongue that made Donal's eyes go wide in astonishment. But I could not afford to alarm him. "Was there anything more?"

His face screwed up with concentration and confusion.

"I did not understand. They spoke among themselves and I could make no sense of it. They said Tynstar wanted the seed of the prophecy—me!—and my *jehana* for a woman. A woman to use in place of the one he lost to you." Donal stared up at me. "But *why* does he want my *jehana*?"

"Gods—" I shut my eyes, seeing Alix in Tynstar's hands. No doubt he would repay me for sending Electra to the Crystal Isle. No doubt he would use Alix badly. They had opposed each other before.

It was Rowan who drew Donal's attention away from my angry face. "How did *you* win free?"

For a moment the boy smiled. "They thought I was a child, not a warrior, and therefore helpless. They counted my *lir* as little more than pets. And so Taj and Lorn kept themselves to the shadows and followed across the river. One night, when the men thought I slept, I talked to Taj and Lorn, and told them how important it was that I get away. And so they taught me how to take *lir*-shape, though the thing was too early done." His face was pinched again. "*Jehan* had said I must wait, but I could not. I had to do it then."

"You came all the way in *lir*-shape?" I knew how draining it could be, and in a child . . . I had seen Alix, once, when she had shapechanged too often, and Finn as well, after too long a time spent in wolf-shape. It upset the human balance.

"I flew." Donal frowned. "And when I could not fly, I went as a wolf. And when it sickened me, I walked as myself. It was hard—harder than I thought . . . I believed *lir*-shape was easy for a warrior."

I held him a little more tightly. "Nothing is done so easily when it bears the weight of the gods." I rose, lifting him to stand. "Come. I will see you are fed and bathed and given rest in a comfortable bed."

Donal slid down to the floor. "But my *jehan* is here. *Jehana* said he was."

"Your *jehan* has gone to Hondarth and it is too soon for him to be back. Another week, perhaps. You will have to wait with me." I tousled the heavy black hair which had already lost some of its childhood curl. "Donal—I promise we will fetch your *jehana* back. I promise all will be well."

He looked up at me, huge yellow eyes set in a dark

Cheysuli face. No Cheysuli trusts easily, but I knew he
trusted me. Well, he would have to. I would make him into
a king.

Donal braced both elbows against the table top. He
rested his chin in his hands. He watched, fascinated as always, as I traced out the battle markings drawn on the map
of Caledon. In the past ten days we had spent hours with
the maps.

"It was here." I touched the border between Caledon
and the Steppes. "Your *su'fali* and I were riding with the
Caledonese, and we went into the Steppes at this point."

"How long did the battle take?"

"A day and a night. But it was only one of many battles.
The plainsmen fight differently than the Homanans—Finn
and I had to learn new methods." Well, *I* had; Finn's methods were highly adaptable and required no reorganization.

Donal frowned in concentration. He put out a finger
much smaller than mine and touched the leather map. "My
su'fali fought with you—so has my *jehan* . . . will *I* fight
with you when I am made a prince?"

"I hope I may keep the peace between Homana and
other realms," I told him truthfully, "but does it come to
war no matter what I do, aye, you will fight with me. Perhaps against Atvia, does Osric wish to task me . . . perhaps
even Solinde, should the regency fail."

"Will it?" He fixed me with intent yellow eyes, black
brows drawn down.

"It might. I have sent Electra away, and the Solindish do
not like it." I saw no sense in hiding the truth from him.
Cheysuli children are more adult than most. Donal was also
a clan-leader's son, and I did not doubt he already knew
something of politics.

Donal sighed and his attention turned. He pushed away
from the table and got off the stool, sitting down on the
floor with Lorn. The wolf stretched and yawned and put a
paw on Donal's thigh as Donal reached to drag him into
his lap. Taj, perched upon a chair back, piped excitedly and
then Duncan was in the doorway.

"Jehan!" Donal scrambled up, dumping Lorn, and ran
across the room. I saw Duncan's smile as he caught his son
and the lessening of tension in his face. He scooped up the

boy and held him, saying something in the Old Tongue, and I knew he could not know. They had left the telling to me.

"Have you been keeping Carillon from his duties?" Duncan asked as Donal hugged his neck.

"*Jehan*—oh *jehan* . . . why did you not come sooner? I was so afraid—"

"What have you to be afraid of?" Duncan was grinning. "Unless you fear for me, which is unnecessary. You see I am well enough." He glanced at me across the top of his son's dark head. "Carillon, there is—"

"*Jehan*—" Donal would not let him speak. "*Jehan*—will you go now? Will you go up across the river? Will you fetch her back?"

"Go where? Why? Fetch *who* back?" Duncan grinned and moved across the room to the nearest bench. He sat down with Donal in his lap, though the boy was too big to be held. It seemed odd to see Duncan so tolerant of such things; I knew the Cheysuli did not profess to love, and therefore the words were lacking in their language. And yet it was manifest in Duncan's movements and voice as he sat down upon the bench. "Have you lost someone, small one?"

"*Jehana*," Donal whispered, and I saw Duncan's face go still.

He looked to me at once. "Where is Alix?"

"Alix was—taken." I inhaled a careful breath. "It appears it is Tynstar's doing."

"*Tynstar*—" Duncan's face was ashen.

"You had best let Donal tell you," I said quietly. "It was he who won free and came to me here, to tell me what had happened."

Duncan's arms were slack around the boy. And then suddenly they tightened. "Donal—say what has happened. All of it. Tell me what you saw; tell me what you heard."

Donal, too, was pale. I doubted he had ever seen his father so shaken. He sat hunched in Duncan's lap and told the story as he had told it to me, and I saw the struggle in Duncan's face. It made my own seem a shadow of true feeling.

At last Donal finished, his voice trailing off into silence. He waited for his father to speak even as I did, but Duncan said nothing at all. He merely sat, staring into the distance, as if he had not heard.

"*Jehan*—? Donal's voice, plaintive and frightened, as he sat on Duncan's lap.

Duncan spoke at last. He said something to Donal in the Old Tongue, something infinitely soothing, and I saw the boy relax. "Did they harm her, small one?"

"No, *jehan*. But she could hardly speak." Donal's face was pinched with the memory and he was frightened all over again.

Duncan's hand on his son's head was gentle in its touch. The tension was everywhere else. "*Shansu, Shansu* . . . I will get your *jehana* back. But you must promise me to wait here until we come home again."

"Here?" Donal sat upright in Ducan's arms. "You will not send me back to the Keep?"

"Not yet. Your *jehana* and I will take you there when we are back." His eyes, staring over Donal's head, were fixed on the distances again. Duncan seemed to be living elsewhere, even as he held his son. And then I realized he spoke to Cai. He was somewhere in the link.

When he came out of it I saw his fear, though he tried to hide it from Donal. For a moment he shut his eyes, barricading his soul, and then be held Donal more tightly. "*Shansu*, Donal—peace. I will get your *jehana* back."

But I knew, looking at him, he said it for himself and not his son.

"Duncan." I waited until he looked at me, coming out of his haze of shock. "I have spoken to your second-leader at the Keep . . . and the Homanans as well. We are prepared to go with you."

"Go where?" he asked. "Do you know? Do you even know where she is?"

"I assumed the *lir* could find her."

"The *lir* do not need to find her . . . I know where Alix is. I know what he means to do." Duncan set Donal down and told him to take his *lir* and go. The boy protested, clearly frightened as well as offended, but Duncan made him go.

At last I faced him alone. "Where?"

"Valgaard." He saw the blankness in my face. "Tynstar's lair. It is a fortress high in the canyons of Solinde—you have only to cross the Bluetooth and go directly north into the mountains. Cross the Molon Pass into Solinde and you have found it. You cannot help but find it." He rose and paced across the floor, but I saw how his footsteps hesitated. "He would take her there."

"Then we will have to go there and get her."

He swung around. One hand was on the hilt of his long-knife; I saw how he wanted to shout, to bring down the walls, and, yet he kept himself very quiet. It was eerie. It was the intensity I had seen so often in Finn, knowing to keep my distance. But this time, I could not.

"Valgaard houses the Gate," he said in a clipped, hissing tone. "Do you know what you say you will do?" He shook his head. "No, you do not. You do not know the Gate."

"I admit it. There are many things I do not know."

Duncan prowled the room with a stiff, angry stride. He reminded me of a mountain cat, suddenly, stalking down its prey. "The Gate," he repeated. "Asar-Suti's Gate. The Gate to the Seker's world."

The words were strange. Not the Old Tongue; something far older, something that spoke of foulness. "Demons," I said, before I could stop.

"Asar-Suti is more than a demon. He is the god of the netherworld. The Seker himself—who made and dwells in darkness. He is the font of Ihlini power." He stopped pacing. He stood quite still. "In Valgaard—Tynstar shares that power."

I recalled how easily he had trapped me in my bed, seeking to take my life. I recalled how he had changed the ruby from red to black. I remembered how it was he had stolen Homana from my uncle. I remembered Bellam's body. If he could do all of that while he was *out* of Valgaard, what could he do within?

Duncan was at the door. He turned back, his face set in stark lines of grief and determination. "I would ask no man to risk himself in such a thing as this."

"Alix risked herself for me when I lay shackled in Atvian iron."

"Alix was not the Mujhar of Homana."

"No." I did not smile. "She carried the seed of the prophecy in her belly, and events can change events."

I saw the shock of realization in his face. The risk he

spoke of was real, but no greater than what Alix had faced. Had she died in my rescue, or somehow lost the child, the prophecy might have ended before it was begun.

"I will go," I said quietly. "There is nothing left but to do it."

He stood in the doorway. For a long moment he said nothing at all, seemingly incapable of it, and then he nodded a little. "If you meet up with Tynstar, Carillon, you will have a powerful weapon."

I waited.

"Electra miscarried the child."

Chapter Seven

As one, my Homanan troop pulled horses to a ragged halt. I heard low-voiced comments, oaths made and broken, prayers to the gods. I did not blame them. No one had expected this.

No one, perhaps, except the Cheysuli. They did not seem troubled by the place. They merely waited, mounted and uncloaked, while the sun flashed off their gold.

A chill ran down my spine. I suppressed it and reined in my fidgeting horse. Duncan, some distance away, rode over to ask about the delay.

"Look about you," I said solemnly. "Have you seen its like before?"

He shrugged. "We have come over the Molon Pass. This is Solinde. We encroach upon Tynstar's realm. Did you think it would resemble your own?"

I could not say what I thought it might resemble. Surely not this. I only dreamed of places like this.

We had crossed the Bluetooth River twelve days out of Mujhara: nine Homanans, nine Cheysuli, Rowan and Gryffth, myself and Duncan. Twenty-two men to rescue Alix, to take her back from Tynstar. Now, as I looked around, I doubted we could do it.

The Northern Wastes of Homana lay behind us. Now we faced Solinde, having come down from the Molon Pass, with Valgaard still before us. And yet it was obvious we drew closer. The land reflected the lair.

Icy winds blew down from the pass. Winter was done with in Homana, but across the Bluetooth the chill never quite left the land. It amazed me the Cheysuli could go bare-armed, though I knew they withstood hardship better than Homanans.

Snow still patched the ground beneath the trees, mantling

the rocky mountains. Great defiles fell away into canyons, sheer and dark and wet from melting snow. All around us the world was a great, dark, slick wound, bleeding slowly in the sunlight. Someone had riven the earth.

Even the trees reflected the pain of the land. They were wracked and twisted, as if some huge cold hand had swept across them in a monstrous fit of temper. Rocks were split open in perfect halves and quarters; some were no more than powder where once a boulder had stood. But most of them had shapes. Horrible, hideous shapes, as if nightmares had been shaped into stone so all could share the horror.

"We draw close to Valgaard," Duncan said. "This has been the tourney-field of the Ihlini."

I looked at him sharply. "What do you say?"

"Ihlini power is inbred," he explained, "but the control must be taught. An Ihlini child has no more knowledge of his abilities than a Cheysuli child; they know they have magic at their beck, but no knowledge of how to use it. It must be—practiced."

I glanced around incredulously. "You say these— shapes—are what the Ihlini have made?"

Duncan's horse stomped, scraping iron-shod hoof against cold black stone. The sudden sound echoed in the canyon. "You know the three gifts of the Cheysuli," he said quietly. "I thought you knew what the Ihlini claimed."

"I know they can make life out of death," I said sharply. "One Ihlini fashioned a lion out of a knife."

"There is that," Duncan agreed. "They have the power to alter the shapes of things that do not live." His hand swept out to indicate the rocks. "You have felt another of their gifts: the power to quicken age. With the touch of a hand, an Ihlini can make a man old, quickening the infirmities that come with years." I knew it too well, but said nothing. "There is the possession I have spoken of, when they take the mind and soul and keep it. And they can take the healing from a wound. There is also the art of illusion. What is, is not; what is not, seems to be. Those gifts, Carillon, and all shadings in between. That is a facet of Asar-Suti. The Seker, who lends his magic to those who will ask."

"But—all Ihlini have magic. Do they not?"

"All Ihlini have magic. But not all of them are Tynstar."

He looked around at the twisted trees and shapechanged rocks. "You see what is Tynstar's power, and how he passes it on. We near the Gate of Asar-Suti."

I looked at my men. The Homanans were white-faced and solemn, saying nothing. I did not doubt they were afraid—*I* was afraid—but neither would they give up. As for the Cheysuli, I had no need to ask. Their lives belonged to the gods whose power, I hoped, outweighed that of Tynstar *or* Asar-Suti, the Seker of the netherworld.

Duncan nudged his horse forward. "We must make camp for the night. The sun begins to set."

We rode on in loud silence, necks prickling against the raw sensation of power. It oozed out of the earth like so much seepage from a mudspring.

We camped at last behind the shoulder of a canyon wall that fell down from the darkening sky to shield us against the night wind. The earth's flesh was quite thin. Here and there the skeleton broke through, stone bones that glistened in the sunset with a damp, sweaty sheen. Tree roots coiled against the shallow soil like serpents seeking warmth. One of my Homanans, seeking wood for a fire, meant to hack off a few spindly, wind-wracked limbs with his heavy knife and pulled the whole tree out of the canyon wall. It was a small tree, but it underlined the transience of life near Valgaard.

We made a meal out of what we carried in our packs: dried meat, flat journey-bread loaves, a measure of sweet, dark sugar. And wine. We all had wine. The horses we fed on the grain we carried with us, since grazing was so light, and brought water from melting snow. But once our bellies were full, we had time to think of what we did.

I sat huddled in my heaviest cloak for too long a time. I could not rid myself of the ache in my bones or the knowledge that we all might die. And so, when I could do it inconspicuously, I got up and went away from the small encampment. I left the men to their stilted conversations and gambling; I went to find Duncan.

I saw him at last when I was ready to give up. He stood near the canyon wall staring into the dark distances. His very stillness made him invisible. It was only the shine of the moon against his earring that gave his presence away.

And so I went near, waited for acknowledgment, and saw how rigid his body was.

He had pulled on a cloak at last. It was dark, like my own, blending with the night. The earring glinted in his hair. "What does he do with her?" he asked. "What does he do *to* her?"

I had wondered the same myself. But I forced reassurance from my mouth. "She is strong, Duncan. Stronger than many men. I think Tynstar will meet his match in her."

"This is Valgaard." His voice was raw.

I swallowed. "She has the Old Blood."

He turned abruptly. His face was shadowed as he leaned back against the stone canyon wall, setting his spine against it. "Here, the Old Blood may be as nothing."

"You do not know that. Did Donal not get free? They were Ihlini, yet he took *lir*-shape before them. It may be that Alix will overcome them yet."

"Ru'shalla-tu." He said it without much hope. *May it be so.* He looked at me then, black-eyed in the moonlight, and I saw the fear in his eyes. But he said nothing more of Alix. Instead he squatted down, still leaning against the canyon wall, and pulled his cloak more tightly around his shoulders. "Do you wonder what has become of Tourmaline?" he asked. "What has become of Finn?"

"Every day," I answered readily. "And each day I regret what has happened."

"Would you change it, if Finn came to you and asked to take your *rujholla* as his *cheysula*?"

I found the nearest tree stump and perched upon it. Duncan waited for my answer, and at last I gave it. "I needed the alliance Rhodri would have offered, did I wed my sister to his son."

"He gave it to you anyway."

"*Lachlan* gave me aid. I got no alliance from Rhodri." I shrugged. "I do not doubt we will make one when all this is done, but for now the thing is not formal. What Lachlan did was between a mercenary and a harper, not a Mujhar and High Prince of Ellas. There are distinct differences between the two."

"Differences." His tone was very flat. "Aye. Like the differences between Cheysuli and Homanan."

I kicked away a piece of stone. "Do you regret that Donal must wed Aislinn? Cheysuli wed to Homanan?"

"I regret that Donal will know a life other than what I wish for him." Duncan was little more than a dark blot against the rock wall. "In the clan, he would be merely a warrior—unless they made him a clan-leader. It is—a simpler life than that which faces a prince. I would wish that for him. Not what you will give him."

"I have no choice. The gods—*your* gods—have given me none."

He was silent a moment. "Then we must assume there is a reason for what he will become."

I smiled, though it had only a little humor in it. "But you have an advantage, Duncan. You may see your son become a king. But *I* must die in order to give him the throne."

Duncan was silent a long moment. He merged into the blackness of the wall as the moon was lost to passing clouds. I could no longer see him, but I knew where he was by the sound of a hand scraping against the earth.

"You have changed," Duncan said at last. "I thought, at first, you had not—or very little. I see now I was wrong. Finn wrought well when he tempered the steel . . . but it is kingship that has honed the edge."

I huddled within my cloak. "As you say, kingship changes a man. I seem to have no choice."

"Necessity also changes," Duncan said quietly. "It has changed me. I am nearly forty now, old enough to know my place and recognize my *tahlmorra* without chafing, but each day, of late, I wonder what might have happened had it been otherwise." He shook his head. "We wonder. We ever wonder. The freedom to be without a *tahlmorra*." The moon was free again and I saw another headshake. "What would happen did I *keep* my son? The prophecy would be twisted. The Firstborn, who gave the words to us, would never live again. We would be the Cheysuli no longer." I saw the rueful smile. "Cheysuli: children of the gods. But we can be fractious children."

"Duncan—" I paused. "We will find her. And we will take her back from him."

Moonlight slanted full across his face. "Women are lost often enough," he said quietly. "In childbirth . . . accident . . . illness. A warrior may grieve in the privacy of

his pavilion, but he does not show his feelings to the clan.
It is not done. Such things are kept—private." His hand
was filled with pebbles. "But were Alix taken from me by
this demon, I would not care who knew of my grief." The
pebbles poured from his hand in steady, dwindling stream.
"I would be without her . . . and empty. . . ."

Near midday we came to the canyon that housed Valgaard. We rode out of a narrow defile into the canyon
proper and found ourselves hemmed in by the sheer stone
walls that stretched high over our heads. We rode single-
file, unable to go abreast, but as we went deeper into the
canyon the walls fell away until we were human pebbles in
a deep, rock-hard pocket.

"There," Duncan said, "do you see?"

I saw. Valgaard lay before us: an eagle on its aerie. The
fortress itself formed the third wall of the canyon, a pen-
dant to the torque. But I thought the fit too snug. I thought
the jewel too hard. No, not an eagle. A carrion bird, hov-
ering over its corpse.

We were neatly boxed. Escape lay behind us, Valgaard
before. I did not like the feeling.

"*Lodhi.*" Gryffth gasped. "I have never seen such a
thing."

Nor had I. Valgaard rose up out of the glassy black basalt
like a wave of solid ice, black and sharp, faceted like a
gemstone. There were towers and turrets, barbicans and
ramparts. It glittered, bright as glass, and smoke rose up
around it. I could smell the stink from where we stood.

"The Gate," Duncan said. "It lies within the fortress.
Valgaard is its sentinel."

"That is what causes the smoke?"

"The breath of the god," Duncan said. "Like fire, it
burns. I have heard the stories. There is blood within the
stone: hot, white blood. If it should touch you, you will die."

The canyon was clean of snow. Nothing marred its surface. It was smooth, shining basalt, lacking trees and grass.
We had come out of winter into summer, and I found I
preferred the cold.

"Asar-Suti," Duncan said. "The Seker himself." Very deliberately, he spat onto the ground.

"What are all those shapes?" Rowan asked. He meant

the large chunks of stone that lay about like so many dice tossed down. Black dice, uncarved, and scattered across the ground. They were large enough for a man to hide behind.

Or die under, if it landed cocked.

"An Ihlini bestiary," Duncan explained. "Their answer to the *lir.*"

We rode closer and I saw what he meant. Each deposit of stone had a form, if a man could call it that. The shapes were monstrous travesties of animals. Faces and limbs bore no resemblence to animals I had seen. It was a mockery of the gods, the *lir* defiled; an echo, perhaps, of their deity. Asar-Suti in stone. A god of many shapes. A god of grotesquerie.

I suppressed a shiver of intense distaste. This place was foulness incarnate. "We should beware an obvious approach."

Duncan, falling back to ride abreast, merely nodded. "It would be unexpected did we simply ride in like so many martyrs, but also foolish. I do not choose to die a fool. So we will find cover and wait, until we have a plan for getting in."

"Getting in *there?*" Rowan shook his head. "I do not see how."

"There is a way," Duncan told him. "There is always a way to get in. It is getting out that is difficult."

Uneasily, I agreed.

It was, at last, Gryffth who found the way in. I was astonished when he offered himself, for he might well be boiled alive in the blood of the god, but it seemed the only way. And so I agreed, but only after I heard his explanation.

We knelt, all of us, behind the black-frozen shapes, too distant for watchers to see us from the ramparts. The white, stinking smoke veiled us even more, so that we felt secure in our place of hiding. The stones were large enough to offer shade in sunlight as well. In the shadows it was cool.

Gryffth, kneeling beside me, pulled a ring from his belt-pouch. "My lord, this should do it. It marks me a royal courier. It will give me safe entrance."

"*Should,*" I said sharply. "It may not."

Gryffth grinned a little. His red hair was bright in the sunlight. "I think I will have no trouble. The High Prince has said, often enough, that I have the gift of a supple tongue. I will wind Tynstar around this finger." He made a rude gesture with his hand, and all the Homanans laughed. In the months since the Ellasian had joined my service, he had made many friends. He had wit and purpose, and a charming way as well.

Rowan's face was pensive. "When you face Tynstar, what will you say? The ring cannot speak for you."

"No, but it gets me inside. Once there, I will tell Tynstar the High King of Ellas has sent me. That he wishes to make an alliance."

"Rhodri would never do it." Rowan exclaimed. "Do you think *Tynstar* will believe you?"

"He may, he may not. It does not matter." Gryffth's freckled face was solemn, echoing Duncan's gravity. "I will tell him High Prince Cuinn, in sending men to the Mujhiar, has badly angered his father. That Rhodri wishes no alliance with Homana, but desires Ihlini aid. If nothing else, it will gain Tynstar's attention. He will likely host me the night, at least. And it is at night I will open the gate to let you in." His smile came, quick and warm. "Once in, you will either live or die. By then, it will not matter what Tynstar thinks of my tale."

"*You* may die." Rowan sounded angry.

Gryffth shrugged. "A man lives, a man dies. He does not choose his life. Lodhi will protect me."

Duncan smiled. "You could almost be Cheysuli."

I saw Gryffth thinking it over. Ellasian-bred, he hardly knew the Cheysuli. But he did not think them demons. And so I saw him decide the comment was a compliment. "My thanks, Duncan . . . though Lodhi might see it differently."

"You call him the All-Wise," Duncan returned. "He must be wise enough to know when I mean you well."

Gryffth, grinning, reached out and touched his arm. "For that, clan-leader, I will gladly do what I can to help you get her back."

Duncan clasped his arm. "Ellasian—*Cheysuli i'halla shansu.*" He smiled at Gryffth's frown of incomprehension. "May there be Cheysuli peace upon you."

Gryffth nodded. "Aye, my friend. And may you know the wisdom of Lodhi." He turned to me. "Does it please you, my lord, I will go in. And tonight, when I can, I will find a gate to open."

"How will we know?" Rowan asked. "We cannot go up so close . . . and you can hardly light a fire."

"I will send Cai to him," Duncan said. "My *lir* can see when Gryffth comes out and tell me which gate he unlocks."

Rowan sighed, rubbing wearily at his brow. "It all seems such a risk . . ."

"Risk, aye," I agreed, "but more than worth the trying."

Gryffth stood up. "I will go in, my lord. I will do what I can do."

I rose as he did and clasped his arm. "Good fortune, Gryffth. May Lodhi guard you well."

He untethered his horse and mounted, reining it around. He glanced down at Rowan, who had become a boon companion, and grinned. "Do not fret, *alvi*. This is what I choose."

I watched Gryffth ride away, heading toward the fortress. The smoke hung over it like a miasma, cloaking the stone in haze. The breath of the god was foul.

Chapter Eight

The moon, hanging over our heads against the blackness of the sky, lent an eerie ambience to the canyon. The smoke clogged our noses. It rose up in stinking clouds, warming our flesh against our will. Shadows crept out from the huge stone shapes and swallowed us all, clutching with mouths and claws. My Homanans muttered of demons and Ihlini sorcerers; I thought they were one and the same.

Duncan, seated near me, shed his cloak and rose. "Cai says Gryffth has come out of the hall. He is in the inner bailey. We should go."

We left the horses tethered and went on by foot. Cloaks hid our swords and knives from the moonlight. Our boots scraped against the glossy basalt, scattering ash and powdered stone. As we drew nearer, using the shapechanged stones to hide us, the ground warmed beneath our feet. The smoke hissed and whistled as it came out of the earth, rising toward the moon.

We worked our way up to the walls that glistened in the moonlight. They were higher even than the walls of Homana-Mujhar, as if Tynstar meant to mock me. At each of the corners and midway along the walls stood a tower, a huge round tower bulging out of the dense basalt, spiked with crenelations and crockets and manned, no doubt, by Ihlini minions. The place stank of sorcery.

The nearest gate was small. I thought it likely it opened into a smaller bailey. We had slipped around the front of the fortress walls and came in from the side, eschewing the main barbican gate that would swallow us up like so many helpless children. But the side gate opened, only a crack, and I saw Gryffth's face in the slit between wall and dark wood.

One hand gestured us forward. We moved silently, saying

nothing, holding scabbards to keep them quiet. Gryffth, as I reached him in the gate, pushed it open wider. "Tynstar is not here," he whispered, knowing what it would mean to me. "Come you in now, and you may avoid the worst of it."

One by one we crept in through the gate. I saw the shadows of winged *lir* pass overhead. We had also wolves and foxes and mountain cats, slipping through the gate, but I wondered if they would fight. Finn had said the gods' own law kept the *lir* from attacking Ihlini.

Gryffth shut the gate behind us, and I saw the two bodies lying against the wall. I looked at him; he said nothing. But I was thankful nonetheless. Like Lachlan, he served me as if born to it, willing even to slay others.

We were in a smaller bailey, away from the main one, and Valgaard lay before us. The halls and side rooms bulged out from a central mass of stone. But we seemed to be through the worst of it.

We started across the bailey, across the open spaces, though we tried to stay to the shadows. Swords were drawn now, glinting in the moonlight, and I heard the soughing of feet against stone. Out of the bailey toward an inner ward while the walls reared up around us; how long would our safety last?

Not long. Even as Gryffth led us through to the inner ward I heard the hissing and saw a streamer of flame as it shot up into the air from one of the towers. It broke over our heads, showering us with a violet glare, and I knew it would blast the shadows into the white-hot glare of the sun. No more hiding in the darkness.

"Scatter!" I shouted, heading for the hall.

My sword was in my hand. I heard the step beside me and swung around, seeing foe, not friend, with his hand raised to draw a rune. Quickly I leveled my blade and took him in the throat. He fell in a geyser of blood.

Rowan was at my back, Gryffth at his. We went into the hall in a triangular formation, swords raised and ready. The Cheysuli had gone, slipping into the myriad corridors, but I could hear the Homanans fighting. Without Tynstar's presence we stood our greatest chance, but the battle would still be difficult. I had no more time left to lose.

"Hold them!" I shouted as four men advanced with

swords and knives. I expected sorcery and they came at us
with steel.

Even as I brought up my sword I felt the twinge shoot
through both hands. In all my practice with Cormac I had
not been able to shed the pain of my swollen fingers. As
yet they could still hold a hilt, but the strength I had taken
for granted was gone. I had to rely more on quickness of
body than my skill in elaborate parries. I was little more
than a man of average skill now, because of Tynstar.

Gryffth caught a knife from a hidden sheath and sent it
flying across the hall. It took one Ihlini flush in the chest
and removed him from the fight. Three to three now, but
even as I marked their places I saw Rowan take another
with his sword. Myself, for the moment, they ignored. And
so, knowing my sword skill was diminished, I decided to
go on without it. Did the Ihlini want me, they could come
for me. Otherwise I would avoid them altogether.

"Hold them," I said briefly, and ran into the nearest
corridor. The stone floor was irregular, all of a slant, this
way and that, as if to make it difficult for anyone to run
through it. There were few torches in brackets along the
walls; I sensed this portion of the fortress was only rarely
used. Or else the Ihlini took the light with them when
they walked.

The sounds of fighting fell away behind me, echoing
dimly in the tunnel-like corridor. I went on, hearing the
scrape of sole against stone, and waited for the attack that
would surely come.

I went deeper into the fortress, surrounded by black basalt that glistened in the torchlight. The walls seemed to
swallow the light, so that my sword blade turned black to
match the ruby, and I felt my eyes strain to see where I was
going. The few torches guttered and hissed in the shadows,
offering little illumination; all it wanted was Tynstar to
come drifting out of the darkness, and my courage would
be undone.

I heard the grate of stone on stone and swung around,
anticipating my nightmare. But the man who stepped out
of the recess in the wall was a stranger to me. His eyes were
blank, haunted things. He seemed to be missing his soul.

Silently, he came at me. His sword was a blur of steel,
flashing in the torchlight, and I jumped back to avoid the

slash that hissed beside my head. My own blade went up to strike his down. They caught briefly, then disengaged as we jerked away. I could feel the strain in my hands, and yet I dared not lose my grip.

Again he came at me. I skipped back, then leaped aside, and the sword tip grated on stone. And yet even as I moved to intercept, the Ihlini's blade flashed sideways to stop my lunge and twist my sword from my hands. It was not a difficult feat. And so my weapon clanged against the black stone floor and I felt the hot pain in my knuckles flare up to pierce my soul.

The blade came at me again, thrusting for my belly. I sucked back, avoiding the tip, and felt the edge slice through leather and linen to cut along my ribs. Not deeply, scraping against one bone, but it was enough to make me think.

I jumped then, straight upward from the floor, grabbing the nearest torch and dragging it from its brackets. Even as the Ihlini came at me again I had it, whirling to thrust it into his face. The flame roared.

The sorcerer screamed and dropped his sword, hands clawing at his face. He invoked Asar-Suti over and over again, gibbering in his pain, until he slumped down onto his knees. I stepped back as I saw one hand come up to make an intricate motion.

"Seker, Seker. . . ." He chanted, rocking on his knees while his burned face glistened in the torchlight. "Seker, Seker. . . ."

The torch was still in my right hand. As the Ihlini invoked his god and drew his rune in the air, the flame flowed down over the iron to caress my hand with pain.

I dropped the torch at once, tossing it toward the wall while my knuckles screamed with pain. The flame splashed against the stone and ran down, flooding the floor of the corridor. As the Ihlini continued to chant, his hands still clasped to his face, the fire crept toward my boots.

I stepped back at once, retreating with little aplomb. My sword, still lying on the stone, was in imminent danger of being swallowed. The flame poured across the floor like water, heading for my boots.

"Seker, Seker—make him *burn!*"

But he had made a deadly mistake. No doubt he intended only his enemy to burn, but he had not been clearly distinct. He himself still knelt on the floor, and as the stone caught fire from the river of ensorcelled flame so did he. It ran up his legs and enveloped his body in fire. I kicked out swiftly and shoved the sword aside with one boot, then ran after it even as the river of fire followed. me. I left the living pyre in the corridor, scooped up my sword and ran.

It was then I heard the shout. Alix's voice. The tone was one of fear and desperation, but it held a note of rage as well. And then I heard the scuffle and the cry.

I ran. I rounded the corner and brought up my sword, prepared to spit someone upon it, but I saw there was no need. The Ihlini lay on the ground, face down, as the blood ran from his body, and Alix was kneeling to take his knife. She already had his sword.

She spun around, rising at once into a crouch. The knife dropped from her hand at once as she took a two-handed grip on the sword. And then she saw me clearly and the sword fell out of her hand.

I grinned. "Well met, Alix."

She was so pale I thought she might faint where she stood, but she did not. Her eyes were huge in a bruised and too-thin face. Her hair hung in a single tangled braid and she wore a bedrobe stained with blood. It was not her own, I knew, but from the man she had slain.

I had forgotten the gray in my hair and the lines in my face; the altered way I had of standing and moving. I had forgotten what Tynstar had done. But when I saw the horror in Alix's eyes I recalled it all too well. It brought home the pain again.

I put out one hand, ignoring the swollen knuckles. "Do you come?"

Briefly, she looked down at the dead Ihlini. Then she bent and scooped up the knife, moving to my side. Her free hand was cool in my own, and I felt the trembling in it. For a moment we stood there, soiled with blood and grime and in the stink of our own fear, and then we forgot our weapons and set arms around each other for a desperate moment.

"Duncan?" she asked at last, when I let her free of my arms.

"He is here—do not fret. But how did you trick the Ihlini?"

She glanced back briefly at the dead man. "He was foolish enough to unlock my door. To take me somewhere, he said. He did not expect me to protest, but I did. I took up a torch and burned his knife-hand with it."

I put out my own knife-hand and touched her hollowed cheek. "How do you fare, Alix?"

Briefly there was withdrawal in her eyes. "I will tell you another time. Come this way with me." She caught up the hem of her bedrobe and went on, still gripping the knife in one hand.

We hastened through the corridors and into a spiral stair. Alix went first and I followed, falling behind as we climbed. We went up and up and I grimaced, feeling the strain in my knees. My thighs burned with the effort, and my breath ran short. But at last she pushed open a narrow door that I had to duck to get under, and we stepped out onto the ramparts of the fortress.

Alix pointed. "That tower is a part of Tynstar's private chambers. There is a stairway down. If we get there, we can go down unaccosted, then slip into the wards."

I caught her hand and we ran, heading for the tower. I heard the sounds of fighting elsewhere, but I knew we were badly outnumbered. And then we rounded the tower, looking for the door, and I stopped dead. Out on the wall walkway stood a familiar figure—*"Duncan!"*

He spun around like an animal at bay. His eyes were startled and fearful. "No!" he shouted.

Alix jerked free of my hand and started to run toward him, calling out his name, but something in Ducan's face made me reach out and catch her arm. "Alix—wait you—"

The moonlight was full on Duncan's face. I could see the heaving of his chest as sweat ran down his bare arms. His hair was wet with it. "Go from here—*now* . . . Alix—do not tarry!"

Alix tried again to free herself from my hand but I held her tightly. "Duncan—what are you saying? Do you think I will listen to that—?" Briefly she twisted her head to glare at me. "Let me *go*—"

Duncan took a step toward us, then stopped. His face turned up toward the black night sky. Then he glanced back at me, briefly, and put out a hand toward Alix. "Take her, Carillon. Get her free of this place—" He sucked in a deep, wavering breath and seemed almost to fall on his feet. I saw then, in the moonlight, the blood running down his left arm. "Do you hear me? Go now, before—"

What he intended to say was never heard in the thunderclap that broke over our heads. I recoiled, flattening against the tower, and dragged Alix with me. With the explosion of sound came a burst of light so blinding it painted everything stark white and stole our vision away.

"Do I have you all, now?" came Tynstar's beguiling voice.

I saw him then, moving along the wall from another tower. Duncan was between the Ihlini and us. He put out a hand in my direction and cast a final glance at Alix. "Get her *free*, Carillon! Was it not what we came to do?"

I ran then, dragging her with me, and took her into the tower. I ignored her protests. For once, I would do what Duncan wanted without asking foolish questions.

I did not dare take a horse for Alix from our mounts for fear of leaving another man afoot. So I swung up onto my own, dragged her up behind me and wheeled the horse about in the shadow of shapechanged stone.

Alix's arms locked around my waist. "Carillon—wait you. You cannot leave him behind."

I clapped spurs to my horse and urged him away, sending him from the smokey, stinking haze that clung to black-clad Valgaard. *Away* I sent him, toward the defile and freedom.

"Carillon—"

"I trust to his wits and his will," I shouted over the clattering hooves. "Do *you* not?"

She pressed herself against me as the horse slipped and slid on basalt. "I would rather stay and help—"

"There." I interrupted. "Do you see? *That* is why we run—"

The nearest stone shape reared up just then, shaking itself free of the ground. It lurched toward our mount, reaching out its hands. No, not hands: paws. And claws of glassy basalt.

Alix cried out and pressed herself against me. I reined in my horse with a single hand and jerked our mount aside, shouting for Alix to duck. We threw ourselves flat, avoiding the slashing claws, and the sword I held outthrust scraped against the beast. Sparks flew from the blade on stone: steel against a whetstone, screeching as it spun.

We rode past at a scrambling run as the horse tried to keep his balance. Chips of stone flew up to cut our faces as iron-shod hooves dug deeply into basalt. I saw then that all the stone shapes were moving, grating across the ground. They had none of the speed or supple grace of fleshborn animals, but they were ghastly in their promise. Most were hardly recognizable, being rough-cut and sharply faceted, but I saw the gaping mouths and knew they could crush us easily.

Yet another lurched into our path. I reined in the horse at once and sat him on his haunches, knowing he scraped his hocks against the cruel stone. Alix cried out and snatched at my doublet, holding herself on with effort. I spurred relentlessly, driving the horse to his feet, and saw the lowering paws.

A bear; not a bear. Its shape was indistinct. It lumbered after us, hackles rising on its huge spinal hump, ungainly on glassy legs, and yet I knew it might prevail. The horse was failing under us.

Smoke shot up beside us: the breath of the god himself. It splattered me full in the face and I felt the blood of the god. It burned, how it burned, as it ate into my beard. But I dared not put a hand to my face or I would lose control of the horse. And I refused to lose my sword.

The smoke shot up with a screeching hiss, venting its wrath against us. It stank with the foul odor of corruption. The horse leaped aside, nearly shedding us both; I heard Alix's gasp of surprise. She slid to one side and caught at my arm, dragging herself back on the slippery rump. I heard again the scream of the smoke as it vomited out of the earth.

The canyon grew narrow and clogged with stone. The defile beckoned us on. We had only to get through it and we would be free of the beasts. But getting to it would be next to impossible with the failing horse beneath us.

Another vent opened before us. The horse ran directly into it and screamed as the heat bit into his belly. He twisted and humped, throwing head between knees, and then shed us easily enough. But I did not complain, even as I crashed against the stone, for the horse was caught by the bear.

I pushed myself up to my feet, aware of the pain in my bones. I still had my sword and two feet and I did not intend to remain. I went to Alix as she sat up from her fall, grabbed her arm and dragged her up from the stone.

"Run," I said, and we did.

We dodged the stone beasts and jumped over the smoke, threading our way as we ran. We gasped and choked, coughing against the stench. But we reached the defile and ran through, knowing it too narrow to give exit to the beasts. We left behind the smoke and heat and went into the world again.

The ground was laced with snow. Twisted trees hung off the walls and sent roots across the earth, seeking what strength they could find in the meager soil. Behind us reared the canyon with its cache of beasts and smoke.

Alix limped beside me, still clinging to my hand. She was barefoot; I did not doubt it hurt. Her bedrobe was torn and burned away in places. But she went on, uncomplaining, and I put away my sword.

I took her to a screen of wind-wracked trees that huddled by a rib of canyon wall. There we could hide and catch our breath, waiting for the others. I found a broken stump and sat down upon it stiffly, hissing against the pain. My aching joints had been badly used and I felt at least a hundred. No more was I able to perform the deeds of a younger man, for all I was twenty-five. The body was twenty years older.

Alix stood next to me. Her hand was on my head, smoothing my graying hair. "I am so sorry, Carillon. But Tynstar has touched us all."

I looked up at her in the moonlight. "Did he harm you?"

She shrugged. "What Tynstar did is done. I will not speak about it."

"Alix—" But she placed one hand across my mouth and bid me to be silent. After a moment she squatted down and linked both hands around my arm.

"My thanks," she said softly. "*Leijhana tu'sai.* What you have done for me—and what you have *lost* for me—is more than I deserve."

I summoned a weary smile. "Your son will be Prince of Homana. Surely his *jehana* has meaning to us both."

"You did not do this for Donal."

I sighed. "No. I did it for you, for myself . . . and for Duncan. Perhaps especially for Duncan." I set my swollen hand to her head and tousled her tangled hair. "He needs you, Alix. More than I ever thought possible."

She did not answer. We sat silently, close together, and waited for the others.

One by one the warriors returned, on foot and mounted on horseback. Some came in *lir*-shape, loping or flying as they came through the trees; we were not so close that the magic could be thwarted. But I saw, when they had gathered, that at least four had been left behind. A high toll, for the Cheysuli. It made it all seem worse.

Rowan came finally at dawn. He and Gryffth were mounted on a single horse, riding double from the defile. Blood had spilled from a head wound to stain Rowan's leathers dark, but he seemed well enough, if weary. He prodded Gryffth with an elbow and I saw how the Ellasian drooped against Rowan's back. I got up, feeling the pop in both knees, and reached out to steady Gryffth's dismount. He had a wound in one shoulder and a slice along one forearm, but both had been bound.

Rowan got down unsteadily, shutting his eyes as he put one hand to his head. Alix knelt beside him as he sat and parted his hair to see the wound. He swallowed and winced as her fingers found the swelling.

"This is not from a sword," she said in consternation.

"No. His sword broke. So he grabbed down the torch and came at me. I ducked the flame but not the iron." He winced again. "Let it be. It will heal on its own."

Alix moved away from him. For a moment she looked at the others, all wounded in her rescue, and I saw how it weighted her down. Of us all, I was the only Homanan. The others, save Gryffth, were all Cheysuli.

The Ellasian leaned against a boulder, one arm pressed against his ribs. His freckled face, in the pale sunlight of dawn, was ashen, streaked with blood and grime, but life remained in his bright green eyes. He pushed a hand through his hair and made it stand up in spikes. "My thanks to the All-Father," he said wearily. "Most of us got free, and the lady brought out as we meant."

"And for that, *my* thanks," said Duncan from the ridge, and Alix spun around.

He stepped down and caught her in his arms, crushing her against his chest. His cheek pressed into her tangled hair and I saw the pallor of his face. Blood still ran from the wound in his left arm. I saw how it stained his leathers and now her robe. But neither seemed to care.

I pushed myself up from my tree stump. I moved stiffly, cursing myself for my slowness, and then stood still, giving them their reunion. It was the least I could do.

"I am well," Duncan answered her whispered question. "I am not much hurt. Do not fear for me." One hand wove itself into her loosened braid. "What of you? What has he done to you?"

Alix, still pressed against his body, shook her head. I could not see her face, but I could see his. His exhaustion was manifest. Like us all, he was bloodstained and filthy and stinking of the breath of the netherworld. Like us all, he was hardly capable of standing.

But there was something more in his eyes. The knowledge of terrible loss.

And I knew.

Duncan put Alix out of his arms and sat her down on the nearest stump, the one I had vacated. And then, without a word, he stripped the gold from his arms and set it into her lap. With deft fingers he unhooked the earring and pulled it from his lobe. He was naked without his gold. Still clothed in leather, he was naked without the gold.

And a dead man without his *lir*.

He set the earring into her hand. *"Tahlmorra lujhalla mei wiccan, cheysu."*

She stood up with a cry and the gold tumbled from lap and hands. "Duncan—*no*—"

"Aye," he said gently, "Tynstar has slain my *lir*."

Slowly, tentatively, trembling, she put out her hands to touch him. Gently at first, and then with possessive demand. I saw how dark her fingers were against the flesh of his arms that had never known the sun, kept from it by the *lir*-bands for nearly all of his life. I saw how she shut her hands upon that flesh as if it would make him stay.

"I am empty," he said. "Soulless and unwhole. I cannot live this way."

The fingers tightened on his arms. "Do you go," she said intently, "do you leave me, Duncan . . . *I* will be as empty. *I* will be unwhole."

"*Shansu,*" he said, "I have no choice. It is the price of the *lir*-bond."

"Do you think I will let you go?" she demanded. "Do you think I will stand meekly by while you turn your back on me? Do you think I will do *nothing?*"

"No. And that is why I will do *this*—" He caught her before she could move and cradled her head in his hands. "*Cheysula,* I have loved you well. And for that I will lessen your grief—"

"No!" She tried to pull out of his arms, but he held her too well. "Duncan—" she said, "—do not—"

As she sagged he caught her and lifted her up. For a moment he held her close, eyes shut in a pale, gaunt face, and then he looked at me. "You must take her to safety. Take her to Homana-Mujhar." He tried to steady his voice and failed. "She will sleep for a long time. Do not worry if, when she wakes, she seems to have forgotten. It will come back. She will recall it all, and I do not doubt she will grieve deeply then. But for now . . . for us both . . . this ending is the best."

I tried to swallow the cramp in my throat. "What of Tynstar?"

"Alive," Duncan said bleakly. "Once he had struck down Cai—I had nothing left but pain and helplessness." He looked at Alix's face again as she slept in his naked arms. And then he brought her to me and set her into mine. "Love her well, my lord Mujhar. Spare her what pain you can."

I saw the tears in his eyes as he moved back. Then one foot struck an armband on the ground, sending it clinking against the other, and he stopped short. He touched one naked arm as if he could not believe its loss, and then he walked away.

Chapter Nine

Donal's young face was pinched and pale. He sat quietly on a stool, listening to what I said, but I doubt he really heard me. His mind had gone elsewhere, choosing its own path; I did not blame him. I had told him his father was dead.

He stared hard at the floor. His hands were in his lap. They gripped one another as if they could not bear to be apart. The skin of his knuckles was white.

"Jehana," he said. That only.

"Your mother is well. She—sleeps. Your father gave her that."

He nodded once. No more. He seemed to understand. And then his right hand rose to touch his left arm, to finger the heavy gold. I could see it in his mind: Cheysuli, and bound by the *lir*. As much as his father had been.

Donal looked up at me. His face was starkly remote. He said one word: *"Tahlmorra."*

He was an eight-year-old boy. At eight, I could not have withstood the pain. I would have wept, cried out, even screamed with the grief. Donal did not. He was Cheysuli, and he knew the price of the *lir*-bond.

I had thought, perhaps, to hold him. To ease what pain I could. To tell him how Duncan had gotten his mother free, to illustrate the worth of the risk undertaken. I had thought also to assuage his guilt and grief by sharing my own with him. But, looking at him, I saw there was no need. His maturity mocked my own.

Alien, I thought, *so alien. Will Homana accept you?*

I lifted Alix down from her horse. She was light in my arms, too light; her face was ashen-colored. She had come home at last to Duncan's pavilion—six weeks after his death—and I knew she could not face it.

I said nothing, I simply held her. She stared at the slate-colored pavilion with its gold-painted hawk and recalled the life they had shared. She forgot even Donal, who slid slowly off his horse and looked to me for reassurance.

"Go in," I told him. "It is yours as much as his."

Donal put out a hand and touched the doorflap. And then he went inside.

"Carillon," she said. No more. There was no need. All the grief was in her voice.

I put out my arms and pulled her against my chest. With one hand I smoothed the heavy hair. "Now do you see? This is not the place for you. I would have spoken earlier, but I knew it would do no good. You had to see for yourself."

Her arms were locked around me. Her shoulders shook with the tears.

"Come back with me," I said. "Come back to Homana-Mujhar. Your place is there now, with me." I rocked her gently in my arms. "Alix—I want you to stay with me."

Her face turned up to mine. "I cannot."

"Do not fret because of Electra. She will not live forever—when she is dead I will wed you. I will make you Queen of Homana. Until then . . . you will have to content yourself with being merely a princess." I smiled. "You are. You are my cousin. There is a rank that comes with that."

Slowly she shook her head. "I cannot."

I smoothed back the hair from her face. "All those years ago—seven? eight?—I was a fool. I lived in arrogance. I saw what I was told to see by an uncle I abhorred. But now I am somewhat older—older, even than *that*—" I smiled a little, thinking of my graying beard and aching bones—"somewhat wiser, and certainly less inclined to heed such things as rank and custom. I wanted you then, I want you now—say you will come with me."

"I owe Duncan more than that."

"You do not owe him personal solitude. Alix—wait you—" I tightened my arms as she tried to pull away. "I know how badly you hurt. I know how badly it bleeds. I know how deeply the pain has cut you. But I think he would not be surprised did we make a match of it." I recalled his final words to me and knew he expected it. "Alix—I will not press you. I will give you what time you need. But do not deny me this. Not after all these years."

"Time does not matter." She stood stiffly in my arms. "As for the years—they have passed. It is done, Carillon. I cannot be your *meijha* and I cannot be your wife."

"Alix—"

"By the gods!" she cried. "I carry Tynstar's child!"

I let go of her at once and saw the horror in her eyes. "Tynstar did *that* to you—"

"He did not beat me." Her voice was steady. "He did not harm me. He did not *force* me." Her eyes shut for a moment. "He simply took my will away and got a child upon me."

I thought of Electra, banished to the Crystal Isle. Electra, who had lost the sorcerer's child. An heir. Not to me or to my title, but to all of Tynstar's might. He had lost it, and now he had another.

I could not move. I wanted to put out my hands and touch her, to tell her I did not care, but she knew me better than that. I could not move. I could only think of the Ihlini and his bastard in her belly.

Alix turned from me. She walked slowly to the pavilion. She put out one hand and drew back the doorflap, though she did not look inside. "Do you come in? Or do you go back?"

I shut my eyes a moment, still aching with the knowledge. Again, I lost her. But this time not to Duncan. Not even to Duncan's memory. That I might expect.

But not this. Not losing her to *Tynstar*. To a bastard Ihlini child!

By all the gods, it hurt. It hurt like a knife in my loins. I wanted to vomit the pain.

And then I thought of hers.

I let out my breath. Looking at her, I could see it hurt her worse. And I would not increase the pain by swearing useless vows of vengeance. There was already that between Tynstar and me; one day, we would end it.

I went to her. I took the doorflap out of her hands and motioned her inside. And then we both turned to go in and I saw Finn beside the fire.

The light was stark on his face. I saw again the livid scar

that marred cheek and jaw; the silver in his hair. Then he rose and I saw he had grown thin. The gold seemed heavier on his arms.

"*Meijha,*" he said, "I am sorry. But a *tahlmorra* cannot be refused. Not by an honorable man. And my *rujho* was ever that."

Alix stood very still but her breath was loud in the tent. "You *knew*—?"

"I knew he would die. So did he. Not how. Not when. Not the name of the man who would cause it. Merely that it would happen." He paused. "*Meijhana,* I am sorry. I would give him back to you, could I do it."

She moved to him. I saw the hesitation in her steps. I saw how he put his arms around her and set his scarred cheek against her hair. I saw her grief reflected in his face.

"When a *lir* is lost," he said, "the others know at once. Storr told me . . . but I could come no sooner. There was a thing I had to do."

I was wrung out with all the emotions. I needed to sit down. But I did not. I stood there, waiting, and saw Donal in the shadows. He sat between two wolves: one a ruddy young male, the other older, wiser, amber-eyed Storr.

Alix pulled out of Finn's arms but she did not move away. I saw how one of his hands lingered in her hair, as if he could not let it go. An odd possessiveness, in view of his actions with Torry. But then I could not blame him; Alix needed comfort. From Finn, it would undoubtedly be best. He was her brother, but also Duncan's. The bloodlink was closer than that which cousins shared.

I sighed. "Electra has been banished. She lives on the Crystal Isle. There is no question about her complicity in Tynstar's attempt to slay me. Did you wish it—you could take up your place again."

He did not smile. "That time is done. A blood-oath, once broken, is never healed. I come home, aye, to live in the Keep again—but nothing more than that. My place is here, now. They have named me Cheysuli clan-leader."

Alix looked at him sharply. "You? In Duncan's place?" She caught her breath, then went on. "I thought such things were not for you."

"Such things were for my *rujho,*" he agreed, his gravity an ironic measure of Duncan's, "but things change. People change. Torry has made me different." He shrugged. "I have—learned a little peace." He used the Homanan word. I liked *shansu* better.

"I am sorry," I said, "for the time you lost. I should never have sent you away."

He shook his head. "You had no choice. I saw that, when Torry made me. I do not blame you for it. You let her go with me. You might have made her stay."

"So you could take her from me?" I shook my head. "No. I knew the folly in trying to stop you."

"You should have tried," he said. "You should have kept her by you. You should have wed her to the Ellasian prince . . . because then she would still be alive."

I felt the air go out of my chest. The pavilion spun around me. The fire cairn was merely a blot of light inside my skull. "Torry is—*dead?*"

"Aye. Two days before Duncan lost his *lir*. It was why I could come no sooner."

"Finn," Alix said, "oh, Finn—*no*—"

"Aye," he said roughly, and I saw the new pain in his eyes. It mirrored that in my own.

I turned to go out. I could not stay. I could not bear to see him, knowing how she had loved him. I could not bear the grief. I had to deal with it alone.

And then I heard the baby cry, and the sound cut through me like a knife.

Finn let go of Alix. He turned and pulled the tapestry aside. I saw him kneel down and gather a bundle from the pallet. He was gentle. More gentle than I had ever seen him. Incongruous, in him. But it seemed to fit him well, once I got over the shock.

He brought the bundle to us and pulled away the wrappings from a face. "Her name is Meghan," he said. "She is four months old . . . and hungry. Torry—could not feed her, so I became a thief." Briefly he smiled. "The cows were not always willing to be milked."

Meghan continued to cry. Finn frowned and shifted her in his arms, trying to settle her more comfortably, but it was Alix who intervened. She took the baby from his arms and sent Donal to find a woman with an infant. She cast a glance back at Finn before she followed Donal out. "No more the milk-thief, *rujho*. I will save your pride by finding her a wetnurse."

I saw a shadow of his familiar grin as she slipped outside the pavilion. It took the hardness from his face and lessened the pain in his eyes. I saw it now, where I had not before. He had lost more than a brother.

And I had lost a sister. "Gods," I said, "what happened? How did Torry die? Why . . . *why?*"

The smile dropped away. Finn sat down slowly and motioned me down as well. After ten months, too long a time, we shared company again. "She was not bred for privation," he said. "She had pride and strength and determination, but she was not bred for privation. And carrying a child—" He shook his head. "I saw she was ill some three months after we left Homana-Mujhar. She claimed it was nothing; a fever breeding women sometimes get. I thought perhaps it was; how was I to know differently? I did not expect her to lie." He threaded one hand through his hair and stripped it from his face. He was gaunt, too thin; privation agreed with him no more than it had with her.

"Say on." I said hollowly.

"When I saw she got no better, I took her to a village. I thought she needed the companionship of women as well as a shelter better than the rude pavilion I provided. But— they would not have me. They called me shapechanger. They called me demon. They called her whore and the child demon's-spawn. Sorcerer's get." The anger was in his eyes and I saw the beast again, if only for a moment. But I also saw the guilt he had placed upon himself. "Shaine is dead and the *qu'mahlin* ended . . . but many prefer to observe it. And so she bore Meghan in what shelter I could provide, and weakened each day thereafter." He shut his eyes. "The gods would not hear my petition, even when I offered myself. So I gave her Cheysuli passing when she was dead, and brought her daughter home."

I thought of Torry, weak and ill. I thought of Torry bearing the child. I thought of the Homanans who had cursed her because of Finn. Because of Shaine's *qu'mahlin*. And I thought how helpless a king I was to stop my uncle's purge.

"I am sorry, Carillon," Finn said. "I did not mean you to lose her twice."

"Blame Shaine," I said wearily. "My uncle slew my sis-

ter." I looked at him across the fire. "Do you mean to keep
Meghan here?"

"This is her home," he repeated. "Where else would
Meghan live?"

"At Homana-Mujhar," I said. "She is a princess of
Homana."

He stared at me. "Have you learned nothing? Are you
still chained by such things as *rank?* By the gods, Carillon,
I thought by now you might have learned—"

"I have," I said. "I have. I do not mean to take her. I
merely wanted you to think. You have admitted Torry died
because the privation was too hard. Do you give the same
life to your daughter?"

"I give her a Keep," he said softly. "I give her what her
blood demands: the heritage of a Cheysuli."

I smiled. "Who speaks now of rank? You have ever believed yourself better than a Homanan."

He shrugged. "We are as the gods have made us."

I laughed. I pushed to my feet and popped my knees,
trying to ease my joints. The ride had tried my strength.
Finn rose as well, saying nothing. He merely waited. "Privation has rendered you less than what you should be," I said
gruffly. "Have Alix put flesh on your bones. You look older
the way you are."

His black brows rose. "Who speaks of age should look
in the silver plate."

"I have," I said, "and turned it to the wall." I grinned
and put out my arm, clasping his again. "Tend Meghan
well, and bring her to me often. She has other blood besides
the shapechanger taint, and I would have her know it."

Finn's grip was firm. "I doubt not *your* daughter will
need a companion. As for the Mujhar of Homana, he requires no single liege man. He has all the Cheysuli clans
to render him aid when he needs it."

"Nonetheless," I said, "I would have you take the knife
back." I slipped it from the sheath. The gold hilt gleamed
softly in the light from the fire cairn: rampant Homanan
lion and a blade of purest steel.

I thought he would not take it. Another was in his sheath,
one of Cheysuli craftsmanship. But he put out his hand and
accepted it, though there was no blood-oath to accompany
the acceptance.

"Ja'hai-na," he said quietly.

I went silently out of the tent.

My horse still waited. I took up the reins but did not mount at once. I thought of Alix, tending to Meghan, and the child within her belly. She would need Finn. She would need Meghan. She would need all the strength of the Cheysuli when Tynstar's child was born. And I knew she would have it in abundance.

I waited a moment, aware of something familiar. I could not put name to what it was, and then suddenly I knew. It was a flute, a sweet-toned Cheysuli pipe. The melody was quite simple, and yet I knew it well. The last time I had heard it, it had been upon a harp, with a master's hands upon the strings. Lachlan's hands, and the song *The Song of Homana.* And now it had come to the Keep.

I grinned. Then I laughed. I mounted my horse and turned him, ready to go at last, but Donal was in my way. He put up his hand and touched the stallion's nose as I reined him to a halt. Lorn sat at his left side.

"Cousin," Donal said, "may I come?"

"I go back to Homana-Mujhar."

"Jehana has said I may go." He grinned a grin I had seen before.

I leaned down and stretched out my hand, swinging him up as he jumped. He settled behind the saddle. "Hold on," I said, "the royal mount may throw us."

Donal leaned forward against my back. "Make him *try.*"

I laughed. "Would you like to see me tumble?"

"You would not. You are the Mujhar of Homana."

"The horse does not know titles. He knows only your substantial weight." I kneed the stallion out and felt the arching of his back. But after a moment he settled.

"Do you see?" Donal asked, as the wolf trotted beside the horse. I looked for Taj and found him, a dot against the sky.

"I see," I admitted. "Shall we gallop?"

"Aye!" he agreed, and we did.

THE END

Kinspirit

A Cheysuli Short Story

The mists of dawn brought the aftermath of battle: the screams, moans, and sobbing of the injured; the screeching of carrion birds settling among dead and living; the curses of the captured. But to the boy crawling belly-down over the lip of the hillock, the silence of the dead was worse.

His homespun woolen tunic and trews had once been dyed maple-gold. Now the cloth, redyed in blood, was stained mahogany-brown. Thank the gods none of the blood was his; he had managed to avoid swords, knives, spears, and the deadly accuracy of Atvian arrows.

He curled stiffened fingers into the earth, absently marking its unpleasant dampness beneath his body; thinking it was dew and mist without realizing it was the legacy of the dead. He stretched himself out in wet, crushed grass and slowly lowered chin to hands.

As far as he could see lay bodies: some moving, some not; some whole, some in pieces. He gagged and retched, but he was dry, belly cramping on emptiness. His eyes, itchy and burning from the smoke and stench, ached with unshed tears. He lay belly-down on the bloodied soil of Homana and realized, for the first time, what war really involved.

And realized, for the first time, his homeland had lost.

A hand caught him by the tunic behind his neck and jerked him up from the ground. He wobbled unsteadily, shocked by his capture and the unexpected weakness of his knees. It was all he could do to make himself stand erect.

It was all he could do to look his captor in the eye.

A man. Brown-haired, brown-eyed, brown-faced; he was weathered from wind and rain. But his ringmail was washed with gold, and gem-set rings glinted on his hands. Large, competent hands, callused into hardness by the demands of sword and war.

The man smiled. He showed large teeth, and none missing. But his Atvian mouth formed the Homanan syllables harshly. "A ratling," he said. "A young Homanan ratling searching for a bolt-hole."

The boy saw the others. All soldiers, all toughened veterans in leather-and-mail with helms tucked under arms. No one else spoke. They left it to their leader in his gold-washed mail and glinting gem-set rings.

"Ratling, what is your name?"

He summoned a tight-throated voice. "Rowan. Of Homana."

The Atvian grinned. "Rowan. Of Homana. Lacking weapons of any sort—what kind of warrior are you?"

Rowan wet cracked lips. "A soldier of the Mujhar."

The other laughed. "King's man, are you? From out of the cradle into war?" Teeth flashed briefly. "Have we harried Shaine so harshly that he breeds ratlings in place of men?"

He was, Rowan thought, entirely too free—and disrespectful—with the name of Homana's king. Shaine deserved better.

The Atvian's smile dropped away. Hard dark eyes narrowed. "Do you know who I am?"

Rowan admitted he did not.

Dark eyes glittered. "Thorne of Atvia, ratling. Does it mean anything to you? No? Then let me instruct you, ratling . . . I am son and heir to Keough himself, who has destroyed all of Shaine's puny troops. Destroyed them and taken Homana; pay homage to your new lord, ratling. *On your knees,* ratling—I am Crown Prince of Atvia, and now heir to Homana herself."

Rowan fell to sore knees, but only because Thorne's hand was so heavy on his shoulder. He stared blindly at the man's boots and wished Rowan of Homana had never left Mujhara, where his father's shop was tedious but never dangerous.

"What shall I do with you, boy? What should I do with ratlings?"

Slowly Rowan looked up the expanse of chest to the face above it. He thought the answer implicit. "Take me prisoner."

Thorne of Atvia grinned. The men with him snickered.

Rowan, humiliated, stared hard at the gold-hilted knife tucked into Thorne's heavy belt and wished he had courage enough to grab for it. He would die in the doing, of course, and probably painfully, but it would be worth the dying if it meant he could wound—or even kill—the heir of Atvia.

But Thorne seemed to know his mind. His hand fell to his knife hilt. "Not man enough," he said scathingly, then added something more in a harsh, guttural tongue that made the others laugh.

In the space of a single breath, Rowan learned to hate.

"Up," Thorne commanded. "You are a ratling, and insignificant, but ratlings grow to rats. Enough of them can bring down a healthy man. So I will do as you suggest and take you prisoner."

Rowan winced as the Atvian prodded him to his feet. Thorne said something in his ugly tongue and one of the other men came forward. He pointed down the hillock, then gave Rowan a shove that sent him stumbling down the ridge. Rather than disgrace himself by falling, or allow the enemy to touch him a second time, Rowan went where he was directed.

He was put into a massive cluster of Homanan prisoners. All lived, though most were wounded. The strongest men were chained; those weakened by wounds were left unchained but closely supervised by Atvian archers and pikemen.

Rowan, hugging his knees, wiped a filthy hand across a grimy face and tried to ignore the dry ache in his throat. He could not recall when last he had eaten, or taken a drink. His appetite was banished by events of the day, but thirst remained strong.

He ached in every muscle, but could not recall falling or being tossed down; the soreness of his bones must come from days spent running messages between Homanan captains. It was the sort of work he had scorned at first, thinking himself good enough to fight with the rest, but he soon learned the only work boys were given was to act as a pair of legs. Horses could not be risked, so Rowan and others like him ran messages back and forth, back and forth, until he believed himself inches shorter than when he had begun.

He couldn't remember when he had begun.

Don't think about it, he told himself. *You are alive and healthy; others are not so fortunate.*

And so they weren't. Those nearest him were wounded, some badly; they lay twitching and groaning in pain, calling curses on the Atvian hordes that had overrun Homanan encampments just prior to dawn; cursing the mounts that went down beneath them, or the sword that broke, or the eyes that couldn't see through clogging mists, or the Mujhar himself for sending them to fight. They also petitioned the gods for ransom, rescue, or release, depending on the severity of their wounds. Rowan, looking in horror on the broken strength of Homana, wondered what would become of the realm.

"Are you injured?"

Rowan, startled, jerked around and stared at the speaker. A moment earlier he had been an island in the center of a sea of pain; now someone else had arrived.

"No," he answered at once, staring up at the young man towering over him.

The other, seeming to realize he threatened by his posture, knelt carefully and sat. His words held familiar Homanan cadences, but the intonations and accents were of the nobility. And his clothes, now Rowan could see them without the prejudice of apprehension, were far too fine for the plain harness and gear of the Homanan army. He wore ringmail and leather, but all was new and strong, even beneath the gore and blood. On his right hand flashed a ruby set in gold; the signet bespoke his station. And while he wore sheaths for knife and sword, both were conspicuously empty.

The stranger smiled, though it was little more than a weary stretching of his mouth. His face was grimy, one side streaked with blood, and a spreading bruise colored his left cheekbone. Blue eyes were red-rimmed and bloodshot. Tawny hair, sticky with sweat and blood, clung closely to his head.

He assessed Rowan again. "In all that blood, there is no wound?"

Rowan fingered his blood-soaked tunic and realized for all the gore clinging to him, he might be dead as well. "No wound," he answered quietly, ill at ease before a man so obviously bred to higher rank.

The other sighed and scraped absently at his grimy face. Rowan saw no visible wounds, but he moved as if he had been buffeted once too often about the ribs. His broad hands were bare of gauntlets, and Rowan saw calluses broken and bloodied by swordwork. But mostly he saw the chains.

Iron shackles were locked around boots and wrists. A length between his ankles let him walk, but not run; a length from ankles to wrists allowed him to stand, but not erect. The flesh of his wrists was already raw from chafing.

Rowan ventured a question. "Are *you* hurt, my lord?"

The other did not dismiss the title, which made Rowan believe he deserved it. "Only my pride, but that, I think, is sometimes the most painful of wounds." A quick glance at others, truly wounded, made him clench his jaw, as if he regretted the inappropriateness of his comment. "Thorne took my sword, then me."

Rowan nearly gaped. "The Atvian crown prince?"

"Aye." One tawny brow was raised in elegant curiosity. "You know Thorne?"

"He took *me*, as well." The bitterness came so easily it startled even Rowan.

An answering bitterness in the other's brief laugh dwarfed Rowan's emotion. "Then we are *kinspirits*, my friend, caught in like circumstances. Perhaps we are meant to share them."

Emboldened, Rowan edged a little closer. "Why are you chained so heavily?"

His companion grimaced. He was, Rowan thought, eighteen or nineteen, with a big man's height and weight. "They have no wish to lose me. I am too valuable." Strong emotion wracked his mouth, then he controlled himself. "My father is dead, slain by the hand of Keough himself; and I am taken prisoner. The Atvians will send me back in chains to Mujhara, when they take her, to show me off to the citizens. I will provide a means, they hope, to help keep the people cowed." He stared fixedly beyond Rowan. "We should have known," he murmured. "We should have *known* they would creep in and attack before dawn, less than a day after the last battle. But we slept, so many slept . . . and so now the war is lost." The voice died out briefly, then renewed itself in despair. "If only we had *known* . . ."

Rowan realized his presence was forgotten, lost in painful recollection. He missed the brief kinship they had shared, thrown out again on his own to battle despair and misery. He was not yet willing to relinquish that bond. "Surely you will be ransomed . . ." he ventured.

The stranger's attention returned. He shook his head. "They will ask none for me. I am more valuable kept close at hand." The blue eyes grew intent. "What of you?" he asked. "Have you people in Mujhara?"

Rowan did, but no one who could scrape together enough to buy him free. His father's shop in the city barely earned them enough for meat twice a week. And he had, after all, run off to war against their wishes, stealing out in the night like a thief.

"Nc," he said thickly, swallowing painfully.

"Ah well, there is enough in my own coffers to see you free." The other shrugged, smiling wryly. "The Atvians will take it all, of course, but I think they may overlook something. I have my resources . . ." His voice trailed off as he looked more closely at Rowan. "Has anyone ever said you have the color of a Cheysuli?"

Astonishment blazed. Rowan gaped at him, then answered emphatically. "I am not a shapechanger!"

"Black hair, yellow eyes—even the dark skin—"

"I am not a demon!"

"Neither are they." The other shifted. Chains chimed. "Oh, I know . . . you have been taught how terrible they are, men who turn into beasts. But that is all because of the Mujhar, who branded them demons and outcasts because of a personal matter. Shaine's purge—the *qu'mahlin*, the Cheysuli call it—accounted for many deaths. There are few Cheysuli left. If there is Cheysuli blood in you—"

"No," Rowan declared.

His noble companion sighed. "They are not beasts. I thought so, too, until I met them. Until they made me see they are men like you and I, except for a special gift—"

Rowan's eyes were wide. "They turn into wild animals."

"They assume animal form. Cheysuli call it *lir*-shape. Each warrior, when he becomes a man, links with a magical animal. That allows the warrior to take on a like shape, but it does not make him a beast."

Rowan shook his head emphatically. "They are accursed. The Mujhar himself offers coin to any man killing a Cheysuli."

The other sighed. "For now Shaine would do better to pay men to kill *Atvians*."

Reminded, Rowan glanced around. Wounded men lay dying. Dead men did not move.

He swallowed and looked back at his *kinspirit.* Curiosity intervened between conviction and aversion. "You have met one, then? A Cheysuli?"

"I have met several. I lived with them a while. Not long, but long enough . . . certainly long enough to know the Mujhar's purge is wrong."

"But they have *always* been accursed."

"For twenty-five years," the other corrected. "Longer than you *or* I have lived . . . but that does not make it right."

Rowan supressed a shudder. "To take on the shape of an animal . . ." He could not reconcile it with reality. "I am not. Am *not.* I cannot shapechange. And if I could, I would not. I am not a beast."

But his companion was no longer listening. Someone had joined them. Thorne of Atvia, flanked by a guard of six.

"So," he mocked derisively in his ugly accent, "are you fallen so far you keep the company of ratlings? Is this what you do in Mujhara?"

Rowan's companion straightened. "What I do in Mujhara is no concern of yours."

The Atvian prince grinned. "It is now, Homanan. Mujhara will soon be mine."

The Homanan contempt was delicate. "And I assume that once she is, you will give me leave to keep company with *real* rats—in the dungeons."

"That is for my father to decide. As for now, you will have to concern yourself with *Atvian* company; my father desires your presence." A simple gesture to guardsmen resulted in Rowan's companion being dragged to his feet. Iron chains clashed.

As they put rough hands on him, he glanced back to Rowan. "Your name, *kinspirit?*"

Rowan sucked in a deep breath. "Rowan of Homana, in service to Shaine the Mujhar."

His *kinspirit* smiled, and then the others forced him away. Rowan watched him go, stumbling in chains, and felt a surge of pride and gratitude so powerful it nearly choked him. He was proud a captured man could remain undefeated, even in chains; proud he would not bow his head to the man who ordered his disposition. He was grateful he himself was Homanan and of the same dedication to race and realm. But most of all Rowan was grateful that such a man could call a tattered, bloodstained boy his *kinspirit*. It made the bondage more bearable; the fear worth beating off.

Rowan finally fell asleep after dark, but the Atvians came then and pulled him from the ground, much as they had pulled his chained friend. He was frightened and disoriented, but they set him on his feet and prodded him toward a scarlet field pavilion glowing richly in the torchlight. Pennons and banners hung limply in the stillness.

He was stopped at the doorflap of the pavilion, then shoved through when given entry. He stumbled into the torch-lighted canvas cavern and stopped dead just inside the doorflap, gaping at the man who sat at the head of an oaken table.

He was huge. His body was so massive Rowan was put in mind of a bear without the hair, although the man had his own share. It was red and thick, threaded with white. A bushy beard sprang from his face as if it burned his flesh. Blue eyes were deep-set and small, but the size and placement of them did not hide the cunning intelligence. He wore a black tunic threaded with gold overlaid with fighting leathers, but no ringmail, ceremonial or otherwise. Rowan thought perhaps the metal was unnecessary. The man's hide looked tough enough to withstand blade or arrow.

Rowan wet his lips. He knew very well whom he faced: the big man wore a circlet of gold upon his brow, and a knife studded with thumb-sized jewels hung at his belt. On thick fingers rich rings blazed.

Thorne of Atvia moved into Rowan's line of vision. "On

your knees before Keough, ratling. Pay homage to Atvia's king, and Lord of the Idrian Isles."

Rowan started to obey, wishing to save knees and shoulders from Thorne's heavy hand. But before he dropped down he looked past Thorne and saw his Homanan *kinspirit* present, seated at the massive table. The bruised cheek showed deepened color.

Rowan stopped in arrested realization and intense shame. If his *kinspirit* could behave with dignity and decorum—and defiance—so could he.

He looked again at the Atvian king as he sat in his ironbound chair, and then he looked at Thorne. "No. I am Homanan. I do not kneel to my enemy."

Thorne's hand came down across Rowan's face and knocked him reeling into the entrance pole. His hands snagged in the fabric, searching for support, found none; he sprawled on the carpeted floor in an undignified heap. His head rang with the blow and his teeth bit through his tongue, spilling blood into his mouth.

The hand returned, jerking him upright, and dragged him toward the head of the table. Rowan struggled to regain his balance but the momentum made him stumble; Thorne dropped him easily to his knees before the ruddy-haired giant.

Thorne's voice was contemptuously solicitous. "What say you now, ratling?"

Rowan hated himself for shaking, but he could not help it. He swallowed blood, tried not to gag, stared fixedly into hard blue eyes as the enemy king waited. From his *kinspirit's* presence, he took courage.

"I am a runner, my lord—nothing more. I carried messages from one captain to another." A deeper breath gave him more courage. "I saw what you did when you crept in at dawn like a pack of ravaging wolves, attacking men who had fought you honorably only hours before. *I* may be insignificant—a ratling, like he says—but your cruelty makes you no better. If you think I will kneel—*willingly*—to a man who has no honor, you are also a gods-cursed fool."

He prepared himself for the blow, knowing it would fall like a tree and crush him into the ground. But it did not fall as Keough himself reached out to stop Thorne's hand.

"No," Keough rasped. "You do not silence a yapping

wolf-pup by killing it. Instead, you tame it." The eyes were very blue as he looked at Rowan. "But first you must humiliate it, so it knows to obey its master." He pointed at Rowan. "On your feet, boy."

Rowan got up unsteadily, trying not to flinch as Thorne moved restlessly behind him.

Keough pointed to a jug and cup resting on the table. "Pour the wine, boy. Pour the cup full."

Rowan longed to refuse, but something in Keough kept him from it. Defiance of Thorne was one thing, for Rowan judged him little more than a cruel, spoiled young lordling, but the father was another matter entirely. He was wise and cunning and dangerous; Rowan realized instinctively he should not press Keough.

The Atvian giant smiled when the wine was poured. "Now take it to your prince."

Rowan stared at him blankly, thinking he meant Thorne.

Keough elaborated. "The prisoner," he declared, grinning in satisfaction. "Shaine the Mujhar's own nephew— his heir in lieu of sons—styled the Prince of Homana." Strong teeth shone briefly in the depths of his fiery beard. "Do you not know your own lord?"

"Let him be," the Homanan rasped. "Do not play with him like this."

Rowan stared at his *kinspirit,* watching dull color rise slowly in the bruised, battered face. The fine clothing and mail now made sense, and the ring he wore on his hand, which his captors had inexplicably let him keep. A lord Rowan had believed; *that* lord, he had not.

He dropped to his knees so quickly the wine spilled out of the cup.

Thorne's hand dragged him up. "You do not kneel to *Carillon* if you will not kneel to Keough!"

Rowan lost the wine cup entirely. At the table, Carillon rose. "Leave the boy alone! He has no stake in this . . . if you must pleasure yourself by laying hands on a Homanan, lay them on me." Chains clashed as he raised impotent fists. "Or is the pleasure increased in reverse proportion to the boy's youth?"

Thorne released Rowan and rounded the table. "It was I who ripped the sword from your hands, Homanan! I who drove you to your knees in the bloodied fields, and made you know what it is to be put in chains! Do you dare defy *me* while you stand in Atvian iron?"

"Aye!" Carillon shouted.

"Enough!" Keough roared, striking the table with a huge fist. "No more of this. Thorne, do not shame me by playing the fool before the prisoner. As for *you*, Carillon of Homana, you would do well to keep your mouth closed before we find iron for your tongue as well."

Carillon's tone did not waver. "He is a boy. Let him be, and I will wear all the iron you own."

Keough displayed big teeth. "You wear enough for now, I think." He gestured. "Sit down. You as well, Thorne. I desire to eat without further interruption." The cold blue eyes settled on Rowan again. "As for you, my loyal Homanan wolf-pup, you will serve your new masters. To make certain you know our names."

The evening wore thin, but Keough did not weary of eating and drinking. He consumed enough food for three men and drank enough for five, but he did not grow befuddled with the wine. He sat sprawled in his iron-bound chair and watched his noble prisoner, smiling now and again at some private amusement, or speaking to his son in his harsh Atvian tongue.

Thorne's temper improved with food and wine, but to Rowan's detriment. The Atvian prince's idea of an entertainment was to trip his exhausted young servant at every opportunity, laughing uproariously when the boy fell. Rowan dropped two platters of venison and one loaf of bread, each time dragging himself to his feet with the humiliating sound of foreign laughter in burning ears.

The laughter, Rowan decided, was worse than the frequent cuffs meted out by Thorne's ever-ready hand. He understood now why Carillon had said damaged pride could hurt as much as or worse than a real wound.

The Atvians, in their celebration, made him serve Carillon as well. Rowan would have done it willingly and happily under other circumstances, but he found the required service hideous because it was intended as a mockery of the captured Prince of Homana. Keough even invited favored captains inside the blood-colored pavilion to witness Carillon's plight, then announced Rowan was the Homanan's only remaining soldier still loyal to the fallen cause. Carillon himself did not respond, but Rowan sensed his tight-reined rage and humiliation. He felt his own measure of both.

In the shadows, Rowan blinked hard, trying to clear his vision. He was exhausted, hungry, thirsty. His tongue grew thick and unwieldy in his mouth when they made him say *my lord* this and *my lord* that; if he did not answer quickly enough, or forgot to give them expected courtesy, one or more of the captains fetched him a buffet on the head that sent him reeling to his knees. Wobbly and disoriented, Rowan knew he was a single step away from fainting, which would be the ultimate humiliation.

Perhaps that is what they want—

Thorne's booted foot snaked out yet again and snared his ankles. Rowan tripped, lurching against a corner of the table. He felt the flash of pain as wood bit into his hip, but it was nothing compared to the shock and uprushing fear he felt as the winejug he carried crashed against the table and shattered, spilling pungent red wine into the massive lap of Keough himself. Rowan stared, transfixed, and clung to the table with all his might.

Silence filled the pavilion. No man moved. Not even Thorne.

Keough did not even bother to look at the dark stains spreading across the silken fabric of tunic and breeches, soaking into the fine formal leathers. He glanced at Thorne briefly, as if acknowledging his son had won some bizarre form of wager.

"Scourge him," he commanded.

"No!" Carillon was on his feet, chains crashing against the oaken table. "My lord, I ask you—I *beg* you—" He tried to school his tone out of desperation into discussion. "No scourging, my lord . . . it would kill him."

Thorne's smile was cool. "He begins to understand."

Carillon ignored the son, staring at the father. "What do you want from me? Do you desire me to kneel, as I refused before? Do you wish me to bow my head like a properly cowed prisoner?" He dropped to his knees, head upthrust defiantly. "Is this enough for you? If not, then I beg you: let him be. Scourge me in his place if you must have blood,

but do not whip this boy. In the name of my gods, my king—
even the rank that makes me so valuable to you. Do not—"

"Enough!" Keough roared. Slowly he rose. The tunic
was a sodden mass dripping blood-colored wine. Rowan
wished it *was* blood, and that Keough would die of it. The
massive man looked at his expectant son. "You have my
orders."

Thorne caught and lifted Rowan. Two of the captains
restrained Carillon physically as Thorne carried the boy
toward the doorflap.

"No!" Carillon shouted. "I will take his place—"

The sound of a blow cut off the words.

Rowan thrashed once, impotently, and felt the hard mus-
culature and ringmail that made Thorne so contemptuous
of his struggles. The Atvian carried his stunned captive to
a large post set in the ground fifty paces beyond Keough's
pavilion and lashed him to it face-first, wrists and ankles.

Rowan could see nothing but the post. He could *taste*
nothing but the post, ground so cruelly into his face. His
heart lurched in his chest like a smith's hammer, banging
against his ribs. Each time he drew breath his belly met
the post, compressing flesh. Already his hands felt numb.

Thorne spoke to someone Rowan could not see. A moment later the long lash curled gently around the post and
his ankles. Rowan shuddered convulsively and clenched his
eyes shut tightly, trying to swallow back the bile crowding
up from his belly.

*Oh gods, make me wake up—make me wake up and
know all of this is a dream—*

They did not bother to strip the tunic from his back.
Within two lashes the whip tore it from his flesh. Rowan
cried out, then fought his bonds frenziedly.

Make them stop—

He could hear, in his mind, Carillon's words. Scourging
would kill him, the prince had said. Thorne had made it
clear that was the intention.

Twice, thrice, four times the lash fell. The leather of his
bonds stretched far enough for him to slide down the post
into a huddle at its foot, bowed back bared. He ground his
face into wood.

Make—him—STOP—

But the whip sang on.

*   *   *

He roused spasmodically when the hand touched his shoulder. The fingers were infinitely gentle, but the contact cut through him like a flame. Rowan moaned aloud, not caring who heard. Pride was no longer important.

The hand went away. Rowan, breathing noisily, heard someone move from behind him to the other side of the post, where he could see. He stared in shock: it was a woman.

She put silencing fingers to her lips. "I am not an enemy. I am sent from Carillon, to set you free."

Rowan stared blankly. How could Carillon send anyone? The prince himself was a captive.

The woman sliced his legs free with a silver knife glinting in the moonlight. "Your prince knows you have served his House. He knows what loyalty you have offered. He will not have you so poorly treated in return for honorable service."

Heat boiled into Rowan's face. "I did *not* serve honorably," he hissed. "When the Atvians came, I ran. I *ran* . . . and was captured." He spat blood from a bitten lip. "What manner of service is that?"

Her voice was calm. "Carillon also was captured." She bent closer, sliding the knife beneath the leather binding his wrists. "He gave me your name and told me to come straight here, to cut you free."

"How?" Rowan croaked. "Keough has him in his pavilion."

"Not any more. They took him out and bound him into a tumbril, to take him to Mujhara. We freed Carillon earlier."

"But—"

"The Atvians do not yet know he has escaped. They do not fully understand about us, and what we can do . . ." She caught him as his arms fell free of the post. "I know," she murmured. "I know it hurts, Rowan—I promise, it will pass. The blood will flow again, and the lash marks will heal."

He shuddered, gasping, trying to control the immensity of his pain. He stared hard at the woman as she slipped her knife back into a wolfskin boot.

"Who are—?" He cut it off, seeing amber eyes and

black, short-cropped hair. The face was angular, made of hollows and planes with high, sculpted cheekbones. It was intent in the darkness, and oddly feral. It was very like his own.

She stared back, fully as astonished as he. Breath hissed sharply. "Cheysuli!" she gasped. "He did not tell me *that*—"

Rowan recoiled. Crusted lash marks tore. "No!" he croaked. "I am *not a demon*—"

Her hand, reaching toward his face, trembled. "No—oh no—not a *demon* . . . I promise you, it is not a curse. That much I know myself . . . oh, Rowan—" But she did not finish because Thorne was, suddenly, *there*.

She leaped to her feet, man-clad in homespun shirt, leather jerkin and leggings, cross-gartered boots. Except that he had seen her close and heard her voice, he might have believed she was a boy.

Rowan clung to the post, trying to banish the giddiness that threatened to overwhelm him. He saw Thorne catch her arm, clutching her to him so tightly her protest was lost against ringmail. He said something about taking her to Keough, and dragged her toward the pavilion.

No one came. No one appeared to see if he was still tied to the post. He was, Rowan realized, entirely inconsequential.

Carefully, he looked around. He sat hunched very much as he had hunched before, but even though he gripped the post no leather tied him there. Thorne, looking at him—or anyone else, for that matter—would believe the woman's rescue bid failed.

Free— Rowan thought in wonder.

In all but scourged flesh. His back was afire, aching to his bones. Rowan bit his broken lip and worried it deliberately, hoping that small pain might deflect some of the worse pain of his back.

"Carillon," he murmured weakly. "My *kinspirit,* the Prince of Homana . . ." He drew in a breath of astonishment, overwhelmed by the realization. "*He* did this for me."

There was no answer. In the darkness, torches hissed and flared. Rowan clung to the post and repeated in his mind all of the things Carillon had said, the promises made to a young Homanan ratling.

Into darkness, Rowan grinned. He wanted to laugh aloud, to exult, but he knew better. If he stayed where he was, he was sure to be found out. And that would dishonor the great service Carillon had done him, making the gesture empty.

He drew in a deep, meticulous breath, biting his abused lip against the pain of his back, and dug rigid fingers into the wooden post. Inch by inch he dragged himself up from the ground. When he stood again, still clinging to the post that bore the dark stains of his blood and flesh, Rowan knew he would succeed if it killed him.

"That much . . ." he whispered. "That much I will give him—" Carefully, Rowan left the security of the post. Slowly he made his way through the darkness, heading for the perimeter of the encampment. "I will find someone, even Cheysuli, and tell them about the woman . . . and then I will go," he murmured, creating a litany by which he could force his aching body to move when all it wanted to do was collapse. "I will dedicate my life to his service. I will speak of his honor and courage to every Homanan I meet. I will say how he defied Keough himself within the lord's own pavilion, and how he thinks of even a *Homanan ratling* like myself!" He flung back his head and stared fixedly at the moon, strengthening his vow. "I will go into every village and say to anyone who will listen that *Carillon* set me free—that Carillon set *me* free—"

He lost his breath, gasping, and paused to steady himself. The moon was a baleful eye, staring down. Beyond the encampment, shrouded in deepwood darkness, lay the wooded hills of Homana offering safety and concealment.

Rowan laughed softly. "Oh my *kinspirit*, what I will do for you . . ."

He fixed his eyes on the treeline rising above the moonlighted plains and murmured a brief prayer to the gods, invoking their aid and strength in the name of his newfound friend.

Then he threw off the bloodied, shredded tunic and walked softly toward the shining darkness beyond the Atvian torchlight.

APPENDIX
CHEYSULI/OLD TONGUE
GLOSSARY
(with pronunciation guide)

a'saii (uh-SIGH)—Cheysuli zealots dedicated to pure line of descent.

bu'lasa (boo-LAH-suh)—grandson

bu'sala (boo-SAH-luh)—foster-son

cheysu (chay-SOO)—man/woman; neuter; used within phrases.

cheysul (chay-SOOL)—husband

cheysula (chay-SOO-luh)—wife

cheysuli (chay-SOO-lee) (*literal translation*)—children of the gods.

Cheysuli i'halla shansu (chay-SOO-lee i-HALLA shan-SOO) (*lit.*)—May there be Cheysuli peace upon you.

godfire (god-fire)—common manifestation of Ihlini power; cold, lurid flame; purple tones.

harana (huh-RAH-na)—niece

harani (huh-RAH-nee)—nephew

homana (ho-MAH-na) (*literal translation*)—of all blood.

i'halla (ih-HALL-uh)—upon you: used within phrases.

i'toshaa-ni (ih-tosha-NEE)—Cheysuli cleansing ceremony; atonement ritual.

ja'hai ([French *j*] zshuh-HIGH)—accept

ja'hai-na (zshuh-HIGH-nuh)—accepted

jehan (zsheh-HAHN)—father

jehana (zsheh-HAH-na)—mother

ku'reshtin (koo-RESH-tin)—epithet; name-calling

leijhana tu'sai (lay-HAHN-uh too-SIGH) (*lit.*)—thank you very much.

lir (leer)—magical animal(s) linked to individual Cheysuli; title used indiscriminately between *lir* and warriors.

meijha (MEE-hah)—Cheysuli: light woman; (*lit.*): mistress.

meijhana (mee-HAH-na)—slang: pretty one

Mujhar (moo-HAR)—king

qu'mahlin (koo-MAH-lin)—purge; extermination
Resh'ta-ni (*resh-tah-NEE*) (*lit.*)—As you would have it.
rujho (ROO-ho)—slang: brother (diminutive)
rujholla (roo-HALL-uh)—sister (formal)
rujholli (roo-HALL-ee)—brother (formal)
ru'maii (roo-MY-ee) (*lit.*)—in the name of
Ru'shalla-tu (roo-SHAWL-uh TOO) (*lit.*)—May it be so.
Seker (Sek-AIR)—formal title: god of the netherworld.
shansu (shan-SOO)—peace
shar tahl (shar TAHL)—priest-historian; keeper of the prophecy.
shu'maii (shoo-MY-ee)—sponsor
su'fala (soo-FALL-uh)—aunt
su'fali (soo-FALL-ee)—uncle
sul'harai (sool-hah-RYE)—moment of greatest satisfaction in union of man and woman; describes shapechange.
tahlmorra (tall-MORE-uh)—fate; destiny; kismet.
Tahlmorra lujhala mei wiccan, cheysu (tall-MORE-uh loo-HALLA may WICK-un, chay-SOO) (*lit.*)—The fate of a man rests always within the hands of the gods.

Jennifer Roberson